Semper Silence

Semper Silence LLC,

7460 Plantation Rd, Plantation, FL,33317

Semper Silence

Copyright © by M. G. Rigau

For information, address: Semper Silence LLC., 7460 Plantation Rd, Plantation, FL 33317

Visit our website at sempersilence.com

Semper Silence and its design are registered trademarks of Semper Silence Limited Liability Company.

Printed in the United States of America

First Edition: December 2021

Library of Congress Cataloging-in-publication data

Rigau, M.G.
Semper Silence / M.G. Rigau – 1st ed.

ISBN 979-8-9854219-0-3
979-8-9854219-1-0
979-8-9854219-2-7
979-8-9854219-3-4

*To my Sister **Kowinna,***

I promised you I would finish the book. I hope you are watching down from heaven with a smile. Your little brother did it!

Acknowledgments

To: *Gliss, Kevin, Sherrie, Konane, Jeff, Mark, Mike, Dean, Jimmy, Ernie, Yolanda, Tory, Karen, Dawn, Debbie, Reenie, Jorge, Joe, Fletcher, Julia, Robbie, Michelle,* ...and all the other great Marines, and friends who made it sparkle for all those years, especially those with a little more flair! Thank you for the memories!

Melanie Smith, you are a brilliant and amazing woman! Your persistence, belief in me, and your ability to see past the clutter and keep pushing through made this book happen. Thank you!

Paul Rigau, thank you for all the hours of listening, and being my sounding board. You have kept the reins pulled in and have been my voice of reason. You know me best! Thank you for your sacrificial and unconditional love.

Yolanda Mayo, thank you for always being there in a pinch, and for the steadfast friendship through all these years! You're my number one cheer leader!

To my Parents and siblings, being the youngest, each one of you had a hand in teaching me life's lessons! I love you all!

Ruby and **Stewie,** I promise we are going to go for more walks!

Table of Contents

Introduction

2010's
The cold winds of Indiana …

  The straight cold winds of January blew across the frozen plowed fields, rustling up the light snow that was just beginning to accumulate on the ground. It was the type of wind that cut to the bone regardless of what one might wear. The winds and snow were nothing unusual for this time of year, January in Indiana could be brutal. The only thing to stop the wind's momentum were the patches of trees, fence lines, and homes placed sporadically.

  A lone vehicle, in the distance, traveled down the rural road. The roads were a little more than mere paths, garlanded by electric lines hung from telephone poles, helping to divide the wide-open space. Large sycamore, walnut, and maple trees, all leafless, appeared baron from the winter's cold crisp air, towered above a cluster of homes. They, along with the occasional pine that sprang up, added a touch of color, and life, creating a frozen oasis. The vehicle, a gray Toyota Four Runner, slowed at one of the brick ranch style homes that were so common in this area. Turning slowly into the ice-covered driveway, it paused briefly to allow the garage door to open.

  Once inside, the door closed preventing the brisk air from getting in. The car door opened, a tall blonde, large build, forty-something man hopped out and walked around to retrieve some bags and headed inside. Opening the door, he could hear barks, and soon see tails waggling as he was greeted by two small dachshunds. "All right, all right, Ms. Scarlett, Mr. Archie, I missed you too," and continued to the kitchen to set the groceries down. "Come on, let's go potty!" He moved to the kitchen back door as the two quickly juggled to get first dibs at getting out. Stepping out onto the small back porch, only briefly, he got a sample of the freezing cold winds. The dogs were done, and all three were headed back into the house.

With the groceries put away, still in his coat, he rubbed his hands together trying to warm them as he returned to the living room fireplace. Adding a log to the fire, still not warm, he blew into his hands as he headed to the foyer closet, checking the thermostat along the way. The door behind him flung open and he could feel the freezing wind once again blow in. He quickly turned to see Cal closing the door, stomping his feet, and brushing the snow from his coat. "Man, it's getting cold out there Nollie." Noah turned and smirked. "My family is rubbing off on you, they're the only ones who call me that anymore. I haven't gone by Nollie in years." Anxious to hear about his C.P.A. exam, Noah continued, "Well, how did it go?" Cal, putting away his coat, shrugged a bit, "I don't know, about what I expected. I'm not sure." Noah quickly replied, "What do you mean you're not sure?" Cal, more preoccupied on getting settled in, "I don't know, I'm still processing it. Don't really want to talk about it right now," and headed to the kitchen. "They make you wait 3 to 4 weeks to get the results, talk about keeping you on edge."

Wandering around the living room tidying up, Noah continued, "I just got back from the grocery, they're predicting 8 to 10…," Cal interrupted, "That's what she said." Noah rolling his eyes, "I think you watch too much of 'The Office.' I figured I'd better get supplies case we get snowed in. There's some beer." Cal reappeared, "I know, I found it, thanks there Nollie!" sarcastically, as he held it up passing by on the way to the bedroom.

Noah took a glance out the front picture window to see the snow accumulating rather quickly, before settling down in his easy chair. Just as he turned on the TV, a severe weather warning was beeping across the screen. He reached for his laptop, from the stand beside him, when Cal returned to the living room and sat on the sofa now comfortable in his folks-pants. The two dogs joined them as they all settled in.

The new thing to do was social media: Facebook, Twitter, and, of course, the old fashion emails. While logging in to Facebook, Noah notices his refection on the computer screen. Looking at the reflection, he touches his face showing a three-day growth of unshaven beard and becomes self-conscious of the slightly developing double chin. He grabs his cheeks, pushes them back to see if he can still see some resemblance of what he used to look like: shakes his head in disgust and lets go.

Finally, Facebook opened, with two new messages. The first one is from his sister; an invite to play a game called Farmville. He deletes it, "I'm going to block her if she keeps sending me shit!" He quickly moves on to the next message. Opening it, he suddenly recognizes the name Joel Hammond. What? Why would he be writing? He hesitates and contemplates deleting the message. After all, it had been ten years since he had last seen Joel, and when he left it wasn't a favorable situation. Hopefully, it wasn't any bad news. What could this guy want? The curiosity took over and Noah gave in and opened the message. Quickly, he can remember Joel's soft-spoken voice, tall stature, and the young man's blonde hair surrounding his baby face coming back to him. Noah read the letter to himself:

Hey,

Hope all is well! It's Joel Hammond.

I recently returned to school and will be a Senior next quarter at the University of Iowa's journalism school. I thought of you the other day and I'm HOPING that you can help me!

This quarter I am doing extensive research on the "Don't Ask, Don't Tell" policy. Before the end of the quarter, I will have written an 800- and 1600-word essay, turned in a 15-picture presentation, and edited a short video on the subject. I am well aware that the topic is of interest to you as I can see posted under your interests on Facebook and having worked for you in Yuma.

Hope you don't find this email intrusive, but I would be extremely interested in hearing your perspective on the matter.

Once again, hope all is well and that things are going good for you!

Thanks
Joel Hammond

After reading the email, Noah sat for a moment staring at the screen. What memories this triggered off in his mind. He read the letter again and started to delete it but hesitates. "Don't Ask, Don't Tell" was something he didn't care to talk about with strangers or someone he wasn't comfortable with. Although Joel wasn't a complete stranger, Noah wasn't sure if he was ready to trust or engage him in conversation with such a personal topic. Struggling with his own internal strife, Noah had been committed to being silent about the subject years ago. He thought it best, at that time, to work or speak only behind the scenes. Making himself a lightning rod by speaking out was not an issue he wanted to create or face. No matter how he pushed, and walked away, the issue of "Don't Ask, Don't Tell" would find its way once again front and center.

He laid his head back, contemplating what action he should take. So many things were to be said about the topic. He turned toward the picture window with a mile away stare. His thoughts started wandering; suspicious of Joel, what is the real reason he is asking? Should he let his guard down and talk openly, or put up his normal facade, and say thank you, but no thank you. I can't help!

A crackle and shuffling of the logs in the fireplace caught his attention. The fireplace needed poked and stirred to get the flames going once again. Setting the computer aside, he walked over and knelt in front of the fireplace, moving the fire screen to allow exposure to the small flame as he added a log. Grabbing the poker, he stirred and poked until the fire was ablaze once again. He grabbed the screen and put it safely back in front of the flames. Still in a bit of a trance, he glared into the fire in deep contemplation as it started to climb.

Just like he added a log and stirred the fire, did he have anything to add, or want to stir the issue by revisiting the memories and heartbreak of "Don't Ask, Don't Tell," or should the screen remain closed, and the fire contained safely? He rubbed his hands together and faced his palms toward the fire.

In the office, a large rectangle shadow box hung on the wall. The box held various military items mounted on display over a red felt background. In the top left corner, folded in a triangle, was the U.S Flag, on the right, the Marine Corps'. Separating the two was a large brass Marine Corps emblem. The shiny brass name plate engraved with the name Master Sergeant Noah G. Barlow, and the dates Oct 1980 to May 2006 jumped out from below. Accompanying the name plate was a rack of various military medals flanked by the Marine Corps rank insignia. The bookcases in the room, displaying various statues, books, and photos surrounded the desk that sat center. On an easel by the window was a painting in progress.

Noah entered the office through the double doors leading from the living room, closing them behind him. He turned and approached the shadow box on the wall. Looking into it, he could remember the day it was given to him, along with every item on display. How funny the thought, the history of twenty-six years of loyal and faithful service to the Country and Corps were all held and displayed in one little box. At least part of the history, the part that had been allowed to be seen.

"Semper Fidelis" was the Marine Corps motto meaning "Always Faithful." To the best of his ability, during his career, he tried to always live up to it. On the surface, his career looked great, but not without flaw. Anyone really knowing Noah, knew the full story wasn't being told. The other side was hidden secrets, secrets forbidden to be spoken. The more bright, favorable, joyous, good, and loving ones, but also the adverse, dark, devious, treacherous, and sinister ones. All were kept well-guarded within his memories and heart.

Reaching up and touching the shadow box, he pauses and smiles, before releasing his hand and moving away. In a wide-eyed glaze, he walked around and sat down in the chair behind the desk. Placing his feet up on the corner of the desk and cupping his hands behind his head, he contemplated: How long should he remain silent? Being a retired Marine, if he spoke out, could he still be held accountable and punished? If he didn't, was he being fair to himself and his fellow comrades in arms? Those who demanded silence from this unjust law, if allowed to stand, would also control history. It would be a shame for the real history, the real story, of the saga, struggles, valor, and contributions of so many men and women who gave up so much to serve their country, to not be told. The real history of the aftermath from the discriminatory practices and policies of "Don't Ask, Don't Tell," imposed on patriots who did not seek fame, fortune, or notoriety. Those who only wanted nothing more than to serve their country. The memory of those muzzled, yet who paid the ultimate sacrifice, could never speak out again and would be lost to the hands of time.

Noah sat up and reached over to a picture on the desk. It was the last picture of him in his dress blue uniform. Thinking back, it had only been five years since it was taken yet seemed a world away. Time was already starting to fade the memories. So much had changed, including his hair that now had a touch of gray.

He set the picture back down, turning to the window, he watched as the wind rustled up the accumulating snow. Was it now time to break the restraints, remove the invisible gag, and let real history be told to the world? A quote he heard so many times came to mind, "Those who do not learn from the past are condemned to repeat it." Some had spoken out in defeat before. Would this time be the same? Regardless of the outcome, for posterity, the names and stories needed to be recorded. It was time to speak out for them. These warriors' voices should not remain in "Semper Silence."

1960's

Chapter 1

Vietnam

Sitting in back of the truck as rain poured from the sides, Lance Corporal Williams was miserable, and had been for days. This morning he and the rest of the unit were snagged for a mission to go recover some General he had never heard of. They were in a convoy, on the Highway 1, headed to Hue City. More specifically, a place called the MACV compound.

This was Williams' first trek away from Phu Bai since his arrival. Meric, sat next to him on the deuce and a half. "Tet Mau Than," he said out loud. Williams looked at him with a smirk and looked away. "Tet Mau Than," he said again. Williams, not understanding, was a bit agitated and turned to him, "What the hell are you saying?" Meric smiled, "Tet Mau Than, …It means the year of the Monkey. It's Vietnamese." Williams shook his head. Hogan, sitting across from the two, overheard and chimed in, "What the hell does he care? Don't be spreading your propaganda bullshit, just because your dipp'n your stick in some G**k!"

Hogan, who had been in country for a while, was at the end of his tour. He had become hardened from all he had seen. Addressing Williams, "You're a newbie, …" Williams trying to seem cool, "No, I've been in country for a while." Hogan, who had been chewing tobacco, …spit, "That wasn't a question, you're a newbie. … I can smell'm a mile away. Just like I can smell these rat bastard Vietcong." Spitting again, he continued, "I've seen your kind before, just like so many of the others, too many new guys."

About that time, they passed a burned-out tank, and the convoy almost seemed to go into slow motion. The charred bodies still remained in it. Williams, along with the others, stared on at the wreck. When he returned his view back to the vehicle, Hogan was grinning. "Got your attention, huh?" Williams was starting to feel uneasy. Hogan started back in, "If you are going to make it here, you got to pay attention to the small stuff. It's not the big stuff you have to worry about." Williams was puzzled by the comment. Hogan had his attention. "What you mean?" he asked Hogan, who now held his rifle with one hand and started pointing out things around him. "For the last few miles there's been no traffic, …no activity, …no people. It ain't right. These mother fuckers are busy all the time. When shit is quiet, it ain't right." Hogan had Williams' ear, and he was taking in every word, this guy was making sense. "You see any action?" Hogan chuckled, "What kinda fucking question is that? …Does a bear shit in the woods? Fuck, … all you newbies are the same." He shook his head and pointed out the side of the truck, "If this shit stay's the same, you'll have your answer. All you newbie's ask the same question. What you are really wondering, …do you have what it takes when the shit happens." Hogan paused long enough to spit out his tobacco. "Time comes, ... trust me you're going to have more action, and see more shit, than you'll ever want to! You won't be asking those questions; all you'll be doing is trying to forget!" Williams looked on at him in a stare. He was right. Williams was questioning himself. Did he have what it would take? He sat quietly along with the others looking out the back of the truck as it rained.

The Marines sat quietly for a while. Williams noticed a bridge they had crossed and were just leaving a village area when he heard it. Pop, pop, pop, and a few ricochets. The Marines ducked and hit the bed of the truck. The convoy had stopped. One Marine peeked out the side and pointed where the shots were coming from. Williams lifted his head briefly and could see the flash of the machine gun. The Marines jumped from the truck in a haste and took up a defense perimeter. Williams lay in the prone at the rear side of the truck. Off in the distant tree line, he could see movement, but wasn't sure what he was looking at. Meric yelled, "It's them!" Hogan hollered back, "How the hell do you know?" Meric, hollering back, "Because I dip my stick in some fucking G**k, asshole. Mother fucker, I can see the pith helmet, it's their uniform stupid ass!" Williams and the crew started returning fire. This was Williams' first time seeing the North Vietnamese in action, these guys knew what the fuck they were doing. The shooting continued, but word was given to move out on foot. As they maneuvered, the convoy trucks crept forward.

Mid to late afternoon the convoy made it to the compound. Williams wasn't impressed. He sat by a berm wall and changed his socks. Of all things from his boot camp training, changing his socks was what he had remembered to do after a long hump. After putting his boots back on, he took a piss, and refilled his canteens. The Staff Sergeant came around the berm wall, "Come on, we got some wounded to attend too." They carried the wounded into the triage area. Williams watched what was going on around him. He had never seen so much confusion and wounded bodies. The site of the bloody and the bandaged was unimaginable. Williams found himself in a trance. It was surreal. Things seemed to go by in slow motion. Not just now, but the entire day had seemed foreboding, as if something more ominous was yet to happen.

The Staff Sergeant gathered the crew. They were heading back out. For some reason, it seemed there was a miscommunication. They were going further on into Hue City to a place called the Citadel. This supposed General they were to escort was there, and the compound was just a stopping point. As the Marines grumbled, the Staff Sergeant grumbled back, "Well, they say a bitch'n Marine is a happy one, …glad I could make your day. Now get your shit together, we head out in twenty mikes!"

As they stepped off, second platoon, which was Williams' platoon, was the point. Other than an occasional sniper offering a pop and a crack, they made several turns and met little resistance. Williams was third back on the left column. He wasn't sure how much further they would have to go. They were given brief and vague directions and were playing mostly by chance. They reached Truong Tein bridge and huddled off to one of the side buildings. He could hear the pop from rounds flying. The Marines paused, checking gear, and getting a last-minute word from Bernie, who was acting lead. "Keep your distance, and no matter what keep going- even if someone goes down."

One by one they peeled off; Williams was up next. Across the way he could see bodies lying in the street. Williams, not realizing he was speaking out loud, "Holy fucking shit! It's Hogan. Is he dead?" Within seconds he heard the breakout of machine gun fire. The Marine behind him gave him a nudge. He took a quick glance; it was now or never. Off he went running. In his mind he kept thinking, …up, …you see me, … I'm down, until he could take cover by one of the iron pillars of the bridge.

The green tracer bullets were flying all around. Williams kept his focus on the Marines in front of him. He could see forward movement from Bernie making it across the bridge. Once again, Williams stood up and advanced forward. He saw one of the Marines in front of him fall, but he kept moving, taking a brief stop again behind one of the pillars. Bernie signaled to Williams to hold fast. About that time, he heard the M60 machine gun coming from behind. He looked back to see three Marines laying down suppressive fire. He looked in the direction of fire seeing a North Vietnamese machine gun bunker. Meric was off to his right and was carrying a radio. Meric dodging left, then right, came over to him. "Hold fast," he said as he approached, pointing to an army guy in the rear. From behind, an M55 .50 caliber duster started firing, clearing the street.

Once the firing ceased, Bernie, from up front, and another Marine, stood up and rushed the bunker throwing grenades and reeking all kinds of hell. As the fighting continued, Meric told Williams, "Come on let's get the wounded out of here." Williams spoke up, "But they told us to keep moving." Meric looked ahead, "Those guys got that shit under control, these guys need our help, …so fuck that." Meric started grabbing the wounded and taking them to a truck. Following Meric's lead, Williams started going after the wounded. One by one, he would grab and carry them to the rear of the bridge to safety, taking them out of harm's way. Williams wasn't sure how many trips he had made, he just kept retrieving the bodies. In his mind he kept saying, "I'm up, you see me, I'm down." He felt a sharp burn hit his back. He reached back trying to feel the burn when a ricochet bullet bounced off one of the steel pillars. He quickly ducked beside a guy laying below. The guy tried to speak but Williams couldn't understand what he was saying, other than the guy was a corpsman and was wounded. Williams grabbed him and threw him over his shoulder and took off running.

He was almost to the truck when an explosion happened. The blast threw him to the ground. He lay there for a moment looking up at the sky. The Corpsman he was carrying was still cradled around his shoulder. Williams' head was pounding, and his ears rang. He slowly uncoiled from the Corpsman, only to see a Marine, on the truck, firing a .50 caliber. Williams got himself together. The Corpsman he had been carrying was still alive. He picked him up and made it to the truck.

The guy firing the .50 caliber was the driver. He stopped firing, grabbed his crotch, and started screaming in the direction of the bridge, "Fuck you mother fuckers! Eat this you fucken bitches!" He turned to see Williams loading the Corpsman onto the truck. "You're hit man!" Williams looked up seeing his mouth moving but could not hear. The driver climbed over to him and pointed to his chest and arm. "You're hit man." Williams looked down seeing the blood, he became dizzy and nauseous. "Hop on man, we got to get the hell out of here!"

Later, Williams walked along with the truck. They came upon a movie theater. Ironically, the billboard outside was of American Cowboys. It seemed so out of place. For some reason though it had brought Williams back into check. He was seeing things clearly now. He lifted his head and focused forward. In the middle of all the chaos and confusion, he was totally aware of what was going on around him.

1970's

Chapter 2

The early years

Bratty kids

As the guests' paid their last respect to Marigold, they slowly trickled away. Beck stood in the distance overlooking the grave. Elana, Beck's sister, stood by the car at the edge of the graveyard, with the three young children. A middle aged, black-haired woman approached. It was Pat, Beck's sister-in-law. She was the sister of Marigold, Beck's wife, who had just passed. As she approached Elana, she started speaking, "You've taken a big chore raising those three kids." She turned and looked at Beck in the distance, "Look at him, he's all upset now, kind of crocodile tears now, isn't it?" before stopping in front of Elana. Elana, not wanting the children to hear what might be said, "You kids, go on now, go and get your father." Roman and Trina took off, but Noah stepped aside and hid behind Elana. Pat continued, "I hope you're not looking for any help with them. Hell, he was barely around when she was alive." Elana was an immensely proud woman. " I know my brother. If I need him, he'll be there! Besides, I gave my word to Marigold. I told her I would see these kids raised. No need to make these children suffer any further. As long as I'm alive they'll have a home. She knew Beck couldn't do it alone, and that is why she came to me." Pat smirked, as her and her husband started to hobble along. "Good luck with that, …I hope you're right. Tell that to his ex-wife with his other six children. If it weren't for that woman in the grave right there, …they would have never received anything. Marigold was the one who made sure those kids had food on the table." Elana was agitated, "I'm doing it for the children. You know being a Christian, it's the right thing to do." Pat continued to move along to her car. As she opened the door she turned to Elana and raised her voice. "All I know is I have raised my kids, and I don't have room for three trashy, bratty, snot nose kids in my home. Like I said, good luck with that." As she got in the car, Elana realized Noah was standing behind her and heard what was going on. "Honey don't pay her no mind. She is just a bitter old soul, and we'll have to pray for her."

Beck and La Mora

Her beauty was noted by several pageant titles she had won, most of them, the first for a woman of color. La Mora was a tall, slender, long black haired, African American woman in her late 30's. Having studied engineering at the University of Texas, she was well educated. She was confident and comfortable in her smarts, and beauty. An original hire out of Detroit, she transferred to the Blotch location to be close to her retired parents. She was of mixed race, her father being African American, and her mother was white. She was often referred to as Mulatto. If asked what race she was, she would just say La Mora. She refused to be put in a box and would often say, 'Let them choose whatever they want me to be.' As Supervisor, she had a different set of rules; The big one was she wasn't in a Union job. That being said, the visible perks were she had a separate desk overlooking the ladies on the line and wasn't required to wear any uniform or hair covering. These perks were good, however at times, her beauty and position could draw unwanted, unwarranted attention, and entanglements from the gentlemen folk passing by.

As Zone committee man, it was routine for Beck to walk the departments throughout the day. He spent most of his time enforcing and negotiating contract discrepancies between Supervisor, Foreman, and Union employees. Many times, it was minor things like making sure employees were getting their proper break, lunch time, or the proper safety gear to do the task at hand. Other times it could require real skill and tact on his part to save some from being fired. Today, in particular, was a busy day as Beck stopped by various assembly lines to inspect and take in any concerns. He had just come around the corner of the electric starter department when he saw La Mora standing at her desk. Was she new, or had he just not noticed her before? He couldn't be sure without seeing her face. He continued to walk by trying not to make an obvious stare. At the next line over, he pulled out a clip board and pretended as though he was reviewing a checklist. While he held on to the board, he was more preoccupied with admiring La Mora and her doings. Hoping for a chance to get a glimpse of her face, he was contemplating how he could introduce himself. Another Foreman came up and spoke to her, as they exchanged conversation, she was now facing Beck. She was even prettier than he thought and quite stunning. Her jet-black hair went straight back in a slight bouffant and fell to shoulder length with a flip curl at the very bottom. Her smooth olive-skinned, heart shaped face, complimented by the golden necklace and earrings she wore, was perfection. Exotic in looks, with her red, thick, full lips, along with large green eyes that could have been stolen from a wild cat, she beamed from across the room. She must be Mediterranean, he thought. He had never seen the likes of her around here before.

While admiring her beauty, he realized she was looking at him. He had been caught. He nodded and smiled at her, she grinned and returned to the conversation with the Foreman. He hovered in the area as though observing the workers, giving an occasional glance to La Mora. She had finally finished, and started speaking to Big Red. This was his chance; he knew Big Red.

He immediately seized the moment and headed over. "Good morning, ladies, welcome back! Hope you all got to enjoy your time off." Dot, working on the line was briefly startled, quickly turned, and let out one of her big laughs, "Scream'n Barlow I just love you, how the hell are you?" He knew each of the ladies by name and spoke to them as he worked his way toward Big Red and La Mora. Once he arrived, Big Red stopped talking and made the first move reaching out to give Beck a hug, "Well there's my handsome man, how you doing honey?" Beck hugged her back, "I'm doing well, got to see your Daddy. He came out to look at a few dogs." Big Red responded back, "I know Momma told me. She isn't too happy about him getting an ole coon hound, but she said if it stays outside, she'll be fine with it. She isn't happy with you either. She's going to take part of your ear the next time she sees you. It's a topic of much contention. Hah, after all these years, ... she's worried he might get away from her, and he'll use the excuse he's going hunting to hang out in bars." Beck chuckled and looked at La Mora, noticing she was taking in the conversation. "Hello, I'm Beck and you must be?" Big Red, realizing they had not met, "Oh I'm sorry, here I am just carrying on like a fool. Beck this is La Mora Thompson she is our new Supervisor. La Mora this is Beck Barlow, our Zone Committee man, or better known as 'Scream'n Barlow'."

La Mora held out her hand very lady like, "Nice to meet you Beck." Beck, not looking away from her eyes and smile, "Nice to meet you. So, you're new here?" La Mora replied, "New to the factory, but not to GM. I'm a transfer from Detroit." Beck hung on every word as she spoke "Detroit, so you must be in a bit of a shock, leaving a big city to come here to Blotch." "My parents live and work here. You might know them, Ollie, and Lola Thompson. They both worked for GM for years but have now retired." Beck was a bit confused because he knew Ollie, a black man, that worked in plant 15. "I know an Ollie that worked over in plant 15 years ago when I was just starting out, but I don't think he's the one." La Mora quickly validated with a smile "Daddy worked in 15 back in the sixties. I'd come home from college on break, I remember going over to meet him on his lunch hour. He worked in skilled trades." Beck, still a bit confused, was totally smitten by her. "I remember Ollie talking about his daughter. How proud he was to be able to give her a good education. I believe he said she was in college down in Texas, somewhere, and she won all kinds of beauty contests. I remember, whenever she won, he came in and said she's done it again." La Mora blushing with a grin, "Oh yeah, that's my Daddy."

Beck decided it was best not to address the question that piqued his curiosity Was she black? Regardless, it didn't matter. Beck having taken up enough time, "It was a pleasure meeting you and welcome to your new town. Tell Ollie, Scream'n Barlow says hello!" He turned to Big Red, "And you, always nice seeing you! Tell your mom, Barlow hasn't sold him one yet, last time I checked, I have two ears, and I would like to keep them." She chuckled with a grin as he went on his way.

At the exit door, he looked back, and La Mora was still looking at him with a grin. He smiled, nodded his head with a wave disappearing through the double doors.

Chapter 3

The heart doesn't always know what is right.

Combat Correspondent

The kitchen door flung open and what had been a quiet room was now filled with laughter and antics. Trina, Roman, Don, and Noah, all bustled to get their winter coats and boots off. From the living room came Elana, with Bill behind her, the kids could not help but hear the end of the conversation between the two of them. As they approached, the kids quieted. Bill was furious, "Elana, I'm telling you, he better not bring that N****r here to my house!" Elana stopped in her tracks and turned to him. "Bill! ... not in front of these kids!" Bill pointed his finger at her and came a little closer, "What? You think that is bad? ... What do you think they'll hear if he marries her. Well, I got news for you, what they'll hear is a lot worse, and who knows what will be done to them!" The kids were startled by the conversation never hearing Uncle Bill talk in such a manner. Roman tried to intervene, "Aunt Elana, what's going on, is everything all right?" Elana turned to him, and Bill stormed off in the other direction. Elana put her hand on Roman's shoulder, "Hush, now, ...don't worry, it's a comment that should have been left between adults." She turned and looked in the direction of where Bill once stood, pausing briefly before returning her focus on the kids. "You kids make sure you hang up your wet socks by the register so the warm air can dry them out. Once you're done, go change into dry clothes and bring down the wet stuff. I'll need to get them washed, and in the dryer. Lunch will be ready soon, and I have some things I need to talk to you kids about. That can wait for now. So, off you go!"

Lunch was ready in no time, and Aunt Elana was calling for the kids to come help set the table. Soon they were all sitting down. Uncle Bill always sat at the head with Aunt Elana to his right, while the rest took their seats around the table. As a requirement, Uncle Bill approved the meal, and asked, "Mother shall we say grace?" Elana smiled and directed one of the kids to say grace. "Trina, why don't you say the blessing."

Trina said Grace, and Elana prepared Bill's plate first, before passing the dish. Once this was complete, conversations were permitted to begin. Everyone's participation was encouraged.

Lunch was almost over, and Elana asked for Trina, Roman and Noah to stay seated, she wanted to talk to them. Beulah, one of Beck's daughters from another marriage, lived with Elana as well. Elana had already briefed her on their father's situation, and she decided not to visit for the weekend. Everyone else had been dismissed and Uncle Bill had excused himself from the table.

Aunt Elana liked to smile and had a comforting way about her as she spoke. "I spoke to your father this morning, and he is wanting to come and get you three for a weekend visit. Does that sound good?" All three shook their heads, as she continued, "He tells me he has met someone and wants you three to meet her. Is that going to be all right?" The three sat quietly.

This would be the second time they had seen their father with another woman since their mother's death. The first one was a lady named Sandy, and when they went to visit, they stayed at her house the whole-time watching TV. During the day, their father and her stayed in the bedroom, and at night, the two went out to the bars.

Roman smarted off, "Is that the N****r Uncle Bill is talking about?" Elana was stunned by Roman's words. "You know I don't tolerate that kind of language, and your Uncle Bill should have never used it. I believe the word your dad called her is mulatto. She is half black and half white." Roman smarted back angry at Elana, but angrier at his father, "So, she is, a N****r!" He stood up and started to walk away from the table. Elana stood up, "You stop right there young man! Do I have to call your uncle in here?" Before she had finished her sentence, Uncle Bill was standing at the other end of the table. "Boy stop right there!" Roman stopped, and looked at him, "What, you're allowed to say it, and I can't?" Bill looked at Elana, "I told you this was going to amount to no good!" Beulah returned to the room teasing Roman, "You're going to have a colored woman as your Momma. " knowing she was adding fuel to the fire. Roman angrily started to speak, "You can whip me, beat me, I don't care, I'm not going to visit, and she will never be my mother." Elana still standing across the table, shook her head at Bill and waved her hand, hollering out, "Beulah Ann, why would you come in here and do that?" She tried to calm things down. "…Roman, of course she won't be your mom, …and if you don't want to meet her, I'll let your dad know. You don't have to. No one is going to force you." Roman looked at Uncle Bill, "Can I be excused now?" Elana nodded to Bill, Bill calmly spoke, "It's ok, you can go."

Elana looked to Trina and Noah, "Do you two feel the same? If so, I'll tell your dad not to bother." Trina spoke out, "I would like to see my dad." She looked to Noah, "and you?" "I would like to see my dad Aunt Elana, but I don't want to make anybody mad." Elana smiled, as she came over and gave him a hug. "You are always welcome to go see your dad, and no one has a right to be mad at you for doing so." She motioned for Trina to come over as she grabbed both, giving a huge hug. "He's your father and that is something no one can ever change."

It was the weekend and Beck had arrived. He gave the keys to Noah and told him, along with his sister, to get their bags and load them up in the trunk. Elana sat down; Beck joined her. "I suppose you have noticed by now that your other son is missing and hasn't changed his mind." Beck looked around, "Where's he at? I'll go talk to him." Elana, interjected, "He's not here, and I thought it best not to be. He is dealing with bigger things than you think right now, and this new woman has just added to it. Beck, he's a growing boy and is becoming his own man. Losing his mother and not having his father around is affecting him a bit more profoundly than the younger two. He'll need time. He is resentful of you right now." Beck interrupted, "That's hogwash Elana, spare the rod and spoil the child. You're being too sensitive and allowing him to push you around." Elana, interrupted with a bold stare down, "They're your children Beck…, if you don't like the way I'm raising them, then step-up!" Beck realized he had ruffled some feathers, "Elana, that is not what I'm saying, I'm thankful for what you're doing, and when I get back on my feet, I plan on bringing them home. I just need more time." Elana reached across the table and grabbed Beck's hand. "You mean you need more time to find a suitable mother. Beck, I know it's hard on you right now, but you don't have to rush to find another woman. I have grown fond of these children and love them just as my own. I made a promise to their mom, as long as I live, I will make sure these children have a home." Beck lowered his head and she raised it with her hand on his chin, "… I would never allow them to go with just any woman. So don't marry the first one that comes along, just so you can try and get the kids back home. Take your time and the right one will come along."

It was early evening before Beck made it back on the road, with Trina and little Noah in tow. The drive back to Blotch was about 45 minutes, so Beck decided to tell them about La Mora, after all, they would be spending the weekend with her.

"So, what's been happening at school? Your Aunt has told me you both have been doing well." Trina spoke up. "All the girls in my home economics class made dresses. When we finished at the end of the project the mothers were invited in for a fashion show, and we all got to model our dresses. Aunt Elana came, being that mom isn't here." Beck smiled, "So how did it turn out?" Trina perked up, "I got an A on the project. Cousins Shelly and Paige helped me. They both are really good at sewing." Beck focusing on the road, "I bet it was beautiful. Your Mom would be proud of you." Beck changing the subject to Noah, "What about you, what have you been up to?" Noah, sitting in the back seat looking out the window, turned his attention inward and sat up. "Oh, …not much. Just getting used to the kids in my class. …I don't like David, he's mean. But he treats me fine, I think he's afraid of me because I'm bigger than him. But he picks on other kids." Beck frowned a bit. "Don't be getting into fights. …But if he picks on you or you see him doing it to others, let the teacher know. What about your teacher, do you like her?" Noah looked back out the window. "Yeah, her name is Mrs. Christensen, she's old. We're doing reports on famous people in Indiana history." Beck, focusing on the road ahead, "I believe I met her, she came to your mom's funeral. That was nice of her. So, who are you doing your report on?" Noah looked back at his dad. "Ernie Pyle. He was a combat war correspondent during WWII." Beck puzzled, not familiar with who he was talking about. "That's kind of a big word for a young fella like you. Can you help an old man out? …Was he in the military? … like Gomer Pyle?" Noah chuckled, along with Trina. "No, Gomer Pyle was in the Marines, and isn't real. Ernie Pyle was a real person who photographed and reported on the war. He traveled with the military guys reporting on how they were doing. I think it would be exciting to do that. I would like to be like him when I grow up." Beck was surprised by what he was hearing. "That sounds kind of dangerous, are you sure you can handle that?" Noah started losing interest, "Yeah, I suppose so." As he turned and looked back out the window.

Beck decided now was the time to bring up the subject of La Mora. "I have some news. I have met a new lady, and we have started dating." Trina spoke up. "We know, Aunt Elana told us about her." Beck nodded his head. "So, what did she tell you?" Trina started in. "Not much really, it was more of what we overheard her and Uncle Bill arguing about. We weren't supposed to hear." Beck was now listening "And what was it you heard?" Trina continued, "Well, he said some things it wouldn't be nice for me too repeat, but he said you're dating a black lady. Aunt Elana said if we didn't want to go with you to meet her, we didn't have too."

Beck sat for a moment contemplating what to say, before speaking. "Really, … I can imagine what Ole Bill Butler said. …Mr. Christian, … right!" as he shook his head in disbelief. Trina started back in, "he says he served with them in Korea, and they have a stench, and no matter how much they wash, it won't go away, and they won't come clean. Then he says the bible is against it. Says that's what happened at the Tower of Babel. God didn't want the races to mix, so he separated them, and they all started speaking separate tongues."

Beck turned and frowned at her, not sure how to take what she was saying. He was ambiguous as to whether she was telling him or schooling him. Regardless, he didn't like it, and he didn't like what they were being taught. "Listen to me, …There is more than one way of seeing things, and not everything is exactly how you hear, or made to believe. Bill Butler is not the last word on these matters. God loves all his people. Regardless of race. God wants us to love our neighbors as we love ourselves. I'm your father and as far as dating a woman, it doesn't matter what race she is, what matters is if we love each other. You understand me?" Trina nodded her head in agreement. Beck spoke out to Noah, "How about you young man, you understand?" Noah turned to look at his dad driving, "I guess, ... I mean, I don't know, ... it sounds like a bunch of grown-up stuff. I find it boring. I like everybody, ... well not everybody, I don't like Kevin at school. He's a bully, and he picks his nose when he thinks nobody is watching and then he wipes it under his desk" Trina, laughed turning to look at Noah before speaking, "That's gross, ...I caught you picking your nose before." Noah came back, "You did not!" Trina, "Oh yes I did, I seen you wipe it on the couch." Noah came back, "That's a lie! You take it back, Dad she is lying, make her take it back." Beck chuckled, "I'm not in it." Noah turned to Trina, "You take it back, or I'll pick one right now and wipe it on you!" Trina leaned forward trying to get away as Noah moved forward like he was going to do it, when Beck interrupted. "Alright, alright, calm down. Noah knock it off!" Trina turned around and straightened up. "I'm trying to drive here, don't make me pull this car over!" Both shut up and sat up straight in their seats, knowing if the car was to be pulled over, things would get serious very quickly.

Beck sat thinking; it was more of a conversation than he had really planned on. Neither Trina or Noah needed to be bothered with this, and really were not old enough to comprehend. "Well, La Mora and I are dating, and I really like her. I hope you two will as well." Trina asked, "So is she black?" Beck turned to her, "It doesn't matter now does it?" Trina thought for a moment. "No, I guess not. ...Is she nice? What about us, will she be nice to us? Does she have any kids?" Beck interrupted, "Whoa, whoa, whoa, ... Slow down Sally Jane... Whoa, allow me to answer the first one. Yes, she is nice, and she treats me very well. As for how she will treat you, this was her idea. She wanted to meet you kids, and she is excited, and thrilled you are coming. She does have one child, a daughter, her name is

April. She is about your age, and she will be there as well. So, we will all be together at one time." Trina interrupted, "Except Roman, ...Roman won't be there, ...so we won't all be there." Beck nodded, "No, Roman won't be there, but that's because he chose not to be, ... but that might change over time." Trina turned and looked out the window, "I don't think so." Paused, "...April, I like the name April."

You have a beautiful daughter

As the evening sun was setting, Beck pulled the Cadillac into the drive of La Mora's small ranch style home. From inside the car Beck spoke, "We're here. This is La Mora's and where we'll be staying the weekend." The front screen door opened and there appeared a tall black-haired woman. Trina spoke up, "Is that her? She's beautiful!" Beck was amazed himself, "Yes, ...yes she is beautiful." He quickly focused back on the kids. "Now I want you two to be on your best behavior. She's nice, but don't take advantage of her, and Nollie, don't be asking a bunch of questions. It's not polite."

Beck opened the door and hopped out. Trina and Noah both followed behind him. He walked to the door and gave her a slight kiss and gentle embrace before she spoke. "It'll be alright," as she looked him in the eye and smiled. Beck turned to Trina and Noah, "La Mora, these are two of my children." Trina stepped forward, "Nice to meet you Ma'am," and stuck her hand out. La Mora reached for her hand and shook it. "Nice to meet you, ...Trina, did I get that right?" Trina shook her head yes. La Mora continued, "You're just as pretty as your dad said you were. My, you are a pretty one now, aren't you?" Trina smiled, "Thank you Ms. La Mora. I told Daddy I thought you were pretty as well." Trina giggled and shied away. "I have a daughter also, she is just about your age, you'll get to meet her in just a minute." La Mora turned to Noah, "And who is this handsome young man?" Beck spoke, "This is my son Nollie." Nollie grabbed onto his dad's coat and cowered a bit behind him. Beck pushed him forward. "Go on now, introduce yourself." Noah put his hand out hesitantly, "Hi I'm Nollie, nice to meet you ma'am!" She shook his hand, "Nice to meet you..." but before she could finish, he quickly took it back and hid behind his dad again. "You must be shy?" Beck, chuckled, "Oh, just when he first meets someone. Once he knows you, he won't be quiet." Noah looked at her still deciding whether he liked her or not. La Mora, turned to the house, "Welcome to my home, and you kids sure are welcome here. Let's get in out of this cold." They started walking to the door when Noah whispered to Trina, thinking only they would hear. "She doesn't look like she is black to me." Beck turned and shushed him, but La Mora heard, "That's alright, I get that all the time. No need to be quiet about it." She smiled and opened the door and they entered. Noah softly said, "I don't understand why everyone is so upset."

The next day at breakfast, plans were made for the day. It was decided Beck would take Nollie with him to attend a hunting event at the local Hunters club, while La Mora would take Trina and April for a lady's day out.

The afternoon at the mall seemed to be going well. La Mora noticed Trina and April getting along quite nicely. They decided to go into the shops and look at dresses. After ruffling through, Trina found one she really liked, "This one is pretty, I like it!" La Mora smiled, "Honey, would you like to try it on?" They took it to the dressing room attendant. The lady attendant unlocked the room and waited with La Mora and April. Trina made herself ready and, after a few moments, appeared in a light blue lace dress. La Mora held her hands up, "Oh how pretty! Do you like it?" Trina blushed but before she could reply, the attendant spoke, "I think you are the prettiest little colored girl I've ever seen. Why if I didn't know better, I wouldn't even suspect she's colored." The attendant looked at Trina, "Oh, I see it now, … you do look a lot like your Mommy, don't you?" Trina looked at La Mora not knowing how to respond. April chuckled, "Oh, that's not her Momma. That's mine, …she is my Momma's boyfriend's daughter." The lady looked at her, and then back at La Mora, "Oh I'm sorry, but she does resemble you. …with that pretty black hair, and that olive skin, I just assumed she was your daughter. But you must admit for a black child she sure is pretty."

Trina realized what was being said, and started to frown, realizing this lady was assuming she was black. La Mora, trying to move past the awkward encounter, decided to ignore the lady's comments, "Trina, why don't you go ahead and change back over, honey. If you want the dress we can get it, I'm sure your daddy won't mind." Trina's mood had changed, "No thank you Ma'am, I'll be fine." She returned to the room. On her way out she hung the dress back up on the clothes return and passed the attendant and stopped briefly, "Just so you know, I'm not colored, neither is my daddy! If I was it wouldn't really matter, pretty is pretty now, isn't it?" The attendant was startled a child would speak to her in such a manner. La Mora overheard and approached, placing her hand on Trina's shoulder. The attendant gasped and without any shame, "Well honey, if your daddy is dating a colored woman, you might as well be! You better get used to it." La Mora nudged Trina, "Come on now, no need for this, …nothing we want in here anyway!" The three left the shop as Trina gave the attendant a brow beating stare.

La Mora couldn't help but notice Trina had hardly spoken since leaving the store. She had hoped it hadn't scared her away leaving any negative feelings or resentment toward her. As they arrived at the house, Beck and Nollie were waiting inside. The kids scattered into various rooms as La Mora made her way to the kitchen. Beck had noticed the quietness when the three had arrived back home. He walked into the kitchen, "Hey welcome home." La Mora smiled as he gave her a kiss. She smiled and began putting things away. "How was your day at the hunters' club?" He grabbed tea from the fridge and fixed a glass. "Good, Old Frosty Wise made it down. Haven't seen him since he had his stroke. His son brought him. I think it did him some good to see all the fellas. He has some trouble getting around, and it's kind of hard understanding what he is saying, his speech is a little affected. Other than that, it was just a bunch of men talking bull, …What about you?" La Mora paused for a moment at the counter, and smirked, "You're not the only one trying to understand someone's speech, …the difference being, …I could understand every word she said, but can't understand how someone can be so ignorant. Unfortunately, your daughter had to experience it too." Beck looking confused and concerned, "What,

…what are you talking about?" La Mora stopped what she was doing. "Your daughter, she experienced what it was to be black firsthand today, …Oh I don't want to get into it again. It was nothing, just a stupid lady at the mall, talking out of her head. She thought she was paying a compliment but had no idea she was being insulting." Beck looked puzzled, "Ok La Mora, I don't understand, you're going to have to explain, is everyone alright?" La Mora, chuckled, "Of course I'm alright, it was just a normal occurrence for me, but your daughter, I don't think she understood. She was awful quiet on the ride home." Beck was still confused, "Ok, break it down, what happened." La Mora chuckled, "Of course you don't, you're white. You've never had to experience unaware, back handed compliments." Beck interrupted as he moved over to her and grabbed her hands, "Whoa, whoa, whoa, look you're right, I may not have the experience, but I won't learn if you don't tell me. Come on now, explain it to me, if we are going to be together, I need to understand."

La Mora smirked and began explaining the event that had taken place at the mall. When she finished, Beck, finally understood, "So, … did you try to talk to Trina?" La Mora continued, "I did a little, but I didn't want to push it, …I couldn't tell if she was upset with the lady, or with me. I think maybe a little of both." Beck sat quiet for a moment, "Well you didn't do anything wrong, …the lady was out of line. As for Trina, I'll have a talk with her. But the lady was right, she is a pretty girl, and although you may not be her mom, you're a beautiful lady as well." As he grabbed La Mora and brought her close to him, La Mora pushed back gently, trying to resist a bit, "You forgot to add, for a colored lady…" Beck pulled her close and face to face, "No, I didn't forget," as he softly kissed her, "because you are beautiful period."

Sunday afternoon came and it was time to gather the kids' things and get ready to take them back home. La Mora walked them to the car. Nollie spoke up, "Thank you for allowing us to stay at your house Ms. La Mora." La Mora smiled and gave him a hug, and turned to Trina, "And you, can I get a hug from you as well?" Trina gave her a hug and quickly got into the car without saying anything. Beck, noticing her cold reaction, kissed La Mora goodbye, "Give it time…" He pecked her on the cheek and hopped in the car. As they pulled off, La Mora waved until they were out of sight.

The drive home was quiet. For the kids, it was a realization they now lived with Aunt Elana, and no longer at home with both parents. There was an unspoken absence, a reality their mother was gone, and she was not coming back. About halfway through the ride, Trina spoke out. "Do you miss her?" Beck was taken off guard. "Who me?" Trina spoke up, "Yes, you. Do you ever miss her?" Beck responded without hesitation, "Of course I do, all the time, and more than you could ever know! Why, do you think I wouldn't?" Trina sat for a moment, "Well, sometimes it seems like you have forgotten her, and maybe you have forgotten us." Beck was stunned, but at the same time, surprised how mature she had become. "No, I haven't forgotten her, and I have definitely not forgotten you kids, why do you think that?" Trina, deciding not to hold back, "Because you say you'll show up to get us, then at the last-minute, change your mind, then we find out you've been with some other woman and her kids doing things." Beck became defensive, "I have had to cancel, but where do you get, I am spending it with other women and people's kids?" Trina quickly spoke up, "Aunt Elana, she tells us everything, she doesn't do it intentionally, but we overhear her talking, and we find out…" Beck interrupted, "Hold up young lady, …first you shouldn't believe everything you hear. I'll have a talk with your aunt. …and am I supposed to start answering to you now? Don't forget you don't know everything. Who I see and what I do is not of your concern, don't forget I am the adult here and your father!" Trina turned her head facing the window and said quietly, "Then act like it…" Beck could hardly hear." Excuse me what did you say?" Trina shrugged and ignored his question. Beck let it go as he focused back on the road.

Upon arriving at Elana's, Beck opened the trunk, and the kids began bringing in their things. Beck walked to the door and the kids rushed in. Elana was waiting to give them a hug, before sending them on their way. Beck spoke, "Can we speak for a moment?" the two went into the kitchen. Beck opened his wallet and gave her some money before he began to speak. "The visit went well. They seemed to get along well with La Mora." Elana smiled, "Well, I'm glad to hear. I'm sure she is a nice lady." Beck interrupted, "Elana, I need to ask you to be careful what you might say around the kids, regarding me. Trina is at a stage where she is absorbing everything and isn't afraid of sharing her own opinion, but it's not quite accurate." Elana gasped. "Well, if she is hearing it from me, I can assure you it is correct. … and by the way, she is becoming a beautiful young lady, and smart too. So, don't discredit her observations as someone else's. She is quite able to form an opinion. She is growing up Beck. All these kids are. They're not up here at my house just sitting on a shelf until you figure the world out. Their lives continue whether you're in it, or not. They know when you're supposed to be here, and they know when you don't show up! I'm not going to make excuses when you don't." Beck raised his hand stepping back, "Ok, Ok Elana, I get it, … just please, I'm asking, can you be a little more aware of what is said in front of them?"

Elana stood quiet with her head tilted in disgust. Beck paused and stared back for a moment, realizing this was a battle he could not win, "I should let you know, there was an incident when Trina went to the mall with La Mora." Elana quickly came to life, "Oh no Beck, you didn't… use your head." Beck interrupted, "Elana, Elana, calm down, let me finish, please let me finish!" Elana rambled for a moment before letting him continue. Beck explained the episode to Elana. He finished with "There was a little bit of a confrontation. That's all. La Mora handled it." Elana rolled her eyes, "Beck are you listening to yourself. Really, La Mora handled it? Your daughter is being mistaken for a black girl, and you think that is no big deal? Really? Is, this how you want your kids brought up?" Beck sat down at the table while she continued. "Thank God Bill isn't hearing this, … I'm not sure how he would react. Is this how you want them to be treated when they go somewhere with her. It might have just been a slur, …a misunderstanding, or something that was really no big deal this time, but Beck it is. You don't know what could happen to them. You think this is about you dating a black woman! I don't care about her being black. I care about the prejudices you and your kids will be put through. Prejudice, that you and your love can do nothing about. You can't control it, and after all these kids have been through with losing their mother, you can't ask your kids to go through that as well. Beck you have got to slow down. Stop, just stop, and think about what you are doing." Beck sat for a moment, "I love her Elana, I can't help it." Elana stood across the room and stared at him before speaking. "The heart doesn't always know what is right. You fell in love, learn to fall out, … Use your head Beck, my God use your head!"

1980's

Chapter 4

Why the Marine Corps?

The military recruiting offices were housed in a former Motel. It still had that mid-century modern look with open staircases, and doors all opening into the courtyard. The pool had been replaced with cement benches, planters, and trash cans. At the end of the courtyard, Nollie and Von walked out a glass door with a big Navy sign above it.

Von sat down on a bench and looked up to the sky in exhaustion. "Wow, …I mean WOW, …that was intense!" Noah chuckled, "What did you expect? They're serious, …get used to it! My sister says they are all in it for themselves and, not to be trusted. Don't believe anything they have to say, you aren't anything but a number." Von, a bit perturbed, "Yeah! …. well, what'd you expect from someone who likes to smoke pot, braid her hair and parade around all day in tie-dyed shirts! You know, I'm not sure if she even knows the war is over or is she still on an acid trip?" Nollie replied in her defense. "You do know she lost quite a few friends in Vietnam, including an uncle? She says those friends who made it back are all fucked up or messed up in the head." Von stopped looking around and focused on Nollie. "So what? Become one of those people who don't believe in war?" Noah looked at him, "I believe they're called conscientious objectors, and I'm not saying run to Canada to avoid war." Von continued, "There are no jobs around here. GM is closing down. All school did was push us through to get a factory job. Who knew they would all be going away? We are not prepared for college. Everyone thought we would just graduate and go work in the factory. You know my dad was in the Navy, back in the day? I think it would make him proud." Nollie let out a sigh, "Who you trying to convince, you or me?" as he leaned on the planter box. Noticing the Marine recruiting sign, he reads it out loud, "Join the Marines, they're looking for a few good men." He sarcastically responded, "Hell, if you're going to join the military, why pussy around? Join the fucking Marines! If you want a death wish, they're bad ass! Just do it and get it the fuck over with!" Von interrupted, "Yeah, and first to die!"

Nollie stood up and started walking briskly toward the Marine recruiter's office. Von shouted out, "Point made! Hah, hah, ...very funny." Nollie turned to Von as he opened the Marine recruitment door, "Besides they have the best uniforms!" Von caught up, "Yeah, yeah, I know you won't do anything, 'cause they don't allow homos in!"

Are you a Homosexual?

It was dark outside, and Noah stood in the dining room looking down the country road for any sign of visible head lights. Gunny Kincaid said he would be there around 3:30 AM to pick him up. Today was the day he would be going to take his entrance exams into the Marine Corps. Noah heard some noise and turned to see his father heading to the kitchen. "You're up early. Better get used to it, they get up early in the Marines." Noah smiled and stared on down the road. His father rustled around the kitchen for a moment, returning with a cup of coffee, and looked at his watch. "He better get here soon, Indianapolis is a long drive," and joined Noah in staring down the country road. Noah, gave him a brief glance, "He said he had another guy to pick up first, and then me." Beck looked at Noah, "You sure this is what you want to do? You know you can still back out." Verifying, one more time, that Noah still had a choice. Noah didn't say anything, just nodded his head yes. Beck started to walk away, "As long as you know it's your choice, not anyone else's." Noah continued standing at the window until he saw head lights coming down the road. The car was soon pulling into the drive. Noah turned to Beck sitting in his living room chair, "It's him. It's supposed to be a two-day process. I should be back tomorrow if all goes well. Wish me luck." Beck got up, pulled out his wallet, "Here take this, you might need a soda or something to eat down there today." Noah chuckled, "No dad, I'm good, they provide us with a lunch." Beck pushed it at him, "You never know, here take it anyway." Noah took the twenty, "Ok, Thanks," and headed out the door. Beck returned to his chair and took another sip of his coffee and stared into the quietness. With Noah leaving, this was the way things were going to be. For the first time in 28 years, he would have a house without any kids in it. It would be just him and Claudia home alone.

Once in Indy, Noah was checked in and the paperwork began. It seemed endless and kept coming so quickly, he wasn't even sure what it was he was signing at times. The instructor handed out one form called "Character and Social Adjustment." He would read each statement and explain it. Noah was to answer yes or no. A couple of questions in, the instructor read out loud. "Next, Question C. Are you a homosexual or a bisexual?" He went on to define it. "Homosexual is defined as sexual desire or behavior directed at a person of one's own sex. Bisexual is defined as a person sexually responsive to both sexes." Noah paused, as thoughts ran through his head. He had never been asked this question directly. How would they know whether someone was or not? How could they tell if he just said no. The next question went one step further as the instructor read it out loud. "Next, Question D. Do you intend to engage in homosexual acts? Defined as 'Sexual relations with another person of the same sex'." Deep down, Noah knew the answer. He had never been asked directly or requested to make a statement on the topic. He couldn't say for sure; he had never been with anyone, male or female. Even if he was, he would be too terrified to admit it, especially with all the jokes being made in the room from other candidates. He answered no, and quickly sat back in his chair and gave hollow laughs along with the others making sure he blended in.

The rest of the day consisted of the ASVAB test and then onto the physical exam. All was complete and Noah was now a qualified candidate for the United States Marine Corps. His scores qualified him for the job he wanted, Photography. As long as he maintained his current situation and graduated from high school, he would be guaranteed entry, and that specific job. The recruiter explained everything to him on the ride back home. For now, he was delayed entry, and would be required to check in monthly and maintain contact with the recruiter. Once he graduated, he would be given a departure date and be sent to recruit training. Noah couldn't wait to get home to tell everyone.

Noah looked out at the cornfields as they drove by. Wow, he was actually going to become a Marine. If he could just maintain the status quo for the next year, he would be given the chance to prove himself. He still had the biggest obstacle of all, Marine Corps Recruit Training, or "Boot Camp."

It was October and fall had set in. The cornfields were tilled and barren, and the seasonal changes of the trees were taking hold. Things had not gone as planned. Noah and his father had a falling out. He had been staying with his sister Trina and driving to work and school. He had not seen his father in over a month. He was no longer able to complete the required chores at home. Going to school during the day and working at night took its toll on Noah. His attendance had dropped to a point where he had gotten himself in trouble at school. His father grew angry dealing with empty nest syndrome, realizing this is what it would be like once Noah had gone. Upon his father finding out, he called the recruiter hoping to stop Noah from going into the Marines. Receiving a call from Beck sent up a red flag with the recruiter. The recruiter reached out and called Noah to find out what was going on. Noah explained his father was going through empty nest syndrome. With Noah in jeopardy at school, the recruiter offered him a solution. If Noah quit school, he could still join the Corps, but he would lose his guaranteed job. The Marine Corps would decide where they needed him the most. All this could be done without his father's approval. He would leave for recruit training immediately. Noah agreed.

Noah sat at the airport waiting on his plane. He wasn't sure if he would get to see anyone from his family or not. He had told Trina he was leaving, but still had no communication with his father. He looked at the clock when the TWA flight attendant came across the speaker and started pre-boarding for his flight. Noah had never flown before. This would be his first flight. Unfamiliar with the process, he got up and started moving toward the gate when he heard his name called out. He turned to see Trina hustling to make it to him. He smiled as she approached. Giving him a hug, "I thought we were going to miss you!" Noah laughed and stepped back, "What do you mean we? I only see you." Trina turned to look behind her and started waving. Noah looked in the distance and could see his father and stepmother Claudia, along with his sister Beulah approaching. Trina turned back to Noah. "Don't say a word! He really is upset you're leaving." Over the speaker, final boarding for his flight was announced. Noah turned to his father. His Dad was fighting back the tears. "Did you think we were going to let you get outta here without a goodbye?" Noah teared up, "No Sir!" The two hugged quickly. Noah stepped back, "Sorry, I can't stay any longer, that's my flight they're calling." Beck smiled, sniffled, but stood proud. "You make sure to write. Call if they let you. Oh, and be sure to let us know when you graduate, I want to be there!" Noah grinned; he was happy to hear it. He nodded his head, "I sure will!" He smiled and headed to the gate. After checking in, he turned, taking one more look, all four were still watching. He waved goodbye one more time and turned and headed onto the plane.

Chapter 5

MCRD San Diego

It was dark when the plane landed. The flight had been good, they made it alive. Noah was anxious to get off the plane, the cigarette smoke was giving him a headache. A couple of the other guys had taken advantage of the free alcohol knowing they were on their way to recruit training.

As he approached the hatch, Noah could smell the jet fuel in the air. On the ladder down, he viewed the skyline in the distance getting his first glimpse of California. One of the recruits pointed across the air strip. "That's the recruit depot right there." Noah paused briefly, taking in as much as he could, before he was quickly guided into the airport and directed to the military liaison for check-in. The liaison took Noah's paperwork and directed him to the phones. "If you're not making a call, you'll need to stay in the area." They were still expecting other arrivals. Once all were there, the depot would send a bus to pick them up out front of the terminal.

Noah sat in one of the airport chairs when he saw the automatic doors open, and there he was-Noah's first glimpse of a Marine Corps Drill Instructor. He walked straight over to the liaison. He went over some paperwork, then gathered all the record packets brought by each recruit. Noah watched, knowing any minute he would be calling for them. "Alright, listen up, as I call your name you need to sound off, 'Here!' Once I give you the ok, I want you to fallout and get on the bus right outside those doors. Any questions?" "Alright, get on your feet." One by one he went through the packets, reading the names and they loaded the bus. It was getting near the end when Noah finally heard his name called. "Here!" He sounded off. The Drill Instructor gave him a once over. "Go!" Noah got to the bus and took a seat about halfway back. Soon they were all loaded.

They sat there quietly for a few minutes, not sure what was going to happen next. The Drill Instructor boarded the bus and stood in the front center aisle. "Ok, listen up, here's what's going to happen. You're going to keep your eyes to the front, and your mouth shut! I don't want to hear a peep out of anyone." He turned to the bus driver. "We're good, let's go!" Once out of the airport, Noah watched as they passed the bay, with it boats and ships neatly docked. In the distance, he could see San Diego. The skyline was beautiful. About that time, one of the recruits spoke loud enough for the Drill Instructor to hear. The D.I. stood up, "Oh, so you just want to run your mouth! Who was it?" One guy raised his hand, "Up front now!" He pointed to a seat next to him.

The rest of the trip was silent. Arriving on base, the bus made a few turns and there it was "The Grinder." The parade deck, the place where boys were made into men, and men into Marines. Noah had heard so much about it. It got its name because of the countless hours the recruits would spend grinding their boots into it marching. It was surrounded by old Spanish looking military barracks. All connected, looking like a fort. The base was pristine in its keep, and the buildings were all yellow and trimmed in brown, with red terracotta tile roofs. Noah noticed the giant palm trees lining the buildings. It was the first time he had seen one outside of television. He was amazed. The bus made a turn and then pulled up behind one of the buildings. Everyone started to get up when the D.I told them to hold fast. He went into the building for a couple of minutes, and returned with another D.I. The guy sitting next to Noah spoke softly, "Standby, shit is about to get real." The D.I. got back on the bus. "Ok, listen up, you are now at the United States Marine Corps Recruit Depot, San Diego. This is what you are going to do. You are going to get your things and get off my bus. You are to stand on the yellow footprints right outside. You will remain on said footprints until I tell you to do otherwise. Do you understand?" It was a half-hearted response from the recruits. The D.I. was not happy. "No, I believe I asked a question! When I do, I need to hear it as loud as you can. So, we are going to try this one more time. Do you understand?" Everyone on the bus yelled as loud as they could "YES!" The D.I. retorted, "That is more like it. Now, get your shit and get off my bus!" The recruits started unloading, while the drill instructor screamed, "Hurry up, get off my bus, get off my bus!" Noah had no idea what he was saying, other than this guy seemed like a mad man. The D.I. yelled, "Stop!" Everyone stopped right where they were. He spoke again, "Get back on the bus! Try it again, you didn't do it quick enough!" Noah lost count how many times this repeated itself, before they actually stood on the yellow footprints.

Once standing, they were quickly taught the position of Attention; head and eyes directed to the front. Feet required to be positioned at forty-five-degrees. Fingers were to be tucked and thumbs pointed down along the trousers' seams. This was the position they should remain in until told to do otherwise.

Next came the barbershop. Those with long hair were singled out first. Noah was in the back row when the D.I came around and pointed at him, "You, Goldie locks, up front now." Noah went up to the front row and stood behind the last guy in line. The D.I. came back around, "Did you not hear me? I said up front Goldie locks, you're first." Noah moved to the head of the line. Once inside the room, there were four barbers waiting as the drill instructor hollered, "All the way down, move it all the way down, there Goldie locks!" The barber directed him into the chair and had a bib over him in no time. Both drill instructors came over to the chair, "Oh, look it's Goldie locks, he likes to have his hair parted down the middle. Go ahead give him that part." The barber took the clippers and ran it straight down his part. He sat there with a cut strip smack center of his head. The drill instructors started laughing, "Oh, there you go, Goldie locks, you have a real part know."

Once finished, the recruits were herded off to another room and given a basic issue of uniforms and directed to change over into them. Camo blouse, pants, and boots. Next, they were given a form called a MARS gram, and instructed to fill it out. It read, "Dear whoever, I made it here to the Marine Corps Recruit Depot safely and will contact you soon. Your Name." While they completed it, the D.I. walked around and got up in different ones faces, asking if they were from Mars.

It was 3:00am by the time they all made it into their racks. The lights were out except the light coming from the streetlamps outside the window. Noah went to one of the squad bay windows and looked out at the recruit grinder. He was here. It was the first moment since he had arrived that he didn't have someone yelling and screaming, telling him what to do. As he looked out, his thoughts wandered. What the hell had he signed up for? And was he going to have what it would take to become a Marine.

The training begins

The first week went by quickly, doing in-processing. They were given their graduation date, but were told the date could change slightly, depending on their actual training day pickup. Noah was finally given a chance to call home. The phone rang once when Claudia picked up, "Yes, we've been wondering if you're ok?" Noah explained some of the things that had already taken place and was only given a few minutes to talk. He gave her the dates, and the Battalion he was going to be assigned to. His dad was not there, but she would pass all the info on to him. Beck was excited and they planned to come out for the graduation, along with his aunt and uncle, and possibly even his sister Beulah. All planned to stop in Las Vegas on the way and drive over to San Diego. Noah was happy, but cautioned her not to make any final plans, things on his end were not definite.

The following week was filled with classes and processing. Once again, he sat in a room and went over his contract, and the moment of truth, was on him. The instructor stood up front and went over things such as illegal drug use, criminal backgrounds, or any outstanding warrants. Then, one more time it came up, "The Homosexual statement." The instructor explained, "This is your last moment to come clean! If you lied to get here, or were told to lie from your recruiter, or someone else, now is the time to come clean.

If you don't tell the truth and it's found out later, you are punishable by the USMC and could do time in prison. This is your last chance to come clean." A few guys raised their hands and came forward. They were taken out of the class. Noah wondered how many times he was going to have to answer the question.

He was finally assigned to 3rd Recruit Training Battalion, only to be there for a week, before he was set back in training after spraining his ankle and could not complete the initial Physical Fitness test. Noah was upset and hoped plans had not already been made at home. When things changed, he was given an opportunity to call home. Getting a hold of Claudia, he let her know the new dates. She had already bought tickets but seemed to think there would be no problem getting the date changed. All seemed to be set now that he was going to be graduating a week later than originally planned.

The training continued and his ankle recovered, allowing him to complete the Physical Fitness test. Soon, the first phase of recruit training had ended, and the platoon was off to Edson range. The major requirement of being a Marine was being able to complete marksmanship training. It was not a choice, either you pass this portion, or you go home. The Marines took pride in, "Every Marine is a Rifleman." Physical intensity had increased daily. He had gotten accustomed to the proper way of military protocol and addressing the Drill Instructors. The classes continued. Things seemed to be going his way. He was cut off from the world and found himself writing different family members each night. A letter from anyone back home, that offered any kind of news, was welcomed. The isolation forced him to focus on the task at hand: A strict diet, working out daily, and knowledge. He felt himself growing stronger and smarter every day. He had gotten to know a few of his bunk mates, but really getting to know any one was almost impossible. They were so busy, that bonding only took place with the few guys next to your bunk. Talking was limited most of the time. Tomorrow was the final day at Edson range, or Qualification Day. It was his birthday, but he didn't tell anyone. He was only 17 when he arrived, and soon learned he was the youngest in the platoon. Most of the guys let him know it. All offering their years of experience on how the world operated.

It was commanders time. Noah sat quietly going over his notes for the next day. Trying not to think about his birthday, out of nowhere he heard his name summoned to the D.I. Hatch. He beat on the hatch, "Private Barlow reporting as ordered Sir." From the hatch, he could hear SSgt Strickland's voice, "Isn't there something you'd like to share with us?" Noah thought maybe he had done something wrong. "Sir, the private doesn't understand Sir?" About that time, the Staff Sergeant walked out the hatch, with a cup cake, and a lit candle. The platoon behind him sang happy birthday. Noah, using all of his willpower, held back the tears. When they finished, the drill instructor told him to blow it out. "Now get down and give me one for each year, and one to grow on." Noah did the pushups and came back to attention. The drill instructor gave him the cup cake and told him he had one minute to eat it. Noah grabbed it and it was gone in seconds.

Reveille came very early. Up, shit, shower, shave, and dressed, then form it up and off to the chow hall. The Platoon was told this morning's menu was "Russian Duck." Which meant, you rushed in, and you ducked out. In other words, no time to sit and eat. They arrived at the range while it was still dark. Everyone fell out and waited by their assigned targets, until the butts were sealed, and the range was called hot. Today was qualification day. This was where you had to put up or shut up. And by put up, meaning putting rounds on the target. You were given one chance to qualify, if you failed, they would recycle you and give you one more chance, if you failed then, you were sent home. Noah thought the best birthday gift would be to qualify. The stress was high. Noah would be shooting third on his target. Third relay was called, and one by one, he shot off his rounds, making every round count. Every time he loaded a round; he went through the same sequence. Finally, at the 500-meter line, after this, if all went well, it would be over, and he would be moving on to third phase of recruit training. In the prone position, he loaded his last round: aimed in, breathed, relaxed, aimed, stopped, and squeezed. Bang! Off went the round before he even realized it. He was questioning it. He watched as the target was pulled. He waited anxiously, …why was it taking so long. Finally, the target reappeared, Bullseye! He was done. He verified one more time his score, if the pits had the same, he was moving on to third phase. Once all the shooters were finished, the D.I. gathered them and went over their scores. Barlow, 215. He was a Sharpshooter. He had qualified.

Third phase brought them back to MCRD San Diego, briefly, to do swim qualification, the obstacle course, repelling, and hand to hand combat fighting, or puggle sticks. It was Noah's turn with the sticks. He stood in the center ring, as the other recruits cheered. Noah didn't know the recruit on the other side. All he knew was the guy was bigger than he was. The two sparred, bumping each other here and there with a tease. Then bam. Noah took a blow hard on the head. Noah backed away trying to gain his composure. He could hear his drill instructor yell, "You going to let him hit you like that! Hit him hard, get back in there." Noah went back in swinging, left, right, then a butt stroke, and then Boom! The other guy was on the deck. The whistle blew and Noah was out of the ring.

Noah had taken his head gear off and was getting ready to watch the next two go at it when his Drill Instructor hollered, "Private Barlow!" Noah reported in and his Drill Instructor told him to get down and begin. Noah was very familiar with what that meant, get down and start doing pushups. His Drill Instructor hovered over him. "Private Barlow you need to learn to speak up! Be more aggressive! The meek shall inherit the earth, but not in the Marine Corps. If you want to make it in the Marine Corps, you better find your voice and learn to speak out fast. You hear me Private Barlow?" Noah sounded off, "Yes Sir!" as he continued to do pushups. The Drill Instructor continued, "What was that? I can't hear you!" Noah yelled at the top of his lungs, "Yes Sir!"

The following day the Platoon returned to Camp Pendleton to complete in-field training. To apply and demonstrate what they had learned in the classroom, military squad tactics, maneuvers, and the gas chamber. The final task had come, the one everyone talked about, "Humping Mount Mother Fucker!" It started out steep and stayed that way. Noah would look up to see if they were almost at the top, only to find out it continued. The pain in his legs grew along with the weakness. He refused to give in as he watched others fall by the wayside and into the bowels of the Drill Instructor's furry. Noah kept his head down and continued grinding forward till finally they had reached the top.

They arrived back at the recruit depot when it was dark out. It had been a few weeks since their last mail call, everyone was tired, but motivated. In two weeks, if all went well, they would be graduating. Saturday was a slow training day. They were going to be given a mail call, and Sunday they would get to make a phone call home. Mail call came, Noah had several letters, one from Claudia, and another from his sister, and a couple from friends just catching him up on things. His Dad and Claudia wrote in the letter, they were going to be there for visitor Sunday, and then come back for graduation the following Friday. Noah was hesitant to start daydreaming about graduation day, because there were still several events, he needed to complete in order to graduate. Not wanting to jinx it, he put it out of his mind.

Sunday came and he made his way to the phone booth and called home, but there was no answer. He tried a few more times, but the recruits behind him were anxious to use the phones, so he gave up his spot and headed back to the barracks. On his way back, he saw a recruit walking with his family. Today was visitor's day for the next graduating series. Thinking the recruit looked familiar, he realized it was one from his old platoon. Then it dawned on him. His old platoon series would be graduating next. If he hadn't been set back, he would be graduating this coming Friday.

He was sitting on his footlocker spit shining his boots for the upcoming week, when he heard his name summoned to the D.I. Hut. He reported in, and SSgt Strickland appeared. He gave Noah a once over, "…Is that the best camo's you got?" before Noah could respond. "…never mind" Looking at his watch, "It'll have to do!"

He gave Noah instructions that he needed to report into the Battalion Sergeant Major's Office. ASAP.

The whole purpose of the trip

Noah entered the building and turned the corner to beat on the Sergeant Majors' hatch when he almost froze. His Dad, Claudia, along with his aunt and uncle, and sister and her husband were all standing in front of him. He didn't say a word but knew they had seen him. Stunned, he realized he had to report in and continued on to beat on the hatch. "Private Barlow reporting as ordered Sir." The Sergeant Major told him to enter.

Noah was at a loss for words. Why were they here? He told Claudia; his graduation date wasn't for another two weeks. The Sergeant Major put him at ease. "I take it you know those folks right outside my hatch?" Noah sounded off, "Yes Sir." "Now, this is not normal procedure, but we can't turn them away without seeing you. So, I'm going to give you my office, for a few and let them visit with you. Son, did you tell them when you were graduating, because for some reason they thought you were graduating today?" Noah came to attention." Yes, Sergeant Major, I told my stepmother, she made arrangements." Sergeant Major stood up, "Go ahead and come to attention, I'll bring them in, I'm sure she has a good reason, but it doesn't matter now." He went to the door and called, "Mr. and Mrs. Barlow you can come in now." They came in and stood off to one side of the office. Sergeant Major spoke to Noah's Dad, "Sorry for whatever confusion, we normally don't allow this type of visit, but your son will be graduating and is doing well! I know you folks have traveled a long way to see him. Private Barlow, I'll be stepping out, you have 30 minutes." Sergeant Major left and closed the door.

Noah was dumbfounded, he didn't know whether to be mad, or glad. He was in shock; his family was right in front of him. He was still at attention; this was the first time he had been left to his own accord since arriving there. He was almost afraid to respond. His sister looked at him and started crying. His Dad had a hanky and wiped away his tears. "Nollie is that you? Is that really you?" It hadn't dawned on Noah how much he had changed in appearance since they last saw him. He had lost weight, gotten in shape, but most importantly, he had no hair. He was in uniform. Noah, almost afraid to talk, and not sure how to address him. "Yes Sir," was all he could get out. His Dad gave him a hug, "I'm proud of you son!"

Afterward, each one hugged him or shook his hand. They talked about his time left, and his dad asked, "What happened, why the set back? Noah if you knew, why didn't you let us know?" Noah realized his father was out of the loop. "I did, I let Claudia know the moment I found out." This was news to his father. He turned at Claudia, "You knew and never told, me? You knew and let us drive all the way here, …knowing he wasn't graduating today?" She stepped back a bit and nervously giggled, "Well, I just thought, …I mean, (she grew nervous) well I knew, but figured they would let you see him anyway! Besides, we already had hotel reservations for Las Vegas, and all! What was I supposed to do cancel or rearrange the entire trip?" Noah's father was angry, "The whole purpose of this trip was to come see him graduate! Not anything else!" Claudia smirked and shrugged, and looked to Beulah, "What? Next time Beck, you can just make your own plans!"

Noah was embarrassed hearing the conversation and hurt knowing she had caused his father to miss one of the most important days of his life. He turned his head away, as he kept silent, and kept to his thoughts. It was never about Beck's kids, it was always about her, and her kids. This was just a slap in the face for Noah! They visited a while longer and soon the 30 minutes were up.

Noah arrived back at the barracks, surprised and happy to see them, but heartbroken at the same time. It opened old wounds, and he remembered why he had left home. The one thing it did was motivate him. He was now more determined than ever to graduate.

The next two weeks went by quickly. Final drill, final inspection, final everything. The platoon sat down, and one by one were given their orders. Upon graduation, Noah was being sent to motor transport school at Camp Pendleton. He would be attached to Base Motors until he received his school date.

Graduation Day had arrived. He had spent most of the night awake, too excited to sleep. He was up before reveille, packing and making sure everything was ready to travel. With their gear staged, they formed up and marched onto the grinder. "Lean back, set'em down," the Drill Instructor's voice sang out, as heels hit the deck. The uniforms, with their razor edge creases, and spit-shined shoes sparkling. In the distance, the guests gathered in the stands. This is it; Graduation was finally here! They arrived at their spot on the grinder after a pass and review, allowing their families and guests to see their marching skills on display. The audience grew quiet, and the colors were brought forth. The National Anthem played. The tears were hard to hold back. He had taken an oath to support and defend his country and the Constitution of the United States of America. Here he stood to fulfill it. The National Anthem had never held so much meaning as it did now. Colors were rendered and soon a guest speaker gave a few words, and then recognition to the overachievers. Then it happened, what they all had been waiting for. Finally, for the first time since their arrival, they were called "Marines." The speaker went on, "It is not a title that is given away, it is a title that is earned. Once you have earned it, ... it can never be taken away!"

Chapter 6

Dangling Marine

Noah was now in his third week of motor transport school. The crew had just gotten off work and started the long walk back to the barracks. Over the ocean, the sun was starting to set. Noah intentionally slowed his pace, taking a moment to admire the sunset in amazement. He took a breath, released it, and closed his eyes. He's in California and the challenging work of the last year is finally starting to pay off. One more day and he will get to spend his first weekend of liberty in southern California. His thoughts were interrupted by Owens, his bunkmate, "If you keep on daydreaming you ain't going to make it back in time to hit chow before field day!" Noah started shuffling to catch up as Owens continued, "Still getting used to it all huh?" Noah slowed his pace to walk, "It's beautiful, hard to believe a smalltown boy from Blotch, Indiana is actually here!" Owens, looking toward the barracks, "I know, stopped earlier today and had to look around. Wait 'til you get out in town and off this base. I'm told there is some wild shit past them gates." Noah grinned, "Well, that right there my friend, is what I intend to find out."

The group arrived at the old WWII barracks and filed up the stairs. In the hall was a young guy huddled in a corner with one hand on his ear and the other holding the phone trying to be as private as possible in his conversation. Behind him were a couple of guys fidgeting and impatiently waiting to use the phone. The hall bustled with traffic of young men, some in uniform, others in PT gear, hollering, joking, and yacking. Corporal Haggerty was standing next to a desk with his duty belt on. He sounded off at the young Marines filing in through the door, "You boys are running late … better hurry up or you'll miss formation …it goes 1800, sharp!"

Field day was underway, and Noah was put in the head, along with Owens, Potts, Richards, and Hodges. Potts was known as a complainer, and already had an attitude toward the Marine Corps. Noah steered clear of him when possible. Hodges was a hard head, and hard to read. He made it difficult to know whether he was serious or joking. Originally from Los Angeles, he spent his spare time in the boxing ring. Richards was labeled a partier. Even though liberty was only on the weekends, he would often sneak out of the barracks window to go party. He would return right before reveille, pounding on one of the windows until someone could help hoist him back in. The windows were too high, and it required someone to reach down and pull him up before he could reach the seal and climb the rest of the way in.

They had been cleaning for a good hour or so, before Richards and Hodges grew tired of each other. Hodges was one to pay attention to detail. Richards was one to do only what was necessary to get by, or even worse, he would disappear letting others do the work. He was known as a "skate." Hodges wasn't having any part of it and was riding his ass all evening making sure Richards was doing his fair share. Words broke out between the two. Hodges told him he was tired of his lazy ass and to stop waking up the entire barracks with his late-night antics. Richards responded, "Fuck off, it's not my fault you want to be a barracks rat!" The others had to separate them, before an all-out fist fight broke out. Hodges threatened, "You better hope I'm not the one who comes to the window to let you in. Mother Fucker, you'll never need to be let in again!" Noah had never had the experience of Richards's doings, but several in the barracks had. Potts changed the subject to the weekend, defusing the situation. Each one talked of their weekend plans. Hodges was headed to LA to go see his fiancé and family. Owens and Noah had not decided what they were doing, other than to hangout in Oceanside. Richards gave them all the ins and outs of where to go. He jokingly brought up the pier and warned them that is where "she-she" boys hung out. The field day lingered on, and it was almost 11 pm before they were given the ok and could hit the rack.

The morning was filled with written tests and preventive maintenance on the vehicles. It was almost noon when pay call was sounded and each lined up for their checks. Once paid, liberty call was sounded. They did not have to be back until the 5:30 am reveille call on Monday morning.

Noah and Owens hopped off the bus on Hill Street. After hitting a burger joint, they stopped by the USO and checked out some of the free games, pinball, pool, and darts. Neither was old enough to drink, so their options were limited. They walked around for a while before stumbling into a topless stripper joint which only required its patrons to be 18 to enter. Noah was bored and soon told Owens he was headed out. Owens was infatuated with one of the strippers and decided to stay.

Walking out, Noah noticed to his right at the end of the street was the pier. He walked down to look. He had never been on a pier before. About halfway down, he gazed at the moonlight reflecting over the water. His attention was caught by the noise of laughter, whistles, and hollers back up on the street. He stood a bit longer before walking back up to the street where the noise was coming from. As he walked, the darkness turned into a glow from the streetlamps. There were a few groups in huddles talking and laughing. He continued on, finding a few guys standing alone, leaning on the palm trees that lined the road. He was getting a few stares, and quickly realized this was the area Richards had spoken about. The "She-She boys" were here. Noah didn't say anything as he continued on. Eventually, a couple of blocks down, the light dimmed, and he turned and headed back. As he walked by this time, he recognized one of the guys standing and leaning on a car. He wasn't there the first time Noah passed. This was Sergeant Rose. He knew him from base Motor-T, and just seen him picking up some guy at school. Noah ducked his head and looked the other way, hoping he wouldn't be recognized.

He was almost past when he heard, "Hey, don't I know you?" Noah ignored him, but he spoke again, a bit louder this time. Noah stopped and turned. "Excuse me?" Rose approached him. "Don't I know you?" Noah couldn't deny it. So, he looked at him a bit closer, "Yeah, ...Yeah, I think you do. Base Motors, right?" Rose smiled, "Yeah, and you are?" Noah introduced himself, and Rose reintroduced himself, before asking, "So what brings you down this way?" Noah not sure how to answer, "Oh, just taking a walk, and checking out the area. Haven't been down this way before." About that time a car passed by, with a guy hanging out the window waving. "Hey girls!" Rose blushed. "This might not be the right place for you if you get my drift." Noah chuckled and shook his head in agreement. Rose quickly gave the excuse he was down here waiting to meet someone, and they should be showing up soon. Noah realized Rose might be gay. Not knowing how to break the ice, he decided to go on. Rose nodded to him. "Nice seeing you, I'll catch you back up on base."

Noah was a few feet away when he heard a car door slam and what he thought was a loud man's voice yell. "Richard Rose you better come give Mama a hug!" Rose responding, "No, if it isn't, Miss Champagne herself." Noah took a few more steps and turned to see what was going on. It was a Drag queen, and Rose was giving her a hug. Rose continued to speak, "Darling look at you, you never fail, …Always a star." Champagne stepped back and did a twirl, showing herself off, then taking Rose's head and shoving it between her oversized boobs, and shaking them. Rose played along and laughed. Noah, amused watching the two, was fairly sure Rose was gay. This was the first time he had even an inclination someone in the Marine Corps might be gay. Once finished, Rose turned to notice Noah had stopped and seen what had just taken place. Noah smiled at him, nodded his head then turned and walked away. He wanted to go back and talk to him, but it was getting late, and he was worried he would miss the last bus to base.

Sunday was a day for catching up. Up early, Noah got dibs on the washing machine and knocked his laundry out of the way. With his uniforms pressed, and his studies complete, the rest of the afternoon was his. Some of the guys were headed to the beach and asked Noah to come along. The beach was a slight walk from the barracks. One of the guys was from California and offered to show some of them how to surf. Noah took his turn at it, but wasn't successful, getting the wind knocked out of him. He tried to take it a bit easier by playing volleyball. One final round of chicken in the ocean, and it was time to head back. Noah stopped by the phone booth along the way and made his routine call home. First talking to his stepmother, then his father, catching them up on all he had been doing and finding out what was new at home.

At the barracks, he went over his schoolwork one more time, and worked on spit shining his boots, as he observed the trickle of different ones returning from their weekend away. He had just finished showering when the lights went out and taps sounded. Noah crawled in the rack and lay awake staring at the moonlight shining through the windows.

It was around 3:30 am when Richards stumbled up to the barracks. With it being well past Cinderella liberty, he tried sneaking up to the barracks door. The duty was at his desk. He waited for a few moments thinking he might be able to get in without being seen. He stood outside watching but the duty was steadfast at his desk.

Richards looked at his watch. "Fuck it!" and took off around the outside of the barracks. Finding the window above his rack closed, he grabbed a small rock and kept hitting it. Almost breaking it, he gave in when no one showed. When that failed, he decided to take his fist and hit the side of the wall. Finally, the window opened. Richards spoke "Hey can you help me in?" A voice from the inside, "Sure, let me get a couple more guys, …give me a second." Richards waited for a minute or so, when one hand came out the right side of the window and another came out on the left. "Come on man hurry up!" Richards took a leap, grabbing on to both hands, "Ok man, I'm ready, pull me up." They started to pull him in but stopped about halfway up. He was dangling from the window. Too low to go up any further, and too high to be able to reach the ground. He spoke again. "Come on man, pull." About that time, he felt warm liquid running down him. "What the fuck?" He tried to shake away, and break loose, but soon realized it was urine. Someone from the window was pissing on him. He started screaming. "You motherfucker, you motherfucking son of a bitches, (choke, choke) I'll fucking kill you for this shit, you Motherfuckers!" Then, BAM! he hit the ground, as the window slammed closed above him. He turned and ran for the front door of the barracks where he was met outside by the Duty. "What's going on?" Richards ran past the duty and into the barracks squad bay, slamming on the lights. "I'll kill you Mother fuckers! Who did it… who did it?" Noah, startled, was now wide awake along with the entire squad bay. Richards paced up and down the center aisle, like a mad man, making accusations, covered in piss. Everyone was just starting to get an understanding of what had just taken place. Some in laughter, some sympathetic, some saying he got what he deserved. The duty came in and calmed him down. For now, no one was living up to the deed. All remaining silent.

In the morning, during company physical training the Marines were on their jog, when Hodges jumped out to sing cadence. He started in, "Don't let your dingle dangle, dangle in the dirt…" The platoon knew he was making fun of Richards. The Marines chuckled, and they all sounded out loud! Later that day, the entire Company was scolded for what had happened. The Commanding Officer offered a 96-hour pass to any Marine who could identify the culprits who had done such a despicable deed. There was a code of silence amongst the platoon. Richards' ordeal did not escape the CO's wrath. He was written up for being out past curfew. The CO showed leniency because of what happened and confined him to the barracks for two weeks. Richards was never out past curfew again.

Once again it was field day night at the barracks. Noah found himself cleaning the head along with his bunkmate, and the rest of the crew. About an hour into the cleaning, Noah got a holler from the duty. He had a visitor at the front desk. It was Sergeant Rose. He met up with him and the two stepped outside the barracks.

"Hi, how can I help you Sergeant?" Sergeant Rose chuckled, "At ease, at ease, …I hope I didn't scare you? After running into you last weekend, I thought I would stop and check in on you. How are you doing?" Noah thought it a bit odd, but knew there was an ulterior motive, and was sure it had to do with what he had seen at the pier. "I'm doing well. I have about two weeks left before graduation. Then I'll be back to base." Rose didn't waste much time cutting to the chase. "Look I'm going to be around this weekend, if you need any help with anything. Here's my number…get a hold of me. I'm going out on a limb here, but I kind of think I might know you, … I mean, I know what you saw last weekend, and not sure but, if you think you have any questions you might need to ask, go ahead" Noah was trying to follow him, but he was being very ambiguous. He was sly and the meaning could be taken different ways. By no means was he coming out, but here he stood in front of him. Noah smiled, "I appreciate that. No questions." Noah knew why he was there, "Look, I'm not sure what this is about, but I have an idea. If it is what I think, I didn't see anything I would consider wrong, or offensive last weekend. If that is what you're getting at." Rose seemed a bit relieved, "SO, … we are talking the same language now. I wasn't sure how much you saw, but was worried you might have been offended, but I was betting you might be familiar with that environment. I want you to know, I plan on getting out in a few months. I hope you are not going to turn me in?" Noah was taken by surprise, "Hold up, that is what you thought? I might tell on you. For What?" Rose stood there perplexed, "You know," … he nodded his head with a tilt, trying to get Noah to understand without saying it. Noah shook his head, "No, I don't," Rose did it again, "You know, …for being gay?" There it was, Rose had just came out to him. Noah smirked, "No, it hadn't even crossed my mind. I wouldn't even consider doing that to you or anyone." Rose exhaled, "Thank you! I mean I wasn't sure if you were cool with it, straight or gay," Noah looked at him, "I'm not anything, but whatever you are it's cool. I kind of wanted to hangout and see what was going on, but when I saw you, I figured I needed to move on." Rose smiled, and perked up, "Really, so you were not just out and stumbled through the area." Noah laughed, "Well not quite, but yes, I did go down to check the area out. I had heard the rumors about the pier at night." Noah heard his name come from the hatch, "Barlow, are you coming back man, we need you in here!" Noah, "Yeah, I'll be right in!" Rose quickly spoke up, "Hey, if you like, maybe we can hang out this weekend, …I can pick you up, and, and show you around?" Noah smiled, "Yeah, I think I might." Rose grinned, "Great, I'll give you a call." Noah chuckled, "I look forward to it," and took off to the barracks.

It was Saturday evening, and the sun was setting across the jetty as Noah waited on the barracks steps. Rose pulled up in what Noah called a led sled. A 1972 Cadillac, burgundy, but cherried out. Rose hopped out, "What you think? Just had it cleaned and detailed." Noah laughed, "You know this was the childhood car I grew up with. My dad is a GM guy. He has had a Cadillac since before I was born." Rose laughed, "I love'em! They are so cheeky, and cheesy at the same time! Come on let's get this party started!" Noah got in the passenger seat. This was the first time he had really got to see Rose in the day light, and out of a baggie uniform. He was actually not a bad looking guy. He was a small guy, only about 5'5 at best. He was slender but had huge muscular arms, almost disproportionate for his size. Noah chuckled to himself. He reminded him of a real-life Popeye. Noah remembered meeting him in the motor pool, and never once thought he would be gay.

Being Noah relied on public transportation, Rose decided to show him around the area. First Carlsbad, and the mall. Then, on out to Vista, and back to the coast, stopping at the small ocean towns along the way, ending at Delmar before heading back to Oceanside. It was an opportunity to see the area, but also time for the two to get to know each other. Rose was originally from Ohio and had been in the Marine Corps for 12 years. He was passed over for Staff Sergeant, so he was being forced out. Noah asked, "How can you be in for so long and the Marine Corps not know?" Rose explained, "I keep to myself. I try to be good at everything they ask me to do. Some people know, or figure it out, and every now and then, I run into someone who isn't cool, or a hater. I stay away from them. I've seen several friends be discharged. There are others, in the Corps, and they all try to support each other, 'Family' you know, ...whenever possible."

Noah changed topics, "I'll be going to Okinawa once I graduate." Rose chuckled, "Yeah, that is no surprise, that is normal. They either get you your first year, or they send you your last year. I've been there once, years ago. Do you know a guy named Giselle?" Noah thought for a moment, "I know of him, but have never really spoken to him." Rose continued, "He is a friend of mine, he just left to go there. He is Motor-T, and just graduated. I can give you his information, let him know you're a friend. Maybe you two can hang out." Rose finally asked "So, you don't have to answer, but are you gay?" Noah chuckled. "I don't know what I am. I guess I just don't like labels. I mean, I have met some guys, prior to coming to the Corps, but I never liked being called the girl thing. You know, the way they spoke to each other. I just think I'm more than a label. I mean I don't know, I really haven't been with someone, or could say for sure one way or another. Hell, I just turned 18 in recruit training. It seems like everybody is caught up on, … are you straight? …are you gay? You have a girlfriend? Hell, can't I just be me. I'll figure it out in time." Rose smirked, with a half laugh, "I get it, didn't mean to pressure you. No labels here except, I think you're good looking!" and put his hand on Noah's leg and gave it a squeeze. Noah gave a nervous chuckle and looked down at the hand on his leg. He didn't move it. Noah knew where this might be heading and wasn't sure he liked the direction.

The two ended up at the pier and stood alongside the car. Different ones would drive by and honk. Others would park and get out and stand. Rose knew several people and spoke to them. He introduced Noah as a friend, but never really allowed anyone to get too close to him. Noah couldn't tell whether he was trying to protect him or trying to keep him for himself. Noah had an idea where the night might lead but didn't want to get ahead of himself. It was getting late, and Rose suggested it was time to go. In the car headed back to the base, Rose offered Noah to spend the night. They could go to breakfast in the morning, and he would have him back by mid-afternoon. Noah thought about it and spoke, "Sure why not!"

Chapter 7

Marine Corp Motor T, Truck company

Noah touched down at Kadina Air Force Base in Okinawa. The seventeen-hour flight gave him plenty of time to think about his time home on leave. He attended several high school graduations for old classmates. Noah had already graduated and received his diploma. Thankfully when he arrived at Pendleton, his Lieutenant noticed he had not graduated from high school and told him to go to the base education center, and don't come back until he finished. He was back on track and ahead of the game. Well sort of, he was motor transport, but what he really wanted was to be in the photographic/television field. Off the plane and through customs, Noah was finally able to pick up his luggage and was directed to the holding room, awaiting further transportation to Camp Foster. He was going to 3rd FSSG, which was the Service and Support side of the house. He would not be with the ground pounders, or so-called grunts. He was trained as a Heavy Vehicle Operator meaning he could be stationed at a multitude of places.

The transportation cattle cars arrived, and all the Marines were herded in. Noah grabbed a seat looking out one of the open portholes. He was anxious to get a view of this strange land he had found himself in. He couldn't see much, just a blur as things passed by. At the stops or when the vehicle slowed, he would get a glimpse of the outside. It definitely wasn't what he had expected. He thought it would resemble some of the old WWII movies with grass roof huts or "Minkas" In actuality, it was more like a Godzilla movie. The streets were crowded with vendors, banners, and signs. Multi-level cement structures were connected by overbearing and prominent electrical wires. The signs were all written in Japanese, with an occasional one that might be bilingual with English added to it. It was hot and muggy inside the cattle car, but once set in motion, it generated a cool breeze bringing with it the smell of the East China Sea.

In what seemed a short ride, they made it to Camp Foster. He would be staying here for three days of in-processing and training before given his permanent unit assignment. The Joint Reception Center, or as most called it the JRC, was not an enjoyable occasion and could be a roll of the dice. The orders were often designated by quotas and, depending where one's name was on the list of arrivals, would determine where they would be stationed; five for this unit, 3 for this unit and so forth. Also, the needs of the JRC had to be met. The 3-day processing could be extended to 30 and require the Marines to be assigned to mess duty, before being sent on to their permanent duty station. For those not chosen, it didn't mean they would get off free. They would be required to field day, clean the barracks, and any other shit detail that might come along. When not in class and after hours, they were confined to the barracks, except for going to the chow hall, or local exchange. There was no need to turn them loose without being schooled on the culture, customs, and the laws of the locals.

While standing huddled in a group outside during one of the breaks, Noah observed some of the Marines walking by. He heard them making a mocking sound of a cow mooing. One of the guys looked over at them, puzzled. "What the fuck is he doing, mooing like a cow?" Another one laughed, before speaking up. "He's not mooing, he's calling us Neeewbies… Anyone new to the island, or the rock is called a newbie." The group chuckled as the guy realized what was being said. "So that is what we are now? Newbies on the rock…"

The next day was spent in the classroom, with long and drawn-out presentations. People getting up and going to the back of the classroom to keep from falling asleep. The change in time, and jet lag was catching up to the new arrivals. The third day everyone was excited. This was the day they found out who hit the lottery, and who was left washing dishes. One by one names were read out, and their destination given. Some would cheer, and others not so happy.

Finally, 3rd FSSG was called out, "All those going to be stationed with the 3rd FSSG listen up." The admin clerk started in with the names, First the As, and then the B's. Noah was the first one called out. "Barlow, 9th Motors, Truck company. However, there is a condition on yours. You'll be back here tomorrow and are required to complete an additional class to earn your international driver's license stamp. Not to worry, you will be our neighbor." The clerk pointed out the window. "They're just two buildings up above us on the hill." Noah let out a sigh of relief, he was going to be here at Foster. Most importantly, he would have no mess duty.

The following day the international driving class was full of about thirty Marines. All were going to different locations on the Rock. There were six of them going to Truck company. He knew all of them from Pendleton when he was going thru Motor Transport School at Camp Delmar. Jim Manaus and he were in the same platoon and worked together on the night drive course in school. They would now be working with each other for the next year.

Noah felt lucky getting Camp Foster, when he found out where some of the others would be stationed. The other bases were more remote and not so well situated on the island. Camp Swab and the Northern Training area was the furthest north, and the least populated, but was known for its great beaches, but no real activity outside the base. Camp Hansen was the home of the grunts and boasted Kenville, a small village right outside the gate. It was known to be a bit of a rough house with all the grunts being stationed there. Camp Courtney was northeast of Camp Foster, the Headquarters for the III Marine Expeditionary Force. It was well disciplined with high visibility within the officer ranks. The Marines referred to it as a lot of dog and pony shows and, kiss ass going on. The Marine Air Wing was just southeast at Futenma and was considered one of the best duties if you were going to be on the island. The term, 'the wing takes care of its Marines,' held true because they usually had the best facilities and work hours. South was Camp Kinser, the supply and logistics hub. It was closest to Naha, making it the most congested and difficult to get around. For the truck drivers, it was considered the arm pit for traffic, and the most dangerous area to drive. Most wrecks happened there. Camp Foster, however, was the center hub of the island. Truck Company was strategically placed here to give it easy access in dispersing anywhere. After a long day of intense classroom training, the group all passed their international exams and looked forward to checking in to Truck Company the following morning.

The lights came on in the barracks at 0530 sharp. The Marines all hustled and bustled to get ready. Showered, shaved and with "attention to detail" they all dressed in the prescribed alpha uniform. Before putting on their jackets, they all staged their sea bags outside for pick up. As 0730 rolled around, a camouflaged Dodge pick-up pulled into the parking lot. The driver came in and hollered out, "Anyone headed to 9th Motors better get your bag on the truck, or you'll have a long hump to carry it." The Marines fell out and loaded the sea bags on the truck. The driver gave them directions to the Battalion, and they were left on their own to hike over to it. The group formed up and marched in sync down the hill and across the grass grinder arriving at the Battalion. After checking in with admin, the clerk called truck company, and they were told to stand fast outside the building and wait for their ride. The group huddled up with their sea bags, and those who smoke lit up while waiting. About 20 minutes later, a deuce and a half showed up. The Marines loaded up and headed to Truck company.

The center hall of the company had highly shined floors and smelled of cleaner and Brasso. Noah could tell the military appearance was impeccable, which meant a tight ship. As he and Manaus made their way down the hall, they stopped outside the Company Gunny's office, and gave each other a quick once over. Noah noticed Manaus' hair. "Man, you're pushing the regs on top, looks close to 3 inches." Manaus shrugged as he turned to the mirror outside the hatch. "No man, it's cool, …I just had it cut, the sides are in reg, and the top is too. I can't wear it short man, I lose that surfer look." Noah shook his head and chuckled. "Ok, I'm just saying you only get one chance to make a good impression. If you want, we can go to the barber, and come back." Manaus gave another glance in the mirror. "No, I'm good." He blew it off, before knocking on the hatch.

They were welcomed in by Gunny Rosette sitting behind his desk. He got up, came around and gave a quick checkout of their uniforms. "You two right out of school?" Both answered yes. He then asked for the service record books and check-in sheets. He perused the books, before stepping in front of a large white board of Marines names, identifying what platoon they were in. He added both names and pertinent info. "You both will be in first herd; they are short on personnel right now. So, I'm sure they'll be glad to have you on board. If you have any problems, I expect you to use the chain of command, but if you can't get results, my door is always open. You understand?" Both sounded off, and he took their packages into the First Sergeant's office. He came out, "Barlow, you're first."

Noah walked in, snapped to, and reported in, and was quickly put at ease. First Sergeant Holmes gave a quick once over and started going through his service record book, when they heard a yell coming from the office next to him. The First Sergeant lifted his head up for a moment to listen…, "Don't worry, that's just the Company Commander having his breakfast," before returning to his inspection of Noah's service record book.

Noah tried to block it out but couldn't help hearing the "ass chewing" that was taking place. Noah had gotten the gist of it. The Marine had broken restriction. The Company Commander was brutal in his chastising, and the only thing Noah could think was he really didn't want to get on the bad side of this guy. It was a one-way conversation; the Marine being scolded was quiet.

The First Sergeant, looking through the book, noted his Physical Fitness score, and his pros and cons. He thought both were high. A new voice sounded off from the Company Commander's office "Aye, Aye, Sir," and a Marine opened the door and came out of the CO's office. The Marine was disheveled in appearance with wrinkled cammies, hair out of regs, and no shine on his boots. The

First Sergeant told him to stand fast, he would deal with him in a moment, before getting up and going into the Company Commanders Office. He closed the door behind him.

The Marine that had come out looked at Noah, "You're just getting here, … I feel for you man, …unless you're a smack ass, this place sucks the big weenie man. Make sure you sound off loud, this guy is on a power trip, and is known for busting people. I was a Corporal when I got here, he's a fucking dick." Noah remained quiet, not knowing what to say, but noticed the guy was now a private.

The First Sergeant opened the door and stood fast as he called Noah into the CO's office. Noah walked in, centered on the desk, and reported in almost at a yell. Major Dee, the Company Commander, looked up from his record book in front of him. "Pipe down son, I'm only sitting right here." Noah sounded off, "Yes, Sir." The Major looked at his hair cut and then gave him a once over. He returned to his record book for a minute or two. Looked up at him, "You have arrived here with a clean record book. Do what you are told, and it will remain that way. My NCOs are my extension, and if they tell you to do something, it is as good as me telling you. You understand?" Noah sounded off again, "Yes, Sir." The Major closed the book, signed off the check-in sheet, and handed him the book. "Welcome aboard, dismissed" Noah stepped back, "Have a Good Day Sir," then did an about face and left the office.

Manaus was now on deck. Noah was in the hall for a few minutes when he heard hollering coming from the Major's Office. "What kind of haircut is that? You want to come in my office looking like a shit bag. You got one more chance to come back and report in, there Candy Pancakes, and when you do, make sure you get a goddamn haircut. Now get out of my office." Noah's eyes lit up as he listened, and his only thought was thank god it wasn't him. Manaus just got reamed by this guy and did not set a good first impression.

Noah moved on down the hall wanting to get away from the offices for fear of any fallout. He found what was a TV room and vending machines and stood by keeping an eye out for Manaus. A few minutes went by before Manaus came out of the company office in a hurry with his tail between his legs. He saw Noah and headed his way. As he approached, he looked at Noah, rolled his eyes, and let out a breath, "Come on man, get me the fuck out of here before this guy finds something else to bitch about. Fuck that mother fucker, Candy Pancakes, jeez…" Noah held back a laugh, but a chuckle escaped anyways. "Well, I guess the base barbershop is now in order." He grabbed his satchel and cover and the two took off out of the back entrance, avoiding the office area all together.

Coming into the barracks, the duty, seated at a small desk, stopped them not knowing who they were. Both explained they were new joins and were let through. Most of the Marines would be getting off by now, so this would be their first time meeting the guys in the platoon. They turned down the main corridor and could see the barracks were now full and hopping with action. Manaus came to his cubicle first as Noah walked on to his. When he arrived, a light skinned, black Marine, with a dew rag on his head, was sitting by himself on the rack up front. Noah walked in, put his stuff on one of the empty bunks and turned, stuck his hand out and introduced himself. The guy spoke with a broken Puerto Rican accent. "I'm Carree. You must be the newbie that is taking one of doze racks." Noah wasn't expecting to hear the accent, "Yeah, I was going to take the top. So, no one else is in here?" Carree smiled, "No, just me and you mon!" Noah liked the accent, "Cool," he smiled and turned to getting settled in.

Noah had changed over, and was unpacking, when a tall blonde, fit guy came in. "You Barlow?" Noah spoke as he turned from his unpacking. "Depends on who's asking?" The guy smiled and stuck out his hand, "I'm Corporal Miller, you'll be in my platoon, I'm the acting Platoon Sergeant. So, where you coming from?" Noah couldn't help but notice this guy was extremely good looking and looked like he was a poster child for the Marines. "I'm coming from Pendleton, Delmar, but originally from Indiana."

Corporal Miller smiled, "Hoosier boy, we have several of you guys here,"

A voice from a few cubicles down spoke out. "Did I hear Indiana? We got us another basketball guy?" A tall guy, about 6'4", appeared from around the wall locker. "How's it goin' man, ... Sedan here, ... You from Indy?" He walked in, slapped Noah on the hand, Noah looked up at him, "Yeah, Blotch, Hokum, but most people know Blotch". Sedans eyes lit up, "Yeah, Blotch, they got some basketball champs there. You play ball?" Noah didn't want to get committed into playing ball, "I play some, ...but not that good." Sedan chuckled, "You can play some ball, anyone not that good in Indy is great anywhere else. I'll check you out later, hey you got a good platoon, we got several of us all from Indiana, anymore and they'll call us the Hoosier Platoon."

He walked out of the cubicle, and Corporal Miller laughed, "That's Sedan, he's not shy. Look, once you're checked in, I'll get you up to speed, but get ready to hit the ground running. We need drivers, we're putting in some miles, and long hours. But that's good, ...it makes the time here on the Rock go fast."

Noah turned back to unpacking, and it wasn't long before he was settled. He made his rack and decided to kick back and relax a bit to wind down from the day. Okinawa, the Rock, he was excited to be here. To think he was a Marine, on the other side of the earth, far from Indiana, far from the cornfields, and far from family. Life was changing and moving quickly. This was his doing, and no one else's. He was officially living on his own.

After a week of bureaucracy, checking-in, Noah was finally able to make it to the motor pool. Manaus's rocky "check in" with the Company Commander didn't go unnoticed. "Candy Pancakes" was assigned to mess duty for the first 30 days.

Noah arrived at the Motor pool and reported to Corporal Miller where he was taken around to meet the rest of the Platoon. Some he had already met, like his cubicle buddy Carree, and Sedan, but today he would meet everyone. Stubblefield was a small framed, blonde-haired guy from Tennessee and had a deep southern drawl.

Duncan, or as everybody called him Dunk, was a tall black guy in decent shape, from Texas. He and Stubblefield were amigos, and where you saw one you would find the other. Dominguez was a hard-core Marine. She was Hispanic, from Los Angeles, and very street wise. She tended to be a bit manly, very athletic, and made no bones about who she was. She insisted on being treated like one of the guys. Some of the Marines, both male and female, tended to shy away from her, out of intimidation. She would call you out if you were messed up. Finally, there was Giselle. Noah did not know him but had heard of him through Sergeant Rose before leaving Camp Pendleton. Noah was supposed to contact him once he arrived on the island. Wasn't this a coincidence? They were going to be in the same platoon. Giselle was one of Sergeant Rose's adventures. Rose was a chicken hawk, and he and Giselle had tricked a couple of times. Noah was glad to know there was someone else in the platoon he could talk openly with, but for now he would play it cool and not open that door.

Corporal Miller showed Noah the vehicle line, and then like all permanent drivers, he assigned Noah his own vehicle. It was a five-ton truck. Each Marine was assigned a vehicle when they checked in, some were drivers, others were assistant drivers. Not every vehicle had an assistant. First herd was short on drivers. Only those with suspended or lost licenses were assistants. Noah was given his place in the lineup; he was next to Giselle. This was great and would give them a chance to make friends. Noah started doing his preventative maintenance and inspection of the vehicle. It was a nice one. The 5 tons were new upgrades from the old deuce and half that he had learned to drive in school.

While putting his canvas on the truck, he was called back front by Corporal Miller. The entire platoon was standing in front of his vehicle. Noah was a bit confused. What was taking place? He came forward, "Yes Corporal?" Miller told the Marines to form it up in two lines. Noah started to fall in, before he was halted. "Not you, come with me." Noah followed Corporal Miller to one end of the platoon. The Corporal called them to attention, then commanded

"About Face," to the first row. They were now facing each other. He put them at ease, and they all started yelling, "Wahoo, ... I'm first, ...let me at him." They started punching their hands as though they were warming up. Noah had seen this before; it was called a "gauntlet". Usually done for a promotion; some called it pinning on the stripe. Noah was confused, he wasn't getting promoted. He looked at Corporal Miller and the corporal could tell he was puzzled. "We are getting ready to tag your 5 ton." Noah shook his head in confusion, "...You're getting your name put on the bumper. But first you must walk the gauntlet." Noah looked down the line at the anxious Marines ready to pounce on him, and he stepped off. One by one he moved toward his vehicle. There were roughly six Marines on both sides. Some gave it all they had, and Noah's arms were getting pretty beat up. Resolute, he was not going to be the one who quit. Finally, the last punch was thrown. Corporal Miller was standing there waiting on him. "You're not done yet." He walked to each side of Noah punching each shoulder.

When he finished, the Platoon gathered around the bumper of the truck. Noah's name was formed in stencils, and Giselle, with some black spray paint, placed them to the bumper and sprayed "Lance Corporal Barlow" on the truck. He then pulled it off and stepped back. The platoon let out a cheer. Corporal Miller turned and shook his hand, "Welcome to first herd, best in the west and east of the Mississippi." He chuckled and stepped off as the rest of the platoon stepped in line, shook Noah's hand, and welcomed him aboard. Dunk got in front of him, "You got the truck, now don't fuck it up!" Stubblefield stepped up, "You know what they say, 'If you can't truck it, ... fuck it.' ...I'm glad you're here, now maybe some of us can get off at a decent hour." Dominguez smiled as she stepped up and shook his hand, "Welcome aboard." She let go and paused, giving him a once over before commenting, "... Aren't you a sweet pea. ...Don't let these assholes fuck you up." Giselle, was behind her and overheard, "One of us assholes, hah, hah, ... you'll be the one to corrupt him..." She replied instantly, "Shut the hell up Giselle." She turned back and laughed as she walked on. Giselle reached out to

shake his hand, "Welcome aboard, I'll be right next to you on line."
Noah shook his hand and let go; this was the first time he had spoken
to him directly. He looked Noah directly in the eye. Noah quickly
turned away, trying to avoid eye contact. He looked over to his truck
before looking back, "So, you're the lucky one. Nice to meet you,
…you'll probably get tired of me asking questions, by the time it's
over, or at least till I get familiar with everything." Giselle smiled
and started to walk on, "No problem, I still have a lot of questions
myself." He looked back at Noah with a smirk and a wink, taking
him by surprise. Maybe he already knew. Could Rose have already
told him? Noah smiled back and shook the next Marine's hand.

A long way from the cornfields of Indiana, he was now at his
first duty station. Living his oath to support and defend, this is where
the country called to have him serve. He took a mental snapshot of
those around him. He was in the presence of grace and grit with the
doers, the courageous, and the compassionate. All serving with
gratitude to better humanity. They all had made him feel welcomed.
Holding an unspoken connection, he was now part of the team.

Rainy days playing cards

Truck Company's barracks sat high on top of a hill on
Okinawa's Camp Foster. It looked out upon the beautiful waters of
the East China Sea. On a bright sunny day, one couldn't distinguish
between the baby blue sky or its refection on the waters. Walking to
the Motor-pool, Noah stopped briefly to put on his raincoat and look
upon the sea as the rain started to trickle down. Today was not one
of those sunny, picturesque days Okinawa was known for. The early
morning sky was gray and hazy, with shuffling ominous clouds. He
was still high enough on the hill that he could look down and see the
Motor-pool in the distance coming to life as the streetlights began to
fade to a twinkle. The vehicles maneuvered to get their position in
the lineup before leaving out on the early morning runs. He quickly
finished putting on his raincoat and started down the hill. At the
bottom of the hill, he saw Manaus walking from the cross street and
waited for him to catch up. Although the two had arrived together on

the island, they had two distinct paths. The island had not been kind to Manaus. Since his arrival, he had run into a string of mishaps. A bad first impression with the Company Commander landed him 30 days on mess duty. It also left him with a label of a shit bird, with a bit of attitude. After a month or so on the island, he got a "Dear John" letter from his girlfriend back home. The poor guy also wrecked his 5-ton truck, hitting a Japanese local, causing his license to be suspended. Not being able to drive, he had been transferred to maintenance company, working in the dirty and hard labor tire shack until cleared of any wrongdoing.

Manaus recognized Noah from across the street and spoke out in surprise, "Yoh, B, how's it going?" Noah smiled as he approached, thinking how Manaus always seemed to be in a good mood, regardless of what was thrown at him. "Well, no shit dog," as Manaus reached him, "… How's the new gig?" The two started walking on to the Motor-pool as they conversed. Manaus started in, "Awe man, …You know, I'm surprised, I really like it. I thought being off the road would be boring, and the tire shack would be back-breaking fucking work. But man, the Staff Sergeant there is so cool, and he likes me. When I got there, the place was a cluster fuck, … a bunch of shit bags, all short timers, doing only the bare minimum. …I figured it's hard telling how long I might be there. So, it would be easier to get it squared away. The Staff Sergeant noticed and put me in charge. He tells me if I keep doing an excellent job, he might even put me in for a meritorious mast. I thought the work would be hard, its dirty, I'll give ya that, but hey, … lifting heavy tires is putting on some guns for me."

Manaus stopped and curled his arm and grabbed his bicep. Noah rolled his eyes. Manaus started laughing. "Huh? …I'll show ole girl what she missed out on. …She's gonna love these bad boys when I get home." Noah chuckled, shaking his head. "You're not giving up on her, well you're not a quitter …fucked up in the head, maybe, but definitely not a quitter." Manaus responded, "No man, I don't want her, just want her to see what she could have had." Noah laughed, "Well good luck with that…" and changed the subject to the rain. "Well, I'm envious on days like today, Bud. You get to be inside out of the rain." Manaus came back "Yeah, I don't miss having to work out in this shit, but you know what I do miss?" Noah looked over to listen in closer. "I miss being able to get up in the back of the trucks and hide out under the canvas with everyone." Noah adding to the conversation, "Nothing like a good game of Spades." Manaus perked up. "Big Mo, Little Mo. Hah Ha, ...Man I love that game. And Dunk, awe Dunk, he would get so pissed when he would get his ass kicked. He hates losing at anything. I loved playing cards, ...man we used to play for hours, the jokes, just the shit everyone talked, even sitting it out to catch a snooze." Noah sensed Manaus might be feeling a bit left out, "We still play, yah know?" Manaus eyes lit up. "Oh man next time it happens come get me! I'll see if Staff Sergeant will let me get away." Noah responded, "Cool, the way it looks now, we might be under the canvas today, but I don't know man, we have the I.G. inspection coming up and Gunny is ramping up the PM's to make sure we're ready." The two arrived at the Motor-pool. As they parted, Noah spoke out, "Great seeing you Man, any Spades games, I'll let you know."

When Noah arrived, the rest of the platoon was just starting to cluster, but no one was falling out for formation. He went to his vehicle and started doing his morning routine. Giselle, in the truck next to him, hollered over, "I wouldn't get too far ahead man. Word has it we are going to be secured early if it starts to rain." Noah stopped what he was doing, "Really? Who is saying that shit? You know we ain't getting outta here." Giselle looked to the dispatcher shack. Corporal Miller was headed their way. Dunk, hollered out, "Everyone fall in!" and it was echoed down the line.

Standing in formation, Corporal Miller arrived. Dunk asked "So, Boss what's the word? Are we getting out of this place?" Corporal Miller shook his head no. "Gunny thinks this stuff is going to blow over, and we can continue after it's gone." As the group listened, the rain started picking up to a downpour. Corporal Miller took the initiative and told everyone to get in their trucks, hang out, and try and stay out of sight. He would let them know if anything changed. Dunk agitated, "This shit ain't stopping! Fucking Gunny, …so what, he's a meteorologist now?" Everyone knew what that meant, they were not getting out early. Some of the drivers would sit in the cab of their truck and snooze. Others would gather up in the back to chill, talk smack, and play cards till they were given the word to get back to work. Noah went to his truck and sat in the cab. He looked down the line and most of the others were doing the same. After a few minutes, he slouched and pulled the brim of his cover over his eyes.

Dozing in the truck, he was awakened by a pounding on his door. It was Giselle, "Hey come on man, everyone is getting together in the back of Dominguez's truck."

Dominguez was one of the female Marines in the platoon. Her truck was in line next to Giselle. She was well liked by the guys and comfortable enough that she was out about her sex life. It was no secret in the platoon that Dominguez was into women and was rumored to be a stud in the lesbian community. The female Marines lived in separate barracks. The guys called it Alice's Palace, or the Green Mattress Ho-tel. It was a slight on female Marines. Alice's Palace referred to Alice from the Brady Bunch. She was a spinster on the TV show, and the female marines were considered to be just like her. The other, Green Mattress Ho-tel, referred to all female Marines as walking mattresses. Unfortunately, a lot of young Marines liked to talk smack and label their female counterparts as either lesbian or whore. Dominguez didn't help that situation. She was known for sharing gossip about different women in the barracks, including her own conquests.

Noah sat up and looked down the line, then up to the dispatcher shack; no one was around. The rain continued to pour. Giselle was waiting outside getting soaked, and squinting trying to look up at him, "Hurry up man! …You coming?" Noah flung open the door and jumped to the ground. "Come on, …let's get the fuck out of this shit." Both took off running. They arrived at the back of Dominguez's truck and the back tailgate was already down. Giselle grabbed the chain hanging on the side of the truck and jumped into the back. Noah was right behind him. The trucks side boards were down and acted as seats. Stubblefield, Pedro, and Dowdy were already in as Noah and Giselle jockeyed for their places. Dominguez came around the side of the truck, and hollered, "Hey, one of you assholes, give me a hand getting up in this bitch." Stubblefield got up to help when Dowdy jumped in his seat behind him. Stubblefield reached down to give her a hand but was confused why she could not get up on her own. "What the fuck, it's your truck, how the hell you get up in it when you're out on the road?" Dominguez pushed back, "Fuck it! … I'll do it myself!" Grabbing the chain, she rolled into the back of the truck. Watching her make it in, Stubblefield started bitching at her. "See, what did I tell yah! You can do it; you were just being lazy. Damn, why you making me get up and shit, … One of these motherfuckers is gonna try and steal my seat." As he turned back around to sit down, "Dowdy, get the fuck up, you know that ain't your seat." He moved over next to him, and nudged him on the shoulder, "Come on man, don't be like that, you know that's my seat." Dowdy got up and moved back to his old seat, "I was just keeping it warm for you." Stubblefield, chuckled, "Yeah, is that what they're calling it now." Dominguez moved a toolbox center and broke out some playing cards, "Who is the first to get their ass whipped?" Giselle curious, "Depends who's your partner?" Dominguez smiled. "It's a surprise, he'll be here in a minute!"

A deep voice outside of the truck spoke out. "I know you all ain't up in their without me?" Dunk, appeared from the side of the truck, and flung himself up. He high fived everyone, before stopping at Stubblefield, "We got this man?" Stubblefield piped up. "Hell yes, Dominguez count us in. We'll take your ass on, … I don't care who the fuck your partner is!" From the back of the gate, Manaus appeared, "What up you all?" The truck broke out in laughter. "Oh, hell nah!" Noah started laughing, "Man, we were just talking about this, this morning." Manaus laughed, "I know, Dominguez came back this morning to have a tire fixed. We got to talk'en; she came up with the idea." Stubblefield interrupted, "Hey, we gonna sit and kiss ass all morning, or are you going to get up in this bitch and get your ass kicked?" Dunk chimed in, "Come on, let's play some Bemo, hah!" He rubbed his hands together, and Dominguez shuffled the cards. She finished and offered a cut to Stubblefield. He waved his hand no. "Be... mo... careful, pass." She dealt and the game began, Noah and the others looked on.

Dominguez and Dunk shared a storied past that could, at times, make everyone around them a bit uneasy. Rumor had it the two had a common love interest and Dominguez won out. Dunk had a chip on his shoulder losing out to a woman.

Dominguez and Manaus were losing. She grew agitated and decided to make it personal, attacking Dunk. "Yeah, like I spanked your girlfriend's booty last night!" Dunk couldn't let it go. He reached down and grabbed his crotch. "I know you ain't talk'en bout my girl, she loves the dick!" Dominguez mouthed back, "Oh is that what she tells you, ...that's what they all say, ...fake it till they make it. But I say they fake it till they make it BACK TO ME! They come to Mama, when they want it done right." She started laughing, along with Manaus who spoke up. "Damn girl, hah ha, ...you're putting it out there." Dunk grew angry, "Yeah, well it's like I told yah, ...show me your dick, ...my girl likes the dick, and unless you can show me a dick, you ain't shit!" Stubblefield, noticing the conversation was hitting a nerve with the two of them, decided to defuse the situation. "Come on, would you two knock it the hell off! You know neither one of you has got shit going on. So, pay the fuck attention and let me show yah how it's done." Stubblefield gloating, "Lookie there! I'm calling a Bemo, a big ass Bemo. Not no little shit, but a big ass Bemo!" Looking to Dunk, "And Buddy, I'm going it alone!"

He had the group's attention, and they gathered around to watch. The focus was back on the game, as Stubblefield led each round. One by one, he slowly led the cards out. Everyone was in amazement but remained quiet when he made it to the last round. Before he laid the last card down, he looked around the table, smiled and spoke out knowing he had taken the game. "And that my friends, is how you play a Bemo!" The group leaned back, as Dunk and Stubblefield high fived, and Dominguez got up and kicked the toolbox, as the others chuckled. About that time, they heard Corporal Miller, yell from outside the truck. "Time to get back to work."

Arriving at the Motor pool the next morning, rain was forecast for the entire day, and the group found themselves back in the truck under the canvas once again. It wasn't long before Dominguez was ready to make up for yesterday's loss. "We going to sit and kiss ass all morning or are we going to play some Spades?" Dunk smirked, "What, you didn't get enough of an ass whipp'en yesterday?" He rubbed his hands together, "Come on, let's play some Bemo, hah!" Manaus wasn't with the group, so Dominguez looked to Noah. "Come on Sweet Pea, you any good? You can be my partner." Dominguez shuffled the cards. A few rounds went on, before Dominguez called a Bemo. The group watched as she played the cards one by one. Finally, as the last card was revealed, she stood up and high fived Noah, they had done it! The group hooted and hollered. Dunk decided to make it personal again. "Yeah, that's all right, because I spanked your girl's booty last night!" He reached down and grabbed his crotch. "She loves the dick!" Dominguez kept her cool, looking down to where his hand grabbed his crotch, "Yeah, from what I hear, you can barely call it that." The others chuckled as they looked on. Stubblefield spoke up again. "Goddamn, would you two kiss or go fuck or something! Every time you two get around each other, you have to go at it!" Dunk, ignoring Stubblefield, "Yeah, well it's like I told yah. Show me your dick! Unless you can show me a dick, you ain't shit!" Stubblefield, trying to diffuse, "Ah shit, Dunk would you knock it the hell off!" Dominguez stood up, and the others cleared back not sure what was going to happen. "No, he's right! Mother fucker you want to see my dick, I'll show you, my dick!" Stubblefield tried to stop her. "Come on Dominguez, you don't have to do this, you don't have to prove shit." Dominguez undid her belt and unbuttoned her trousers. Their jaws fell open, what the hell was she doing? Dunk sat back, with a provoking smirk. She looked at Stubblefield, and then back to Dunk. "No, I'm gonna show this Mother Fucker!" She dropped trouser to reveal men's Fruit of the Loom, tighty-whity underwear. The guys' eyes were wide open, mesmerized, and confused at the same time. They couldn't look away. She lowered the tighty-whities, and out popped a strap-on dildo. She busted out laughing as she started waving her hips, and it wobbled side to side. The guys gasped, before exploding with laughter. Dominguez taunted them with it as she moved closer to them. Shocked, they needed to escape! They started hustling to get out of the truck, stumbling over each other.

As they fell out of the back of the truck, they rolled around on the ground laughing in tears not even aware of the pouring rain. Dominguez came to the back of the truck with her pants down, her strap-on still out, and stood towering over them flashing her pride. "I told you Mother Fucker, ... I got a dick, don't fuck with me!" Dunk walked up from behind and stuck out his hand, "You win, I'll never question you again!" The two shook hands.

Somewhere, through the hazy gray sky releasing the rain, there was a truth unspoken. Her need for trust, compassion, and wanting to be heard, may have been broken by the laughter, but wasn't lost. Dominguez's persistence to be accepted pushed on.

Chapter 8

Gay Club Tony's

If you didn't know you were in another country, the open mall in Okinawa would let you know immediately. It was the quintessential stereotypical Asian market, unless one spoke Japanese, it was all confusing. It catered to the locals as opposed to Americans and tourists. As one walked by, the vendors would show you merchandise, or say something catchy to get your attention, hoping you stop so they could make a sale. Every now and then, an unsuspecting customer would give in and buy something, realizing later, they could have bartered for it from another vender for much less. Everything from trinkets, clothes, music, or high-end electronics could be found. One area offered exotic foods, strictly off limits to the military or tourists. When those who were curious ventured in, the locals would swish them away, letting them know they were not welcome. Past the mall, the road opened slightly leading to what was known as "B.C. Street." There were several takes on what the B.C. stood for. Depending on whom you talked to, some called it "Bad Conduct Street" others "Before Christ." Regardless, the suggestion was well received by most of the Marines. This is the place where the party was.

The night was muggy, and the crew was just leaving the mall when another group appeared from a side alley. Were it not for the group's sudden entrance, the alley would be passed by without notice. The group was obviously military, but Noah couldn't tell which branch. Air Force, Army, and Navy were all stationed there. The Marines comprised most of the U.S. military on the island. The group was loud and boisterous. One tall black guy, being a bit flamboyant, caught Noah's attention. He recognized this behavior and realized, not just the tall black man, but the entire group were probably gay. He wasn't the only one to notice, some of the others did as well. Dunk spoke out, "Wow! That one's a Flamer!"

Stubblefield chimed in, "Fuck'en faggots." Noah kept quiet as the group moved on. As they reached B.C. Street, Noah took a quick glance back, making note of where they had come from. The flamboyant group disappeared as quickly as they appeared. The crew moved on a bit, but Noah had paused without realizing it. Hopkins hollered back, "Hey, you gonna stay there all night or are you coming?" Noah turned and quickly caught up to the crew of Marines as they headed into "Club Sgt Pepper's." The music was loud and poured out the door as they climbed the steps to get into the club. At the top, they began the push and shove to get through the crowd to the bar. Finally, they got their drinks and began to mingle.

Sgt Pepper's was one of the hotspots on the island for Americans. The military and their dependents hung out there because it catered to them. It had the latest information, music, videos, and trends from the states. It was also the place where the local Japanese women, who fancied Americans, came as well. Unlike so many of the other bars, which had "Buy Me Drinky Girls", the ones who came here were not prostitutes and not trying to make a buck off of the G.I.'s. As the crew mixed and mingled, a fight broke out in the back of the bar. The J.P.'s arrived quickly and had the two guys contained and removed. Noah had his fill of the loud music and the constant pushing and shoving. He decided it was time to head out. Besides, this would give him an opportunity to investigate the alley and the group they had seen earlier. He found both Hopkins and Stubblefield sitting in a booth with a couple of locals. He gave them a heads-up and took off down the stairs.

Once outside, the recent rain caused the dark street to hold the reflection of all the different neon lights that hung from above. The smell of the rain mixed with the open sewage created a stench only to its own. It was payday weekend and B.C. Street hustled with spirited young participants, ready to spend their money, and release pent up energy. The dollar converted to Yen made the coins tango in their pockets; only to be dispersed to the bars, merchants, and women who "recruited" in front of the hotels of Whisper Alley.

Noah stayed focused on the route, steadfast on getting back to the road leading to the mall. An occasional horn interrupted the voices of the ladies in front of the bars whispering for him to come inside. Once back on the mall street, he noticed a couple of guys heading down the small alley where the group appeared from earlier. He hung out for a few minutes to see if they would return, or if anyone else would leave or enter. A few minutes went by before a few more guys entered the alley. They were too ambiguous in appearance for him to tell if they were straight or gay. He started to pace back and forth between the alley and the mall. He had just turned away from the mall when he heard a ruckus from behind. Looking over his shoulder, the flamboyant group from earlier had returned. Not wanting to draw attention, he moved over to one of the store windows, pretending to be interested in its merchandise. Once they passed, he watched out of the corner of his eye to see where they went so he could follow. They had gone down the alley again.

Noah paused briefly and went over to see where it led. The group was slightly ahead and silhouetted from the light in the distance. The light from the mall dropped off quickly, and once on the street, it remained dimly lit. Noah moved further down the alley without getting too close to the group in front of him. It was flanked with small lights that illuminated the backdoors, scattered trash, stacked boxes and garbage cans. Noah noticed a rat jumping from one as he passed by. The moonlight and occasional streetlamp lit up the upper sides of the building, showcasing the black metal fire-escapes with ladder wells hanging from one side. He was now far enough down to notice the alley lit up at a dead-end clearing and turn-around parking lot. He remained in the shadows as the group entered the clearing. As he watched, they walked through the lot and over to the left side buildings to one of the back entrances. Noah thought they were going to go in when they walked past it and on to one of the ladder wells hanging down. Each one started climbing the ladder well and landed on the platform above.

Noah moved a bit closer. He could see the platform was lit up and had a red door that entered the building. In front of the door was a small Japanese man sitting in a chair. He could hear some laughter coming from the group as the gentleman stood up and opened the door to let them in. He was a door man.

Noah heard someone coming from behind and quickly acted as though he was just leaving. As he passed by, the two young military guys exchanged looks. When they thought Noah couldn't hear, one said, "He's hot." Noah was quite sure he had just found a gay bar. He continued a bit and stopped to return and see where these guys went. Once again, they headed to the building, up the ladder well, stopping to talk briefly to the doorman, and then on inside.

Noah was nervous and still hadn't the courage to go up. Besides, how would he get passed the doorman? Maybe it was a private club and you had to be a member, or referred by someone to get in. He stood in the shadows watching; trying to get the courage up, but still wasn't sure. The door on the platform opened and out walked some guys. One stopped and spoke to the door man then kissed him on the cheek as he said goodbye. Bingo, that was enough to convince him. Straight guys don't kiss goodbye. As they came down, they passed Noah. Noah looked back at them briefly to catch them doing the same. He let out a chuckle and thought to himself, how long had this been here? He had been on the island for almost a year.

He finally made up his mind to try and get in. Two guys walked by him and headed to the entrance. Noah decided he would follow them. He walked a few feet behind and paused briefly as they made their way up the ladder well. While waiting, a small sign on the wall caught his attention, "Club Tony's" with an arrow pointing upward to the ladder well. It definitely is a club he thought, as he started his ascent. Once at the top, the two just finished with the doorman and were headed inside. The doorman closed the door and turned to see Noah approach. Immediately without hesitation, "No, no, no, you can no come in!" Noah dumbfounded and a bit embarrassed, quickly asked "Why?" He responded, "This not your kind of club… you no like! … Only members! (Shaking his finger) …you no come in!" Noah responded, "How do you know I won't like it, (he leaned in) I can assure you I will." The guy moved back a bit, "You go…" and shooed Noah away with his hands.

Noah could see this guy was not going to budge. He thought about how he could convince this guy. Maybe he should just turn around and go, until he could get someone to vouch for him. Noah thought it's now or never, then it hit him; he spontaneously reached over and grabbed the doorman by the shoulder and kissed him on the cheek. Letting go, the doorman was in shock, stepped back, and put both hands to his cheeks. His mouth fell open and he sat down briefly on the seat. With a great big smile, his manners changed, and he became very flirtatious and girly. He stood up, batted his eyes, "Oh I like you!' he took Noah by the arm, "You come in, you come in!" as he escorted him to the door. Pushing a button, Noah could hear a buzzer as the door clicked open and the doorman let him in.

Toadvine

Tony's was a gay bar that operated clandestinely off B.C. Street and was known only by word of mouth. Naval Criminal Service probably knew of it, but unless one was proven gay, or at least gay friendly, they could not get past the backdoor man. The dimly lit, smoked filled room at Club Tony's was a bit more than Scott could bear. He and Jarrod had been watching a pool game between their friend L.J and another guy. Now that L.J. had gone to the bar to get a drink, it was time to refresh their drinks as well. A wall ornament long enough, Scott reached over to Jarrod, tapped him on the shoulder and motioned for him to follow. It was just a few months ago that the two met there at Tony's. Both Marines, Jarrod was a supply clerk with Landing Support Battalion, and Scott was an admin with Headquarters, Marine Corps Base. As Scott and Jarrod worked through the maze of people, they stopped briefly to chat with the owner of the night club, Tony Nakamura.

Tony was a small, older gay Japanese guy who owned several different night clubs. Club Tony's was the only gay one. He had opened it in 1979 to fill the void of gay clubs on the island as well as his fondness for blonde Marines. Catering to gay American military members, he was familiar with the risk they faced with being outed. He tried to create a haven for their special need of privacy. On any given Friday or Saturday night, it wouldn't be uncommon to see him in the bar making his rounds introducing himself, laughing or chatting it up with his patrons.

Seeing Scott and Jarrod walking hand and hand, Tony stopped them. "Oh, you two, …too much in love, …look at you love birds! Get a room!" He stuck his finger in his mouth, like he was going to get sick, before letting out a chuckle, as he reached to hug and kiss each on the cheek. Scott and Jarrod, both giggled, as they reciprocated. They exchanged pleasantries and moved on to the bar as Tony went about greeting other customers.

Once at the bar, they found L.J. still talking to the gentleman he had been playing pool with earlier. There was an opening next to them so the two moved in. Jarrod, addressing L.J. as he approached, "There you are…." L.J. turned slightly to greet him. Making sure the young guy couldn't see him, he gave a frown, nodded in the young guy's direction, and mouthed, "Noooo…" Jarrod picked up his message but decided to have some fun with him. Responding loudly, "What, what, what was that you were trying to say? The music is a bit loud in here." L.J. snapped back with a frown. Jarrod turned and introduced himself to the young man, "Hi, I'm Jarrod, this is Scott, and you are?" as he stuck out his hand. The young man, smiled with a big smile, showing his yellow teeth and the bit of chewing tobacco tucked behind his lower lip. He quickly grabbed a cup from behind, and spit in it, getting a little bit on his hand. He wiped it on his blue jeans and reached to shake their hand. With a deep southern drawl, "Howdy, I'm Bob, pleased to meet yah!" Jarrod, who was exceptionally clean and self-conscious of his appearance, was taken aback by his behavior and withdrew his hand. Pulling it back to his neck he responded with a bit of resistance, "Nice to meet you Bob…" He immediately looked at L.J. who was now staring back giving him a sarcastic smile of, 'I told you so.' Scott was amused, "So where you from Bob?" Bob smiled, "I'm from Alabama, a small town outside of Tuscaloosa, a place called

Toadvine. Few folks have heard of it." Scott, stunned, unsure if he had heard him right, "I'm sorry, did you say Toadvine?" Bob shook his head, "Yes sir, you got it right." In amazement, Scott let out an unwitting chuckle, "You are not serious?" questioning Bob, "Toadvine, …really?" All three were now listening to Bob. "Sure thang, not many have heard of it." Jarrod, a bit uppity, was still standoffish, "I never knew a place called Toadvine could even exist. I would hate to think how it got its name…?" Bob started in, "Oh it's not what you think… It really is an interesting…" Jarrod rudely interrupted, "I was only joking, I didn't…" When Scott interrupted him, "Jarrod let him speak, …No, no, come on now, I want to hear this, come on, a place called Toadvine? … you've got to be kidding me. How often do you meet someone from Toadvine, Alabama?" Jarrod gave a questioning frown and looked at L.J. still grinning. "Oh, this is going to be interesting!" Jarrod bemused, "He has a story, oh my God he really is going to tell the story! You can't be serious?" Jarrod waved to the bartender, "Hold up, bartender, oh bartender, I'm going to need a stronger drink for this one." Bob started in. "There were a big guy back in the day, a stout fellow, but not too good look'en; folks say he was covered in warts and his Momma found him under a vine where the toads hid. So, they nicknamed him Toadvine." Jarrod and L.J. both let out a laugh, but quickly received a frown from Scott. "Come on you, it's not right to make fun of someone because of their looks, you don't know what was wrong with this guy…" Bob interrupted, "Wait, wait, hold on now, before you get all bent out shape…" Bob continued, "Ole Toadvine might have been ugly, but was big, and had a big heart. Having been made fun of all his life, he also had to learn to defend himself and fight. He was a bit scrappy. So, one day a friend of his was being bullied, and shoved around, and before he knew it, was getting beat on by a guy three times his size. Ole Toadvine tried to stay out of it, but it wasn't a fair fight, the guy had pretty much already won the fight, but wouldn't give in and kept beating his friend. Some thought he was going to kill him. So, Ole Toadvine was the only one to stop it and stepped in. The guy didn't like it and turned on him. Ole Toadvine, being big and scrappy, won the fight defending his friend. That friend later became a war hero because of his military prowess, and the folks wanted to name the post office after him. But, remembering what his buddy had done, told them none of his accomplishments would have been possible if it weren't for Ole Toadvine. So, he told them to name it after him. That's how it got its name." Scott, along with the other two, still looked on in amazement. Jarrod chimed in, "Thank God, it has a good ending…," L.J., now with sarcasm, was bored and over the whole thing, "And there you have it folks, all the way from Toadvine, Alabama to Okinawa Japan." Jarrod started laughing, turned to Bob, "Honey, not meaning to be rude, but how would I have ever made it through life without knowing about, Ole Toadvine." L.J. turned to the bar and flagged the bartender, "I need a refill, and make it a double, …, (under his breath) …something has got to get this night going," …he paused briefly to look at Bob, "Toadvine Alabama!"

While L.J. was waiting on his drink, he looked down to the end of the bar, where he noticed a tall blonde guy. He reached back to Jarrod, tugged on his arm, and pointed toward where the guy was standing. L.J. walked up next to him to order a drink. The gentleman did not notice. While he was ordering, L.J. started making a face at Jarrod, and nodded his head, "Look who's next to me." Jarrod decided to help the situation along, reached up and grabbed the blonde's arm from behind. He quickly turned to see who it was. Jarrod, smiled, "It was just there, …the bicep, … you know, …I couldn't help it." The blonde chuckled and smiled turning back to the bar for his drink. With Jarrod coaxing him on, L.J. turned to the guy, "I'm sorry my friend doesn't get out much, please forgive her!" The blonde turned and smiled, "No harm, it's alright, takes the edge off, nothing wrong being friendly." L.J. smiled, thinking, this guy has really pretty eyes and a good smile. Jarrod, in the back, pointed to the guys' buttocks, and mouthed in silence to L.J. "Oh my God!" then acted as though he was going to grab them with his hands. L.J frowned and, turned to the guy quickly and grinned, "Nothing wrong with being friendly," waving Jarrod away. The guy received his drink, when L.J stuck his hand out, "Nice to meet you, and you are?" The blonde answered back, "Oh, that's not fair, you haven't told me who you are yet? You go first…" as he reached out to shake L.J.'s extended hand. "Larry Joe Cohen, but they call me L.J for short."

The blonde came back "Well Larry Joe, ...L.J. that is, I'm Noah, nice to meet you!" L.J's eyes lit up, "You say Noah?" Noah replied, "Yes, I know I get it all the time." L.J grinned, "So is your family religious?" Noah knew where this conversation was going, "No, not religious, not Jewish, and no I didn't build an ark." L.J smiled, "Guess you have been asked a few questions before," and chuckled, and continued, "You know why there are no unicorns?" Noah puzzled grinned, "No I give..." L.J. continued, "Well, Noah gathered one male and female of all the animals, except the two unicorns, they were a gay couple!" Noah laughed, "Ok, haven't heard that one before." Noah was curious about this place he now found himself in, "This your first time here?" L.J. replied with a smile, "No, we've been coming here since we first got on the island. I was told about it from a few friends who used to be stationed here." Noah told him about the group of flamboyant guys, and his adventure of building up his courage to get in, and finally having to kiss the doorman. L.J sympathized with him, before asking, "I take it you're a Marine, at least you look like one." Noah perked up, "Yes over a year now." He could tell L.J. wasn't a Marine, "How about you? Are you in...?" L.J. chuckled, "Yes, of course, who else would come to the Rock. I'm a Navy Corpsman, stationed at Camp Lester. Where you at?" Noah told him, but wasn't comfortable talking about the Marine Corps. He was more interested in the others sitting at the bar, "So, you here alone?" L.J. had forgotten to introduce him to the rest of the group. "Oh, ... Oh my God no, ... excuse me ...," as he introduced them, "This is Jarrod, and his partner Scott, and our new friend Bob, he was just telling us about his hometown." Jarrod was anxious to meet him, "You are the first Noah I've met." L.J interrupted, "Uh yeah, we already went over this, ... So, first time here?" "Yes, just discovered it by chance," and then proceeded to tell them about the awkward entrance. Scott, provoking the other two, asked, "I hear a bit of an accent, where are you from in the states?" Jarrod interrupted being afraid of the prior response from Bob, "No, no more, you don't have to answer that?" as he pinched Scott. Noah laughed, "It's ok...," as though he was being left out on something. "Indiana, a town called Blotch." L.J. spoke up, "Thank God you didn't say Toadvine!" Noah puzzled, "What, Toadvine?

What the hell is Toadvine?" Jarrod interjected, "Ask Bob, when you have more time, he'll explain it." Bob laughed, "The night is filled with different names, …your name, …and my hometown, don't worry it's a long story I'll share sometime." Changing the subject, "So, you going to stay for the show?" Noah not familiar, "What show?" L.J., attracted to the innocence of Noah, explained, "They have a drag show here on payday weekend, it is a lot of fun! Tony usually MC's. The Drag Queens are usually guys stationed here, but sometimes they have a local performer as well. He provides a room and place to get ready, so they can keep their things here and not on base." Just then, a loud boisterous group came through, interrupting the conversation. They all paused to see the ruckus. Noah immediately recognized the group, he leaned over to L.J., "That is the group I saw earlier, the one that I was telling you about." He recognized the tall, flamboyant black man, and the other few flocking around him. L.J laughing excitedly, "No wonder!" as he pointed to the tall black man, "...That is Martin," pointing to a well-built muscular guy, "...and that is David, … they are the ones performing tonight. No wonder you could tell they were gay, they're out there, … how no one knows about them is beyond me, how could you not!" Jarrod asked, "So how long you been out Noah?" Noah was a bit taken back by the question, "Out, I'm not sure, (as he stuck his hand up and did air quotes) …that I am out." Jarrod laughed, "Well, whenever you decide, we have this group in the Corps we call family, its code for being gay. It can come in handy at times when you're trying to feel your way around." Noah perked up, "Family? I've heard a few at work talk about family." L.J grabbed Noah by the arm, "Come on." The group moved further into the bar and closer to the stage, parking it off to one side, when Tony, the owner, took center stage.

"Good evening, ladies, and gentlemen! And I use those words lightly. Tonight, we have an incredibly special treat for those of you who haven't found their trick!!! (The audience chuckles) It brings me no joy in telling you this, but tonight will be her last performance here at Club Tony's. (The crowd does an augh!) Like so many of you that arrive on the island as a newbie, she has done her time here on the rock, and will be leaving to go back stateside to reclaim the title as, 'The Whore from Baltimore!' But for you here on the island, she serves you from the Kinser Chow Hall, and is better known as 'The Queen of Camp Kinser!' Ladies and Gentlemen, 'Ms. Allined Isaman!" (All- I- need-is-a-man)

The lights went dark on the stage. The audience was quiet as a soft man's voice came across the sound system. "To all my children, this song is the message I leave with you. Sang by Ms. Diva herself, Diana Ross. "Ain't No Mountain High Enough." A single spotlight came on center stage on Allined. She had her back toward the audience and wore a long white feathered floor length smock coat, her black kinky hair cascading down the middle of her back. As the song kicked in, she turned around and looked up into the spotlight and in perfect lip sync she continued with the song. Two young guys came from behind as she slipped out of the feathered smock. She was now revealing a strapless, full length, silver sequined gown, with long silver gloves. Diamond earrings burst from black hair on both sides matching the huge diamond necklace choker surrounding her neck. She moved from side to side working the audience and being tipped as she went. L. J turned to Noah, "What do you think?" Noah was in amazement, "Oh my God! …Unbelievable, this is the guy we just saw?" He turned back to watch the performance, which was extended a bit because so many had lined up to tip her and say goodbye. When she finally finished the line, she returned to center stage and gave a cue to the D.J to lower the music, "I just want to say how loved you all have made me feel this evening. Where's Tony?" … Someone pointed to Tony standing off to one side of the stage, as she continued, … "Tony, I can't say how thankful we are to have you. You have created a place for us to get away. Even if just for a few minutes, you have allowed us to escape from our everyday lives, and come here and be open, free to be who we are. For that, I can't say enough how much you and Club Tony's has meant to me, and so many others while here on the island." The audience let out a round of cheer and applause. Allined continued, "Yes, yes, a well-deserved round of applause," as he turned to the audience, "… Now let's finish this song. Are you ready to twirl girls?" The crowd let out a cheer as the song came back up loud, she picked up the lip sync, where she left off and as a finale' broke out in a full twirl, with the crowd going crazy. When she finished, the audience gave a standing ovation.

Tony returned to the stage, "Tank you, Tank you, tank you, …she never fails to excite, …the dog that is." Allined gave a frown to Tony and bowed to the crowd as she left the stage. Tony, "Oh I'm going to miss you!" As he blew kisses to her. "Let's hear it one more time for Ms. Allined Isaman…" Tony continues, "Ok, ok, you all enjoy yourself? (The audience cheers) If you no enjoy then you do not drink enough… 'Buy me drinky!!'" as he laughed and grinned. "What you no feeling tonight? Come on, any sailors, let's here for the Navy!" as he stuck the mic out to the audience. L.J., along with others in the crowd, let out cat calls, and whistles, with a few boos' mixed in. Tony laughed, "That more like it!" He then broke out in a slow cadence singing as he passed by studying some of the ones, he thought might be sailors, "Navy, Navy, … I'm in doubt," …he then raised his voice… "Why you belly hang'en out!" He slumped and pushed his belly forward. The audience laughed and played along. He quickly came back center stage and looked out, "What about my Marines?" The audience got real loud with applause, cat calls and whistles… Tony, laughed and cheered them on, before he tried to calm them, "Shush, shush, shuuuuush," as the audience slowly faded. Once the room quieted, Tony took the opportunity, "Well now we know where the bottoms are…" The room grew into laughter and boo's simultaneously, as Tony laughed along. He then asked, "I need a sailor, raise hand if sailor?" A guy close to the stage raised his hand. Tony walked over toward him. "So, you know why they have Marines on ship?" With the mic in his face, the sailor replied "No." Tony then asked, "Have you ever been with Marines on a ship?" The young sailor answered "No." Tony gave him a frown, "Oh, (pausing) ... how unlucky for you," as he moved away, "Everybody want to be on ship with the Marines." The Marines in the room let out a big howl. Once center stage, he looked back to the sailor, "I going to tell you why they have Marines on ship, …. because sheep would be too obvious!" The crowd oohed and awed with laughter. He then picked Noah out of the audience, who was with L.J., standing close to the stage. "Oh, you pretty one. You been here befow?" Noah, a bit shy, shook his head, "No this is the first time." Tony smiled, "Oh, you Cherry boy!" As the audience laughed, Tony continued, "How long you been on Okinawa, you newbie?" Noah replied, "No, been here nine months." Tony appeared a bit shocked, "Nine months? And you just find Club Tony?" Noah shook his head in agreement. Tony, noticing L.J., pointed at the two of them, "You two together?" Both replied, "We just met." Tony addressing the audience, "Oh young love." As he clutched over his heart, he quickly addressed L.J.… "He's been on the island nine months, … girl you hit jack pot, you are getting laid tonight!" L.J. leaned into Noah and smiled, and grabbed his arm, both laughed. Tony noticed, "Oh look, she wants to make sure he not get away, (he lets out a gasp, as if he was taken back) … you want it, you a ho!" The audience was bursting with laughter. Noah and L.J. were both a bit embarrassed. Tony smiled, "You two good sports, I leave you alone now, and wish you best on you long relationship, …and see you again in here looking for new love tomorrow night." The audience laughed again, Tony continued, "I won't ask your name, but you go to bar, tell them Tony buys your drink." He turned to the audience, "Everyone, tanks to these young guys for being so kind."

"Up next, all the way from Raleigh Durham, when she's not deployed taking care of the Marines on ship, she takes care of the horny boys of Camp Hansen. You can find her at the U.S.O. restroom, in the last stall on the left. Ladies and Gentlemen please welcome Ms. Day Nish."

The lights went dark, and a deep southern drawl could be heard from across the sound system. "Hey ya'll! I hope you all are having a fun time! Well, if not, I hope I can help change that! You all, I just want you to know how sad I am that my good friend and bitch sister is leaving the island! I'm going to miss her, how about you?" The audience cheered. "Well, I just want to show her how much I care. So, tonight I won't be lip syncing, I'll be singing in my own voice. You all know "Freebird" is the anthem for leaving the island, tonight I'll be saying, 'Fly High!' to Ms. Allined. Please bear with me, and, if you like, feel free to join in." The stage went dark. The audience heard in a cappella, "If I leave here tomorrow, would you still remember me…" The spotlight came up center stage with a bit of smog rising, the background music kicked in. A small bird-like figure, dressed in black, crouching with huge black wings, appeared. The song continued as the figure slowly started to rise and the wings opened revealing Day Nish. She wore a black skintight body suit with a form fitting hood, with a bright red ponytail coming out of the top. Her face was completely made-up in full drag. The high heeled, black patten leather stiletto boots she wore caused her to tower when completely upright. With the wings full span, the audience applauded, as she continued to sing, slowly hovering very seductively while working her way around the stage. Noah watched her intensely, and caught how she remained very much in character, to her costume, and mimicked a bird on occasion. Her voice was actually genuinely nice as she sang. L.J and Noah, along with the audience, watched mesmerized by the performance. Noah whispered to L.J., "I don't think I've ever seen anything so creative." L.J. whispered back, "She makes her own costumes." Noah gave a gesture of surprise as he turned to watch her break out in a creative dance, before bringing the show to a close.

Day Nish finished her performance and took her bow to a standing ovation, as Tony came back on stage. "Give it up for Ms. Day Nish, … who wouldn't want her with your coffee in the morning!" The audience continued to applaud as Tony walked on center stage, he sang cadence as the applause faded, "… Who's that woman dressed in green? That no woman, that a gay Marine," while Day Nish exited the stage. "Ladies and Gentlemen tank you so much! You have been a wonderful audience! Join us again at midnight for late show. In meantime, drink up, love you long time G.I. no shit!"

Noah turned to L.J. amused by what he had just experienced, "Wow, that was just fucking crazy! I don't think I've ever seen anything like that before." L.J. laughing, "I told you, it was worth staying around for." Noah looked around the club mesmerized. He was taken aback, not just about the show, but the fact he was in this club and the whole gay experience. He wasn't alone. There were others just like him, and they were not just getting by, but they were surviving, and flourishing. Being able to laugh about the whole experience made it feel safe to let go. It was like being at home, being with 'family.' Even if it was just for a minute, all the hate and bigotry seemed to fade away inside the bar.

Chapter 9

Chicken

Kitamae was a small village just outside the gate of Camp Foster. It was a mixed community of U.S. military and Japanese nationals. It catered to its Japanese locals, but businesses closest to the gate seemed more interested in making a quick buck from the Marines. There were mostly bars, restaurants, and massage parlors. On occasion, you could find a transient street food vender. They would place their carts up and down the street at various locations, serving chicken yakitori, fried rice, or yakisoba. Sometimes they served fried chicken, in an effort to replicate what was found in the U.S. deep south. Dunk finished picking up his order from one of the carts and caught up to the others huddled on the sidewalk. They had all stopped briefly to grab a bite to eat before heading on to Club Kitamae. Dunk approaching, "Ya'll, know I come from Texas, ...and you know we take pride in what we grow 'Everything's big in Texas,' but I want yah to look at this." Dunk held up the breaded chicken leg he had just ordered. It was unusually large. The group started to laugh. "Now, I'm no expert, but I'm just saying, I've seen some big chickens, but I ain't never seen a chicken big enough to have a leg like this!" The other Marines continued to laugh as they listened. "So, you gonna tell me, they have a secret to growing giant chickens here on this island? I drive every day on this island, and I can't say that I've ever seen a chicken." Stubblefield decided to harass Dunk a bit, "That ain't no chicken, that's a goddamn cat's leg Dunk! They are calling it chicken, just so you'll buy the damn thing. There ain't no American going to buy a damn cat leg. Just shut up and eat the damn thing." Dunk took a bite out of it, "Taste like chicken." Stubblefield laughing, "Of course it does, everything tastes like chicken, except fish, fish don't taste like no chicken." Dunk took another bite, "Well, we'll just go along with chicken, 'cause I ain't eat'n no cat." Giselle, laughing in agreement, "That's right, …that's what they say, everything tastes like chicken. We tried rattle snake out at twenty-nine stumps, taste just like chicken." Noah a bit surprised, "You've eaten rattle snake?" Giselle taking pride of his accomplishment. "Sure did, the thing snuck up on us while we sat around the hooch. So, we killed it think'en it might get one of us. One of the guys in our squad said he knew how to filet and cook it. We had been out there for a month living off of C-Rats, so we fired that bad boy right up over the fire. It tasted just like chicken." The group continued to laugh. Noah shook his head, "I get the killing part, …I hate a snake, terrified of them! I don't think I could eat one, and definitely not a poisonous one. Were you afraid of getting sick?" Giselle smiled proudly, "No, it's all about how you kill it. You got to get behind the venom sacks, about an inch or so behind the head, and cut it off." Noah shook his head. "No, …I don't think so, …see that's the problem. You assume I would touch it …huh, …nah, …that ain't going to happen!" Dunk curiously asked, "So Barlow, what's the strangest thing you've tried?" Noah laughed, "Let me think about it." While he thought for a minute, the group finished their meals and started to walk toward the club. "I would have to say coon. I tried coon once." Barlow grinned. Stubblefield, a Tennessee guy, was surprised. "Coon, now coon is some good eaten, if it's cooked right." Noah was a bit surprised that Stubblefield had tried it. Dunk inquisitive, "It taste like chicken?" Noah along with the group laughed, "No, no I don't think it did. I think it kinda tastes like beef, …just a bit more gamey." They were almost at the entrance to the bar, when Dunk asked Stubblefield the same question, "What's the strangest thing you've eaten Stubb?" Stubblefield, paused for a minute before answering, "That'd be Sally Mae Gothenburg, and don't ask me if she tasted like chicken." The group, taken by surprise, broke out in laughter as they entered the bar.

As the four entered the bar, the ladies who worked at the club escorted them to their tables. Dunk and Stubblefield sat at one booth with two of the girls. They were regulars at Club Kitamae. Noah and

Giselle sat in a booth, telling the girls thanks, but no thanks. Neither were interested in their company or buying a drink for them. These girls were called "Buy Me Drinky Girls." Their purpose was to keep the Marines company, get them to buy their drinks, and stay longer. They kept their drinks watered down so they could last all night without getting drunk. Tonight, was an opportunity for Noah and Giselle to catch up. They met when first arriving on the island. Sgt Rose, a common friend back stateside, had told Noah about Giselle and to look him up. It turns out they were stationed together at Truck Company. Giselle was gay and, like Noah, still very closeted. Although they were both stationed together, they seldom saw each other because of their work schedule. Over the next few days this would change as the "Big Inspection" truck company would be going through. Once every two years, the Inspector General and his staff inspected the Company, making sure it was abiding the regulations set forth by Headquarters Marine Corps. This required all hands-on deck, and most of the drivers would be in the motor pool helping to get ready. Giselle's truck was next to Noah's in the lineup. It was common to talk about work when they did see each other, but never anything gay or compromising. At the Club, Noah suspected the "Buy Me Drinky Girls" in the bar knew what was up with the two of them. The two had been in before and got use to them sitting alone. As they spoke, Noah noticed an older, large black man come in and sit in the booth next to them. Noah nodded to Giselle making him aware to keep his voice down in case the gentleman might hear. It was unusual to see an older Marine out and about. Most were married or had family and didn't frequent the local bars. Because of his age alone, Noah suspected he must be high ranking. They best be on good behavior while he was here. The conversation had been mostly about truck companies' portion of the inspection before Giselle changed the subject to Sgt Rose. Noah welcomed the conversation, "I haven't heard from him since arriving on the island." Giselle made a joke about Rose being the 'Chicken Hawk' of both Camp Delmar and the Oceanside pier. Both agreed how aggressive Rose was when pursuing them. It was probably the same with other young unsuspecting guys. Noah curious, "Have you found Club Tony's?" Giselle spoke quietly, "No, I know about it, but have been afraid to go there on my own." As they continued, both shared who they thought might be gay.

Noah looked up from the table to see Corporal Miller, his boss, walking through the door. He caught a glimpse of Noah and came over to the table. "Man, I've been looking for you all over." He had been searching for Noah and Dunk. Both were the only two with ammo license. They had been assigned a last-minute run leaving early in the morning. Corporal Miller went to inform Dunk, as Noah said his goodbye. Giselle, still wanting to hang out, stayed with Stubblefield and agreed to walk back with him. Corporal Miller came back with Dunk and the three were off to the motor-pool to get the trucks ready for morning.

Giselle grabbed his drink and moved to a stool. Sitting down, he looked over to see what was happening with Stubblefield. He was talking with Akie. Akie was the girl he came in to see a couple nights a week. Although she was a "Buy Me Drinky Girl," he would pay Mamasan up front for the entire evening. Akie could then sit with him for the night. Akie and Stubblefield had a genuine affection for each other, and he spoke about trying to marry her. This would require buying her contract from the bar. Most of the girls were from the Philippines and were brought here on rotation. Some were brought for prostitution; others were here just as bar help. It was a sordid underground of sex trafficking, but if you knew and paid the right people, it was overlooked. Either way, Akie was indebted to the Club. A contract had to be purchased for her freedom; this was a risky venture with no real guarantee.

Giselle turned and waved for another drink. The older black man came and leaned on the bar next to him. Sitting his empty glass down, he motioned for another. Mamasan came down and refreshed their drinks. Giselle acknowledged the older man with a nod. The guy took the opportunity to speak. "So, I couldn't help but hear you guys are getting ready for an inspection." Giselle was a bit hesitant to speak. "Yeah, …we are having an IG inspection." The older man smiled at him with a chuckle, "Oh, I don't envy you there! I've been through a few of those myself." Giselle continued "This is my first one, I'm not sure what to expect." The older man pulled the bar stool out and sat down. "Oh, they're not too bad, if you know what you're doing…" as he took a swig of his drink, "… and you have been doing what you're supposed to on a regular basis." Giselle in agreement, "I guess you're right. Staff Sergeant and Gunny, they keep us tight. Both have been through a couple. They seem to know what the inspectors are looking for." The older man took a drink and continued, "They're pretty much all the same. A list comes out with the changes, and of course the routine stuff, that always stays the same. But it is mainly the changes we're looking for." Giselle picked up on the "We're looking for" part. "Wait, did I hear you say that correctly? 'We are looking'…" The older gentleman chuckled and gave a quick glance to Giselle. "You're quick. Yes, you heard right, probably shouldn't have let that one slip out. I'm on the IG inspection team." Giselle instantly was intimidated, "Oh, I'm sorry I probably should…" Before he could finish his sentence, the older man interrupted. "It's all right, relax, keep your ass sit'en down. You didn't do anything wrong." Giselle calmed down and grabbed his drink tossing it back. The older gentleman did the same, and then waved at Mamasan, "Give us another round, this one is on me." He continued, "I don't like hanging out at the SNCO Club on base, it's to stuffy, and I can't be myself, everybody gets uptight or tries to kiss your ass, they know I'm on the IG staff, and of course my rank." Giselle hanging on every word, "So who are you, if you don't mind my asking?" The older guy gave a look of contemplation, "I'm Gunnery Sergeant Phobos, I'm the lead inspector for Motor-T." Giselle, impressed, "Gunnery Sergeant, I've never spoken to one, other than briefly in passing. I mean, they're never around, and when they are you better be on your best behavior, you speak only if spoken too." Gunny stuck his hand out. Giselle shook it. "I never would have thought, most of ours, they're old and decrepit. Sorry no offense, but you look like you're in good shape, …and no ways near old enough to be one." Gunny Phobos chuckled, "Oh, I take care of myself, try to eat right and work out. I think being around you young guys keeps me young at heart and in shape. So, you know who I am, so what about you?" Giselle surprised and almost ashamed, "Oh, sorry, I'm Lance Corporal Anthony Giselle, but everyone calls me Giselle. I'm a truck driver at 9th Motors." Gunny Phobos smiled. "Well Lance Corporal Giselle, nice to meet you. You know, I'll probably be the one inspecting your truck." as he chuckled, he waved over Mamasan and ordered a couple of shots for the two of them. They toasted and threw it back. Gunny gave a once over on Giselle, "You seem like a pretty squared away one, are you ready?" Giselle felt the alcohol hitting him a bit. "Ready for what, …I'm ready for anything…" and laughed. "Oh, it's my turn, to buy you a drink…" He waved to Mamasan. When she came over, Gunny, interrupted the order, "Thank you, but I still have one." Giselle insisted, but the Gunny was firm. "I still have one to finish, along with a walk home." Giselle looked around to see Stubblefield was still in the booth wrapped up in Akie. "Yeah, I got a walk home too. The hill is a killer, and truck company, it is at the veeeery top." Gunny chuckled, "Well mine isn't at the top, but it is still a bit of an ass kicker." Giselle curious, "You stay in that new SNCO barracks?" Gunny could see Giselle was a bit drunk and had loosened up. "Yeah, we even have our own rooms." …he chuckled with sarcasm… "I'm stationed at Camp Courtney; my wife and kids are here with me, and we have our place in family housing. I stay at the temp SNCO barracks overnight when I travel for inspections." Giselle was impressed by the fact the Gunny had his own quarters. His speech was becoming slurred. "They got us in an open squad bay, … It's divided into cubicles, fucking cubicles, like what kind of privacy is that … if anyone lets a fart, you can still smell it… Oh, …and the snoring." Gunny let out a chuckle, as Giselle continued, "No, you have not heard snoring until you have been in my barracks. Oh my god, you can't get away from it. So, we have this one guy we call "Hog Head Horine," he revs it up, so you kind of turn to get away from it, then from the other direction, another guy, Borst, he kicks in. I swear one night they were in competition with each other. One would let out a snore, and just a few minutes later, the other would do one louder. I had to go sleep in the TV lounge it was so bad." He started laughing when Gunny joined in. "I remember those days, and I wouldn't want to live through that again." He looked at Giselle and patted him on the leg. "With that my young friend, I need to get going, and I would recommend the same for you. You'll want to be up bright and early, and ready to go tomorrow." Giselle looked over to see Stubblefield still occupied, turned back to the

Gunny, "I'm with my buddy over there. I think he's going to be awhile." Gunny looked over to the booth. "Yep, I think your right. You're welcome to walk back with me." Giselle surprised, "You mind, the gate guards can be dicks if you're a bit tipsy." Gunny shook his head. "No problem, I can assure you they won't say anything with me." Giselle let Stubblefield know he was leaving and came back over to the Gunny.

The two crossed the street at the Kitamae cross walk heading to Camp Foster. The gate Sentry came out of the guard shack once they approached. They made their ID's ready, and the Sentry waved them through. While passing by, Giselle put on his best sober act. Once on the base, the alcohol kicked it up a notch and he stumbled. Gunny grabbed and held him up to keep him from falling. "Hold on there, big guy, you'll make it." Before they knew it, the climb up the hill was in front of them. Giselle paused to take a glance at what lie ahead. He gathered the motivation to complete the task at hand. "Did I say I live at the very top of this bitch!" He let out a laugh and Gunny gave a push on his back, "Come on, a young stud like you should be able to handle this with no problem." Giselle pushed on. "Now I know why they had us hump Mount Motherfucker in recruit training, ... it was to prepare us for this." About halfway up was the SNCO barracks, where Gunny stayed. "Well, this is it for me. ...I tell you what, I have an inspection checklist inside my room. Come on up and get it, ...besides you'll get to see what the SNCO barracks look like." Giselle, excited and still feeling the effects of the alcohol, "Awesome! You sure?" He started to stumble along with the Gunny as they walked to the barracks. Giselle asked, "Won't I get in trouble for being in here?" The Gunny answered with a question. "For what? ... you're with me, ...If anyone asks, you're getting a check list." Gunny held his finger up to his lips, shushing him to be quiet, "We don't want to wake anyone."

Once inside, Gunny told Giselle to make himself at home. If he wanted a drink, there was beer or alcohol in the fridge. The room was a small efficiency type studio. A large bed sat in the middle of the room. Off to one side was a bathroom, on the other side was a small efficiency kitchen. Gunny went to the restroom, "I'll be just a minute, hang on and I'll have that inspection sheet for you." Giselle went to the fridge, opened it, but decided he'd had enough for one night and closed it. He looked around checking out the studio and finally sat at a small table by the window. He was ready to get home and get in his own bed. He didn't want to be rude. Gunny was being cool, and willing to help the crew out for the inspection. The door opened and Gunny came out in a Dashiki robe and kufi brimless hat. It looked very African and tribal. Gunny was a huge and very dark black man. The bright orange Dashiki, lined in a tribal pattern, made him appear even darker and larger. Seeing him in his robe made Giselle feel uncomfortable, but he didn't say anything. Gunny turned on some low music which matched the robe he wore. The tribal sounds filled the air. Giselle had never been to a black person's home, other than sharing a cubicle with some of the black guys in the barracks. Maybe this was a cultural thing he wasn't familiar with. Gunny went to his satchel and pulled out some papers, shuffled them, and brought one over stopping in front of Giselle. He laid the paper on the table. His crotch was right in front of Giselle's face, and he couldn't help noticing the Gunny had an erection pushing the robe out. Giselle was now extremely uncomfortable. He realized this was not about him getting a checklist, or the Gunny being kindhearted. This man had been working him from the moment he came up to him at the bar. Giselle was now scared. How did Gunny know, or did he? Was he that obvious? Regardless, he wasn't into him. Giselle decided to play off being straight. Giselle grabbed the checklist and began to look over it. Gunny had seen Giselle look at his crotch and his erection hidden beneath the robe. He got very bold, "So do you like what you see?" Giselle knew what he was referring to, but didn't acknowledge it, and commented on the checklist instead, "It looks good! Thank you so much for it, I think I need to get going, still have that hill to climb and I need to sleep this one off." Giselle went to stand up, hoping Gunny would step aside. Instead, he pushed him back down on the seat. "What, you think you're just going to come up here and lead me on like that." Giselle was taken aback and, quietly, looked up at him not sure what he should do. "Uh, I'm not quite sure what you mean?" Gunny got a bit angry, "Oh, you think I sat there and bought drinks and talked all night being nice to you just because, … Oh, yeah I do that with every Lance Corporal who comes along, come on. Listen here you little twink, …I know your story. You think I didn't hear you and your buddy earlier talking about guys and Club Tony's? You think I only heard about the inspection portion?" Giselle was astonished, how could he have been so naive, so stupid, how did he not put two and two together? What was going on, this guy was being a jerk. "Look, I'm sorry if I gave you the wrong signal or something, but as for my friend, that was us just having fun. I've had a really good time, but it's time I get outta here." Giselle got up and, before he knew, Gunny had him thrown on the edge of the bed. "You ain't going anywhere bitch!" Giselle got quiet, as Gunny towered over him in his African garb. "This is what you're going to do, … you're going to keep your mouth shut, and do whatever I ask, … if not, … I'm going to turn you in for being a fag. I'll tell them what I heard from you and your buddy. Or I'll tell them you came on to me. Who they going to believe? Me, a Gunnery Sergeant on the Inspector General Staff; … married with a wife and children, or a little peon bitch, …a little nothing?"

The effects of the alcohol, plus this, was not letting Giselle think clearly. He didn't want to be investigated and worse yet, he didn't want Noah to be either. This guy was right, if he didn't do what was asked or if he went for help, they would never believe him over the Gunny.

Just then the Gunny grabbed him by the legs and pulled him to the edge of the bed. He tried to kick, and the Gunny let go and shushed him. "What did I tell you?" Giving Giselle a warning, he once again grabbed his legs and pulled him closer. Once Giselle was on the edge of the bed, he opened his robe and let himself be exposed. His huge erection pushed out to Giselle. He grabbed Giselle by the head and pushed it into his face. Giselle, tried to resist, but was futile. Before he knew it, he was flipped over, and his pants were off. The giant African man was having his way with him. Giselle could feel the extreme pain, and the abrupt force trauma being rampaged as he faded into a dream like state. All he could hear was the African tribal music play on as he tried to block what was taking place.

Giselle wasn't sure how long it went on before realizing it was over. Still in a trance, and just starting to come back around, he felt his underwear and clothes hit his face. They were being thrown at him from the Gunny. "Get dressed, get your shit and get the hell out." Giselle got dressed and could feel the wetness between his legs from the blood, shit, and semen oozing out his ass. He didn't care, just so he could leave, that was all that mattered.

Once he was dressed Giselle grabbed the checklist to take it with him before Gunny grabbed it out of his hand. "You won't be needing this, you stupid little fuck! Your SNCO and command already have it. They get it well in advance, so they know what we are looking for. You think I'll let you take anything out of here, that even says you have been here, … you're wrong. Get your shit and go!" He walked over to the door and got ready to open it, "Like I said, this is between us, you say anything or go to anybody, I will deny it and tell them about you and your little homo buddy. So, don't think you'll outsmart me." He opened the door and laughed as Giselle walked out. It was as though he wanted to rub salt in the wound. One more chance to show conquest of what had just taken place. Giselle refused to acknowledge anything he said, and as soon as the door was open, he was out and down the hall.

Once on the street, Giselle stumbled and heaved into the bushes that lined the side. He stumbled a few steps further and fell to his knees and wept. What had just happened? He laid face down on the ground before turning over and facing the sky. Car lights hit the street in the distance, catching his attention, so he got up and gained his composure. In a blur of tears and drunken confusion, he made his way to the barracks. Once there, he went to his locker, trying to keep quiet, he grabbed his toiletries and a towel and went into the barracks shower. He didn't care how late or how early, or who was even around. He didn't want to think, he just wanted to be blank. He stripped naked, got under the hot shower, and stood letting the water cover his body. Let it wash his body clean, if he could still call it his body after everything that had just happened.

Chapter 10

What would I tell them?

Noah's alarm clock woke him up at 2:50 am. He hit the snooze button a few more times before finally getting up at 3:00am. He grabbed his gear and was off to the head to get ready for the early morning run. On his way up, he could see Corporal Miller ahead in the lighted area. He was talking briefly to the duty, before leaving the barracks. Noah stopped by Dunk's cubicle to find him in the rack. He went in and gave him a nudge, "Hey man, it's time to get up." Dunk groggy, "Yeah, got it man." Noah headed on to the showers. Once inside he set his gear down and went to take a leak. He heard the shower running and thought it unusual for someone else to be up this early. He assumed whoever it was must have an early run as well. He finished and went to shave. He took his time, hoping whoever was in the showers would finish.

The community showers were not private. Six shower heads; three on one side, and three on the other. To take a shower by himself, for once, would be a treat. He finished shaving and thought, whoever was in there has been taking a long time. Regardless, he couldn't wait any longer. He set his belongings on the bench and stripped down and went into the shower. Walking in, Noah found Giselle. He had his back toward him and was hunched over with the water running down. Noah couldn't help but notice what looked like a mixture of blood and water running down from underneath him. Concerned and shocked he asked. "You all right man?" Giselle lifted his head, but really didn't move, or acknowledge him. Noah could tell something was wrong. Not sure if he had heard him, Noah went over and touched his shoulder. "You alright?" Giselle exploded upward and away from Noah, "Don't fucking touch me!" Noah backed away "...Ok, ok man, ... didn't mean to touch you. It's just that, you are bleeding man..." Noah pointed down at the blood running down. He still wasn't sure where it was coming from. Had Giselle tried to cut his wrist? "Giselle let me see your wrist man," Giselle not caring, "Fuck you man! ...I know what you're thinking,

...I didn't try to kill myself." As he continued to weep, he knelt back down with blood still seeping down the drain. Noah was trying to figure out what was going on. "Hey Giselle, it's me man, it's Noah, you can let me help, ...I'm one of the one's you can trust." Giselle lifted his head and came up pissed, "Fuck you maaan, fuck you, ...you're the fuck'en reason, ...you're the motherfucking reason, this shit happened! You motherfucker, you left me out there by myself. Fuck you!" as he started shaking his hands and turning around crying frantically. "Fuck you, Mother fucker, fuck everyone, Trust! ... what the fuck is trust? Yeah right, my ass! ... You can't trust anyone!" Noah stayed calm. "Look I don't know what happened Anthony, ...but it'll be all right! ... I can call you Anthony, yeah?" Giselle shrugged his shoulder and nodded his head. "My mother calls me Anthony." Calling Giselle by his first name seemed to open a bit of trust again. "Look, I need you to calm down and stay a little quiet, it's early and everyone is still asleep. The duty will come in if you don't. Besides, we don't want to wake everybody up. Can you do that for me Anthony?" Giselle agreed as Noah continued, "The way you're talking man, they'll put you in the nut ward." Noah walked a bit closer, holding his arms up like he had nothing to hide. "Now, I just want to help. You're bleeding and I don't know where its coming from, but we got to get it stopped, you with me?" Giselle shook his head, as Noah shut the shower off. "Come on man, let's get you a towel and dried off." Giselle walked with Noah out of the shower. Noah grabbed his towel sitting on the bench and gave it to Giselle. He started drying off. Noah could see a bit of blood running down Giselle's leg. "Man, where is the blood coming from?" Giselle was calm and mono-toned as he looked down at his legs. "My ass, it's coming from my asshole." Noah did not know how to respond. All he could think about was how to stop the bleeding. "Here let me get something to help." Noah went to the sinks and a grabbed a bunch of paper towels, folded them, and brought them back. "Put them between your cheeks, tuck them, they'll help absorb." Giselle did as Noah asked. Noah grabbed some more, "Here, replace those and put your underwear over them to hold them in." Noah wasn't sure what had happened but knew enough to know it was traumatic. Giselle was calming down, and

Noah had now gotten his underwear and T-shirt back on as did Giselle. Noah trying to lighten the mood, "Goddamn Giselle, you try and fuck an elephant?" Giselle, laughed. They both sat on the bench, Noah patted him on the back. "Look, I don't know what happened, but just know if you need to talk, I'm here." Giselle leaned over and put his head on Noah's shoulder. Noah not knowing what to say, or do, put his arm around him, and held on as Giselle cried.

Noah heard the door to the showers open. Both gained their composure, and started gathering their things, as Dunk appeared. "Hey man, Corporal Miller left a message with the duty, we're supposed to have an A-Driver. I already woke Stubblefield; he's going with me. You need to find someone." Giselle looked at Noah, "I can do it man, let me go with you. I don't have anything going on. We are supposed to get our preliminary inspection today, and my truck is in the shop. They'll be trying to snag me for shit details." Noah witnessing what had just happened, thought it was probably best to keep Giselle away from the motor-pool. "Yeah, that'll be cool."

Noah and Giselle arrived at the Motor-pool, picked up their vehicle and all three trucks were on their way. They were headed to Camp Schwab, stopping by the ammo dump along the way. It was a good hour's drive. It didn't take Giselle long to curl up in the passenger seat and fall asleep. Noah was still in the dark about what had happened the night before and wasn't sure if he would ever know. What he did know was that Giselle needed a moment of space from the Marine Corps right now. Anthony did not want to be alone and didn't want to let Noah out of his sight; he obviously felt safe and secure around him.

They completed their drop off and were on the flip side heading back to Foster. Noah tried not to disturb Giselle and let him sleep through most of the run. Noah had his portable boom box in the front of the truck and was listening to the local Armed Forces' Radio. The sun was out and starting to heat up the truck. He rolled down the window to let in some fresh air, helping to keep him awake from boredom.

The air brought Giselle around as he adjusted, yawned, stretched, and sat up. Noah noticed, "Morning sunshine! Thought you were going to sleep the whole trip." Giselle looked around to see where they were. "We're headed back already. Man, you let me sleep through, why didn't you wake me?" Noah laughed, "Don't worry man, Stubblefield is out back in Dunk's truck as well. We're good." Giselle seemed rested and in better spirits. He lit a cigarette and cracked his window. They cruised on down the road listening to the radio. Noah noticed Giselle had finished his cigarette and lit another off the first one. The stress had him chain smoking.

A few more miles went by and then, out of nowhere, "I know you're curious about what happened." as he looked out the side window. Noah, busy following the road, glanced over briefly, "I don't know, am I?" Giselle glanced over and turned back away, "Well, I figure I'm obligated to tell you, your name was brought up." Noah confused, "My name was in it?" Giselle, "Well, your name wasn't, he didn't know your name." Giselle had peaked Noah's curiosity, "He who? Ok, you need to come clean. What the fuck is going on?" Giselle slowly looked to the front as the truck rolled on, "You remember that guy that came in last night at the bar, the one who sat in the booth next to us?" Noah shook his head, "Not really." Giselle continued to jog his memory, "Yes you do, the big, … big, black older guy. He sat beside us. … You shushed me, to not talk so loudly, cause he might hear." Noah shrugged, "Vaguely, but go on." Giselle continued, "After you left last night, I moved up to the bar, he came up and started talking to me. Turns out he's a Gunnery Sergeant, married with a wife and kids, …But wait, get this, he is on the inspection team that is coming through doing our inspection." Noah perked up, "Really?" Giselle continued, "So, we talked, and before I knew it, the drinks were being lined up. He kept buying me drinks. Next thing I know, I have got a serious buzz going on. Well, it started getting late, he was staying at those new SNCO barracks, so we walked together. We get to the barracks, and he tells me he can give me a checklist of what he'll be looking for in the inspection. So, I figure what the hell. Why not? I go up to get the checklist. Shit was a bit of blur for me with the fucking buzz I had going on. So, that is when shit started getting fucking weird. Before I knew what was happening, he's got some bright-ass, African fucking garb shit on. Now get this, he walks up to hand me the checklist, and he's got this huge fucking erection pushing his fucking robe out, right in front of my face. I'm like, you couldn't help but see it. It dawned on me; this guy is fucking coming on to me. Now, I ain't into it, and tried to play it straight, and he got pissed. That's where you came in. He says he heard everything we were saying at the bar. You know about guys, and Club Tony's and shit. Said if I didn't go along with him, he would turn me and you in for being fags. I was like fuck this, I'm out of here...got up and tried to leave, ...bam! ...He nailed me and threw me on the bed, ...threatening me again, while slapping me around and calling me a fuck'en twink, bitch, and shit. All I know is that's when I drew a blank. It was a blur from there, but you get the fucking picture. When it was over, he threw my shit at me, told me to get fucking dressed, threatened me again if I told. Bragging, he's a Gunny and married, and I was a nobody and some shit, and no one was going to believe me. Then when I was about to walk out, he grabbed the inspection sheet, telling me I wasn't getting anything to show I was even there. Top it off, he laughed about it as I walked out. Why? Because he knows he's right. Ain't no one gonna believe me. If I said anything, they'd say I either wanted it, or I was just trying to get him in trouble, or I deserved it. But you know and I know, I would be the one thrown out the fucking Marine Corps."

Noah was dumbfounded. Holy shit what did he just hear. He looked over at Giselle, "I'm so sorry man! I don't know what else to say... Other than it pisses me off to hear." Giselle looked over at Noah briefly, "Look I don't want you feeling all sorry and shit. I know it's not your fault. I was just saying that this morning in the shower because I was fucked up, and all. But what happened, that motherfucker is the only one to blame." Noah being concerned, "Don't you think you need to see a doctor? You were bleeding pretty bad." Giselle grudged his head, "No, besides, what would I tell them?" Mockingly, Giselle imitated himself telling the doctor what had happened, "Oh excuse me Doctor but can you sew up my bum hole, because I got pounded by a big black dick. Oh, by the way, can you throw in an extra stitch for good measure for the next guy who comes along." He and Noah both started to laugh. Noah, realizing he was laughing, paused, "Sorry I know it's not funny, but you're right, they would start an investigation, and I don't think you want to go down that road. Probably best to remain silent." Giselle continued on, "I'll just buy some women's fucking Kotex and wear them until it heels up a bit." Noah laughed, "Oh, I want to see you go in the store to buy them." Giselle chuckled, "I'm so glad to not be in the motor-pool today, thanks for letting me come along. You know he is supposed to be there doing the pre-inspection." Noah got pissed immediately, "Fuck that mother fucker, won't he be surprised when he finds you're not there." Giselle smiled looking at Noah, "You know he is looking around for me, fuck him! I hope he's fucking scared. I really don't want to ever see him again. If I did, I don't know what I would do."

Noah focused back on the road, as Giselle turned back to the window. Occasionally, he would glance over at Noah. How strange when the cosmic universe can send someone into your life at just the right time. Giselle was thankful. He was glad he could call Noah a friend.

A hard Inspection

Arriving back at the Motor-pool, Corporal Miller hopped on the sideboard of the truck, "Go ahead and do your ops checks and spray it down. I'll meet you over on the line." Noah and Giselle continued to the wash rack. While there, Giselle started to get a little worried, "You think the inspection team has already been through?" Noah spraying the truck, "I would think so. They were having all hands-on deck at 8:00am." Giselle looked over at the line, "Hey, …they have my truck back on line from the shop. Sweet!" Noah paused briefly to look over at the line. "Yeah, I think you're right…" Giselle was excited, "Hey, can you finish up here? I want to go take a look."

Giselle arrived at his truck, inspecting it to make sure everything was ok. He noticed all the other vehicles were still perfectly aligned from this morning's inspection. The space next to him was where Noah's truck belonged. He hopped up on the front bumper to open the hood when Noah pulled through the open space from behind. "Hey, can you help me get this aligned." Giselle hopped down and guided Noah until he was in perfect alignment with the other trucks. Noah powered down and started his after ops check. When he walked around the front of the truck, he noticed Corporal Miller was down the line talking to Dunk and Stubblefield. It dawned on him. None of the other drivers were there. Had they been secured already from the inspection? It was only 10:00 am. The inspection must have gone fast not to have anyone still around.

He had just started to drain the air-tanks when he heard Corporal Miller's voice holler for him and Giselle. He walked back to the front. Corporal Miller and Giselle were waiting. Corporal Miller started, "Man, you two are not going to like this." Noah approached a bit closer, as Corporal Miller continued. "The inspection hasn't gone yet. It's been delayed until 1300." Noah confused, "Yeah, so what does that mean?" Corporal Miller was hesitant, "It means you two, along with your trucks have to be in formation and ready for inspection by 12:45." Giselle couldn't hold back. "That is messed up!" Noah was not ready to hear this, "Embrace the suck! …that's just not right!" Looking at Corporal Miller, "…it's not too late, I haven't closed out my trip ticket, we can go back out in our trucks." Corporal Miller shaking his head, "Gunny has already seen you and told me to have your shit ready to go." Noah looked over to Giselle wondering how he was going to take this. This was not cool. How would he react if Gunny Phobos was the one to inspect? He had thought they had dodged a bullet. Corporal Miller continued, "Let's finish up here, make sure the trucks are good to go. Giselle, I know yours just got out of the shop, it should be alright. If not, it is what it is. Help Barlow finish up, and you two guys head to the barracks. You'll need to be back here squared away and ready to go by 11:30. Sorry, no chow today guys."

Noah, waiting until Corporal Miller was out of hearing range. "Giselle, are you going to be alright? … You ain't going to do anything crazy are you?" Giselle shrugged, as he waked away. "Don't create any drama." He mocked Corporal Miller, "... It is, what it is. …Just hope that motherfucker isn't the one inspecting."

Later at the barracks, Noah and Giselle were showered, clean shaven, and dressed in their highly starched inspection cammies. Both had the sparkle on their spit-shined boots. Fresh haircuts and razor-sharp creases completed their look. Each gave the once over, making sure the other was inspection ready. Their checks included:

no Irish pennants, chevrons in proper place, brass buckle seated and aligned, correct belt length, and no nose or ear hairs sticking out. Corporal Miller came in to do a pre-inspection and gave them the go ahead.

Catching a ride with the Corporal back to the Motor-pool, they arrived just in time to fall in for inspection. This inspection was different in the way it was conducted. Normally, they would fall in as a platoon, but today they would stand aligned in front of their individual vehicles. Both the Marine and the vehicle would be inspected. The Marine would be inspected on appearance, military bearing, and basic knowledge of the Corps, job, and the vehicle. One never knew what might be asked during the inspection, so they would need to have well rounded knowledge on all topics.

Aligned in front of his 5-ton, Noah leaned forward taking a glance to see how everything looked. It was a rare and amazing sight. The motor-pool was clean and pristine due to the many police calls that had been conducted. The trucks were perfectly aligned, and washed, with newly painted camo. Their appearance matched the smartness of the Marines in their highly squared away uniforms. The expression, "If it doesn't grow, pick it up…" was forever embedded in Noah's head. The curbs, street signs, and parking lines were all vibrant from being freshly painted for the occasion. Noah faced back front as the Company Gunny, along with the Platoon Sergeants, came out of the head shed and took their respective places in the formation. Shortly thereafter, they were joined by all the higher ups of Truck Company's chain of command. Noah knew the arrival of the inspection team was getting close. The anticipation and stress were high.

Within minutes, a caravan of vehicles arrived through the gates of the motor pool. Circling around, the lead car, with two flags on the front, stopped just center of the head shed. The Company Commander called the Company to attention, echoed by the Officers in Charge. Noah snapped brilliantly to the position as he watched the sedan door open. Out stepped the Inspector General. He made his way to the CO exchanging customary greetings before the company was put at rest. The inspection team exited their vehicles, greeted their respective counterparts, and deployed throughout the motor pool. Noah gave a quick glance to the front of the 5-ton line to see if they had begun, and who might be inspecting. He noticed Giselle looking as well. "Can you see who it is?" Noah said under his breath, just loud enough for Giselle to hear. Neither could make out the inspector. He was still too far away. Both stood patiently, but Noah had concerns it might be the Gunny. He didn't know Noah's name but might remember his face as the one talking to Giselle the night before. If recognized, he would now learn Noah's name as well. If he wanted to pursue anything, he would now know who Noah was.

The inspector was three trucks down and had just finished with Dunk before stepping in front of Stubblefield. Stubblefield sounded off, "Good afternoon, Gunnery Sergeant, Lance Corporal Stubblefield ready for inspection!" Stubblefield was known for a big mouth and sounding off loudly. It drew Giselle's attention, causing him to glance down the line. Giselle quickly looked at Noah, without a word and nodded yes. Noah got a good look at the inspector; he fit Giselle's description of Gunny Phobos. The panic on Giselle's face was obvious. It was Gunny Phobos, the one who had raped him. Noah's heart went out to Giselle. How crazy of a joke had the universe played, making someone endure this asshole. Once was enough, but twice? As much as Noah wanted to punch this man, now wasn't the time to be anyone's hero. Although they both wanted to, neither could just walk away. How were they to maintain military bearing with this guy in front of them? The two continued to wait patiently. It would take all of their discipline to remain calm and keep silent.

Gunny was now inspecting Lance Corporal Dominguez and was just finishing up. She was the truck next to Giselle, which meant Giselle was next. Listening to the conversation, Noah could hear what was being said. Telling her she looked outstanding, the Gunny noted to the Staff Sergeant her vehicle and knowledge were both noteworthy. Staff Sergeant scribed it down. Giselle gave one final glance to Noah. It was one of reassurance, pulling strength and courage from him. Noah nodded his head in affirmation and stuck his hand out with a thumbs-up. Giselle returned the thumbs-up. Now was the moment to stand tall.

Gunny stepped in front of Giselle as he came to attention and sounded off. "Good afternoon, Gunnery Sergeant! Lance Corporal Giselle ready for inspection."

Normally when Giselle was standing in front of an inspector, he would look through them as if they weren't there. Sometimes he would pick a spot on their face, like the forehead, and on occasion, glimpse in their eyes. He felt by looking into someone's eyes you could see into their soul. Likewise, they could see into yours as well. Giselle made a point to look Gunny Phobos directly in the eyes. He wanted him to feel uncomfortable. He wanted him to know he had no control; he was not defeated. He wanted him to see the hatred and contempt he had inside.

Noah observed what was taking place. Gunny didn't acknowledge Gisele's greeting. He, instead, looked him in the eye, held his composure and smirked. The two exchanged stares, before Gunny Phobos stepped back and started inspecting. His two assistants moved on to the vehicle behind him. Pulling out a small ruler, he measured Giselle's rank chevron placement on his collar. "You see that? They're off." Staff Sergeant started taking notes. Gunny told him to lift his blouse. He did as he was told. While Giselle held his blouse up, Gunny measured the belt, stating that the buckle was not shined nor properly seated. He stepped back and told him to lower his blouse. Moving down to the trousers, he looked to the sides and noted an Irish pennant. There was a slight scuff on Giselle's boot top. Gunny directed him to look down at it, pointing to a slight mark. His assistant acknowledged it and wrote it down in the book. The Staff Sergeant could tell it wasn't going well for Giselle and gave a frown. Gunny stood back up in front of him, "Did you even spend any time getting ready for this?" Giselle knew he was being picky, but couldn't respond with anything other than, "Yes, Gunnery Sergeant." Gunny smarted back quickly, "Well it doesn't show!" as he glared into Giselle's eyes. "Let's see if your knowledge is any better than your appearance?" He rattled off several questions and Giselle answered them quickly and correctly. The final one was intentionally done to stump Giselle. "So, what is the mileage on your 5-ton?" Giselle had no idea what it was. "Sorry Gunnery Sergeant, I do not know." He wasn't even going to pretend.

He wasn't going to chase this rabbit down the hole any further. He realized that no matter what, there was no passing this inspection. The Gunny was hell bent on failing him, and there was nothing he could do. It just added more salt to the wound. One more conquest, one more 'I told you so!'

Noah felt Giselle's pain. He could see firsthand this guy was manipulating and trying to humiliate Giselle even further.

Giselle didn't care. There was no other humiliation this man could do to him that had not already been done the night before. Fail, as it may be, he stood looking this prick in the eye. He had not run away. Beaten, battered, and torn, he was standing his ground.

Gunny came back to attention as the two assistants came forward. They handed him the inspection sheet. He went over it briefly. The Staff Sergeant spoke up that the truck had just returned from the shop the day prior. Anything wrong was not Giselle's fault, and it would be rectified. Gunny looked at Giselle one final time and stepped off to the next Marine in line, Noah.

Noah popped to attention and sounded off loudly. Gunny Phobos was taken aback by the loudness, and enthusiasm. "I think they heard you up at Camp Hansen with that one." He looked Noah up and down, quickly. Turned to his assistants and they deployed onto Noah's truck. Gunny stepped up beside him as he started to inspect. While inspecting he paused and looked Noah dead on. "You look awfully familiar. Do I know you?" Noah knew this guy recognized him as the one with Giselle at the club last night. He maintained his composure, "No Gunnery Sergeant, I don't believe we have ever met." Gunny went item by item, like he had done on Giselle. Noah just knew he was going to nitpick him as well. Before Noah knew it, he was done with the uniform part, and was now being asked questions pertaining to knowledge. All were general and basic, nothing unexpected. Noah breezed through them.

Finally, he looked Noah up and down one more time, before asking once again, "You sure we have not met, what state are you from Lance Corporal?" Noah could tell he was trying him. Gunny Phobos was puzzled wondering if Noah knew what had taken place the night before. "Indiana, Gunny." Gunny quickly responded, "Oh, midwestern guy. I'm from Chicago myself." Gunny gave a quick glance over to Gisselle. "You work with Lance Corporal Giselle much?" Noah was surprised at the question, "Sometimes Gunny." He stared at Noah and grinned, "You should take him in under your wing, he didn't do so well. He needs someone like you to help him out." Noah acknowledged him, "Yes Gunny, I'll do my best." Gunny Phobos turned to the Staff Sergeant, "This Marine right here is outstanding, make a noteworthy next to his name." It was clear at this point Gunny definitely knew it was Noah with Giselle the night prior. To anyone else listening, it sounded as though he was talking about the current inspection, but Noah knew the real hidden meaning. He was talking about raping Giselle. He addressed Noah once again, "I'm sorry, if you'll forgive the Old Gunny, with so many Marines today, I can't remember them all, what was yours again?" Noah knew what he was doing, he was a master game player. He begrudgingly gave his name again "Lance Corporal Barlow, Gunny." Gunny Phobos repeated it, as if to record it, "Lance Corporal Barlow, …I'll remember that one." As Noah stood at attention, Gunny came to attention, "Outstanding job Marine." grinned and moved on.

Noah went to parade rest and turned to Giselle. Shook his head, and mocked under his breath, "He's fucked." Witnessing his passive aggression, Noah knew this guy thought it a conquest to stomp on Giselle. After what he had done, it was to his benefit to intimidate and make Giselle suffer and destroy him. The worst Giselle appeared, the less likely anyone would believe his story. Although he wasn't as aggressive with Noah, he made his message clear. Should he go to the authorities, Phobos had his number as well.

The inspection of the Motor-pool was over. Unfortunately, Giselle would need a lot of time and space for healing. Any chance of vindication for him had yet to show itself. The crimes committed by Gunny Phobos, for now, would remain silent.

Chapter 11

Outside looking in

The sun was just starting to set as Noah and Beulah pulled
into Oceanside. After hours of driving, Noah was tired and ready to
get to one place and settle down for the evening. He knew of a cheap
hotel, close to Camp Pendleton, that would work. Noah found the
hotel right off the I-5, not far from base, pulled in and went in to find
out if they had a vacancy.

The hotel had seen its hay day in the 1960's. Noah walked
into the small office at the front of the hotel and noticed a sign to
ring the bell. Ringing the bell, he heard a voice of what sounded to
be an older woman coming from the back, "Be right there." Noah
stood at the counter and looked around at the dated décor of brown
wood paneling, green flowered wallpaper and a hanging swag light
that looked to be layered with a film of smoke from days gone by.
He noticed a pay phone just outside the office, "Can I help you?"

Noah quickly turned back to the counter to see a tall, slender
black woman emerging from a bead draped doorway. He couldn't
help but notice how pretty, yet eccentric, the approaching woman
was. Her hair, done in a stacked black curl beehive with single
flattened curls that came forward, appeared to almost be glued to the
cheeks of her face. She had bright white, plastic hooped earrings that
hung down contrasting with her skin. She wore a white mini skirt
and white go-go boots with heels. She was a bit busty, and you
couldn't help but notice her under garments which shown through
her free flowing translucent white and blue flowered shirt. Around
her neck she wore a white scarf and a strand of long pearls. He
smiled and thought how surreal and appropriate, she matched the
décor and probably had been with the hotel since it had opened in
the 60's. Noah quickly asked if she had any rooms available. She
laughed and sternly responded, "How many you want?" She laughed
again, the whole time eyeing him up but also looking suspiciously

out to the parking lot at his car. Noah noticed she had a name tag on her shirt when she adjusted the scarf that had fallen a bit from her neck. The tag read 'Violet.' "One room if you got it, but a double… if you please, Violet." He smiled at her. She chuckled and quickly changed her attitude to let him know she was not easily schmoozed, "Oh child, you're a sweet one, huh? It'll take more than saying my name to get you favors here. Now, you want a smoking or non-smoking?" "Non-smoking Ma'am." She looked to a board on the back, with a group of cubby hole boxes, which looked to be for notes or mail for the guests. "I have a double. That your car out there?" Noah looked out the window, "Yes Ma'am." Violet in a sweet but sexy voice, "That sure is a pretty car, and T-tops on it as well. I don't think I've ever seen a car so pretty." Quickly she changed her attitude and sternly asked: "Who's the lady with you? I'll need her name if you get the room." Noah quickly got the vibe that she might think they were a couple. "Oh no, she's my sister, just getting stationed here at Camp Pendleton. We drove across country." Violet quickly responded, "Where yah coming from?" he responded, "Indiana, just getting back from Oki." Violet chuckled, "Oki, well good for you! Bet you glad to be back?" "Yes Ma'am." Having decided she would rent to him, she looked at her watch and quickly turned to business, "That's your business child, I don't get caught up in all that." As she placed her elbows on the counter leaning over, "Everyone's got a story when they come here, and a different one when they leave, …someone, or something. All I know, the room is 23 dollars, checkout goes at 10:30. You break anything in the room, you buy it. Any trouble, we call the cops. No guests in the rooms, only who's registered." Noah was glad to get the room, "We'll take it!" Violet smiled, "Good, I'll need an ID from you and anyone else in the room." Violet paused, looked out to the car, with a bit of sarcasm. "That includes your sister out there, …uh-huh." Noah looked out to the car and motioned for Beulah to come in. She got out and started toward the office. Violet commented, "You know we get Marines in here all the time. I can tell you're still young and new, you'll be alright though." She turned to get the paperwork and keys.

Beulah walked in the office. Noah turned to her, "They need IDs for both of us to check-in." Beulah reached into her purse, got her ID as Violet returned to the counter. She handed it to her. Violet took it, wrote her info down on the paperwork, took Noah's and did the same. Violet told them the room was available for a second night, if needed. but would need to know first thing in the morning. Violet held the key up in the air so he would have to grab it. He took the key and she pointed out the window giving directions to the room. Violet watched them exit, letting out a small chuckle and mockingly said out loud, "Sister, alright... um huh, ok, now? You two have fun."

Noah and Beulah made it to the room and settled in. He wanted to call Bob, a Marine he had met while in Okinawa. Bob was now stationed at Camp Pen. and was part of the gay group who called themselves "family". He had let Noah know he was welcome to stay with him, if he needed a place to crash when they returned. Tomorrow would be a busy day. They needed to get to base and get his pay so they could head to Las Vegas the following day. They were to spend two nights there and then Beulah would fly home from Las Vegas. Beulah decided to use the phone in the room to call home. Noah was hungry and decided to venture out to get a bite to eat.

On the way out, Noah stopped at the pay phone to call Bob and let him know he had arrived back in CA. As the phone rang, he made a quick decision to stay at the hotel for a second night and not take Bob up on his offer. Beulah could be a bit nosy, and he wasn't ready to answer any of her questions. Even though Bob was a Marine, and just a friend, he was not familiar with how Beulah would react around him, or worse yet, have her find out they were gay. The phone picked up on the third ring. Noah heard a deep southern male voice on the other end, "Hello." "Bob, hey this is Noah." "Hey Noah, how's it going?" Noah replied, "Doing well! Just letting you know I made it back to Cali." Bob, happy to hear from him, "That's great! What kinda car did you buy?" Noah excitedly, "Oh man it's beautiful! A 1978 Oldsmobile. It's white with white and red interior, two door, T-Top. It's used but has low miles." Bob replied, "Oh, it sounds nice! Are you going to need a place to stay?" Noah anticipated he would ask, "Glad to hear the offer still stands Bob, but no, I'm good! We rented a hotel room off the I-5, close to base. Just wanted to touch base and let you know I'm back." Bob, a bit taken back about the offer, was still curious about their plans, "Awe man, I was hoping to meet her, and see your new car, but thanks for letting me know. You got any plans while she's here?" Noah continued, "No, she can be a bit to deal with, too many questions. What she doesn't know, she can't ruin. I really don't think I'm ready for all that right now. So, it's best to pass and keep her at bay… just going to show her the base tomorrow. Besides, we're supposed to head out to Vegas once I get paid." Bob, still a bit disappointed, "I get it. Well, let me know if you need anything, or if you have any problems." Noah, "Great, appreciate it Bob, talk to you when I get back."

Noah finished and headed out to the local burger joint just down from the hotel. After dinner, he and Beulah went and sat by the hotel pool. Beulah took a quick dip. Noah, sitting in one of the pool's lounge chairs started to doze off. Beulah finished her swim, came back over, grabbed her towel, and kicked Noah's chair, "I'm headed up to the room." Noah got up and moved to the table and chairs sitting at the far end of the pool. The light from the sun was being overshadowed by the surrounding neon lights of the hotel. Noah propped his feet up on the chair across from him and laid his head back with a sigh. He had made it back to California.

As Noah sat, he started watching the different guests of the hotel coming and going. One family, just across the pool, had the door open, TV blaring, and a child that kept running in and out. He noticed a Marine, in uniform, pull in, hop out of his car, and walk over to the room. The young child started hollering, "Daddy, Daddy" before he made it to the room. A young woman appeared in the door, with a towel wrapped around her head, as though she had just gotten out of the shower. The child, a little girl, not able to contain her excitement, ran to him and leapt into his arms. He picked her up and carried her into the room. The lady and he embraced while he continued holding the child. Noah could hear the laughing and feel the joy filling the air as they disappeared into the room.

The surreal feeling of being in California had returned. The traffic sounds coming from I-5 was loud and meant rush hour was in full swing. Noah got up, looked out to see he hadn't put the tops back on his car and headed out the pool gate. While putting the T-tops on, a woman came out from the room in front of the car. A black woman, a little on the tall side, with straight reddish-brown hair, that appeared to be a wig, falling just past the shoulders. She was wearing a short, black leather mini skirt, gold belt, and a dark form fitting long sleeve sweater that accentuated her overly large breasts. Around her neck was a thick black choker with a pendant hanging down. She leaned slightly forward, having a little trouble with stability from the high heels she wore. Her body was disproportionate to her appearance. Not only did her breasts seem overly large, she seemed a tad bit large in the arms and shoulders, but yet the hips seemed exceedingly small. Noah thought something looked a bit off. She quickly put on dark sunglasses when she realized Noah was looking. She shuffled off, holding her purse close by. Violet, the attendant came out as the lady tried to hurry past. "Champagne, you got my money, I've got to have the rent. I can't keep covering for you!" The lady stopped in the shadows past the office, "Girl, I'll have your money tonight! Don't be hollering, …putt'en all my business out here. Now hush girl and go on back in your office. You know I'm good for it. I gots to go make some money." Violet, not happy, "I'm telling you, …you better have it soon!" She turned to go in the office, pausing to take a look at Noah. "That sure is one pretty car!"

Noah, finished putting the T-tops on, closed and locked the doors. The hotel lights were now in full illumination. In his mind, he thought: Why do you where sunglasses at night? He remembered hearing the name Champagne before. He looked down the parking lot and the woman was gone. Maybe she walked so funny because her boobs were so big. He laughed at the thought, turned, and headed to the room.

The next morning, Noah was awakened by hearing Beulah talking on the phone. He assumed it was her husband, by the way she spoke, telling him the plans for today. He sat up on the bed, still in a half slumber. Beulah turned to see he was sitting up, spoke out, "You up?" Noah waved his hand without speaking. "Herman says hi!" as she continued on the phone. Noah took the advantage to go ahead and get in the shower. The plan for the day was to show her around Oceanside and Camp Pendleton, and later stop by work to pick up his check and run a few errands. The rest of the day would be a lazy one. Tomorrow they would be driving to Las Vegas, which was part of the deal for Beulah helping with the drive from Indiana. She would catch a flight back home from there.

After breakfast they headed to base, where Noah worked. They pulled in and both got out and walked through the Motor pool. A few of the Marines called out to him, looking curiously at the lady with him. Once inside the dispatch shack, SSgt O'Dell came out of his office with his check in hand. "Suppose you're looking for this?" Noah grinned, "Yes Staff Sergeant." He turned his focus to Beulah, "Who's this?" Noah quickly introduced them. After the greeting, the Staff Sergeant turned back to Noah, "Before I forget, while you were gone you won a gift from one of the Navy-Marine Corps fund drive tickets you bought." Noah grinned, "Really, what did I win?" The SSgt continued. "You won a watch; the only problem is it's a woman's watch." He went back in his office and came back out with it. "It's a pretty nice watch." As he handed it to him, Noah opened and looked at it, along with Beulah looking over his shoulder. "What am I going to do with a woman's watch?" Beulah spoke up, "Oh that is gorgeous, let me look at it!" She took the box and glared at it, "Are those real diamonds?" The Staff Sergeant spoke up, "Yes, the value from Navy Relief was $1200." Noah was shocked at the price, "No way!" Beulah all starry eyed, "How much do you like your sister?" Noah came back, "No, no, I know what your think'en. Sorry, can't do it. I just bought a car; I need the money." The Staff Sergeant spoke up, "I was hoping you would say that. My wife stopped by the other day and seen it. She loved it. We would be willing to give $700 for it." Noah paused for a minute. Thinking about the trip to Vegas and his promise to buy Beulah's ticket home. "Can you go $800?" The Staff Sergeant studied for a minute, "...Alright you have a deal!" They shook and Noah gave him the watch. The Staff Sergeant said, "Look come back by after lunch, and I'll have your money." Noah and Beulah headed out to tour the base.

After touring the base and settling with the Staff Sergeant, they headed back to the hotel. Once at the hotel, they called to see how much an airplane ticket for Beulah would be to fly home from Vegas. Speaking to customer service they were told the ticket cost was $280. Noah relayed it to Beulah, and she agreed for him to just give her the $280 and she would take care of the ticket. The day had been long, and both were tired. Beulah called back home to check in and Noah decided to go sit by the pool for a few to chill out before hitting the sack.

The sun had already gone down, and the neon lights were giving an amber glow to the whole hotel. The sound of the freeway in the distance was faint. While sitting by the pool, he was beginning to relax when he noticed the same black lady coming back to her room. This time she was accompanied by a young guy that appeared to be a jarhead. They arrived at the room, unlocked the door, and went in. She was pretty, but he still noticed that something was out of place. His thoughts were interrupted as Beulah yelled out from the room. "I'm headed to bed." Guess it was time for him to hit the rack as well. The drive was at least 4 hours to Vegas, and he needed to be well rested.

The hot desert sun of the Mojavi beat down on the Oldsmobile as they made their way to Vegas. They stopped only to gas up and use the restrooms. With the T-tops off, music blaring, and the wind in their hair, the two dreamed of the big jackpot in the sky. As Noah drove on, the heat waves rose from the scorching pavement in front of him. The openness of the desert, the reflective blur of the heatwaves and the excitement and lure of Vegas, created a sense of freedom. After four hours on the road, he became impatient to get there and pushed on the accelerator! Coming up and over a small hill, a state trooper had a car pulled over. Noah immediately slowed, taking a quick glance at the speedometer. Ninety-five miles per hour! Wow! It didn't feel like they were moving that fast. After slowing down, he looked in his rearview mirror. "That was close." Beulah with her sunglasses on and her hair pulled back, shook her head, "You better watch it. They patrol this area heavily." Then pointing at the sign ahead "Area patrolled by air." Noah maintained the speed limit the rest of the way. Soon the Vegas skyline was in the distance and Beulah sat up in her seat, "Yeah, come on twenty-one! I'm ready to win some money!"

They were staying at the Fremont Hotel and after checking in, and freshening up, they were out walking the streets of Vegas. Both had been here before. Noah wasn't an enthusiastic fan of gambling, instead he preferred the unspoken excitement that was in the air. For Beulah, Vegas had a hypnotic effect. She seemed to throw all common sense out the window when it came to gambling. Like so many who come to Vegas, the opportunity to hit it rich was overwhelming. As they walked, they ventured in and out of the casinos, dropping an occasional coin in the slots. Now late in the afternoon, they decided to stop for dinner inside the Four Queens. The restaurant was familiar, both having been there with their father on previous visits. Their father loved Vegas and they reminisced over dinner about how envious Beck would be of their trip. Dinner was over, and Noah tired from the drive, decided to head back to the hotel room. Beulah coaxed him in to staying a bit longer. Walking by the Blackjack tables, Beulah sat down. Noah, not wanting to gamble, agreed to stay and watch for a few minutes. Placing her first bet, Beulah was soon caught up in the game. Noah watched on. She was having good luck. "Win, …win …win." Wow, she was on a roll. Her excitement was catching the attention of those passing by and soon the table was full. Noah tapped her on the shoulder. "You have fun, I'm headed up to the room. I'll be back down after a nap." She nodded, "Ok, look for me in this area when you come back down." Turning back to the table, she let out a yell of joy, having hit again.

Noah woke up and went to the window to see the view of the neon capital lit up. Checking his watch, it was just past eleven at night. He showered, got dressed and headed out to enjoy the night. Down on the street, he walked over to the Four Queens to find Beulah. Once in the Casino, he headed to the table and saw Beulah still playing. Noah snuck up behind her. "Are you winning?" Beulah, a little startled, turned. "Hey, you get some rest?" Noah nodded, "Yeah, the rooms are nice. How about you, …you still winning?" Beulah smiled and pointed to the stack of chips in front of her. "What do you think?" There were around fifteen chips in front of her. Noah, not familiar with their value, "It looks like a lot, how much they worth?" Beulah looked at them briefly before she spoke, "Right around eight thousand…" Noah's jaw dropped. "Are you serious?" Beulah grinned, shaking her head as she motioned for the dealer to hit her again. "Yes!" and chuckled as she looked at Noah. "I'm done if you want to go hang out." Noah agreed. She cashed her chips in and the two walked to Fremont Street, checking the oddities and street acts as they strolled. After a complete tour of the area, they landed back at the Four Queens. One of the bars had a "lounge lizard" playing the piano, so they sat down, ordered drinks, and listened to music. The singer was the quintessential male Vegas singer. Dressed in a vibrant, sequined tux, black pants, ruffled shirt, and bow tie. Singing everything from Frank Sinatra, Engelbert Humperdinck, and Neil Diamond. Changing it up every now and then, he would throw in Elvis or Conway Twitty. There was a clearing by the stage with a dance area. An older gentleman came over and asked Beulah to dance. It must have been obvious they were not a couple. Beulah accepted, as she handed Noah her purse. "Watch this, and don't let it out of your sight." The unspoken word she conveyed to Noah was 'here is eight-thousand dollars, watch it for me'.

Noah watched on, as the couples slow danced. He took a look around, observing all that was taking place. Everything from the couples dancing to the high skirts of the waitresses, bending over to give drinks. The occasional kiss on the cheek of the girl standing next to the guy at the bar. The couples walking by holding hands. And, of course, the girl two tables away giving him the eye. The only thing he could think was please don't come over. I really don't want to make this any more uncomfortable. He was alone in the crowd. Like so many times before, he was on the outside looking in, and with this crowd, he was ok with that. He was different, and it was ok. The set was over, and Beulah returned to the table, thanking the guy, and sitting back down. It was now after 3:00am and Noah was feeling groggy, and the effects of the alcohol made him even more tired. He was over the whole Vegas thing and just wanted to rest. "I'm ready to call it quits." He told Beulah. She was surprised, "What do you mean? It's Vegas, you don't go to bed until the sun rises." Noah wasn't in agreement. "No, that ain't going to happen." She was disappointed and started to quote the cliché, "Come on, 'every party has…'" Noah interrupted, "A pooper and it has to be you! Yeah right, …I know, but I have a long drive back home." The two got up from the table and headed out when Beulah stopped. "Well, you can hide out in the room by God, but this is Vegas, and who knows when I'll get out here again. I'm going to have some fun!" Noah was confused and agitated. He was tired of the peer pressure. "What? What do you want from me Beulah? … My God I have went out of my way to make you happy since we've left Indiana. And now I'm tired, that's all, I'm tired." Beulah was snippety. "Fine, …I'll just go play cards by myself. You haven't gambled since we've been here. Why did you even come?" Noah was taken aback by her comments and tried to remain civil. The length of the trip and the time they had spent together was starting to take a toll. He didn't want to say something he might regret later. "I haven't gambled because I don't have the money. I've put a few dollars into the slots. So, I have gambled. I just don't want to throw my money away." Beulah rolled her eyes. "That ain't gambling." Noah pushed back. "It is for me. I don't get off on it like you." Beulah grabbed her purse and started walking toward the Blackjack tables. "Fine you do what you want. I'm going to play…" She took off as Noah stood debating whether he should go with her. She arrived at the tables and sat down. Noah walked past her when he heard her say. "I'll be up when I'm done." Noah waved without looking back. He arrived at the room, hit the rack, and was out in minutes.

The morning sun was peeking through the curtains when he opened his eyes. Looking at his watch and looking over to the other bed, he sat up immediately. Beulah had not made it back. The bed had not been slept in. What the hell did she do? Did she stay up all night gambling? Then he worried maybe something happened to her. Getting up, he got dressed and headed back down to the last place he saw her, the Blackjack tables. When he arrived at the casino floor, the air was stale, and hazed with the smell of cigarette smoke. He came around a row of slot machines to see Beulah sitting at a table alone with the dealer. He watched without saying a word as he approached the table. She played the last of her chips. Boom, the dealer had a perfect twenty- one. It was over, Beulah had lost all of her chips. She got up, and looked at Noah, "Well shit. That was the last of it!" Noah wanting to make sure of what she was saying. "You lost all the eight thousand from last night? You put some up, didn't you?" Beulah looked at him, and shook her head no. She walked on, as she straddled her purse over her shoulder and crossed her arm. "I'm tired, but I'm hungry, you ready to get something to eat?" Noah was in disbelief at how she could be so calm. She was up eight thousand dollars when he left to go to bed. Was she completely broke? Noah let it go for now, but he wasn't going to forget. They headed to the diner and sat down for breakfast. After getting coffee, Noah asked again, "So you lost all the money from last night?" Beulah shook her head again yes without saying a word. Noah reemphasized how much it was. "You know that was eight thousand, right?" Beulah's words rolled out of her mouth nonchalantly. "I know it, can't get it back now." Like oh well, nothing was wrong here. Maybe it wasn't anything to her, but for him it was quite a bit of money. The waitress brought the food. They were about finished when Beulah opened her purse and looked to Noah. "You got any money to pay?" Noah looked at her purse. "Yeah, I got it covered. Why are you broke?" She wouldn't answer. He could tell the way she looked away he was right. She was embarrassed, "Are you serious? You had all that money, and now you can't even afford to pay for your own breakfast." Beulah sat quietly. Noah shook his head in disbelief, as he finished his meal. He thought how irresponsible and inconsiderate of her. She had not offered to help with any expenses the entire trip, then winning that kind of money and not even buying him a meal. She was either self-centered or had a gambling problem. At least today was the day they both were leaving. Noah had money to get himself back and enough to last till next payday. Thank goodness he had already given her the money for the plane ticket home. Then it dawned on him, did she gamble that away? "Beulah, do you still have the money for your ticket home?" Beulah looked at him, "Yeah, it's right here." She opened her purse and started rummaging thru. "It's right here, I put it right here…" Noah knew she didn't have it. She looked up at him. "I swear, I put it right here separate from the rest of my money." She back tracked in her mind to validate her actions. "I must have grabbed it not realizing it." Noah was now upset. "Beulah, I don't have any more money to get you home." Beulah sat there for a minute quietly. "If you have some you can loan me, I can try and win enough to pay for it." Noah was taken aback. "Are you serious? … what? … and if you don't, then we are both stranded. No, bad idea. Girl, you got a serious gambling problem! That's how we got into this situation; you need some help!" Beulah's eyes teared up. "You said you would get me home?" Noah was appalled at the arrogance of her. "Really, are you trying to blame me? Look I gave you the money for your ticket. I didn't agree to pay for your gambling. If you decided to gamble it away, that is your problem. But I can tell you, I will be leaving Las Vegas today. Whatever you do is your business. So, you better figure it out." She sat and wiped the tears as she cried. "I guess I'll have to call Herman. I can't tell him I lost the money, he'll be pissed" Noah held firm. "Well, that's on you, you gotta do, what you gotta do." Beulah went to the phone booth while Noah stayed to drink another cup of coffee. He was just finishing when Beulah returned. "Well, is he going to do it?" Beulah was smirky in her answer. "It's done. He's taking care of it. I told him you were broke and couldn't afford a ticket home." Her smarminess came across. She was proud of tricking Herman into believing Noah had broken his promise of getting his wife home. Noah now looked bad from Herman's point of view. He didn't care, as long as Beulah was out of his hair and on her way home. That issue was hers to deal with now.

They finished at the diner, and Noah was ready to get back on the road and head home. He didn't care how tired she was, Beulah was no longer calling the shots. He was taking her to the airport, and she could wait it out there. Her lack of gratitude and concern had worn thin, and his guard was now up. He dropped her off at the curb. Getting out long enough to unload her luggage and give her a hug goodbye, he was back in the car and on the road. The ride home was quiet and peaceful. It allowed plenty of time to contemplate and reflect on all that was and would be: the trip back to Indiana, purchasing his own car; the trip to Vegas and then standing his ground with Beulah. Something was changing inside of him. Although he couldn't put his finger on it, …it was right. Arriving back at the barracks in the early evening, it was good to be home.

Chapter 12

Child, I'll call you Noey

After a week back at work, it was Saturday and Noah had spent most
of the day doing chores: dropping his uniforms off at the cleaners, getting his car washed and then a haircut. Now he was bored. He decided to take a cruise around Oceanside, maybe see if his uniforms were done. He remembered the gay cruising spot where he met Sergeant Rose just past the Oceanside pier. Maybe he would drive down there and see if it was still happening. He always liked the area because a scene from the movie "Top Gun" had been shot at this location. In his daisy duke shorts and flip flops, he contemplated whether to go as is, or should he shower and make himself presentable. He looked in the mirror. "No, …just no!" The daisy dukes were not for public consumption. If you're going to do it, do it right, besides, you never know who you might meet.

Noah cruised by seeing who was hanging at the pier when he saw his friend Jay. He pulled further down the street and made a U turn to take a parking space right in front of the blue and white house that appeared in the Tom Cruise movie. Though a bit unkempt, the house was still identifiable. Noah parked and headed down the sidewalk and found Jay talking to a young black man. Jay, a former Marine, had gotten out of the Corps but had stayed in the area. Noah wasn't sure what Jay did now, other than being a bit of a punk rocker. Jay had been one of the first "family" members Noah had met prior to going to Oki. They hung out a few times at the pier and both had a common acquaintance, Sgt Rose. Jay had offered to take Noah to the clubs in the area, but the two had never managed to work it out. The last time Noah had seen him was for a brief hookup in Oki, before Jay returned to the states. As Noah approached, he could see Jay had really started sporting the punk rock look. He was wearing ripped, bleached, and rolled up jeans. He sported black combat boots, a razor blade earring in one ear, and a black leather jacket. His dog tags hung around his neck over a white 'wife beater' T-shirt. Jay turned from his friend to greet Noah. "Well, well, well, look at you motherfucker, what brings you out tonight?" Jay was always a bit rough around the edges. Noah laughed as he stopped where the two were standing, reached out and shook Jay's hand, then gave a brief hug. Noah couldn't help noticing the dark makeup around his eyes and wasn't going to let it go. "What's all that shit around your eyes?" Jay laughed, took a couple of steps back to parade his latest look, turned around so Noah could see everything from both sides. "Hey, it's subterranean, freedom from pain and suffering. I'm just helping to elevate the cause." Moving back to where Noah and the young black man were standing. "Semper Fucking Fi…" Noah laughed at him, "You look good man," Jay shook his head and gave an aloof smirk, "Yeah man, no fucking regs, fuck the suck, …nah, but it's all good!" He quickly did a once over of Noah, "You're looking good too man! You're starting to fill out." He briefly grabbed Noah by the bicep, "You're getting some guns going on. Shit man, I remember when you first got here, …skinny little toothpick." Noah being a bit embarrassed, pulled his arm away, and quickly pushed him back a bit. "Lay off man…" Jay grabbed Noah's arms, pushing them down, and started laughing, "Hah, hah, it must be all that good fucking Marine Corps PT," as he stepped back away, "that I don't miss, hah, …I'm just fucking with you man you look great!

The young black man Jay had been talking to was now standing next to Noah. He started looking around at the cars going by. Noah had noticed the young man was wearing dark sunglasses, slightly pulling them down a couple of times checking the cars that had slowed to cruise. Noah couldn't make out if this young guy was a Marine. His appearance was a bit ambiguous. He looked like a Grace Jones knock-off. This guy had an extreme flat top, but the rest was shaved like a Marine's haircut, zero around the back and sides. He fit the check list for off base regs, wearing a tucked-in, bright pink polo shirt with the collar up. Noah noticed the jeans he wore. They were well-kept, skin-tight designer jeans and were highly pressed with razor sharp creases. His white belt matched his shoes, which looked like ladies' slippers.

Waiting for Jay to introduce the two of them, Noah quickly gathered Jay may not know this guy's name. So, the unspoken rule was to introduce yourself first to take the awkwardness off the guilty party. Noah trying to be polite, "Hi, I'm Noah. Sorry, I didn't get your name?" Noah stuck his hand out to the young man. The young guy stepped back and dropped his glasses down a bit, lowered his chin, and with a straight face, gave a once up and down of Noah's entire body, "Do I know you?," not as a question, but more like 'how dare you talk to me!' Noah felt he had just been completely judged within a half second. The young guy quickly pushed his glasses back on his face, snapped his head away and almost simultaneously put his hand on his hip. Noah had seen this before in some of the gay clubs he had been to but had never really been one to take part. It was a warning from this young man to Noah; "I'll talk to you when I'm ready, and I'll tell you what I want you to know about me." Some called it attitude, or a precursor to what was called a 'reading' if you pushed your luck. Jay quickly laughed as he saw what had just transpired. "Ooooh, better watch out Noah. Don't push your luck, you're about to get read." Noah was completely caught off guard at what just happened, "What the fuck?" The young guy posed with his hand on his hip, moved his head up and down, giving Noah the once over again. He quickly snapped his head away and simultaneously moved his hand from hip pose, then made a low snap at him. Jay, laughing again, "Come on Glenn behave! Noah, this is Glenn. Glenn, this is Noah." Noah, hearing the name Glenn, looked at Jay and then turned. "Glenn? I don't think I've ever met a Glenn." Noah looked to see how the young man reacted. Glenn turned again toward Noah and, very lady-like, stuck his hand out with a limp wrist expecting Noah to shake it. Noah quickly responded, "No fucken way… you ain't gett'en me again!" Glenn withdrew his hand, laughed, and said, "Ya Biatch." Noah realized this was all an act, and it was Glenn's humor. Jay interjected, "I take it you two have never met. Glenn is up at Pendleton as well." Glenn turned the attitude to Jay, "Don't be telling people my business bitch." Noah looked at him, "It's cool. I'm not going to do anything," Jay explaining himself to Glenn, "Me and Noah go back a couple of years, it's cool Glenn, he's "family." Glenn lightened up and let out a "Heeey!" and snapped his fingers in what was known as a gay pop. "Child, how did ya get the name Noah, are yah parents religious?" Noah familiar with the question, "No not really, it's been in the family from way back." Glenn put his hand out as though he was saying stop, "Child I don't know if I can call ya that? Feels like I gots tah go to church or something. Hayah!" he raised his hand up in praise, "Like I gotta get down on my knees and pray. Yes lord."

Noah was finding his reaction a bit amusing. He had learned early on in life not to be offended when people learned his name. It was uncommon to hear someone with his name. Getting a reaction out of someone had become normal. Noah looked at it as a positive. As an adult, he realized it caught one's attention and was a name most could easily remember.

Glenn continued with concern, "Child, I know you got it as a kid growing up…?" "No not really," Noah explained, "A lot of people didn't know my real name. My nickname is 'Nollie.'" Glenn's face responded in confusion. Noah laughed and was tickled to see his reaction. Glenn suddenly thought Noah might be pulling his leg, "Child are you messing with me…?" Noah responded, "No seriously, it's Noah." Glenn was confused, "What'd you say… Nollie, do you have brothers or sisters?" Noah nodded, and chuckled, "Oh yeah, there are eleven of us." Glenn was in awe, "Are you serious child, eleven? Boy your parents must have been busy! Which one are you?" Noah laughed, "I'm the youngest." Glenn was still curious, "So any other names like yours?" Noah shook his head, "They're not all from the same parents, some are half. Mom and Dad were both married before." Glenn shaking his head in disbelief, "Well, no wonder they called you Noah. Child, they ran out of names. I'll just call yah 'Noey.' When I talk to yah that's your name, 'Noey.'" Noah shook his head, laughed, and changed the subject, "How long you been at Pendleton?" Glenn, with attitude, "Long enough, and you?" Noah amazed with the attitude this guy was showing and wondered how long he could keep it up. "About the same... just got back from Oki, Motor-T here." Glenn's interest just perked up. "Motor-T, heeeey! Well alright... you know what they say? 'If you can't truck it, fuck it!" Noah, realizing Glenn was familiar with the job, "So where you at on base?" Glenn replied, "Oh, I didn't tell you?" Noah a bit confused, "No, you didn't." Glenn raised his hand and did a snap and pop, "We'll I guess that means it's none yah bizzzz." Noah holding up his hands as though he was giving up, "Fine, just trying to make new friends."

Tired from the attitude, Noah directed the conversation back to Jay. "So, where you at now Jay." Jay started telling him he had an apartment a couple of blocks away and had just started a new job. Noah curious, "Ever hear from Rose?" Jay grinned, "Nah, last I heard he moved back to Ohio after leaving the Suck and that's the last anyone has heard from him."

Noah's thoughts were interrupted by a whistle, and callout. "Jay, what's up guuurl!" Noah turned to see a light blue Chevy Citation packed full. One young guy hung out the back window hollering out to catch Jay's attention. Jay, laughing, cupped his mouth and let out a yell, "Hey girl, pull over!"

The car slowed to start looking for a parking place, while the crew in it was still letting out whistles and cat calls at anyone who might be standing by. Noah, watching the car, "I take it you know them?" He stepped off the curb to get a better look at his own car making sure it was alright. Jay's eyes followed the blue Citation, "Yeah, that's Dan hanging out the window. I think he's with Reggie and they're in Ms. 'Sher-am-moi's' car." Noah, a bit puzzled and curious, came back up on the sidewalk, "Sher-am-moi?" Jay chuckled, "Yeah, she's a Fag Hag. She loves the gays, loves the guys, and loves to party." Jay turned his attention away from the car as it parked, "If you want to know the happenings, or the drama, she'll be the one to know it. Miss Chatty Cathy right there, but don't push it with her, she'll read your ass in a heartbeat!"

Noah looked down the street just as the passengers exited the car. Jay started telling Noah who they were. "The blonde skinny one getting out the back is Dan. The dark-haired guy next to him is Reggie." Then a dark-haired Hawaiian looking lady emerged out of the front passenger side. Jay squinted to try and get a better look at who it was, "Holy shit, is that fucking Kauli?" He followed up with, "She got her hair cut." Another passenger then exited the driver's side. It was a heavy set, curly blonde, with big eyeglasses. Jay hollered out, "Sher-am-moi!" The ladies walked up on the sidewalk, breaking out into their best runway strut. A few steps away from Jay, they turned, went back a few steps, and turned again, snapping their fingers in the air as they posed. Jay, excited about what he was seeing, bent over laughing, let out a "Woohoo, you go guurl!" and did a snap of his own back to the ladies. Kauli, Dan, and Reggie, made it to the group. They all exchanged pleasantries by giving Jay and Glenn hugs, fake kissed each other, "Mwah," turned and introduced themselves to Noah. Miss Queen herself Sher-am-moi waited a little behind the rest of the group to make her own grand appearance in front of Jay. It consisted of a cheezie imitation of Olivia Newton John's scene out of the movie "Grease." She stuck her finger out to Jay's chest, moved it down a bit and hissed in a seductive voice, "Tell me about it stud." Jay rolled his eyes, laughed, and gave her a hug. Noah, amused by the flamboyant pageantry the group had portrayed, stood by as the group caught up with each other and reminisced. Dan and Reggie, seemingly bored of this, moved on to what was happening around them. Both were now hollering and whistling at the cars passing by.

Noah, realizing the group was drawing attention, started feeling a bit anxious. He went to where Jay and Sher-am-moi were and poked him in the side, "Hey I'm gonna get going." Jay, a bit disappointed, "Ah come on stay, you all just met." Noah, "Yeah I know, just not real comfortable standing out here. Anyone could pass by." Jay, looking to where the others were standing, realized the group had been joined by a few others. The hoots and hollers were starting to get loud. "Yeah, I get it. Hey we need to hang out some time." Sher-am-moi spoke up, "You need to come down to San Diego with us." Noah's eyes lit up, "I've never been out to the clubs in San Diego, I'd love to!" "Sher-am-moi" grew excited, "Oh those guys will eat you up honey, but don't worry, I'll tell them your mine!" Noah blushed with a big smile, "Just let me know when."

Jay pulled a card out of his back pocket with his number on it and gave it to Noah. He took a glance at it and started to put it away when Sher-am-moi snatched it away, "Oh Honey, you ain't getting away that easy, here's mine too." With a pen pulled from her bra, she wrote down her number on the card. She handed it back to him. "I come ready doll! We have a group going down Halloween. You should join us. If you've never been, that's the time to go. It's hard telling what you'll see." Noah took the card from her hand and put it away. "What do you mean it's hard telling what I'll see?" With excitement in her eyes, shaking her head in disbelief, "Oh honey I'm not even going to try, you just have to come and see!" Glenn overhearing the conversation, "I know that's right, Heeeeeey!" and did his snap and pop. Noah started to part, when he stuck his hand out to Glenn once again to see if he would shake his hand goodbye. Glenn had let his guard down and went to shake his hand. Noah quickly yanked his hand away before Glenn could follow through. "Gotcha!" and started laughing as he walked away.

Noah had reached about fifteen feet or so and he heard Glenn say, "Horno." Noah stopped in his tracks and turned back not quite sure what he was saying. "What?" Glenn looked at him, "Horno, …You asked where I was at. I'm at Camp Horno, … yah Biatch!" Glenn snapped his hand with a pop. Noah chuckled, "I'm at Delmar, maybe we'll run into each other …" Glenn let out a chuckle, "All right now."

Blacklist Strumen

After cruising Hill Street for a while, Noah decided to drive back to the cleaners to see if his uniform was ready. It had been more than an hour since he had dropped it off at Mattie's one-hour cleaners. He hoped it was done because it was starting to get late, and he still needed to get back to finish his boots for inspection the following day.

Mattie's was one block west of center Hill Street and could be a bit dicey late at night. The bus station next to Mattie's was on the corner and brought many transient people, hoping to make a buck off young Marine arrivals trying to find their way to the base. On the other side next to Mattie's was a bar. It had a stucco facade with two separate doors on each side of the establishment. A metal awning extended across the entire front where a white wooden sign hung down the center with scripted letters "The Capri." There wasn't much illumination and made one wonder if it was done intentionally to not draw attention. Noah had never been in the bar before, but knew it was a gay hangout from rumors heard on base. He had tried going in once but was turned away for being underage. Though still underage, it was now the fear of being seen entering or leaving by someone from base that really kept him away. He had also seen reports in the local paper of people being jumped or harassed when coming out of the bar. To make matters worse, it had also made the so called "Blacklist" posted on base.

The list, published and updated by the Staff Judge advocate and the MP's office, placed civilian establishments in the local community off limits to Marines. It was posted in all the units on the base and all Marines were expected to read it. Institutions that targeted young naïve Marines with rip off scams were the primary reason to make the list. Some were loan shark companies that would loan money to Marines who couldn't manage their funds from paycheck to paycheck. Unfortunately, when they would take a loan with one of these places, they would end up losing their entire paycheck just to pay it. Once on the list, many of these places would change their names to trap unsuspecting Marines. Other places would be placed on the list due to frequent occurrences of Marines being harassed, robbed, rolled, or arrested. Many of these places were bars, hotels, strip joints or houses of ill repute. There was still one more group. Last, but not least, establishments known to cater to the gay community. Gay bars, cruising places, trans community hang outs, and bathhouses were all targeted. Naval Investigative Service, the crime unit who investigated any possible gay service members, often patrolled, and performed undercover work at these locations. Most Marines laughed at the "Blacklist." It was an ongoing joke. NIS had done the work for them. It listed all the fine establishments a young Marine would want to go.

As Noah pulled on the street, he slowed to look for a parking space. Most of the businesses were open 24 hours and parking was a nightmare. If one found a space, it had to be scooped on immediately. He was in luck! A car was just pulling out right in front of the cleaners; it was true "Doris Day parking." Disgruntled, he found the line at Mattie's reached out the door and flowed into the street. Underneath the flashing bulbs and neon lights, he was close enough to slightly hear the disagreement going on at the customer desk. Suddenly, the sounds of the street were overpowered by the music and laughter coming from the open door of the Capri lounge. It caught Noah's attention and he looked to see the ruckus. Out came a heavy-set middle-aged man laughing and carrying a bar stool. He sat it down and propped the door open. At the same time, what appeared to be three ladies walked out. One tall, white woman and two black women. Noah couldn't quite get the gist of the conversation other than they told the guy good night. The ladies moved closer to the curb and huddled. One lit up a cigarette as they stood in conversation. Noah looked back into Mattie's to hear the conversation of the dissatisfied customer and was beginning to wonder if he was going to get his uniform tonight. Intrigued, Noah turned back to the bar. The ladies were saying their goodbyes as two turned and started walking toward Noah and the third walked in the other direction. The two walking toward him were laughing, chatting, one even hollered out at a car passing by. As they passed by, Noah got a better look. The smaller black one looked familiar to him, but he wasn't sure from where. He quickly looked away but heard the two commenting, "Child I could do his laundry." The other chimed in, "Alright girl, and you know I don't need an iron to make them wrinkles fall out…" Noah, thinking they had passed, turned to get a quick glance, only to realize they both had turned and were looking back at him. The taller one said, "Alright now, I know you was listening." Both giggled as they moved on their way. The line finally moved forward after another clerk came to the counter. Noah was now inside and could hear the conversation with the guy at the counter. The Asian lady holding his ticket explained in broken English, "So sorry not ready yet." She hollered back in another language to a woman working at a commercial iron. The two women had a brief conversation. After they finished, she turned back to the young man "Yes, so sorry not ready yet." The young, slender, dark-haired man was not liking what she had to say. Very firmly and to the point, he chose his words wisely. "Ma'am you told me they would be done in an hour. You charged me an extra $5.00 for expedited service. It has now been an hour and a half, and they are still not done. Exactly when will they be done and am I going to get my $5.00 back?" The Asian woman responded, "Yes, Yes, done soon." The young man asked, "What's soon?" The lady in the back at the iron hollered to the front "15 minutes" and the Asian woman at the counter repeated, "15 min." He looked at his watch and repeated to the woman, "Ok, 15 minutes, I'll be back." She handed him his ticket and he turned and started toward the door. As he passed Noah, they briefly caught each other's eye. Noah quickly looked away and the man went out the door. Once Noah thought the man was away, he glanced back to find the man had also made a quick glance back as well. Noah grinned and slowly looked to the counter. Not bad looking Noah thought. He must be a Marine because of the way he spoke and dressed. Marines had standards in civilian clothes, and he fit the description. He wore jeans with a belt and tucked his pastel orange Polo. The walk, the hair cut helped give it away.

Noah reached the counter and had the same Asian woman. He gave her his ticket and she went to retrieve his items. She quickly returned and told him it wasn't ready. Noah could hear where this conversation was going as Deja vu kicked in. She told him it would be another 15 mins. Noah took his ticket and returned to his car. While sitting in the car, Noah started noticing the different people going in and out of the bar. He noticed people walk by the bar, go further down the street checking out the area and return to the bar and quickly dash inside the door. There was one guy parked across the street who ran from his car and entered abruptly. It was warm out, so he turned the car ignition on and rolled the windows down.

While he continued to wait, he heard laughter coming from further down the street and looked to see what appeared to be a small group haphazardly dancing and walking. They appeared to be enjoying themselves. Once across the street, he could hear them coming closer and soon realized they were headed to the bar. As they came to a stop in front of the bar, someone came out, stopped, and spoke to them. After a brief conversation, they went into the bar and the person started walking down the sidewalk towards Noah. As he approached, Noah recognized him as the young man who was just at the counter at the cleaners. Noah looked at his watch and it had been about 15 mins since he had left. The handsome man turned and went back into the cleaners. Noah turned the ignition and rolled the window up and got out of the car heading back into the cleaners. He was right about the Marine part. When the man turned to leave the store, he went past Noah, they once again gave each other a glance. This time he smiled and nodded his head toward Noah. Noah thought the guy was far enough away and gave a quick glance back to see where he went, only to find him looking back at Noah. He smiled, knowing he caught Noah looking. He slowly turned and walked toward the bar. Noah, caught up in the moment, was brought back when the woman at the counter announced. "You gonna wait all night?" Noah headed to the counter, grabbed his uniform, and headed to his car.

Just as he reached the car he heard, "What's your name?" He ignored it, fearing it may be one of the vagrants in the area. He walked around the car to the driver side and put the key in to unlock the door when he heard it again. "What's your name?" He looked up and, on the sidewalk, stood the young Marine he had just shared glances with. Standing with one hand holding the uniform slung over his shoulder and the other he had hanging by a thumb in a front belt loop. Noah stopped what he was doing and looked him in the eye before answering, "Depends on who's asking?" The young man smiled. "I am." Noah paused but continued to look at him for a second, contemplating if he should respond or just get in the car. He knew he was a Marine; he just saw him pickup his uniform. Not sure what he should do, he looked back down to the car door, unlocked it, and hung his uniform in the back. The guy spoke up "My name is Dodge, …Dodge Strumen." Noah responded, "Hello Dodge, Dodge Strumen." Still not sure if he should give him his name, Noah was being extra cautious. Could this be one of those NIS traps he had heard about? He did just see him come out of the bar. They both had checked each other out, but still this guy was taking a lot for granted. He was a bit aggressive to ask Noah his name. Noah wondered if he had been that obvious and had he really done anything wrong if this guy was NIS. Wow, how paranoid had he become? Dodge quickly came back, "Sorry, didn't mean to startle you, just thought I might have known you. You look like someone I use to know from base, haven't seen in a while… Guess I was wrong. Once again, sorry to bother you man." Dodge turned and started down the sidewalk toward the bar. If this guy was NIS, he was giving Noah an out. Noah watched him as he walked past the bar and on down the street. He crossed the street and disappeared.

Noah got in his car and took off. As he got to the corner, he looked across the street. Dodge was standing a short distance away from the rest of the Marines waiting at the bus stop. Noah said to himself, "What the fuck." He pulled up next to the curb where

Dodge was standing and rolled down the passenger window. Dodge, still holding his uniform over his shoulder, bent down, and looked in the car. Noah held his hand out, offering a handshake, "My name is Noah." Dodge stuck his hand in the car, "Nice to meet you Noah," Holding on to Noah's hand a bit too long, Dodge was clearly indicating his interest. "That's a different name." "Yeah, I get that..." as Dodge grips his hand tight one more time and let go. They both look at each other with big smiles and nervousness. Noah notices Dodge's jitter, "Look, sorry to give you the brush off back there, you can never be too sure." Dodge replied, "No need to apologize, I shouldn't have asked your name. It was a bit bold...you had a right to jump the fuck back." "Yeah, it scared the shit out of me, didn't know what to make of it." Dodge tired of beating around the bush, "Look I'm going out on a limb here, and if I am, fuck it! I think we both know what's up here and if not, I'll deny it happened. When I saw you in the cleaners, I wasn't sure, but when I looked back, I thought maybe. When I came back and saw you again, I was like, yeah." Noah asked, "Sure of what?" Dodge paused and contemplated how he should answer without blurting the gay word. With sarcasm, Dodge blurts out, "Someone I could talk to, you know, like 'family.'" Noah familiar with the term 'family,' repeats to Dodge, "Like 'family'? It's always nice to have 'family' around." Dodge said with a sigh of relief, "Cut the shit." Noah laughs. "I saw you leave the Capri Bar back there." Dodge rolled his eyes, "Ass, you knew and made me stress?" Noah, "I had to be sure." Dodge looks up to see the lights of the bus turning on to the street a couple of blocks down. He tells Noah, "Hold out your hand." Noah, puzzled, "What for?" Dodge hastily, "Just hold out your hand." Noah begrudgingly holds out his hand. Dodge reaches in his pocket and pulls a piece of paper out and puts it in Noah's hand. Noah looks, "What's this?" Dodge, seeing the bus getting closer, starts to pull away from the car. "It's my number. I wrote it down in the bar in case I saw you again." Noah laughs as Dodge starts to walk away and shouts, "Use it!" He ran up to where the rest of the people were waiting to catch the bus. Noah smiles, looks in his rear-view mirror seeing the bus coming up behind him, looks out to his left and speeds away.

Chapter 13

Plan the weekend

Camp Pendleton 22 Area was the central location of the logistics, supply, and maintenance facilities. During the work week, it was busy with the hustle and bustle of Marine trucks working to keep the world's finest at top speed. Noah just finished doing a drop off when he heard a voice behind him, "Ya Biatch!" Noah stopped in his tracks to look. It was Glenn standing on the loading dock. He was in his cammies, looking squared away with razor sharp creases and spit shined boots. Noah let out a chuckle, "What are you doing here?" Glenn smiled, "Just dropping some paperwork off, where are you headed?" This was the first time Noah had seen Glenn on base. "I'm done for now but have to hang around until after lunch for a pickup to take back." Glenn, inquisitive, "Same here, you want to do lunch?" Noah was taken by surprise, Glenn was being so friendly, "Sure…" it would give the two a chance to get to know each other a bit more. Glenn grinned, "Ok, let me finish this paperwork, you can leave your truck here. I'm in that van, (as he pointed to it) No need to drive this beast," Referring to the 5ton. "I'll be about 5 minutes," and took off into the bay area doors. Noah climbed up into his truck and, as he waited, he noticed all the buildings in the area. There were rows of warehouses that lined both sides of the street. The loading docks and awnings all faced the roads making it easy to load and unload all the many items being shuffled and transported. One building looked the same as the next. If one wasn't familiar with the area, the only way to define a location was either by the red and yellow signs located on the building or knowing the building number. There must have been a master plan back in the day, because this was the normal layout at most of the bases. These buildings had been around since WWII, meant to be only temporary, now looked like they had long been overused. Glenn came out and

Noah heard him hop down from the loading dock and asked, "Child these people are about to work my last nerve, …So where do you want to go?" Noah, not knowing of too many places for base, "Well, it's the club, or exchange…" Glenn, "Come on gurl…"

Once in the van they headed to the chow hall. On the drive they noticed a few guys jogging. Glenn lowered his dark sunglasses to get a better look and let out a "Haaaay!" Noah was a bit paranoid, "They can hear you…" Glenn waved his hand doing a swish away. "Noey, you too wound up, … they don't know what I'm talking about, hell …, You need to lighten up child … calm down!" Noah shakes his head, "I have a job, I'd like to keep it…" As they got closer to the chow hall, Glenn's attention was caught by a Marine walking down the street. "Child, is that who I think it is, let me turn this thing around." Glenn pulled over and did a quick U-turn. As he got closer to the Marine, "That's my good friend Telly, child he's a hoot! You gots to meet him."

Glenn slowed the van as he got close to him. "Ya Biatch!" The Marine stopped in his tracks to see who was hollering. When he recognized who it was in the van, he chuckled, "Oh no you didn't Queen!" as he snapped his finger in the air at Glenn. He let out a laugh. Glenn looking in the rearview, "Where you headed?" Telly noticing the car coming from behind, "Pull this thing over, and get out the road." Glenn pulled over to the side of the road, letting a car go by, and Telly came to his window. "I was going to the barracks, how about you?" Telly wasn't sure if he could speak openly in front of Noah, "Who is this child? Didn't your mother teach you any manners…" Telly looks over to Noah, "This child is rude, I'm Kalvin, but you can call me Telly." Noah nodded his head, "Hi, Noah here, nice to meet you Telly.." Glenn interrupted, "You two are safe, you're both "family." Telly looked at Glenn… "Child, can we have our business…" Glenn asked again, "So are you coming or not, I gots to get out of this road?" Telly rolled his eyes, "I don't know child, I got to keep this figure in shape, so I's can get the cookies Girl!" Telly struck a model pose, "You know Halloween is coming up and I have to look good for the children down in Hillcrest!" He started to chuckle. Glenn smirked and took the opportunity to be catty, "Biatch, it'll take more than not eating to make that happen." Telly had made his mind up to come along. "Hush Child! ...Now how do I get in this thing?"

Once in, they were off to the chow hall. Telly was curious about Noah, "So where you at child?" Noah leaned over a bit so Telly could hear. "I'm at Camp Margarita." Telly smiled, "They gots some trade up there, Heeey! Those men are hot child. All of them grunts. You know there some shit going up there in those barracks." Glenn chimed in, "Ok now, preach Sister." Noah, chuckled, but was curious from the comment earlier, "So what is Hillcrest?" Telly was surprised, "Child, you never been to Hillcrest?" Noah shook his head no. Telly sat up, "Laawwd help me up in here! (Raising his right hand to Noah) As a gay queen it is my obligation to tell you, Child, that's where all the children are, Huuuun-nay! ... it's the gay ghetto of San Diego, and the children are there, ...Hear- me-now!" Noah was amused by Telly's accent and chuckled a bit. "So, what happens on Halloween." Telly, realizing Noah may be a bit new to the gay community, "Where you from originally child?" Noah spoke, "Indiana, a small town called Blotch. Why, where you from?" "Baltimore" Kalvin laughs a bit, "Child did you say Blotch? Like a stain?" Noah nodded his head, and Telly tucked his head and frowned. "Well child, no wonder you got the hell out of there! Indiana, hmm ...child I'm sorry...do they even allow gays there?" Noah, "No, not really, I mean they do have a few gay bars in Indy, but not really." Kalvin, getting back to the subject at hand, "Yeah, I figured as much, you probably don't know much about the gays huh?" Noah, a bit perplexed, "I'm kinda' getting used to this gay thing, really just since California." Telly excited to school him, "Well child let me tell yah, ...Halloween is when the children come out to play. Straights have Christmas Honey, but the gays own Halloween. It's one of the biggest parties of the year. They shut down the whole neighborhood. They have several bars, all within walking distance, so the children will parade their costumes, doing a pub crawl from bar to bar. If you have never seen it, you have got to go. Nobody does Halloween like the gays honey."

Telly started talking about the different costumes of years past and the crowds, festivities, and parade in the streets. Noah hung on every word Telly was saying. Glenn spoke up, "Let's make plans to go?" Noah excited, "You serious?" Glenn excited as well. "Yes, we'll have to get costumes together, it's less than two weeks away." Noah thought a bit, "I can think of something…" Telly cut in, "Child I already got mine together, but can't tell you. But you have to do it right, or the children will talk about yah!" Noah with a bit of concern, "Oh man, I can't get in, I don't have an I.D." Telly a bit confused, "Child you got your military I.D." Noah interjected, "No, no, I mean yes, I have my military ID, but I'm only 19. I can't get in without a fake I.D. Telly laughed, "Honey you just a baby, don't worry child, most places don't care if you're in costume. Haaay! Let Mother work on it." As he patted Noah on the shoulder. "Child, we got this, we're going to do Halloween."

Halloween night

The group met up at a place called Ten-Pen-Allie's. It was Friday night, Halloween weekend. The drinks started flying in anticipation of the wild weekend ahead. Adding to the festivities, they celebrated Glenn and Lilly tying the knot! It was nothing unheard of for gay and lesbian members to get married to each other, usually for professional reasons, or to throw off suspicion and questions. Marriage was often viewed as maturity within the workforce, and the military was no exception. If one was to be promoted or attain a higher rank, it was expected they took on a spouse. Monetary benefits and personal freedoms followed if you were married. Lower ranking service members were required to live on base and subside at the chow hall. If they were married, they were granted permission to live off base. They'd be given a spousal housing allowance and spousal pay, provided they resided with their spouse and took care of their wellbeing. In addition, because they would be eating most of their meals at home and not at the mess hall, they were given a subsistence allowance. There were a number of benefits one could go into, but the point was they did it to be able to live a life in private, away from the Marine Corps. It was something to take seriously, with the many benefits or perks, there were just as many pitfalls. The marriage is real, and it is legally binding. You can answer for the other person, and they can answer for you. You really have to trust them. The bigger reason is the military frowns upon it. One could laugh and say they do not like any marriage. So, the saying, "If the Marines wanted you to have a spouse, they would have issued you one." They really frowned on what they called a marriage of convenience. If a couple was suspected of it, it was hard to prove. After all, what goes on in a married couple's bedroom is private, and a couple doesn't have to testify against each other in court. However, if it could be verified, this marriage of convenience, the Marine could be discharged, and both could be prosecuted for fraud. They would be required to pay the money received back to the government, and even sent to prison. Although they would rather marry the person they loved, this was a remedy. It wasn't an ideal situation, but some thought it was worth the risk to be with the one they loved. It was nothing new in the gay community. During WWII, the Hitler regime persecuted and condemned lesbian and gays, putting them in concentration camps, and sentencing them to death. They would frequently marry as a cover to prevent being found out.

Tonight however, all that was set aside, Lilly and Glenn had considered the risk, and decided to join together and create a home where both could be with their significant other. Glenn and Charlie, Lilly and Patsy, all living in one big house. The bar was hopping. It was not often so many gay military members were in one location outside of a house party. For the most part, lesbians and gays ran in separate circles. They had their own bars, and hangouts. On occasion, like tonight, the two circles merged.

Noah was enjoying himself; he was meeting so many people. Everyone was open and being real, the walls were down just briefly. Glenn introduced Noah to one of Lilly's friends, Dusty. She was a tall, strikingly good looking, light skinned black woman. Her partner, Gloria, was a shorter version of Dusty. Noah awkwardly spoke out, "I don't think I would have ever guessed, …" Dusty chuckled, "Honey, …some of us can give you fish baby!" She paused and seductively kissed Gloria. Then she held up her drink to toast, leaning to Noah, "Oh, …is that 'her' lipstick I'm wearing?" Noah chuckled as he held his glass and toasted, "Well Cheers, …shows you how much I know." Both chuckled, he really enjoyed talking with the two of them. She and her partner had been together for a while. She hinted to Noah they were looking to do the same as Lilly and Glenn and find someone to get married. The thought had never really crossed Noah's mind.

Saturday night came and their motel room was a disaster, between their bar clothes, costumes, and shopping bags from a day at the mall. Glenn, Noah, and Telly were all in a room together; clothes and shopping bags were thrown in every direction. The drinks were pouring, and so was the music out of the room. The no-tell motel was full of the crew he had met in Oceanside. They had all booked their rooms in advance. The block party included Jay, Sher-am-moi, Reggie, Dan, Kauli, Lilly, Patsy, Dusty, and Gloria. and several others he had never met. Being close to Hillcrest, the hotel catered to the gay community, and those attending the festivities for the weekend. When the party crowd was ready, they even offered a shuttle to and from various activities.

The evening had set in, and the neon lights and streetlamps were all that illuminated. It was Halloween and the festivities were underway. On University Ave, in front of Mr. Dillions, the small shuttle pulled up. The door to the bar flung open and out walked an entourage of men dressed as brides, in full white wedding gowns. To vamp it up a bit, the main bride wore a head piece, designed as a several tiered wedding cake, with a veil flowing down from the bottom. To make it clear they were men, they all had handlebar mustaches. The shuttle passengers applauded as they unloaded, the brides curtsied and moved on down the street. The Oceanside crew were amongst the passengers. All were in costume. Glenn, as no other than Ms. Grace Jones. Telly was in a tux, went as one of the

Carrington's off the show "Dynasty." Sher-me-moi was Raggedy Anne. Kauli was in a Hawaiian grass mini-skirt and a coconut shell bikini top. Noah supported a modified Elvis look with dark glasses and sideburns; he wore his collar flipped up. As they finished unloading, they heard a holler and ruckus from the bridal party just down the street. They turned to look at the brides facing them with pulled up dresses showing their combat boots and jock straps. A couple of them had turned and were shooting the moon. Sher-am-moi, full voice, "Oh Honey! ... you need to come back here so I can get a close up!" as she did a snap and pop. As the group started to enter, Noah paused noticing Jay was not with them. "Anybody know what happened to Jay?" Sher-am-moi grabbed him by the arm, "Come on honey, Jay is a big boy, he'll find his way home."

The group arrived early enough so they were able to get a good place to watch and see the others arrive. A figure wearing a Grim Reaper cloak, with a skull mask and crown, walked by. It puzzled the group because of the blonde hair poking out from the hood, the princess sash laying across it's chest, and the steering wheel it was holding. The mysterious figure gave them all a creepy feeling, as it waved a scepter in front of the group. The costumes were amazing. A guy dressed as a pirate came up to the group. Even in costume, Noah could tell he was good looking.-His one eye patch, mutton chops and goatee made him appealing. Why did he look familiar? When he spoke out to Sher-me-moi, she recognized him instantly. "Oh my God, Dodge! You- look- so- good. Honey, everyone is going to be all over you tonight!" The two hugged, along with a few others in the group. When he got to Noah, he stuck out his hand, "You kinda look familiar, but I can't say for sure, if it's the Elvis thing or is it you that seems familiar?" Noah lowered his dark glasses, and said his name, "Noah." It hit him. Dodge recognized him. "I remember you!" Noah was surprised, "I'm sorry, have we met? Can you remove that patch thing on your eye, sorry, I just don't recall?" "Sure." Dodge pulled his patch off and removed his pirate hat. "I met you one night at the laundry, right outside of the Capri Lounge. We were both picking up our uniforms." Noah smiled, "Oh my God! Yes! Yes, I do. We talked a bit…" Dodge interrupted, "I gave you my number, …and you never called. Yeah, yeah, I get it" Noah on the defense, chuckled, "No, no, it's not what you think. I mean, I really liked you, it's just that I wasn't sure, … you know, the military and all. I'm still kind of new to all this. and got cold feet." Dodge was inquisitive, "What? You thought I might be NIS or something?" Noah chuckled, "No, it's just, we met, you know, out on the sidewalk, Oceanside, who knows you could have been anybody." Sher-am-moi interrupted, "Ok, you two boys can chat it up, but we're headed to get our place for the costume contest" In another environment, Miss Sher-am-moi would probably go unnoticed, or even be shunned for her weight, but here she reigned Royal Queen. She snapped her fingers and the group moved on. Dodge and Noah stayed behind. "You know sometimes I don't know whether to love her or hate her?" Dodge chuckled and turned back to Noah. "Where were we? Well now you know, …I'm gay …and we're here, so let's make a night of it…I would like to buy you a drink, if that's ok?" Noah liked Dodge from the first time they met. He wasn't going to pass it by a second time. "Yes, I think I would like that."

Later in the evening, after dancing and chatting most of the night, Noah and Dodge joined the group by the stage as they watched the final contestants. The Drag Queen MC held up her hand for the last time and the decision was made. From the overwhelming crowd applause, they had a winner. The figure on stage was the one wearing a Grim Reaper cloak, the costume named, "Miss Afterlife Grace Kelly." Although campy, it mocked in bad taste the late actress and Princess of Monaco, who had perished the year earlier, when her car went off a cliff. The MC spoke to the contestant, "So what made you think to do this?" The response was muffled, "I'm sorry honey, we can't hear through that mask," The winner took it off. Surprising everyone to learn it was Jay. He had been there the entire evening. He had won the contest. Only Sher-am-moi had known prior and was able to remain silent. Of course, it was Jay, who else could have been so dark? Jay came from the stage and was greeted by the crew with congratulations. He had taken his mask off. "Finally, I can breathe." Noah and Dodge went to the bar with him to get a drink. The three did a shot, and Jay chuckled, "I have been watching you two all night! I was wanting to say something but didn't want to give myself away. Now that I can, …You guys make a really cute couple. I've known you both, and I get it! So, when I saw you talking, I thought, yeah, it makes sense. I mean you guys look really good together." Noah laughed and he and Dodge looked at each other and grinned. Noah jokingly commented with Jay still in costume, "Thanks Jay, but I don't know if having the grim reaper's approval is a good thing!"

Call home for the Holidays

Christmas had arrived and Dodge and Noah were looking for a place to move into together. Noah and Dusty had come to terms with each other and gotten married in a private little ceremony with just her and her partner Gloria as maid of honor. Dodge stood in as best man. Although he didn't like it, telling his family about Dusty was part of the facade. If the Marine Corps ever questioned the marriage, it made it more believable. It also took the question from his father, and the rest of the family, about when was he going to finally settle down.

Christmas Eve was the night everyone gathered at his father and Claudia's home. It was a big deal, and this time of year was the hardest being away from family. The family would spend the day doing last minute preparations, primarily shopping, cooking, and decorating. Noah's father would complain about all the money being spent, but when the evening came, all that was put aside, and he enjoyed it the most. His tradition for the adult folks was his "Coon-dog Punch," and for the young ones, he would slip off and reappear as Santa, only to handout all the gifts from under the tree. The gifts, at times, could be a bit over the top. He remembered the first big Christmas they had done after Beck and Claudia were first married. He bought two miniature Shetland ponies for the grandkids. When it came time to give them as presents, he brought them in the house to show to everyone. Claudia went in a rage, telling him to get them out. He laughed, "Those little ponies aren't going to hurt a thing, let the grandkids enjoy them for a minute." It wasn't the gifts that Noah remembered though, it was the fact everyone got together, setting their differences aside, and enjoying each other. Noah had been gone for three Christmases now, but he always liked to call home on Christmas Eve. This year would be no different.

Noah waited till he knew they would all be there and made his call. Claudia started the conversation, and soon, one by one each of his siblings would get on the phone and speak, all happy to wish him a Merry Christmas and tell him they missed and loved him. Beulah got on the phone and wished him a Merry Christmas. Being she was one to instigate, and stir up trouble, she began to speak her mind and inform Noah that she was angry and displeased with their father and Claudia. She spoke, "Give me a moment while I go into the other room. There are too many ears in here, besides I can barely hear you." She paused briefly, and Noah could hear the crowd through the phone grow quieter. "There can you hear me now?" Noah, calmly, "Yeah, what's up?" She continued, "You have been gone for three years now, and it burns me up that you don't have the money to fly home for Christmas, and they know it. But that messed up son of hers, moved to Seattle, and has been barely gone six months, and they go and paid for his way home."

Noah sat quietly. This hurt, but it wasn't something he needed to hear right now. It was Christmas. All it did was open old wounds that were better left buried. It did no good to allow the negativity to take control, it was something that would not change. Noah spoke up, "Beulah, Claudia works and makes her own money, if she wants her son there, then by all means, she should be able to do it." Beulah continued, "Yes, but it still ain't right! It just burns me up! You wait till the holidays are over, and I get Dad alone. I'm going to let him know about it. It's just not right!" Noah really didn't want to hear anymore, and why was Beulah even bringing this up, was she hoping to stir trouble? "Well thank you for looking out for me, Beulah, but I really prefer to not even know things like that. …Is dad around? He's the only one I haven't spoken to yet?" Beulah responded, "Yeah, one second let me get him, you know he's out there having a good time!"

Noah could hear the shuffling and the crowd noise growing louder, soon he heard his father's voice. "Yeah, Nollie is that you?" "Yeah, dad, just calling to wish you all Merry Christmas!" Beck continued, "Merry Christmas to you too! We miss you, sorry you couldn't be here! One of these times we are gonna have to get you back here for the holidays, along with that new bride of yours. You wouldn't believe all the presents under the tree. You know I still dress up as Santie Clause, the young ones, the kids they love it. I remember doing that for you kids when you were still young." Noah chuckled, "I remember too dad!" "I think some of the teenagers are sneaking into the coon-dog punch, and they think no one knows. It reminded me of you when you were still at home. You would sneak a glass and thought I didn't know." Noah laughed, "Who? Not me dad. That was Roman, you know I was always the good one!" Noah's father laughed, "Yeah, I know, all three of you boys got it in!" Noah laughed, "Those were some good times. They'll be all right, might have a headache in the morning." The phone call lasted only long enough for the two to say Merry Christmas one more time and then they hung up.

Chapter 14

Home Coming Out

The flight from San Diego to Indiana was about 4 hours. Noah had tried to doze in flight, but anticipation of what lay ahead kept him from any real rest. Thoughts of his grandmother mixed with his own situation, kept tussling over and over in his mind. His emotions of grief and loss were confusing. The grief and loss from the death of his grandmother was very real, but also, he found himself mourning the loss of the home and life he had once known. He knew any chance of the life he had once known was no longer an option, nor had it ever been. The heterosexual dreams, standards, and expectations of a wife and children placed on him from his family and society were never his. He had finally come to terms with who he was and knew there was never a chance of going back. His Grandmother had once told him, "Sometimes in life, in order to move forward, you have to let go of the past." How prophetic her words had come back to him at this time. Her smile, hugs and loving embrace of life would never be forgotten; however, it was now time to let her go. The part he was having a problem with was the status quo of "living a lie" with his family and friends. It bothered him to lie and have to hide who he was in love with. The longer this went on, the bigger the lie became, and it was just getting increasingly out of control. It was time to put this behind him, and move on, but it was a matter of mustering up the courage.

Coming off the plane, Noah looked around not sure who would be there to greet him. With everyone being so busy with the funeral arrangements, he was told someone would be there, they just weren't sure who it might be. Not recognizing anyone, he headed to luggage pick up. Just as he came down the escalator, his sister Lois and brother-in-law Earl were waiting by the luggage carousel. Lois excited and waving to make sure she wouldn't be missed, came running to give him a hug. It was great to see her. He was glad it was her and Earl who came to pick him up. It meant the two-hour ride home would not be a boring one. Quickly, the luggage had come, and they were on their way.

The ride home was filled with the latest talk of family, friends, and trends. What was most important was it allowed for a time to catch-up. Lois was excited to tell Noah about her recent "Boy George" concert adventure. "Oh Noah, I got dressed up just like him, dread locks, make up, and all. When we arrived to go in, there was a bunch of protestors outside, because you know he dresses like a girl and all. My girlfriend was worried, I didn't care, I walked right through them. I got stopped by a reporter from the newspaper. He took a picture. Next thing I know it was on the front page. Who cares? It is all stupid! Besides, I think he's sexy! And I love his music!" Lois changed the subject, curious, asked about his wife. Noah glazed over the topic, leaving it at work would not permit her the time off.

Time went by quickly and, before they knew it, they were pulling into the circle driveway. Noah could see his dog Jodie come running out and barking, to meet the car. Once the van side door opened, Jodie came to a standstill not expecting Noah to step out. Noah spoke up, "What's a matter girl, you forget who I am?" Jodie, recognizing him, began jumping on him, licking, and whining while wagging her tail. Noah was in tears at the greeting she had given him. The door opened, and his father stood in the doorway. "Yeah, …She ain't going to let you out of her sight, she knows who you are." Once inside, he gave his father a hug, along with the family waiting in line to see him.

After he settled in, it wasn't long before Beulah popped the question, "Where's your bride? Thought we were going to get to meet her." Leave it to Beulah to always be poking into everyone's business. Noah once again blew it off, "Work would not permit her the time off." He knew this would not be the last time he would be asked about her and was already getting tired of it. This was going to be a challenge to keep up the charade. His father, from out of nowhere, "I dated a black woman once." Claudia, being a bit surprised, "What does that have anything to do with?" His father realizing, she might be a bit jealous, "Nothing, just wanted him to know it's ok." He sat down at the kitchen table, and quickly changed the subject to the biscuits sitting on the table, "Look at them biscuits I made Nollie, you need to try one of them." as he broke one and started to eat it. Claudia, knowing she made them, rolled her eyes, and let out a laugh, shaking her head in disbelief. Beulah, having to be part of the conversation, "Yeah right, Claudia don't let him do that to you. We know you made them." Noah joined him at the table laughing. He missed the pranks and humor of his father.

The next day was a long and emotional one. The funeral was nice, or at least nice as funerals go. Extended family and friends had gone and a few of the siblings remained. Noah was in his room finishing talking to Dodge, when his sister Beulah knocked on the door. Rushing in before he could answer, "How are you doing?" Noah not surprised, remembered how pushy she could be. "Doing fine, … I guess, …if you're talking about Grandma, glad to know she had a nice turn out." Noah sat down on the bed, Beulah came over and sat down as well.

Noah could sense she was wanting to talk about something, but knew it wasn't the funeral. Was she going to try and pry into his business? His guard went up, so he immediately reverted the conversation to her, "What about you, what's going on with you?" She teared up, "I don't know, somethings not right. …all this has caused me to think. I'm so sick and tired of trying to make everyone else happy. I just want to live my own life for me and quit trying to be what everyone else wants." Noah wasn't sure where she was going with this conversation. "Ok, what are you talking about Beulah. You're going to have to do better than that if you want me to listen." Beulah, now crying as Noah reaches to the nightstand, grabs a Kleenex, and hands it to her. "Dad… I've tried talking to him. He doesn't listen, just tells me to stay, I'll get past it." Noah still confused, "Get past what?" Beulah still crying, "Me and Herman have been having problems. I can't take the drinking. I told him if he doesn't get help, I'm leaving." Noah enquiring, "So what does Dad have to do with it?" The tears had started to subside as Beulah started to explain, "Dad says I had a good man once with the kids' father. He thinks I jumped the gun and ran off because things got hard. He says I'm too young and wild and still wanting to sow my oats, and that no man will do. So now with Herman, he says I just need to calm down, grow up and deal with it instead of trying to run off all the time." Noah, unsure what she was asking, "So what is it that you want to do? Not dad, not Herman, not anyone else, but you?" Beulah paused for a moment thinking to herself and looked away before answering, "I don't know what I want...I want Herman, but not like this. I'm simply confused and think it might be easier to just walk away. Part of me thinks Dad is right. I...I...I just don't want someone telling me what to do." Noah could see she was gaining her composure back, but, at the same time, understood exactly what she was saying. "Look if you're relying on other people's opinions, then you'll never be right. Come on look at Dad, he's not necessarily the best to give advice when it comes to love or relationships. Hell, he's been married four times." Beulah let out a chuckle, "You're right about that."

Noah decided to be open with her and be a little more honest. "Look, you have got to do what is right for you, and live for yourself, not the family or anyone else." Beulah was puzzled, "Are you talking about marrying a black woman?" Noah gets up and goes to his suitcase and pulls out a framed picture of his wife Dusty. He hands it to Beulah. "How pretty, I hope we get to meet her." Noah smirked, "Well, that is who I married." He then took the picture frame, opened it from behind and pulled out another picture and hands it back to her, "This is who I am in love with."

Beulah looks at the new picture, it is of Dodge. She frowns a bit with confusion, "Oh shit!" Quickly to cover up her own thoughtlessness, "But you're married?" Seeing it was confusing her, Noah continued, "Look it's a long story and it's complicated. Simply put, she is a cover up. She is a beard, and he is who I am with." Beulah, still in a state of confusion and shock, "Does anyone else in the family know? What about Dad, oh my God, have you told Dad?" Noah puts the frame back together as he replies, "No, and I'm not sure if I want him to know." Beulah insistent, "You got to tell him before he finds out by someone else." Noah's guard went up and now wished he had not said anything. "Look, I'll handle it. As far as I'm concerned, he doesn't need to know. It's my decision and I'll tell him when I 'm ready." Beulah was still insistent and as usual, she offered up her services to be the one who tells their father. "Look, I can help if you like, you don't know how he'll take it. I can let you know if he doesn't like it, that way you won't have to face him, or you can just act like nothing has happened." Noah looked at her knowing this was no longer in his control. He would have to talk to his father. Beulah would make it a point to tell him. He was angry with her and angry at himself for trusting her. She had always been known as the family tattletale, anything she thought would give her one up in their parent's eyes, she would be sure to tattle to them. "Really Beulah, that sounds absolutely absurd. What, go around on eggshells, ignore it like it doesn't exist. Yeah right! I'll be the one to tell, he deserves to hear it from me, and I deserve to hear his views. Do me a favor and at least keep your mouth shut, until I can have a talk with him?" Beulah trying to act innocent and insulted, "What, I won't say anything."

The evening had set in and was Noah's last night at home. The visit was subdued, but several of the family members still wanted to have an impromptu get together to make sure they had a chance to send Noah off right. The VFW was the next town over and was more centrally located for everyone to attend. Noah rode with Lois and Earl just in case Beck and Claudia wanted to leave early. When they arrived, neon glared from the patches of ice in parking lot. The cars were sporadic, which meant the place wasn't busy and they should all be able to sit at the same table. As they walked in the brisk air, the band music would make an occasional outburst when the door was flung open. Once inside, Aunt Biffy, had already claimed a table and as different ones arrived, they would take their place. The table with its folding chairs in the back of the dimly lit, smoke-filled room, wasn't far from the dance floor. Lois and Earl headed to the bar, as Noah sat down at the table. Within minutes, a song came on causing Beck to grab Claudia, while hollering to Herman and Beulah, "Let's hit the floor."

Noah watched the couples dance. Lois and Earl arrived with drinks from the bar. A pretty, young, black woman came over to the table, a friend of Aunt Biffy, and started speaking to her. "Hey darling, how are you doing?" The conversation carried on for a minute before Aunt Biffy introduced her as the waitress for the table. "Hey ya'll, this is Sheena, she'll be our waitress tonight, let her know if you need anything. I've known her since she was this high (as she held her hand up, displaying a young child's height)." The song finished, and the couples returned to the table.

Noah had been sitting quietly, off to himself, like so many times before, an outsider looking in. His mind and heart were back in California. Yet once again, he found himself observing all the different couples enjoying their partners in life. He would never be a part of this no matter how he tried, at least not now in this time or at this moment. Although they were his family, they were oblivious to the one-sided relationship they shared. This was the norm. It was the way it was and always had been but was this the way it was supposed to be. Claudia interrupted his thoughts, "Come on Nollie, let's go get a drink."

While at the bar, she asked, "You doing all right? You don't seem like your normal self." Noah nonchalantly shrugs, "I'm doing alright, just a lot of change going on right now." Claudia wasn't happy with the answer, "Well all I know is you've been preoccupied about something the whole time you been here. It's ok if you don't want to talk about it, but it's not like you to be so distant from everyone. I'm not the only one who has noticed."

Although she could be caring, he instantly grasped this concern was out of character. Noah turned from the dance floor and faced the bar, "Beulah has spoken to you?" Claudia looking at him with concern, "Yes…" (she reached over and put her arm around him and gave a slight hug) "But I already knew and have known for many years." Puzzled by her comment, "Why haven't you ever said anything?" Claudia smirked, "Really now, what was I to say? You would have denied it. If I was wrong, what kind of mess would I have made?" He looked at her and chuckled, "I suppose you're right. It really is not something you could have brought up." She reached over and gripped his forearm. "I may not have given birth to you, but I helped raise you just like you are one of my own. I've been around you long enough to know. Mothers tend to know these things, it's just whether we choose to acknowledge it." Noah, curious how far the news had traveled, "Does Dad know?" Claudia took her hand away from his arm, "It is not a conversation we've had. However, Beulah did speak to me, and you know how she is. So, I really don't know."

The bartender brought the drinks, as Claudia paid, she continued, "If you decide to tell him, do me a favor and give me advance warning, so I'll know." Noah looked over to the table where the family sat, wondering who all Beulah had already told. Claudia grabbed the drinks in front of her and they headed back to the table. Noah, knowing the conversation with his father would have to happen soon, "I fly out in the morning, and I will tell him before I go."

As they walked, Claudia looked over to the table and paused briefly, noticing Noah's father talking and laughing with the young black waitress at the table. She leans slightly to Noah, "I'm so glad to hear you didn't marry that colored girl because you loved her!" She turns and walks away.

Noah was confused and bewildered about what he just heard. What an awful thing to say. Did she think she was paying him a complement? Looking at his father talking to the young black woman, he realized she must have been made aware of La Mora, the woman his father had fallen in love with long ago. It must be coming from a place of jealousy.

The ride home was quiet. Upon arriving home, Noah immediately went to his room and readied for bed. As he laid in the moon lit room, he contemplated the next morning and how it would all transpire. What if his father decided to go to the Marine Corps and tell them? What if he is banned from home; what if his father gets violent? All the wrong answers just kept filling his mind. Maybe his father won't care? What about Dodge? Is this all worth it? How would they get by without the Marine Corps; all they had worked for. Would this all really be worth it? How can the world play such a dirty joke! Why couldn't he just be like everyone else? What kind of freak of nature had he become? It was all ready to be exposed. He realized he must go through with telling his family. No more lies! It was hurting the people he loved the most to have to look at them and lie. If he would just leave it as is, and not speak at all, he was only being untrue to himself. All the tossing, turning, and thoughts were overwhelming. Before he knew it, the sun was starting to come in through the window, a new day had begun.

He had been awake most of the night, Noah realizing he would not get any more sleep and needed to get his head cleared, decided to get up and get dressed to go outside and watch the sun rise.

The barn was his safe place. This is where he had come so many times as a child. The place where he could escape, clear his mind, and dream of how big the world was and all that it could be. As he walked around the barn, he noticed his father's bedroom light was on and the house would soon be stirring once again. Looking out to the open fields and trees, he was reminded of how much he loved the place where he grew up. What was about to take place might change his welcome to this place forever. Noah sat down on one of the doghouses and looked out at the frost covered fields, where the sunrise was just starting to break through.

He wasn't sure how long he had been sitting before he was startled by the family dog Jodie, who came up and sniffed and jumped to play. Noah responded, "I miss you too ole girl." They played a bit when Noah looked to his left to see his father walking toward them. He was in his bib overalls, with his Carhart jacket over them, chewing tobacco, with his hands tucked behind the bib portion. He started to talk from afar, "You know that dog just sits on the porch and mopes for weeks every time you leave, can't get her to eat or do much of anything. She normally doesn't pay any mind to the cars that pull in and out of here, but the moment you go, she'll sit up and look at every car for the next month, seeing if you get out. You know she loves you!" He said with a smile on his face as he approached. "I remember the day we brought her home, the guy told me she was mean and couldn't be tamed, … liked to bite. I told him you don't know that boy of mine. You are the only one she would let near her; she took a liken to you and has never stopped!" Beck paused long enough to spit out the chewing tobacco juice. "She's getting old you know. She tolerates me, but it's you she likes. …One of these times she may not be here when you come home. You better enjoy her while you can." Noah continued to pet Jodie and let out a half laugh, "Is that right ole girl, you hear what he is saying about you? Soon he'll be telling me he taught you to coon hunt."

Noah stood up, and walked to his father, noticing the hat he was wearing. It was the Marine Corps hat he had sent him through the mail. "I see you got your hat?" Beck replied, "Yeah, pretty nice one too. Some Jarhead sent it to me all the way from California." He pulled it off to push his hair back and put it back on…and laughed. "So, I came out to get you for breakfast, before they clear everything up in there. You know those women they can't stand any mess; they have to get it cleaned up right now. So, I figured I would come on out and get you. They all thought you were in your room. Beulah went to get you and came out swearing that you had done left in the middle of the night. I don't know what the hell happened with that girl. Some'en ain't right. She has always gotta stick her nose into everything, and always jumping to conclusions. She's just like her mom, a goddamn troublemaker!"

Noah was surprised by what his father was saying about Beulah and could tell she had done something to agitate him this morning. "I told them he's out back, he'll be back in. But then I started wondering if you were ever going to come back in. Didn't know how long you would be out here staring out at them empty fields." He paused for a minute "You know you use to come back here as a kid, if you thought you was going to get in trouble. I'd let you stay out here till you finally would get brave enough to face me. All I can say is something must be bothering you or weighing deep on your mind. Nobody looks out there at nothing that long."

Noah took a couple of steps toward his dad, and looked back out over the fields, and let it out, "You know what I have to say don't you?" His father replied, "Maybe, but I want to hear from you, not a bunch of cackling hens who have nothing better to talk about."

Noah let out a halfhearted laugh, turned a bit to look behind at his father. "You mean Beulah and Claudia," His father quickly snapped back "You know who I'm talking about, now don't try and change the subject. Be a man, speak your mind! I ain't getting any younger, and I'm not a mind reader, now speak."

Noah took a deep breath, "I'm gay, … I'm gay Dad... do you know what that is? Do you!" Beck replied with a bit of resentment, "I know, I know, I didn't get off the bus yesterday." He paused for a moment, "And this other, who's he? His name is Dodge, what kind name is that anyways? I mean who names their kid after a truck? Is he a Marine?" (Noah chuckled.) His father continued, "And how long you been?" Noah confused by all the questions, "What gay or with him?" His father looks down and frowns a bit, "I guess both." Noah in disbelief was finding the whole thing to be surreal. "All my life." As he knelt to pick up a rock and throw it, "…and just a few months with Dodge." Beck asked, "His family, they know?" "Yes, have for some time, he is older." Beck looks at him, "How much older?" Noah looks away, chuckles at his father's tone of concern. "Don't worry, I'm not looking for a daddy, He's only 28."

Beck gave a frown, took a couple of steps away from him and paused for a moment to look out to the field. Noah couldn't read his expression, "Who's looking out at the field now?" His father continued his stare, "You know the bible doesn't agree with it." Noah disagreed, "That is subject to interpretation." Beck turned back at him trying not to get off topic "Yes, and no." Shakes his head as if he had enough, "Oh hell, I don't know what the bible says. I haven't tried to figure it out." His father looking away to the fields again, "Well, I guess that's my fault. I never pushed the Bible on you kids, just supported it if you chose to follow. So, no need to go there now." Beck looked at Noah, "Well shit, … what I'm trying to say is, it ain't going to be easy." He paused struggling for words "…you know when you go against the norm, people aren't as quick to accept things as you would like, or maybe not even at all. It takes a strong person, or couple to not get broken from it all." (Beck paused to spit.) "I've been married four times and only loved one of them."

He walked up and put his hand on Noah's shoulder, "Ah, I suppose I cared for all of them in one way or another, but I only had that burn in your belly, that heartthrob into your soul twice. Your mom was the first. I loved her whole heartedly. I was young and didn't treat her right and to this day I think the good lord took her away! … But the other, …La Mora, …" Beck paused as though he could see her standing in front of him. "… I knew the moment I laid eyes on her. We had our go at it, but she was black, and I was white, and it was a different world then we're living in now. People and family with small minds were never going to accept us. She got it from her end, and I got it from mine. Bigotry got the best of us, so we walked away."

His father turned back to the house, leaned his head in and looked Noah straight in the eyes, "After this conversation, as far as I'm concerned, it's a mute issue. I don't know if I agree, or disagree, and maybe just don't understand. I do know this; When it comes to love, the mind lies, but the heart doesn't." Beck reached up and put his hand on Noah's shoulder and gave him a shrug. "Yesterday I didn't know, I was a proud father of a Marine and a man that loves his son. You're the same man I raised you to be, and you are still my son. I loved you yesterday and I love you today, ask me again tomorrow and I'll still love you. This is who you are, I just didn't know. So today I know, doesn't change who I am, and it doesn't change who you are." Noah reached up and put his hand on his fathers and patted it as a tear came down his own face.

His father pulled his hand down and took a couple of steps and paused. "Now don't be jumping the gun, it might take some time to get used to it, and eventually, maybe you'll trust us enough to bring your beau home. It took some time for you to come to terms with it, I ask the same, I'll get used to it in my own time."

Beck headed toward the house, when he was a good distance away, he yelled back, "Breakfast is getting cold, and you've got a ride to catch. Make sure you say goodbye to Jodie."

Chapter 15

Valentine's Day Massacre, it's a thing

Noah parked his car, excited to be home early. It was Valentine's Day, and he had a special evening planned. He was going to surprise Dodge with matching rings and a nice dinner to follow. He started up the stairs of his apartment when someone on the first floor caught his attention. He looked familiar but Noah couldn't get a clear view of his face. Noah paused; no this can't be. What the fuck? He looked again making sure he wasn't noticed. No fucking way. He stood at the top of the stairs until he was sure the guy was inside his apartment. Once he knew it was safe, Noah went down and took a look at the mailbox. Oh my, what was he going to do now? His fucking Lieutenant lived right below him. Even if Noah was straight, he wouldn't want his boss living right below him. How long before he figures out it is Noah living above him? Why hadn't Noah noticed it before? Then it dawned on him, he's been on leave. He had moved off base for privacy. Now, it's not just the Lance Corporals he had to worry about, it's the man himself. The one who can actually get him thrown out. Noah rushed back up to the apartment before he was seen.

While unlocking the door, a letter had been posted on it from the landlord. What the hell did she want? Noah rushed in. He was in a panic. He had to let Dodge know about his Lieutenant. He changed clothes and came back to the kitchen. Hearing a knock on the door, Noah answered it, and it was Glenn. "Oh my God come in, come in!" Noah told Glenn what he just found out. Glenn shrugged, "Oh no, I'd be outta this place tonight, Huh-uh, ...no child!" Glenn raised his hand and waved no. "Here, let me get on up out of here, this place is got bad juju!" Glenn got up and acted like he was leaving, before he chuckled. "No child, I'm just messing with you but seriously, I don't know what to tell you, that's just a shit show waiting to happen right there."

Noah calmed down as he opened the landlords' letter. "What? What is she talking about?" Noah read the letter aloud:

"Dear Mr. and Mrs. Barlow, I need to speak to the both of you about your living situation, and it has been noted that Mrs. Barlow has yet to be seen. Specifically, I need to address your roommate Mr. Strumen. Please contact me immediately, or I will be required to contact the base and your command in the morning."

Glenn's jaw dropped. "Noey, you need to get out of this place. She knows what's going on up here. Who is this nosey bitch anyways? Child drama!" Glenn snapped and popped his fingers. Noah shook his head and sat down at the dining room table. "What the fuck kind of letter is this? The worst timing and bad luck, on Valentine's Day no less. I'm going to have to call Dusty and get her over here. I hope she can come." Glenn shook his head in disbelief. "Child what kinda dirt she got on Strumen that she needs to talk to you about him. That must be pretty bad for her to write it down. Child, what did I tell you about him, when you first started dating? You know some neighborhoods look better when you're just passing through. I knew there was something off about that guy." Noah shook his head, "I don't know…"

Noah got his thoughts together and contacted Dusty. He explained what was going on and read the letter. She agreed to stop over. When Noah hung up, he looked at Glenn, "You're not going to leave, are you?" Glenn laughed, "Child, I ain't going nowhere. I'm fixing me a drink, …uh-huh, I'm staying right here, … I am watching how this plays out."

Dodge was working late and wouldn't be in until later. When Dusty arrived, the two walked down to the rental office. Dusty grabbed Noah's arm, hanging all over him just to make an appearance. The landlady was a heavy-set woman, with light brown hair, and a plain Jane. Once in the office, they were brought into a private room. She greeted them, "Hi, I'm sorry I needed to be so abrupt in the letter, but you'll understand my position in just a minute. Glad to see you Mrs. Barlow, we were beginning to wonder if you really existed." Dusty didn't like that comment at all. "You do know I'm a Marine, and I deploy for weeks at a time just like the men do. I didn't know when we signed for this place, I would need to check in with you!" The landlady sat back in her chair. "I'm sorry, I didn't mean it that way. It's just..." Dusty interrupted her, "I know what you meant, now that you have us in here, what is it that was so urgent that you must see us tonight, of all nights, Valentine's Day. What is it that a simple phone call wouldn't do?" The landlady continued, "Well, I have something to show you." She opened her desk drawer and pulled out a stack of letters. She handed them over to Dusty. Dusty fumbled through them. "Yes, these are all addressed to Dodge Strumen. That's our roommate, not us. Why are you giving them to us? Isn't this illegal, or an invasion of privacy." The landlady sat up, "No, it's not, when he threw them in the trash can, but missed, and a young child brought them to us. But that is not the point I'm getting at here. Mrs. Barlow, your so-called roommate is a homosexual. These are all love letters from his lover in Memphis, Tennessee. The most recent one is post marked just a few days ago. So, this is still going on right under your noises. This is a family complex, and I can't have that kind of activity going on here. Now, I don't care if you and your husband stay, but he'll need to leave. I don't want to cause any trouble, but if not, I'm going to have to contact the base about this situation."

Dusty looked at Noah, he was dumbfounded. Dusty could tell he was hurt and confused. He just found out Strumen had been in another relationship the whole time they had been seeing each other. She couldn't read him. Trying to keep up the façade, "What do you want to do about this?" She asked. Noah shook his head, "I don't know. ...wow, that's a lot to take in." The landlady spoke "Like I said, I have no problem with the two of you staying here, but he'll have to go. Now, I don't know if you two can handle the rent on your own. I have one-bedroom apartments come available all the time. They run a little cheaper. I know when you applied you were counting on his income." Dusty spoke up, "And if we don't stay will we get the deposit back?" The landlady did some kind of twist with her head, "Well, you did sign a six-month lease, and now you'll be breaking it. If you go with a smaller apartment, …I might be able to work with you, but I'll have to have your old apartment cleaned, so you won't get your full deposit back."

Noah's thoughts were running rampant. What a fucking bitch. She is fucking us over and knows there ain't shit we can do about it. Who the hell wants to stay knowing his boss lived right below him? And what the fuck was up with Dodge, was he betraying Noah? At this point he would go back to base. He didn't know what he was going to do. Noah shook his head, "I think it is safe to say we are done here. We'll find another place to stay." The landlady looked surprised, "You know if you do, I can't give you your money back?" Noah stood up. "Oh, you could, …but you won't. Because you're a bitch. As for our roommate, what he does is his business. And for myself, and my wife, why the hell would we want to live in an apartment complex knowing we have some nosey bitch watching our every move. Furthermore, don't ever threaten me again about contacting the base or my command. You assume we have something to hide, and we don't. So, go ahead and contact my command, hell, I might save you the time. You won't have to go far, because my boss lives in the apartment right below us. I think if we were hiding something he would already know. Last time I checked our rent is paid up until the end of the month. We'll be here until then." Noah looked at Dusty, "Come on, let's get the hell out of here. I don't like the company this place keeps."

Promotion of Jealousy

The list was out for the meritorious promotions. Noah, the kid from Blotch, Indiana, population forty thousand, had been selected for meritorious promotion to Corporal! His dedication to his demanding work and studying had paid off. The Battalion Commander had the final say and chose Noah. He had been impressed by Noah's demeanor and the military bearing displayed while being interviewed by the board. Staff Sergeant congratulated him and soon the word had spread. He was being congratulated by everyone in the motor pool. Mainly from those wanting to know when the wet down would be. Marines and their booze. Wow, he had done it! He could now say he was a Noncommissioned Officer, a leader of Marines, able to carry the NCO sword and add blood stripes to his dress blue trousers. Noah's thoughts then turned to Dodge; had he been selected as well? The extra money would be welcomed and the two of them promoted to Corporal would be a step in the right direction. Their relationship was now strained and on life support. Dodge had helped him with his studies and deserved partial credit for his promotion.

Noah walked into an empty apartment. He was eager to tell Dodge his news, but knew he should hold off his excitement, in case Dodge wasn't selected as well. After an hour, Dodge finally arrived. His entrance was a sad testament. He stumbled on one of the bar stools, grabbing the chair to brace him from falling, before pushing at it in anger. Noah spoke up, "Hey calm down, those cost money you know." Dodge, mocked him, "Those cost money you know." A few moments went by before Dodge started to speak, "I didn't get it, I didn't get selected to Corporal." Noah was at a loss for words. "Sorry to hear, did they say why?" Dodge continued, "Due to keen competition, too many others were more qualified." Noah shook his head. "Well, I would like to see the others, … Really. If it matters, I think you deserve to be promoted, but I'm not on the board." Dodge smirked, "Thank you!" Noah decided he would hold off on telling him about his own promotion. Let it rest a few days. Hopefully, he wouldn't ask about it.

It was the next morning and the doorbell rang. It was Glenn. He made his entrance as grand as ever. Giving fake kisses on each cheek, before walking to Dodge and turning away. "I see the garbage is still here. Child you need to do something about that, it's starting to stink." Noah knew he was referring to Dodge. Glenn liked to take jabs at Dodge whenever he could. There was always an unspoken tension between the two. Noah, not letting it slide. "Glenn, you need to play nice." Dodge got up from the dining room table, "That's alright, I don't need you to defend me with Ms. Thing, I pay her no mind." As he took his breakfast dishes into the kitchen. Glenn didn't let the opportunity slide. "That's because you would have to have a mind first," then made a face as he stuck out his tongue. Noah, trying to get Glenn to stop, smacked him on the arm, and gave him a frown, not wanting to provoke Dodge any further. He knew he would hear about it later. "Glenn why do you insist? I swear your incorrigible."

Glenn chuckled changing the subject, "When we going shopping? Guurl we gots to spend them promotion dollars! Child I can't wait to call you at work. ...Um yes, can I speak to Corporal Noey?" Glenn continued on excited for Noah. Noah raised his hand, trying to shush Glenn. Shaking his head, and mouthed "No" Glenn continued, "Child what's wrong with you, what you trying to say? Aren't you excited you're getting promoted?" Noah turned noting the look on Dodge's face. It was too late; he could tell Dodge heard everything.

Dodge was aggravated, "So, are you going to tell me? ...or do I have to continue hearing it from this queen." Noah replied, "I was going to tell you, it's just that when I found out you didn't get promoted, I wanted to wait a couple of days. I had planned to tell you today, but Glenn seemed to help things along" Glenn listening, "Child, you mean you haven't told him. And you, ... oh, Mr. Marine himself, ... child you didn't get selected, but Noah did?" Glenn tried not to chuckle. "Haaaay, there's drama up in here. I gotta have a seat and see how this plays out." Glenn's comment had provoked Dodge. "Yeah, well, I still know more about the Corps. Shit, I've forgotten more than you ever learned." Why Dodge insisted arguing with Glenn, Noah could not understand. He was outmatched when it came to Glenn's wit. Glenn had to get in the last word, "Really, and remind me what good does it do for you?" There had always been a bit of tension between the two and Noah felt like he always had to walk on eggshells. When it came to the Marine Corps, Dodge being the son of a retired Sergeant Major, always felt he had one up on the matter. Often condescending, he would correct others, and come off as a know it all. Noah turned to Glenn, "You guys are acting like children, Glenn can you give us a minute?" Glenn gave a stone-cold bitch face to Dodge, before giving one last jab, "Why yes Corporal, (as he smirked) go ahead and talk to the Sergeant Major's son. I gotta run a few errands. Don't let him be a kill joy. This ain't about you Dodge, Noah has worked hard to get this promotion. I'm proud of you Noey, don't let him trick you into believing otherwise. You haven't done anything wrong." Noah smiled, "Thanks Glenn!"

Glenn left and Noah turned back to Dodge. He sat quietly, as Noah explained. "As for not telling you, well I had stopped and bought beer, thinking we could celebrate together. But when I found out you weren't selected, I didn't want to gloat. So, I figured I would give it a couple days, before telling you."

He started to go in the other room, when Dodge finally broke the silence. "Congratulations, …you worked hard, you deserved it. …I'm glad at least one of us made it." Noah paused in his walk, before speaking. "Thank you! It's not me, it's us, and the work we put behind it."

Chapter 16

Marine Corps Admin, Staff Sgt Williams

Walking down the halls of the admin building, Noah noticed how clean everything seemed. The floor was highly buffed without so much as a foot scuff. The walls sparkled; all the brass was shined. You could smell the Pine-Sol and Brasso in the air. The only thing Noah could think was how glad he was not to be working in this building. This was the administrative building, and it also housed the Battalion Commander and Sergeants Major, along with their entire staff. It was the pinnacle of leadership and they set the standard for the entire Battalion. All those that worked there were always immaculate, or as Noah and most of the Battalion coined "Smack." Noah was summoned for this visit today because of an issue that came up on his life insurance policy. The PFC admin clerk called Noah to the counter. "How can I help you today Corporal?" "Yes, I was informed that I needed to sign some paperwork dealing with my life insurance." The PFC asked his name, "Give me a minute." He left and came back with Noah's service record book. Once there he pulled a note and started to read. "Yes, there are some questions on your choice of beneficiary." Sergeant McGuire stopped what he was doing and looked up, "So you're Barlow?" Noah, surprised, "Yes?" Sergeant McGuire started in with a bit of a sarcastic tone, "Yeah, you're the one who wants to list someone besides family as your next of kin and beneficiary, can't do that." Noah responded, "Why not?" "Because the Marine Corps says you can't that's why. Regulation …"

That's when Noah started blocking him, and everything McGuire said was blah, blah, blah… McGuire was the Marine's "secret weapon" known for destroying customer service and finding errors, often to the benefit of the government. His reputation of obstruction was legendary throughout the Battalion. When he finally finished, "Well, who can I put on it? Why does the Marine Corps ask us if they have already decided who they want it to be?" McGuire, "Look don't get smart, or you can come back tomorrow with a new attitude." Noah raised his eyebrows, "I'm not getting smart with you Sergeant, it just seems I'm being told who my beneficiary is, when it is supposed to be my choice." McGuire seemed to back down a little, "It is your spouse or your parents." What if I'm not married or if my parents are deceased?" McGuire smirked, "But you are married" "Yes, I have her listed as half and I really prefer not to go into this, my reason is personal. I'm sorry Sergeant but is there someone else I can talk to who has the authority to allow this. Surely, I'm not the first Marine to have this problem." McGuire, turned and looked back toward the glass enclosed office. "You can talk to the Staff Sergeant."

Noah knew to whom he referred, Staff Sergeant Williams. He was known around the Battalion as being a Marine's Marine. His military bearing and presence alone were intimidating. He had combat time in Vietnam and was the talk of many stories of valor. He wore a bronze star and purple heart on his uniform. Being a former Drill Instructor, he was often the one to call cadence on the Battalion PT runs. Physically well-built and always impeccable in uniform. Noah responded, "I have no problem talking to him." McGuire pointed over to the chairs lined up at the wall. "You might have a bit of a wait; he is busy." McGuire turned and walked back toward the Staff Sergeant's office. Noah went over to the chairs and took a seat. As he sat there, he noticed Sergeant McGuire return to the counter, grab Noah's service record book, and head back to the Staff Sergeants office. He entered and handed the book to the Staff Sergeant. Noah could see the two engage in conversation before Sergeant McGuire returned to his desk. Noah sat there patiently.

Another Marine had arrived and was being helped. He appeared to be young and had his family with him. A motherly woman and three children. She held one child in her arms, a little girl by the hand and the little boy was standing by his father. She was speaking in baby talk to the children and moved over to the seats to sit down. Her husband turned from the counter, asked her something and she quickly opened her purse and pulled out documents and gave them to her husband. The little girl, in a dress and a bow in her hair, was chewing on what appeared to be a cookie with more on her face and hands than in her mouth. She had been a few chairs over and was curiously and slowly moving toward Noah one chair at a time. When she arrived, she held her hand out with the cookie, as to offer him some. Noah smiled and replied, "For me?" Her mother, who had been preoccupied dealing with her husband and the baby in hand, called out her name, "Rosita!" The mother pointed to the chair where she was now sitting. The little girl shuffled to her quickly and turned around smiled and giggled at Noah. It was about that time Noah heard his name called out from the back of the room.

Noah navigated the desks in the admin pool toward the Staff Sergeant's office. As he passed one desk, a Corporal, without looking up, spoke softly for Noah to hear. "Make sure to go to attention and report in." Noah quickly looked at him as he moved toward the office. The young female Marine at the door gave Noah his service record book and waved him to go on in. Noah entered and the door closed behind him.

The Staff Sergeant sat at his desk, with his back turned, working on a typewriter. Noah centered himself at the Staff Sergeants desk and sounded off, "Corporal Barlow reporting Staff Sergeant." Staff Sergeant Williams didn't budge or turn from his work, but boldly announced. "Next of kin is spouse, blood relative, child, parent, sibling, etc. …not friend. Got it? You can choose who you want on your insurance, but questions will be raised if your friend, and not spouse is on there." At that point, the Staff Sergeant turned his head and gave a stare to Noah. "Is there something wrong that you don't trust your wife?" Noah was at a loss for words, as the Staff Sergeant continued. "I'm trying to ward off some embarrassment for you. I may not personally care, but there are others in this office who will make an issue of it. I know because they have already brought it to my attention. Things like this we are supposed to flag and bring it to the chain of commands attention. If I turn my back and let it go, it won't stop." He turned and gave a glance to Sgt McGuire, hinting by and nodding his head without saying a name. "Let's just say I have seen this before, you're not the first. I don't know your personal life, and I really don't care. Trust me, if something ever goes down, the first place they look is at paper trails. Get what I'm saying?"

Noah was taken aback at how candid SSgt Williams was being. It was as though he could see right through everything. But Noah still played coy. "What do you mean, something ever goes down Staff Sergeant, I have nothing to hide?" "Really, you really want me to go there?" The Staff Sergeant gave him a direct glare. Noah paused... this guy was looking out for him. "No, Staff Sergeant, I think we are on the same page." "Good, now, save yourself trouble, put your parents or your wife on there." The Staff Sergeant was protecting him, but why?

Noah hesitant for a minute, "No, you're right. I trust my wife it's just if something happened, I would want to protect her and have a friend talk to her, and of course she'll be on my insurance." The Staff Sergeant responded, "The Marine Corps likes things legal, and by the law, they don't like people to create waves. Any questions Corporal?" Noah in a subordinate tone, "No Staff Sergeant." "Good, then we're done here, sign the docks as the law sees it. Anything changes bring in the legal documents to support it. Now get out of my office."

As he left the office, Noah couldn't help but think, why the Staff Sergeant seemed so familiar, like he had met him before? Walking back through the desks, he passed the Marine who gave him the heads up to report in. Noah looked over and nodded at him. The Marine smiled back and leaned back in his chair "So you survived?" Noah gave a bit of a chuckle, "Yeah didn't go so bad, I've heard horror stories." The Corporal laughed "Yeah, we've replaced the hinges on the door many times. He must have liked you." Noah reached out his hand, "Corporal Barlow and you?" The Marine shook his hand "Corporal Schmitt, but they call me

Schmitty" Noah responded, "Noah here, I work down at the Motor T." Schmitty responded back, "Cool you know us corporals are like, …family, and need to look out for each other." Noah was amused and smiled, 'You bet!" Noah had picked up the code word "family." The Corporal was letting him know he was gay and looking out for him. Schmitty continued, "Next time you come in here ask for me, I'll be glad to help you," He gave a slight glance to Sgt McGuire. "If you understand what I'm saying. By the way, SSgt Williams is cool, he keeps McGuire in check." Noah realized McGuire was causing the stir. He smiled, "Thank you!" He shook his hand and took off past the front counter. As he turned to leave, he paused to notice Sgt McGuire at the counter.

The couple with the children had left and had been replaced with another young couple. The Marine was a short blonde guy, and his wife looked barely out of diapers, let alone old enough to be married. The Marine Corps made it easy if you were a straight couple. Yet, here Noah was having a problem getting Dodge as next of kin on his life insurance. The young Marine had brought his new bride in to be indoctrinated into the world of Marine dependent. For her, the Marine Corps opened the golden gate of benefits, all she had to do was walk down the aisle and they would be laid at her feet. She was a willing participant and had no hesitation. She expected them, and accepted them proudly, it was her right. The Marine Corps gave them to her. After all this was the love of her life, and she too would be required to make sacrifices alongside her Marine. Besides an increase in his paycheck, the benefits provided her medical and dental, on base housing privileges, and access to all the recreational activities, including buying groceries at the commissary, and shopping the big Exchange in the sky. Noah chuckled, the system was really geared to promote marriage, if one was a heterosexual. Who wouldn't want to get married with all the benefits? He and Dodge both married women they barely knew, and lived a lie, a ruse, just to be able to have permission from the command to live off base. It allowed them to be able to live and create a life with the one they cherished the most. On its face alone, if any rumors came up about either one's sexual orientation, it was discounted for the most part by the comment, "He is married." Any extra money might have been an added perk, but the point was, unless one was married, they were still required to be at all field day formations and maintain a room at the barracks. They were still required to eat and subsist at the chow hall. They paid taxes just like everyone else! Was their love and relationships any different than anyone else? Why were they treated like second class, and not afforded the same benefits of married couples? Oh, that's right they weren't allowed to marry each other.

Noah, lost in his thoughts, was brought back to reality by Sgt McGuire's voice. "Is there something else you need Corporal?" Noah realized he was being looked at suspiciously and turned and walked out of the office. When he and Dusty had first gotten married, he was very hesitant, and felt ashamed of what he was doing. Tainting the sanctity of marriage. He felt it was deceit. Not only to himself, but to everyone around him. However, there were so many other gay people who did this for the very same reason. But today actually woke him. Who was actually committing the deceit? Him for marrying someone he barely knew, or the government for not allowing him to marry the one he loved? He remembered the saying, "Love will always find a way." If he had to sign a paper, live a lie and a life of silence, so be it. One would move heaven and earth to be with the one they loved, and Noah wasn't any different. Hell, hath no fury for the one who might get in the way. It was the story since the beginning of time. Who was the government to tell him to love? No one controls where Cupid points his arrow!

Chapter 17

Sleeping with a snake

The convoy left out the Fallbrook gate of Camp Pendleton headed to Twentynine Palms. Noah was in the tail in Charlie, with only the wrecker behind him. It was his responsibility to ensure if any vehicles broke down, he would stay with them and keep communication with the lead. Ultimately, making sure the vehicles made it to Twentynine Palms and the Delta Corridor for training. This was his first big responsibility since he had pinned Corporal on.

As he sat in the open jeep with the wind and heat hitting from all directions, he thought briefly about the ceremony. It was in front of the Battalion, and the Colonel personally pinned each Marine, before giving a speech that it was a privilege to be able to meritoriously promote the best of the best. Noah called home to tell his father. Beck wasn't familiar with the rank structure, but knew it meant a promotion, and Noah must be doing something right. Strumen did not attend, and Noah felt relieved that he didn't.

Things were getting a bit uncomfortable at home, and he wasn't sure if it would get better. The drinking was getting worse, and it brought to surface Strumen's darker side. His actions were becoming toxic, and Noah was worried about him, believing he could hurt himself, or even do harm to others. The confrontations, or sarcastic remarks, made it almost impossible to be around him. Noah would find him making off colored comments, "Like maybe I'll just end it all." When Noah would try to console him about how stupid it would be, he would accuse Noah of not really caring about him. Noah ignored his drinking and tried to remain positive, but it was now almost impossible. Strumen would start drinking when he got home and when bedtime came, Noah would try to lay down, only to be woken by the light being flipped on, and Strumen yelling at him, "Get up, get up, I have some things to say." The time apart might do some good, letting him find some self-worth.

Still, Noah couldn't get out of his head the conversation they had that very morning. Noah had finished setting his things out on the curb waiting for Davis to pick him up. He went back in to say his goodbye to Strumen. He opened the door to the bedroom and approached the bed. Noah leaned down and kissed his head and turned to walk away, when he was startled by Dodges voice, "Are you coming back?" Noah turned and looked at him surprised and thought it odd. "Of course, I'm coming back, at least I hope so! Why would you ask?" Dodge turned in the bed so he could see Noah directly, "Just making sure, you never know what could happen out in the desert. Besides, I didn't know if you really wanted to come back?" Noah was puzzled. "If you think I'm wanting to leave, you're wrong. I'm looking forward to getting this thing over and having a nice 96 with you when I get home." Strumen smiled before looking Noah straight in the eye. "Ok, if that's what you say. I'll miss you." Noah stood quietly not sure to hug him or just walk away? The pause was awkward before Strumen finally spoke, "Just so you know, if you ever decide to leave me or cheat on me, I'll go to the Marine Corps and turn both of us in." Strumen stood up and pecked Noah on the forehead. "Go, I'll see you when you get back," and acted as though he had said nothing. Noah stayed quiet to avoid having an argument. He knew it was something that couldn't be resolved at this moment, he had to be on his way. Besides, what was he supposed to say? It wasn't a threat, it was a warning, and one Noah felt Strumen would act on. Strumen had said it trying to get in Noah's head, and he was quite successful, because it continued to eat at him.

Staff Sergeant's voice coming across the radio. "We are at the halfway point. We'll be pulling these bad boys over. It'll be about 20 mikes, …Make sure everyone does a walk around, and checks their vehicles and Marines, we still have another hour to go.

It was late afternoon before they arrived at Twentynine Stumps. The first night would be spent at Camp Wilson before heading on out into the Delta corridor. Camp Wilson was tent city as the Marines called it, with showers, pay phones, and a hot-food chow hall. In the morning, these luxuries would not be seen again until their return three weeks later. Noah stood in line to use the payphones. He was going to call Strumen to let him know he had made it safely. Noah waited patiently, before getting into a booth.

The phone rang, no answer, he hung up and tried again, but still no answer. There was a line outside the booth with other Marines. He was being coaxed to hurry up. He gave it one more try. As the phone rang, he patiently waited, he let it ring on, before there was a "Hello?" Noah was relieved. "Hey, it's me, just calling to let you know I made it here." Dodge seemed happy that he had called. "I was wondering if you were going to call, … I'm glad you did! I'm just getting home myself, thought I might had missed your call." Noah chuckled, "Almost, I thought I was going to get overran by this guy behind me. We are here at Camp Wilson for the night, and head out to the Delta Corridor tomorrow." Dodge chimed in, "I'm very familiar with it all, I don't envy you." Noah with a nervous laugh, "Yes I suppose you do." It was still an awkward moment; both could tell there was much more before Noah spoke up, "Well I guess I'll see you in three weeks, I should probably get going." Dodge hesitated as he spoke, "Hey, …you know, don't you?" Noah paused, "Yeah, …yeah, I do." Dodge nervously chuckled with a sigh of relief, "Be safe, …I'll be here waiting for you when you get back." The phone was quiet before Noah heard him hang up.

The first few days in the Delta Corridor seemed to go by slowly. The temps were easily in the hundreds, because of this, the battalion would do most of it's maneuvering at night. This meant a lot of arduous work and late evenings, in low visibility. However, it was worth it to remain out of the hot desert sun. Mornings were nice because there was no rush to get up and get going. It was always interesting to wake up and see where they had landed during the night before. Other than morning chow, roll call, and special assignments given out, they were on their own time. They were required to stay in the area, and most would sit around and relax until late in the afternoon. Some would play cards or tell stories, while others took advantage of gaining much needed sleep. It was amazing how quickly one could fall asleep anywhere and wake up on a moment's notice.

One evening the battalion had an extended night move. The Marines didn't make it to their designated spot until early morning hours. They quickly found a place for the night and took cover. They pulled up through a ravine, parking the vehicles close to one side of the cavern wall. While still dark out, they draped the camo nets on the top side of the cavern wall and down over the vehicles so, from the air, it looked as though the ground continued. Any low flying aircraft would not recognize the convoy. Once finished, the Marines were ready for the rack. They pulled out their sleeping bags and most slept in the back of the trucks. Noah slept in front of one of the five-ton trucks. As he sat curled up in the front seat, he could see out of the truck windshield and see the stars peeking through the silhouettes of the camo net. He was just starting to calm down. Being in the desert forced him to focus on work. He was starting to get his priorities aligned. He still needed to do the wet down. Once that was out of the way, he needed to be more present in his and Strumen's relationship. He slowly faded off to sleep.

It was 0630 and reveille was being sounded. The Staff Sergeant came around and needed help getting everyone up and accounted for. There were some last-minute tasks that had come in and he would need to have everyone present. Noah started off walking the convoy line of vehicles behind him. He climbed on the back of the trucks, checking to see if everyone was up and moving. A few trucks behind him he climbed up and it was Sgt Mallard, and Guiterez, with Dewey and Stewart, and a few others from the motor pool. Noah sounded reveille and relayed the Staff Sergeant's message to Mallard. As Mallard was getting up, he nudged Stewart who was still inside his sleeping bag. "You heard what the man said, get your ass up, and get moving." Guiterez started to hop out of the truck, before stopping in his tracks. "Holy fuck, check that shit out!"

He was pointing to the embankment wall next to the truck. There was a rattlesnake on the wall, while another was slowly slithering away. Guiterez moved over to one side of the truck and hopped down.

All three Marines looked on. Mallard pointed over to another one just a few feet further down. Guiterez spoke up, "Man this is a rattlesnake bed!" Sgt Mallard reached up and grabbed Stewarts sleeping bag, "Man come on get down from there, get your ass up and get moving." There was no sound and Stewart didn't move. Guiterez spoke up, "Come on Stewart get your ass out the rack." Still nothing. Noah chimed in "Stewart are you alright man, come on, your ass is going to be UA, it's a mandatory formation. Get up!" Still no movement or sound from Stewart. The three looked at each other.

Dewey was still in the truck, sitting on the railing away from the snake wall. He looked down at Stewart, "Are you alright man?" Looking at him he could see his eyes and his hands holding the sleeping bag by his chin. He was pointing down very gently with his finger. As he lay inside his sleeping bag, he kept pointing downward toward his feet. Dewy spoke out, "Hey Sergeant, he's awake, but I think he is trying to say something, he keeps pointing toward his feet."

Sgt Mallard got back up on the truck and looked down at him, "What the fuck are you trying to prove fool, get your ass up!" Stewart, with hands holding the zipper part of his sleeping bag to his chin, pointed with his finger, downward. Sgt Mallard watched, "Are you trying to tell me something, just fucking speak, and quit playing games. This ain't no charades motherfucker, what the fuck is wrong with you? If there is something wrong with your bag, what, what the fuck man, I don't get it, what?"

Stewart pointed once again, this time trying to communicate by moving his head yes to what Mallard had just asked. Dewy spoke up, "I think he's trying to tell us there is something wrong with his bag, but that wouldn't stop him from speaking, man I think there is something in there, try unzipping his bag." Mallard stepped back, "Motherfucker you unzip his bag. … if he won't, I sure the hell don't want to! Whatever the fuck is in there sure the hell ain't going to get me."

Guiterez climbed up, "Step back mother fuckers! I'll do it." Sgt Guiterez bent down and grabbed the bag zipper and slowly started to unzip it, before Dewy spoke out, "You need to undo it quick, whatever is in there might get you!" Guiterez grabbed the bottom of the bag and held on as he did a quick jerk on the zipper, opening the bottom portion of the bag. He quickly let go and jumped back with everyone else. Coiled around Stewart's legs, was a large rattlesnake, now hissing and rattling. They had startled it and it was pissed off.

Noah watched from below on the ground. He couldn't see it but could hear it. Stewart remained calm. Guiterez and the other two jumped toward the front of the bed. "Everyone remain calm. We just gotta get it to uncoil and away from Stewart without biting him." Mallard chimed in, "Motherfucker, who said we." Dewey went up over the side rail and hopped down to the ground.

Noah looked around, trying to figure out what to do, "Dewey, go get the Staff Sergeant and the Lieutenant, they have pistols." Noah looked around for a stick or something but couldn't find anything. "Man, we need a stick or something long to get it off." Mallard turned and hopped out over the rail, "There is a GP tent in my truck, we got poles in there, I'll get a couple." Guiterez looked at Stewart, and could see he was stressed, "Stay calm man we're going to get this thing off you."

The Staff Sergeant arrived and looked on, "Is he alright, has anyone been bitten?" Noah spoke up, "No, we are okay, Mallard's getting some poles from his truck, and we are going to try and get it off him." Staff Sergeant spoke out, "Hang in there Stewart. We are working on getting help!" Mallard came back with the poles and the Lieutenant arrived with his pistol. "Everyone ok, no one has been bitten, right?" Staff Sergeant spoke up, "Well I think Stewart might be a little fucked, but everyone else is good, sir."

The lieutenant investigated the truck, "I sent Dewey after the corpsman. They should have the anti-venom. Hold off until he gets here. We don't want to make that thing any more pissed off than it is. As long as it doesn't move or strike at him, we'll be ok."

Noah watched, along with the others, anticipating what might happen. Stewart had to have discipline to not move with that thing around him. How the hell did it get into his bag without biting him? Dewy returned with the corpsman in tow. He had the anti-venom with him. Although rare, rattlesnake bites happened in training in the Delta corridor.

The Staff Sergeant and Sergeant Guiterez grabbed the poles. They would be the ones who would try and get the snake off Stewart's legs. The rest stepped back away from the truck. The plan was to get the snake to uncoil, get it away from Stewart, and off the truck to shoot it. The two climbed up on the truck bed, one on each side with the poles out in front of them. It was coiled around Stewart's leg and focused on Sgt Guiterez's pole. It rose and leapt at Sgt Guiterez. The Staff Sergeant was able to strike it, this time flipping it to the back of truck. It tried to slither over to one side, but Guiterez took the pole and scooted it off the truck as he shouted, "Get ready, here it comes."

As soon as it was on the ground, the Lieutenant fired his pistol. It bounced up from the impact, it was dead. The Staff Sergeant felt relieved, "You alright Stewart, you hear that? It's dead, it's off you and it's dead."

Stewart lay quiet for a second, in a daze. Then with a sudden burst of energy, he got up and let out a yell, and jumped off the truck. Everyone watched in amazement, as he ran frantically before stopping and falling to his knees. He sobbed and howled at the same time. He was glad to be alive.

The Staff Sergeant and Lieutenant and the rest of the crew surrounded him. He stood up and started thanking each of them. The Staff Sergeant patted him on the back. "You're one brave soul. How long did you lay there with that thing on you?" Stewart explained, "It had been there all night. I lay there looking out at the stars when I noticed it slither onto my bag. I was afraid to move and thought if I was still, it would move on. The next thing I knew, it was slithering into my bag. I lay there all night afraid to move, shit afraid to breathe. When everyone started getting up, I was afraid to speak or anything. I knew it was around my legs but didn't know where its head was, so I just stayed still."

The crew investigated, and the embankment turned out to be a nest for rattlesnakes. Stewart was the talk of the entire Battalion for the rest of the exercise. After the incident, it wasn't uncommon to see folks with walking sticks, or banging two rocks together if they were walking in unchartered territory.

The last few days in the field went by quickly, the maneuvers had picked up to a culmination, and now things were on the downside. The last night was back at Camp Wilson, and the lines for the showers, hot chow and phone booths were at their peak. Noah passed the phone booths for a hot shower and food. By the time he had finished with both, the phone lines were still twenty men deep.

He headed back to the GP tents and hit the rack for a decent night's sleep.

The next morning the Battalion was on the road and back to Pendleton and secured by noon. Davis dropped him off at the curb of his apartment in Oceanside. He unloaded his gear on the front porch and headed in. Once in, he did a walk around, it had been kept clean. He was there only long enough to run a hot tub of water before he was stripped and sat soaking, relaxing in silence. Every part of his body ached.

When finished, he hit the rack and must have dozed for a couple of hours before he was woken by his legs being massaged. He briefly looked behind to see Strumen already out of his uniform and in his tighty-whities. Noah lay there as Dodge continued to massage his legs, working his way up to his buttocks and soon Noah had been covered by him. Noah turned to kiss him, and both were soon amidst the throws of passion.

Once they finished, both lay quietly in each other's arms without saying a word. This was what it had been like when they first started dating. It had been a while since both seemed to be present and not just going through the motions. Maybe the absence had made them both more aware of each other, and there was some kind of emotion behind all the chaos after all. It was late in the evening before they got dressed and headed to the kitchen to grab munchies before sitting on the sofa to cuddle and watch TV.

The next morning, they gathered themselves together and went out for breakfast. The topic of conversation was the plans for the wet down. After three weeks in the field with the Motor T crew, the last thing anyone wanted was to get together their first weekend back. Strumen seemed to be on his best behavior, even asking if Noah would like to go out for a drink or dancing. Noah opted for the two of them to stay in and rent videos and nest on the sofa. Come Monday, Noah had the day off and Strumen returned to work. Noah spent the day getting caught up on phone calls, handling bills, and doing laundry. By the time Strumen had gotten home, he had dinner prepared. Things seemed to be calming down. The time away gave them a new appreciation. Whatever was happening Noah liked it.

The following morning, Noah returned to work. He dropped Strumen off, before heading on to his. Once he arrived, it was back to the grind, all the vehicles had to be cleaned and preventive maintenance completed. The entire week was doing recovery from the prior three weeks in the corridor. It went by fast, and the weekend was once again on them. Before securing, everyone was asking if the wet down was still on. Noah gave out directions and the wet-down was set for Saturday night.

The next morning both were up and cleaning the house, making a list of all the things they needed to get completed for the nights big event. Alcohol run, munchies, and of course music selection. Noah had invited Dusty, along with Gloria, for appearance. Glenn, Sherry, Telly, and Kauli, and several friends besides the motor-t crew. He let the neighbors know they would be entertaining and even invited them.

Glenn had arrived early to help get things together and kept the music going. Davis was one of the first guests to arrive, and before long the house was buzzing. All seemed to be going well. The tale of the snake made its return when Stewart arrived. Mallard, who was all but freaking out, stood tall and portrayed the hero who remained calm, cool, and collected during the episode. Noah looked over a couple of times and caught Strumen staring back. Both exchanged eyes, in which only the two held the secret.

The night seemed to go by, and before long different ones were hitting their limits, it must have been around midnight before Sgt Mallard and Guiterez left, both holding each other up arm in arm. Finally, Dusty and Gloria were glad to be able to leave. The door closed; Noah leaned back on it as it shut. He looked to Dodge who was standing across the room with hands on hips. "Well Corporal you did it!" Noah smiled and walked to him, gave him a hug, and held him, briefly kissing. "Wrong, we did it!" Noah smiled kissed him on the forehead, and looked him in the eye, "Thank you!" Dodge leaned over and grabbed a bottle of wine, "Well, I saved this for the two of us!" Noah smiled as Strumen broke away and poured the two of them a glass. They went outside to the dark front porch and sat on the steps looking up at the stars. Noah felt good. He was happy, at least this very moment in time. He was living his dream.

He was in the Marine Corps, and was excelling, meritoriously promoted, living in California, food on the table, good friends with a guy he loved. If someone had told him just a few years earlier, while back in Indiana, that he would be doing this he wouldn't have believed them. This was just the beginning, there was no going back. This was who he had become. He had a taste of leadership and he liked it.

The two sat on the steps a while longer, until Noah found himself shaking off sleep. "I'm tired, and it's been a long day. I am calling it a night. You coming in?" He stood up, Strumen spoke. "Why didn't you tell me they made you squad leader?" Noah stopped and sat back down. "No reason, I guess things have just been going so crazy. Staff Sergeant made it official, once I was promoted. You already knew I was doing the job." Strumen took a drink, "Yeah, but you didn't tell me it was official. You know the first rule of leadership is never assume anything. Is that how you are going to handle your squad?" Noah wasn't sure where he was going with this, ignored the comment and got up to leave. Strumen spoke again. "Oh, I must have hit a sore spot. What, you just going to walk away?"

Noah stood for a moment contemplating. Strumen could become very agitated when drinking. Tonight, had been a great evening and he didn't want things to escalate. Noah decided to stay and talk, "Did I ever tell you about my pet rabbits?" Strumen looked up at him, "What, where the hell is that coming from? Rabbits, what the fuck does that have to do with what we're talking about?" he chuckled and took a drink, "So, I'll go with it. No, I don't believe I have ever had the privilege of hearing about your pet rabbits. …"

Noah sat back down. "Well, when I was in the eighth grade, a friend of mine offered me some free rabbits. I wanted them. I thought oh how cute and cuddly, … they are not. At least I didn't think so. So, I went to my father. Dad, Dad I got to have these. At first, he said no. But I begged and begged, and finally he gave in. But when he did, he made conditions. I would be the one totally responsible for them. Buying their food, feeding them, watering them, making sure their cage was clean, and so forth. I wanted them so bad, I agreed. So, the first week or so went by and I was out at their cage every day. But as I got bored, I would miss a couple of days. I noticed when I went out there, someone had fed them, and they had water. Next thing I know a couple of months had gone by. One day I wondered how they were doing. I went to the cage. Oh my God! I was in tears. The rabbits were dead. They were half rotten skeletons, sitting waiting at their feed bowl. They had died. I ran to the house to my father. What happened, you let my rabbits die! He looked at me. "No, I didn't, I told you from the word go, they were your responsibility." He was right. They were my responsibility and I let them die. No one else. What a cruel and awful way to go. I grieve over them today. Whether it was intentional or not, my father taught me the best lesson I could have on responsibility. So, from that day forward, when I'm asked to do something, ...I think about it before I ever agree. So, if you think I haven't thought about those Marines in my charge, I have! And yes, I take it very seriously."

Dodge took a drink and chuckled, "Damn, I'm going to have to call you a bunny killer." He was heartless. Noah stood up, "Why do I even bother, I think I'm done here." Noah headed to the door and paused, "You coming in?" Strumen turned and gave a smirk, "No, I think I'll sit here for a while longer. You go ahead, I'll be in, in a bit."

Noah made his way in, grabbing some of the glasses and cans, to tidy up a bit before heading to the bedroom. He undressed and laid out across the bed in his green onionskin PT shorts. The open window allowed the breeze to fill the room with the ever so distinct smell of the eucalyptus trees that were so common to southern California. It was an added therapeutic calming to the otherwise warm night. Noah lay on his stomach, and within minutes was asleep.

Strumen sat outside continuing to drink. The more he drank, the more he became agitated with Noah. Who the fuck does he think he is, he thought to himself. The day's events had become too much for him to handle. The fact he wasn't chosen to be promoted, but Noah was. How could that be?

Strumen got up and stumbled his way in the apartment, managing to lock the door and shut things up, before he made his way into the bedroom. Noah lay asleep across the bed. How is it he could love someone as much as he did, but still not be happy for him. He stood looking at Noah one minute in admiration and the next angry and insecure. How was he so worthy of this guy? What did he do that was so worthy? Noah was handsome, smart, and yet so innocent. The fucking world is given to people like him. Little fucking golden boys, fuck him! He'll probably just up and leave anyway.

Strumen moved on to the bathroom, and was peeing, before he started to get sick. After throwing up a couple of times, he lost his balance and went to grab the towel rack and shower curtain. Both came crashing down as Strumen fell to the floor. He had woken Noah. "Dodge is that you?" Dodge spoke up, "Yeah, I'm alright, the bathroom towel rack fell the fuck down." Noah concerned. "You need me to help, …you alright?" Strumen got agitated, "No, no, no, I don't fuck'en need you to help. I got it. I told you I'm alright!" Noah could tell he was drunk and agitated. "Geeze I was just trying to be nice." Strumen stood and was bobbing, "Go back to bed, I'll be there in a moment." Noah sat for a moment hearing him fiddle around. He flipped back on his stomach and lay on the bed and dozed off.

BAM, SLAP, HIT, BANG, … Noah woke to extreme pain across his legs, and immediately flipped over only to feel a strike of the medal towel rod hit him across the forehead knocking him back. "WHAT THE FUCK? …What the fuck? What the fuck are you doing?" He raised his hand and arms to block and shield himself from the blows. He began ducking and dodging, the slaps, hits, and punches, along with the occasional whack of the towel rod. He was at the head of the bed now curled up and blocking any attempted hits by Strumen. "Stop! …fucking stop! … What the fuck? …Have you lost your mind? ... Strumen stop, what are you doing?"

Strumen continued to scream, "...You Mother fucker! You Mother fu…" Noah interrupted "Would you quit?" Strumen paid no mind. "Shut the fuck up! Shut the fuck up!" he began crying and sobbing, "You think you're all that, … Mr. High and mighty. Oh, I'm second squad leader, … oh, oh, oh I'm Mister Corporal, …I'm in charge here, …Yeah, fuck you Corporal. Look at your ass now. Look who's begging. I'll kill your fucking ass Mother fucker! Huh, what you gonna do?"

As Strumen threatened to hit him with the metal rod again, Noah flinched. He was still only in PT shorts, and the blows from the hits, and the rod were already starting to welt. Strumen started pacing back and forth spouting off things that made no sense to Noah. Noah looked over to the corner and saw his trousers. If he could get them on or grab something to help protect him until he could get Dodge calmed down.

Noah tried to get his trousers on, but Strumen struck him with the rod across his back and it broke. Noah continued on as Strumen fled the room. Noah got dressed, and started to put his shoes on, he needed to get the fuck out. Glenn would let him crash if he could get away. Just then Strumen showed back up in the room with a large butcher knife. Pointing it at Noah. "What? ...Where do you think you're going? You think your leaving?"

Noah stood up and backed away, only to be trapped between Strumen and the door, his only way out. Noah spoke calmly. "Put the knife down Dodge. You're not thinking straight. You don't really want to do this. You'll regret it in the morning. Come on now!" Strumen continued toward him pointing the knife. Noah had his back to the wall. He loved Strumen. Why would he want to do this to him? What had he done that was wrong to make him this angry?

Strumen held the knife point up to his throat. "That's been your plan the whole time. What use me for rent, get what you can from me. I see the way you look at other guys. Don't tell me you don't. I've seen the lust in your eyes." As he held the knife to his throat, he got right up into Noah's face "I got news for you buddy. You ain't going anywhere. I'll kill your ass first." Strumen's stare was manic, before he backed away from Noah. "You might as well take your clothes off. You aren't going anywhere. Just get back in bed."

Noah stood there not saying a word. He had never seen this side of Dodge. This wasn't the alcohol talking. He had delt with drunks before. This was something more. Strumen meant every word he said. Noah felt something run down his face and wiped his head, only to realize it was blood. He started toward the bathroom, only to have Strumen jump at him with the knife. He stopped as Strumen let out a deranged laugh. "Scare yah? Did I scare yah? I hope so. Cause

I mean to keep you scared." As he jumped at him again, Noah stood and stared, until he finally allowed him to pass to the bathroom.

Noah took a look in the mirror. He was covered in blood. His forehead would need stitches. The guy who lay in the sleeping bag with the snake came to mind. He had to lay calm and cool, hoping not to get bit. When the opportunity came along, he needed to be ready to escape. Noah washed his face and checked the rest of his body out. The welts were everywhere. The black and blue marks were all over his body. He was sore. He dressed the wounds with what he had. Making a butterfly bandage, he fixed his forehead. That would have to do for now, until he could get further medical attention. But that would not be tonight. For now, he had to allow things to calm down.

Chapter 18

Champagne March

The Jeep convoy class just turned onto the last leg of the road heading back to the Motor pool after completing an all-night training session. Lance Corporal Pope was driving while Noah slouched with his cover pulled down taking an opportunity to catch a few zees. It was still morning, and the sun was just beginning to cut through the haze. Camp Margarita sat on a bluff overlooking the Santa Margarita River floodplain and Marine Corps Air Station Camp Pendleton. The rainy season was just ending, and the landscape was at the beginning stages of turning brown. In the distance, an occasional military helicopter would make an appearance. Camp Margarita was the home of the Glorious Fighting, First Battalion Fifth Marines, and the Fifth Marine Regiment, known for valor, and one of the Marine Corps most decorated units.

Arriving at the motor pool gate, Lance Corporal Pope reached and nudged Noah. "Hey we're here." Noah sat up and pointed to the right lane of the wash rack, "Pull all the way forward. I want to get as many on the wash rack as we can. Hopefully when we're done we'll be outta here." He hopped out and immediately started directing traffic into the wash racks. "Get'em washed and get them online."

Noah worked his way through the maze of jeeps toward the head shed. In the hall, he passed Fritz. "You better turn the other way if you don't want snagged." Noah puzzled and agitated, "For what, I just got back, what the fucks up?" Davis continued walking, "I just heard Staff Sergeant on the phone, word has it Battalion piss test at 1300." Noah let out a sigh, "Fuck, fuck, fuck." He knew a piss test meant staying until it was over. There wasn't any chance of getting out early. He quickly turned back thinking he could get out before being seen. "Where are you headed?" Noah turned to see the Staff Sergeant. "That's right, my door was open and I'm not deaf. 1300 on the Battalion grinder, and you can also let Sgt Davis and the rest of the Marines know. Anyone not there is UA (Unauthorized Absence)."

Noah returned to the line and gave the word. After the Marines finished their vehicles, they secured until the 1300 formation. Noah got in his car and headed over to the Battalion grinder. He parked, cracked a window, and reclined in his seat. Noah was awakened by Sgt Guiterez tapping on the door. "Wake up skate, they're forming up." Noah yawned and looked at his watch. It was 1245. Sgt Guiterez, still waiting for him, "Come on man let's go! We got to get the platoon formed up." Noah got out grabbing his camo cover, giving the once over in the car window, he and Guiterez headed out.

While walking, Sgt Guiterez noticed the PA system. "Why do they need a PA system?" Noah, glanced ahead as they walked, "I know right? That was what I was thinking…" Guiterez brushed it off, "Probably going to give out an award or something." Once they arrived, Sergeant Guiterez formed up the platoon. Noah, as 2nd squad leader, took his position and the Marines started falling in beside him. Most of the Marines were talking smack about various things while they waited for the entire Battalion to arrive. Some worried about the piss test, while others were just disgruntled about standing in formation. Across the deck, Noah saw the Lieutenant arrive. Sgt Guiterez took a quick glance and brought the platoon to attention, turned, and saluted as the Lieutenant walked past taking position next to the Staff Sergeant.

While at parade rest, Noah noticed military police cars pulling onto the grinder. Something was up. What was going on? The formation was starting to look increasingly different than a surprise piss test. It was right about that time the Sergeant Major called the Battalion to attention. Colonel Keller, the Battalion Commander, walked up, and the officers all took their place. The Colonel put the Marines at parade rest, looked at the Sergeant Major and said something in a muffled voice. At that point, the Sergeant Major motioned for the military police cars to come forward. The Colonel started in on his speech.

"Good afternoon, Marines. At ease!" The Marines sound off, "Good Afternoon Sir!" "Well, most of you are wondering why we are here this afternoon. For those of you studying for a piss test, sorry to let you down!" Two military police cars pulled up behind him and the MP's hopped out and stood beside their vehicles. One MP was plain clothed. At the second vehicle, an MP opened the back door to let a K9 police dog out. After they were in place, the Colonel began. "Marines, it brings me no great joy in what we are about to see! Trust me, I plan on doing everything I can in my power to see this is handled with the dignity and respect it deserves." At that point he turned and nodded to the MPs at the front vehicle. "Bring the goddamn thing out!" The MPs reached and grabbed the arm of the lady sitting in the back seat. Out came a tall black slender woman. At first glance, Noah thought she looked familiar, "No way…" not realizing the words slipping out of his mouth. The woman's face was too far away to see. Everyone was a bit confused as to what was going on. What the fuck was the Colonel doing? She appeared well made up, with shoulder length reddish hair, a tight white long sleeve shirt, partially buttoned, revealing a well-endowed bust. She was handcuffed behind her back, barefoot, holding on to her high heeled shoes. The Colonel sounded off once again. "This does not belong in my Marine Corps, and I'm going to do whatever I can to get it out!" He had peaked the Marines attention. He looked back at the Marines and started pacing. "Look at it! I SAID LOOK AT IT! Look at this goddamn thing!" The Marines were shocked and not sure what they were seeing. They looked on, wondering what the hell the Colonel was babbling about. The Colonel spoke to the MPs. "Bring it here. Bring the damn thing here!" The MPs grabbed her by the arms, she stumbled a bit as they forced her forward to the Colonel. The Colonel continued to sound off. "This thing has the nerve to call itself a Marine. It makes me sick! A MARINE!" The woman was now next to the Colonel, "But while out in town it's masquerading as a woman, I SAID A WOMAN!" He reached up and snatched the wig from her head and threw it to the deck, turning back to the Marines and shouted out. "Now, tell me what do you think of that? Let me hear yah!" The Marines started shouting and calling out names. "Queer, fag, fucking freak, Homo…" etc. The Colonel broke the chants and name calling by interjecting, "He calls himself a Marine, you might know him here in the Battalion as Staff Sergeant

Williams, who works in admin. Believe me you won't be calling him that for long!"

The Motor T platoon stood in disbelief at what they were seeing. Staff Sergeant Williams, the admin chief was dressed as a woman. What was he a Drag Queen? It didn't add up! Noah looked around to observe what was taking place. He overheard Lance Corporal Huck, "Hey Monte is that the girl you been humping?" and started laughing. A few others were making cat calls. Noah turned to look at Fritz, shaking his head in disbelief, "Told you that motherfucking Colonel is a circus."

The Colonel continued; the humiliation wasn't done yet. He looked to the MPs and pointed over to the first platoon. They grabbed Staff Sergeant Williams by the arms and started toward the first platoon. Staff Sergeant Williams resisted a bit, but gave in, knowing resistance was futile. The Colonel hollered, "Now here's what we're gonna do. ...I'm having "IT" paraded in front of you. Because it wants to be a woman so bad, we're going to make sure everyone gets to see it as one." The Colonel stopped what he was saying when he realized the wig was on the deck, "Hold up now..." pointing to the wig "You forgot its wig, somebody get its wig," The MP grabbed the wig, and returned with it. The Colonel, paying close attention, "Gotta have its wig. Make sure to put it back on. These Marines deserve the full affect." The MP took the wig and put it on SSgt Williams' head not caring how it looked just as long as it was on. They continued to the first platoon. One by one they paraded the Staff Sergeant past a platoon and paused. The Colonel would shout out, "Tell it, tell that thing what you think about it!" If the Marines weren't loud enough, he would holler, "I CAN'T HEAR YOU!" They arrived in front of the Motor T platoon. Noah got a good look at what was now a disheveled mess of Staff Sergeant Williams. Oh my God, he recognized him, or rather her. It was Champagne from out in town.

When he first saw her step out of the police car, he thought, just for second, it looked like Champagne and discounted it.

Champagne wouldn't have been up on base and most definitely not at Battalion formation. Now, Staff Sergeant Williams is Champagne. How fucking crazy is this. It clicked! All the different times Staff Sergeant Williams had helped Noah. The advice he had given, he was just looking out for him. All the time he knew about Noah, yet Noah never put two and two together. Noah had met him as Champagne out in town and never once had a clue. Staff Sergeant Williams was an awesome Marine! A Marine's Marine. He was admired and often emulated, and most everyone in the Battalion looked up to him. He was always being recognized with awards and honors. Yet all the greatness he was known for had been tossed aside, and now here he was being hauled across the parade deck being humiliated. For what? Because he dressed as a woman afterhours.

Noah looked at him with tears in his eyes. Staff Sergeant Williams/Champagne, either one, it didn't matter, his heart wept. There was nothing he could do to help her without throwing himself on this crazy fire. Champagne lowered her head, but it couldn't remove the shock, horror and fear on her face which was now embedded in Noah's memory forever. He wasn't sure if she was aware or coherent anymore. The traumatic event had become the equivalent of what was a modern-day lynching. Noah stood in silence. Just as they tugged her to move on, Champagne lifted her head and gave a glare from left to right as though she was recording the Marines in front of her. The name calling continued. When she looked in Noah's direction, Champagne stopped briefly, and they caught eyes. She recognized him. She adjusted her body to stand tall, lifting her head up with mascara running down her face. She stood proud, turning away looking straight out past the platoon toward the sky with defiance. The MPs tugged again, but she kept her head high as she turned and moved on to the next platoon. Noah stood in silence, and suddenly felt alone and out of place in this crowd. He lost himself in thought until Fritz tapped him on the shoulder. "Hey man, you ok? They called the Battalion to attention." Noah, lost in thought about what had happened, was still at parade rest. He quickly came to attention just as the word was given to dismiss.

Worn out from pulling an all-nighter and the crazy shit show that had just taken place, Noah headed toward his car on a mission. He was pissed! All he wanted was to get the hell off base and far away from this, whatever this was, and as quick as possible. From behind Fritz yelled, "Hey, wait up man!" Noah didn't slow and kept walking. Arriving at his car, he got in, put the keys in the ignition and leaned forward putting his head on the steering wheel. He sat there for few minutes before finally leaning back.

The ride home was numb, and he was despondent, it was as though the car had been on auto pilot and got him there. He let himself in, Dodge had duty and was gone for the night, he was thankful no one was home. The last thing he wanted this evening was to deal with another night of arguing and fighting. The light over the stove was on in the kitchen offering just enough light to make his way around. He took off his cammie blouse, hung it up on the coat rack and walked to the kitchen. Noah stopped and picked up a note. It was from Dodge, "Don't forget I have duty, Love you! See you in the morning." He laid it down and headed to the refrigerator. He opened the door and grabbed a beer. In the darkened living room, he sat down center of the sofa, placed his feet up on the coffee table, took a swig and sat in silence. Two more weeks, and he would begin his escape from Dodge, but escaping to what? He was escaping from an abusive relationship. However, from what he had just witnessed, not the hate or bigotry that was ever so present in the Marine Corps.

Chapter 19

Deployment on the Tarawa

The Motor-T crew had just finished inspecting all the vehicles in the cargo hold of the ship and were headed back to the berthing area, when Staff Sergeant Higgins stopped Barlow, "You need to report to the armory for Guard duty." He already knew he was going to be on guard duty while on ship and didn't mind. It got him out of the berthing area and gave him a chance to roam more freely on the ship. Noah went by his rack, grabbed his gear for duty, and headed to the armory. Once at the armory, he reported in to find out he had been made Corporal of the Guard. This entailed roaming the ship making sure all was well, along with supervising the sentry's and assisting while they stood watch at their post. Anything out of order, he was to act and report all violations back to the Sergeant of the Guard. The posts were four-hour shifts. Noah knew the Sergeant of the Guard and convinced him in giving the eight to midnight shift to him. This meant he would have normal sleeping hours. The other good thing was, other than a couple of evenings of Night Ops, most of the Marines and crew would be confined to the berthing areas. Because he was on duty, he was on 'Mid Rats,' which meant he ate chow outside the normal rush when everyone else stood in line. In the mornings, he got to sleep in when the rest of the Motor-T crew sat in classes or completed daily maintenance checks on the vehicles down below. Being pretty much on his own, out of boredom, he would often find the rest of the crew and lend a hand, or check-in with Staff Sergeant to get the latest word.

One night, while on duty, he had gotten a radio call from one of the Sentry's in the cargo hold. The private asked for backup and wanted him to come down. Noah, not sure what was happening asked, "What's going on?" He came back over the radio, "I've just seen a couple of guys take off down in the cargo bay here. I hollered, but didn't get a response, and can't quite make out what's going on." Noah replied, "Stand fast I'll be right down."

Noah took off down the ladder well, through a couple of hatches and out into the large open maintenance area. He continued further down the cargo ramp into the cargo area. When he arrived the young Private came to attention, "Good evening, Corporal!" Noah quickly put him at ease. "Have you seen them come back up or are they still there." The private spoke, "I heard a noise down one of the halls and went to check on it. When I came back, I saw the two guys walking down the ramp. One looked like a Marine and the other a Sailor. Both disappeared further down into the cargo hold, before I could get their attention." Noah thought for a moment. "Ok, what I'm going to do is have you wait here. If I don't come back in a few minutes, get ahold of the guard shack and let them know I'm here."

Noah headed down the ramp. It was dark once he got past the lights of the first ramp. He grabbed a flashlight from his duty belt, turned it on, and headed on past the lowered ramp further down into the cargo hold. On the right, vehicles were strapped down to the deck to keep them from moving. He had to go slow, so he didn't trip over the straps. Once past the jeeps and military vehicles, back to his left, was the beginning of the next ramp opening to the lower cargo bay. The area had a few security lamps which dimly lit the way down the ramp. He walked slowly trying to see or hear anything out of the ordinary. At the bottom, he shut off the flashlight, stood quiet, and observed. He heard nothing but the sounds of the ships humming, churning, and creaking.

Just as he was getting ready to turn his light back on, he heard something rustling back behind him, and it sounded to be coming from under the ramp. He stopped and listened again. Without turning on his light, he crept around the ramp toward one of the Amtrak's. As he stood by the Amtrak, he looked further up into the darkness. He could really hear the rustling now; it was coming from under the ramp. It was too dark to get a glimpse. He could hear the rustling getting louder. With his left hand, he grabbed the flashlight and with his right, opened the holster on his pistol. He slowly proceeded forward to the opening under the ramp, trying to be as quiet as possible. He reached the opening of the ramp and quickly flipped on the flashlight. He was not ready for what he had just found. Two men were lying almost completely nude, frozen, one on top of the other.

Once the initial surprise of Noah's presence wore off, they both jumped up hurrying, awkwardly, to grab their trousers and pull them up. The one who had been on top held his hand up to block the light, trying to see if he could identify who had just found them. The other, still struggling to get his trousers on, had tripped hitting a loose bar causing a crashing sound when it hit the deck. It must have been loud enough to hear a couple of decks up, because the private hollered down. "Are you all, right?" Noah was not quite sure what he was going to do. He hesitated, looked up the ramp to see if the private was coming, and quickly looked at the two young men. Both were frozen and staring in a daze toward Noah. Noah took another look up the ramp and looked back at the two men, "Yeah... I'm all right!" He rushed them, "Come on, get dressed and step out here in good light."

Once completely out, both came to a position of attention. Noah took their ID's and looked at them. One was Lance Corporal Alfonso Morello, and the other was Petty Officer Mark Hudson. He asked both, "Where you work?" The Marine replied, "For Comm." the Sailor replied, "The ships galley." Noah, contemplating what to do, asked for more information from the Marine. "Are you with the ships Comm. or 5th Marines?" The Marine, nervous with a bit of a stutter, replied, "Fu, fu, Fifth Marines, a radio repairman with communications." He was in Noah's unit. The Petty Officer was permanent personnel on the ship and worked in the ship's galley. Noah could tell they were both scared and embarrassed at the same time. The Petty Officer nervously asked, "What's going to happen?" Noah, in a dilemma, was torn between his duties to report them or let them go. He couldn't help but think how it would be if he had been found in the same situation. On the other hand, if it was found out he hadn't reported the incident while on duty he could get in to trouble as well. It's not like he ran across two people out in town and would never see them again, this was on ship, a government vessel. For that very reason, if he reported it, the charges against these two could be harsher. Committing a homosexual act on a base or on a government vessel, could bring additional charges.

Noah looked at the two of them, "You know what will happen if I turn you in don't you?" Both replied, "Yes." Noah shook his head contemplating what to do, decided. "I tell you what I'm going to do... Nobody else saw what happened down here. My Private up there knows you were here. So, what's going to happen is we are going to walk up and out of here together. I'm going to tell him I've got it taken care of and all is under control. We are going to walk up a couple of decks and I'm going to let you go. If any questions are asked, you came down to check on some gear and brought your buddy. You understand?" Both shook their heads. Noah looked them both in the eye, "Good! Come on let's go."

They headed back up the ramp and turned when they heard the Private call out, "Is that you Corporal?" Noah hollered back, "Yeah it's me, I found'm it's ok," as they continued up. The three approached the Private, Noah pointed for the two to stand over by the ladder well while he spoke to the Sentry. Noah looked at him, gave a quick inspection, and commented, "You done well. He's with our unit Comm. and was just checking on the gear he had worked on earlier. Couldn't remember if it was secured or not." The private looked over to the two standing by the ladder well, smiled and responded as though he was a bit embarrassed about calling for backup. "Sorry to bother you Corporal." Noah replied "No need for sorry, you did your job. Do you need anything or have any questions?" The private sounded off, "No Corporal!" "Very well, carry on." Noah stepped off, walking over to the two waiting by the ladder well, "Follow me." They took the ladder well up a couple of decks and walked through a hatch into a corridor not far from the berthing areas. Noah looked to see if anyone was around as one Sailor passed. No one else was around. Noah stopped, "Tonight was your lucky night! Be glad it was me and not someone else. You're free to go. Oh, and stay the fuck out of the cargo bay and don't let this shit happen again." The Lance Corporal said quietly to Noah, "Thank you Corporal" and quickly took off. The Petty Officer reached to shake his hand. Noah looked at him but did not shake it, "Just take your ass and go before I change my mind." The sailor did an about face and quickly disappeared from the end of the corridor. Noah did a quick scan around and went the opposite way.

The 30 days seemed to flash by, thanks to being able to stand guard duty. There had been a couple of mail calls. Noah hadn't received any mail from back home, so everything must have been ok. He was starting to see things more clearly now. The path ahead of him still had a few bumps in the road, but he could see the commitment with Strumen was going to finally come to an end. The time on ship had done some good. Most of the Motor-T crew were getting cabin fever because they were being confined to the berthing areas most of the days. There were few places on ship to be able to get a view outside and a bit of fresh air. One area was a large porthole on the side of the ship where those who smoked all congregated.

One evening Noah had free time and decided to go down to the porthole where the Marines often would take a smoke break. He worked his way through the ladder wells and hatches and finally came out to the huge opening that looked out on to the vast body of water, the East China Sea. As he walked toward the opening, he was surprised to find it wasn't crowded and there was just one Marine standing at the rail silhouetted by the sunlight beyond the porthole. As Noah walked closer to the opening, he recognized the Marine standing at the rail. It was the young Marine caught with the sailor under the cargo ramp. The one he had previously let go when they first set sail. Noah walked to the rail and wasn't going to say anything, until the Marine turned and recognized him. He quickly nodded his head, addressed Noah, "Corporal," and started to walk away as if he was still embarrassed from their previous meeting. Noah quickly replied, "Don't go, at least not on my part, you were enjoying the view." The Marine stopped, looked at Noah then returned to the rail. Noah, breaking the ice, "I believe it's Morello, right?" "Good memory," he replied nervously as he stood and looked out. "You know I'm thankful for what you did. It's, it's been such a long deployment and I, I can't justify it and all…" Noah could tell he was still worried, "At ease, no need to explain, and I'm not a God, so don't put me up there… I did what any decent human being would have done… for you or anyone else in that situation. So, your thanks are not needed." As they looked out at the water Morello continued, "Well I know a lot of others would have turned us in." Noah turned and looked over at him and decided to take a chance and put him at ease. "Well maybe, I'm not like everyone else.…" smiled and looked back out to the water. Morello snapped his head toward Noah and paused before he realized what Noah was saying. "Wait, … no, … no way, you mean, … are you saying?" Noah turned his head and chuckled with a smile while Morello was trying to find his words. Morello got very inquisitive of what Noah was really saying. "So, you're telling me you're like me?" Noah looking out at the water "Well, … I wouldn't go that far… I'm not just like you, … I don't think I would have gotten up under a cargo ramp. (He laughed) …or better yet, get caught. … (as he continued to chuckle) …What the fuck were you two thinking?" Morello, now able to laugh about the situation, chuckled as well. "I know, right? I guess all I can say is boys will be boys. You can't imagine how fucking scared we were… I just thought holy fucking shit! …My entire life over, for what… a quick lay." Noah chimed in "You wouldn't be the first one to have done it!" Morello starting to trust him, "You know if it wasn't for being on ship, I was thinking about just fucking running." Noah quickly replied, "I'm glad you didn't, it would have made it harder for me, and worse for you. It would have been out of my hands." Morello was now confiding in Noah, "It was a wake-up call, damn! …All I could think about was what the Marines in my Platoon would be saying. The jokes, the cat calls, and humiliation, but worse yet… my dad, my family, they don't know. How would I explain it, …(sarcastically)Your son has been thrown out for being a fag? …Fuck, what was I thinking?" Angry with himself he looked down while shaking his head. "What's worse, … I have someone waiting for me back in Oceanside. How would I explain to him that I got caught, I cheated?" About that time a couple of sailors came out through the hatch way. Noah and Morello both paused in conversation until they passed by. Noah started the conversation back up, "Well look, it's in the past now. Just use your head from now on. It's behind you." Changing the subject, "So you have a beau back home?" Morello's eyes lit up. "Yeah, we've been together just over a year." Noah, "Yeah I had someone too." Morello, "What you mean had?" Noah decided to share, having not been able to talk about his situation openly since they arrived aboard ship. "Well technically, we haven't called it quits, but that will happen when I get back stateside, … if not sooner. I begged for these orders just to get away from him and out of the relationship. He is a bit of a nut job and an abuser. He threatened to turn us both in if I ever left him. I believed him. So, I spoke with a friend of mine, who helped me out with the plan of getting orders. We thought if I had to leave, and it was no fault of my own; he might be willing to let go." Morello was curious, "He's a Marine?" Noah smirked, "Oh yeah, bulk fuel, his old man was a jarhead, Sergeant Major. So, he feels like he has something to prove. He's still trying to live up to the old man's reputation, 'Hard ass.'" Morello curiously, "What makes you think he'll let you go?" Noah, now glaring out at the smooth reflective waters, "I don't, but have to take the chance. I figure me being away will allow him time to get used to not having me around and maybe lighten the blow." Morello, "Wow this guy must really care for you?" Noah, "Oh no! It's a control thing for him. Besides, I haven't had much communication with him since I left. As usual, quite a few letters at first, but then the trickle down, now it's been a month, if not longer, and nothing." Morello still listening, "You think your plan is working?" Noah sighed, "Oh I don't know, I hope so. The good news, I have spoken to several friends from state side, one just came to Oki right before we came on ship. I got to meet up with her and catch up on all the latest dish from the states. She tells me Dodge has moved on. Supposedly, he already has moved someone else in the apartment with him." Morello turned a bit stunned, "Awe man that is fucked up! You cool with that?" Noah in discuss, "Abso -fucking-lutely cool with it! … just as long as I get my car back, everything else he can have." He paused briefly, "Enough about me. What about your boy?" Morello grinned, "Oh, we're good, I hope. The deployment and being gone has taken its toll. We have talked and have agreed to just not talk about what happens while gone. We're not going to dwell on it. Boys will be boys, and what happens at sea, stays at sea." Noah looking out to the water, "But what about him, he's not at sea?" Morello, "I know, but I just gotta believe that he loves me, I do love him, and neither would do anything to jeopardize it. Don't get me wrong, I'm not looking through rose-colored glasses. Neither of us are Saints, obviously not me." As Morello was talking, Noah turned to him, noticing Morello had lightened up and seemed transported to another place far away from where they were standing. Noah could hear the love pour out as Morello spoke. "It was just us, … two friends, … partners and so much more. We're more than shaved whiskers left in the sink, … by the way I hate, …also, more than a burnt meal, or a second glance by another man. Most of all, definitely, we are more than what the Marine Corps, along with the rest of the world, says we are! I get so pissed the way we're treated. We are no less, or different than any straight couple the Marine Corps supports. My father and mother have a great love story. All my life I have admired them. I don't think there is anything wrong with wanting the same. A love that will last throughout time." Morello went quiet for a moment lost in thought. Noah, who had been observing him, broke the silence, "You really love him…" Morello a bit teared up, "I do, and I get tired of holding it inside. I think one day, I'll just scream it out, so the entire world knows." Noah interrupted, "Ok, I think you're getting a bit carried away. You can do that, let the entire world know, but I don't think on this ship, right now, is a good time." Noah moved over to Morello, pausing briefly to put his hand on his shoulder, he then faced the rail and stood next to him. Both gazed out at the reflecting sun upon the great vast body of water.

Whirly Birds

The Motor-T crew had started working full time again. Noah had returned all his gear to the armory the night before, after standing his last security watch and was now working along with the Motor-T crew. The time on ship had come to an end. They were getting the equipment and supplies ready to debark from the ship. The helos had started deploying and staging gear for the beach landing getting ready to take place. All that was left for the Motor-T Marines to do was wait to board their helo and depart the ship. The ones assigned to vehicles as drivers and "A" drivers had already gone to the cargo bays. They would be arriving via the landing craft and driving their vehicles onto the beach. Over the past few days, the jeeps, the Gama-goats, and the 5-tons were fitted with forging gear in case the landing boats should fall short on the beach head. The ship lowered its back gate deploying the landing craft. As they departed the ship into the ocean, they formed up and headed to shore. Noah supervised the last of the vehicles as they departed and then headed topside to the berthing area to grab his gear and wait with the rest of the Motor-T crew for their helo. They would be flown to shore. Once there, they would secure the beach head, move inland, and make a 360, and wait for word.

A Marine, from debarkation, arrived and gave the word to follow him, the transition was on. In single file, the Marines headed out to the ladder well, up two decks and were just ready to exit the hatch onto the flight deck, when they were temporarily halted. Gunnery Sergeant Holland, from S-4, came in from the flight deck closing the hatch behind him to drown out the noise and wind of the helo's. He informed Motor-T that they had been bumped back one bird. The Battalion Commander wanted more Comm on the ground to get better communication established. Gunnery Sergeant Holland directed his Marines to run and get the Comm Platoon and tell them they needed to report to the flight deck immediately. Motor-T backed up against the bulkhead to make way for the Comm Marines to get through.

As they stood there waiting, the Comm Marines came through and started lining up on the opposite bulkhead waiting for the 'all clear' to go on deck and board their aircraft. Noah, standing on the bulkhead, looked across and saw Lance Corporal Morello. Noah stepped out and tapped him on his shoulder. He turned around, recognizing Noah, "Hey how's it going?" Noah grinned, "Doing great, you ready for all this?" Morello replied, "You bet, glad to be getting off ship. Man, this thing is so fucking big when you first get on it, but after a month at sea it seems so small." Noah chuckled, "You got that right! Just another day in paradise and a day closer to home." Morello grabbed his pack and quickly started digging to find something, "I got something to show you. A letter from home with pictures." Noah responded, "Pictures? Woohoo come on, I gotta see!" Morello pulled out an envelope and started sharing the pics. "This is who I was telling you about." He handed Noah a stack of pics and Noah started shuffling through them. He recognized the guy in the picture. Noah pointed at the picture. "I know him. It's J.D." Morello in shock, "Say what, no way!" Then it dawned on him that he might know him from a past acquaintance. Morello suspiciously, "Wait a minute, how?" Noah, realizing Morello was suspicious, "No, no, no. not like that! I've known J.D. for a while. I met him through Reggie and Dan, J.D. is a good guy. We have hung out several times." Noah paused "... Wait, wait, wait, oh my god, it makes since, you're Alfie." Morello smiled, "Yeah, my real name is Alfonso, but J.D. didn't like Alfonso or Al. So, with my jarhead haircut, he said I look like Alf, so he started calling me Alfie and it stuck." Noah shuffling through the pics, noticed others. "Look there's Reggie, and wait I know almost all these people... I've known J.D. for years. Last time I saw him was at a party of Reggie's just about a week before we left. He said he had been seeing someone and kept saying Alfie, ...Alfie, Alfie, Alfie...."

Gunnery Sergeant Holland shouted out, "Comm Platoon your up, make sure your gear is packed good and tight. We got high winds out there today. Now move it out!" Noah started to hand the pictures back to Morello, but he was fumbling to get his gear together. Noah was holding the pictures when the Marines started pushing Morello from behind to get going. Gunnery Sergeant shouted, "You're holding the line." Morello, flustered, looked at him, "Keep'em," referring to the pictures, "I'll get them on the other side." Noah was hesitant, "Whoa, whoa, wait… what about …" Morello cut him off, "Look you know most everyone in them, so enjoy them, besides," punching his fist on his chest over his heart, "I got the best one right here!," and quickly shuffled toward the hatch. Noah hollered out to him, "You got it, … Alfie!" Morello stopped in his tracks, looked back with a big smile, gave Noah a salute and disappeared out the hatch.

There seemed to be a bit of miscommunication, and a long wait, but finally the guide motioned for the Motor -T troops to come out on deck. The guide stayed in the hatch keeping the door open against the high winds. When Noah arrived on the flight deck, a single file line had formed leading to the helo. As they waited to board, the Comm Marines were finishing loading the bird in front of them. He could see Morello was one of the last to board. There were a few Marines from S-4, in front of the Motor T crew, still left to board when one of the flight crew waved his hand horizontally across his upper chest signaling there was no more room. The Marines from the front of the line motioned to go back. Arriving at the hatch, Noah and the Motor-T crew huddled on one knee, as the bird took off. The wind picked up and the Marines lowered their heads. Once the bird was gone and the wind and noise had subsided, Noah could see the birds flying off the bow in formation toward shore.

From the rear of the ship came another group of helos returning from a completed drop off to pick up more Marines. As the birds got closer, the winds and noise started to pick up again. Noah, and a few others around him, turned their focus to the shore

watching the whirlybirds that had just left. The first one and second
had landed, the third one was hovering and doing a slow decent. The
fourth helo, the one they were originally supposed to be on, was last.
It seemed like it was having trouble with the high winds, which
probably meant a bumpy ride for the Motor -T Marines when it came
to their turn. Noah had ridden on these types of birds many times
before and hated it. Somewhere along the line he heard the term 'it's
like flying in a tuna can.' For him, it was always a risk and he never
felt safe in any of them. He looked out aft of the ship to see if the
returning birds were within close range when out of nowhere a large
BOOM! came from the direction of the bow. It was so loud that
everyone ducked, before looking toward the direction of the blast. It
had been on shore. You could see a ball of fire at the landing site. No
one was sure what had happened, until one Marine hollered out, "It
went down!" The Motor -T Marines stood up looking at each other
in confusion, trying to make sense of what just happened. Noah
couldn't tell if this was the helo the platoon had almost gotten on or
if it was another. Sgt Guiterez, one of the Motor-T Marines, "It was
like watching in slow motion. It flew a bit to the left, then to the
right, did a spin and BOOM!, an explosion happened when it hit the
ground." The gasps and disbelief came from the huddled Marines.
"Did that shit just really happen?" The group slowly tried to validate
if what they had just seen was real. Noah hollered to the flight deck
crew, "Does anybody know what bird it was?" Everyone had
different opinions. One guy thought it was the third, but Sgt Guiterez
sounded off, "The third helo had already landed motherfuckers, it
was the fourth helo, the one we were supposed to be on." Noah,
along with the others, were in shock as they looked on. Sgt Guiterez
continued his rant, "You all better get down, and say a good prayer!
After that, you better kiss Gunnery Sergeant Hollands ass when you
see him for moving us back. Otherwise, we wouldn't be here talking
about it!" All kinds of thoughts were going through Noah's head.
Who was on it? Was it the Supply Marines, the Comm Marines?
Were they ok? It didn't look like anybody could survive the blast, or

the ball of fire it made. Then, it hit him, oh no, Morello was on that bird.

The moment of confusion was broken when a returning bird flew in low to land. Within minutes of seeing the crash, the Motor-T platoon was being instructed to board. A couple of Marines panicked and freaked out trying to get back below. Noah overheard arguing and a ruckus at the hatch, with the guide telling a Marine, "Get out on deck and get on board the helo." The Marine was yelling back, "Fuck that mother fucker! Court Martial my ass, I ain't getting on one of those pieces of shit!" The wind, noise, and confusion seemed to add to the surreal feeling and shock. The bird was loaded full, and a couple of Navy Corpsman had been brought to the front of the line and were added in. The flight crew did their checks, and the bird was in the air. Noah looked across at the Marines on the other side, sitting solemnly in their seats.

They were quickly rushed out to hit the ground, and the helo was gone. No sooner than they had gotten off the bird, he could see and smell the smoke coming from the crash. While he lay in the prone position waiting for the word to form it up, Noah could see the ocean and the U.S.S. Tarawa in the distance. He looked to the right where the crash had taken place. The crash crew and medical personnel were now on the scene working to control it. With a closer look, he could tell it would have taken a miracle for anyone to have survived. He couldn't help thinking how he, along with everyone around him, were just footsteps away from being on that helo. He lowered his head and said a prayer for those in the crash. All the petty stuff he had been worried about, seemed insignificant now. He was grateful to still be alive.

Chapter 20

Return from Korea, Marcus meets Glenn

All was quiet in the Motor pool due to the upcoming Memorial Day weekend. This would be their first weekend back on the island since deploying to Korea. The crash still imbedded in everyone's memories. Morello, along with everyone else on board, had perished in the crash. Noah contacted his partner, J.D., and sent Morello's pictures to him.

Today, most of the troops were tidying up the area, trying to look busy, as they anxiously waited for liberty (libo) to be sounded. Noah and Davis were shooting the shit as they put the last of the equipment away. Davis, getting impatient about libo, shouted out loud hoping they might hear in the staff shack, "Lord what are these fools doing? I gots my girl out in town, along with many mother fucking hoes waiting on me, it's time to go!"

Davis turned to razzing Noah, "Sweeeet Thaang! I know you're ready to get out of this sweat hole. You headed to B.C. Street? Oh, you better watch out for those little Mamasans, they'll take ALL your money." Davis chuckled as he went about his work, knowing Noah had already told him of his weekend plans of traveling to Camp Lester.

Noah went along with Davis's charade. However, the real deal was he and Marcus were going to meet up and travel to meet Glenn, who had arrived from the states. Noah finished going over paperwork in the tool room when Monte stuck his head in, "Staff Sergeant is on his way down." Sergeant Guiterez hollered out for everyone to form it up. Just as they started out of the tool shop, the phone rang. Davis, the one closest to it, looked at it as it rang. A late call on Friday afternoon was never good. It usually was someone having a last-minute schedule for the weekend. Meaning, whoever answered was usually the sucker who would have to work it. Both paused, seeing who would make the first move. Davis coaxing Noah,

"You answer." Noah responded back, "Fuck that I got plans."
Neither was budging as the phone rang on. From the maintenance
bay outside, you could hear hollers, "Somebody shut that fucking
noise up!" Davis hollered back, "Fuck that mother fucker," as the
two continued to hold out. "Here it is closing time and they want to
call last minute, don't answer, we're already gone." The phone quit
ringing. Noah looked at Davis and laughed, "Man, we can't do stuff
like that. You'll get our asses in trouble. Besides, if they want us for
something, they'll just track our asses down at the barracks, and
we'll be right the fuck back here."

Davis, struggling to put on his cammie blouse, "So fuck'em!
Piss poor planning on their part doesn't constitute an emergency on
mine!" He left the room to head to formation, "They'll have to find
my ass first." Noah grabbed his blouse and started to follow behind
when the phone started to ring again. "Fuck!" Noah hollers to Davis,
"Tell them I'll be there in one minute." He moves to the phone and
picks it up, "First Battalion Fifth Marines motor pool, Corporal
Barlow speaking. How may I help you?" On the other end, he hears
a familiar voice, "Yes, this is Corporal fucking Hall, yah biatch!
When the fuck are you getting your ass down here!" Noah burst out
laughing. "Bitch, how the fuck are you doing?" Glenn chuckles,
"We've already started drinking, waiting on your slow ass!" Noah
was glad to hear from Glenn, "When did you get in?" Glenn
continued, "I got here Monday, but child they been work'n my last
nerve with this JRC, bullshit!" Noah laughed aloud, as Glenn
continued, "Tried to check in, but they've all packed up and gone for
the long weekend! The duty signed me in, said. 'I'll see you Tuesday
morning.'" Noah was curious, "What about Lilly?" Glenn replied,
"Ah the wench, she's here with her fat ass!"

Noah could hear Lilly in the background, "Child I will fuck
your black ass up!" Glenn shushed her. "We're stay'n at the hostess
house until we get our new place." About that time, Monte stuck his
head in the hatch. "Hurry up man, Staff Sergeant, ain't going to let
us go until everyone is in formation, hurry the fuck up! We're ready
to get out of here!" Noah pulled the phone away from his ear, covers

it with the other hand, "I'll be right out, got a last-minute request." Monte took off as Noah returned to the call. "Hey man I gotta get going, I'll be down to Lester tonight. What's your room number?" Noah grabs a pen and paper and writes the number down. Finishing, he tells Glenn, "Got it, cool man, I'll be knocking at your door in about three hours. Have your ass ready when I get there, cause we're hitting the motherfucking town." He hangs up, rips the info off the paper, puts it in his pocket and hurries out the hatch.

After stopping by the barracks long enough to change and grab his duffle bag, he was off to go meet Marcus. The walk to Marcus's barracks was a short two blocks away. As he turned the corner in the distance, he could see Marcus ready and waiting in front of his barracks. He wasn't sure where this newfound friendship with Marcus was heading. Noah had been honest and open about his current relationship with Strumen. Both had agreed to take it slow, one day at a time, and just enjoy it for whatever it was without any labels. Whatever it was, it was real, new, and exciting. This was ok for now, however, each time he would see Marcus, the more he wanted to see him again. He reminded Noah of everything Dodge wasn't. Whatever feelings were developing, they were genuine, and the last thing he wanted to do was entangle Marcus up in any of the drama of Strumen.

The situation with Dodge had to be dealt with for this to go on any further. Marcus's smile lit Noah's day up, and it took full self-control to keep from grabbing him and smothering him with kisses. Any public display of affection was strictly forbidden. They both would be thrown out of the Marine Corps. Something as a mere holding of the hands, let alone a kiss, would be an investigation and discharge.

When he arrived, both paused and gazed into each other eyes for a moment without saying a word. A simple look that conveyed the others' bursting emotions hidden deep inside. Marcus commented, "It's about time, I was beginning to think you might have headed out without me." Noah looked at him with a flirting smile. "You know better." Marcus smiled and blushed as Noah rushed him along, "Come on, we have to get to the USO before the next bus leaves, or we're not going to get there till after midnight." They both grabbed their things and headed out.

After a marathon run, the two arrived at the USO just as the bus was starting to turn into the parking lot. Noah excited, "Oh no, come on man! We're going to miss it. Hubba, Hubba!" as he hurried Marcus along. Being a bit ruffled and tired of Noah's insistent quick pace, Marcus noticed all the Marines waiting to catch the bus, "Oh fuck no, I will have a seat! Someone is going to give up their seat or I will lay down in front of that bitch! It isn't going anywhere unless we're on it." Marcus ran up to the curb and just by luck the bus stopped right in front of him.

While the bus let passengers out, Noah jostled a place right behind him. The USO bus was a free service that ran between bases to allow service members to get around. All you had to do was just show up and get on. The last person was off, and Noah nudged Marcus to hurry as they got on. "Sweet!" Marcus laughed. The bus was already a bit crowded, Marcus tapped Noah on the shoulder and pointed to the rear of the bus where there were a couple of open seats. Noah took the seat by the window and Marcus sat beside him. They stashed the bags, and settled in. They were lucky, not everyone who had been waiting made it on, as the driver announced, "Sorry, no more inside." They both looked out to see a line of people still waiting; glanced at each other as Marcus let out an "Oops, sucks to be you," along with a sigh of relief as the bus drove off.

Camp Lester was south of Camp Hansen on the island of Okinawa and was a 45-minute drive, but with the bus stopping at all the different bases, and the local traffic, it became two-hours.

As the bus cruised along, Noah reflected while looking out the window as traffic and lights passed by. He couldn't help but remember the night at the Oceanside Pier when he had first met Glenn. His Grace Jones appearance, grand walk and gesture of a full hand circle accompanied by a snap and pop, were hard to forget. The slight introduction of the two was inconsequential, like so many other strangers who meet. The two had no idea how much each would have an impact on the other's life. At a time when Noah needed a friend the most, Glenn had come into his life. After navigating turbulent waters, and failed relationships, Glenn made him laugh once again. Most importantly, although he appeared flamboyant, he had a level head and proved to be a devoted friend.

Who knew he and Glenn would both end up on this little island, in the Pacific, let alone at the same time? Glenn's arrival had worked out perfect, with Noah's return from Korea, and the long weekend. He looked forward to a much-needed break. The stress of all he had been dealing with at work, the crash in Korea, and the ever-present fact of the gloomy and dreaded breakup that was to take place with Strumen. He hoped Glenn brought with him some good news about the affairs of the family stateside.

Noah met up with Lilly on her arrival to Oki just before he deployed to Korea. She had updated him on the latest dirt and drama that had taken place since his departure, but nothing unexpected. She did mention Dodge was still drinking heavily and quote, "Child, you know when the cats away the mice will play." She raised her eyebrows and followed with an "oops!" While putting one finger to her mouth, jokingly implying, she accidently said it. Noah had pushed her a bit, trying to find out more, but she pushed back, insisting she didn't want to be put in the middle. Lilly's girlfriend, prior to coming to the island, was friends with Dodge, so Lilly was aware of his doings. Noah, knowing Glenn did not care much for Dodge, hoped he had more info to share.

An unintentional nudge by Marcus getting a tape from his bag, brought his attention back to the bus. Noah observed in silence as Marcus put his Walkman on. He liked everything about him. They shared a love for music, and fashion, along with a good sense of raw humor. But most importantly, Noah had already noted this guy wasn't a push over. He stood his ground with Noah and with others, he kept it real. His dreamy looks would catch your attention when he walked in the room. Looking at his hair, the light brown hair pushed the Marine Corps' regulation limits. He kept up with the latest trend in fashion and often broke with the norms, he was very stylish.

Today he was wearing a white Polo shirt, with another under it colored aqua blue, both shirts had their collars turned up and were tucked into his gray cargo pants. Noah was excited for Marcus and Glenn to meet. He hoped the two would have a better friendship than the one Glenn and Dodge had experienced. Too many times he had to run interference and separate the two. But who knew?

Glenn was totally unpredictable. He could take a punch and hold his own. Although he could appear a bit fragile, when he got you to believe it, when you least expected it, bam! He would dish back and not bat an eye. He didn't make bones where he stood with you, he liked you or he didn't. Noah appreciated Glenn because he had a way of keeping it real and pushed Noah to leave his own comfort zone.

At Camp Lester, soon Noah and Marcus were off the bus and walking into the so-called temporary housing. It was for transitional families who were deployed to the island awaiting their permanent home. Noah reached in his pocket and pulled out a paper with the room number. Following the signs, they were on their way down a long hall, almost to the end was room 214. Before knocking, Noah looked at Marcus, "Are you ready?" Marcus smiled back with a big grin, and nodded his head, "It'll be alright."

Noah heard voices and laughter coming from inside the room as he knocked on the door. The room quieted and shortly the door opened up slightly, it was Lilly, peeking out. She let out a small gasp, "oh…" along with a giggle and tried acting shy. All a show of being more feminine than she really was. Noah started laughing, knowing this was out of character. Lilly started laughing as well, and invited them in. "Child you better get in here and do something with this child! He's already driving me crazy; you hear me. I swear we're gonna end up in divorce court with his stupid ass." She looked around seeing Glenn wasn't in the room. "Where did that child go now?" There was another couple in the room Noah did not know. They spoke out, "He rushed into the restroom." Lilly headed over to the restroom door. "Glenn quit your goddamn prep'n and get your ass out here, Noah has seen your ugly ass!"

Noah stuck his hand out to the two guys sitting on the edge of the bed. "Hi, I'm Noah, this is Marcus." They responded by getting up. "I'm Tony and this is Anthony," as they shook hands and sat back down, just as the restroom door flung open. Out walked Glenn in black sunglasses, a black and red polo with the collar turned up, and black parachute pants with a red belt and red slippers. "Haaay!" Strutting as though he was on a fashion runway, walked center of the room stopped did a twirl, turned, and walked up to Noah. "Noey guuurl, it's been so long!" Leaning in, gave a fake kiss on each of Noah's cheeks and stepped back. Now focusing on Marcus, he turned his head and immediately lowered his glasses peeking out over the top while holding them with one hand. "Hmm…" Noah spoke up, "This is Marcus." Marcus, amused at what he was witnessing, stuck his hand out to shake. Glenn, still peeking over his glasses, looked down at Marcus's hand and snubbed him. Putting his glasses back on, turned to Noah, "What'd I tell you about bringing strangers to my house?" Noah tried to interject, "Glenn..." Glenn took a couple of steps back from the two of them. Putting one hand on his hip and the other one he pointed at Noah, "Biatch, where's my Tupperware, I want it back!" and did a complete circle with his hand and one of his notorious snap and pops. The room burst out in laughter, Glenn broke character and started laughing as he ran up to Noah and gave him a hug, "I missed you Noey!" He turned to Marcus, apologizing, "Hi I'm Glenn, so sorry, I'm just having fun," and gave Marcus a hug. "How nice to meet you!" He then turned to Noah, "Child he's cute, Haaay!" Lilly, laughing chimed in, "Glenn I ought to slap your faggety ass. Marcus don't pay him no mind. Noah help me, I told you he ain't right, and been like this all day! … wearing on my last nerve." Noah looked over to Marcus smiling back at him, the ice had been broken. It looked like Marcus was going to fit in.

The monkey show

The crew made their way out to B.C. Street, touring the area, showing Glenn the notorious festivities in which it earned its' name. Tony, the bar owner of Club Tony's, had opened a new club called E.T.'s and opened his old club to the straight crowd. This was a common practice for him, and he did it to keep the Naval Criminal Service at bay. The entourage eventually landed at new Club E.T.'s. It was at the opposite end of B.C. Street from Club Tony's, but like Club Tony's the front entrance was closed and entry was from behind in the alley. Once in the bar, the dance floor was much larger, and the lighting and sound system much better. The crew had their drinks and were sitting at a cluster of tables. Noah was anxious to speak to Glenn about the situation back stateside, but waited patiently, not wanting to ruin the evening if Glenn had brought any unwelcome news.

The bar grew packed, as the evening went on. Finally, about 1:00 am the crew grew tried, and were ready to call it a night. Lilly had met a friend and had decided to hang with the ladies. The boys headed back out to B.C. Street to get a Honcho. As they walked, they passed the street vendors who offered up their merchandise at the "best price just you." The respectable stores were closed at this hour. What remained was the food cart vendors, along with the last call bars and hotels with girls batting their eyes for a drink, with a promised whisper of a fun time. Different ones in the group spoke of the activities that went on in the bars. Glenn played hard to get with the young ladies as he passed by the bars. His curiosity got the best of him, and he decided to go into one called "The Zoo." The group played along but gave him fair warning that it was not for him. Once in the bar, they were seated at a large booth. The buy me drinky girls were interwoven between each of them. Noah paid close attention to Glenn as the girl next to him spoke, "You buy me drink?" Glenn, not familiar with the customary expectation, was taken aback, "Child why would I want to buy you a drink?" He quickly looked to Noah in disbelief, "Noey, she wants me to buy her a drink..." Noah rolled his eyes, and smirked, "Just play along with it, I'll pay for her drink." He nodded at the waitress to go ahead with the drink. Once the drinks were delivered, they did a toast to welcome Glenn to the island. The bar was starting to get a late-night crowd as guys kept coming in. The music went low, and over the speakers came a woman's voice, in broken English. "Otay boys, please, we ask you to clear edge of stage. Now I know you all excited, please feel free to eat banana, but try to stay off stage for performance."

Noah looked over to Glenn to see his reaction. Glenn asked, "Noah what is she talking about? Huh-uh child, what's going on here?" Noah chuckled, "You wanted to see what these places were about, so just sit back and take it in." The woman's voice spoke out, "Please, please, welcome to the Zoo stage, our very own Monkey Girl," The audience applauded, and a small Asian lady dressed in a jungle prehistoric-type dress appeared from behind the curtains and started to dance. She danced for a few minutes and, before the end of the first song, was completely naked.

The woman's voice came back over the speaker. "Oh, this monkey work hard, she hungry!" The audience cheered, "...You all the Zookeeper, did she earn banana?" The crowed let out a cheer, "Oh I don't think she get fed, you not loud enough." The crowd let out a roar, and continued, while some started moving closer to the stage. "Oh, you been a good Monkey Girl, you get banana." The crowd roared again, as the voice continued, "Oh you really good, ... you get two bananas." A small Asian man came from the side and handed her two bananas. The voice came back over the speakers. "You boys gave them to her, now watch, Monkey Girl enjoys her banana. Remember Monkey Girl like to share some banana with Monkey boys, if she shares feel free to eat."

Noah turned to Glenn watching him take in everything going on around him. He could tell Glenn was totally out of his element, and shocked at what was taking place. Noah nodded to Marcus, to check him out, as they both chuckled. Noah asked Glenn. "Are you ok?" Glenn, too caught up in what was taking place, gave a glance, and shushed him with his hand. As much as Glenn detested it, he couldn't look away.

The show continued. The little Monkey girl started doing her dance, gradually peeling the banana, then teasing the crowd and her vagina, before sitting down on it, taking it all the way inside of her. She moved to the edge of the stage, and lay down, expelling part of it out, and cutting it off with the lip of her vagina. The Marine at the edge went face first down on the banana. When he came up, he held it in his mouth, turned to show the crowd and then swallowed it.

Noah was startled by Glenn's sudden movement. Noah turned to see Glenn move away and frowning at him. Noah thought he was disgusted by what had just happened on stage, but he was wrong. Glenn spoke out, "Child this thing (referring to the buy me drinky girl next to him,) just grabbed my leg." Before Glenn could finish, the girl, reached and grabbed Glenn's crotch. Noah saw Glenn pop up in the booth trying to get away from her. Noah was shocked and amused at the same time. Glenn was freaked out. "No child, huh-uh, you got to let me out…, come on, …move, let me outta here." He nudged and pushed trying to get up and away from the girl. He was trapped in both directions being in the back of the booth. Noah in shock, along with the others, started laughing. Glenn at this point was now frantic. "Child this ain't funny, let me out!" Glenn was now standing in the booth, trying to walk over those around him to get away. The buy me drinky girl, spoke out, "You no like girls?" She and the other girls were laughing at Glenn's expense. Glenn made it out of the booth, angry, "Noey, this ain't funny!" He took off out the bar.

Laughing hysterically, the group fell out of the bar. Glenn was steaming and headed down the sidewalk. Noah begged, "Come on Glenn, we told you, you probably wouldn't like it." Glenn continued, giving Noah the middle finger. Noah took off running to catch him. Once he caught up, "Come on man, … sorry, but you know that shit was funny." Glenn stopped and crossed his arms, turning his head in a pout as Noah calmed him. "Look I don't like those places either. I think they're degrading. Both for the women who work there, and what does it say about the guys who visit." Glenn was listening, as Noah continued, "Look I'm sorry, we should've told you in advance what happens in those joints. I kind of thought you knew what you were getting into." Glenn was pissed, "Child I was raised right! I don't know about you, but my momma taught me not to go to places like that! Those girls are somebody's daughter, sister, hell by the looks of some of them, are even moms and grandmas." Noah put his hand on Glenn's shoulder and pleaded. "Come on lighten up." Glenn stood for a minute, contemplating, before he let out a laugh. "Child, I was just sitting there minding my own business, when I felt her hand on my leg. I thought ok, I'll just let it go. But then she started moving her hand up my leg even further… And with that Monkey thing on stage, and the guy eating the banana, … she moved up next to my crotch…Oh no child, …I was through." Noah reliving it, tried to muffle his laugh. "What, did you think we would let her rape you? Come on we were right there…" Glenn shook his head. "No child, huh uh…" The rest of the group caught up. All still laughing and chuckling, Glenn was now calmed down and laughing along. They walked a bit further, before hailing a Honcho to head back to base.

The first weekend on Oki was now one to be remembered. Getting back to the hotel, the others made their makeshift beds and were off to sleep. Not ready for bed, Noah and Glenn grabbed a beer and headed to the roof to watch the stars and chat. On the roof, they sat on the ledge, looking out. Noah asked Glenn what he thought of Oki. "Ah, it'll be alright. Lilly and I will be getting our apartment in a few days. She already knows everyone at work, so I kind of know what to expect when I get there." Noah looking out over the water in the distance. "Look at that reflection of the moon on the water…," Both paused, before Noah continued, "You guys going to be here a year huh?" Glenn took a drink of his beer. "Yeah, seems like a long time, but I'm glad to be here, glad to get away, …for a while." Noah chuckled. "I know what you mean." Glenn coughed several times, as Noah looked on. "Damn you gonna be alright?" Glenn was not too concerned. "I think I'm getting a cold, with all this traveling. … I need to slow down."

Both sat quietly for a minute, when Glenn spoke up about the elephant in the room. "Well, the Psycho has a new boyfriend…." Noah remained quiet, knowing he was referring to Strumen. Glenn was definitely not a fan of Dodge and seldom called him by name, but always had a nickname to call him. Noah use to get on him about it, but now found the names amusing, because most of them fit. Noah not sure what to say, looked at Glenn, "You're talking about Dodge, right?" Glenn smirked, "Of course, who else is Psycho, …and by the way, who fucking names their kid Dodge?" Both chuckled, as Noah spoke, "I guess it fits, he is kind of Dodgy." Glenn continued, "I haven't seen him that much, but I was staying at Lilly and Patsy's, before coming over here. He stopped over with his new boy. Didn't know I would be there. I came out to the living room where he and the new boy were sitting. He was chatting up Patsy and hushed when I came in the room." Noah, now listening to every word, "Did you say anything?" Glenn smiled, "Child you know I did!" as he chuckled. "I told him, 'I see they now let you out on chaperoned visits from the psych ward. How lucky for you.'" He spoke back, "Nice to see you too Glenn." I turned to the little boy, and child I couldn't even tell you his name, other than he is some scaggy thing from the Capri lounge." Noah smiled a bit, even though he knew Glenn's opinion was biased. Glenn continued. "He introduced me, to the little tart; This is Glenn, he's a friend of Noah's. I'm sure he'll tell Noah now. Like he was going to offend me. Please!" Glenn chuckled. "I snapped and popped, and told that bitch, Noah already knows, and if he doesn't, I believe he'll be glad. Regardless, he ain't stupid, only when he chose to date your stupid ass. I stared that bitch down, before walking away." Noah laughed, Glenn had never backed down from Dodge, and had defended Noah's honor several times. Glenn had Dodge's number from day one. He was never shy about letting Noah know there was something off about him. "You think he'll be ok with the breakup. What do you think will happen when I get back?" Glenn, surprised at the question,

"Hell no, you ain't never going to be safe from that psychopath! But you ain't never going to have a better chance than you do right now. … Just don't provoke him Child." Noah knew he had to face him when he returned. "What do you mean? I have to get my car; he still has it. I don't want to talk to him or see him period." Glenn concerned. "Then don't. You don't need to see him to get your car. Besides I don't think he is driving it anymore. Patsy said something about the transmission being out, and his little boy is driving him around." Noah astonished, "Really, do you think she can find out where it is? … How ironic, so now he is driving the boy's car. Oh, doesn't that sound familiar. I almost feel sorry for this new piece." Glenn continued, "I don't know if Patsy will get involved, child her and Lilly got their own problems. I haven't said anything to Lilly yet, but that is a time bomb as well."

Noah was shocked, "Say what?" Glenn realizing what he had just said. "Huh-uh Child, I ain't getting into that mess. But let's just say, her and Dodge are hanging out for a reason." Noah looking back at the stars. "Lilly will be heartbroken…" Glenn in agreement, "I know."

They sat quietly for a moment when Glenn continued. "All I can say, you'll be alright, you'll get your car. But you got to promise me, …once you get your things, you have got to keep away from him. I mean you can't let Dodge know anything, …I mean nothing about you. Noey, I think he'll try and come back on you if this little fly boy he's with doesn't work out. He's a nut, hell, he's liable to try and kill you. I'm telling you he ain't right!" Noah took a deep breath, "I hear you, and I can tell you, …I can promise you, once I am away from him, he'll never hear from me again." Noah finished his beer, and stood up, "I believe you're right, about the killing thing. You forgot; I have lived it, and he has already tried."

Noah looked out at the moon's reflection on the water. "You know if we were a straight couple, the Marine Corps would have had his ass locked up for abuse by now! But we don't have that kind of support. We can't go to them for help! It's up to us to deal with it. Always silent." Glenn stood up when Noah turned, smiled, and grabbed him, giving him a hug, "Did I ever tell you how glad I am that you are here right now, and part of my life." Glenn hugged him back for a moment before making light of the seriousness of the moment, "Ya Biatch!" The two grabbed their empty beer cans and worked their way down from the roof.

The next morning, the friends said their goodbyes and were off on their journey home. Noah and Marcus caught the early bus and were back at Camp Hansen by noon. With good timing, it allowed both to be able to drop off their belongings, change over, and head for the beach. Stopping at the exchange on the way, they grabbed some drinks and were soaking up the sun in no time. The beach was more rock than sand, and not very large. It didn't take much to get crowded on a sunny day but today it was fairly empty. With a blanket sprawled out, both lay side by side basking in the sun. Starting to burn, Noah rolled over and asked Marcus to put lotion on his back. Before too long both dozed to the sound of the ocean.

Kenville was a small village just outside the gate of Camp Hansen. There they stopped at Dave's, one of the favorite restaurants of the Americans, to get 'chicken taco rice.' After finishing, they hung out for a couple of drinks at Club Shangri-la, before getting a hotel room to spend the night. It had been a wonderful weekend, and neither was ready to go back to base. For the first time in a while, Noah felt he was able to let go. The stress level dealing with the helo crash, and the death of Morello, along with the uncertainty of the relationship with Dodge had taken its toll. This weekend, with good friends, allowed a respite and time for gratitude for all that was good in life.

Chapter 21

Grounds to slander

The phone rang with the morning wakeup call from the front desk. Marcus answered and hung up. Slowly the two rolled out of bed, not in a hurry to get back to Camp Hansen. On low speed, both were up, dressed and out the door.

Heading back to base, they had made the most of the weekend. It was dusk out and Kenville was just waking. The walk to base was quiet as both remained silent observing the morning rituals of the villagers. Although they were in a foreign land, the rituals were not any different to those in the U.S. One building Papasan was rolling up the metal coverings revealing the doors. Another, Mamasan was cleaning and threw water out from a bucket. Once at the gate of Camp Hansen, they were stopped long enough by the sentry to look at their ID's and let them through. They arrived at Noah's barracks first, said their goodbyes and Marcus continued on.

Noah came in the barracks, passing the duty, and nodded his head. "Hey how's it going?" He had always hated the open squad bays, but more than that, he hated the community showers and toilets. He made it to the cubicles when the lights came on in the squad bay. He unlocked his locker and started his morning routine of getting his uniform laid out before heading to the showers. Stopping to use the urinal, the end one was opened. As he approached, both guys using it stopped and left. He finished and went to the sinks, to shave for Monday morning inspection. The week ahead was a simple one. They were on the downside of being on the island, and in just a month or so, would be packing up to go back stateside. Sergeant Mallard came in and sat his shaving kit down. Noah acknowledged him, before he said he had forgotten something, and headed back out. Noah finished and moved across the hall to the showers. He set his shaving kit down on the bench, grabbed his gear, stripped down and headed into the showers. When he walked in, Knox and Wilson, both of supply, were already under the shower's heads. Noah thought it odd, as though he were intruding when both stopped, quit talking, and grabbed their gear and took off upon seeing him. Noah figured it wasn't his business. He continued to shower when Dowdy came in and saw Noah in the shower, turned and went back out. Noah started to feel a little uncomfortable, like maybe they knew he was gay or something, but discarded it as being paranoid. He finished, got dressed in his shorts and headed back to the cubicle.

Passing the cubicle next to his, he heard, "Hey did you hear about Barlow?" He stopped in his tracks, hiding behind the locker where he couldn't be seen to eavesdrop. Baxter was telling Huck, "Yeah Sergeant Fisher said he seen Barlow and that guy he hangs out with at the beach, kissing and shit. That the guy went down on him, and they started having sex on the beach." Huck, cut him off, "Awe man, that's bogus! If it was true, so fucking what, …that's his business." Baxter, continued, "Hey, I'm just saying what Sergeant Fisher is telling everyone." Huck was aggravated to be hearing the nonsense, "Yeah, well that's the problem, fucking Sergeant Fisher. Like he has room to talk about anything. Man, he stirs shit up all the time. Besides, think about it. You've been to that beach, it's busy all the time. If all that shit was going on, don't you think somebody would have said something? Why didn't Fisher say anything….?" Baxter chimed back in. "Hey, that's not all, …I also heard the dude he hangs out with is already under investigation for being a fag."

Noah was pissed, turned, and went into his cubicle. This explains what he had experienced all morning. The low whispers when he walked by, and the silence when he walked into a room. Corporal Loose came in from the shower and started putting on his uniform. Noah couldn't hold back. "Loose, should I be aware of anything?" Loose was levelheaded and didn't get caught up in a lot of the scuttlebutt of the barracks. He sat down to put on his boots. "Look, I wouldn't worry about what these motherfuckers say! But if you're talking about Sergeant Fisher, and the sex on the beach bullshit! Yeah, I heard it, … I didn't want to say anything, look at the source." Noah threw his uniform on his rack and headed out to Sergeant Fisher's cubicle.

Sergeant Fisher was sitting down on the rack, when Noah came in. Noah was pissed. Fisher got up quickly and backed up against the bulkhead holding his hand out for Noah to back off. Noah sounded off so the entire squad bay could hear. "What's this bullshit, you are starting Fish? Come on, tell it to my face, you motherfucking prick. Tell me what you saw? You can't because you are a fucking liar." Sergeant Fisher, interrupted, "Let me explain man, let me explain." Noah sounded off, "Yeah you fucking do that! Come on let's hear! Let's all hear it! And say it loud enough so all you motherfuckers, who believe this stupid shit, can hear!" Fisher started in, "Look, a buddy of mine is in your boy's unit, you know that Romano dude. Well, he says he's under investigation for being a homo. You two are hanging out, and I saw you two down at the beach, he was rubbing your back, you seemed to like it man."

Noah exploded and lunged at him but Loose and a few others grabbed him and pulled him away. Noah screaming and kicking at him. "You're a stupid fuck, he was putting suntan lotion on my back, who gives a fuck!" From over the cubicle wall, Noah could hear. "Someone better shut that white boy up, before he gets his ass whipped!" Noah, hearing, sounded off. "Fuck you! You want it, come, and get it mother fuckers. You all think I'm a faggot, you'll find out what it is to have a faggot boy beat your ass."

Sergeant Fisher grabbed his camo blouse and tried to scoot past, while Noah was being held back. "You better watch out, that Motherfucker is crazy!" Loose looked to Fisher, "You better leave, before you get hurt." Fisher took off out of the barracks. The duty hearing all the commotion came down. "Hey, what 's going on?" Fritz and Mallard blocked him in the center hallway. Mallard spoke calmly, "It's nothing man, …it's all under control. Everything's cool." Loose calmed Noah down and got him back into his cubicle. Standing by, he waited a few minutes, before speaking to him. "You got it under control?" Noah was sitting on the rack, with his head in his hands. What the fuck had he just done? Lifting his head, he took a deep breath and let out a sigh. "Who knows? … Yeah, I'm cool for now, …that stupid fuck!" Loose patted him on the back. "Look nobody believes anything he says…don't let him get to you." Noah turned, gave a half-baked smile, "I'm cool, you're gonna be late man, you better get outta here" Loose took off. Noah couldn't help wondering if anything was going to come of this. He knew of people investigated just for the mere accusation of being gay. This was the kind of stupid shit that caused people to be investigated. Once NIS started digging, they would keep on till they found a way to get you out.

Noah made it to the motor pool, and was handing out PM kits, when Staff Sergeant came in. "Barlow, my office." Noah grabbed his camo blouse and put it on as he headed out. Walking in, Loose and Mallard were both already sitting down. Staff Sergeant Higgins told him to grab a seat. The Staff Sergeant started in. "So, I hear there were some problems this morning in the barracks?" Noah looked over at Loose and Mallard, knowing where this conversation was headed. "Yes, Staff Sergeant." The Staff Sergeant continued, "Well son, I've already heard what happened, but I want to hear your side of the story?" Noah, irritated, began to explain his side of the story and included what had taken place on the beach with the suntan lotion. Staff Sergeant sat and listened intently. When Noah finished, he took a moment to gather his thoughts, and gave a glance to Mallard and Loose to see if any reaction came from them while they listened to the story. "This is what is up. I've already been called by the First Sergeant; He wants to know what the hell is going on. Gunny Ramos, Sergeant Fisher's boss has called saying you threatened Sgt Fisher and made racial slurs. They want your head. First Sergeant knows Fisher's reputation and wants to know your side of the story. I've told him I would speak with you and get back to him. Let me give him a call."

Staff Sergeant called getting the First Sergeant on the speaker phone. Noah explained his side of the story. When he completed, the First Sergeant started to speak. "Son let me tell yah. Normally I would have you front and center, but because of your outstanding reputation, and you know the Battalion Commander's fondness for you, I'm not. This seems to be out of line with your character. Now I know what's being said, I understand why you did what you did. Son I want you to know we stand behind you. Now, all that said, it does not solve our problem. Sergeant Fisher, as much as we may not like it, has a right to be heard. So, let's make him heard. If he wants to slander you, let's make him put it down in writing. If he doesn't, I'll have grounds to put slander charges on him, and I have the witnesses that have all heard his bullshit. But Son, I must tell you. I know Fisher, if he thinks he's going to get charged with slander, he'll write a statement, whether it is true or not. If he does, then I'll have to let it go up the chain of command, which means you may end up being investigated. I personally don't give a shit who you sleep with. You're an outstanding Marine, but others may not see it that way. Now are you ready for that?"

Noah shaking his head in disgust, "Yes First Sergeant," he sat quietly as the First Sergeant continued. "The other option is you'll get charged with threatening another Marine, and disrespect to a superior. Now, I can tell you the charge of threatening is serious, but being you are a Corporal, and a Non-Commissioned Officer yourself, it would probably be nothing more than a page eleven. Either way, it doesn't look good for you. So, I'll call this piece of shit in and see how it goes. Corporal Barlow, I'm saying this as politely as I can, without using a dog whistle, make sure you have your shit together. You understand what I'm saying?" Noah sounded off, "Yes, First Sergeant!" First Sergeant closed. "I'll get back with you."

Noah was embarrassed about the whole thing. This train has left the station without a destination, there was no telling where it would go. Regardless, he was a passenger on it wherever it went. Noah thanked the Staff Sergeant and returned to the tool room. Monte had finished handing out the PM bags and was sitting behind his desk. Noah's mind was racing. He needed to get ahead of this thing. He needed to let Marcus know, and he needed to get rid of all the letters from Strumen, or any other evidence that might be incriminating, or proof he might be gay. He wasn't even sure what to say, if asked, other than to deny any accusation. How would he get word to Dusty? As much as he didn't want to talk to Strumen, he would need to let them him know as well. It was time to close ranks and enlist any help he could. Now was the time to call on anyone that was gay, or a friend of the "family". Noah knew some would not risk being discovered and would turn a cold shoulder. He didn't care, now was the time to find out who really had his back. They all wanted to call themselves "family", now was a time to find out who would live up to it.

He thought quickly, Monte was getting ready for his morning route around base. Monte wasn't aware of the whole story but knew Sgt Fisher was stirring shit. Monte being gay, had a stake in this. Any discovery of Noah being investigated, could turn into a witch hunt, and could ultimately lead to him being discovered as well. Noah decided to come clean and let him know what was going on. Monte was sympathetic and understood the risk and was willing to help. On his morning run, Monte was going to get word to Marcus, so he could fend off any incoming attacks. Noah couldn't call stateside. The phone lines in the motor pool could only be used to call stateside via overseas operator, which meant he couldn't call Strumen or Dusty without a record of the call being made. He would need to get to the USO to make a call ASAP, and he needed to get back to the barracks and clean up any loose ends that might be incriminating.

Davis (Fritz) wasn't gay but was gay friendly. They had each other's back on many occasions. He was someone Noah could trust. Noah looked out to the maintenance bay and saw Davis working on a jeep. Hollering to get his attention, Davis came in the tool room. He told Davis what was getting ready to take place. Davis having dealt with Sergeant Fisher in the past, agreed to cover for Noah and came up with an idea for Noah to do a morning breakfast run to the USO. Noah took orders from around the motor pool and headed to the USO.

Stopping by the barracks, Noah quickly went to his cubicle and gathered anything he thought could be incriminating, proving he was gay. Putting the items in a duffle bag, he was back in the jeep. On his way to the USO, Noah spread the ripped-up letters, photos, and such throughout different dumpsters. This was in the event if someone was to find them, they wouldn't have them all.. Finally, he made it to the USO. Once there, he signed up for the oversea phones, and grabbed a seat to wait. He was third on the list, which was actually rather good, meaning he didn't have a long wait. Noah sat anxiously, looking at the clock, both trying to figure the time back in the US, and to keep track of how long he had been out of the motor pool. A few minutes went by, and his name was called. He picked up the key and went into the booth. Finding Dusty's number, he dialed, one ring, two ring, three ring, under his breath, "Come on Dusty pick up." Four rings, finally he could hear a groggy voice on the other end. Noah responded knowing she had been sleeping, "Dusty, Dusty it's, Noah." The phone went silent... "What, who is this motherfucker? (The phone went silent for a moment) Noah what, ...what the hell are you doing calling me at this time?" Noah still anxious, "Dusty, listen to me, I don't have long to talk. I need to tell you shit is starting to happen over here. You understand me." Dusty stayed calm, "Go ahead." Noah continued, "Listen, none of the shit is true, and I'm not going to go into it. Other than a guy in my unit is making accusations against me about being gay. Just know we have been in contact and our marriage is fine, that's all you must know." Dusty went off, "Motherfucker I told you to cover your ass, now look what you've done... Oh you can guarantee if they call me," She changed her tone and began to speak sarcastically. "I'll be, Oh I love my husband, what, what did you say? He's a homo, Oh I'm shocked to find out just like you, and I'll boo-hoo-hoo, right there in front of them." Noah chuckled patronizing her but didn't find it amusing. "Dusty just trust me; I need your help right now. If anybody asks you any questions." Dusty interrupted him, "Noah, calm down, listen to me. You'll be alright. Look by law neither of us must speak to anyone about the other. We are husband and wife. We can't be compelled to be a witness against the other." Noah wasn't aware of this. "Really?" Dusty was now reassuring. "Look, I don't know what is going on over there, and I don't need to know the details. I have your ass covered on this end. Just make sure you know, you have rights motherfucker, and they should read them to you. At that point you do not have to say anything. Just know it is almost impossible to prove without a picture, or you admitting to it. Of course, unless someone is saying they slept with you?" Noah shrugged, "No, nothing like that!" Dusty continued, "Just keep calm and remain quiet." Noah felt like Dusty being removed from the situation, had her head on correctly, and took her advice seriously. "Look I just wanted you to know. Sorry Dusty, I appreciate this." Dusty laughed, "We cool motherfucker, we cool. Now it's the middle of the night here and I'm getting some sleep." She hung up the phone. Noah leaned back on the wall of the booth and let out a sigh. Up next was Strumen, he started to call when he hung up. He struggled for a few minutes debating in his mind whether to call him. Noah's address was the same as Dusty's, and the Marine Corps had no record of the two ever living together. Other than some checks in his check book made out to Strumen, there was nothing at this point linking the two. He finally concluded; it was best to not call. Having to explain, would just further complicate an already strained relationship, and besides, finding out about Marcus, he might go to NIS himself.

Arriving back at the Motor pool he passed out the orders to the Marines and went to his desk. Trying to catch up on his work, he was overwhelmed with thoughts and stress. How could this be happening.

The morning went by slowly, and Noah's ability to concentrate waned. Right before lunch, Staff Sergeant came in the tool room. "Look, the First Sergeant called, Fisher did what we expected. He has made a pretty damning accusation about you. First Sergeant read it to me; Just to let you know, it's hard to hear. I don't want to go into it right now, but he's saying it's more than just rubbing suntan lotion on your back. We're expected to be at the First Sergeants office at 1300. You'll be going in front of the CO. He'll be reading your rights, and charges against you at that time. It'll be up to you to make a statement, or a plea. Just so you know you don't have to say anything." Noah sat quietly shaking his head, acknowledging what was just said. Staff Sergeant continued, "Myself, and the Lieutenant will be there with you. Keep your head up, you'll get through this."

If you find my check book

Noah arrived at the Company office a few moments early. Not knowing what to expect, his thoughts were everywhere. The blinders were off. He was ready to fight, and if he didn't win this battle, it had awoken him to the bigger war. The rumors had run rampant. He couldn't go anywhere without whispers in the background. There was no putting it back in the bag. His reputation was already tarnished, and he was already convicted in the world of public opinion. The only thing he could do now was fight. Fight to keep his self-respect, and to keep his dignity intact. Nothing about to take place, in the Company Commanders office, could damage him any further than the humiliation he was already experiencing.

Noah sat at a picnic table under the pavilion next to the company office. He stared at his watch, waiting till the last minute to report in. The Company Commander entered from the side door, and the First Sergeant and Staff Sergeant arrived together and walked in. The Lieutenant followed a few minutes after. All the players were there, and now it was Noah's turn to make his entrance. Finishing his soda, he straightened himself up, and headed in. He was greeted by the Staff Sergeant and went into the First Sergeants office. While there, he went over how the proceedings would be conducted. Once finished, he had Noah wait in the hall as he and the Staff Sergeant went into the CO's office.

The CO sat behind his desk, center of the room. Noah reported in and was read the accusation of being a homosexual, possible sodomy charges and his rights. The CO put him at ease and asked if he would like to make any comment or if the accusations were true. Noah withheld any comment. The CO further read his requirements until the investigation was completed. He was to have no further contact with any person involved, which meant Sergeant Fisher, and Lance Corporal Romano, (Marcus). Any interaction, other than in the line of duty, would be considered an act of interfering in an investigation. The CO told him he would be turning all pertinent information over to legal and the Naval Investigative Service. Their findings would determine what charges would be applied, if any, at that time. The CO made note; he knew Noah was up for reenlistment, and it would be postponed until he was cleared from the investigation. Noah was dismissed and left the room.

Outside, the Staff Sergeant informed him he would need to report to NIS immediately. Two Military Policemen were standing by to escort him. He wouldn't be allowed to go anywhere other than straight to the NIS office. This thing was growing legs and moving fast. Wow, he felt like a criminal. What happened to innocent till proven guilty? He knew what they were doing. This was an ambush tactic. The element of surprise. They were on the offensive, making things happen quickly, before Noah would have time to react, or in this case, get rid of any evidence. Thinking about his earlier actions, getting rid of any compromising information immediately was the right thing to do.

Arriving at NIS, the MPs registered him. He sat waiting. A mirrored window off to one side of the room, left Noah wondering if they were observing him. He sat patiently. Finally, the door opened and a woman wearing a blue blazer, white top, and gray dress pants came out. She called Noah by name. He stood up. "Here Ma'am." She gave him the once over. "I'm Detective Krasinski. I'll be handling your case," as she pulled out a badge and showed it to him. "Come with me." Noah followed her down a hall until he came to a small room, where she stepped aside and told him to go in and have a seat. She was average height, Caucasian, light brown hair, and, like most women in law enforcement, carried herself professionally. She told another detective down the hall she was conducting an interview, please refrain from any calls. She entered the room and closed the door behind her. She came around the desk, sat down, and offered Noah a drink if he wanted it. Noah didn't accept. Pulling a couple of files, and a tape recorder from the desk, she set it down and began reading through the file. Once again, she read him his rights. When she finished with the formalities, she became a bit more personable. "Ok, just to let you know, we have been briefed on this, by your command. They think highly of you and seem to think you really shouldn't be here. You're well thought of." She smiled, and paused, with an inquisitive look on her face. "But yet here we are. Why is that?" Noah sat quietly. He had no intention of engaging in any form of conversation. Not in the least. Whatever they wanted to know they were going to have to work for it, and nothing would come from him. Friends who had been investigated said the way to deal with NIS was to say nothing. That is exactly what he intended to do. If you spoke, they would take it and try and trip you up, so best to say nothing. Detective Krasinski continued. "You mind telling us what happened on the beach that day?" Noah smiled and said nothing. She continued, "Can you tell us how you know Lance Corporal Romano?" Noah sat quietly. "Do you know he is being investigated for being a homosexual? Do you know anything about that?" Noah remained silent as she rattled off a few more questions and said nothing. She wrote a few things down on a pad of paper in front of her. Looking up to Noah, "I know you're not going to say anything, and that is fine. You are not the first one to sit in that chair and remain quiet. But I can tell you it will go a lot better if you cooperate. Now, if this goes on further, it could mean the difference between an Administrative Discharge, or are you doing brig time and getting a BCD. You know what a BCD is? …It's a Bad Conduct Discharge. It will follow you for the rest of your life. No matter what. You go to apply for a job, and boom there it is. Oh, you may think it will go away in time, but it will stay with you, even 60 years from now. So, what do you say, you want to talk? I know you want to get it off your chest. If it isn't true, don't you want us to know. If it were me and someone was lying about me, I would want everyone to know the truth. You can trust us. Don't you want us to know your side of the story?" Noah sat quietly. She was good, but he still knew best to not say anything. Detective Krasinski continued, "What about Sergeant Fisher, why would he want to say something like this about you? Most people willing to sign a written statement are usually not liars. Yet, you want us to believe he is. If so, then why?" She paused and sat back in her chair. "I'm going to step out for moment, …maybe you need some time to think about it." She got up and left the room.

Noah sat quietly, before taking a breath and exhaling. He got up and stretched, before sitting back down, lowered his head with his elbows on his knees. Thinking to himself, say nothing. They knew what they were doing. Just then, the door flung open, and another Detective came in. This time it was a guy, fortyish in appearance, and dressed like Detective Krasinski. He popped out his badge. "You have already had your rights read to you. I'm Detective Hermanson, I'm not going over them again." His demeanor was abrasive. He sat on the edge of the desk towering over Noah. "So, why are you wasting our time? You know what you did, … so do we! Now, sign the statement admitting to it, and this will all be over. You'll be on your way. We can have you out of the Corps, and back home by the end of the month. We have a way of making things move quickly, and quietly. No more harassment, an administrative discharge, no bad paperwork to follow you. Hell, we can have you out of the barracks, and in temporary quarters, until you're discharged. You won't have to face anyone you work with or explain anything. Pack your bags, and we'll have you gone tonight. Just say the word. It'll be all over." Noah sat quietly thinking this must be the "Good cop, Bad cop" thing going on. What the Detective was saying would be a simple answer. However, it wasn't for Noah, he wasn't giving in. If they wanted him out, they were going to have to prove it. The whole policy, and regulation, was simply wrong. Why does it matter who he sleeps with anyways? If being dragged through the mud would change one person's opinion, it would be worth it. He wasn't getting out on an administrative discharge. He had worked too hard, to not get an Honorable. As far as he was concerned, he hadn't done anything wrong to begin with. It was the system that was broken, not him. It was all or nothing at this point and best to remain silent.

Noah's silence, frustrated Detective Hermanson, and he left the room. Noah sat by himself for twenty minutes, before Detective Krasinski came back in the room. The good cop bad cop thing continued. She was nice and professional. "Did anything Detective Hermanson say help you make up your mind?" Noah shook his head no. She continued on, "Well I think we are done here for the day, …except one more thing." She paused looking at him in contemplation, before speaking. "… We are going to take you to the barracks and go through your belongings." She stood up and pointed. "So, grab your cover and let's go get this over with." Noah was surprised, but really wasn't sure if they had a right to do this.

They took her car and went to the barracks. Inside, they arrived at his cubicle. Corporal Loose was already there. He needed to be there to validate what was his and what wasn't. Detective Krasinski was shown everything belonging to Noah in the cubicle. She began going through his wall locker. Item by item, she would inspect. The clothes hanging up, she would go through the pockets. Noah started getting a little nervous. He had already purged everything, but what if he had missed something. He wished he could have found his check book. It had been missing for a day or two now. He needed to pay some bills, then it hit him. How could he have been so stupid? The check book had the receipts of all the checks he had been sending Strumen. If she found it, it would show a connection to him. It recorded every monthly rent check, car maintenance, and so on. Maybe she wouldn't find it. If she did, he needed to play it off. Act like nothing was in it and she might just go past it. Noah decided to go with it. "If you find my check book, let me know. I've been missing it for a couple of days and need to get some bills paid."

The cubicle was crowded, she asked the two to step aside in the hall. They could still watch, but Corporal Loose was not liking the idea of the search. "Isn't this illegal? Don't they need a warrant, or something?" The Detective spoke up. "Just to let you know, we don't need a warrant. You are in a government building, on base, and we are within our right to do a search and seizure. The moment you came on base, you left that behind." Noah had taken so many things for granted. He had read the signs posted at the gate, saying subject to search and seizure, but never really gave it much thought. She set a few items out, one a shoe box of photos, nothing he was concerned about that would be incriminating. She went to work again in the wall locker, and soon pulled out his check book and showed it to Noah. He spoke up, "Oh man, I've torn this place apart, looking for it." The detective flipped through it, giving it a quick glance, and held it up in front of him. "See, something good can come out of this…" and handed it over to him. "Thank you!"

Noah was relieved and put it in his pocket. She went through some drawers and looked around the cubicle one final time. Huck and Baxter, who both worked at the motor pool, came in the barracks. Walking by the cubicle and seeing Detective Krasinski, Baxter spoke out. "What the fuck? What's a woman doing up in here?" Startled, Corporal Loose motioned him to keep it down. The noise triggered the Detective's attention causing her to give a quick glance at her watch. "I think that will about do it." Noah confused, "So what? Is that it? That's all?" She looked at him, like he was being naive. "Oh…, (as she tucked her chin and smiled at him) …Oh No. We're just getting started." And chuckled again. "We still have a lot of unfinished business to discuss, so I'll be giving you a call tomorrow. We're going to get to know each other really well, …you and I." Stepping out from the cubicle she continued. "I need to emphasis one more time, in case your command didn't. You are to have no contact with Lance Corporal Romano, or Sergeant Fisher. Any contact can be considered tampering with a witness or interfering with an investigation. You understand?" Noah acknowledge her. She took off, making it to the end of the squad bay. "I'll be in touch."

Chapter 22

The Homophobes

It was Saturday afternoon, and Noah had finished all his weekend chores. Laundry done, uniform squared away, a good workout at the gym, and a long run completed. Now showered, it was time to make it to the chow hall before it closed. Noah came around the barracks and onto the main drag of Camp Hansen. The sunshine was kicking in, along with the humidity. Having just showered, it was as though he had not even dried off, and his clothes were already moist with sweat.

Walking by himself, he had now gotten used to doing things on his own. The investigation had been underway for a couple of weeks and had a way of weeding out those who were his true friends. Oh, he didn't view everyone who shied away an enemy. Some were just intimidated and wished not to be associated with fallout around the whole thing. Others were right out homophobes and made no bones about it. He would walk by and hear the whispers, but others didn't hide it, and made it a point to call him a fag, homo, or queer. It was always some derogatory term, however, Noah started looking at it as a badge of honor. He decided not to take the bait knowing they were looking for a fight. It became so common, that it would be futile to try and take on everyone who thought they were being cute, or funny. Besides, if he did, it gave more fuel to the command as to why gays should not be in the Marine Corps. They called it a morale problem. The violence, the fighting, and the hate toward gays, from other Marines, proved it was not acceptable, or conducive to good morale and welfare. Rather than report it, Noah tried to ignore it, and remembered what the real threat was and avoided any situation that could prove to be confrontational.

He made it to the chow hall, through the line and now was looking for a place to sit. Normally he would be asked to have a seat, but now most turned a cold shoulder if he passed by. It reminded him how juvenile so-called adults could be. The not so cool kid in high school that no one wanted to sit at their table. So rather than be turned away, Noah found a table to himself. Almost finished with his meal, Monte and Fritz came through the line, and were looking for a seat. Seeing Noah had seats at his table, they came over and sat down. Not asking, they were not going to give him a chance to say no. Fritz was a good sport and knew of the contempt that was being shown to Noah. "Bitch, why didn't you tell us you were coming to chow? We could of came over together?" He was straight, but was a lone wolf, and a very independent free thinker. He did not like what was happening. It was common for him to talk back if he heard one of the derogatory comments about Noah in his presence.

No sooner than they had sat, a couple of guys walked by. Noah had never seen them before. "Let's get the fuck out of here, I see the freak show is in town!" and walked on. It didn't go unnoticed by Davis. He stood up and turned toward them, "Hey you!" The guys stopped and turned back, Davis continued, "The only freak I know is your girl, when I was fucking her!" The tables around overheard, and a few gasps were heard. Davis was calling the two out. The one looked around and hesitated before responding. "Yeah, … whatever, keep hanging with your fag buddy." They gave Davis the finger, turned and moved on. Davis continued to stand, before he heard Noah speaking, "Davis, come on man, let it go! Just ignore'm. They're not worth it." Davis slowly turned back before sitting down, as Noah apologized. "It ain't the first-time man, and it won't be the last, I'm just sorry you guys had to experience it." Monte was wired now as well. "Fuck them assholes! I'm so fucking sick of all this bullshit, who gives a fuck?" Noah just shook his head in disbelief and decided to make light of the situation. "That one in the front was cruising me, I guess he wanted my attention. If I had known he was going to get nasty about it, I would of gave him my number…" Davis wasn't sure how to take what Noah just said, "Oh girl you better control yourself." The seriousness of the moment was broken, and the table broke out in a laugh.

The three finished up and headed back to the barracks. On the way back, Davis asked, "When's the last time you been out?" knowing Noah had been staying in the barracks and isolating. He didn't want the harassment, along with the fear of his every move being followed, he figured he might as well isolate and stay in. Noah smirked, "It's been a couple of weeks." The three decided they would head out to Kenville later that evening for a few drinks. The time on the island was growing short, and so was the opportunity to enjoy all it had to offer. It would do him some good to get out.

He had traded a few messages with Marcus, via Monte, and a few other friends at the chow hall where Marcus worked. He had seen him a couple of times in line serving food, but they didn't speak. They would acknowledge each other with a nod and an extended glance. Noah thought it was amazing how a thousand words could be exchanged in one look. Marcus's time on the island was growing short and soon he would be rotating back stateside. Noah figured whatever had begun of their relationship, was now probably behind them. Although he thought about defying the order of no contact or communication, he knew the risks were too great for either to take. A nod at the chow hall would suffice for now. He couldn't help but wonder how much longer this investigation would go on. He was contemplating re-enlisting, but now wasn't sure. Even if he was cleared, was this an environment he wanted to stay in. They sure didn't welcome his kind. If he re-enlisted, he would still have to hide his identity.

Noah woke from a late afternoon nap, showered, and made himself ready for the evening. Casual was the attire for the night. He still had to conform to Marine Corp standards, so no flip-flops. A shirt with collar, closed toe shoes, and belt were required even in shorts. Noah was finishing up when Fritz and Monte showed up. Fritz seeing Sergeant Fisher across the hall in the cubicle across from Noah, decided to be sarcastic. "Oh girl, don't you look mighty fine! Give me a kiss!" He looked back over to Fisher. "There motherfucker, go report that shit. I saw that female investigator bitch. I'd like for her to investigate me, … I'll fuck her." Fritz had gotten Fisher's attention, giving him a snarly look, he got up and moved. Noah spoke up. "Fritz, chill man, if he goes to the CO, I'll be the one to get in trouble." Davis looked back at Noah, "I'm serious, I'd like to fuck that investigator bitch." Noah, along with Monte, rolled their eyes and chuckled. "You ain't right man."

Sergeant Fisher hearing the laughs, got up from the cubicle and left. Noah concerned, "Seriously Fritz, they can take away my libo, or put charges against me for harassing him." Fritz had moved on. "Come on bitch you ready? We gots to go." Noah locked up his wall locker and the three were out the door.

Kenville was hopping. Saturday nights were always busy. As they walked down the main street, Noah observed all the happenings taking place. Stopping at one of the local restaurants and getting some fresh hibachi squid, they made a feast of it. Once finished, they stopped at a pirated cassette tape shop, looking at some compilations. Noah was bent over the counter perusing, when the door opened, and Marcus came in. Monte, standing next to Noah, wasn't sure if Noah had seen him and nudged him to look over. Noah looked up, did he dare say anything, or ignore him? Davis seeing him, "Lord the children are up in here tonight!" and gave a mocking face. He walked over to Marcus, and exchanged a halfhearted high five, which was more of a hand slap. Marcus laughed. "What's up Fritz?" Fritz chuckled, "Notta, just hanging out with your gurl over there. Look at her, ain't she sweet!" Marcus chuckled, Fritz was always so out there and wound up, no one ever knew how to respond. Fritz decided to take advantage of the moment and hollered over to Noah. "Oh guuurl! Now you know you two ain't getting out of here without talking." He nudged Marcus, "Now, go on over there and give your gurl a hug. You know you want to, go on, ain't nobody going to say shit." Marcus wasn't sure how to read Noah and moved begrudgingly toward him. Monte went over by the door and stood, to keep an eye out. The only people in the store were the three of them, and the owner.

Noah gave Marcus a hug. "Why do I get the feeling this was a set up?" Marcus laughed. "Monte stopped by this afternoon, and we worked it out. We figured if we said anything you wouldn't go for it. You, ok?" Noah looked over at Monte and Davis, with a happy smirk. "Yeah, I'm good. Thanks for coming out. How you been?" Marcus smiled, "I'm doing fine. They called me in a couple of times wanting me to talk. I just kept quiet and said nothing. That Hermansen is an ass though. He tries to grandstand; he obviously doesn't have anything, otherwise he would quit asking. He keeps telling me he's going to get me thrown out." Noah, watching the door, "I know, he has tried the same with me. Just keep saying nothing!" Marcus changed the subject. "Well, I got orders finally. I'm leaving the beginning of June. …thirty days leave back home in Pennsylvania, before I have to report in." Noah was confused. "I thought they wouldn't transfer you if you are being investigated?" Marcus laughed sarcastically. "Oh, they are transferring me, but get this, NIS, is sending a package to my new command informing them of my case. Nothing like going to a new command, checking in, saying "Hi, I'm the gay guy you have heard so much about." Noah chuckled in agreement. "I know this whole thing is just insane. Where did you get orders to? And more importantly, am I going to get to see you again before you go?" Marcus sighed, "Yes, but I don't know how. I'll be going to Bridgeport, California, Mountain Warfare Training Center," Noah not hearing of it before. "Where the hell is Bridgeport California?" Marcus chuckled, "I know right, …It's up north, on the California-Nevada border. Close to Lake Tahoe, I'm told it's isolated." Noah thought for a minute. "Well, it's California, where I'll be, once I get back. Maybe we'll be able to meet up!" Marcus liked the idea. "I think we can figure it out, I have never been down to southern California. I can't wait, woo-hoo!" Noah changed back to the here and now. "As for here, before you go, I might be able to figure something out. You able to make it to Foster?" Marcus's eyes lit up. "Yeah, I think I have to go to the JRC down there when I leave the island." It clicked in Noah's mind. "Look, Glenn and Lilly have their place out in town. I can get you their address. I think we can work something out with them, without being seen." The door opened and a few Marines came in. … Noah looked at Marcus, smiled. "We got this. I'll be in touch, stay strong. If anything changes or you need to get a hold of me, call Monte." Marcus stayed behind looking at cassettes as the three took off. At the door, Noah turned to find Marcus looking back at him. He smiled and gave a thumbs up and was out the door.

The three lingered around Kenville, bar hopping as the night moved on. Coming out of the Moonlight lounge, Noah noticed the two guys from chow hall. The ones that called them freaks. They were with a group of four or five Marines. The one saw Noah and tapped his buddy on the shoulder and pointed to him. Noah didn't turn away, but gave a stare, only to be returned with a finger coming from one guy. The other one grabbing a handful of his own crotch and shaking it at Noah.

They were far enough away he couldn't hear what they were saying, but figured it was best. He could only imagine, as they pointed towards him, causing the rest of the group to turn and look his way. Davis and Monte were slightly behind him coming out of the bar. Noah, not wanting any confrontation, quickly directed them away before they could see what was going on. The three ended up at one of Fritz's favorite clubs, "The Ken Blue." It was a "buy me drinky" bar.

Upon entering, the girls all gathered around, they knew Fritz. He wasn't the most handsome guy, and the attention, whether real or bought was welcomed. They hung out for a couple of drinks and danced a few songs with the girls. Davis was now in a booth with his favorite girl. Noah and Monte were both ready to head out, when a friend of Monte's showed up. Seeing Monte, he came over. "I've been looking for you?" Monte jokingly spoke. "Damn, I thought I had gotten away from you." And acted like he was going to walk away, before stopping and giving him a hug. Noah was familiar with the guy. He was in their unit, working in admin. His name was David, and he and Monte had a thing going on since back in the states. Noah exchanged greetings but, figured this would be an all-night thing and decided it was time to bail. He made his rounds saying goodbye and headed back to base.

Making it through the gate, he decided to take a short cut, through the supply area, to save time and make it back quickly. He made it past the supply buildings and nature called, he needed to take a leak. Man, he should have used the restroom before leaving the bar. There was a wooded area just past the buildings, not so well lit, so he made his way off the road and slipped into the woods. Doing his business, he hurried back out to the road. Just as he passed by the supply building, from out of nowhere, he heard voices and turned to see a group of guys walking his way. He went ahead and started walking along the roadside. Before too long he could hear them getting closer. Then a cringe ran down Noah's spine, as heard from behind, "Hey, isn't that the faggot?" Noah didn't turn around, he was by himself, and picked up the pace. Within a second or two, he heard footsteps running up behind him. Now under a streetlight, one of the guys had caught up to him, and was walking backwards hollering back, "Yeah, it's the faggot ya'll." The rest of the crew had ascended upon him, Noah was stopped in his tracks. Trying to keep anyone from coming up on his back, he turned to face them. It was the guys from the chow hall. The one spoke, "Where's your little bitches? … What, they leave your ass behind?" Noah, didn't know what to expect, knew he was outnumbered, and tried to defuse the situation. "Look, I don't want any trouble." The outspoken one was a white guy, about Noah's height, light brown hair, with a muscular build. He chuckled, "Well fag, you should've thought about that before you decided to become a dick sucker!" Noah, looking around, tried backing up a bit as they moved in on him. These guys were serious. He needed to think of something quick. They had every intention of beating the shit out of him, if not kill him. He looked past them to see if anyone was coming, or within hearing distance. Nothing in either direction. He put his arms and hands up trying to keep them at a distance and moved slowly backwards. Before he knew what had happened, a couple of the guys grabbed him from behind and pulled his arms back. He started yelling for help. One of the guys socked him in the mouth, knocking a tooth loose. "Shut the fuck up!" Noah hollered out only to be hit again. Another grabbed his head and put his hand over his mouth. The others started kicking and punching him wherever they could. Noah tried to break free; kicking a couple of them allowed him to break loose, but only briefly. He tried to run, before being caught again, and this time knocked to the ground. The mouthy guy seemed to be the one leading the lynching. "Hold him down." The guys pinned Noah's arms and legs to the ground. The mouthy one straddled over him and started undoing his pants. Noah tried to shake his head, before it was pinned and gagged by a hand. The mouthy one pulled out his dick, kneeled and tried shoving his cock in Noah's face. "You want a dick, faggot, is that what you want?" The others coaxed him on, while laughing. Noah tried to squirm away, as they all started laughing. The one's hand slipped off Noah's mouth and he spoke out. "Go ahead you prick!" as he spit at the guy "…Do it, …you'll never do it again," He looked at him in defiance, and did an intentional laugh. "…Look at you, …is that all you got, that little mother fucker. I thought a guy like you would have so much more. …Hah, I thought you were a man, … I've seen bigger dicks on a gnat! …Hah, Hah... Come on, do it! I'll bite that fucker off!" Then BAM! A backhand landed across Noah's face, throwing his head back to the ground. He was bleeding from his mouth, and now had ringing in his ears. Blood was all over his face. The mouthy one got back up and kicked him in the groin, which started a kicking frenzy, with the others taking their turns. Noah, now curled in a fetal position, was no longer aware of what was taking place. He felt a few kicks to his back, and ribs, before a blow to the head again. Looking out he saw the blades of grass and feet moving around in front of him. Not able to raise his head, he became nauseous, dizzy, and faded to black. He now lay unconscious. The guys continued to kick him before one spoke up. "Man, I think we killed him." They stopped and stared at him lying there motionless. A few minutes went by, before they started discussing what they should do with him. Deciding to pull his body off into the wooded area, they left him lay. They looked around making sure no one had seen them and took off.

Noah wasn't sure how long he had been lying there before coming back around. He tried sitting up, but the pain in his stomach from being kicked grabbed a hold immediately putting him back down. He rolled over on his side, and looked around, he could barely see out of his right eye. He raised his hand up to his head, feeling the swollen area and crusted blood. He rolled completely over on all fours and tried standing again. First getting up to his knees, and then standing completely. His left shoulder was sprained and hurt badly if he tried to raise it. Still nauseous, he stumbled a few steps and threw up. Bent over he waited a moment, before getting the will to stand again. He made it to the edge of the woods and stopped. He did not want to take a chance of these assholes still being in the area. Noah was convinced it was their intent to kill him. He did not want to come out until he was sure no one was around, and he was safe. Looking around, he finally stepped out of the woods and stumbled along, stopping every so often due to the overwhelming pain. He would gain his composure, and breath, before moving again. It seemed like it took forever to make it to the barracks.

It was well late into the night, if not early morning when he stumbled onto the front steps of the barracks. He laid there just a few moments before passing out. He was awakened, being carried in by Fritz, and a couple of other guys from the motor pool. The duty had found him passed out on the steps and got concerned because of the blood soaked, torn up, and soiled clothing. The duty recognized him and got Fritz, knowing they worked and hung out together. Fritz had already made it back from out in town, and was surprised, assuming Noah was in his rack asleep. They took him in the head and sat him down on the sinks.

The duty started to call the MPs before he was stopped by Fritz. "No man chillout. We got this, …don't even log it in." He grabbed a cloth, wetted it, and started wiping the blood from Noah's face. Noah, overhearing it, "Thanks Fritz, I don't need another investigation." Fritz was concerned. "Man, whoever did this, really fucked you up!" Noah was totally aware of what Fritz had just said and got pissed. "It ain't whoever man, …It was the asshole from the chow hall. The one that called us freaks. Him and his cronies, they did this." Fritz was not surprised, "I knew I shouldn't have let you take off on your own." Noah laughed, "I know, … you dick, it's all your fault." Fritz laughed knowing Noah was being sarcastic. "Oh, gurl you're still the sweet one." Huck was still in the restroom watching on when Davis asked him to get some ice. Huck took off.

Noah started telling Fritz what he could remember. Fritz was concerned, some of the injuries were serious, and maybe even a concussion. The gash by his eye, and the protruding lip would probably need to have some stitches. "Man, you are going to need to go to see the Doc." Noah immediately refused it, before thinking a bit longer. "Get Nelson, get Doc Nelson, the corpsman, he's cool, you understand. He can help. He lives in the barracks next door." Davis, shook his head, "You got it man." About that time, Huck came back in with an ice bag. Fritz took and held it up to Noah's eye, as he flinched. It was now completely swollen shut. He sent Huck to fetch Doc Nelson the Corpsman. Huck was reluctant. "Man, the lights are all out, do you know what time it is? I don't even know where his rack is." Fritz, agitated at Huck's remarks, "Who gives a fuck? Figure it out man, he's got to have some help." Huck took off.

Within minutes Corpsman Nelson walked in the restroom. "What the fuck happened to you?" Noah grinned and ouched at the same time. "It's a long story Doc …you're familiar with what's been going on with me?" Doc was aware of Noah being investigated for being gay. "Don't tell me somebody beat you up over that shit?" Noah chuckled, "Well, let's just say not everyone is a fan." Doc started examining him, as Noah continued. "Listen Doc, I can't have this get out; this has got to remain silent. Can you help me?" Doc stopped examining him and stepped back, "Look we have got to get you in the Clinic, tonight! You are going to need stitches, …I can get you some pain meds there as well. That head, and ribs, have got to be x-rayed. I'm laying money on it that you have a concussion if you were throwing up." Noah confused, "So, what do we do Doc?" Doc, trying to put Noah at ease, and more concerned about getting him treated. "Look, I can keep it out of your medical record, but in order to get help, you have got to come into the clinic. I know the duty Corpsman, and Doctor. I'm quite sure if I tell them, they'll help us out." Noah, foggy and in pain, "I trust you Doc, thank you!" Fritz and the two others helped Noah out of the barracks. The duty agreed to keep it out of his logs. They got him into the duty vehicle and took him to the clinic. Getting out of the jeep he was now delirious but was thankful at the same time. As they put his arms over their shoulders to carry him in, Noah started to speak, "Thank you …" But was interrupted by Fritz. "Shut the fuck up man. You would do the same for us." Noah chuckled. "You sure about that?"

After a full checkup and X rays, the Doc had Noah on his way back to recovery. He had been beaten up badly. A concussion, bruised ribs, a few stitches on the inside of his lip, and a sling for his arm. The eye was swollen and would need to be monitored as the swelling went down. He had lost his glasses and a new pair would need to be ordered. The doctor wanted Noah to report it to the MPs, but after hearing Noah's plea, he agreed to go along with it on one condition; he did not develop any further complications. For now, the story would be he fell from a bike ride. After two days of bedrest, he would need to return for a follow up.

It was mid-morning before the crew had Noah back to the barracks. On his way in, the stares and rumors began to fly. Noah didn't give a shit. He was tired and ready to hit the rack. The two days of bedrest were much needed. With no one around the barracks, it gave Noah plenty of time to sleep, rest, and recover.

The next morning brought on the full effect of his injuries. The pain, and soreness could be felt all over. His emotions surged. One-minute anger and another sorrow. He contemplated going to the authorities. These guys deserved to be punished and it should not go unnoticed. However, if he went to the authorities, once again, they might or might not prosecute them. The accusers in these situations were usually harassed by the authorities, and often discredited. It was understood, or the unspoken word, if you were gay, you got what you deserved. All the traditional views, against man and nature, and, of course, against God and religion, tended to prevail. These guys were just doing what was natural to protect themselves, God, and their way of life. This had been taught to them their entire life, and it was deeply rooted in their being. Forget Noah's rights. Forget the beating. It's not a crime, if it is done to a homosexual. After all, that was the only real crime to be found here and that made it alright. Even if the guys were reprimanded, it would go down as another reason why gays should not be allowed to serve. It upset the morale of the troops, so much that they had to take actions into their own hands. Even if he spoke out, the leadership needed in the command was not there to support him. He finally concluded; he'll stay silent, and not go to the command, but it would not go unpunished. He just hadn't figured out what to do, yet.

The two days of bedrest went by quickly. He was given the ok to go back to work, but would be on light duty for two weeks, and needed to return for a follow up. The good side was the bike story seemed to be holding.

On his way out of the Doctors office, he was surprised to find Marcus at the front desk. This was the first time seeing him since all this had taken place. Noah, was hesitant to acknowledge him, nodded his head and went on out the door. Once outside, Noah heard the door fling open. Marcus's voice came from behind. "Noah, …Noah, …would you stop? I know you can hear me." Noah stopped and turned to face him. Marcus came up. "I know what happened, I saw Monte and Davis. They have been keeping me posted. I'm so sorry, no one deserves this!" Noah smiled, "Thanks, I appreciate it." Although Noah was smiling, Marcus could see the pain, both emotional and physical that he was experiencing. "Do you know the guys who did it?" Noah nodded his head yes. "Yeah, from the chow hall. I don't know them by name, but somehow they know about me and what's been going on." Marcus took a breath, "Ugh, …yeah, I might be able to help with that. I think they are in my unit. If it is the same ones, they have harassed me. …But nothing like what they have done to you." Noah eyes lit up. "Why do you think it's them?" Marcus continued, "One of the guys in my unit, told me he overheard a couple of them bragging about it. Bragging, they beat the fuck out of the fag, who hangs around with Romano. He came to me worried. Wanted to know if it was true and thought they might try and do something to me." Noah concerned. "Have they tried to do anything?" Marcus smirked, "Here you are fucked up, and wondering if they have done anything to me. No, not really, the one threw me up against the wall locker, and called me a fag, but walked on. His name is Benson. He's a Corporal in legal with my unit. He's a bit of a loudmouth, and a homophobe. To be honest, I think he is a closet case." Noah chuckled, "Yeah, it sounds like one of the guys. If it's the one I'm thinking of, you're right. If I didn't know better, I would say he is a closet case. I've thought it every time I've seen him. I don't even know the guy. Before all this happened, I mean before I even knew you, I would catch him staring at me. You now, like he was cruising me. I've seen him at the gym, and at the chow hall. He followed me into the gym locker rooms one time. I almost said something because he made me uncomfortable." Marcus frowned. "Figures, always one of our own, that gets caught up in this shit. Who do you blame, him or society? Him, because he is so fucking scared of what society thinks, so he represses his own sexuality. He doesn't have the courage to face it, so he tries to destroy it and make it go away" Marcus struck a nerve with Noah. He wasn't feeling the same. "Fuck that bullshit! I blame him. Fuck the psycho analysis shit! We all have issues dealing with this, but to gang fuck someone and beat the shit out of them… Don't make excuses, because there isn't an excuse! Whatever he is, I don't care! You don't do this to another human being, to anyone!" Marcus, backtracked. "Sorry, that wasn't what I was wanting to say. I'm just saying, if you want their names, I think I can get them for you, at least a couple of them." Noah calmed a bit realizing this whole thing brought out strong emotions. "Look, I know you're trying to help. I'm not hollering at you. I'm not mad at you. I'm pissed about the situation. Ok?" Marcus with a stern face stared him straight in the eye. "I know." Noah broke the stare and looked around. He had gotten so engrossed in the conversation, that he lost track of his surroundings, and track of time. If NIS had seen the two talking, they could be in trouble, but he didn't care. He grabbed Marcus by the shoulder. "Look, I know you're trying to help. I appreciate it. Yes, if you can get me any names, that will be great. I don't know what I'm going to do yet. But I can assure you, this isn't over." Noah let go of his shoulder and turned and walked away.

The next two weeks went by, Noah returned to sick bay. His eye was almost completely back to normal, but his front tooth would need some work. Other than some signs of bruising, he was returned to full duty.

Making it back to the Motor Pool, he checked in with the Staff Sergeant and gave him the news. What perfect timing he sarcastically thought, when the Staff Sergeant informed him that the entire Battalion had a surprise physical fitness test. Shit just keeps happening. It was being conducted in a week. It was one of the series of obligations to be done prior to their rotation back to the states. Finished with the Staff Sergeant, he headed back to the tool room. Fritz came in. "So, what's up Bitch?" Noah shrugged, "Notta. Got the ok to return to full duty." Davis grinned and walked over to him. "You go gurl!" Raising his hand, he high fived Noah. "I saw those motherfuckers at chow this morning." Davis had Noah's attention. "Yeah, they say anything?" Davis proudly spoke, "No, but I did! Fuck'm," as he grinned and sat on the edge of the desk. "It wasn't just me. It was me, Mallard, Loose, Guiterez, Baxter, Monte, and Huck, pretty much Motor-T. We were all sitting together and were almost finished when those asses came in and sat down. I pointed out to the guys; those were the jerks who had done all the bullshit to you. Mallard, got pissed and got up, told everyone to cover his back. So, we all got up and walked over to the table. We surrounded it. Mallard started in, "So, you're the bad asses, beating up a guy by himself." The mouthy one started to stand up, before Mallard pushed his shoulder, and told him to sit the fuck down. He sat there, as Mallard told him, "We know what you did, don't think we have forgotten. If we find you even coming close to him, or anyone of us again, it won't be one you're dealing with, you'll be dealing with us all. You may think you got away with it for now, but I can assure you, you haven't. Oh, by the way, go try and report us. I'm sure they'll be glad to ask you questions about our buddy's medical record. Speaking of that, what's in your medical record?" Mallard walked away. "I told him Karma is a bitch. That Mother fucker was shit'en in his pants." Noah laughed, "Holy fucking shit. I wish I could have seen his face. ...Man, the guys did that for me?" Noah paused for a moment, getting a bit emotional, "Seriously, ...Man that gets to me." Davis noticed. "Oh gurl, don't be so sensitive!" He got up and laughed. Noah chuckled along with him. "I still haven't thought of a way to get these guys. I've been thinking, sometimes, there is no revenge, sometimes, there is no hero. Sometimes life sucks and assholes get away with it, Fritz. I don't want anybody fighting my battle, you get me. I just don't see where it ends. They did this to me, we go and fuck them up, and then what? I appreciate what everybody has done, especially you. Man, you have stood by my side, but I can't allow this shit to go on any further. Someone is going to get hurt or killed. We're not gangs man, we're Marines. Let Karma work this shit out." Davis paused, giving Noah an ambiguous glare, before walking out.

Chapter 23

A Bad Goodbye

The work week went by quickly and remained quiet with no major incidents, NIS had not called, and there were no flare ups or agitations. Thursday evening was field day at the barracks, and Monte came into his cubicle with a note from Marcus. He would be leaving for Camp Foster to the Joint Reception Center, in the morning. He wanted to meet up with Noah and say goodbye in person. With field day not getting over until late, and having a PFT the next morning, Noah needed to figure out how he could swing it. He couldn't just show up at his barracks, NIS was watching, and they were still not to have any communication. Noah got Monte to relay the message to him to meet at 10pm at the sports field, behind his barracks. Field days always seem to take forever. No one really wanted to do them, and they dragged out, sometimes all night. Noah waited anxiously to pass the inspection and get out. Once the ok was given, Noah was gone and out of the barracks. The sports field was big, a couple of baseball diamonds and a football field combined. There were bleachers, several restrooms, huts, and dugouts. It was lit up in the evenings for those wanting to use it.

Noah was not sure where Marcus would be. It was a few minutes before 10pm when he arrived. Wearing PT gear, just in case anyone was to ask, he came out for a late-night jog. He walked onto the field, looked around, and did not see anyone. He did a slight jog, ending up by the dug outs. An MP patrol car drove by slowly. Noah, trying to not look suspicious, did a light jog back up the field again, while the MP car looked on. The car left and Noah walked back to the dug outs, this time he went in and sat down. He sat there for a few minutes, starting to wonder if something happened, or maybe Marcus wasn't able to make it. He would give it a few more minutes, then he was heading back home. While sitting there, from behind the cinder block wall of the dugout, Noah heard Marcus's voice but could not see him. "Give me a few minutes and meet me in the restroom at the end of the field." Noah did not say anything, but looked over toward the restrooms, and watched as Marcus went in. He sat and waited before getting up. He walked to the end of the dugout and looked around. He did not see anyone. As he began to exit, the overhead field lights went out, and it was now dark out. The moonlight took over and the stars were now visible in the sky. Noah slowly walked behind the dugout and headed to the restrooms. One final look before he went inside.

Marcus was standing by a urinal acting like he was using it, just in case it was not Noah who walked in. Seeing Noah, he quickly broke free and ran to give him a hug. The two held their embrace not letting go and saying nothing. All seemed well just for a moment. Marcus, shed a tear, "I didn't think I would be able to say goodbye." Noah shushed him, "It ok, I'm here now." They stood quietly for some time. Before Noah noticed a light flash from the outside. Oh shit, someone was coming. He let go of Marcus, "Hey someone is out there." The two stood quietly, trying to listen. A small window showed a flash of light again. Then they heard voices. It was coming from the women's side of the restrooms. Whoever it was, was just outside.

Noah held his finger up to his lips, signaling for Marcus to keep quiet. He then motioned for him to follow. As they got close to the door, they could hear the voices clearly. "Man, I told you we should have locked these up earlier, now I can't see shit. You got the keys for these locks." Noah slowly peeked outside, and could not see who it was, but seen the MP car, parked just beyond the restroom. Shit, it was the MPs, and they were locking up the restrooms. If the two of them did not get out, they ran the risk of being caught together, or being locked up in the restroom all night. If the MPs caught them in there, it would look too suspicious. Two guys in a dark restroom late at night. They might just call their names in or create a log. If so, NIS would have record of the two of them being together. They had to get out now.

Noah looked out again, this time to see where they could run to without being seen. The nearest thing was the bleachers, if they could make it there, they could hide under them without being seen. Noah heard the voices again. "I got this one man. Go ahead and check out the men's side, before we lock it up. You have to make sure no one is in there." Noah looked at Marcus, and whispered, "We got to run for it. No matter what, don't look back. We'll get through this."

Noah peeked out quickly, no one was there, and took off in a full sprint. He headed to the bleachers. Once there he slid down, like he was sliding into home plate. He rolled up under them and Marcus was right behind him. The two low crawled until they were far enough under them to not be seen. On their stomachs they looked out and could barely hear the MPs. One was shining his light over in their direction. "Did you hear that man. It sounded like someone was hitting the deck or some shit." He pointed his flashlight out over the bleachers, looking around. The other one stood quietly as they listened for noise. The one carrying the light came over by the bleachers and stopped again, listening. Noah and Marcus ducked their heads and got as low to the ground as possible. The MP bent down and flashed his light up under the bleachers. Noah and Marcus were facing each other and could look into each other's eyes. There was no panic, both smiling as the flashlight loomed over them. Finally, the MP moved on, "I don't think it was anything, if it was, they are gone now. Come on. …get this thing locked up and get outta here."

They two MPs finished and were gone. Noah and Marcus chuckled, and then started laughing, how crazy this was and what they were going through. They continued to lay under the bleachers for some time, holding each other, until early morning light before emerging. Both said their goodbyes for now but, this would not be their last.

It was Friday morning, and everyone was at the Battalion PT field, lined up and waiting for the whistle to blow, to begin their three-mile run. It was the second event of the Physical Fitness test. Having maxed out the pullups portion first, Noah and Davis were within the first few rows of runners. The whistle blew, and the runners were off. The course was comprised of a few roads on Camp Hansen and ended with a final lap around the PT track on the back side of the base. Once finished, they would be given a few minutes to catch their breath before doing the third portion, sit ups. Both had made it to the final track portion when Davis pulled ahead of the pack. Noah, seeing Davis pull away, expanded his stride, and soon both were out front in the lead. Davis was ahead, with Noah slightly behind, they came around the final bend. Noah looked back to see they were the only ones out front and had a significant lead. Davis came across the finish line first at 17 minutes. Noah was ten seconds slower at 17 minutes and 10 seconds. They were the first ones across and were cheered on by the personnel monitoring the event. They were directed over to the area where the sit-up portion was to be conducted.

It was a few minutes before some of the other Marines started arriving. They organized and were ready to do sit-ups. One guy would hold the feet and ankles, why the other did the sit-ups. Once finished, they changed over, and the other guy completed theirs. The max credit being given to 80 sit-ups completed within two minutes. Noah held the feet of a Marine he didn't know. The whistle blew and the guy began, down-up, down-up, down-up etc. The whistle blew and they changed over, and it was now Noah's turn. The command to begin was given and Noah kicked in. Down-up, down-up, down-up, so it went, until he completed the full 80 sit ups in a minute 20 seconds and waited for the whistle.

Noah started to get up, when he was halted by one of the monitors. It was Lieutenant Hummel, he worked at the S-4 and had been a witness at the Company Commanders office, when Noah's rights were read, and accusations were made. He was also the Officer in Charge of Sergeant Fisher, and the main one pushing the homosexual issue against Noah. Noah stood in place, as he approached. "How many sit-ups did you do?" A bit confused as to why he would need to know, Noah responded, "I did 80, Sir." He immediately asked who his partner was. Noah pointed to the Marine. The Lieutenant instructed the Marine, "Hold his feet again, I didn't see it. I'll count, you need to re-do them." Noah realized he was being harassed but had agreed to do them again. He sat down and the whistle blew and once again Noah kicked it as the Lieutenant counted. Down-up, down-up, down-up, every so often, he would tell Noah, "That one doesn't count." Noah hit 80 sit-ups at the 1-minute mark and stopped. The lieutenant was agitated, but there was nothing he could say. Noah stood up at attention and sarcastically asked,

"Does that do it for you, Sir?" The Lieutenant did not respond, but instead gave Noah an evil glare, turned and walked away.

Once the lieutenant had gone, Noah reported his numbers to the monitor who had observed what had taken place. "What the fuck did you do to him?" Noah looked on to where the Lieutenant was in the distance. "Not a damn thing, other than I merely exist." Noah signed the roster next to his name. "…some people are just that way." With the PFT behind them, they returned to work, only to be cut loose early.

Noah's weekend plans were already set in motion, and this allowed him to get to it. This was Marcus' last weekend on the island, and they were going to meet up at Glenn and Lilly's house. Keeping clandestine, it would have to appear as though they were not together and traveled separately. Marcus was leaving this morning and was already in route to begin his checkout at the JRC. Noah was taking the bus, and once there, would be on foot to Lilly and Glenn's place in the village of Kitamae. Being Marcus' schedule was unknown, they would play it by ear, and hopefully connect some time over the weekend. Noah made it to Glenn and Lilly's place and got settled in. Glenn spoke to Noah briefly, telling him he needed to talk to him about something, but was interrupted by Lilly, and her new friend Camille. Glenn went quiet and told him they could speak later. Camille was in the Air Force and was new to the island. She had been stationed at Kadina Air Force Base. Glenn told Noah he came clean with Lilly, on what was happening back in the states with her partner. He didn't want to be the one to tell but couldn't be the one who stood by and watched her being made a fool of. Regardless, Lilly was going to be on the island for a year, it was a bad goodbye for now, but with a year, things could change and might get better.

Not far from base, Glenn, and Lilly's one-bedroom apartment was large by Japanese standards. The building was a faded white, three-level complex, furnished, with no more than twelve apartments. Full of non-English speaking locals, Lilly, and Glenn, were the only Americans. They lived on the end; neighbors on one side, and a staircase going all the way up to the roof on the other. On a nice day, they would grab the boom box and cooler, and chill on the roof that overlooked the small village and ocean. Today was one of those days.

Glenn and Noah grabbed some drinks and music then headed to the roof. Glenn led the way through a maze of clotheslines, with white laundry flowing in the breeze, before the two made it to some chairs already in place. Glenn turned on some music, sat in the chair and looked out. Glenn was rattling about Lilly, and all she had been doing to get on his nerves. Noah leaned back and zoned off in thought. After chill'n for a few minutes, and small talk, the real reason Glenn wanted to come up to the roof came out. "Noey, I need to talk to you, and you have got to promise me you won't say a word, not even to Lilly." Glenn noticed Noah was not paying attention and poked him. "Noey!" Noah startled, "Oh my God! Are you still talking? I don't even know where this conversation is going. Ok, I guess, what is it?" Glenn hesitated, "No, I'm serious! You have got to tell me you won't say a word. Not to anyone, I mean no one."

Noah could tell something was really bothering him. He sat up in his chair and turned to him. "Not a problem, ok! I promise, but make it quick, you have been talking non-stop for the last twenty minutes." Glenn started in. "I got a letter from Charlie, back in the states. He says he has been diagnosed with the gay man's disease; you know that AIDS thing." Noah sat quietly listening. Charlie was Glenn's partner back in the states. Glenn had gone quiet, so Noah coaxed him on. "So, what are you saying Glenn?" Noah looked over at Glenn, and saw he had a tear coming down his check. This was so out of character for Glenn. Noah got up and moved down on one knee beside him, putting his hand on Glenn's knee. "It's alright Glenn, it'll be alright." Glenn sat for a moment, without saying a word, he grabbed a napkin off the cooler next to him and wiped the tears away. Embarrassed, he looked away from Noah. Glenn pushed him away. "I'll be fine, Noey." Noah figured it was time to just listen, and let Glenn talk, and say what he needed to say. Glenn finally decided to speak. "If he does have it, I'm sure I do too. How could I not? I don't know what I'm supposed to do. Do I go to sick bay? If I do, what do I tell them? How do I tell Lilly, and what will they say on base if I test positive and she doesn't?"

Noah sat and listened; he didn't have the answers. This was the closest the disease had come to hitting home. He had known others who had contracted the virus but didn't know the ins and outs of what happens to someone who gets it. Noah, for a lack of words, "I don't know Glenn, I don't know what happens." Glenn turned his thoughts to Charlie. "Charlie is in the hospital; this letter was written over a week ago. He says in the letter they don't give him much time. I don't know where he is or where to call or write. He says he wanted me to not worry about him, just that he wanted me to know, so I could get checked." Noah wanted to say something smart, something calming, to help Glenn, but was lost for words. "I think he's right; you're going to have to find out." Glenn was agitated by what Noah had to say. "What, find out, then what. They don't have a cure. So, find out that I have this crud and can't do anything about it." Glenn stood up, shaking his head in confusion, "… Fuck that! …Every fucking time I cough, every time I sneeze, every little bump, or rash, I'll freak out. No, I don't need to know." Noah stood up, "Glenn, …Glenn." Trying to get him to calm down, as Glenn went on. Finally, he yelled. "Stop it! …Stop it, damn it, just fucking stop it!" Glenn turned to him; he was quiet. "Look I don't know what the fuck is going to happen to you. Hell, you don't even know if you got it right now. How about calming down. If you do, then you'll know, and you can plan your life according. If not, you still do the same. Either way, at this point, you are going to always question whether you have it or not. So, don't let it rule you, find the fuck out. Don't live blindly, find the fuck out. If you like, we'll find out together. Know this, you are not alone; you hear me, you are not alone."

Glenn lowered his head and started crying. Seeing him break down, Noah wrapped his arms around him, and hugged him. Glenn needed a friend right now, and that's what mattered. The two remained on the roof for a while, finishing a few rounds, before they were joined by the ladies. Noah sat quietly as Glenn decided to tell Lilly. Lilly remained calm and asked many of the same questions and experienced the same confusion. But in the end, she was going to stand by Glenn's side. Things went well with her, after the tears they cried. Noah stayed the weekend, listening to Glenn, and calming him down.

Before leaving, the three had come up with a plan, on how to go forward. Glenn had agreed to get tested, and Lilly would be there for him, both for the testing and results. When Noah arrived back in the states, he would contact Charlie for Glenn, and let him know he was getting tested, and would send notification when he found out the results. Noah waited to hear from Marcus, before leaving back to Camp Hansen late Sunday evening. He gave Glenn and Lilly hugs saying goodbye. Whatever problems seemed to be going on in Noah's life, just seemed to be dwarfed, and was nothing compared to Glenn facing the fight of his life.

The last few weeks on the island went fast. Finally, the day came for the flight home. The motor pool crew was now headed out of the waiting area, on to the runway. Taking inventory of all the things that had taken place, since his arrival. He was not the same person, who arrived at this island. It had been a long tour. So many things had happened, and so many things had changed. The death of Morello, the investigation, and the relationship with Marcus was up in the air. Strumen was over, and the final goodbye lay just ahead. The AID's thing was growing more and more prevalent, and he had a feeling Glenn was just the beginning. Noah made it up to the top of the ladder well and took one final look around. He was now standing jaded, worn, and confused. He was beaten and torn, and no longer naive, and feeling robbed of his innocence. He had no idea what life held for him. The next few months would be challenging and could go in so many directions. He spoke out. "Goodbye Okinawa." He turned and stepped inside the plane.

Chapter 24

Cushy Tushy

Since his return to Oceanside, a lot had changed. He found his car was being held ransom by some auto shop Strumen had left it to be repaired and never returned to get it. In order to get it back, Noah had to pay the repair bill, along with the storage fee. Strumen had long moved on and already had another guy living with him. As far as Noah was concerned, it was "Goodbye and Good Riddance." The only thing that concerned him, was he felt sorry for the new guy he was with. Noah really felt Strumen was mentally unstable and needed help but could only hope this new guy would never experience what Noah had gone through. Noah was back to living in the barracks and didn't mind. After some coercion between mutual friends, the two had a brief interaction, long enough to get belongings. Thank goodness Glenn was already back when the time came and wouldn't allow Noah to go it alone. Glenn and Lilly had returned early from their tour in Oki. Once Glenn was diagnosed with HIV, the Japanese had strict guidelines, and would not allow them to stay on the island. So, they were transferred back to southern California. There was no tell, tell signs. He looked healthy, he was a bit thin, but Glenn maintained himself. If one didn't know better, they would just assume he might be working out a bit too much. Physically, he hadn't begun to show any signs.

It was Friday night, and the air felt a bit cool blowing in with the T-tops off. Glenn and Noah were cruising the pier. The two were just finishing a tour of cruising the strip and pulled over in front of the Capri Lounge. The night was getting chilly, Noah hopped out leaving the car running, opened the trunk grabbing one of the tops and began attaching it back on the car. Glenn was sitting in the car reached over and turned the music down. It caught Noah's attention, when he heard Glenn holler. "Hey yah Bitch!" Noah looked up from what he was doing to see Champagne, along with another, appear from the Capri, and were now on the sidewalk smoking a cigarette.

Noah grinned, "Haaay guuurl." Champagne was wearing dark sunglasses, lowered them, and looked at the two. She clutched her chest and gasped in surprise. This was the first time Noah had seen her since the humiliating fiasco on base.

She quickly came over to the car and Noah walked around to greet her. Glenn opened the door and got out. Champagne gave Glenn a slight grasp on the shoulder and mock kisses on each cheek, "Mwah, Mwah," before doing the same to Noah. Noah had gotten a bit too close and bumped her check. "Mind the makeup honey, it takes Momma a good hour to put this pancake on." She chuckled and grabbed a tissue from her clutch purse and dabbed Noah's cheek removing the dark makeup, before pulling out a compact and touching up her own makeup. "Honey a gurl has gotta do, what a gurl has gotta do!"

Once finished, she gave full attention back to the two. Immediately she looked at Noah, "Honey, how are you? I have not seen you since that God awful day up on base!" Noah didn't know what to say. "I'm doing well, we made it back from the West Pack Tour." Without saying too much, "I got put under investigation for being gay. But they tell me it's not going to stick, because they have found no reason to believe the accusation." Noah's comments hit a nerve with Champagne. "Child don't believe anything they say. Once NIS gets you in their target, they don't let go until they get you out."

Noah changed the topic "So how have you been, what happened after that day on base? Champagne, I'm so sorry what happened to you. I stood there so dumbfounded and helpless, …and they pushed …" Champagne interrupted, "Hush Child, no need to relive it! You don't owe me an apology, those motherfuckers up there on that base, The United States Marine Corps, they're the ones who owe me an apology. Child, I saw you that day. I was about to collapse, until I saw you. I knew someone else here was just like me. Not everyone was against me. Seeing you gave me the courage to raise my head and stand proud. Remember, they only have the power over you that you allow them. They tried their best to set me aside, humiliate me, but I thought fuck these motherfuckers. Show them what a proud black queen is. Show'em a proud trans-gender woman, and show them what a proud, gay, outstanding Marine is." Noah asked, "Are you doing alright?" Champagne lit a cigarette and looked away seeing a couple of Marines walking her way, when she pushed her glasses back to her face.

As the Marines walked by, they stared at the group. One made a cat call, thinking Champagne was a girl. "Look at the tushy and the cushy on that one!" Champagne paused, wondering if they would approach her. Once they passed, Champagne motioned for Glenn and Noah to follow. "Child, step over here, it's too bright and I don't want them to see me in this bright light." They moved into a dim lit cubby hole of one of the closed stores. Champagne looked up the street seeing if the Marines might turn around and come back. "Shit, Cushy and Tushy, come on back little boys. Let Momma show you the cookies. For fifty dollars, shit otherwise shut the fuck up." Champagne turned back to Noah, "Child I'm doing alright, having a hard time finding legit work. I miss my Staff Sergeant pay. They gave me a court martial, 6, 6, and a kick. Six months in the brig, six months forfeiture of pay, and a dishonorable discharge. So now if I apply for a job and they do a background check, boom immediately not qualified. I keep hoping something will change, but you never know." Noah curious, "What about your family, don't you have anyone back home?" "Child, I was rejected by my family years ago. I don't even know if my momma is still alive. The only one who helps me is Ms. Dee, and Violet, at the hotel. If it wasn't for them, child I'd be on the street."

She paused to take a quick glance out of the cubby hole, when she turned back "You all gotta go!" She gave them a hug, "Now, you know Momma loves the children, now go before Cushy and Tushy get here. I don't want them to be afraid to talk to me. You know some guys won't talk to a group." Noah, realizing he left his car running, "Shit…!" and he took off as Glenn moseyed behind. Noah finished putting the T-tops on, and before he got in the car, he looked over to Champagne. She spoke up just loud enough for them to hear. "You take care of yourself baby brother, don't you give up. Make them prove it. Stand your ground and be a proud Marine. We aren't no second-class citizens." Champagne glanced to see the boys cross the street. "Now go, child I might have scored a trick for the evening." Noah hopped in the car and the two waved, as Glenn hollered out, "You go girl!" As they pulled away.

With the tops back on, they turned the music up and jammed. Back down by the pier, and down by the beach, Oceanside was happening. Noah told Glenn about back home when he was in high school. He and his buddies all had cars and would meet and cruise what they called the L. It was more to show off their cars, but the unspoken motive was a chance to meet and talk to the girls. Glenn laughed, "They didn't know you was a homo?" Noah smirked, "Hell Glenn, I don't think I knew I was a homo…" Glenn being a bit of a smart ass, "Child they must be some really backwoods folks." Noah surprised at Glenn's comment. "Why would you say that?" Glenn snapped his head directly at Noah, "Child one look at you, how could they not know, YOU'RE A FLAMING QUEEN!" and laughed at his own joke. Noah was tickled at how proud Glenn was at his own comment, and it was nice to see him laugh.

The two completed a lap and were now back in front of the Capri lounge. Glenn told Noah to slow down, he wanted to see if Champagne was still around. As they passed slowly by, Glenn spoke out, "Oh my God, is she doing what I think she's doing?" Noah tried to pay attention to the road and look at the same time. He noticed Champagne and a guy in the cubby hole. She was facing one corner bent over, back to the street, and it looked as though the guy was screwing her from behind. Champagne turned and noticed them, as the guy was going at it. She stuck her hand out behind her motioning for them to move on. Glenn turned to Noah, "Child go!" Noah sped up and turned at the corner to do another tour, when Glenn chuckled and started laughing, "Oh no she didn't, Noey she was fucking the child right there in that cubby hole. Right out in public. How can she do that, ain't she afraid someone might see her." Noah was saddened, but tried to justify it, "Glenn, she said she couldn't get a job, with all that happened, and was turning tricks to get by." Glenn interrupted, "Noey, I heard her talking about turning tricks and all, but has she lost all self-respect, doing it in the street? I mean, my gosh! I thought she meant going to a hotel. I used to have all kinds of respect for her. I thought I had seen it all…" Noah was angry, "What do you expect. I mean you didn't see what I saw that day on base.

Man, she went through hell. The Marine Corps had no reason of doing what they did to her. I'm surprised she didn't end it all." Glenn sat appalled, "I know, but man she had so much going for her. Boom, overnight it seems, one giant fall. She has lost her way." As they cruised, Glenn became saddened, "Noey, I'm tired, but I've had a good night. Seeing that back there, …No Child, that didn't sit right with me. I think it's time to head home."

Noah stopped by Glenn's car, letting him out. The two said their goodbyes, and Noah headed back to his barracks on base. As he was waved through by the guard at the gate, he thought about the evening. Seeing Champagne, Noah felt empathy toward her. Seeing what the Corps had done to her, being thrown out after so many years, and left with nothing. The music on the radio station was fuzzy and cutting in and out. Noah decided to scan to something else when he came across a Christian station, pausing just for a moment he listened "If you did it to one of the least of these, my brothers and sisters, you were doing it to me." How ironic, Noah thought. The universe was speaking. If the Corps had done this to Champagne, it would think nothing of doing it to him.

Coffee, Donuts, and News in the morning

After completing his Saturday morning rituals, Noah stopped, grabbed some coffee and donuts, and headed over to Violet's. Glenn was there, and they were going to get together for breakfast. Noah pulled up in the back-alley driveway of Violet's house. It was only about 9:00am but the heat for September was very unusual. Jolie, Violet's 8-year-old daughter, was waiting inside the rickety screen door and hollered to let everyone know that Mr. Noah was here. She took off, slamming the screen door, to greet him. Noah reached in the back seat and grabbed the box of donuts and some chocolate milk, closing the door behind him. Jolie, excited to see him. "Mama and Glenn are in the house. She said to tell yah to come on in. What you got in that box, Mr. Noah?" Noah laughed; she knew it was a donut box. "You know, I stopped at the store, and there was a lady who gave me these donuts. She said she had bought them for her kids, but they got rowdy in the store and wouldn't behave, so she gave them to me. You know any kids that have been behaving?" Jolie's eyes were fastened to the box of donuts, "I have Mr. Noah. Honest, you can even ask my Mama."

As the two started walking to the house, Violet came to the back door. "Hey Noah, …Jolie don't be pestering him now, let Mr. Noah make his way." Noah chuckled, "Oh, she is alright, Violet, I told her I have some donuts, but only for kids that behave. I hope that's ok?" Jolie looked to her mother for approval, "Mama can I have one, and he's got some chocolate milk." Violet looked at her daughter with hesitation, "Noah you are going to drive me crazy giving her all that sugar." Jolie interrupted, "Please Mama, I promise to mind. I'll be ok." Violet, not wanting to be the one to say no, "Ok, but you know how you get on sugar, and you best behave. Child, go wash your hands and face. I'll let you have one, but you are going to sit right out here and not say a word."

Violet stood holding the screen door open, as Noah gave her the box of donuts and chocolate milk. "Sorry…" He gave her a quick hug, "Child you'll be ok." The two made it through the cluttered house to the dining room. Glenn was sitting at the table, "Good morning, Noey, I see you finally got your tired ass up and made it this way. We was beginning to wonder." Noah laughed, "You are always such a bitch. Besides you know I have been up for hours; Saturday morning is my day to run errands." Violet came in with a hot pot of coffee and a pitcher of orange juice. She had made a skillet of scrambled eggs, some bacon, and fresh fruit, along with the donuts. Jolie helped her set the table. Violet told her to get the morning paper off the front porch, and then go wash up for breakfast.

Violet always liked Noah's car and commented on it as she set the table. "I see you are still driving my car?" and chuckled. She didn't know it was a sore topic with Noah. "You know I'm lucky to have it. The transmission messed up, and Strumen took it in to the mechanic to have it repaired. He never returned to get it. When I got back from Oki, I had to pay for the cost of repair, plus a storage fee. They were just getting ready to sell it, thinking it had been abandoned." Violet shook her head. "I don't know what happened to that child. I used to think he was ok. But, after all the things he's done to you, I can't say. You know, after you left, I would see the child, you know out and about and things. I saw him one time in your car, and he had some little sweet pea, just sitting in it right outside of the Capri. I was walking by, noticed, and deliberately stopped. "How you been?" and immediately asked, 'How's that Noah been?' He didn't know what to say, with the little sweet pea sitting right next to him. 'I see you been taking loving care of Noah's car. You know I have always loved this car of his.' I smiled, knowing I had stumped him. Leaving I told him, 'When you talk to Mr. Noah you tell him Ms. Violet misses him and hopes he's ok!' … Ha-hah. I know that sweet pea was just full of questions, and Strumen was just wanting to get away."

The group chuckled, when Jolie returned with the paper, laying it on the table. Violet quickly instructed her, "Now Child, I'm not going to tell you to go wash your hands again. Don't think I've forgot. Now off you go, when you come back, your donut and milk will be sitting on the kitchen table. The TV's on so you can sit in there while the grown-up folk visit." Jolie left the room, and the adults made their plates, "Thank you for having us over Violet, this looks great!" Glenn made his plate and reached for the newspaper. As he opened it up and read the front page. "Body found slain behind dumpster." Glenn perturbed, "Why do they put that stuff on the front page. Huh uh, who wants to start the day off reading something like that first thing!" Noah chuckled, "I know, I quit watching the news before going to bed. Everything bad, crime, and train wrecks, doesn't sit well when you're trying to sleep."

The phone rang, Violet got up and went to the kitchen to answer it. Noah and Glenn could partially hear, "Saaay what? … Oh my, …any idea who? …yeah, yeah ok, well listen, I've got Glenn and Noah here, let me call you back, ok?"

Violet hung up, and came back to the table, "Child that was Ms. Dee, she's saying they found Champagne murdered in the alley, just a couple of blocks down from the Capri, behind some dumpster. That must be what the article is about in the paper. Let's see what it has to say." Noah and Glenn looked at each other in shock, "Oh my God are you serious Ms. Violet?" Noah and Glenn sat quiet for a moment, when Glenn spoke, "Child come on read us the paper, what does it say?"

Violet read as the paper explained. "A known prostitute, and transvestite, was found behind a dumpster in what appeared to be a hookup gone astray. The guy, thinking he was with a woman, must have found out he was actually with a man. He lost control in a rage, pulling out a knife, stabbing her and slitting her throat. He tried to hide the body by stuffing her behind a dumpster, before getting away. It further says, they are in search of a person of interest, seen in an image pulled from a video camera, from one of the local stores nearby. There were no witnesses, only a friend, who had seen her leave with a young man, walking from the Capri lounge. They do not think this is a related crime, to anything else." Violet laid the paper down.

The three sat quiet. The silence was only broken by the sound of the washing machine, just off the kitchen. How did this happen? How did Champagne land here? Was there something they could have done? Was there anything anyone could have done? A hero, decorated for his bravery, tossed aside as trash, from the very country he swore allegiance to. The silence broke with the sound of sobs coming from Violet. Noah stood up and went to her kneeling and putting his arm around her. Glenn grabbed a tissue and knelt by her. Neither said a word, "I looked out for that poor child, from the day he arrived. At first, I kept my distance, you know he wasn't easy to get to know, and he didn't trust folks. He was Staff Sergeant Williams when I checked him in at the front desk and didn't think much about it. Then, one night I had to work late, and I saw Champagne come outta the room. At first glance I thought he had brought a woman back to the room, but when that child walked past me, …she looked away, and put her dark sunglasses on, like I couldn't tell who it was. I never said anything, till one night I got tired of her wearing the same thing over and over. So, when she came out the room, I was waiting and stopped her. 'Child, if you are going to do this, you got to do it right. Come on.' You know she could wear my clothes; she was about my size. So, I had her try some outfits on, and the child looked fine. I helped with the makeup, taught her the right way, and the wrong way, and before you knew it, when she left here, she looked beautiful.

The padding and breasts came later. Child would double up water balloons, putting them in her bra. Then she cut up an old seat cushion adding padding to her hips. I told her to calm down on putting so much upstairs, but she would say, "The boys like it, beside it makes it feel more real. When I walk, they just move all over."

Violet chuckled at her own words. "We had a cheap bottle of Champagne, drinking while we played makeup. We had been sipping on it all night. She looked at it when I asked her what she was going to call herself. She smiled, looking at the bottle, "Honey, …I want you to meet Ms. Champagne." She stood up and twirled. "You can call me Ms. Champagne, cause I'm bubbly and I go down easy!" Noah and Glenn both laughed.

Noah shook his head as he stood up and returned to his chair while reminiscing. "I remember the first time I saw her at your hotel. I had just made it to California with my sister. I was sitting by the pool, and she came out of the room, it must have been later in the evening. I noticed her, and she noticed me, and quickly put her glasses on, and hurried off. I never met her, until I was with Glenn and Telly. We stopped by the hotel to her room, and she came to the door, in a wig with curlers in it rolled up to the scalp. She had a face mask on, a house coat and furry slippers. It was like she was having a spa night all to herself.

Not once did I ever put Staff Sergeant Williams and Champagne together. I saw Staff Sergeant Williams on base, and he was an impeccable Marine. He was what they called a Marine's Marine. Every special team or inspection that came along, he was called upon for his military prowess. I think that was what bothered them the most when they found out. They were humiliated, their 'Golden child' was a cross dresser. I think the Battalion Commander couldn't handle the fact that someone he thought such an outstanding Marine, could be, in his eyes, so flawed as to be queer, and such a freak of nature. It didn't fit in his box. He hated her, felt betrayed and had to make Champagne pay."

Glenn, now standing across the table from Noah. "I think that is why he was so good. Most of us are. There is no room for error. We try and do our best, try to be better, as a deflection, to throw them off. They're so quick to say we can't do the job, we're sissies, so we must prove ourselves. If they find out, or even suspect that we might be gay, or a homosexual, …Just maybe, … just maybe, they might, overlook it, …maybe they will be forgiving."

Glenn paused, in a stare, before changing the subject "…So now what?" He turned to Violet. "Doesn't she still have a room at the hotel?" Violet shook her head no. "No, she couldn't afford to pay, so she moved out a month ago. I felt bad, but she was already behind, and the owner wouldn't let her stay. Supposedly, she had stored her things in Ms. Dee's garage and had been sleeping on her couch." Noah curious, "What about arrangements, are they being made?" Violet shook her head, "I don't know how that will work, child. I'm just finding out like you. I guess they'll try and contact the family, and it will be whatever they say. Hell, they may not even claim the body. We may never hear anything."

Noah was aggravated, "It's just awful! Staff Sergeant Williams, … Champagne deserved better than this. My God, he had served the country, he was wounded in combat. How could he not even be honored at his own grave." Noah, looking at the two with conviction. "Let's do something. Let's do something for Champagne. We can do the memorial. We don't have to have the body. We'll invite the family if they want to come, but if they don't, fuck them. There is no law saying we can't remember our friend. She deserves to be recognized for her contributions, regardless of what the military says. Hell, if the family doesn't claim her, we do. She was one of our own. As messed up as she was, or as good as she was, we accepted her, and she knew it. Glenn you and I have served on many burial details, we know how to conduct one. If the VA won't do it, we can do it ourselves. Who needs the Marine Corps permission, let's pull this together?" Violet, smiled, "Child you're crazy, but you're right. We have the banquet room at the hotel, I can use it anytime I want." Glenn smiled, "We can pick a date, we'll have to get Dee's help. She has known that child for years! She can tell you more about him than anyone. We can even post it at the bar. Anyone wanting to pay their respects, can come."

Dee Solved the Puzzle

"What is it we are looking for again?" Glenn asked. Dee was busy rustling through boxes, "Anything to do with the military; awards, medals, anything like that? Something we can display at the service. These children need to know the real Champagne!" Dee continued on, searching through boxes, "This child ought to be glad she is gone, …I could beat the shit out of her right now! How does someone keep so much shit?" Glenn spoke up, "Child she was squared away at work, …but she looks like a hoarder at home. …you know she had to keep that stuff!" Violet got excited. She came around some boxes and pointed to the corner. "What's that right over there?" Noah spoke, "A footlocker…" Violet asked, "And what do you keep in a footlocker?" Glenn chuckled, and both he and Noah simultaneously said, "Your military gear." They chuckled and grabbed it, sitting it up on top of other boxes. When they opened it, there was the treasure chest, Champagne's/SSgt Williams' medals lay in front of them. The citations, awards, and letters completely filled it to the top. Noah started going through them one by one. So many different ones he couldn't even begin to read them all. As they got to the bottom, Glenn paused in surprise, "You got to be fucking kidding me!" Slowly he brought forward the Purple Heart and The Bronze Star. "I never knew he was awarded these." Noah interjected, "I saw him on base in uniform. He was wearing them. Everyone always wondered what they were for, but no one really knew. He never talked about it." Dee shuffling some papers, pulled out a citation. "He didn't talk much about it, but he did to me. This is the one I was looking for; I knew about this one. We spoke of it many times. On the day he received it, as a Lance Corporal, he centered himself on the Battalion Commander and saluted. They read this citation:

"The United States of America

To all who shall see these present greetings. This is to certify that the President of the United States of America has awarded

The Bronze Star Medal

To: Lance Corporal Anton L. Williams

Second Platoon, Company G, First Battalion, First Marines,

For: For exceptional meritorious achievement and heroic actions under hostile fire while engaging NVC at the risk of his life above and beyond the call of duty as a rifleman. On 30 January 1968, Company G was advancing in dense population near the Perfume River in an effort to extract the General of the Army of the Republic of Vietnam from Hue City and return him to Phu Bai. Lance Corporal Williams' platoon was the point lead element. Upon crossing the Phu Tong Bridge, they were brought under intense enemy small arms and automatic weapons fire. The platoon reacted swiftly, getting in columns they proceeded on foot crossing the bridge and returning fire. With the Marines tightly bunched together Lance Corporal Williams with the other Marines found themselves only meters from the enemy position. As the fire fight continued many men were wounded by the deadly assault. While lead members of the squad fired and maintained a suppressive cover, Lance Corporal Williams unhesitatingly and with complete disregard for his own personal safety, stood up and began evacuation of the wounded. Taking rounds himself did not detour his efforts. These actions saved countless numbers of his fellow comrades lives and minimalized injury and possible death of the wounded. His personal heroism, extraordinary valor, and inspirational sacrifice reflected great credit upon himself, and the Marine Corps and upheld the highest traditions of the United States Naval Service.

"Once he finished getting his award, Champagne returned to the rear of the platoon. He was numb, he didn't feel like a hero. At least that was what he told me. Although everyone told him he was a hero, he felt he had done what anyone would do, … you know, the right thing. Once the formation was over, he started to walk away, when he heard a voice from behind. "Excuse me, Lance Corporal Williams." He stopped and turned, a young Navy Corpsman on crutches was standing there. "Um, I know you may not remember me, but I remember you. I was on that bridge that day. You saved my life." LCpl Williams told me he was puzzled and didn't remember the young Corpsman. The Corpsman reminded him what happened that day on the bridge. "I remember you. I was hit almost immediately once on the bridge. In my mind I thought this is it! … this is where I'm going to die." The Corpsman said he lay there watching as Champagne started evacuating the wounded. The Corpsman tried talking, but his voice wasn't loud enough. He was fading in and out from blood loss. But the Corpsman kept seeing

Champagne going by and bringing another to safety. He told himself, you have to hang on, he'll not forget you, when another round hit him in the shoulder. It started burning, he was barely alive and losing consciousness. He felt an upheaval and was looking at the pavement bouncing below. Champagne had him on his shoulder. Then BAM, …the two hit the ground. Champagne still had him. The Corpsman said he remembered when he was laid out on the truck it was LCpl Williams face putting him there. That Corpsman was the last one, he picked up. He stuck out and shook Champagne's hand. Thank you!"

Dee turned to the boys. "So, you see, that is who the real SSgt Williams is, …the real Champagne! He never really talked about it, because he didn't feel like he had deserved the award. I always begged to differ. That young Navy Corpsman whose life he saved, got it right! …I know, because I am that young Navy Corpsman."

Chapter 25

Revival

Living in southern California in the summertime, you were pretty much guaranteed a bright sunny morning. Saturday, along the Pacific Coast Highway, in Carlsbad, was festive with joggers running the trails. Along the beach, in the parking lot, the surfers would park, changing over into their wetsuits before catching a few waves. If one was paying attention, they might see more than they bargained for.

Noah and Glenn had gotten up early to do a jog. It was Noah's last weekend in southern California before transferring to a reserve unit in Pennsylvania. He and Marcus would be stationed there. Glenn and Noah were now sitting at a seaside café. This was one of their favorite spots overlooking the ocean. Glenn sat in his dark sunglasses, he called them his cheaters. It allowed him to look at unsuspecting victims as they walked by.

Noah was checking out the menu when a young surfer boy waiter arrived. Glenn kicked Noah under the table and lowered his sunglasses as the waiter told the two about the day's special. Noah ordered a Mimosa, Glenn a Bloody Mary. Glenn raised his sunglasses back to his eyes again, as the waiter rushed away. Glenn tilted his head to get a better look, following him with his eyes.

Noah knew what he was up too. "Glenn, stop it!" Glenn straightened up and started singing "I wear my sunglasses at night, so I can, so I can see..." Noah laughed, "Yeah, well the sunglasses might cover your eyes, but they don't cover your body. It's obvious what you are doing." Glenn gave Noah a frown, "Child, what do I care? I swear, you are starting to work my last nerve. Noey, you need to lighten up, and enjoy life."

Glenn noticed the gentleman standing at the next table over. "Noey, look at that child's hair. That tail thing hanging down his back. What is that?" Noah glanced, "It's a braid, I think it is a thing now." Glenn curious, "Why is he wearing something like that? ...Huh-uh, no child, you would never catch me wearing that! It looks like a rat's tail. I just want to take the scissors and cut it off, don't you?" Noah looked at it once again. "It doesn't bother me, … to each his own. You know there are other people in this world, right?" Glenn ignored Noah's comment, "You know what it means?" Noah amused by Glenn's interest in this man. "What, he belongs to some secret society or something?" Glenn was agitated, "Nooo, it means he doesn't have any friends! … If he did, they would have told him to cut it off by now!" Noah did his best to keep from laughing. "Ok Glenn, let's focus back on the waiter." The two checked him out again. Noah continued. "He is cute, isn't he?" as Glenn nodded, the waiter was headed back their way.

He arrived at the table, "Excuse me, but I failed to mention, we have a brunch special of bottomless Mimosa's or Bloody Mary's. Does that interest either of you?" Noah looked at Glenn, "Come on, what do you say?" Glenn was tempted, "It sounds good, but I think I'm going to pass." Noah came back, "Who needs to lighten up now? Come on it'll be fun." Glenn shook his head no, but Noah insisted, "Come on!" Glenn tightened up and remained firm on his decision, "No Noey, I told you. Don't try to make me give in to peer pressure. I don't feel good." He adjusted himself in his seat looking away from the table. Noah told the waiter, "The drinks we ordered will be just fine."

The waiter left, and the table remained quiet. Noah let Glenn have a moment before he spoke, "So what do you mean you don't feel good, are you sick?" Glenn was slightly agitated with the question. "Don't go there, I'm not dying bitch! …don't be such a Drama Queen! Everyone's like, …Oh, you're H I V positive, …Oh, you don't feel well, …Oh, this must be it, you're dying! Why is everybody trying to pick out my funeral song?"

Noah was a bit insulted by Glenn's comments, and the fact Noah was concerned. It was like he really didn't want anybody to care. He was guarded, trying to push people away. Noah gave him a frown, "Fine bitch, I'll never ask about you again. I was only concerned because it's not like you to not want to have a drink." Glenn snapped back, "So what, now I'm an alcoholic?" Noah grew frustrated, "You know what just forget it! …jeez."

Glenn sat there pouting with his head looking away before Noah got tired of it. "So, what now, you going to sit and pout all day? What do you want me to do?" Glenn smirked, "Well right now, … I would like you to shut up!" As he looked Noah straight in the eye. "…But then I would like you to educate yourself. I'm HIV positive, I don't have AIDs. At least not yet anyway." Noah shrugged, "I don't even know what that means." Glenn perked up, "Exactly, that's my point! Educate yourself about this virus, so you understand what I'm going through, but most importantly, so you don't land in my shoes. I am HIV positive; I'm not going to die tomorrow; it takes some time for this thing to develop into AIDs. Every time I get a cough or sneeze, I can accept other people freaking out, my mom, maybe some of my family, but not you. I don't need that reaction from you, you are my best friend. I just want us to be like we've always been, just us, keeping it real."

Noah understood what Glenn was saying, he was right. Maybe he did look at him a bit differently. Noah was ignorant about this new disease. He always looked at it as; … it happened out there, …far away, …to someone else, but not him. But, far away, was no longer that far away. It was across the table looking back at him. Noah spoke in agreement, "You're right, I need to educate myself." As the waiter set their drinks on the table, they both ordered the breakfast special.

After the waiter left, Glenn started to speak again. "You know I just have been feeling a little weird lately." Noah replied, "Oh yeah, only lately? I thought weird was normal for you?" Glenn chuckled, "Hah, hah, no, seriously! I don't know how to explain it. I mean, it's not anything physical, like I'm getting sick or something. But I mean, like Lilly, she has been going to this church. She's begun singing in the choir, and tomorrow, she will be doing a solo." Noah was stunned, "Lilly? For real, …Lilly's going to church? Are you freak'n kidding me? I don't know which is more surprising, Lilly going to church, or that she is singing in the choir, God help us! … Where's she going? So, I can be sure to stay away, …just in case lightning strikes and burns the place down." Glenn chuckled, "I know, right? …Child, now stop. It's not about Lilly, it's about me. I'm thinking I'm missing something. Every time I speak to my mother, she's always preaching." Glenn imitates his mother's voice, "You need to get back in church, I can see you slipping away!" he changes back, "We all know that is a lie on its face. She doesn't know I was sucking cock, in the church basement, while the congregation was singing Hallelujah upstairs."

Noah dropped his jaw and ducked his head, looking around as if someone might have heard. "Glenn, watch what you're saying, … now, go ahead, do tell." Glenn flapped his hands in front of him. "Who cares if they heard," as he looked around. There was a couple just a few tables away, not really paying attention. He looked at them as if they might have been listing. He jokingly spoke, "Can I have my business please?" before turning back to Noah without missing a beat. "As for the B.J. in the basement, I'll save that for some other time. Now, what I was saying, … I'm thinking I might want to go and see Lilly sing. Maybe start going back to church on a regular basis again, you know, make it right with the man upstairs." Noah sat for a moment, as he sipped his drink. "Well, if you wanted to go, I'd go with you." Glenn was surprised, "You would?" Noah quickly responded, "Of course I would, why not? Besides, if nothing else, I would love to hear Lilly sing! Is she any good? Even better, is she going to be in a dress? I'd give anything to see her in a dress." The two were tickled at the thought with Lilly being so butch.

This was their first real conversation where the two really talked about religion. Noah thought it funny how you could be around someone and know them for so long without really knowing how they felt about a higher power. Glenn asked if Noah had been brought up in the church. Noah was a bit hesitant, "Yes, and no, …my dad, or mom for that matter, were not real religious. When she passed, and I had to live with my aunt, it was hell, fire, and brimstone! Scared the living shit right out of me." Glenn laughed, "Obviously not enough!" Noah continued, "She made us go to church every Sunday, Sunday night, Wednesday, Summer Camp, and if there was a revival, we would be there every night for that to."

Glenn laughed, "Revival, you got that right! That's what I need to do. We can go to church tomorrow morning, me, you, and Charlie. We can invite Telly; hell, you can invite anybody you want to bring along with you." Noah laughed, "I'm game, where is this said church." Glenn laughed, "Child, it's Southern Baptist, have you ever been to a black folk's church?" Noah shrugged, "I don't know. I never gave it any thought. I always thought of church just being church, Christian you know, not as a black or white thing." Glenn was excited and interrupted, "Oh no child, no, no, no!" Noah continued, "I guess, they're all the same if they believe in Jesus Christ, I don't see anything new." Glenn chuckled, "Child, … black folk get up and whoop and holler. …Hell, they might feel the spirit and get up and start running around the church, …speak'en in tongues and things. Just sing'en the lord's praise." Glenn, taken away with his own words, "Hay-yah, fill me up in here now Lord! Hallelujah!" as he raised his hand and waved. "Feel the spirit, Child you hear me!" Noah chuckled amused by Glenn's actions. "I have been up at the base Chapel, and their services there. Does that count? There were black people in church with me then." Glenn laughed, "I have been to those services as well. Trust me, that's why I go out in town, they're not all the same. The message of Jesus Christ yeah, maybe, but two separate venues, totally."

Noah grew a little concerned, "Glenn, will I be the only white person in your church, and will I be welcomed?" Glenn noted the concern, "You might be, but it ain't like they never saw white folks before, of course you will be welcomed. You might seem a little out of place, but Charlie, he's white. The two of you might get some looks, but you are with me." Noah chuckled, "I don't know Glenn, a bunch of gay guys, and a couple lesbians going into a Southern Baptist Church, are you crazy?" Glenn laughed, "Always, now who is afraid of living, are you with me?"

The word got out and there was a whole group that was interested in going. Glenn decided to make it a party, having several of them spend the night over at he and Lilly's house. Noah already had plans for the evening and could not attend but agreed to be dressed and ready to go and meet the group the next morning.

For those who were staying at Glenn's house, they were wakened by Glenn, as he walked around in his pajamas and dew rag on his head, listening to gospel. Lilly just finishing her shower, came out in a skirt, topless in front of all the guys. When Glenn turned to speak to her, he gasped, "Augh, Lilly, quick, would you do something about those missiles, quick, cover them up. Do something before you hit one of us in the eye." Lilly kept moving on, "Child, I would if I could find my bra, has any one seen…" When Charlie interrupted, sitting on the couch, he reached down pulling the bra up from between the cushions. Lilly, not batting an eye, snatched it out of his hand. "How the hell did that get there? I must have taken it off in my sleep." Lilly left early so she could get one last rehearsal.

Once she left, the guys, wanting to relieve their morning wood, ended up in an orgy. When it was over, Charlie spoke up about how sacrilegious it was knowing they were headed to church. The crew continued to get ready for the big event. They were now calling it the Revival. They began donning their suits, helping each other with ties, until the entire crew looked like they were ready for Easter Sunday.

Just as they finished with their suits, the doorbell rang. It was Telly and Noah. Glenn showed them the way to the kitchen, before fixing each a cup of coffee. They both looked at each other, crinkling their noses. There was a noticeable funk in the air. Telly couldn't ignore it. "Why does it smell like ass up in here?" The group tried to suppress the chuckles, except for Charlie. He had no problem talking about the group's orgy. Charlie, knowing they were getting ready to go to church, made a pun, letting them know they had already participated in what he was calling CUM-union. Sarcastically, Noah commented, "Sorry, I missed it," as he rolled his eyes at Telly. "And to think, …all we wanted was a cup of coffee." Glenn hit him with the towel he was holding, "Shut up bitch, you've done worse!" Noah smirked, "I guess you really do need to get back in church!"

The crew arrived in different cars. Parking was difficult and it appeared the church would be a packed service. The grey stone building appeared a bit run down and had seen better days. Glenn and Charlie waited in front of the doors as the others arrived. Once all were there, the door opened, the organ music could be heard. They were welcomed and escorted into the sanctuary. The group was slightly late and seated on two different rows. Members shuffled to make room for them. Noah sat between Glenn and Telly.

After a moment or two, the deacon took to the pulpit, and began speaking, as the choir entered from the rear. Once in place, the deacon finished, and the choir began to sing. It was beautiful. The service continued, with prayer, and offerings, before they were informed of special music from Ms. Lilly.

The choir started in, and then went soft as Lilly opened her mouth, her voice filled the room. Noah, along with the rest of the group, sat in awe. Lilly could sing, like really sing. Accompanied by the choir, she had the congregation on their feet. Ladies with their big hats on, and men standing with their hands in the air. Glenn sat listening, before saying Lilly was anointed with the Holy Ghost, as she riffed. Glenn sat intensely on the pew, trying to hold back the tears. He had held himself back from standing up. Noah found him trying to stand up, only to stop himself, and sit back down. Lilly's message in song, was getting through to him. He was letting go. Whatever he was going through, he was letting it out. The tears began to flow. Glenn could not hold back any further as he stood in praise. Noah, who stayed seated for a moment, stood up beside him, handing him a tissue. Glenn raised his hands in praise hearing Lilly's voice. Noah looked at Lilly, as she sang. It was as though she was being an instrument from the great beyond speaking to Glenn's heart.

Glenn stood, tears rolling down his cheeks as the song ended. Lilly came over to their row and worked her way to them. She grabbed Glenn and gave him a hug and sat down. She held him as he cried. Noah was at a loss for words.

The Reverend of the church, from behind the pulpit, noticed and spoke out. "It's ok Brother, it's ok." His voice was soothing, before he turned loud, "GOD! …I said God is speaking to you, …and you cannot run, …LET IT OUT! …let it out, … let it all out. …WE HAVE ALL BEEN THERE, …WE ALL KNOW!" as he turned to a whisper, "Let God in, …let him comfort you." He changed back to deep bravado, "LET HIM TAKE IT AWAY! …I SAID LET HIM TAKE AWAY YOUR PAIN! … let it out, …let it out. I said, God take away his pain, whatever it is that is weighing heavy on his heart. Whatever it is that brought him here today to seek you, Lord, hear his prayer. My Brother, …trust in him. confide in him. God hears you my friend, …God hears you." Several in the congregation were standing in prayer, waving their hands. Echoing the Reverend's word, with an occasional "Yes, Lord" and "Amen." Noah sat quietly beside Glenn and Lilly.

After the service, Glenn asked Noah to walk with him for a word in private. Glenn gave some unexpected news, "I'm in love with Charlie. I think we are going to move in together and take it a step further." Noah grinned. "Are you sure?" Glenn looked at him and let out a laugh, "No, …about the moving in part, that is, but yes, … about the love. He's a good guy, besides he accepts me for me and all my crazy!" The two continued to walk, Noah smiled, "What about him, …what does he say?" Glenn shrugged, "Oh, he would have moved in a long time ago if I would have let him." Noah chuckled, "I agree. What about Lilly, what does she say?" Glenn smirked, "What can she say. Look at all the crazy's I've stood beside her with. She better not say nothing. But nah, she likes Charlie, they get along." Noah chuckled, "Well, only you can make that decision, but whatever it is, I wish you the best." Noah noticed a tear run down Glenn's cheek, before he spoke, "Noey, you know I'm going to miss you!" He had totally caught Noah off guard. Glenn was not one to show his emotions. Was this his way of saying goodbye? Noah smiled and stopped him. "Hey, I'm going to miss you too!" The two hugged for a moment before Glenn straitened himself up. "When you get to Pennsylvania, you and Marcus make sure you have a guest room. We'll be coming for a visit."

Whatever happened that was keeping Glenn away from church, he had reconciled with it. It was between him and his maker. But one thing for sure, come Sunday morning, Glenn could almost always be found on a pew in the church. Noah and he never really exchanged views, on their beliefs, but he knew Glenn felt the church was right for him.

Chapter 26

Move to PA

Once Noah arrived at Pennsylvania, and checked in to his new unit, he had orders awaiting him. He was being sent to Colorado, Lowry Air Force Base, to complete his training as a Combat Motion Picture Photographer. When he re-enlisted, it was under the condition that he be given the job he originally signed up for. It didn't take long for the Marines to fulfill that request. He was checking in and out at the same time. Well, it was a good thing, at least he would not have to settle in for long. Marcus was from the area and would be able to live at home with his father for a while.

Noah headed out to Colorado, stopping off in Indiana for a couple of days to visit with family, then he would be on his way to Denver. Finally, he would be doing what he had wanted since he was a child, a combat photographer. Well sort of, he was going to be doing something even better, Motion Picture Combat Photographer. The setback caused by his father, and high school, when first joining, would finally be set straight. Part of his stopping in Indiana, was not just to visit. His sister Gabbi had spoken to him, and his niece was considering joining the military. He agreed, while he was home, he would go to the recruiter with her. Things might have been different had he known the process and someone looking out for him. He might have been able to avoid those mistakes. Oh well, it is what it is, …no going back now.

Noah arrived early evening and went to dinner with his dad and stepmother. At the restaurant, they met up with Beulah, Lois, and Trina, his sisters. While waiting to be seated, Claudia, and Beulah went to the restroom to freshen up. It wasn't uncommon for his father to run into someone he knew, being he was a union rep for so many years at the factory. This evening wasn't any different. His friend Big Red had shown up and was waiting as well. "Scream'n Barlow, how the hell are you?" Beck smiled and gave her a hug, "Hello Big Red!" They chatted for a few, bringing him up to speed on all that was taking place at the factory. Noah stood by and listened, knowing his father was back in his glory days, talking about old times. It wasn't long before La Mora's name came up. His father paused, "How is La Mora, is she doing all right?" Big Red smiled, "Oh Beck, you know she is just as pretty as ever. She is getting ready to retire. We are supposed to have a dinner for her in a couple of weeks. I'm sure she would appreciate it if you came." Beck, smiled and started to speak, when Claudia showed back up and grabbed his arm. Beck quickly changed the subject, "Claudia, look who showed up. You remember Big Red?" Claudia smiled as Beck continued, "She was just catching me up on the factory." Claudia smiled, "I'm sure there is plenty he would love to hear, …sometimes I can't get him to quit talking about it, even after all these years." The host interrupted to let them know their table was ready. "Nice talking to you Big Red," Claudia walked ahead; Beck paused, "Let me know about what we talked about. I may not make it, but give her my regards, and let her know I still think about her." Claudia, paused, and turned back to him, "Beck are you coming or not?" Beck winked at Big Red and turned and walked on.

After dinner Claudia showed Noah his room and he settled quickly. After a few phone calls with Marcus, and then his sisters, he was in bed and asleep.

Morning came and he was up and out the door. Stopping by only long enough to say hello to his sister Gabbi, and to pick up his niece. They were on their way to the recruiter. Noah remembered this walk from before. It had been years now since he walked through the courtyard of the recruiting station. But this time, it was with his niece Adrian. She was a senior in high school and had taken the Armed Services entry test. The Navy Recruiter had spoken to her about joining, and she was going in to see what they had to offer. Noah, having been through the process, was there for support or to answer any questions. The interview went well. Adrian had done really well on her entrance exam. The recruiter was a bit uncaring and not working with her. He only wanted to offer her data processing. Noah sat quiet. On their way out, she looked at Noah, "No way, I hate data processing!" Noah was curious, had she considered any of the other branches. "What about the Marines? You think you got what it takes to become one?" She giggled, "No, I never really thought about it." He looked at the office, "Come on, let's go talk to them." The two entered the office, and introduced themselves, Noah letting the recruiter know he was a Marine. Soon Adrian sat at his desk asking questions. The interview was going well. The recruiter told her what he could offer her, and the process.

On the way home, the two spoke about both branches, and she had a lot to think about, but had not yet made up her mind. Noah put his two cents in, "Well, just to let you know, this family is a Marine family, if you join, you will be carrying on a family tradition."

After dropping Adrian off, he headed back to his father's house. Taking the long way around, he went by some of his old stomping grounds. At home, he came into a quiet house. It seemed everyone was gone. He started to his room, when he stumbled over a piece of his luggage. Why was it sitting in the living room? He looked around and noticed all of his things had been moved into the living room. He walked into the bedroom, and it was empty. Well, this doesn't make any sense. He heard the front door open, and he stuck his head out. It was his stepmother. She seen him looking out the bedroom door, "Oh, we just went to get a bite to eat. Your dad will be in in a minute, he went to the barn to check on the dogs." Noah curious, "Is there a reason my things have been moved out of the bedroom?" She walked on to the kitchen, as though it was nothing, "Oh that, …I forgot, Nash is coming out here, and he needs that room. He'll be staying the weekend and the others aren't clean. I figured you could just sleep on the couch, being you won't be staying too long." Nash, her son lived close by and had his own apartment, why did he even need a place to stay. It didn't make sense; Noah was from out of state and traveling through. But regardless, if he was going to stay, why not just straighten up another room, or put him on the couch. Then it clicked in Noah's head. She was making it clear, Noah wasn't welcome, and he needed to be getting along. Even if she couldn't throw him out, she could make it miserable for him to stay, or to feel unwelcome. Rather than saying anything, Noah grabbed his bags and belongings and loaded them up. When he was finished and getting ready to leave, his father noticed. "What's going on, are you taking off already?" Noah didn't say anything, he started his car and left.

It was too late to head out for Colorado. He contacted his sister Birdy and crashed on her sofa for the night. Explaining to her what happened, she was appalled. She explained this wasn't the first time that Claudia made them all feel unwelcome. The next morning Birdy called their father. She explained what had happened, and how could he stand by and not do anything. The phone hung up, and a few moments later his father called back, letting them know Noah had a place to stay. He asked if Noah would be coming back out. Noah chuckled, and smirked in disbelief, "You never have to worry about me staying at your home again. It was made perfectly clear, where we stand. She'll never have a chance to humiliate me again!"

The drive to Colorado was roughly a two-day trip. He arrived at the Marine Barracks, and checked in. Classes were not to start for a few days, and the in-processing procedure began.

When classes started, Noah suspected he wasn't the only one who might butter their bread on the other side of the fence. One of the Air Force instructors was a bit effeminate and spoke with a lisp. Another student, a female airman was also a bit manly. With the right words, and a few comments here and there, they all soon knew of each other. It made his time at school go very quickly. About midway through school, they all decided to meet up and do a night out in town, which might have been Noah's downfall. While out, he met someone and ended up going home with him. Not only did he have to worry about Marcus finding out, but it also turned out the instructor had feelings for Noah as well. Thankfully most of the classes he taught were over and Noah only had to see him briefly in the weeks remaining. Noah confided to Steph, his lesbian classmate, about Marcus back home, and she cautioned him to be careful. "They say once you cheat, it's hard to stop!" She was right, the door was open, and Noah started going out on a regular basis. He justified it as, Marcus was far away, and school was long. Nobody would find out, and he would just keep it to himself. All would be kept silent.

The day came and it was time to bid farewell to Colorado. Noah had grown to like Denver, and the area, and he would miss it, but the good side was he was now a Combat Motion Picture

Photographer, or what they called an Audiovisual Production and Documentation Specialist. He would be returning to Pennsylvania, and be working out of Youngstown, Ohio. The difficult part was he would have to face Marcus. They had been together a little over four years now. This was the first major separation. It had changed Noah; he was now questioning the relationship. He was no longer sure this was his forever partner. Marcus was a good guy, but their directions seemed to be growing apart. With this new job, Noah wanted to focus on it and see where it would take him. It would require many more separations, and he wasn't sure how much more their relationship could stand. He was already lying, and he knew eventually it would come out, either Marcus would find out, or Noah would have to tell him. Besides, maybe Marcus had been doing the same thing, and felt the same. Regardless, if this continued, they were both on a destructive path.

The drive back to Pennsylvania was long. He stopped off in Indiana, staying with his sister Gertie this time. He was on speaking terms with his father but refused to stay at his home when offered. While there, he visited with his sister Gabbi. She was excited telling him of his niece Adrian's adventures while at recruit training. Adrian had chosen to join the Marine Corps. She was doing well and had been recognized for platoon high shooter at the rifle range. She would be graduating from Marine Corps Recruit Training at Parris Island, South Carolina in a few weeks, and wanted to know if Noah would be attending. Noah smiled in amazement, "Platoon high shooter, Adrian? Wow, do you know how hard that is?" Gabbi smiled, "That's your niece." Noah continued, "That is an achievement! Of course, I will! I don't think I have a choice. I wouldn't miss it for the world, how could I? ... another Marine in the family." Noah was excited, but quickly realized, Adrian knew he was gay. He had never really spoken to her about it. Now she was going to be a Marine. She knows their policy, and may not agree with him being in. Hopefully, she would be on his side, or at least if she wasn't, then maybe he could get her to remain silent about it. He shook his head, ...this policy, it wasn't just affecting him, but he now had to ask his family to lie about it as well.

The next year or so went by, Noah still had not spoken to Marcus about his time in Colorado. Being silent had become the norm. Silent to Marcus about his feelings. Silent at work about his personal life. Silent to his father about his treatment of his own children. This was becoming the way everything was being dealt with. Put it in a compartment somewhere in his brain housing group. Never to be spoken of again. All forgotten and kept silent. Noah knew this was becoming a destructive behavior, … things never really do stay silent!

Chapter 27

El Paso, Glenn

Lilly walked down the hospital corridor slowly. Exhausted from being up all night, and day after day of sitting in a chair, never completely sleeping. How could she not have seen this coming? Further up the hall she noticed Charlie walking out the door and leaning on the wall. The two had been taking turns holding vigil by Glenn's bedside as he slipped in and out of consciousness. Upon arriving, she handed him a cup of coffee, "I figure you might need this. Anything new?" Charlie took the cup, "Thanks. No, he was awake for a moment, only to take a sip of water, and gripped my hand and fell back to sleep. The nurse came in, along with the doctor, to check up on him, wanting to know who I was. When I told them his friend, they asked me to leave the room while they did their thing." Lilly shrugged and smirked a bit. "I know it's the Naval Hospital, they only allow immediate family in the room when discussing or doing medical things." The two walked back into the room together, Charlie taking a seat on the empty bed, as Lilly went to Glenn, doing a quick check on him before giving him a peck on the cheek. "Glenn, oh Glenn! Child, I know you can hear me. I said I know you can hear me! I'm here now. If you need anything just let me know. Me and Charlie are going to sit right here. You hear me now! You just go on and sleep, we'll be right here." Glenn, groggy, mumbled something but was off to sleep again. She grasped and shook his hand before sitting down by the chair next to the bed. "Child who could have known. Charlie, you know when we got married, I had no idea what I was signing up for. This was supposed to be a marriage of convenience. I have done more with this man than I ever cared too. I have stood by him through good and bad, more so than any woman I have ever been with. You hear me! … Child, you know it ain't been easy. I have been a witness, you hear me, witness, to this child being beaten, called names, investigated, almost getting both of us thrown out of the military. Yet I still stand beside him. No matter what, he has kept going. If anyone can beat this AIDS shit, it'll be him. He has pissed me off more times than I can recall. Yet I keep coming back. You know why Charlie, you know why?" She looked at Glenn, "You know why Glenn, I know you're listen'en?" Charlie shook his head no. "Child because I love him. Not in a lover way. And although he thinks he's sexy, I sure to hell don't! But he's been my best friend, and I know he has been there just as much for me. We're family, the good family, the kind that ya choose. When I needed him, or he needed me, we've been all each other has had." Lilly didn't want to put off Charlie, after all, he and Glenn were a couple, and even though the law didn't allow it, he and Glenn were together. This was Glenn's real partner. "Charlie, I know it must be hard to have to sit back, and be treated like, … like an outsider, and not even be able to have a say in your partner's treatment. It breaks my heart. Just like today, being asked to leave the room because you weren't family. Child you are his family, and don't ever allow anyone to say any different. I can't imagine how that makes you feel. But let me tell you something. If there is anything you want done, or something I can do, by law I'm his wife, but you and I know it is really you." Startling the two, Glenn spoke up. "I hope you mean that Lilly, I'm relying on you."

****

The phone rang once, twice, three, four, … before Marcus finally hung up the phone. Maybe he had the wrong number. He looked at the number again. No, this was the number on the sheet of paper. This was the last number he had for Nina. Maybe it was no longer any good. It had been about three years since he had contacted her. Maybe her and Beatrice had moved, if so, how would he find her now. He called information and spoke to the operator. "Yes, do you have a number for Beatrice Howell, or a Nina Romano." The operator searched for a moment, before responding, "I'm showing a number for a Beatrice Howell in Escondido, would you like that number, and if you like I can connect you?" Marcus perked up, "Yes, and yes please." Marcus wrote the number down, and soon the phone was ringing. One ring, two, three. …the operator spoke." I'm sorry Sir, but there is no answer at that number right now." Marcus sighed, "Ok, thank you operator, I'll try again later."

Marcus hung up. At least he possibly had a new number. How did he allow himself to lose contact with her, after all, this was his wife! He should have gotten a divorce while he could. Right after he had gotten out the first time. Now who knows where she is. The recruiter will want to know where she is, and the Marine Corps will want her address now that he was reenlisting. How will he explain this if he doesn't know where she's at? This whole thing was becoming a fucking mess. He got up and went to the kitchen. Giving the fridge a quick glance, he noticed it was getting late in the day. Why hadn't he heard from Noah? He must be making good progress. No news was good news. He'll probably call once he stops for the night.

****

Late afternoon, and the sun was just starting to shift into the windshield. Noah pulled down the visor as he headed west on US 10 to El Paso. It had been a while since he had seen a town and the gas tank was getting low. The last sign he passed said El Paso 102 miles. This was the first time traveling this far South. It was all new country for him and seemed desolate. The low country was dry and plain, and the rise of the mountains in the distance was brown and rocky. There was a beauty to the openness allowing the mind to wonder and offering the eye freedom to gaze. Hypnotically, the hum and vibration of the truck could cause someone to fall asleep. Noah adjusted his seat and sat up and spoke aloud, "Wake up! Wake up!" while shaking his head and turning the radio on to break the monotony. The tank was riding right on E, and he hoped the truck wasn't going to run out of fuel before he made it. He planned to stop in El Paso to get fuel and hopefully drive on through to Tucson and spend the night. Up the road he could see another update sign. As he passed it El Paso 48 miles. He was really starting to worry that he would run out of gas first. Surely there would be a gas station prior to getting to the city. It was just a few miles further when the truck choked and sputtered a bit, which caused Noah to panic. He turned down the radio to listen. Nothing unusual, as the old F-150 truck kept rolling along. Noah turned the radio back up but slowed a bit to try and save on gas. Now he was focused on the road and looking for any sign of life in the horizon. Nothing for as far as the eye could see. A few more miles had passed when the truck sputtered again. Noah quickly turned the radio down and slowed a bit. This time, however, he noticed the check engine light had come on, along with the hot temperature gauge. He slowed even more, however the truck was now sputtering and smoke was now coming out from under the hood. As he pulled to the side of the road, the engine had stopped completely. Noah sat in the cab for a minute, before getting out and opening the hood. Once opened, the steam and smoke kept rolling off the engine compartment. Noah stepped back from the truck, away from the heat. The desert sun beat relentlessly down as he walked around the vehicle, before kneeling to look under the truck. There was oil coming from under the engine. This did not look good. What was he to do? He sat for a while in the cab, letting it cool down, thinking he might be able to try and get it to start again. After all he was running low on fuel, maybe once it cooled, he could get it to start and drive it a bit further. After a half hour or so, he tried starting it, but nothing. Well, the only thing that he could do was hitch hike to the nearest town or station and see if he could get a tow truck. He closed the lid and stuck a white flag on the antenna made from a T-shirt he had pulled from behind the seat, and down the road he went. Not much traffic had passed by, and the last sign said 48 miles to El Paso, so he figured it was now probably 40 miles or so with the distance he had traveled. He heard a vehicle slow from behind. He turned to see a state police car pulling over behind him, and a slight hit of the siren to let Noah know he was there. Noah stopped and turned back as the car pulled off the side of the road. By the time Noah arrived, the Officer was already out of the car and waiting for him. "It's an awful hot day to be out here walking. Where are you coming from?" Noah smiled with a chuckle, "I agree! I'm having a little bit of bad luck. My truck broke down a few miles back and I'm trying to get to the nearest town to get some help getting towed. I'm in the Marines and driving across country to report into my next duty station in California." The Police Officer smiled, "You're still about 30 miles or so from the nearest station. But your luck just changed. I can get you a ride. Semper Fi, I was last stationed at Pendleton. Always glad to help a brother in need. Got out about 3 years ago myself and became a state trooper. I know a station on the outskirts of town. Ran by an Old Jarhead himself. I'm sure he will help you without breaking the bank. Hop in, let's get out of this heat."

****

Hearing Glenn speak out, Lilly and Charlie rushed to his bedside. "Child you're awake! I knew you were listen'n." Glenn smiled and grabbed her hand softly but jokingly, "Awe, shut up you old dike!" as he chuckled. Charlie looked over his shoulder and listened to make sure no one was coming before leaning over to give Glenn a kiss. "You're awake, so nice to see you! To think I was almost ready to go, and I would have missed it." Glenn smiled, "Nice to see you as well," squeezing Charlie's hand. "Listen up the both of you, I'm serious about what I got to say. I'm awake and I need to get this out now." Both shook their heads and listened. "I hope you meant what you said Lilly. About being my wife by law. My mother will be here tomorrow. There will be a lot of surprises, and much she does not know. For instance, I haven't told her about Charlie, other than he's a friend, but she also doesn't know we're married." Lilly was shocked, "Say what? Child you are going to wreck her nerves. She shows up on your death bed, and I'm supposed to say, Nice to meet you! Oh, by the way I'm his wife, your lesbian daughter-in-law. And this is Charlie his real partner. Glenn what the hell were you thinking?" Charlie trying not to be overly distraught. "Sounds like he wasn't. I thought you had this all under control Glenn, how could you do this?" Glenn was frustrated, "I just kept waiting for the right time! Eventually, I planned to, but I never thought it would be like this. My control was not telling her. She is a strong Christian woman, and I didn't want to cross her. It's hard telling what she might have done." He turned to Lilly, "Look, I don't know how all this is going to pan out. All I know is I'm dying. I don't care about all the other bullshit. All I want is to be able to go in peace. We owe her no explanation. I love her, that's all she needs to know. As for my family, you guys are it. If she doesn't agree, she can go. Lilly, I may not be able to call the shots much longer. I need you to make sure that no one walks over Charlie. Trust me, I can assure you my mother will. That is why I'm counting on you, like you said by law we are married. She can challenge it, but the law is on our side." Glenn started going over all the different things he wanted done. The funeral arrangements. Who was to get what and so forth? Then he stopped. "Lilly, …Do you know how to get a hold of Noah? I've lost his address; He was in PA or something. I think with Marcus, I don't know how to get a hold of him. If you could, can you try and find Noah, track him down and let him know! Even if I'm gone?" Lilly shook her head, "No one's heard from him in a while, but I'll see what I can do." Glenn starry eyed, "Just let him know I asked about him, I miss him, I really do!" Glenn turned his head away, to keep the tears from showing. Charlie grabbed a tissue and wiped them as Glenn began to speak again. "I'm sorry, I'm not going to be a victim here. This isn't how I thought things would be. I just thought I'd see him again one day." Charlie spoke up, "And you will!" Lilly chimed in, "Child, if I know Noah, I'm sure if he finds out, there won't be nothing that can keep him away! But for now, you gotta get your rest, we have a whole bunch of other things to worry about."

****

Noah stood by the station as the wrecker pulled his truck into the maintenance bay. It wasn't long before the mechanic and Carl the owner appeared waving for Noah to come over. Once there, Carl started explaining to Noah what was wrong. "Son, it's not good. You have blown the engine. It overheated in this hot sun, and looks like you blew the head gasket, and the engine fused together. What you have is pretty much a boat anchor sitting in there right now." Noah's heart dropped. "Can you fix it, and if so, any idea how much it will cost, and how long?" Carl shook his head, "Yeah, I can fix her, but that's not the problem, I have to find an engine first. If I can find an engine, I can have her done in about three days. Come on in the office with me." Carl sat behind the desk and told Noah to have a seat while he called. "Danny you old sons a bitch, I have a young Marine here down on his luck trying to get to his next duty station, and this old desert sun, has done wreaked havoc on his truck and he's blown the engine." As he filled him in on the details, Noah noticed a handsome, brown haired guy walking into the office. Handing a note to Carl, he gave a glance to Noah. As he headed into the mechanics bay, Noah noticed he gave him a second glance holding it a bit longer, before disappearing again. Was he just cruised? The second glance was so synonymous of gay men. Do a quick glance, look away, and glance again as to not get caught. Noah brushed it off. Must be wishful thinking because of the young man's extremely good looks. Noah's thoughts were interrupted by Carl's voice. "Your luck just changed. They think they might have one. He's going to go look at his inventory." As Carl cupped his hand over the phone, "An Old Army dog, but we won't hold that against him." He chuckled at his own joke before the phone conversation picked back up. "Yeah, right, right, right, so when would you be able to have it ready to go. …. Right, …. Right… Okie, dokie. Dan, give me about a half hour and I'll let you know what he says." As he hung up, "You're in luck, he's got one, says he can have it ready by tomorrow for pick up. Which is good, because I can have your old one yanked tomorrow and by the next day be ready to have the new one put back in. What do you say?" Noah paused, "I'll need to call my dad, to help with the money. Can I use your phone?" Carl chuckled, "Sure, give him a call and see what he can do. If he can't, we'll work something out, but we have to get you back on the road to serve our country!" Noah gave the thumbs up to get them started. One way or another he would figure something out, regardless, he had to have transportation.

The El Paso sun set low in the sky and was beaming directly into the phone booth outside the station. Noah kept trying to get a hold of his dad, and Marcus, only to get a busy signal from both. Finally giving up, he resigned to try again later. Now to face what was at hand. Because he would be here for a couple days; he would need a place to stay. From the old phone book hanging in the booth, he looked up hotels and found one not far away. Returning to his truck, he grabbed his overnight bag and panicked noticing he had left the Damron's gay guide in the front seat. He quickly grabbed it and tucked it in his bag, hopefully no one had noticed it. He headed out on foot, hiking along the highway, he took it slow. A mile or so into it, a red mustang pulled over. Noah walked up, not recognizing who was in it. As he approached, the window started rolling down. It was the young guy from the station. "Hey, name is Jedd. I work for Carl, I saw you back there and was going to offer you a ride, but you got out of there before I could find you. Where you headed?" Noah was surprised. "Thank you. I'm headed to the Lantana Hotel. You know where that is?" Jedd laughed, "Yeah, just off the road, up a way. Come on, hop in, I'll get you there." Noah walked around the mustang, and hopped in. As Jedd pulled off, Noah was a bit nervous, "I can't tell you how much I appreciate this. Everyone has been so helpful, and kind." Jedd smiled and looked over to Noah with his brown puppy dog eyes. "Carl is a super nice guy, and he demands it from all of us as well. I heard you were in the Marine Corps; Carl has a weak spot for military. He was wounded in Vietnam, doesn't talk much about it. But he goes out of his way for those in uniform." Noah grinned, "I guess I found the right place then. I'm headed to California, going to be stationed in San Diego. Thought my truck would make it." Jedd exited the freeway, "Yeah it was pretty bad. I was one of the ones to tow it. The gauges were frozen, didn't even move. When I looked underneath and seen the oil, I knew it was bad. I've seen this desert eat many cars." Noah listened but was checking out the area around him. After all, this was his first time in El Paso. Most importantly, he needed to know how to get back to where he came from. "You from here originally?" Jedd perked up "No, from West Virginia originally. I've traveled a bit; my dad was Air Force and came here for work after he got out. I did a stint in the Navy myself, San Diego, four years, but got out after my father passed. He's gone, but my mom's here. I live with her or should say she lives with me." He smiled. Noah wondered if he was married, or had kids, "You and your wife must have your hands full with your mom, and kids?" "No wife, or kids, just me and Mom. No wife for me." He turned and looked at Noah, like he was leading him on, his message was ambiguous. Was this guy gay? After all, Noah's first impression was, he might have been. He still couldn't tell. And he sure wasn't going to out himself, with the truck in his shop. Last thing he wanted was to be wrong. It was not worth the risk. Jedd pointed forward, "Your hotel is just up here on the right. Not a bad place. They're decent on price. Convenient location. The Mall is about a block behind it." Jedd pulled into the parking lot and parked outside the office. Noah opened the door to get out before Jedd spoke up. "Do you have a room already? From the looks of this parking lot, they look packed. We have the Hot Air Balloon Festival going. Things can get sold out." Noah looked around, "No I called, she said they still had room." Jedd quickly interjected, "If you like I can wait to make sure you get in, wouldn't want you stranded." Noah smiled, "Thank you, I'll check it out really quick and let you know" Noah hopped out and went in, before returning. "I got a room, but the bad news I don't have it until tomorrow after 11. She's booked tonight. You know of another one close by?" Jedd nodded his head, "Yeah come on I thought as much. We can go on down the road, there's another but I have a feeling you might be out of luck." Noah was starting to worry. Where would he stay, if the next one was booked as well? The red mustang pulled into the Blue Hawk Inn, and soon Noah was out of the car and into the office. Just as he made it to the desk the attendant turned on the no vacancy sign. "Sorry, sold out for the night." Noah sighed, turned, and walked back out to the car. "They're sold out." Jedd with a half grin. "Yeah, I figure most places will be the same." Noah nodded his head in agreement as he walked on to the car. "Thanks man, you've done your best! I can't keep you held up. You've been so nice; I don't want to inconvenience you any further. I'll figure it out." Noah reached in and grabbed his bag. Jedd spoke up, "No inconvenience here, but I understand. There are a few more on up another mile or so, but I have a feeling you're going to get the same." He grabbed a pen and paper and wrote his name and number down. "Look take this and if you can't find something or need any help give me a call. El Paso can be a bit rough in places." Noah took the number. "Thanks again man!" as he stuck his hand out to Jedd for a shake. "You've done enough already. I really mean it." Jedd shook his hand and Noah stepped away from the car as it pulled off.

****

Marcus paced the floor, giving it a bit more time before trying to call Nina again. Hopefully, this would be the right number.

He had tried so many different numbers to no avail, but this one seemed a bit more promising. It was the right name and location. He started thinking what he would ask her and decided to write it down so he wouldn't forget. One, what was her address? Two, did she still want to remain married, if not would she give him a divorce? Or would he have to pay her off or something? She was always on the down low. Oh, he must not forget to ask about Glenn. Noah would want to know where Glenn was, and any of his other friends he might have known. Ok, now that he had all his thoughts in order, the moment of truth had arrived. He sat down and dialed the number. One ring, two, three, four, …Marcus was anxious, "Oh come on pickup already!" He let the phone ring a few more times. Just as he began to hang up, he heard a voice on the other end. "Hello, …hello, is anybody there? Who is this?" Marcus was in shock and almost forgot to speak out, "Uh, Uh, yes I'm calling for Nina, is she there?" The voice on the other end paused, "Um, Nina doesn't live here. Who is this?" Marcus heart dropped, "This is Marcus. I'm an old friend of hers and was trying to reach her. By any chance, do you know how I could find her?" The voice on the other end laughed, "Marcus, huh, I know a Marcus. You are talking Marine Corps Marcus, right as in Noah and Marcus?" Marcus spoke up, "Yes that is me." She continued, "You don't recognize my voice, do you? Man, this is Howell, you know Beatrice." Marcus was astonished, "Oh my God. Of course, I remember you. Beatrice is that really you? Oh my God, I can't believe it! I have been looking for the two of you for years. Wait, don't tell me, you said Nina doesn't live there, are you two still together?" Beatrice laughed, "Child drama! You know that's how we roll. But yes, we're still together. I was just screening her calls; you know bill collectors and shit. She's right here beside me chomping at the bit to talk to you. Here, let me go!" The phone was quiet for a second, before Marcus heard a soft voice, "How are you Hubby, if I can still call you that…?" Marcus laughed, "Yes, you can, unless you got a divorce without telling me." Nina chuckled, "No, not here. Things are still the same." The two started catching up and filling in each other on all the details of the last three years, before Marcus started going down the list of questions he'd written down. When he came to Glenn, Nina paused, "I'll let

Beatrice tell you about Glenn," Beatrice got back on the phone. "Marcus, … hey man, about Glenn, … I don't know how to tell you this, but it ain't good. Your calling is right on time. Man, they have been trying to get in contact with Noah. Glenn has been asking for him." Marcus wasn't sure what Howell was saying. "What do you mean 'asking for him?" Howell continued, "You know I'm friends with Lilly, right? Well, me and her was just talking. You knew Glenn was diagnosed with HIV back in 86." Marcus spoke up, "Yeah I remember." Beatrice continued, "I guess he is not doing too well, and now he's in the ICU at Navy Hospital Balboa. He is dying of AIDS. I haven't spoke to her in a few days, but she was saying they don't expect him to make it much longer. I guess there has been all kinds of drama around the situation, dealing with his mother and such. He never told his mother that he and Lilly had gotten married. Nor had he ever come out to her." Marcus stunned. "Wow, ...just wow! I mean I get that she may have not known about Lilly and the marriage, but my gosh, did Glenn ever really need to come out to anybody? I mean come on; we're talking Glenn here, how could she not have known?" Beatrice chuckled in agreement, "I know, right? Hah, hah, … Lilly was the one telling me Glenn would like to see Noah one more time." Marcus sat quietly, "Give me a moment, that's quite a bit of unpacking." Beatrice spoke softly, "I know, we have had so many of our gay friends pass, it seems almost weekly anymore. I don't know if you remember Telly or not, but we just found out he is in a home in Escondido. Doing bad with that shit they call the gay cancer. Kaposi sarcoma or something like that. So, we went and seen him, man it is bad! If we hadn't been told who he was, we would have never recognized him. When we came out of there, me and Nina just cried." Marcus sat in astonishment listening to the words Howell was saying. Marcus sighed, "Well some good news. Noah is on his way back to Cali right now. He re-enlisted and will be stationed at MCRD in San Diego. He asked me if I got a hold of you guys to find out where Glenn was. He was wanting to reconnect with him. Man, I don't know if I should tell him while he's on the road or wait till he gets to San Diego." Beatrice, shied away, "That's between you two. I know Glenn is still in the hospital, but not sure how much longer. If Noah is driving maybe, he can make it there in time." Marcus agreed and the two said their goodbyes and hung up the phone. Noah was so looking forward to meeting up with Glenn again, to hear this will be devastating.

****

The El Paso strip bustled with traffic, and the sun was setting giving the amber glow of the early evening. The smell of tar and exhaust filled the air. The redeeming feature was the midcentury modern neo motel sign flickering, 'Palms Island' pool and air conditioning. Noah looked around and noticed the pool had an island in the middle of it with fake palm trees. He chuckled, at the concept, as he headed to the phone booth. Still worried about a place to stay, he thumbed through the phone book and tried calling a couple of other hotels. Still no luck. He figured now was a good time as any to go ahead and make the call home to Indiana to see if his father would be able to help. The phone rang a few times before Noah noticed the voice on the other end saying hello. "Claudia, hey it's Nollie." Claudia spoke up with excitement, "Oh hi, how's the road trip going, have you made it there yet?" Noah paused with hesitation but knew she would have to know in order to get to his father. "I've run into a little bit of trouble. My truck has broken down and seems like I'm going to have to get a new engine to finish the trip." Claudia with shock, "Oh my, let me get your father for you, he'll want to talk to you about it." The phone went silent for a moment before he could hear his father asking Claudia questions as he came to the phone. "Yeah, Nollie, what's going on?" Noah explained the situation and told him where he was at. Then he told him how much. The phone remained silent for a brief pause, before his father spoke. "Well, I guess we'll have to get it to you. We can't leave you stranded. Besides, the Marines might not be too happy if you don't show up. Get her done, well figure it out." Noah could hear Claudia in the background complaining to his father, "How we going to afford it? We don't have the money. I swear, there is always one of them calling out here wanting something." His father covered the phone, but Noah could still hear his father. "By God, if it were one of your kids, you'd be jumping in a car and hand delivering it. This boy has never asked us for anything, and unlike your kids, I guarantee if he tells me he's going to pay it back, he will." Noah's father spoke back into the phone. "I might have to sell a dog or two, but we'll get her done." Noah gave him the information to the station, and his dad reminded him before hanging up, "Make sure you let us know when you get back on the road. We'll be worried about you till then." Noah chuckled, "You bet dad, I will, I will, and hey dad, Thank you!" As he hung up the phone, he stood there for a moment. Wow, just wow, …That went way better than he had planned. And his father, what a surprise, how he seemed to be changing. He stood up to Claudia for his kids.

Noah started to call Marcus but delayed it in hopes of finding a hotel room first. He started going down the list of hotels in the phone book again, a blast from a horn honked behind him. He grabbed his ears and hunched, startled by the noise, "My God, what the fuck asshole!" Only to turn and see Jedd parked outside. He had returned. Noah walked over to the car. "Holy shit, you scared the fuck out of me!!!" Jedd smirked with a shrug and a look of please forgive me, before he started to speak, "Um, I know you don't know me that well. I'm not a stalker, or a crazy or anything, …uhm, I thought, well maybe you can spend the night at my house. I made it home and was telling my mom about you. She insisted I come back. We both agreed. We can't see leaving you stranded. I mean, El Paso is nice, but probably not the safest place to spend the night on the streets. It's just my mom and me. We have a guest room. It's taco night and my mom makes the best. We don't get many guests, and I figure I can get you to your hotel tomorrow. What do you think?" Noah was thankful and shocked from the kindness of strangers but was hesitant on accepting. This was a bit of a scene out of "Psycho"; son and mom, freaky hotel, only this was their home. His options were dwindling. After all he knew where the guy worked, and Jedd had already gone out of his way to help. One night wouldn't hurt. "Thank you, but…" Jedd interrupted, "I insist! Come on, it'll be cool. We can hang out and have a few beers on the patio. Mom goes to bed early." Noah threw caution to the wind. "Why not?" Besides, he didn't want to sleep in an alley somewhere, or on a park bench. Noah grinned, "You sure it won't be a problem?" Jedd smiled, "Absolutely!" Noah couldn't help but grin seeing Jedd's face light up. Noah grabbed his bag and flung it in the back seat as he hopped in. "Ok, but only until I can get a hotel room, I don't want to impose any more than I have to."

****

As Marcus dozed in the recliner, a loud noise on the TV startled him awake. Brushing off the sleep, he looked at the clock and grabbed the remote and turned down the tv. It was getting late, and still no word from Noah. He looked at his clock it was almost 10pm already. Sitting up for a moment, he yawned and contemplated if he should go to bed. The phone rang and before the second ring Marcus had already picked up. "Hello!" Noah's voice came from the other end, "Wow, that was quick! What were you waiting by the phone?" Marcus laughed, "Was it that obvious? So, where are you, what's going on? I was beginning to wonder if something was wrong, thinking you might have called by now?" Noah could hear the concern in Marcus's voice, it was nice to know someone out there was thinking of him. "I'm ok, but things haven't gone quite as planned. My truck broke down just outside of El Paso." As he finished catching Marcus up on the current situation, he turned it back to Marcus. "So that is what is happening with me, what's going on with you, you know I miss you right?" Marcus yawned, "Sorry it's getting late, but I do have some news. I was able to find Nina and spoke to her. She and Howell are still together. They were glad to hear from me". Noah perked up, "Oh my god! That is good news. They're still together! So, where are they? What are they doing? What about Glenn? Do they know anything about Glenn?" Marcus was overwhelmed, "Whoa, give me a moment, so many questions. I was just getting to it." Noah impatiently interrupted, "Ok Glenn, Glenn, … what about Glenn, ...is he alright?" Marcus patiently, "Well if you let me speak, I'll tell you. Howell told me Glenn is currently in the hospital with AIDS complications and is not doing very well. They don't expect him to make it much further." Noah hurriedly, "What does that mean, make it much further? A day, a week, a year, what does further mean" Marcus rephrased, "They don't expect him to make it. He has been in and out of the hospital, and they do not expect him to leave the hospital this time. It's what you were afraid of, he's dying of AIDS." The phone became quiet, Marcus couldn't read what was going on with Noah, "Noah you've gone quiet, talk to me, what's going on? … are you still there? …hello, say something!" Noah spoke up, "I'm still here, …just give me a moment…" Marcus continued, "If it's any consolation, Beatrice spoke with Lilly, and she was trying to find you. I guess Glenn has been wanting to see you! He keeps asking Lilly if she has found you?" Noah teared up, "Of course he has, … the jerk… he's always been looking out for me, ...(sobs) … making sure I'm alright." Marcus intervened, "Get a hold of yourself. You'll be alright, he's still alive! You'll be in San Diego in few days, maybe you can go see him." Noah sobered up a bit. "You hope! This truck breaking down couldn't have happened at a worse time. I thought this transfer, coming back to San Diego would be a good thing. You know, allow us to get back on track with Corps. Hopefully, reconnect with old friends, maybe pick up where we left off. I guess nothing stays the same." Marcus spoke up in agreement, "It just seems shit has been happening against us since you decided to do the transfer. Like it was a forewarning or something. I mean, two days after you found out, dad passed away. Thank God you were here for that. Now your truck has broken down, and now Glenn. Maybe we have been living in a shelter, away from all of this." Noah interrupted, "We have been living in a shelter. We have been living away from the gay community. Doing our own thing. Other than your family, that is really all it has been for the last three years. I mean come on, … like this disease has taken its toll. I used to reminisce about catching up with old friends, but now, …now it makes you wonder if you should just keep the memory of what was, rather than to find out what has happened to them. Each time it tears away at you until you just don't want to hear anymore. But Glenn, this hits home. I mean, I know he had gotten sick, but I guess I just wanted to believe it wouldn't affect him." Marcus said his goodbye before hanging up the phone. "Noah don't hesitate to call no matter what time it is. If you just want to talk, I'm here."

Noah hung up the phone and returned to the living room where Jedd and his mother sat watching TV. Jedd spoke up, "Everything good!" Noah smiled with a fake grin, "Yeah, everything is fine. All is well at home." These were not the people to trust in. They had been so nice to him, no need to add to the drama, or bring the house down with more bad luck. The good news tonight was he had a place to stay and tomorrow he would be out of their hair. Jedd got up, "Come on, let me show you where you'll be sleeping tonight." Noah followed him to the far side of the living room, into a hallway, and off to the left to a bedroom. Flipping on a light, "This is it, I just put fresh linens on the bed while you were on the phone. Right outside on the left is the bathroom and the door on the other end is my room. Hope you don't mind sharing a bath. Mom's room is on the other side of the house. It keeps things private that way." Noah thought that was a bit weird, and more than he really needed to know. "Thank you, I really do appreciate this." Noticing his bag was already sitting on the bed. "Oh, yeah you left it by the door, so I set it in here, hope you don't mind." Noah grinned, "No, No, thank you." There was something about Jedd that didn't seem to be adding up. Noah went to grab his bag when he noticed the Damron's guide half hanging out the side pocket. Had Jedd noticed this? Noah was curious to find out more but wasn't willing to expose himself to find out. Jedd offered Noah a beer and the opportunity to sit outside with a fire. This was a chance to relax and learn more about his host.

****

Just as the elevator door started to close, Charlie heard a voice from outside and a hand grab the door. "Wait, wait please." Charlie quickly hit the open-door button and a black woman, dressed to the hilt stepped in. The black and white dress strapped over one shoulder with a large bow, while the other exposed her dark black skin. All this was accompanied by a black patent leather purse with stilettos to match. The white, wide brim hat was crowned with a black satin ribbon and mesh, cleverly displayed, was only matched in contrast with the pearls around her neck. She looked as though she could have stepped out of Vogue. Charlie thought how odd, but at the same time thought of how Glenn would just love this look. He could see him, snapping his finger and saying, "Ok girl, you go right ahead!" He unconsciously chuckled out loud and the lady turned, giving him a look. "Sorry, just thinking of my friend." The door opened and Charlie waited till she stepped out before exiting. She walked as though she was royalty down the hall. The click of her heels made every step. Soon he was at his turn, and she continued on, as he made his way down to Glenn's room. Lilly was dozing in the seat next to Glenn's bed. He walked over to Glenn asleep and gave him a kiss on the cheek "Hey handsome, I'm here." Glenn smiled dozy, "Hey," he lifted his head to see Lilly snoring in the seat. "That child wonders why she can't keep anyone!" Both watched her for a moment when she let out a loud snore. Charlie laughed loudly and Glenn shushed him, "Let her sleep. I have told her to go on home, but she won't." Charlie, leaning close to him, "She's worried about you Glenn. I don't think she likes being at home without you." Glenn laid back and smiled into Charlie's eyes as the two took a moment just gazing. Charlie decided to tell Glenn about the woman he had just seen on the elevator. "Glenn you would of gave her two snaps up, she looked amazing!" Glenn lay with his head back and started to doze again, while Charlie held his hand watching over him. Once Glenn was asleep, Charlie took a seat and started reading. It was just a few moments before Charlie could hear the click, click, click, of heels in the hall getting louder. It must be the lady he had seen on the elevator. He walked to the door and peeked down the hall. It was the same woman, and she was checking the paper she held with the room numbers. Charlie stepped back in the room, so not to be obvious he was staring. As he sat down, he heard the steps right outside the door. Slowly he turned to see the woman walking into the room. She tip-toed, trying to not make a noise. Charlie stood up and she shushed him. She walked over to Glenn's bed and grabbed a hold of his hand and in a soft whisper, "Honey, it's Momma, I'm here now. I told you I would be…" She leaned over and kissed his forehead. As she stood back up, Glenn woke. "Mom…" Both started crying. After tears and hugs, she spoke, "I miss you baby, my beautiful baby." Glenn was surprised, "I thought you wouldn't be here until tomorrow." "Now child you know the president himself could not keep me away from my son." Glenn gave her a once over and laid his head back, "You look amazing." Mrs. Hall perked up, as she removed her hat. "Thank you, …unlike some people, I believe in looking in the mirror before stepping out." Charlie chuckled at the comment, realizing this is where Glenn got his attitude from. The apple didn't fall far from the tree. How did he not recognize this when he first saw her in the elevator? Of course, this was Glenn's mother. Hearing the chuckle, she immediately turned to him. "So now, … I've heard your little chuckle, …laugh, ...twice now. Don't you think it's time I know who you are?" Glenn frowned, "Mom, be nice!" as he stared her down. "…this is my friend Charlie. Charlie this is my mother." Charlie, already on his feet, stuck out his hand. She looked at it suspiciously, before saying, "Uh huh," and turned to put her hat on the table across the room. Lilly, who had been asleep, yawned and growled awake, sitting up disheveled in the seat. "What, what, …" looking around she realized Glenn was awake, and Charlie was there, before she realized there was a stranger in the room. Both were equally stunned by the others appearance, and presence. "Child, whaaaat is this?" Lilly realized she had spoken out loud. Glenn's mother spoke out, "I might ask the same." Glenn quickly intervened, "Mom, this is Lilly, Lilly this is my mother, she arrived a day early, isn't that nice of her." Lilly shook her head, "Well alright then, …" under her breath, "Better late than never." Mrs. Hall heard her. "What's that supposed to mean?" Lilly stood up and yawned as though she never heard her, and walked over to Glenn, "Child I can see you're in good hands, I'm going home. I'll be back in the morning. I know you two have a lot of catching up." She squeezed his hand and he held on mouthing, "You can't leave right now." She leaned in to kiss him and whispered, "You got this, you'll be alright." As she walked around the bed, she asked Charlie if he would join her in getting a cup of coffee down in the cafeteria. Mrs. Hall looked at the two, "Oh, would you mind getting me a cup." She reached for her purse. Charlie spoke out, "Not to worry, I got it!" The two left the room and she moved over to the bedside chair. "So that is the Lilly? I always hear you talking about her. She is on the rough side, isn't she?" Glenn gave a bit of an eye roll. "She is a Marine." "Charlie is nice, but he is kind of small." Glenn noted she was already sizing them up. "I never really noticed his height." She sat quietly. The elephant in the room was ever so present. He didn't want the tension; he had no time for the games anymore. His mother and him sat quietly, both wondering who was going to speak first. "Was Charlie the one?" Glenn turned to her, "What?" She stood up and came to his bedside. "Charlie, is he the one that gave this to you? I know how you get this, I'm not so dumb... well whatever. You're not the first person. A lady at the church, her son, he had it. He was that way, you know, different. So, you're not the first." Glenn sat in astonishment not sure how to respond. She started in again. "What? You don't want me to know? You think I haven't known. I've known for years. A mother always knows her own. You don't think I can handle it?" Glenn sat and listened, before he noticed she started to cry. He reached over and grabbed a tissue and handed it to her. "Mom, this ain't about you. I know you may think it that way, but it's not. What, what do you want to hear? You want to hear me say "I'm gay," does that make it better. Does that change anything? Ok I'm gay. Was Charlie the one? It doesn't matter, because it could have happened from any number of guys. The point is, it's not going to change anything. I'm dying Mom and nothing else at this point matters." Mrs. Hall, sobbing, grabbed his hand, "You're coming home with me! I can't leave you here to die on your, ... you're, you're not thinking right! These people out here don't have your best interest in mind. You're coming home with me so I can take care of you." Glenn grew frustrated but could see her hurt and knew the temptation to give in to her was strong. However, he remained committed to seeing it through. "First of all, you know, and I know, I'm no longer well enough to travel. But most importantly, I don't want to go home and die isolated in some back room in Arkansas. This is my home out here. Charlie, Lilly, they are my family." Mrs. Hall angrily, "Yeah, and they're the reason you're in this mess. My baby left to join the Marines. Made his momma proud. I remember you walking across that parade deck in your dress blues." As she reminisced, "That's my baby, that's my MARINE right there. That's who that is!" She reached and grabbed his hand and squeezed. "You, growing up, ... every time you walked out that door, I said a prayer. A mother worries. God knows there are so many things in this world a mother has to worry about. And when I hear you come in, I'd say a prayer of thanks to the Lord, knowing he answered my prayer and brought you back to me!" She smiled as she spoke, "When I found you was going in the Corps, I thought my baby is going to do something. Going to make some'en of himself. Then it dawned on me, he is putting his life in danger. But it was better than just sitting there, I learned to get used to it. I would trick myself into think'en, well if something happens at least he'll come home a hero. But what about this? How am I supposed to deal with this? Some'en you can't even explain." Glenn gripped her hand, "You don't have to explain anything. … As for me, there is nothing to be ashamed of Momma. This disease is nobody's fault, just those who choose to ignore it and act like it will just go away. I'm still the Marine you were so proud of. I'm still that same boy you prayed for. Don't lower your head to anyone. Don't throw all that away. You walk proud. I'm proud, why can't you be proud for me. You done a fantastic job of raising me. You were and still are a great Mother! I love you and nothing will ever change that." Mrs. Hall wiped away her tears, straightened herself and pulled away. "So, does this still mean you're not coming home?" Glenn sighed, "Yes, Mother it still means I'm not coming home. I'm here. Like I told you, Lilly and Charlie are my family. They know my plans, who to notify, my friends, and what arrangements need to be made. It'll be ok!" Mrs. Hall gave in, but not without one more plea. "Ok, but you're sure?" Glenn smiled "Yes, I'm sure. But there is something else you need to know. You have to promise me you'll keep it to yourself, and not do anything crazy. I mean it. It could cause a lot of legal problems." Mrs. Hall stuck her hand up and turned away, "Enough, I don't need to hear no more. Child you are going to put me in the grave before you get there! Where's my purse, where's my purse?" She hustled across the room and grabbed her purse. Opening it, she started rummaging through it, before she pulled out a flask. "Child, I thought I would save this for later, but I think I need it now!" She threw it back and took a couple of swigs. Glenn went on speaking, "Listen, promise me you will keep it to yourself? Trust me you need to know this." Mrs. Hall sarcastically rolled her eyes and frowned, "It's so important that I need to be told now?" Glenn was desperate. "Mom, it's important. Lilly and I are married, we've been married for years now." Mrs. Hall clutched her chest. "What, you got married without even telling me?" Pointing to the chair where Lilly had been sitting.

"Lilly, the one who was just in here? Is she, is she the one who…?" Glenn laughed, "Oh God no! How could you even think that?" Mrs. Hall let out a sigh, "Oh my God, she's kinda manly don't you think?" Glenn couldn't hold back the laugh. His laugh aggravated his mother. "What, you think this shit is funny? You think what you're doing to me is funny? Oh, hell no! Child, you won't do this to me. I sat back and kept my mouth shut. Have I been blind? I don't even know my own son!" Glenn tried to intervene, "I don't think it's funny. Lilly and I agreed to get married to help our careers. The less people that knew, outside of the Marine Corps, the better. But it turns out we are really good friends. We have been there for each other." Mrs. Hall was pacing the floor when Charlie returned to the room. "I'm back," but stopped in the doorway feeling the tension. Mrs. Hall gave an evil stare at Charlie before turning to Glenn, "I'm done! This ain't happening, No! …not right now! Death bed or no death bed, I'm your mother I deserve better." She paced back and forth furious, "No, no, just no, … I'm done here. … gotta go, I need time to clear my head." She grabbed her purse and looked at Charlie, "I suggest you get outta that doorway unless you want to wear that coffee!" She stamped her heels out of the room. Charlie walked into the room and smiled, "So I see that went well!"

****

Jedd walked out handing a beer to Noah before stirring the fire a bit and sitting down. Noah glared into the fire, letting his mind wander. It was almost hypnotic. Jedd sat quietly looking at the fire before speaking. "You know I sit back here most of the time by myself. Every now and then Mom might join me. Sometimes a couple of the guys from work might stop over. But for the most part, this is my little sanctuary. I sit back here and look at the fire and glare off out into the night sky. Checking out the moon and stars. Most of the time, it's clear and the sky seems mighty. Nothing but the hum of traffic, the voice of the city in the distance. It can be peaceful. A good place to let go." Noah smiled, this guy has a tender side, but he's also lonely. "So, you were in the Navy, what happened, didn't like it?' Jedd pondered for a moment before answering. "Eh, I wouldn't say I didn't like it, 'cause I did. It wasn't enough. I almost re-enlisted, but Dad got sick, and I came back home. My brother lives in Oceanside, him, and his wife. I knew they couldn't come back here. So, it was kind of left up to me." Noah smiled, "That's admirable of you. Not many guys your age would have done that." Jedd stirred the fire again, "Yeah, but now Ma is talking about going back up to West Virginia. She still has family up there, and all. If she does, who knows what might happen?" Noah thought for a moment, "You ever think about going back in?" Jedd grinned, "Yes, matter of fact, I have. Not the Navy though. I have thought about joining the branch you're in, the Marine Corps. I told you my brother lives in Oceanside, and I have visited there quite a bit and have known several Marines. I think they're more in line with what I'm looking for." Noah was surprised, "Really, that is a big change." Jedd cautiously proceeded, "I know right? But I think I want more of a challenge, besides people look at the Marines differently than they do the Navy, or any other branch of the service for that matter. It's a lot to think about, and there is still a lot of things that me and the military don't agree on." Noah took that as an opportunity to dig a little deeper. "Yeah, it can be a hard way of life, I don't always agree on everything, but I try and make the best of it. Every job has some give and take." Jedd, intervened quickly, "Yeah but they are so much into your personal life. I like to do my job, come home relax and do my own thing. But they want to dictate, the way you walk, the way you talk, how you grow your hair, hell, they even want to tell you who to date." Noah was taken aback by the last comment, did he just say what he thought he said, "I'm sorry, I get some of that, but I don't get the date thing." Jedd realized he said something he probably shouldn't have, and quickly stumbled to back pedal. "I mean you know, if a guy was to date someone who was married, or something like that. I mean who cares, who is sleeping with who." This guy was so ambiguous, was he trying to get a feel of what Noah was about. Noah tried to figure how he could bring up the gay thing without being obvious. So, he decided to make a joke about it, "I don't know, I recall a whole lot of the saying "what happens at sea, stays at sea"." Jedd laughed, he had gotten the innuendo, "I know right?" but then an awkward pause remained between the two.

As much fun as it was toying with Jedd, Glenn was still weighing on his mind. So, he decided to change the subject and bring it up. "I have to tell you, today has been a rough day. I appreciate all this. I don't want to sound like a downer. You have been the one good thing all day. But, when I called home, I found out more bad news. An old friend, I was planning on reconnecting with once I got to San Diego, is in the Navy Hospital. I guess they don't give him much longer to live. So now I really want to get on my way. I figure if I can make it there soon, I might be able to say my goodbye." Jedd, paused, "I'm sorry. Was he a good friend?" Noah chuckled, "Yeah, he is one of the best. You know one of the ones you can call in the middle of the night to help bury the body. So yeah, he is." Jedd sat quietly before speaking. "I'll talk to Carl tomorrow to let him know. He might be able to make things happen a little quicker." Noah glared into the fire, "Thank you, I appreciate that," before he turned to notice Jedd had been staring at him. The two locked eyes, neither saying a word.

Jedd looked back to the fire and spoke. "I'm not superstitious or anything. But I do believe sometimes fate brings people together at certain times in our lives to see us through. You know Angels among us." Noah watched him through the smoke and slightly floating embers of the fire while he spoke. It only added credibility to his words. Noah returned his gaze to the fire, realizing Jedd would stay there all night if Noah sat there with him. Although they were complete strangers, the mere presence of each seemed to offer the other comfort. Noah felt secure in Jedd's company and was glad he had taken him up on the offer to spend the night.

****

The elevator doors flung apart, and Lilly stepped out juggling coffee, donuts, and a tote full of files. She arrived in the room, both Charlie and Glenn were wide awake. "Charlie, child grab these coffees before I spill it all over." The Doctor had already been in to see Glenn and the nurse was just finishing up with routine checks before leaving the room. Once gone, Lilly couldn't hold back any further, "Ok, Glenn I brought all this paperwork up here with me, but before we get started, child you need to dish! How did it go with your Momma?" Glenn stared daggers at her without saying a word. Lilly noticed, "That bad huh?" Charlie chimed in. "Let's put it this way, when I came back with the coffee, she told me to get out the way if I didn't want to wear it." Lilly tilted back "Say whaaaat? Oh no, that don't sound good. Glenn what you got to say about that?" Glenn laid his head back., "She'll be alright. What more can I say? I told her and that is that." Lilly didn't agree with what was being said, "Glenn look at your grand ass! Child that's your mother. You need to make it right." About that time a voice spoke out from the door. "Well, I'm glad someone in here thinks so. I was beginning to think I was on my own around here." Glenn's mother walked into the room. All were quiet as she entered. Lilly looked at Glenn, "You want us to give you some alone time?" Glenn's mother spoke up before Glenn could answer. "No, no, from what I understand we are all "FAMILY" here. I think it is time we had a family talk. Charlie can you be a doll and close that door? Family talks can sometimes get a bit loud if you know what I mean." Charlie rushed to get the door. It looked like Mrs. Hall had come in full force this morning. Glenn started to speak, "Mom, don't…" but was hushed by Mrs. Hall. "Child, I have heard enough from you. I think it's time I say my piece, so you just sit there and keep your mouth shut! When I'm done you can say what you want but hear me first!" All three sat quietly. "I'm your mother, you hear me, your mother…! But right now, I'm pissed, hear – me – now! PISSED. I'm pissed that my son is in bed and dying of AIDS, and I can't do nothing about it. I'm pissed because he has the love of his life, and I was denied the opportunity to get to know him! … I'm pissed he got married and didn't trust his mother enough to tell her. But, most importantly, I'm pissed at myself!" She started crying. "My son, my son what have I done, that you would think I would ever walk away from you. What have I done that warrants you not being able to trust me enough to confide in me! And now, only because it is being forced upon you, are you willing to talk to me. I'm sorry, God knows I would walk through hell on earth for you."

Mrs. Hall turned to Lilly, "So you are my daughter-in-law, and turning to Charlie, you, you are my son's love. I don't know how this all works, but I want to be a part of my son's life, whatever he might have left of it. So, you want Ol' Mom to keep quiet about all this. Remain silent! Then let's talk, and by the end of the day, let's agree as a family what is best for my son." Mrs. Hall walked to Glenn, leaned over, and kissed his forehead. "Baby boy, I taught you better, ...have faith!" Lilly stood up and offered her seat to Mrs. Hall.

Wanting to know how everyone had met, Mrs. Hall started asking questions. Before long, the group was laughing and joking. Glenn paused for a moment, taking a slow glance around the room. Everyone he considered family was with him, he thought to himself. Why had he not spoken up so much sooner. He could tell, as much as his mother didn't want to admit it, she liked Lilly. It finally hit him; Lilly was very much like his mother. Not in a womanly way, but a strong woman way. He watched on as both Charlie and Lilly, entertained all the curious questions she had to offer.

Charlie took a break away and came to Glenn's side. "What you think?" Glenn smiled, "That's my Momma!" Charlie chuckled, "By the way I forgot to tell you last night. You know the lady I was telling you about in the elevator. I said she looked like she just stepped out of Vogue, that was her. That was your Momma. I just didn't know it at the time." Glenn looked at her with a smile. He sat there watching them enjoy themselves before he cleared his throat. "Listen up, Listen up." The room was quiet, and he had their attention. "Mom, I told you I don't want to go back to Arkansas, but that is only part true. I want to be buried there. I want to be buried at the family graveyard. If you want to do a funeral there that's fine, Lilly you and Charlie can go back if you like, or you can hold a service or something here. But I want my body to be taken back to Arkansas and laid to rest there. Lilly, Charlie, Mom, I'm counting on you, now don't let me down." Glenn's mother stood up and came to the bed grabbing his hand, pulling it to her face, kissing it. "My baby, ... MY Son, ...My Marine!"

****

Noah woke up to hear the bathroom door close and the shower turn on. It must be Jedd getting ready for work. He got up and gathered his belongings, laying out what he needed for the day.

He made the bed and soon heard the bathroom door open. He turned to see Jedd standing in his doorway, a towel around his waist and one in his hand still drying off. Noah, in his undies, was startled to see him there. Jedd spoke up, "Good morning. There is coffee out in the kitchen. Help yourself, Mom's already up and gone. She's out running around today and won't be back until later this afternoon. If you like, you can chill here, and I can stop back around noon, and take you where you need to go." Noah smiled and nodded his head, trying not to be obvious, but couldn't help but notice the chiseled body with just a slight grouping of brown hair center chest. Jedd turned and walked down the hall to his room and Noah followed him out but stopped to turn into the bathroom. Just as he was turning to the bathroom, Jedd dropped his towel and turned looking back down the hallway. Noah stunned, stopped, getting a full-frontal view. When he realized he had been staring, he glanced up to see Jedd had caught him. Noah quickly went into the bathroom and closed the door.

Oh my god, his heart was pounding. He couldn't get the image of Jedd standing in the doorway completely nude out of his head. He brushed his teeth and got in the shower. By the time he was done, surely Jedd will have been dressed and almost ready to leave. Noah had just finished dressing when Jedd appeared again, fully dressed, wiping his hands on a towel. "I'll talk to Carl this morning about your car. I know we're supposed to pull the engine today. If not, I think I might have a solution to getting you over to see your friend." Noah was surprised, "What do you mean?" Jedd, "Well, I don't want to say anything yet, … so we'll leave it at that for now. By the way, I like the tighty-whities." Jedd smiled and threw his towel at Noah and walked away. Noah was stunned but not surprised. He quickly took off after him. "Wait, (Chasing after him) …Hey you don't get to lay a line like that down and walk away." When he reached the living room, Jedd had his keys and was already at the front door. "I saw the Damron's guide in your truck. I know what it is." Noah smiled "You've known the whole time?" Jedd, "No, I mean I hoped, but wasn't for sure until this morning" Noah's jaw dropped. Jedd grinned, "hah, hah, …Hey, gotta head out, I'll be back around noon."

Noah finished getting himself ready for the day and made a few phone calls. Before he knew it, midday had arrived, and it was time to call on his truck. There would be a delay. The engine they thought was good from the junkyard had to be rebuilt. This was not good news. He tried calling the hotel and got a busy signal. It felt intrusive staying with a stranger, and he really wanted to get his own room. Jedd being gay, was even more reason to get his own room, so there would be no misunderstandings or expectations. Besides, Noah knew Marcus would not appreciate it. Maybe he should see how much a bus ticket would be and go ahead and report into San Diego. Once the truck was done, he could always take a bus back over and pick it up. If he reported in, he might be able to make it to see Glenn.

Noah heard what sounded like a car pulling in. He hoped it was Jedd and not his mother. How awkward that would be to have to sit with his mother. Noah peeked out the front window, "Oh thank goodness!" Jedd came barreling through the door all bright eyed and bushy tailed, "I brought some lunch! Hope you don't mind burgers." This guy was like a God send. Was he for real? Noah shook his head. "Thank you!" Jedd was bursting with excitement, "Come on, come on, come sit down, … you gotta hear this." As the two sat down to eat lunch, Jedd started in. "I take it you spoke to Carl already, and know your car is going to be a few more days than planned." Noah nodded in agreement as Jedd continued, "So, I told you my brother lives up around Pendleton. So, hear me out! I was thinking of going over there this weekend to visit and I can give you a ride, that way you'll be able to see your friend. I'll enjoy the company during the ride. Besides, we might be able to hang out a bit in San Diego." Noah paused, "Jedd, look, I appreciate all that you have done. But I think there are some things we need to discuss before I hop in a car and drive across country with you." Jedd stopped him. "What, you know where I work, for God's sake you know where I live…" Noah interrupted him, "Jedd, hold up. I know that… What I'm saying is I think there are things you need to know, if I'm going to do this." Jedd spouted off. "Your gay, …I get it, … so am I! …I thought we made it clear this morning?" Noah laughed, "Yeah, maybe not so clear for me, but don't you think we should at least acknowledge it. Talk about it, … Not just assume." Jedd chuckled, "Ok, what would you like to know, Noah?" Noah grinned, "Well first of all, … I need to let you know some things so there is no room for misunderstanding. I'm in a relationship, his name is Marcus. Also, the friend that is in the hospital, he's a Marine, also gay, and is dying from AIDS. I haven't seen him in almost three years. So that is me, now what about you?" Jedd chuckled, "Well, thanks for sharing that with me. Just so you know, I'm single, and glad you told me you are in a relationship. I can respect that, but it doesn't change anything on my part. As for your friend, I'm sorry to hear what he is going through. I don't have very many gay friends around here. Hell, I'm barely out to my family, and yes, my family knows. I look at it like this, it never hurts to make a new friend. I've never met a gay Marine. I have heard of them, …would see one out every now and then in San Diego, but never got a chance to meet one. How the hell do you do it?" Noah laughed, "Jedd, Jedd, Jedd, I'll save that for the road!" Both chuckled, "Ok, I'll do it only if I can help with gas. I was just thinking about taking a bus, and now you walk in the door with this. Really, what timing! I think you are a God send. You really are." Jedd grinned from ear to ear with excitement.

Chapter 28

When one door closes, another opens

The drive across the desert seemed to fly as the two chatted and played music. Turns out Jedd had a good sense of humor. The mustang cruised along the barren landscape. At times, they would roll down the windows and let the warm desert wind blow through the car. There was a sense of freedom, and excitement. Just as they crossed the border into California, they came across a sandstorm, pulling over until it passed and could see the road once again. Noah was amazed, only hearing about them in books. Once it cleared, he could see the sand dunes off to the north of the freeway. Jedd coaxed him to get out, "Come on, it'll be fun!" The two hopped out and took off into the desert heat, running up and over the dunes, before tackling and falling over each other, rolling down the dune hills. They were covered in sand, both laughing like small children at play. As they walked back to the car, a calmness had taken over Noah. His stress was gone for now. Jedd could tell Noah was in a brighter spot and his mood had gotten better. "You know, sometimes you got to remember to skip." Noah looked at him in puzzlement, "What?" Jedd, "You have got to remember to skip, you know like you did when you were a kid." Noah smirked, like Jedd was out of his head. "I think the heat is getting to you." Jedd smiling, he was serious. "No, come on, ..." He started to skip down the road. But stopped when Noah didn't join in. "Come on skip with me. Show me you haven't forgotten how to skip." Noah chuckled, "But why...?" Jedd was persistent, "Because if you skip, it'll keep you young! You know, no problems, no worries, no adult stuff, just skip." He took Noah's hand, "Come on now, skip!" Noah laughed thinking how silly it sounded, but somehow it made sense. So, he stepped off with Jedd. The two started skipping alongside the US 8 freeway. The passersby had never been so graced by the presence of the two as they skipped along. Noah let go of Jedd's hand and started laughing. Jedd himself was chuckling and laughing to see Noah let go. At one point, the two joined hands again and the cars drove past honking, even a semi-truck blew its horn. Both waved at every honk. How crazy they must have looked, but they didn't care what the world thought. At that moment, it was only the two of them, in their own desert playground, in good company, having fun, free of adult stuff, and the stresses of the world around them. They made it back to the car, hunched over and out of breath. Jedd breathing heavily, "See, I told you... Don't ever forget how to skip!" Noah still catching his breath. "Oh my god, I can't think of the last time I did something so spontaneous, and fun." Jedd laughed, "Can you imagine what those people passing by thought!" Noah reached over and put his hand on Jedd's shoulder, "I know what you're doing Jedd, and thank you, I appreciate it!" Jedd reached back and gripped Noah on the shoulder. "It's all good, come on we got to get you to San Diego."

****

The sun was just giving a golden morning glow to the Naval Hospital as the mustang pulled in. The fragrance of the eucalyptus trees, so familiar with Balboa Park and southern California, blew through the air. Noah stepped out of the car yawning and stretching, soon to be joined by Jedd. "We're here, we made it!" Noah grinned, "That we are..." As the two gathered themselves, standing and stretching, Jedd noticed a few sailors parking and getting out of their cars and heading in. One was wearing what he called the "Cracker Jack" uniform. Jedd spoke up. "I don't miss that!" pausing for a moment, "I remember this place, it's been a few years, but I remember it. I never thought I'd be here again." Noah listening, "Is that a good or bad thing?" Jedd, "No. Not good or bad, just never thought I'd see it again, never thought I'd have a reason. Huh." Noah looking around for a restroom, "Well I don't know about you, but I need to take a piss, let's see if we can find a head around here." Jedd trying to be cute, "Did you say a head or some head, you know small words make a difference?" Noah chuckled, "Ha, ha, ...a head!"

The two walked around in the courtyard before seeing a sign directing them to the restroom. Both used the head and refreshed themselves with some cold water on their faces, making sure they were squared away. Noah gave himself a once over in the mirror, "Well, let's see if they will let us in this bad boy" They headed to the elevator, once in, Jedd spoke up. "Will they let you in this early to see him?" Noah shrugged, "I don't know, I spoke to Lilly, and she told me to come up no matter what time I got in. So, I'm guessing she must have already taken care of it."

The elevator doors opened, and Noah stepped out, Jedd in tow. The halls seemed eerily quiet, and Noah's shoes seemed to squeak agitatedly across the highly buffed floor. They came upon the room, and Noah could feel the lump in his throat, and the emotions and tears seemed to take control before he even stepped in. He had to stop to gain his composure. He wanted to appear strong for Glenn. Jedd nudged Noah on the shoulder and pointed to the end of the hall at the waiting room. In a whisper, "I'll be down there if you need me."

Noah stuck his head around the corner to see Lilly sitting in the chair. She had on a hospital gown and mask on her face. She looked up and saw him and motioned with a shoosh over her mask for him to be quiet as she got up and came to the door. Noah stepped back and waited.

She came out and closed the door behind her, lowering her mask. She giggled as the two hugged. They held their embrace as she spoke through the tears. "Child you don't know how glad I am to see you!" The two stood there for a moment, each breaking the silence with only tears, and sobs. Noah patted her on the back, "Lilly, I heard you have been by him all the way! You have done a respectable job!" The weeping subsided and Lilly stepped back. "Thank you, Child I never dreamt it would be like this." Noah, who had already came prepared with tissue, handed her one. Wiping her tears away, she gave Noah a once over. "Well look at you! Step back now and let me gets a good look at you, … now twirl, let me see you…" Noah stepped back and turned with a chuckle. Lilly continued with her favorite thing to do when she was acting fem. She would put her finger up to her mouth and let out a soft, "Well child, …. Hehe, ... Look at you! You go child, you look good! Glenn is going to be so happy to see you." Noah stopped. "Well let's see you," as he made over her, "You're looking great girl!" Lilly chuckled, "Hush child you can't even see me with all this garb on."

As they chuckled, one of the nurses stepped out in the hall from a room and cleared her throat, making it obvious she heard them. Lilly got serious again. "We got to be quiet, they'll throw us outta here." She changed the subject, "So let me tell yah, are you ready for this?" Noah braced for the news, "I don't know? So, tell me, how bad is it?" Lilly shook her head, "There ain't nothing, I mean nothing good about this. Child has been through it all. You'll see here in a moment when we go in. I got to tell you, prepare yourself. He weighs nothing. I swear, I don't know how someone can be so skinny and still survive. Child is emaciated. Oh, can barely talk, because his breathing has slowed. We just got him to sleep; the nurses gave him something to calm the coughing. Which is new, because he usually is sleeping most of the time now. He knows your coming to see him. I couldn't keep it a secret. He's in such a bad place, that I wanted him to know, hoping to keep his spirits up. He's been asking for you the last couple of weeks, wanting me to find out where you were."

Noah shook his head and choked up. All this from a guy that could literally out do him in almost any physical sport or activity. Glenn had always been a perfect three hundred on the Marine Corps standard Physical Fitness test and took pride in it. Lilly continued, "Oh, you'll need to wear a mask and gown when you go in, they're right inside the door for anyone who comes in. You need a fresh one every time you go in." Noah frowned at the thought. "What are they afraid we'll catch it from him?" Lilly spoke up, "No child, his immune system is gone. He can't defend himself anymore. You might give him something." Noah apologized, "I'm sorry Lilly, I feel so stupid. I've heard so many things and seen so many prejudices, stupid comments, from people out of fear, I just thought they might be..." Lilly interrupted, "No need to apologize, it happens, and don't get me started, cause child I've heard 'em all! But no, this one is actually to protect him." Noah nodded in agreement. Lilly spoke, "So child let's get ready and go on in. If he is asleep, we'll just have to wait till he wakes up."

Noah entered the room and completed the task of sanitizing his hands at the sink and putting on the hospital mask and gown. Once completed, he walked further in, Lilly stood up and joined him at Glenn's bedside. Noah got his first glimpse of Glenn through the plastic tent over him. Glenn was still asleep. The tubes running from all directions and the machines monitoring, made it a bit difficult to see him and seemed confusing and complicated. Glenn was so skinny; the once rounded face was that of skin covered bone. His sunken jaws made his ears seem larger, but he held onto his notorious extreme flat top and jet-black hair. The disease had taken its toll. Glenn's hand lay at his side outside of the transparent plastic tent. Noah reached down and gripped it and held on without disturbing or waking him. As much as he wanted to not cry, he couldn't hold back the tears. Lilly grabbed a tissue and gave it to him to wipe them away. He stood holding Glenn's hand when Glenn spoke. "You Biatch, it's about time you got your ass here!" Noah smiled through the tears, "I agree, I was beginning to wonder if I was going to make it myself!" Glenn smiled, gasping for air, spoke softly, "Noey, I'm glad you came!" Noah chuckled and cried simultaneously. He was at a loss for words. Just holding Glenn's hand seemed to say more than anything he could find in words, so he gripped it tighter. Glenn opened his eyes, completely turning his head to get a good look at Noah. "It really is you!" Noah chuckled with a smirk, "Of course it is silly!" Glenn gasped for air, "They have me on so many drugs, sometimes I can't tell what is real and what is not. But I'm glad you came Noey. I was beginning to worry I may never see you again, …I wanted to tell you Goodbye!" Noah held on grasping his hand and shook it, "Come on now, we don't do goodbyes!" Glenn snorted a bit, "I know right? But Noey, I want you to know you have been a good friend, … I have many good memories with you." A tear fell from Glenn's eyes and his voice cracked, "I have always kept you in my heart, …You are one of the good ones." Noah lowered his head and listened to what Glenn had to say. Almost feeling guilty because he had not been there for Glenn the way he would have wanted to over the past few years. However, it wasn't till recently they had lost contact. Noah spoke, "I should have been there more for you! I'm sorry!" Glenn continued, "Hush child, …From the day we met down at the pier, we became almost inseparable. Both coming out in Southern Cal, Okinawa, the Strumen mess, Charlie, Champagne, and yes, this crazy stuff they call AIDS. You're a true friend, we can go days, months, even years without talking and pick right back up where we left off. Remember we use to make fun of wearing a condom?" Noah chuckled, "Yes, I know, better wear a condom, ...you might get him pregnant, wink, wink." Glenn gave a brief smile and soft laugh before continuing, "Noah take care of yourself, ... It is real." Noah sat and listened while holding his hand. "Listen, I don't want you to remember me this way. Not this, not this room, not any of this, it is not me. I want you to remember us laughing. We were fierce with attitude." Noah chuckled. "Yes, but I think you did it much better than me." Glenn laughed, "Someone had to teach your country ass, didn't they?" Noah chuckled as Glenn continued, "Noey, I've seen you go from a little skinny naive country boy into a man. You got good things ahead. Don't ever let someone stop you. Straight or gay." Noah nodded, "I won't." Glenn gasped for air as he continued, "We were Marines, Noey, not gay Marines, but Marines! ...Well, maybe with just a little more flair. You learned your lesson with Strumen, don't ever let anyone mistreat you again, and especially because you're different. You may not know it yet, you're a lifer. You love the Marine Corps! You remember me, and I was the one who told you first. One day when you're an old Jarhead, you remember all of us. The ones who didn't get to make it. I'm not talking about just the ones dying because of this shit, but all of us, the ones with a flair." Glenn chuckled as he rolled his head back, "We'll be rooting for you, and we'll be there in spirit. Promise me you'll remember all of us Noey!" Noah's tears fell, "I will, I promise old buddy, I will!" Glenn laid his head back and closed his eyes slowly falling to sleep.

The next couple of days panned out slowly. Mostly spent at the hospital, other than a brief ride to Lilly's place to sleep, shower, and return. It was now Saturday, and Glenn had been asleep for more than a day without even a slight moment of consciousness. Jedd had been in and out, stopping and checking up on him. Jedd was turning out to be a good guy, and Noah couldn't help but notice. He and Lilly hit it off and both joked incessantly. But for now, they were all at the hospital taking turns holding vigil along with Charlie, and Glenn's mother. Noah had met Glenn's mother; Glenn had not fallen far from the tree. Needing a break from holding vigil, it was now mid-day and Glenn's mother would be showing up soon. Noah, with Jedd, decided to get some lunch for the group.

The two arrived back at the hospital and were walking down the hall when they saw Lily standing outside crying. Without a word. Noah handed Jedd his things. He already knew what Lilly was going to say. As Noah went to hug her, she spoke, "The nurses said any moment now. It's over, Noah, it's over, he's gone." Noah held her as she cried. One of the nurses brought some tissue, and the two stepped into the room. Soft Gospel music filled the air. Charlie sat by the bed with his head held low holding on to Glenn's hand. Glenn's mother stood on the other side calmly poised, rubbing Glenn's forearm. Taking a glance to see who had entered the room, she turned her gaze back to Glenn. "Rest now my baby, rest." The plastic tent had been removed along with all the tubes, and Glenn's almost lifeless body lay in the bed. Noah and Lilly walked to the foot of the bed and gazed on, embracing each other. Glenn was surrounded by friends and family. Noah reached down gripping Glenn's ankle through the sheet letting him know he was there. Glenn's body tightened, and almost immediately went limp as he drew his last breath.

Chapter 29

The Reply, 2010

Minus a few boxes, and some paperwork on the desk, the office was almost completely empty. Noah and his niece, Adrian, were in the office emptying it out. He was excited to be getting new floors. It was now spring in Indiana, and the cleaning had begun. Adrian had just returned from taking a few boxes out to the garage. She started to grab the few items from the desk. Noah stopped her. "I'll get that, that's my book stuff, I have to know where I put it." Adrian inquisitive, "Book, what book?" Noah continued, "I thought I told you, you know, the one about my years in the service." It registered with her. "Oh, the one dealing with Don't Ask, Don't Tell. I thought you had decided against that. What changed your mind?" Noah paused from what he was doing. "I received an email, a while back from one of the guys I use to work with. He was writing a paper, you know, because of all the political stuff going on to lift the ban. Anyways, he remembered me and wanted to get my take on it. I haven't written him back, still not comfortable talking about it. But it did get me thinking. I decided to start writing it all down. I'm getting older, and figure I better do it before I forget. Who knows, maybe one day I'll release it." Adrian laughed, "I'm sure, knowing all the stories you have to tell, it will be a best seller." Noah laughed, "If only, …I have to finish it first, and get over my fear from the crazy policy of still being found out. Then it has to get published."

Adrian started to grab the other boxes on the floor, "Are these ok to take out then?" Noah, "Yeah, those are fine." Adrian paused briefly, "Well it doesn't hurt to have a pipedream; besides, I think your story should be heard. Did I ever tell you about the witch hunt that happened when I was stationed at Camp Lejeune?"

Noah stopped what he was doing in shock. "Saaay what? No, …I mean, I remember, something being reported on the news, about a witch hunt, but I didn't know you were involved?" Adrian continued her story, "Yes, so, most of the women Marines at Courthouse Bay were called to the Command building and asked specific questions about their time at recruit training, and the female Drill Instructors. Questions like, "Did we ever witness any untoward behavior between the female Drill Instructors? Did the D.I.'s ever try to touch any of us? Did any of the D.I.'s in the PCP, (Pork Chop Platoon) act too friendly? They never really came out and said lesbian, but it was obvious by the questions, they implied it." Noah was curious, "So, what was your take on it?" Adrian laughed, "My thoughts were how crazy the questions were, …Huh, we never had time to pay attention to what the D.I.'s were doing?" Noah laughed knowing what recruit training was like. Adrian changed the subject back to Noah not responding to the letter from Joel Hammond. "So, you need to respond back to him. He took the time to write you after all these years, … he remembered you. Obviously, something resonated with him. He wants to know your opinion, not everyone is out to get you, quit being so guarded, and let him know."

Later that afternoon, after contemplating what Adrian had said, she was right! Joel deserved an answer. He didn't ask if Noah was gay, he was just wanting to know his opinion on "Don't Ask, Don't Tell." Noah didn't have to out himself but could still give his opinion. He decided to respond.

Good day, Joel,

Nice to hear from you and thank you for your interest! Glad to hear you are finishing your education and hope the best for your success! Sorry for the delay and hope you can still find my response of use. As you may know "Don't Ask, Don't Tell" is not a topic in which I am comfortable talking about due to the nature of my past negative events in my former career in the Marine Corps. That being said, any policy that allows discrimination, unlawful entry, and rape of someone's personal life, due to prejudice, is not acceptable anywhere in our community, including the military. I have experienced this firsthand. I also say, you have experienced and seen the effects of the policy yourself. The results of this unwarranted investigation were an upheaval in leadership, loss of morale and added confusion simply because someone in the chain of command might have been gay. The sad cost to the taxpayers for this investigation was more than $60,000. The ramifications and fallout to a 19-year Marine with an honorable and meritorious service record was immeasurable. I consider myself a professional, but not without flaw. The current laws dealing with discrimination, religion, *sexual conduct, fraternization, and sexual harassment cover any challenge brought forward by the addition of sexual orientation. Being a professional means abiding by these regulations. As for religious views, we have separation of church and state. Our constitution allows for freedom of religion, or lack thereof. To place one's religious views or beliefs over another is to discriminate. In other words, if I am a Jew, or an atheist, or accepting of gays, you as a Christian may not agree with me, but you do not have the right to discriminate because I may not follow your beliefs or agree with you. So, with all this being said, it's not about whether gays can serve, they already are allowed to. It's about a policy that requires a service member to lie or hide their identity. "Don't Ask, Don't Tell" requires gay service members to hide the truth about who they are, which runs counter to the military's ideals of honesty and integrity. You know firsthand the military wants the highest level of honesty and integrity. This policy is saying, "Just don't tell us because we're not mature enough to handle it." I give more credit to our military community, and the individual Marine, Soldier, or Sailor. They are mature enough to handle this, because they handle it every day within their own families, and communities.*

Well, with this all being said, you can see where I take my stand on this topic. The last thing I would say, "If I were in a foxhole, I'm not thinking is this person with me straight or gay. I'm thinking are they on my side, and can they shoot straight and kill the enemy if needed?" So, the question is not, "Who are you sleeping with?" it is, "Can you do the job?"

I know this is a topic of heated debate and don't expect everyone to agree with my opinion. Glad you remembered me and thank you for your interest. Hope I was of some help, and good luck on your paper and future success.

Semper Fi,

Noah Barlow
Master Sergeant, (USMC Retired)

Noah reviewed his response a couple of times, still hesitating, before he finally let it go! He might as well get used to it. If he was going to write a book, it would take far more courage than responding to an email. Time to get over it! He opened a blank page and started the next chapter in his book.

1990's

Chapter 30

Shake it loose and let it fall

Afternoon PT had finished, and the weekend was about to begin. It had now been six months since Glenn had passed. Marcus' reenlistment was approved, and he arrived in San Diego, a few months earlier, and the two had been living in an apartment out in town. Noah had made a few new friends and had run into some old acquaintances. Running into Glenn and Lilly, reminded him, he needed to go ahead and contact Dusty about a divorce. When he returned to California, the Marine Admin looked her up and found she was still in the Marine Corps, stationed in Hawaii. Noah and she had lost contact when he had transferred back east. Both had long since reported the separation to the Marine Corps and neither were receiving benefits. It was time to put this chapter to rest and get divorced.

Looking at his watch, he was behind schedule, and decided to shower at work so he could meet his friend Jedd for a few drinks at Number One Fifth Ave. It was a neighborhood gay bar, on his way home. The two had maintained contact, and Jedd had been coming to San Diego off and on, since they first met. But today's meeting was important, Jedd had something he wanted to tell Noah and insisted he do it in person. Noah walked in seeing Jedd at the far end of the bar, they ordered their drinks, and headed to the outdoor area. After a few words, Jedd interrupted, "Ok, ok, listen you have got to be quiet." Noah smiled and was amazed how excited he had become. "Ok, …go ahead, let's hear it!" Jedd stood tall looking at Noah, "I joined the Marines." Noah surprised, "You did what?" Jedd shaking his hands at Noah, "I know right, …I joined the Marines." Jedd stepped back watching Noah's response. Noah sat with his mouth agape, "Oh my God, you did, …are you serious? But, what about, …" Jedd interrupted, "I know, it sounds crazy, but I have thought it all out! You were part of my decision. I mean, seeing how well you are doing, …and …and, well, not totally you. … I mean, my mom, she is moving back to West Virginia, my brother is here, and it's time I do what I want. I've been thinking about it for some time and dealing with the recruiter and keeping it under wraps until I was sure they would take me." Noah laughed, "Oh my God, of course they would take you! …Look at you, they would be crazy not to." Jedd continued, "That's not all, the reason I'm here this weekend, is I report in on Tuesday to start training." Noah hugged Jedd, in congratulations! "I'm happy for you, if you're sure this is what you want!" Jedd shook his head in acknowledgement. "It is, … I had been thinking about it for a while but put it on the back burner. When you came in the shop that day it brought it back front and center!" Noah, "Don't blame me, this is your doing!" The two chuckled and Jedd gave Noah another hug. When Noah pulled away to get his drink off the bar, he noticed a familiar face looking at him from across the room. "Oh, shit Jedd." He quickly turned away hoping he was wrong. "Jedd is that blonde guy at the bar still staring this way. No, he is walking over. Why do you know him?" Noah, with his back turned from the guy, "Yes, I believe it is my boss. What the fuck is he doing in here? This is a gay bar. I hope I'm not busted. If he says anything, you are gay, and I came in here with you for a drink" Jedd shook his head, when they heard that familiar voice, "Barlow, is that you?"

Noah turned to see his boss Matt Clark standing there in front of him. "Gunny, hey how are you doing?" Jedd shook his hand, "Nice to meet you. You are?" The two exchanged pleasantries, before the subject came up. Directed at Noah, "Do you know this is a gay bar?" Noah stumbled a bit, "Uh, … Uh yeah, I guess, I mean I never asked. I mean Jedd." Jedd realizing Noah was stumbling, "I think what he is trying to say, is I'm gay, and he came here with me, I didn't tell him. We just came out for a few drinks." Matt stood there looking, "Well, I come here off and on. I live just around the corner. It's walking distance from home." Noah realized he might be gay friendly but wasn't comfortable with outing himself. "Oh really, I didn't know you lived in the area Gunny." Matt spoke up, "Come on now, we're out of the shop, you can call me Matt. It makes it a bit awkward. You go by Noah?" Noah acknowledged him, "Yes, Noah." Jedd changed the subject that they had to go.

They said their goodbyes and were off. Noah walked out but looked back to see Matt staring at him. He waved goodbye.

****

Noah turned the lights on to the studio and walked in. It was Friday morning and he arrived early. Today was going to be a busy day. They had several shoot locations, and Noah needed to do a site survey of each. He was on a tight schedule, if he wanted to be back in time for the Graduation. Today wasn't just any graduation. Today would be the day Jedd would become a Marine. Noah was sure it seemed long for Jedd, but for Noah it seemed like it was just yesterday he told Noah he was going in. Noah gathered his gear, and started out the door, when the phone rang. It was Gunny. "Noah, this is Matt, hey, I had a rough night last night. Has Top been in looking for me?" Noah responded, "No, haven't seen him yet this morning." Matt took a breath and sighed, "Good, look, if he shows up tell him I had to go to Balboa. That should hold him off till I can get there." Noah responded, "Aye, aye, Gunny, I sure will," knowing it would irritate him. Matt on the other end, "Goddamn it don't do that shit, you know me man, it's Matt!" and he hung up the phone. Noah laughed. This had become routine for him.

Ever since he saw Noah at the gay bar out in town, he had broken the ranks of professionalism. He would tell Noah to call him by his rank only in front of others. His wall locker was in his office, and he would call Noah in and talk to him while he would change clothes. At times being totally nude and the two in the room alone, which made Noah uncomfortable. Gunny wasn't married and on weekends, he was always curious what Noah had planned. Also, asking if he was ever going to invite him over for dinner. It was like he was trying to press Noah's buttons. Gunny never knew for sure if Noah was gay, but Noah could tell he had his suspicions. Noah thought about coming out to him, Gunny would probably be cool with it. However, Gunny had a drinking problem and was already taking advantage without knowing. Noah could only imagine how lopsided the relationship would be for Gunny to find out. Who knows what he might want Noah to do? Any refusal, he could threaten to hold it over his head? Although it was unspoken, Noah felt Gunny was taking advantage of the situation already. Noah thought he might even be gay and looking to Noah to bring him out. Noah doubted it though. He knew many of the gay military, and specifically Marines. No one had ever heard or knew of him. Oh well, time to focus. With Gunny gone, Noah would need to get going, and rearrange part of his schedule. He was not going to miss Jedd's graduation.

After completing his rounds, Noah arrived back at the Recruit Depot. He had just enough time to walk over to the viewing stand. Upon arrival, he ran into Dean. Jedd and Dean started dating right before Jedd joined. They had maintained contact the whole time during his training. Basically, Dean was Jedd's war bride. When communicating, he wrote his letters pretending to be a girl. He would change the pronouns, in the event someone other than Jedd would intercept the letter. For all intents and purposes, he was Jedd's boyfriend. Visitor Sunday prior to graduating, Noah let the two use his office for some alone time. No one worked on Sunday, and there were no windows. Noah sat outside on guard for the two just in case someone was to show up. They were thankful.

They were beginning to recognize the recruits who distinguished themselves. Noah and Dean cut through part of the crowd and was standing alongside the viewing stand, in front of him were the honor grads in their dress blue uniforms. One by one their names were read. Noah did a double take. Was that Jedd at the end? Finally, the series honor grad name was read. "Jedediah Lauder." It was Jedd, he had distinguished himself as the number one recruit of his series and was meritoriously promoted to Lance Corporal. Noah looked at Dean, "Did he tell you about this?" Dean shrugged, "No, I don't even know what it means." When the honor grads finished, they did a left face and marched by. Noah and Dean could see Jedd had recognized them when he marched by. When they saw him last Sunday, he had not said a word about being Honor Grad. The little shit had kept it to himself.

Later that night, when all had settled, Jedd and Dean stayed at Noah's apartment. It was no surprise when Noah found out Jedd would be a mechanic and assigned to the motor transport field. After all, that was what he had been doing for years now. He had to complete his formal schooling, and then was going to Twentynine Palms.

Jedd, pursuing his dream, had stirred the emotions in Noah. Noah applied for the Naval Advance Motion Picture Photography School in Pensacola, Florida and was accepted. All those things he had been holding onto were building up. Marcus and he were no longer sharing the same bed. Everything was an argument. If Noah went somewhere, Marcus was full of questions. Noah could tell he had lost trust in him, and for good reason. Their once good relationship had now become combative, competitive, and seemed to be spiraling downward. Noah knew it was time to follow through on what he had been contemplating for more than a year. He wanted him and Marcus to remain friends, but the relationship was over. With him leaving for Pensacola, it seemed the right time to breakup. This would allow the both of them a clean break. Noah would be gone for six months, and hopefully, the time apart would allow them both to move on.

Noah had gone over the scenario in his head over and over again on how to tell Marcus. When the time came, it was still not easy. Both cried, Marcus wanting to know if Noah was sure of his decision. Noah stood fast. "Marcus, it's just not fair for you or me to keep doing this. I know we both have dreams, and directions in life. Not pursuing them is only causing resentment for one another. It will eventually make us end up hating each other. In the end, I want to be able to look at you and know I did the right thing by letting you go. We will hurt for a while but eventually we'll move on and be the better for it!" Marcus thought about it and was in agreement. "I understand what you're saying. It's just, you have become such a big part of my life. How do I wake up tomorrow and you're not here?"

The next week seemed to go quickly. Getting his act together had become his priority. He researched and contacted Dusty. She and Gloria were still together and doing well. Like Noah, she agreed, and was willing to make the divorce happen. Because California took so long to finalize a divorce, they could file in Hawaii, and it would be final in 30 days. Noah moved in with Toni, a friend he worked with and her partner. Jedd had come down for the weekend to help Noah with the move and was doing some house cleaning of his own. He was calling it quits with Dean and was making it final this weekend. Misery loves company. But in truth, Jedd was happy being single and didn't want to be tied down this early on in his new career.

It was Saturday night, and after Coco's many attempts to get Noah back into the scene and out from his slumber, he finally agreed to go out with her clubbing. Noah had picked up Coco and she had a new hairweave done to look extra special for the occasion. Out for a light dinner, and a few cocktails at a couple of the known hot spots, they were off to WCPC's for a late night of dancing. Arriving at the club it seemed, within minutes, Coco's popularity with the men immediately put her at the center of the dance floor. Noah didn't mind as he watched on, she was in her element. She loved to dance, and she loved the attention. The guys loved giving her the attention as she cast her spell on them. But it was more about she made them feel like they were part of something, part of the who's who if she recognized them. Anybody that was anyone in the local gay community had to know Coco. No one wanted to look like they were a loner and knowing Coco was a sure way to break the ice at any affair. Standing at the end of the bar, away from most of the crowd, Noah found himself in his own head. The music blaring and the lights from the dance floor illuminating in slow motion the different poses of the crowd as they bobbed and weaved with each flash of the light. At one time in his life, he would have enjoyed this and been center with Coco, but something had changed. He wasn't a bar person. It's what he had feared would happen with the split from Marcus. However, he had come to terms, and resigned to the fact it was career first from now on. The military was not conducive to married life, and it took an incredibly special relationship to make it work. Add being gay to the mix, and it made it even harder. This had grown old, and he did not miss it. Even though it was over with Marcus, he longed for the day he would find the right partner and be able to enjoy an evening at home. Away from being alone in a crowd. Away from the feeling of being on the outside looking in. There had to be something more. A poem he had written years before still held true. From behind he heard a voice speak, "You look about as thrilled to be here as me." Noah turned, surprised to see

Jedd standing behind him. "What, … what are you doing here? I thought you were, …" Jedd interrupted, "I was, and I did, It's over." Noah caringly, "You all right? Want to talk about it?" Jedd tight lipped, "No, not really. You know how these things go. Nobody is a winner." Noah turned back to the bar as Jedd joined him, "It just sucks." Jedd concerned, "What about you, why you all up here at the bar alone. Why aren't you out there with Coco shaking your booty?" Noah laughed, "No, I was just thinking to myself, how I always feel out of place in bars like these. It's like somebody forgot to give me the memo or let me in on the secret." Jedd nodded his head, "I know. I came here hoping I would find you guys. I don't think I would have stayed had you not been here." Noah decided to share, "You know I wrote a poem and was just thinking of it when you walked up." Jedd curious snuggled up to Noah, "Well come on I have to hear it, Mr. Poet." Noah cautious, "Ok, but you have to be honest, and you can't laugh." Jedd smirked, "Ok, promise to be honest, ….and not laugh." Noah paused and he drifted in thought before speaking.

"Even though the night surrounds me. The pink posey and their full spell bound. I turn my head as stranger remembering the night as a hologram, wrapping me in a cloak. Not tangible, just mist and smoke. One touch, one kiss, one glance, one stroke, Napoleon could have designed the plan placing me in the center of your heart and the opposing's in my hand. Oh, the illusion that turns to disillusion seems so real. Yet, I still believe in a thing called forever."

Jedd stood quiet for a moment after Noah finished. Noah waited patiently, "Well???" Jedd acted like he was thinking it thru, "I get it, … I get it, not sure about the "Napoleon" thing. I guess it's good, I'm not really a poetry guy…" Noah smirked, "So, that's it I lost it on you?" Jedd started laughing, the bartender interrupted, "Alright, you two love birds needing another drink?" Both were caught off guard by the comment, and looked at each other, Noah leaned into the bar, "No, no, you think we're together?" being pushed aside from Jedd. "So, you think we're a couple?" The bartender smiled, "Look I don't know if you are, or not, what I'd really like to know, are you ready for another." Noah looked at the dance floor. Seeing Coco in her groove, he decided why not? He answered, "No we're good..." as they headed to the dance floor.

Working their way through the crowd, they arrived at Coco with a dry hump from behind. Coco kept rhythm before turning to realize it was them. She was sweating profusely from being on the floor for so long and showed no signs of leaving soon. She leaned into Noah so he could hear. "It's about time you got your sexy ass out here!" Noah smiled and the entourage continued. As the music played, Noah let go and nothing was happening in the world except the lights and vibration of the music. He was present in his mind, and totally carefree. Enjoying the dance as the music played on. It seemed they had been dancing for a while when Noah felt something fall across his face. At first, he thought it might have been confetti. Then he felt it again and looked around. On his shoulder was what he thought was a black rope. He grabbed it, and took a closer look being a bit surprised. Where did this come from. Then it hit him. It was a braid of hair. He looked to Coco and realized it had fallen from her head. But not only had she lost one, as she moved and bobbed her head, they were breaking free from her scalp. She was losing her weave. By the time Noah could say anything, others were already picking pieces from themselves as well. Jedd held one up showing Noah. Coco continued to dance unaware. Noah tapped her on the shoulder. She turned to look up at him as he held the braid. She was confused and puzzled. The music was loud, so Noah motioned to his head holding up the braid and pointed to her head, before handing it to her. She paused to look at it, she rushed to feel her hair, only to realize she had now lost quite a few. With her jaw open, Coco now stood in the center of the floor grabbing braids, along with others handing them to her. Embarrassed, she quickly left the floor in a rush. Noah, and Jedd followed behind, but couldn't keep from laughing. They waited outside the restroom until Coco finally appeared without any braids whatsoever on her head. She stuck her hand up to her mouth, and blushed, before she broke out in laughter. Noah had been reluctant to laugh in front of her as to not make her more uncomfortable, but now joined in with her. Coco spoke out, "Well I guess they meant what they said." Noah puzzled "Who?" "My hairdresser..., Child they used a new type of glue to attach the braids but told me not to get my hair wet for 48 hours. I guess they were right. All this dancing making me sweat, child loosened the glue. Now come-on child let's get outta here!"

Chapter 31

Pensacola, Desert Shield/Desert Storm

Noah arrived at Pensacola late in the afternoon. Finding his way onto the Navy Air Station, he soon found the Marine Admin and checked in. With the heightened security on the base because of the threat to the nation with Iraq and the middle east, he decided to stay on base. Assigned temporary quarters until the next day, he found the gym and a running trail and headed out. The trail along the water, and open terrain, was quite a bit different than California. Other than passing a few people along the way, it was peaceful. He gave thought to what he had left behind, but more importantly he was excited to begin this new journey here at the Naval School Photography. The base itself was an air station, and home to the Blue Angels, and also the training school for Naval pilot training. He thought how lucky to be here, and what a privilege. The Marines had provided him with more opportunities than he ever dreamed of when he first enlisted. All he knew, it was the time for him to shine. No more procrastinating, and just doing what he needed to get by. Now was the time he needed to apply himself and prove once and for all, to himself and to others, he had what it took to be outstanding, if not one of the best in his field. He decided to make a plan of what it was going to take to remain focused solely on graduating at the top of his class. This would require more discipline than what he had been giving. He would need to cut out partying and drinking and focus more on self-improvement, hitting the gym, running and meditation, and eating right. Homework was first priority over all else.

Noah couldn't help but think of Jedd, now on his way to Saudi Arabia, in support of Kuwait, and the heightened security of the military. Jedd was really given no warning. When he reported back from San Diego, they were briefed and within 72 hours were on a plane headed to the Gulf. Saddam Hussein and his Iraqi Army invaded and was occupying the country. President Bush, along with the UK and several other nations, joined forces in show of support for Kuwait and were preparing for a possible invasion, if necessary, to regain control of the country and expel the Iraqi forces. Noah prayed for Jedd's safety! On their last phone call, Jedd was excited to be going and, in his words, "This is what I signed up for!" Their relationship had become ambiguous. Either out of fear of commitment, or of ruining what they already had in the event it didn't work out, neither was willing to call it more than friendship. They really cared for each other, and who knows maybe at a different time, or place, things might grow into something further. For now, it was nice knowing someone else was out there without expectations, and only wanting the best for the other.

Being deployed can be isolating for any Marine, but even more for a gay one. Noah decided to commit to writing Jedd at least once a week, just to let him know he was not alone. Noah was a few days into training when he first heard of the naval bombardment. Receiving his first letter from Jedd, he found out he was in Saudi at an undisclosed location doing mockups in preparation for what looked like would be a hostile invasion. The bombardments continued every night for weeks, and Noah remained glued to the TV in the evening watching it unfold and waiting for word along with the rest of the world. Iraq continued to provoke the US and coalition forces with Scud missile attacks. It was late February when the US and Coalition forces finally attacked and, within one hundred hours, declared a cease fire. A few days passed and Noah had not heard from Jedd, nor did he know his whereabouts. Noah had just finished his evening run when he returned to the barracks and turned on the news. The reporting of the atrocities the Iraqis committed were becoming apparent, and the show of U.S. forces in country being heralded as heroes by the Kuwaiti people were being displayed. After watching for a few moments, he decided to turn to his homework, when the news showed a U.S. Marine convoy stopped. Noah paused, and sure enough, he saw Jedd hop out of one of the vehicles. A few weeks later he finally received a letter from Jedd. He had been part of the ground assault and saw firsthand the carnage and suffering inflicted from the bombings on both the Kuwaiti people and Iraqi forces. In his words, "I cannot begin to erase the images that are forever embedded in my mind!" He explained the highway of evacuees trying to escape back to Iraq and killed in place as they traveled. He spoke of the mine and booby traps and improvised explosive devices that lay planted along deaths highway. Their movement was slowed as the armored bulldozers busted through. Every day and every inch of movement had become a threat. Jedd wrote,

"*My senses are heightened, and every move has become calculated to the point where it now is routine, and ordinary. But it is not ordinary, I remind myself. This is not a world I would want for anyone. At night I try to sleep, not knowing when or if the sirens will sound for incoming. They say the threat is no longer with the cease fire. Now, if I can just convince my mind to believe there isn't one.*"

Noah sat in contemplation of the words Jedd had written. Jedd, normally upbeat, now spoke with grimness and despair. Noah wrote with compassion. Although he couldn't relate to the pain and suffering Jedd might have witnessed, he reinforced the support the American troops had back home. Most were proud of the job they had done and considered them heroes.

"*Jed, I can't tell you how surprised I was to see you on the news. I know you are in the thick of it, but what you're doing isn't without notice. I must tell you I have seen the outpouring of support, and patriotism this country is currently displaying. Everywhere I go, ...I see 'support our troops' signs, and bumper stickers, along with so many yellow ribbons. All holding onto hopes for their loved ones return. I myself say a prayer each night for your safe return, along with all those currently deployed. I believe in you, and the American people. You and their resolve give me faith we still have a world worth living in. Looking forward to the day we can sit across from a fire and have a beer and contemplate saving the world. Until then, I pray for your safe return. Now buckle up, buttercup, and get this job done! (Laugh, laugh) PS. By the way, when was the last time you tried to skip?*"

With so much focus on the Gulf war, Noah's time in Pensacola went by quickly. Noah and Marcus still had not communicated since the split. He missed Marcus, and thought of calling him, but was concerned of giving the wrong impressions, or false hope. Now that they had spent time apart, he was convinced more than ever, they made the right decision. His routine, he had established at the beginning, was paying off. Now just a few days from graduation, he found his mind clear, and focused, with his physical fitness reaching plateaus he had never achieved before. Most importantly, he had received news he would be the class honor graduate. He was able to attain the goals he had set for himself when he arrived. The future was looking great.

Once he left Pensacola, he headed for a quick trip back home to Indiana. He was ready for a much-needed break, and also to help his father with repairs to the homestead. His niece Adrian had since gotten out of the Marines, but married one, and her husband was deployed to Okinawa. She was staying at the homestead and was due with her first child at any time. Noah found out, while home, there would be another Marine in the family. His nephew, Rodney, Adrian's little brother, and Gabbi's son, had joined the Marines and would be reporting in for recruit training later in the year. Jedd was still in Kuwait, but had finally received a return date, and would be back in California by the time Noah would arrive.

The visit was productive, and the family barn was once again waterproof and ready for another twenty years. As much as he enjoyed his family, it was time to leave. Noah said his goodbyes and was off to California. He decided to take the southern route, and stop off in Toadvine, Alabama to visit his old friend Bob. Remembering meeting Bob and the story he told of his hometown, he couldn't pass up the opportunity to stop and see him. Bob had served two tours in the Marines, but when his father became ill, he left to return to the family farm and keep the business running. He and Noah had become good friends and had stayed in contact over the years. Noah had an open invitation to stop by and see him. Bob was very southern and gentle in his ways. He would always tell Noah, "I don't have many friends, but the ones I do, I call them friends for life." He would jokingly say, "I'm the one they call when they want to bury the body." Noah always felt there was a dark side to Bob but could never figure it out. He learned early on, never let the sweet southern gentle manners be confused for weakness. On Okinawa, Bob had his share of confrontations and fights. When provoked, like anyone, Bob could become a son of a bitch.

Noah pulled down the long dirt road leading up to the old country farmhouse that was right out of a page of American Nostalgia. White siding, big front porch, and, of course, the old hounds coming out barking as he pulled in. In many ways, it reminded him of his father's place, only much more secluded. Past the farmhouse were various barns, a few cattle, and woods. In the pasture, Noah even noticed the family cemetery. There was not another property within miles. Bob's family had owned it for generations. Noah remembered the stories Bob would tell about his family, and the farm. The place was much more beautiful, in person. The dogs soon brought Bob out of the house and onto the front porch. Quieting the dogs, "Dolly, ... Rank, shut up, and get over here! Don't worry they won't bite. They just don't get many visitors back up in here." Noah hopped out and walked up giving a handshake and a hug. "How the hell are you?"

Bob helped him with his bags, and let him settle in, before he took him on a tour of the farm and the area. Driving around for a while, the two ended up at one of the local watering holes. Bob admitted he had never been in the place before, but it was as good as any to get a bite to eat. Because the area was remote, there weren't many establishments around to choose from. After grubbing on the greasy bar food, and a few drinks, Bob moved to the pool table and was quickly into a game. When he started winning, he was confronted by one of the ruffians, who was being a bit of a bully. It started out over a pool game but became personal. Next thing the guy started mocking Bob and belittling him about his gentle manners. Bob started to rear up against him, and the guy's cronies joined in. Grabbing Bob, they punched him in the gut a couple of times, knocking the wind out of him. Noah came over, and they started to go for him, but backed down when the bartender came around with a bat. Bob and Noah stepped away. Instead, Bob went to the bar, finished his drink, and went outside to his car and waited. Noah tried to get him to leave, but Bob wouldn't have any part of it. Shortly thereafter, the gentleman came out of the bar and stumbled toward his car. Bob hopped out and grabbed his tire iron from the back and walked over. The gentleman recognized him, called him a few choice words, and next thing Noah saw was Bob beating the guy senseless with the tire iron. When Noah arrived, the guy lay unconscious as Bob still beat him. Noah pulled Bob away, not sure if the guy was still even alive, he was bleeding so bad. It was like Bob had become this mad man, enraged. Once he calmed down, Bob spit on the guy, "Now, how does it feel to get your ass whipped by a faggot!" and spit again. They heard a noise from the bar, Noah turned to go investigate when, out of nowhere, he felt a blow to his head and went blank.

The next morning, he awoke to one of Bob's dogs barking at him in the face. He sat up to realize he was in the middle of Bob's family graveyard. How the hell did he end up here? His head was pounding, and he reached to rub it when from behind he heard someone approaching. He turned to see Bob with a shovel returning from deep in the cemetery. "It's about time you woke up sleeping beauty, …thought I was going to have to bury you out here!" Noah confused, "What happened?" Bob laughed, "You don't remember? Hah, …One of those guys hit you from behind, but he didn't see me coming. That's ok, I made sure they won't be messing with anyone again." Noah was puzzled and knew Bob could be dangerous, "Bob, ...what did you do? You didn't…" and he was interrupted, "Now don't you worry yourself about all that, but we probably shouldn't go back to that bar again any time soon." As he chuckled. "Come on now, let's get you up and in the house for some breakfast. It looks like that head of yours might need some attending too." Bob helped Noah up, and the two stumbled across the pasture. Noah tried several times to get more out of Bob, but he remained silent. Noah knew from then on, Bob was never to be taken lightly, the soft demeanor, was a facade for a deep dark underside.

Rodney joins the Marine Corps

It was bright and sunny out as the recruits marched on to the grinder. Noah watched from the studio as they lined up in the procession. Time to go, he thought. He walked out and over to the reviewing stands, then looked around. The Marine Corps band had just taken their place, when he saw his sister Gabbi standing, trying to find her new Marine. It was Rodney's graduation day. Noah walked over to the family. His sisters Gabbi and Birdy, along with his niece Adrian, and his dad and stepmother Claudia were all there to see the ceremony. Noah was glad Beck could make it, being he still harbored harsh thoughts toward his stepmother's sabotage of his own graduation. He sat next to his father and answered questions each step of the way.

The next few days the family stayed at Noah's house and toured San Diego with their new Marine, before heading back to Indiana. Dropping them off at the airport, Noah was relieved. He wasn't used to having so many people around. It would be short lived; Rodney would be back in a couple of weeks and would be doing further training at Camp Pendleton. Noah offered him a place to stay when he had time off or on the weekends. Rod was aware of Noah being gay but didn't care. It was never an issue because it was never made one.

When Rod returned from leave, Noah showed him where the spare key was, and he could come and go as he pleased. After a few months, it became normal having Rod around on the weekends. Noah enjoyed his company and Rod had no problem helping out with chores around the house. "It makes me feel like I'm at home." he would say. He always had questions about the Marine Corps and looked up to Noah being a Sergeant. Many of Noah's friends liked Rod and thought of him more of a little brother. Jedd came down, the first time they met, he and Rod hit it off, both being Marines and long-distance runners. They would often go for long runs when they both were in town staying at Noah's. Rod himself was very much straight, and many times Noah would come downstairs to find a strange woman in his house. One morning Noah came down and a really large woman was asleep on the couch. Rod lay next to her on the floor. Later that day when she left, Noah was anxious to confront him. "Rod, I don't mind you bringing a lady home, but do I need to put a weight limit sign on this sofa." Rod laughed, and ducked his head bashfully, "Uncle Nollie, she is a nice lady!" It became a weekend routine for the two to do a long-distance run Saturday morning, often competing who could run the furthest.

A few more months had passed, and Rod's training came to an end, and so did his stay at Camp Pendleton. He was being sent for duty in Hawaii. The day he was flying out, the two got up and had their last long distance run together. Noah slowed toward the end and Rod, in his Marine Corps voice, "Come on, Uncle Nollie, pain is just weakness leaving the body!" Rather than show his emotions, it was Rod's way of saying, he was going to miss him. Noah chuckled, "Fuck that, Pain is pain!"

Chapter 32

Syracuse

The base realignment commission hearings had finished, and the TV section had fulfilled their mission of providing live feeds. All had gone off without a hitch. It was a high-profile project involving Congressmen and Senators, and high-ranking Generals. All advocating to keep their bases open. Noah and the crew had gained quite a bit of visibility throughout the OCC field. Noah was up for reenlistment and chose Tustin for his duty station, keeping him in southern California, at least for a while. It was a wing unit, and he could be deployed on a moment's notice. Besides, he had grown tired of MCRD. It was constant high visibility, with frequent visitors, and having to set the example for recruits. It was eyes on all the time. The Commandant had stated the Marine Corps mission was making Marines and winning battles. He had been supporting the "Making of Marines" side long enough. Now it was time to go to the "Winning Battles" side.

At first, the drive from Oceanside to Tustin seemed long. Day after day fighting traffic, became tiresome. On long weekend holidays, the 45-minute ride could become hours. Originally Noah thought he would be working in Tustin, but turns out, although his unit was headquartered in Tustin, his workplace building was actually on Marine Corps Air Station, in El Toro. He had now been there for several months. The Gulf War went from Desert Storm to Desert Shield and was beginning to wind down. There was talk of him going over, but because of the shortness of the operation, his number never came up. Sitting at his desk, Gunny Clarkson came in and threw some paperwork down. "Read that and let me know your answer. Your name came down from the Head shed at Quantico as a viable candidate for this program. I'll need your answer by tomorrow." Noah reviewed the paperwork. It was an application to attend an advance school at Syracuse University. The program was called the "Military Motion Media Studies Program." Gunny came back in and stood over Noah as he read. "You know this program went away for a while. It's a new DOD School and they are only looking for one Marine candidate to attend, along with the Navy and the Air Force candidates. Whoever is chosen must be the best. How that person performs will determine whether they continue the program. If you decide to go for it, your application will be reviewed along with all other submissions. You meet all the basic requirements, and like I said, your name was requested to be submitted. It's extremely competitive, you are young and low ranking amongst the candidates, but your work has been impressive. I think you should go for it. The Headquarters Marine Corps Audiovisual will determine the candidate." Noah sat and listened. His mind was running rampant. He never knew this program existed, of course Gunny said it was new. Gunny started to walk away, before spouting off, "If the answer is yes, this is kind of short fused. You'll need to write a paper, explaining why you are the best candidate to represent the Marine Corps. Oh, I would mention any prior education, or Honor Grad/class ranking you might have had. That will show them you can compete academically. Have the paper to me for review by tomorrow morning. Sergeant Barlow, I know this needs some thinking over and rearranging in your personal life. If you like, go take the afternoon off and think about it. Talk to whoever you need to talk to and get back to me. We'll revisit this tomorrow. Oh, just in case you don't want to go, you can explain to me why not. Son this is a privilege, and an opportunity of a lifetime. Gifts like this don't come by that often."

Noah gathered the application and headed home. The drive seemed only minutes before he was sitting in his living room reviewing the paperwork. This was a big step. It would be a career breaker if he failed. He wasn't even familiar with Syracuse. He thought about it for a while, who could he call that could talk to him seriously about this. His friend Chris. He was well educated and came from Toronto and was familiar with the Northeast. Noah contacted him and he agreed to stop by later that evening to answer any questions. Better yet, he was familiar with the process, and had actually been to Syracuse University. He definitely could give some guidance.

After talking to Chris and, contemplating his move, going over all the pluses and minuses, Noah decided to give it a shot and go for it. Before he made any rational decisions, he had to be chosen. It sounded as though he might be a long shot. If not selected, at least he let the higher ups know he was ready and willing to grow. The next morning, he turned in his application, crossed his fingers and let it ride. It would be a few weeks before any decision was to be made. His thoughts turned to getting his affairs in order in case of a transfer.

Chris had a connection in the area and did some snooping to find Syracuse had a gay student association. This would be a good starting point if he needed to find housing or a roommate during his stay. He still had never forgotten how a slight slip up could be, like the one he and Dodge had with their first apartment in Oceanside. The last thing he needed was another repeat episode of a nosy landlord asking too many questions. Having a referral of gay friendly apartments would be a plus. But still, Noah had to be careful with whom he communicated, gay or straight. It wasn't uncommon for a gay person to unintentionally out someone in the military. Most did not understand the secrecy required, to be able to continue to serve under the policy on homosexuals. Of course, there were those gays who, for whatever reason, would also intentionally out someone. At times, certain expectations could come from one who helped, seeking ulterior motives. Leaving them to feel rejected or betrayed when the efforts did not reach their expected reward. Not ready to take a risk, Noah put a pause on any communication until he knew for sure he would be going. He would try and keep all thoughts out of his mind, in hopes of not building too much expectation.

The next few weeks went by slowly. He had just finished a shoot, and was offloading the equipment, when Gunny came out and told him he needed to be in his office immediately. Noah finished what he was doing, freshened up and headed for his office. When he turned the corner, he saw his Commanding Officer, talking with Gunny. As he got closer, he could also see Master Gunnery Sergeant. Ok this better be good, he thought, or it's going to be really bad. Noah beat on the hatch, and before he could finish, the Major told him to get in the office. Gunny sat behind the desk. "You think you're really smart, you have really messed up this time Sergeant Barlow. You thought we wouldn't find out. What do you have to say for yourself?" Noah had no idea what they were talking about. So many things passed his mind. Did they find out he was gay? He was sweating, in a panic mode. He had to say something, "Excuse me Gunny, I don't understand what this is about?" Gunny, stern faced, "What is this about? You think you're so smart, well, now you are going to have to prove it. You were selected, you're going to Syracuse!" Noah was silent. Part in awe, and part relief. "Did I hear you right Gunny? I was selected?" Gunny started laughing, "You heard right you big goof, you're going to Syracuse. Congratulations!" He stuck out his hand and Noah shook it. The Major and Master Gunnery Sergeant were right behind him. Both expressing how much of a privilege it was, and how it would change his future. Master Gunnery Sergeant, informed him, "I spoke to Headquarters. It was keen competition there Marine, but they tell me your packet was unanimous. It stood out above all the rest. Outstanding job! We are all extremely proud of you, and the Marine Corps is lucky to have you within its ranks."

Noah arrived at Syracuse with his two sisters, Lois, and Birdy in tow. They were to help with a preliminary house hunt. Checking into the hotel, Lois laughed, "My first time at a hotel with a man, and it's my brother!" The three chuckled. Tired from the road trip, the two ladies stayed at the hotel, while Noah went to meet Steve from the student gay association. The two had spoken a few times, and he was willing to assist in helping to find a place for Noah to stay while at Syracuse. Noah agreed to stop by his home, just off campus. When Noah arrived, Steve met him at the door and invited him in. The two sat and talked for a while. Noah listened to all he had to say. He gave some really good leads and tips about Syracuse University, and the city as a whole. They spoke of local hangouts. Where to go, and not to go, if he ever found time away from his studies. He had compiled a list of potential apartments, and even rated them. He let it be known he would keep an ear to the ground and if he heard of anything of interest, would let Noah know. As Noah stood up ready to leave, Steve became a bit forward and grabbed Noah's crotch. Noah was taken aback by his advances. Had he done something to mislead this guy. Noah reached down and grabbed his hand and moved it away gently, trying not to be cruel. "Sorry, if I crossed signals. It's just I wasn't..." when Steve shrugged his hand away and tried again. "Oh, come on I saw the way you were looking. No one's around, you know you can feel it." He grabbed Noah's hand and placed it on his own crotch. "Feel that, feel how big it is, I saw you looking earlier, come on show me what a real Marine is made of!" Noah jerked away, and grabbed his belongings, "That's it, we're done here! ...What are you? ... some kinda creep, who uses this association to try and pick up guys! Geez, ...give me a break! You want to find out what a real Marine is, push your crotch on me one more time and you'll pull back a nub." As Noah was leaving, Steve followed behind trying to speak, "Look I'm sorry, it's not really like that. I misread, I mean, ...It's just that I thought..." Noah paused, opening the door, "That's the problem, ...you thought!" as he left slamming the door behind him. Noah made it back to the hotel room and Lois and Birdy were waiting. They asked how it went, and when Noah told them, Birdy sat quietly, listening until he finished venting. "Really, hmm, ..." she looked at Lois with a grin, before speaking again. "Was he really that bad, ...I mean come on, a little wouldn't have hurt yah." As she smirked. "I'm just saying..." Noah was shocked by her reaction, "Come on, ... really?" Lois unconsciously laughed catching Noah's attention, he frowned. She quickly changed her attitude to a patronizing one. "Birdy, how could you?" she paused trying not to laugh, "Maybe that was the problem, ... it was a little..." Insinuating about Steve's genitalia. "Hah, hah..." Noah let out in sarcasm shaking his head in disbelief, "You two are just wrong. I mean really." Birdy stood up, "Welcome to a woman's world! We deal with this type of crap all the time. So, can we go get some dinner!"

The following day the three made their rounds looking at different apartments, none were a perfect fit. One last look and if this wasn't it, he would have to settle.

St James Place Studio Apartments, the sign read, as they pulled in. He had already called and spoke to the property manager who lived on premises. Noah followed the sign pointing to the manager's office. As he walked through the center courtyard, and past the Roman fountains, he thought this was a little extravagant for such a small place. Past the fountain, he saw an older gentleman kneeling, tending to some rose bushes. Noah nodded, and before he could say anything, the gentleman spoke, "You must be the guy I spoke to over the phone?" Noah chuckled a bit, he could tell this guy was a bit of an eccentric. He stood up, took his gloves off and offered to shake Noah's hand. Soon his two sisters joined them, and they were off to view the apartment. It was a fully furnished studio, well-kept and close to the campus. It was exactly what Noah had been looking for. After reviewing the numbers again with the landlord, Noah looked at his two sisters, and could read their faces, "I'll take it." The apartment search was over. All was set to attend Syracuse. Now, to get his sisters back to Indiana and return to California, pack up his belongings and drive back across country to Syracuse, all within three weeks.

It was just a few days prior to starting classes and Noah headed to campus. He was to meet the military liaison and pick up a list of books and supplies he would need. Walking up to the classroom building, Noah opened the door, when a flyer caught his attention. He paused to read it. "Gay Marine looking for apartment or roommate, must be discrete, call Noah,' and listed his phone number. Noah read it again! His mind was wandering. Oh my God, who has seen this already? But more importantly, was this some kind of prank? Who posted this, and why? Noah, angry and a little panicky, grabbed it and ripped it down. He immediately went on to the Liaison's office. After picking up the list, he headed on over to the Campus student center, and bookstore, only to find more flyers along the way. Whoever had done this posted them all over campus. Noah went building by building, looking for and tearing them down. He finally gave in and went on to the student center. There was no way he could be sure they had all been torn down. He was steaming! Only one person could be responsible for this, because only one person had any knowledge of this. Steve, at the LGBTQ student association. When Noah walked in the student center he was heading to the bookstore when he saw a sign for the LGBT Student association's office. He detoured and decided to find out if Steve might be there. As he opened the door, a few students worked at the various cubicles. Past the cubicles, in the distance he could see Steve at a desk talking on the phone. Noah didn't waste any time and headed straight to him. Before he reached him, Steve saw him coming, hung up the phone in a panic, tried to get away. Realizing he was trapped, he stopped and started juggling words as he moved back from Noah's approach. "I was only trying to help! I mean, …I wanted you to have a place…" Noah interrupted. "Just shut up, before I shut you up! … You worthless piece of shit! I trusted you and confided in you. You knew I had to be discrete. I gave you the benefit of the doubt, but you're just a creep and a jerk! You think I don't know what this is about, Mister hands-on my crotch!" Steve backed up against the wall holding his hand out trying to keep Noah back, "I'm sorry, I'm sorry!" he pleaded, as Noah continued on, "Are you stupid or are you just fucked up in the head?" Noah grabbed him by the throat, "I want you to hear me and hear me good! You ever even so much as breath my name again, I'll find you … and there will be no conversation, you understand me?" The students, hearing all the ruckus, stood up behind him watching. Noah realized they had an audience and let Steve go. Steve grabbed his neck and was panting. Noah gave a glare at those in the room, all were in silence. "What the fuck you looking at? …You never seen a mad man before?" and he walked out of the office.

Chapter 33

Camp Lejeune, the early days

Noah walked out of the realtor's office holding the lease and keys in the air, "We got it!" he said with excitement. Cole approached Noah and started to give him a hug, before Noah pulled back, "Uh, no, no, not in public. No PDA's now that we are here in J-Ville." Cole blushed, "I know Nollie, I forget we're not in Syracuse anymore. I just can't get used to it, it's so crazy, I keep forgetting you can get in trouble." Noah smiled, as he walked around the car to get in, "It's ok, you will eventually, it'll become second nature after a while. But until then, we got our house, what are you waiting for, get in!" Cole hopped in and the two were off.

Jacksonville was the town outside the Camp Lejeune Marine base. Noah was familiar with the base having visited it before. His niece Adrian and her husband Brock lived here. The constant influx of new Marines made it a remarkably diverse community creating a microcosm of the greater U.S. It was hard to define the character of the town because it was always changing. The one thing remained true; it stayed a military town. One way or another, it was interwoven with the base. Most of its City Council or Mayors, were usually retired or prior military, along with most of its long-term residents. The elected officials always had to keep a good rapport with the Commanding General and the base if they planned on staying in office for any length of time. For those that were not prior military, they were still connected via business. Many owned or worked for businesses that were patronized by the Marines. Many reputable businesses, such as the mall, barber shops, dry cleaning, and retail stores were reliant on the Marines and their families. Even the community college had opened a campus to attract the Marines and their family members wanting to further their education. And of course, one must not forget the common area of ill repute that comes along with most military towns. After all, the Marines were born in Tun Tavern in Philadelphia, Pennsylvania. Jacksonville had its own version offering anything a young naive Marine of 18 could want, and it was conveniently located exactly right outside the main gate of the base. Bars, strip joints, used car lots, tattoo parlors, pawn shops, and the get rich quick payday loan centers were all made available for the young Marines. Most of the Marines lived on base, however, that was not all true, for various reasons, many lived amongst the locals out in town. Jacksonville had a clean appearance, with pocket neighborhoods, and buildings topped by the Carolina pines. It had an exceedingly small downtown area, if one could call it that, and was probably the original town back in the day, until urban sprawl had taken over. It had several parks, rivers, and estuaries. Its proximity to the ocean was one of its redeeming qualities, in a "No, nothing really to see here" kind of town. For most gay guys this would be pure hell, except maybe for the large amount of good-looking straight Marines to look at. Of course, what kind of hell would that be, you can look but cannot touch. Noah had heard of a small gay bar that sat just outside the base but was told it was monitored by NIS. It was called "Shadows Lounge," and he had heard stories of patrons being harassed as they entered or left the bar by young Marines with nothing better to do than harass the local "queers." Noah had not built the courage or desperation of trying to go at this point but knew the longer he was stationed here the chance of going would probably become good. For now, it was off limits to him. There were other towns like Wilmington, and Raleigh they could go to if they wanted to get out and have a go at it. With the town being so small, it was best to lie low and not take the risk of being discovered or outed. It was going to be just him and Cole, and hopefully, they would make a few friends outside away from the gay bar.

The blue siding, brick ranch style house sat a few blocks from the main strip of Western Blvd. A split-level home with a large sunroom off the back, boasted a six-foot wooden fence surrounding the backyard for privacy. Noah left the décor to Cole; other than the old coke machine he had gotten from his father years ago. It was placed in the dining room. Cole filled the house with antique furniture he had brought with him from New York, to make the place feel more like his own, because this was his first major move away from his family. Noah claimed the garage and one spare bedroom in which he used for his military uniforms, and in-home office. He did not mind; After all, Cole had given up his job, and family to move to no nothing Jacksonville to start a new life with Noah. Noah had to focus on his new job, and obligations to the Marine Corps. Cole getting control of the house would keep him busy and occupied, until he himself could find a new job in Jacksonville.

Noah had started work at the Base Audiovisual Center and was back at doing what he had done best, making, and producing television shows, news, and films for the Marines. Reacquainting with some of his old work colleagues and making several new ones, the team was formed setting ground for breaking new territory. His addition to the staff had been welcoming, and he acclimated to the work environment successfully, before he knew it, was taking on more responsibility.

His boss was Gunnery Sergeant Agatha Bjorn, a past acquaintance he had known for years. They had met on several occasions at different functions or joint efforts throughout their careers, but never actually worked together. She had a great reputation as being easy to work with, but most importantly, she supported independence and creativity. One of his first tasks was to observe the making of one of the current news programs, "Tarheel Marines", and give feedback as to how the show could be improved.

The ultimate say on any changes would need to be approved via the Public Affairs Office. However, the Officer in Charge of the Audiovisual Center was CWO4 Rhonda Chuffer. She was revered in the Marine Corps as one of the best in television, and public relations. She had worked for several Commandants, and high-ranking officials, as an attaché earning accolades and awards one could only dream of. Rumor had it she had been married to a now famous producer and Hollywood movie star, and her connections were deep and wide within the industry. However, things must have gone south because they were now divorced. No one ever asked her about her divorce in fear she might get agitated or pissed off. Not many would go against her if she put her stamp on it. Agatha and Noah worked for her directly. She was the one required to put her stamp on everything and getting that meant a superior product. After a few months on deck, all three were called to the head shed to discuss the base station, and production of a new show.

The Commanding General wanted to increase viewership of the base access channel and reach more of the Marines. First thing he was going to do to increase viewership was directing all base TVs in public areas be tuned into the base channel. He wanted to give the entire station a new appearance. To do that, he wanted the programing to be something the targeted audience would want to watch. In his terms, "Make it exciting, fun, informative, and oh yeah, make it sexy." Those words were all vague, and subject to interpretation, but the targeted audience was what the crew focused on. He wanted the new show to run in sequence to the currently produced news program of Tarheel Marines.

The show was to inform the Marines and families of all the happenings, opportunities, and functions of the base so they could take full advantage of the support they were being offered. Noah, being new to the team, was introduced to the General as the new guy with fresh ideas, and was appointed the producer, with Gunnery Sergeant Bjorn and CWO4 Chuffer as the executive producers. He expected to see a pilot within a month and the crew was given till fall to have the show, and new programming, up and running.

Noah walked out feeling like he had just been given a gift, rewarded, and given a wonderful opportunity. All his years of studying and keeping at it were paying off. A few weeks had gone by, and things were starting to come together quite nicely for the production. They had met with several departments on base about getting a consistent flow of content, and the Graphics Department was working on graphics, but the show was still without a name, and without on-air talent. Both major components were still needed to make it a success.

The crew was in the studio taping Tarheel Marines. Noah was on the bridge calling shots when his attention was caught by Corporal Hickman, the floor director, handing a paper to Corporal Devers the News Anchor. "What is he doing?" Corporal Knotts spoke out from the tech switcher seat. Noah started to do a call on the intercom, before he was interrupted by the Anchor reading from the paper script he had just been handed.

Corporal Devers spoke out, "Pardon me for the interruption folks, but we have breaking news from Headquarters Marine Corps. This just in, we are happy to say that Sergeant Noah Barlow has been selected to the next rank of Staff Sergeant in the United States Marine Corps. Also, pending his promotion, all drinks will be on him."

Noah sat down in his chair, quiet for a moment. He looked around and everyone sat waiting for a response. "What is this? Is this a joke?" He stood up and looked through the glass window in the studio, seeing everyone looking back. Was this for real? Corporal Hickman grabbed the paper script and held it up flagging it in the air, while struggling to speak on his headset. "Uh, any word from the peanut gallery? Don't tell me you're speechless, … cause that will be the first time in history Bud." Noah, still in disbelief, knowing the guys were often pranksters, "You're messing with me man, I ain't falling for it. I don't believe you!" Hickman came back. "Look, come out here in the studio and read it yourself. It is the message for selection for promotion to Staff Sergeant."

Noah took off his head set and walked down the steps to enter the studio when he was intervened by the Warrant Officer and Gunnery Sergeant. They had been in the studio the whole time and were the ones behind it. The entire crew knew what was up. It was for real. He had been selected to the rank of Staff Sergeant.

Noah stood there as the crew all got in line to congratulate him with laughs and handshakes. His thoughts were good! Wow, ...this was a big deal! This was the rank where the Marine Corps says we like you and we want to keep you around for a while. After attaining this rank, even if he did not get another promotion, barring no unusual circumstances, i.e. "Don't Ask, Don't Tell," Noah was guaranteed to be able to stay for twenty years. For the first time in his career, he felt like he belonged. The Marines, and crew he worked with, all made him feel like he was part of the team. This was great news for his future.

That evening on the ride home, Noah was excited and could not wait to tell his dad and family. But he quickly had a feeling of guilt and uneasiness come over him. He was reluctant to tell Cole. He felt it would be rubbing his own fortune in his face. He decided to hold off on telling him for now.

A Champagne Promotion

Noah had forgotten about his promotion, since it would be a few months before his number came up, and the actual pinning date would take place. When the time came the ceremony was held in the studio, and he had invited several of his compadres, various officials, and professional acquaintances to the ceremony. He thought about having Cole there. Oh, wouldn't it be nice if he could be part of the ceremony? Like so many other Marines, to have a spouse or significant other there to do the pinning would be great. Nope, not if you're gay, that was a no, no. Too many questions could bring attention causing suspicion. Noah thought it over to himself and concluded it was best that Cole remained in the dark. No one was even slightly aware of him at work anyway. Cole was not in the closet and was very unfamiliar with the military, especially the rules dealing with "Don't Ask, Don't Tell." Cole was a great guy, but he was very nonchalant about his wording, and actions. Knowing him, he would probably say something he shouldn't. As cold as it sounded, Noah preferred it that way. The less they knew, the less questions could be asked. Besides, he still hadn't even told Cole he was getting promoted. Cole's situation had not changed and, if nothing else, was deteriorating or getting worse.

The CWO, and Gunnery Sergeant Bjorn pinned it on, with the Colonel of the Training and Audio-Visual Support Center presiding. Noah stood proudly as the warrant was read. Although he could hear what was going on around him, his focus was making sure he didn't cry. Holding back the tears from the swell of unexpected emotions was all he could focus on. How embarrassing would that be to cry in front of his fellow Marines. Then out of nowhere, the memory of Champagne/Staff Sergeant Williams came to him. He could still remember that horrible day and seeing her in front of the platoon, being called names and yet not one tear. Wasn't it a coincidence, after all these years, today of all days, the day Noah made Staff Sergeant, the same rank that Staff Sergeant Williams was, his memory came to mind? Noah was not sure if the universe was trying to tell him something, or was the Staff Sergeant there in spirit? Regardless, his eyes dried up as he stood tall as the Warrant was read and the ceremony went on. After the pinning was over, Noah had thought hard and prepared what he would say. Now was the time, and all words escaped him, so he had to wing it. "I just want to say thank you to the Colonel, the Warrant Officer, and Gunnery Sergeant for being here for me, thank you! I would also like to thank all you Marines I work with for making my job easy. Also, I would like to thank all those Marines who have been a role model for me along the way. Thank you to the Marine Corps for accepting me as one of your own. But I would like to call out someone special, although they are not here today, I believe they're here in spirit, Staff Sergeant Williams, (Noah teared up) I still hear you, I haven't forgot, and I'm now standing here wearing your rank. I want to thank you all for coming here and trust me, at the wet down there will be plenty of 'Champagne.' Semper Fi." Noah turned back and assumed the position of attention in front of the Colonel and was dismissed to his fellow Marines coming up, shaking his hand, and congratulating him.

A few days had gone by, and the weekend was upon them. Saturday morning consisted of a routine of chores. First thing was to get his uniforms to the cleaners, get a haircut, get groceries, and do any miscellaneous errands before returning home to do house chores and cleaning. Once those were done, it meant the evening could be spent doing the fun things in life, whatever that might be. Noah was loading up his uniforms to take to the cleaners to have his new rank sewn on, when Cole noticed and spoke up, "Why are you taking all of them, you normally only take a couple?" Noah knew it was time to come clean, "Well there is something I've been meaning to tell you. It just seems the time has never been right." Cole took a step back, looked at all the uniforms in the car and fear came across his face, "Oh, Oh, oh my God, you're leaving." as he covered his hands over his mouth, he was taken aback. Noah was caught off guard, and his eyes opened wide, and his chin dropped, as the words slid out of his mouth, "Wow, didn't see that coming …" and before he could finish, Cole broke out "What do you mean you didn't see it coming?

How did you think I would react..." Noah tried to intervene, "Hold up, hold up," but it was to no avail, as Cole started spouting off in a rant, Noah tried to talk over him, "Whoa, whoa, whoa, hold up, you're overreacting, ...calm down, ...Cole would you calm down!" Cole was just getting started and now royally upset so Noah let him vent. Cole continued, "Don't you tell me to calm down there Mr. Jar face, Jarhead, Jareene or whatever you call it, ...You don't know what I have been going through. I have moved all the way down here, gave up a decent job, and my family just to be with you! ...And now you, ...you, you're just going to toss me away like some, some snot rag... You don't know what it's like being me. I'm broke. I don't have any money. I have to ask you for money just to go to the cleaners, or even buy a soda. I've had to call my parents and ask for money because I know I've been a burden on you, and you, you, all you can do is say I have got to get a job and go to work. Well, let me tell you, if you weren't in the Marine Corps and had to find a job in this one hick town you would be losing it too. Mr. Mr., ... he who hasn't had to give up anything." Noah broke in, "Can I speak, would you just let me speak?" Cole stopped and looked at him, "What, ...what more could you possibly have to say?"

Noah was taken aback with all that had just been thrown at him, but tried to stay focused, "What I have to say is, I'm not leaving! I never was, I got promoted. I've known for a little over a month now but didn't want to say anything. I thought it would be rubbing it in your face. I know you have been having a tough time, and things haven't been going your way. If I haven't said it, I'm aware of all you have given, and done to be in this relationship, and right now it seems a little unbalanced. That you are giving up more, but that is the way things happen. Eventually, things will turn around, and I might have to rely on you. But for now, Thank you." Cole, stared at him for a second before turning away, "I feel so stupid, I shouldn't have said all those things." Noah responded with his arms open offering a hug, "What things?" Cole turned to see him with his arms open, and chuckled, remembering they were outside, and the neighbors could see. "I can't, no public displays of affection!" Cole paused, before commenting. "So, you really got promoted?" Noah laughed and smiled, "Yes, Yes I did. You are now looking at Staff Sergeant Noah Barlow." As he grinned, "Can you believe that I'm a Staff Sergeant now." Cole smiled, "Did you have a ceremony and all that?" Noah chuckled, "Yes, I had a ceremony and all that, …it was this last week, sorry you couldn't be there." Cole frowned a bit, "Wish I could have seen it!" Noah picked up on the opportunity to get him involved, "Well it is not all over yet. I still have to plan my wet down, after all that is the real celebration." Cole inquisitively, "Oh yeah, what is a wet down? In gay terms, I can only imagine, God help us for whatever it means to the Marines?" Noah chuckled, "Be nice, besides you'll love it. It's just a big party, with food and drinks. The downside is I must pay for it. You get all your buddies and fellow Marines drunk, using the amount of the pay raise, …but you can spend what you need, within reason, I mean." Cole perked up, "A party, and I get to plan it?" Noah could see Cole liked the idea, and it would give him something to do for the time being. Noah realized he was getting behind on his chores, "Hey, I hope you're ok, I worry about you! I need to get this stuff to the cleaners, or I won't have a uniform for work on Monday." Cole was now focused, "Go, go, go, we can go over all the details when you get back." Cole smiled, as Noah started to get in his truck, "It's going to be the best wet down ever." Noah smiled "I know it is, …you're doing it."

Cole loved to throw a good party, so agreeing to allow Cole the control of organizing his promotion ceremony wet-down party smoothed things over. Things were going well for him, but Cole was not yet able to find stable employment and was becoming increasingly frustrated. The time alone was leading to boredom and the months of no income were taking its toll. He was becoming reliant on Noah. Noah could see his stress level rising, and his confidence level lowering. Noah tried to reach out by taking him out somewhere on the weekends, and even bought him a gym membership hoping it would help him with the boredom. He thought if nothing else he might make a few friends and have someone besides Noah to talk to. It was hard seeing someone struggling knowing you were only a spectator, looking in from the outside, and could do nothing about their happiness. Noah could see the move was not working out the way they had planned. He wasn't sure of what was going to happen if things continued to go in this direction. How long before Cole reached his tipping point, or worse yet, what about himself? How much longer could he watch Cole agonize. Cole had so much going for him back in Syracuse; a successful model, working for his family and standing to inherit the family business. Now, to watch him flounder and ask Noah for money to be able to do his own laundry was so unbecoming of him. Noah was finding himself going without, to make sure Cole had what he needed to try and keep him happy. It seemed the more he did for Cole, the less he did for himself. Cole seemed to like the idea of being kept, however that wasn't what Noah had signed up for when he agreed to let Cole move down to Lejeune with him. Noah had concluded Cole had to get a job, and soon, for this to continue. Now the problem was, he had to tell Cole.

Chapter 34

Getting acquainted

Driving down Western Blvd, Noah saw a new sign at one of the local strip malls, "Java Escape" coffee shop. It was across from the local community college and had just opened. Noah loved Mom and Pop coffee shops and gladly welcomed the new addition to town. Curious, he turned the Jeep around and pulled up in front of the shop. He could see a few people inside as he hopped out and walked up to the door, stopping briefly to read the hours, he entered.

Greeted by a freckle faced young woman from behind the counter, "Hi, welcome to Java Escape. What can I get for you Hun?" Noah looked at her and smiled, "You have a latte?" She smiled back "You bet; how would you like that?" Noah ordered, and stepped aside as another customer came in. He walked around looking at the place. He could tell they were new and just getting the place together. A bit sparse on furniture, but what they had was nice and gave the place a comfortable atmosphere. The typical displaced sofa here and there and a few tables sporadically placed were filled with what appeared to be students studying. The wall in the rear had a white board across the wall where someone had spent some time artistically writing the menu. Noah noted the Coca-Cola memorabilia on the various walls and couldn't help but think how his coke machine would look in here, after all, it deserved to be appreciated. There were a couple of guys sitting on stools talking at one end of the L shaped counter, with their back to the windows, that gave a full display of the community college across the way. At the other end of the counter, next to the ordering area, was a glass container with pastries and baked goods inside. It was nice to see they were making the attempt. The freckle faced girl called out for Noah, letting him know his drink was ready. He came up, sat at an open stool, and began to drink, as he observed what was going on. The girl, spoke, "So you stationed up at the base?" Noah smiled and acknowledged her. "Yes, been here about six months or so." She smiled back, "My husband is stationed here, not a Marine though, he's in the Navy." Noah laughed, "That's alright I forgive him." She laughed, "I know right! I say that because everyone assumes he's a Marine. He's at the Navy Hospital." Noah smiled, "Well, we like our medical field, we love our Corpsman. Corpsman Up!" She smiled, "Thank you, you must be older, or been in for a while?" Noah, puzzled at her observation, "Do I look that old?" She chuckled again, "No, no, the way you answered. The younger guys always say stinking Navy, like it is below them. The guys who have been around for a while always thank the Corpsman." Noah nodded his head, "Good observation, I think you're right." She smiled, took her towel, and dried her hands from washing cups, before reaching out to Noah, "Hi, I'm Sophie, and you are?" Noah looked at her hand and reached and shook it, "I'm Noah, nice to meet you, Sophie." He could already anticipate the reaction; it was always so predictable. Just as he expected, she started to comment. "Oh my, I don't think I have ever met a Noah before. Is your family religious?" Noah smiled, "No, and no to all the other questions you are about to ask... but go ahead, I've heard them all." Sophie laughed, "I'm sorry!" as she chuckled, "I bet you have heard them all. But you must admit it's kind of unusual to hear these days. But how cool. Well, I think it is a wonderful name. If I ever have a son, I'd consider naming him that. Such a strong name."

Noah smiled and changed the subject, "Is this your place, how long you guys been open?" Sophie smiled as she continued to do her work, "Well partially, I'm a joint owner with another gal, Dale. She'll be in later. I work days, and she and her Momma work evenings. We opened about a month ago, both of us are military wives. Since we were new to the area, we decided to bring a little outside fun to Jacksonville. We both talked of the coffee shops and missed them, noticing a hole in the market we decided to open one." Noah smiled, "Good for you two. I'm glad you did! I was just driving by, saw the sign. Use to go to them in San Diego and New York, didn't know I missed them until I got stationed here. I was surprised to see the sign today." About that time two gentlemen sitting at the bar, broke into the conversation, "We love it! Same here, we used to go to them in other towns, and are so glad to see one open here." Noah smiled, "You guys stationed here?" The dark haired one spoke up for both, "Yes, we're both Marines, I'm Jack, and this is Braun." Noah smiled back. "Nice to meet you both, Noah here." Jack spoke up again, "We caught your name when you were telling Sophie, didn't mean to eavesdrop, but sitting so close we couldn't help but hear." Noah's gaydar went off, assuming they were probably a couple. Both appeared to be Marines, similar medium build, the difference was Jack having light brown hair with dominating blues eyes, and Braun was notably a red head. Jack seemed to be the more open one and a bit more talkative. If one were paying attention, you could pick a slight femininity in his actions and talk. Braun seemed a bit more stand-offish and reserved, half reading the book in front of him, and paying attention to the conversation at the same time. He was medium height, red hair and wore a high and tight, not a bad looking guy, and, without a doubt, a Marine. Noah couldn't quite place him but knew he had seen him somewhere before. Jack continued on, "We like coming here, it gets a bit busier in the evenings, a fun group, you should drop back around some time. Also, if you like pastries, they make them fresh, the place smells amazing when they are making them."

Noah finished up his drink before saying goodbye. As he left, he took another look at Braun, why did he look so familiar. Had he seen him on base, or was he stationed with him before? Back in the jeep, he noticed Jack and Braun glance back out at him, giving him the ever so familiar gay return. He was sure the two guys were gay but did not know how to crack the conversation. The ride home was quick, and he was glad to be able to tell Cole he had found a coffee shop. Maybe this was a crack in the case of discovering J-Ville for them, and maybe Cole could start going there to do some networking.

The rest of the day went well. The chores completed and the plans for the wet down were underway. Cole was excited about the coffee shop and had agreed it might be a place where he could possibly network. They were ready for a nice evening. Discussing plans of going out, Wilmington, was 45 minutes south and Raleigh-Durham two and a half hours, plus hotel expense. Neither seemed pleasing.

Cole brought up the possibility of going to the local gay bar. It would be worth a try and possibly give them some connections and friends locally. Noah was hesitant, only because of the horror stories he had heard on base. He had seen and read several news articles about the bar, which had gained some notoriety because of the recent Clinton initiative of "Don't Ask, Don't Tell". Naval Investigative Service was known to stalk the bar, parking just off the property, and recording license plates and using high powered cameras and binoculars to spy on those entering the establishment.

The owner, Emmit Goldman, was a bit of a rebel, as he would have to be, knowing his establishment was going against the grain of the community of Jacksonville, and the politics of the base. It was often considered a blemish on the community, and if the city or the base had their way, they would rather see Shadows Lounge closed. Emmit was a feisty ole queen, by all meaning of the word. He was also known as Fancy. He often held court and long reigned as one of the best Drag performers on the east coast. He was not new to the harassment and didn't shy away or back down from the politics. He had given several interviews and had been candid about his views and was known to run interference helping the young Marines who just wanted to get out and enjoy themselves in a safe environment. When he learned of the spying, they developed a call network getting the word out telling Marines not to park at the bar. Instead, they would pick them up at another location, and when they arrived at the lounge, the van would pull to the door, and a sheet was held up to block view of them entering the bar.

Noah knew if they were going to make friends, and for Cole mostly, he would agree to go, on the condition they drove Cole's car. Noah's truck, with the base decal on it, was not to be seen in the parking lot. The Lounge was on the blacklist of establishments in Jacksonville for Marines. If NIS was watching, Cole's car had nothing to flag it as a Marines vehicle. The plans were made, and both agreed to go around 9:00 pm. That was early enough to get in, and dark enough outside to make it to the door without being seen.

Shadows Lounge was just off route 24 or better known as Freedom Way and ran alongside Camp Lejeune. Noah had Cole drive past the entrance, scoping out the place and the surroundings, before he had Cole turn around and pull in. If they had not been looking for it, they might have passed it. The cinder block, flat roof building wasn't much to look at. The entrance facing the street had been boarded up, almost looked abandoned, and in a state of disrepair. It was on a large, wooded lot. Pulling in, the driveway led around to the back side of building to an overgrown grass and gravel parking lot. There were several other cars already parked, and an attendant giving directions. Noah observed what was going on and noted the car full of women next to them getting out and heading in. It reminded Noah of Tony's place back in the day in Okinawa, using the back entrance. Noah sat in the car hesitant, before Cole spoke out. "Are you ready?" Noah looked at him, looked back to the entrance and gave another quick glance around before saying, "I guess this is it…"

Once out, they were approached by the parking attendant "Welcome to Shadows, we want you to have a good time, but please make sure to lock your doors before going in." Cole replied, "Thank you! Is this the entrance we go in?" The attendant pointed to the door. "Yes, just follow the ladies in front of you. Make sure you have an I.D., … no one gets in without an I.D." Noah and Cole moved on to the entrance. There was a long hallway that entered the building leading to a door. On the side wall a smaller square opening covered in mesh opened. Noah couldn't help but think of the "Wizard of Oz," and being greeted at the door of the Emerald City with the gate keeper. From behind the small opening, one could hardly make out the face, but the voice coming out could etch glass. "Who are you? I've never seen you in here before. You know what kind of establishment this is?" Cole looked shocked and amazed at the same time and quickly glanced at Noah before responding. "Wow, so much for customer service," he responded to the voice behind the mesh. The voice responded, "Look don't get smart with me, you want to get in this place or not. You a troublemaker? We don't have time for troublemakers! Answer the questions or be on your way, there are other people behind you wanting to get in." Cole gasped, he was appalled, just when he started to sound off, Noah interrupted, "Hi, we just moved here, and this is our first time visiting this place. Yes, we know it is a gay establishment, and I can assure you we will be no trouble." Noah reached and grabbed Cole, pulling him close to him. Letting him know they were a couple. Noah could see the eyes behind the mesh giving them the once over, sizing them up before he heard, "Ok, I guess you'll be alright. It figures, …you both are too damn pretty to be straight anyway. It'll be five-dollar cover for each of you, …the first drinks on the house. Now come on, pay up! I don't want to keep these people behind you waiting all day." The look on Cole's face let Noah know he was itching to say something. Noah scornfully gave him a look to not say a word. After paying, he heard a buzz, and they were directed to a door to the left. Cole, still busting at the seams, started trying to justify his remarks to Noah as they entered. "You think they could be a little nicer, after all, they are asking us to pay to get in." Noah thought to himself how naive Cole was at times, and common sense had escaped him. All Cole could see was he was being harassed and treated rudely. It must be hard to have never really traveled and his exposure to the world had been so limited. Noah was perplexed with Cole at times, not knowing whether to like or hate his ignorance or lack of concern with those being prejudice against gays, and oblivious to the threats they posed. It showed how much of a pampered life he had really led. Noah understood the doorman, and the no bullshit position. He was glad to see it wasn't a cake walk to get in, and if taking a little harassment meant being safer, so be it. Knowing the bar was taking its job seriously to protect those inside made him feel safe as he walked through the door.

Once inside, the smoke-filled room overwhelmed their senses. It was lit by a few neon signs, and a light hanging from a pool table just in front of them. Two women were shooting pool. Noah paused a moment to take in his surroundings before continuing. He gave a once-around view to see if there were any familiar faces looking back that he might have to contend with if they discovered him there. No one looked familiar. The bar off to the right was just begging them to get a drink. Both were obliged and took advantage of their free first drink to cut the edge. Once they had their drinks, they wandered around checking out the place. Really not much to it, they found an enclosed outdoor seating area, where Cole took a smoke. Once back inside, they grabbed a chair at an open table near the dance floor. The whole bar room was a big rectangle, one end for pool, and one end for dancing with the bar and tables in between. Noah couldn't help but notice how unusually low the ceiling was. As they sat, the bar was now starting to fill up. Noah looked behind the bar noticing the guy working the small door and could now put a face to the voice. It was an older man, probably in his late forties, or early fifties. A reddish blonde, appearing to have plucked eyebrows and work added to his cheekbones giving him a more feminine look. Several couples moved on and off the dance floor, as the music played on. Before they knew it, the ice was being broken and they were meeting people from all over the eastern coast of North Carolina. They had met a couple of guys from Morehead City just up the cost. Roy, and Teddy. They were just friends who came down to the lounge because they enjoyed the drag show, and because it was the closest gay bar to where they lived. Before long, they had met a group of Marines and Sailors, all stationed on the base. Dan was a Marine and his partner Donald, who was in college to become a musician and considering joining the Corps. He had a friend along with him named Paula who had just moved to Jacksonville to take a position at the community college in the physical fitness department. Another Marine, Ken, was a Sergeant up on base, working as a computer tech, and his boyfriend Noel was a Navy Corpsman working at the Hospital. Bret was a Marine musician and was in the Marine Band in communications. As the night went on, Noah and Cole mixed and mingled with the group, before the dance floor had gone silent and the gentleman at the door had taken center stage. Noel leaned over to Noah and whispered in his ear, "That is Emmit, he's the owner. He is also known as Fancy." Noah shook his head acknowledging him. Suddenly it made since. This is the guy he had read and heard so much about. This was the one who was notorious for helping so many Marines and had been an advocate for the gay community for so many years. He was often cited and interviewed for being the bar owner going against the grain, so the gay Marines had a place to feel safe and enjoy themselves without being harassed. The plucked eyebrows and cheek bones could not hide that he was definitely a female impersonator and performer. From the microphone, he introduced his first performer. Doing 'Lucy in the sky with Diamonds' was Miss Tonna Gay. He stepped down and from the left side of the dance floor, a drag queen came in dressed as Lady Godiva. In a skintight, flesh colored body suit with a long blond wig almost to the floor. Riding a toy pony stick between her legs. The drag show was under way as she worked her way in and out of the crowd. The patrons lined up to tip her. As she made her way around to where they were sitting, Cole tipped her. Toward the middle of the song, a change in music took place and she returned to center stage. Slightly leaning over to drop her hair in front of her, she began making it go around and around. Noah was sure she was going to get dizzy and fall.

After the shows where finished, Emmit made his rounds and stopped briefly at the table. Several got up giving hugs and kisses. Once the hellos were over, Emmit looked to Noah and Cole, "I see you two Honeys have found your way around. Welcome to Shadows Lounge." Noah smiled, "Thank you, we have enjoyed the entire evening!" Emmit looked at the two of them, pointing his finger at Noah, "Honey, I can tell you're a Marine a mile away, but you, (he turned his focus to Cole) with hair that long, you ain't no kind of military, …at least none that I have been in, … and when I say been in, …I mean been in." He chuckled along with the others, "So, what's your story?" as he looked at Cole. "Oh, we're together." Cole motioned with his hand pointing back and forth between the two of them, with a nervous laugh, "No, no, Honey, I'm not in, … I moved down here to be with him." Emmit chuckled, "So you're a military spouse, Hah, hah, …well good for you! Are you guys getting settled in?" Noah smiled and chimed in, "We're making a go of it…" Cole was quiet. Emmit picked up on it, "Well that was for you Hun, …but this one here is being awful quiet." He looked at Cole, "How about you, are you doing alright?" Cole was hesitant, "Well it has taken some getting used to. I still haven't found a job." Emmit laughed, "In Jacksonville, imagine that. That is because you have all the other military spouses to look at. What kind of work are you looking for?" Cole cheered up, "Anything at this point." Emmit chuckled, reaching over to Cole's shoulder, "Child you best be careful what you ask for, hah, hah, … I know several who would pay to be with you, the way you look," Emmit caught the frown on Noah's face, "Calm, down you big Jarhead," he directed his attention back to Cole, "I won't go there, I know that big blonde Marine husband over there, might want to kick my ass. So, seriously what kind of work?" Cole laughed, "Well I did collections, and some sales before, and modeling." Emmit smiled, "Well there isn't much modeling work around here, but I tell you what. I know a couple of places that might need your experience." He gave Cole a card, "Now, you continue to look, but call me in a couple of days, let me see if Mother can help. I can tell you here in old J-Ville it's who you know, and in some cases, who you blow." Cole blushed, "Oh, thank you, thank you so much. You don't know how much I need this right now." Noah was wide eyed and happy something was possibly looking up for Cole. He stuck his hand out to Emmit, "Thank you, and thank you so much for what you do for the Marines." Emmit chuckled, "Well, let's get him the job first, and for the other stuff, don't believe everything you hear. Now, let me finish saying hello to the rest of these bitches, uh, I mean children up in here." He grinned and walked away.

The night was closing in when the lights came up and last call was being held. Noah exchanged numbers with the group of newfound friends, and even found out most all went to the coffee shop as well. On the way home, Noah noticed a change in Cole's attitude or was it just from the many drinks they had consumed. Regardless it was one of the best nights since they had moved to Jacksonville and a much needed one. In just one night, it was amazing how the closed off isolated town had seemed to open slightly and reveal just a few of its many secrets.

A few months had gone by, and Jacksonville was beginning to be much more open. Emmit, (Fancy) did what he said he would, and helped Cole find a job at one of the local car dealers. It was part time collections and part time sales. The pay wasn't great, but it was something to help out and keep him busy. There was one guy he worked with named Jim, who was gay and liked that Cole was there because of his partner being in the Marine Corps as well. The two got along and quickly became friends. Noah's wet-down party was a success. They ended up doing two separate ones to keep the gays and the straights apart. They held the straight one on base at the staff

NCO club. The underground gay one they met out in town at a local restaurant with the guests being treated to dinner. Afterwards, they stopped by Java Escape for coffee and dessert, before doing a pub crawl ending up at Shadows Lounge. While at the restaurant, Sam, a friend of theirs, had brought a young gay Marine named Joe to the function. It was the first wet down he had attended and the first time he had met someone of Noah's rank that was gay. Boosting Noah's ego because the young Marine was awe struck. He looked at Noah, "One day you'll be attending my wet-down." Noah thought it was amusing he could be a role model and laughed, "I hope that one day I will!"

It was common for him to stop and pick up a coffee and chat for a minute with various people at the coffee shop. He and Sophie had become good friends, along with Dale the other owner. One day they were talking about the coke memorabilia they had on display when Noah brought up that he had an antique coke machine at home. Dale was intrigued and came by to see it and fell in love with it. Noah agreed to allow her to use it at the coffee shop but wasn't ready to part with it. She accepted the offer and the Coke machine now sat in full display in the coffee shop.

Work was moving along, but the General, and the CWO had not yet signed off on the exact format or name of the show. They had tried several candidates for the host positions, but all were shot down. They needed both a male and female host that had chemistry with each other and could appeal to the targeted audience. Noah was starting to get worried because they were past the original pilot date, and the original start date was just around the corner. It was Friday evening, Cole would be working late, so he grabbed his file of prospects and headed out. Stopping off at the coffee shop on the way home, he decided to go through the candidates one more time. He ordered his drink and sprawled out with the files on one of the tables, Sophie spoke out from behind the counter. "Noah, I almost forgot, a lady by the name of Gina stopped in and noticed the Coke machine. She is with the Camp Lejeune playhouse and is directing a play on base. She was wanting to know if she could use the Coke machine as a prop." Noah, who had been looking down at the files, raised his head. Sophie had his attention. "A playhouse on base? I didn't even know they had a playhouse." Sophie laughed, "I know, her name is Gina she comes in here throughout the day. I think she works for one of the local radio stations or something. I have her number. She said give her a call if you're willing to let them use it." Noah was excited to learn about the playhouse; it was something he would be willing to volunteer his time and skills to. Noah took the number and gave her a call and had agreed to meet her the next morning at the small theater located on base. He finished his drink and was tired and ready to call it a night, none of the prospects were going to work. He packed up his things and headed home.

The next morning, Noah was up bright and early, completed his jog, and was making breakfast when Cole appeared, dressed, and ready to go. He had to be at work by 9:00. He filled a to go cup with coffee, said his goodbyes and was out the door. Noah was supposed to be at the Base Theater at 10:00 am to meet the lady who wanted to borrow the Coke machine. Noah's hidden motive for the meeting was to find out more about the playhouse. He finished breakfast, showered, and headed out to the meeting. There were several base theaters. This one was in the Mid-Way Park family housing, away from the main side of the base. It was actually an old film theater from the 50's that had been converted into a playhouse. He pulled up in front of the building and saw several people entering and leaving the theater. He parked, got out, and walked up to the entrance when a young slender Marine emerged from the door. Noah interrupted him. "Excuse me, is the Lejeune Playhouse?" The young Marine replied, "Yes, can I help you?" Noah responded, "Yeah I'm looking for a Gina Russo, can you tell me where I might find her?" The young Marine was obliged and turned around to go back in, as Noah followed. In the building, they went through the lobby, before entering the main auditorium. Off to one side was a tall, long brown wavey haired, Hispanic woman, in her late twenties talking to a couple of young Marines. The Marine pointed her out, "That is her over there." Noah walked up and waited as she finished her conversation. After finishing, she turned to him, "Hi, you must be Noah?" as she offered her hand. Noah reached and shook her hand, "And you must be Gina, nice to meet you." She quickly responded, "Thank you for coming out to meet me. So, this is our little playhouse. It's not the best looking but we have a lot of fun, and the Marines like it. Come on, let me show you around."

The two began to walk as she explained what they were currently working on and showed the facility. Noah could tell they were definitely a non-profit community theater and anything they received was from the good graces of people's hearts. He had been involved with theater on and off throughout his life and could tell she was coming from a true conviction with her love of the theater. He asked her if it was a base function, and she explained all the funding and what gave them the authority to operate. This was through Marine Corps Morale, Welfare and Recreation as a service for creative Marines to have a venue to participate in theater just like they provide gyms, baseball diamonds and recreation centers. Noah saw so many things he could bring to help her out. She explained she was newly appointed, and the previous director had left the Theater high and dry. She was hoping the current production was going to be good enough to breathe life back into it.

Noah asked where the Coke machine came into play. She explained she needed it as a prop on stage for one of the scenes in their current production. She was also talking about needing help with the sound system if he knew how to operate it. She laughed when Noah told her what he did for the Marine Corps. Then she asked if he would be willing to help with the sound as well. Noah agreed to let her use the Coke machine and help operate the sound for her show.

As they got ready to leave, she brought up that she worked at a radio station out in town, and she was a Marine reservist. Noah's eyes lit up, he immediately asked if she had ever done any voice over, or broadcast work for the radio. She grinned, replying she had. Noah was already thinking ahead, she had the right look, and if she had any chemistry on camera, he might have found the next host for the show. He explained the new show coming up, and would she be interested in stopping by the studio to do a read. Just so happens she would be able to stop by Monday afternoon but wanted to clear it with her chain of command. How perfect, Noah agreed, and the two would meet on Monday for an audition.

Monday came and Noah was nervous about the auditions because he had already played Gina up to the Warrant Officer, and Gunnery Sergeant. They had scheduled a couple of guy prospects to read with her. Gina called and let him know she was on her way. She was on time, showed up in the camouflage uniform and was greeted by Noah and escorted into the studio. She was introduced to Gunny, but the Warrant Officer was not available. However, the Warrant Officer got a glimpse of her and directed Noah to bring her the audition tape immediately when completed.

The crew was just finishing a couple of public safety announcements, informing the general population what to do and who to call if they were to discover possible unexploded ordinance in the area. Although the focus was training areas and bombing ranges on the base, it was hard to imagine, but people were still finding unexploded bombs or cannon balls from the Civil War. Noah gave her a copy and had the teleprompter set. Gina took her place, and the crew worked with her getting the lighting and sound. At the last minute, the two possible candidates scheduled to read as a male host called and would not be able to make it. Rather than reschedule her to come back, Noah decided to go ahead and have Corporal Hickman do the read next to Gina, they would have her on tape.

The set was ready, the recording light went on and the set was hot. From the control both, Noah did the count down and called action. Gina killed it the first take. She was a natural, but to everyone's surprise, Corporal Hickman was also good. Gina came off as more professional, kind of the big sister you could trust and tell anything to. She was believable. Hickman was more playful with a bit of the mischievous kid brother. The two played off each other well. It was the on-air chemistry they had been looking for. After the audition, Noah thanked her and let her know she had done well, but the final decision would come from the CWO and the Commanding General.

Most of the content was about what Marines could do on Camp Lejeune on their off time. The group tossed around several names before coming up with "Liberty Call." The final graphics were made, and the pilot tape was edited together, completed, and sent up the chain of command. The crew waited patiently knowing no news was good news. A couple of days went by before the tape made it to the Commanding General. Once he saw it, he called the Warrant Officer personally to thank her and congratulate her and the entire team. It was exactly what he had envisioned. It came back with thumbs up, and all was approved, he loved it. They had found their hosts, and the new show was given the green light for production.

Chapter 35

The lack of action is the same as no action

As wonderful as things were at work, it was the opposite at home. Cole had lost his job for not showing up, found another, and was fired for the same thing. Cole seemed to sabotage every job he was getting. Noah questioned him on it, only to hear this was how he had worked for the family business back in Syracuse. Noah was starting to get the bigger picture when the two had taken a vacation to visit Cole's brother in Florida. Noah found out the real scoop on Cole from Cole's sister-in-law.

Cole worked for the family business in name only. In other words, he was on the pay role, but came and went as he pleased. Noah also learned Grandma controlled the purse strings of the business, and in the event, anything happened to her, Cole was set to inherit millions. In Cole's mind there was no reason to worry about work, he just had to get along until Grandma passed away. Then he would be set for life. Cole was a trust fund baby.

In the middle of Cole's hiring and firings, Noah's success continued. He was informed he was being reviewed for a position at the White House working as a videographer for President Clinton's administration. This would require a stable home life along with the scrutiny of an intensive background check called "Yankee White." Noah couldn't handle Cole's situation, the arguments and home life were becoming way more than he could handle. It was too unstable and unpredictable. The problem was Grandma was healthy, doing fine and showed no signs of leaving this earth anytime soon. When Cole moved to North Carolina and quit the family business, she cut him off, but didn't remove him from the will. Noah was not willing or able to be someone's sugar daddy. It was time for Cole to pull his weight, or he needed to move on.

Noah sat down with him and set his terms. The ultimatum was getting a job by July, or Noah would pay to move him back to Syracuse or wherever he wanted to go. If he didn't get a job and keep it, he could no longer stay. Cole was not happy, and when July came, he still had not gotten gainful employment. Noah held true to his words, and Cole chose to move to Florida with his brother.

It was an August afternoon, in the Carolinas, and all seemed to be a typical Saturday. The Jeep's cotton-top was flapping in the wind, and Noah was thinking how nice the afternoon was. Noah was now single and able to focus back on himself. Not knowing where everyone was, he cruised by the Java Escape to see who was around. As he pulled in, he could see Braun. Braun and his partner Jack were guys he had met when he first came to the coffee shop. It turns out they were indeed actually gay, and yes, they were a couple. Noah had been on the rifle range, and Jack was an expert shooter and was his Coach on the Rifle Range. What was even a bigger surprise was the SNCOIC of the range was his old buddy from Okinawa, Giselle. Giselle had made a career out of the Marine Corps as well, and also a Staff Sergeant. What a small world indeed.

Noah kept thinking Braun looked familiar, and it turns out Noah was right. Braun had been on National News for coming out openly gay. He had testified in front of congress at the open hearings dealing with gays serving openly in the military. Noah had thought he had been discharged from the Corps, but for legal reasons, he was still on active duty. Noah remembered sitting at home in Oceanside watching the hearings. Yes, this really was a small world. He and Braun were now acquaintances, not friends because Noah never really knew where he stood with Braun. He remained ambiguous and distant. Noah could understand his cause, but so many were hesitant to really befriend him for fear of retaliation. Braun might still be a target of NIS, and afraid of guilt by association. Not all the gays agreed with him. Many felt Braun had brought it all on himself and didn't respect what he was trying to accomplish. Some felt he was a glory hound trying to get attention and his convictions were not sincere, or very well thought out. Noah remained nonjudgmental and let Braun's actions speak for himself. Regardless of his personal reasons, he drew light to the unjust policy of "Don't Ask Don't Tell." As to whether it was effective was still to be determined.

Noah headed to the bar and ordered a double cap to boost his energy level. Sophie was the barista, spending more time at the shop because her husband Brad was away for training. "Any word from

Brad?" Sophie perked up "No, not today. Last time we spoke, he seemed to be doing fine in his training, …just miss him that's all." While she made his drink, he asked if anyone had been around. "There was a whole group that met here earlier this morning and were heading to the beach." Noah replied, "I thought as much, was thinking about going to the beach myself and maybe on to Wilmington this evening." Sophie, with her back turned continued busy in her work, "It has been a slow day here, can't wait to go home and relax." Braun moved up to the bar and sat down. "Hey Noah!" "Hey Braun," Noah grinned, "Not out and about today?" Trying to keep it light, knowing Braun could be heavy on the ear, and a bit of a downer. "No, I'm busy trying to respond to letters of inquiry and reading legal papers to make my case." Noah being inquisitive, "Oh, how's that coming along?" Sophie handed him his drink and rolled her eyes. With a bit of an attitude, she responded by looking toward the sofa where Braun had left a mess of paperwork. "That is what all that paperwork you have sprawled out over there is about." Noah looked over to the sofa, before turning to Braun, "Time for a break Huh?" Braun, started to speak, when Sophie interrupted. "Be careful if you get him started on all that. You know what you are walking into. Don't blame me if you can't get away." Both Noah and Braun chuckled as she continued. "I have things to do, let me know if you guys need anything. I'll be in the back." Sophie grabbed a few things and headed to the back of the coffee shop.

Noah took a sip of his drink, hoping that Braun would lighten up if he took an interest in what he had to say. "What's happening with your case that has you so intense on a day as beautiful as today?" He took another sip when Braun replied, "Not really anything. It will be a few weeks, if not a month or two before my case comes up again. In the meantime, you know I have been reinstated until the appeal of the outcome. It's complicated. Everyone at my command knows who I am and the name calling, and harassment continues. I've gotten used to it, if that is even possible. At work they don't really know what to do with me. So, they tell me to go home most of the time."

Noah tried to empathize. "I can't imagine your pain bro. It must be humiliating knowing everyone is in your business, who cares whether they approve of you or not. It is not something I would wish on my enemy! I can't, …just can't see it" Braun, in a bit of anger and excitement, "You know that is part of the problem." Noah noticing his tension, "What's that?" Braun tried to remain calm, but his passion was getting the best of him. "If every one of us came out in the open they would listen. They have no idea how many people are gay in the military. What is sad, many of the gays don't stand up and support those who have been prosecuted?" Noah disagreed, "I hear what you are saying Braun, and I understand about wanting to organize, but I don't agree. Some need to stay in to prove we can do the job and be a role model for others. God knows they try and say we can't. For some, this is the best thing they have going and have too much to lose to raise a flag, let alone the rainbow one. Did you not think this would happen when you started barking out? Did you think you would start a revolution against the Marine Corps? It is the United States Government, for God's sake, laws are laws. I appreciate that you took a stand, but not everyone who is gay sees it like you!"

Braun, a bit angry but still wanting to convince Noah and prove his point. "I didn't know what was going to happen. I just thought there would be more of a rally around what I was doing. I had to be true to myself and my own conscience and I took a stance. You know what happened to me can happen to anyone who is gay." Noah sat patiently and listened before speaking. "Braun, you know I have been in for years and I have seen many friends ousted. Some, it was part of their own doings, but for others, it was no fault of their own. Either way, I don't agree with it, so on that we are on the same side."

Noah paused to take a drink of his coffee and exhaled. Braun wanting to stir the fire, "So are you going to come out to the military?" He said condescendingly. Noah, not liking his tone, quickly responded. "Really, so go in and just tell them and let's see, …end up where you are right now? I'm under no obligation to set myself on fire to keep others warm. I don't think so, being that worked so well for you! Not going to happen." So, Braun leaned forward getting a bit anxious. "So, the lack of action is the same as no action." Noah decides to pull back the conversation realizing they were both passionate about the topic. "Braun, I think you really believe your way is the only way. Good for you, but I think we can agree to disagree."

Sophie hollered from the back of the store. "You two ok out there? I can hear you all the way back here." She came to the counter looking to make sure everything out front was ok. "You two need anything?" Noah, being facetious, quickly responded, "Yes, an aspirin and a to go cup!" She gave a half roll of her eyes. "Hush, you're not going anywhere! Behave!" she looked at Braun. "You need to lighten up! You are always taking things too seriously." Noah interrupted, "So what do you think Sophie? Braun thinks I should come out gay to the Marines?" She leaned back on the counter behind her. "Really? I think that's your choice, …and you need to do what's right for you." She looked over to Braun and spoke a little louder. "Just like Braun feels what he has done is right!" She shook her head like she was through with the whole topic. She stood straight, waving a towel in her hand, and looked around like she was searching for something. "I just don't get it any way. Why does it matter who you love to the military? Why can't they just be happy that you do love? Seems we need a little more love in this world to me, not hate! Now, where are those damn aspirin?" She looked to Noah and grinned. Noah chuckled, "Oh no Sophie, I don't have a headache, I was just joking to harass Braun." She looked directly at him. "I know darling, they are for me." She grabbed another towel, wiped down the counter, and moved back to the back of the store.

Chapter 36

An OASIS

Fall had come to North Carolina, and things were happening at a fast pace. The production of Liberty Call was underway, and the show had made its debut with superior results. It would take a while to know if the format and timing would work, but for now the schedule was set. The show was becoming second nature for the crew, and most of the kinks had been worked out. The news came in that Noah had not been selected to go to the White House, and now was a possible candidate for recruiting duty. Noah and Gina had developed a good working relationship and had become good friends. With the extra time off from work, and now being single, he was able to take a bigger role in the playhouse and auditioned for a part in the fall production. Although it was a small part, he was more of an all-around handy man helping Gina and the cast wherever he could. Anything from building sets, helping with costumes, to sound and lighting. He was loving it and had made quite a few new friends during the show. The play was called "Fly Wright" and was about the lives of the Wright Brothers and the birth of aviation. It was written by a local playwright from Wilmington and had gained some fame nationally. Their version was a much smaller version of the play and did not have the budget that was needed to do it justice. The fun of working with small playhouses is when all else is stripped away the talent is what carries the plays.

During the production, one weekend, some of the cast went out for a few drinks at one of local straight night clubs. Gina and Noah sat at the bar, and before the night was over Gina found out Noah was gay. She already had her suspicions, but the two never had an open conversation about it. She made sure Noah knew she was cool with it, and his secret was safe with her. If he ever needed her, she had his back. Noah's part in the play was a small one. He played next to Sophie from the coffee shop, who was in the play as well. They played an older couple who had taken the Wright Brothers in once they arrived in Kittyhawk.

Weeks prior, during production, Sophie had found out she was pregnant and would be due just about the time the show would end. Well, on closing night, Sophie went into labor, and just as she finished her last line on stage, she was headed to the hospital to give birth. Both baby and mom were fine.

After the show ended, the holiday season was upon them, and the TV crew was in production mode making public service announcements for the annual Marine Corps Toy-for-Tots drive. Liberty Call had grown more popular and filling the guest slots was becoming a lot easier. During the Holiday show one guest, a program manager, came on wearing a Christmas tree costume. Come to find out, it was the Managing Director of the playhouse prior to Gina. Envious of Gina's success, she was sniffing out the territory to see if there might be a position for her on the show. There was a bit of friction between the two, however, Gina stayed professional knowing the Commanding General and the crew had her back.

Having made friends and gaining the trust with several of the locals in the community, Noah was cracking the code and Jacksonville was starting to reveal its secrets. Giselle had introduced him to what was a clandestine gay community organization of prominent figures from within Jacksonville, Onslow County, and throughout the eastern North Carolina region. It was formed by a gay philanthropist wanting to do charitable services and give back to the community. Because of the stigma of being gay, they remained as anonymous donors, knowing many places would not accept charity from a gay organization, including many Politicians. Being anonymous allowed them to support common causes. It was formed of many old southerners, coming from families who had long earned their wealth. In other words, old money. However, it was also made up of doctors, lawyers, City Council members, business owners, and even television news reporters. They called themselves "Onslow Area Society in Service," or "OASIS" for short. They met once a month at various member's homes, to socialize and discuss funding and projects. It was also a time where they would invite guests, who were soliciting their support. It was by invitation only and all meetings were considered private. This was to protect members, as well as the guests, many who were gay, and not open, or out within the community. Noah became a member and attended the meetings regularly.

The Good-Looking Team

November 10th was the Marine Corps Birthday, making November the busiest month of the year for the audiovisual center. Every unit on base celebrated, many on different nights, all requiring Audiovisual support. Noah, now a Staff NCO, had been invited to attend the NCO Ball as the Narrator because of his broadcasting background. Noah decided to bring a friend he had met from OASIS. Charles had always been fond of Marines and when he learned of Noah going, asked if it would be possible to attend. Charles was a meteorologist at one of the local television networks and had never attended a Marine Corps Ball. He and Noah had dated off and on, but nothing serious had really developed from it. Charles, working in the public's eye, thought understanding Marine customs would be beneficial. Noah often steered away from having his personal life mix with his professional one. Seeing Charles's enthusiasm, Noah agreed. This would be the first time Noah had brought someone to the Marine Corps Ball. He would be introduced as a friend, and Noah schooled him about not showing any public display of affection, not even a hint, while they were on base. The two arrived at the Ball, Noah decked out in his Dress Blues, and Charles wearing a black tux. As they entered, they were greeted by their host, and introduced to several acquaintances, and shown their table. Charles' amazement of all the Marines, and their significant others, dressed to the nines was apparent on his face. Every time they were approached, he would give Noah a look of "Are you kidding me?" or tap Noah discreetly when he saw something catch his eye. Charles was having a good time. When it came time for the ceremony, Noah had to leave him and take his place at the podium. As the lights dimmed, Noah's voice asked for everyone to take their seats, the Ceremony was about to begin. Once all was calm, the traditional protocols began. It covered portions of history, and messages from famous Generals and Presidents from the past, before listing the many battles the Marine Corps had participated in. While Noah read the battles, a Marine wearing the uniform of that specific time frame would appear front and center. Starting with the Revolutionary war, all the way up to present day conflicts. After the reading and introduction of Colors, the cake was brought in, with the reading of John A Lejeune's message to the Corps. The oldest and youngest Marines were recognized and given a piece of cake. Once completed, the Marine's Hymn played. During some of the long pauses in the script, Noah would look to see how Charles was fairing, watching him take in all the festivities. He was enjoying himself. After it was over, and the two were on their way home, Charles kept reminiscing of the night's events, and speaking of how many good-looking Marines he saw. He jokingly insisted there had to be a good-looking requirement on the application when getting in. Noah laughed and played into to it, "Yep, they arrive at the Recruit Depot. There is a special team waiting for them when they step off the bus. One by one, as they disembark, the team is saying yes, yes, yes, wait, stop, nope you're not good looking enough, you have to go." Charles laughed, "I'd like to be on that team!" as he continued on, relishing of the night events; "It was wonderful, the whole thing, the ceremony, the cake, all of it. But I can't believe how many good-looking men could be in one location at the same time." Looking at Noah, "I don't know how you do it?" Noah was baffled, "How I do what?" Charles smiled, "How can you be gay and be around that all day long and not show it?" Noah shrugged, "I don't know, never really thought of it. I guess I just block it out or have gotten used to it. It's part of being a professional. I mean, I am gay. Every now and then, I'll notice a guy and give him a second look. But it's not like I want to jump his bones or something. Just like anyone, you just do your job, be a professional."

The Marine Corps Birthday Ball season had passed, and work was becoming routine. Being single, and the playhouse now dark until spring, Noah found himself with more time on his hands. He heard of a possible opening for a part-time news journalist and on-air reporter at one of the local television stations. Turned out one of the guys from OASIS worked there and knew the news director. Noah applied and was hired immediately. He worked for the Marine Corps during the day, and moonlighted of an evening, donning a suit, and working as a reporter at night. At first it was exciting, but then the Public Affairs office on base got wind of it and started monitoring his activity. They raised a flag calling it a conflict of interest on any story he did involving the base. Every time he was required to do a news report about the base, the next day he would receive a call from a Public Affairs Officer, wanting to know where he had gotten his information, or accused him of leaking information. The long hours and harassment eventually took its toll, and Noah decided to part ways with the local TV station.

Chapter 37

Knee High Panty Hose

Mid-summer in the Carolina's could be brutal. Between the heat and humidity, one was in a constant state of sweat. Hop in the shower to cool off, get out, dry off, and within minutes, be soaking in sweat again. For the most part, if you worked in an air-conditioned environment, you would be ok. The last six weeks for Noah had been spent at the Staff Non-Commissioned Officers Academy. Two weeks, in field, amongst the wilderness aboard the base of Camp Lejeune. During the day, they would do maneuvers, sit in classes, learn about various weapons, and shoot them. They would divide up in teams and have a competition on land navigation and shooting azimuths. Whoever found all the points first, and made it back to camp, would be the winner. The reward being if you made it back to Camp you were done for the evening unless, of course, one of the teams got lost and you had to go find them. The mosquitoes, gnats, and occasional snake were bad. The area being swampy and close to New River, the mosquitoes were relentless. If one showed up without bug spray, their time in the field would be miserable, at least for the first couple of days. Then the sweat, stench, and dirt, would help repel them away. But the unspoken part for the newbies to the area were the jiggers. Jiggers were absolutely ferocious. The Marines called them sand fleas and were notable reminders of the days they might have spent in recruit training at Parris Island.

Noah had been a West Coast Marine, or "Hollywood Marine" most of his career. Lejeune was his first east and southern most duty station. He had visited, but this was his first time being stationed here. He fit the category of being a newbie. After about the third night, Noah was getting ready to hit the rack, when he noticed his hooch mate, taking off his boots. When he removed his boots and socks, he was wearing women's knee-high panty hose. Noah turned his head away without saying a word. Why was he wearing those? Was he a cross-dresser? Noah didn't want to ask him, so he kept to himself. Whatever he was, Noah remained nonjudgmental.

A couple more days went by, when Noah woke up in the middle of the night, his lower legs were on fire, and he couldn't stop itching them. He applied some bug spray, and some ointment to help, but it did nothing. Finally, he made it back to sleep. This happened a couple more nights, and he was starting to lose sleep, with the itching wreaking havoc on his legs.

Another night went by, and they sat around the campfire. Noah noticed a couple of other guys taking off their boots. Once again, they too were wearing women's knee-high panty hose. Noah thought, this can't be a coincidence. The Marine sitting next to him spoke up. "Man, I see you got your stockings on. They're the best goddamn thing I've found to protect from being ate up from these jiggers. I forgot to bring my stockings, and I'm regretting it. I've been awake the last three nights with these damn things eating up my legs." He had gotten Noah's attention. "That's what has been wreaking havoc on my legs? Man, I haven't had a good night's sleep yet." The group chuckled, when one of them spoke up. "Yeah, they live in the sand and dirt, and get kicked up when you're out walking through the brush. It takes a couple of days before you know you got them. But man, they love to come out at night. Feels like something is digging right inside your leg." Noah spoke up, "Why knee highs, why do they work?" another Marine spoke up. "Jiggers are really small; you can hardly see them with the naked eye." Another Marine approached, only hearing the last part of the story, he interrupted, "Just like your dick." The others laughed, as the Marine explaining the story continued slightly distracted. "Shut the fuck up bitch, we'll see how small it is when I hear you screaming while I fuck your ass later tonight." The other Marines chuckled, with echoes of oohs and ahhs being heard. One threw some grass at the approaching Marine who was now sitting down by the fire grinning. The storyteller continued, "Down in Florida, they call them No-See-Ums, being they are so small they can get through a normal pair of socks, but with panty hose, the size of the netting keeps them from getting in." Noah listing intensively, "How do you get rid of them?" "Hah, …Good luck!" the Marine spouted off… "They go away after a couple of weeks, some say get in the ocean, others say fingernail polish remover. All I know, …Well, the only way you can get rid of them is to smother them. You can buy this jigger rid shit, but I use my wife's fingernail polish, put it right over the bite and smother them." Noah laughed to himself at the thought of these big burly Marines, using knee high panty hose, and fingernail polish. Noah found it humorous. "You mind if I ask you one more question?" "No go ahead." Noah chuckled, "You don't have an extra pair with you?" The Marines all laughed, the storyteller replied, "Sorry man I don't, but you learned a lesson. You'll never come out to the field again without them!"

Once he returned back to his Unit, he was snagged by the Battalion S-3. Because he was a freshly new trained SNCO he could help with getting the Marines caught up on their annual training. He would be working with the Battalion Commander's team, helping with the gas chamber, and running the grenade range. He would be teaching the classes, and, at the end of their training, would supervise as they demonstrated and performed the tasks. For the most part, he didn't mind, it would be a long stint away from the studio, and for a promotion it would look good, since he would receive a special fitness report for it. The gas chamber was no problem, he would be in mop gear the whole time he was inside. He wasn't required to dawn and clear his mask, just ensure the Marines in training did so. There was never a real threat, only if a Marine panicked and tried to run, or escape. If you got in his or her way, you might get clobbered. However, the grenade range was completely different. It involved throwing real grenades. No room for error. One mistake could cost a life, or maybe a few. It was a simple task but needed to be taken very seriously. The Marine might get nervous, or be overconfident, and mess up the throw. Sometimes causing it to fall short, or even dropping the grenade right in the grenade pit. Because of the danger, they had an instructor in the grenade pit with them giving them the command one step at a time. In the event of a short fall or drop, the instructor was taught how to handle the situation. If something went wrong, if they were not focused, and quick thinking it could cost lives. Noah was not thrilled. He didn't like throwing them himself, let alone being responsible for someone else.

Chapter 38

Rifle Range Detail Gisselle's revenge

Finally, after months of being away in training, Noah found himself back in the studio and was thrilled to be able to get back in touch with his craft. So many new projects had come in while he was away. Sergeant Hickman and Gunny brought him up to speed on all the work in house. Noah and Hickman had grown to be friends. Hickman could be a bit rough around the edges, but in reality, he was a nice guy. The gay issue was never really spoken about openly, it was understood. Hickman had a gay brother and was a gay ally. Part of the responsibilities of the video production department was confidential and forensic in nature. Working with the base law enforcement in the acquisition and preparation of video for ongoing criminal and court martial investigations. Sergeant Hickman had called him in to brief him of a sensitive video currently in house and being dubbed. It was a need-to-know situation. There was a chain of custody, and anyone seeing or working with it had to sign in. Hickman was leaving for other engagements and Noah would take over custody and responsibility of the work. As the two reviewed the tapes, Hickman explained what work needed to be completed. Watching the tape, he noticed a familiar face. He paused the tape and reviewed it again. No, no way this couldn't be. He reviewed it one more time, before grabbing the box cover and reading the title caption. "Master Gunnery Sergeant Phobos investigation."

Noah sat stunned. He thought he had seen the last of this guy. This was the same guy who raped Giselle way back in the early 80's in Okinawa. He was a Gunny then, now a Master Gunnery Sergeant. They weren't able to report him because he threatened to turn Giselle in for being gay. He looked to Hickman, "What is this about?" Hickman was anxious to tell Noah about it. "Oh man, you don't want to watch this thing. Dude is a sick Motherfucker!" Noah curious, "Who's the dude, what the fuck is this about?" Hickman, frowned, but went on, "Well don't say I didn't give you fair warning."

Hickman went and closed the editing bay door. "Look, this dude molested his five-year-old daughter, and it was recorded by accident without him knowing. The mother and grandma were gone and left the girl with him. The grandma had been recording video earlier, and set the camera down in the room, but didn't shut it off. When she came back, she went to review the tape and the whole molestation of the girl was recorded."

Noah sat down in disgust, shocked and guilty at the same time. Hickman continued, "Get this, the mother tried to stop the grandma from coming forward. Shit, what kind of mom is she. That poor girl has got two pieces of shit for parents. The agent said he has older daughters, and when the one found out, she came forward. He had done it to her as well. That sick mother fucker ought to be hung by his balls! This dude is a Master Gunnery Sergeant, been in for years. Get this, he works at the Inspector General's office of all places. He'll probably get off. I have a notion, to take this mother out myself, if I knew I wouldn't get caught! Come on, this is a five-year-old girl we're talking about!" This guy needed to be stopped. Noah didn't let on to Hickman he knew anything about the guy. But he did need to let Giselle know this sicko was here at Lejeune.

Hickman was walking out the door, when Noah heard Gina's voice. "I know he's back, where is he?" Noah spoke out, "Back here Gina." Gina stuck her head around the corner, "It's about time, I was beginning to wonder if you were ever coming back." She walked in and gave him a hug, "The guys did a really good job while you were gone, but don't say anything, it wasn't the same without you. I'm glad you're back" Noah smiled, "Well, I'm glad to be back. I hear the show...." Gina interrupted, "What is this? I know this name." She picked up the tape case of Master Gunnery Sergeant Phobos. Noah grabbed the tape from her. "That is for private eyes only, you aren't supposed to see that."

Gina was inquisitive with a plea, "Noah?" Noah pushed away, "Gina, No! I can't. It's a criminal evidence tape. You aren't even supposed to be in here." Gina wasn't taking no for an answer. "Ok, then tell me this, is it the same one at the I. G. Office?" Noah rolled his eyes, "You know I can't talk about it, even if it was, what good would that do? You still don't know what it's about." Gina continued, "Aha, it is him. I'm asking because I know he is not a very nice man." Now Noah was curious, "Gina, you know something about this guy?" Gina frowned and closed the door behind her. "I've known this guy since I was a Lance Corporal. On second thought, …No, no, you're right, let's not go there. Let's just say this guy is a sick asshole and leave it at that. I know more about him than I care to remember." Noah wanted to know more. "Gina, this guy is in some serious trouble. Now's not the time to hold back. If you know something, share it."

Gina stared at Noah for a moment contemplating "Ok," as she sat down in the chair as she began. "Me and some of my friends were at the E-Club one night. This was years back, right after I had joined. There was a group of us. A few guys from work and a couple of my girlfriends, all Marines. I left early with a couple of the other guys and came back to the barracks. My roommate, Lance Corporal Davis, was one of the girls. She and another girl stayed behind…

(1980's Camp Lejeune…)

The E-club was starting to empty out, as Shalika finished her last drink. She stood up, and the room seemed to move with her. "Oh my!" She sat back down, giving herself a moment. As she sat there, she noticed her shoes, and how proud she was to have them. They weren't the most expensive, but she was so proud of them because she bought them with her own money. The Marine Corps had given her independence. She liked them; they made her feel pretty. She looked around the room and didn't recognize anyone. Why didn't she go home with Gina earlier? She knew Marlee was not reliable and was popular with the guys, always taking off with a new suitor at the end of the evening. Oh well, she would have to make it home on her own. Stopping by the restroom to freshen up, she came out and headed for the door when she stumbled into a Marine. "Oh, I'm sorry!" She looked up; it was Gunny Phobos. The staff duty. Of all people, to bump into. "Oh, excuse me Gunny, these shoes, they're new, and can be a bit hard to walk in!" She tried to cover her intoxication. Past problems, and brawls at the E-club, required the Staff Duty to stop by throughout the evening just for appearances. Just the mere presence of a senior Marine, seemed to remind the junior Marines to keep it under control, or as they liked to say, "Big Brother is watching!" Gunny Phobos, saw right through her cover. "You alright little lady? You look like you might have had one too many. Are you here alone?" Shalika blushed, "I think you're right, …No, I mean I wasn't! I was here with some friends, but it seems they have all gone home. …I'm headed back to the barracks now." She turned and started to walk away, before Gunny Phobos stopped her, "You know what, you go ahead and wait right outside by my car, that one right out front." He pointed to it. "Let me finish my rounds in here, and I'll give you a ride. You shouldn't be walking home."

Shalika sat in the front seat, and the effects of the alcohol was starting to weaken. They approached the street where she lived, and Gunny Phobos confirmed once again which barracks it was. Once he got to the street, he made a turn. Shalika noticed he turned the wrong way. "Oh, it's the other way, I must have told you the wrong number." She sat and looked out the window. Gunny continued on, "I'll turn around up here, there is a small turn out at the end." The road became dark and surrounded by woods. Then a dead end with a small turn around. Gunny pulled to the end and stopped the car. Shalika panicked realizing what was going on and started to get out, he locked the doors and grabbed her. She struggled at first, but his power and the alcohol caused her to give in. He pulled her from the car. On the ground he held her down and covered her mouth, threatening her, telling her, "This is really what you wanted, now isn't it?" She went blank, as he thrust on top of her, blocking the rest from her mind. All she could focus on was the stars in the sky above her.

Once he finished, he drove to the barracks, dumping her off at the curb. "There, go on, get out!" He grinned in some sick manner. "I told you, I would give you a ride!" He grinned at her, like it was some joke. Her hair was disheveled and dirty, with scuff marks all over her. "You tell anyone, they won't believe you! I'll deny it! Who are they going to believe, a Gunny, or a little drunk whore! I'll let them know you were drunk and came on to me." Shalika stumbled to the barracks barefoot, holding her shoes. The ones she was so proud of. The ones she had bought earlier in the day. The ones she felt made her look thin, tall, and pretty. The ones that would catch all the guys' attention. She made it to her room door. She leaned over the catwalk, nauseous from what had just taken place, and started crying. How could she have been so stupid! She trusted him. He was a Marine. What the fuck had she done wrong? She looked at her shoes and became aggravated and flung them out into the darkness in front of her and screamed. "Why?" …

(1990's Continued…)
"…When I found her, she was on the floor outside my barracks door. Battered, abused, and had been raped by this asshole. We took her to

the duty NCO and logged it in. We called the Military Police, and they came and took a statement. They even went to him and took a statement. No arrest was made. Instead of thinking to take her to the hospital and have her checked, they told her to go on home and rest it off and get cleaned up. The next day she was called in front of the CO. He listened to what she had to say. When she finished, he started making accusations; 'why don't you really tell us what happened. You had too many drinks, and you came on to him, now, didn't you?' The Command squelched it. She was silenced. She even went to get a copy of her statement and the police report. They said that it was turned over to the command to handle. Nothing ever came of it, but she and Gunny Phobos both soon had orders. She was sent to Okinawa, only to find out she was pregnant. I mean how messed up is that? You get raped by a guy, and find out you're pregnant by him?" Noah dropped his jaw. "Oh my gosh! What did she do?" Gina continued, "What do you think she did? …and it wasn't easy to get done while overseas. After all was said and done, she got out of the Marine Corps."

Noah sat shaking his head in disbelief, "I can't say I blame her." Gina continued. "I lost track of him, until he showed back up here at Lejeune. A year or so ago, I was walking into Headquarters, as he was walking out. I did a double take, before I checked the roster, and sure enough, it was him." Noah sat quietly stunned. This had become more serious than he had imagined. How long had this been going on and how long had the Marine Corps known and turned a blind eye. Noah looked at Gina. "Now, I have something to share with you. She wasn't the first, or the only one." Noah told her the whole story of what had taken place back in the early 80's on Okinawa. Gina sat, just as stunned, as Noah spoke. When he finished, he took the tape and played it for her. It got to a certain point, and she told him to shut it off.

Both sat quietly, processing what they had just learned. This guy was a serial rapist. Hopefully, CID (Criminal Investigative Division) would follow through and put this guy in prison. Sometimes the military had a way of making things disappear, rather than tarnish the Marine Corps' image. They would squash it, silence it, and force the culprit into retirement, making it go away. This was usually done when the figure was high ranking, and the damage could be contained to base. Issues like this were considered a family matter. Noah hoped it wouldn't be the case this time. Gina spoke up angrily, "Why is this guy not in jail, and still out and walking around? I know for a fact; he hangs out at "Mystic" my husband's place. I've seen him in there before. I warned Tony about him, and to keep an eye on him. Who knows how many others he has done this to?"

Noah turned to her, "You know we are part to blame. We knew and did nothing to pursue it. We just accepted it and moved on. We played right into his hands." Gina interrupted, "Don't say we're the blame! He is responsible for his own actions. He knows what he is doing! Look at his victims, what kind of predator is he? He's like a bad shooter on target, this fucker is all over the place, male, female, and now a child. What's his M.O.? I don't get it" Noah shook his head, "His M.O. is he is a sick fuck, that is what his M.O. is!" Gina shook her head, "No, no, he preys on the vulnerable. The ones he knows can't speak, won't speak or they're not believable" Noah was agitated, he felt stifled. "Look, I want to do something, but what? We just have to keep faith in the system. They know what they're doing, I'm sure this time they'll do what is right." Gina smirked. "You really believe that, with all you have been through?" Noah shrugged, "Yes, I do! Besides, we can't just go all vigilante on him. We got to trust in the system." Gina shook her head, "No! …I don't trust them. (Gina looked at Noah and was dead serious, as she spoke softly.) "Noah, … you know we can no longer sit by and do nothing…" Noah looked at her. "You sound like Hickman; he wants to take him out! What's gotten into you guys? There are still laws. I might have broken some of them, but I am not willing to do what I think you are asking me to!"

He didn't like her when she got like this. He knew she had deep connections on the dark underside. When Gina made up her mind, whatever she was scheming up, you could guarantee she would carry it through! Noah wanted no part of this, he was stepping aside, and going to remain silent. He was best to steer clear!

Chapter 39

Kinston Alien

After months away for training, and a few days back at work, the weekend had arrived. Noah had made it home and was ready to get caught back up on things around the house and reconnect with friends. He had finished laundry, and cleaning, and was ever so thankful to be in his own home. It was wonderful to be able to shower and sleep under a roof in his own bed. He retrieved his calls from the answering machine, writing down pertinent information, when he heard Ms. Delta's voice message. "Hey handsome, I know it's last minute, but got a small group getting together later this evening to celebrate Paula's Birthday, thought you might want to attend. Call me when you can Sweetheart."

Ms. Delta or the "Lebanese lesbian" as she liked to call herself, and her partner Marie, lived outside of the small town of Kinston, located a good 30 miles inland from the base. Delta was a talker, and always had good news to share. Spending the evening with the group would be an enjoyable event. Noah gave her a call and told her he would be much obliged to attend, and cleared the way for Giselle, and Bob, an out-of-town visitor, to accompany him. Noah and Giselle had both known Bob since the early 80's. Noah remembered meeting Bob clear back in Oki, at a gay bar where he learned of his Toadvine, Alabama story. Bob had since gotten out of the Marines and returned to Alabama to work on the family farm.

The thick and muggy late night was hazy, only allowing a trickle of the moon and stars to shine through. As the crew fell out of Shadows Lounge stumbling, and laughing, they loaded up the van and were headed home after a long night of dining, drinking, and dancing. Ms. Delta was the designated driver. Marie, her partner, sat in the front passenger seat and they conversed amongst themselves, as the others laughed and reminisced while traversing on the dark back roads of eastern North Carolina. Once underway, the laughs slowly faded and were replaced by the sound of music coming from the radio as the rest of the crew slowly dozed along the way. In the middle row of the van, Noah sat directly behind Ms. Delta, Giselle was in the middle and Vee at the van door. In the very back was Bob, Paula, and Sunny. They were all headed to Ms. Delta and Marie's home just outside of Kinston. One of Ms. Delta's favorite things to do on special occasions such as birthdays, holidays, and such, was to have everyone spend the night, and in the morning cook breakfast before they headed out. This occasion was Paula's birthday, and after a night out on the town, tonight would be no different. Noah sat quietly looking out at the head lamps that silhouetted Delta's head as she drove. It wasn't long before he felt Giselle's head hit his shoulder, sound asleep. Noah looked around; all were asleep except for Paula in the back. With everyone knocked out, Noah found it difficult to take advantage of the opportunity, worrying Ms. Delta left alone would fall asleep at the wheel. He decided to stay awake and keep her company, asking her every so often, "Are you doing all right?" She would reply, "Child I'm fine, don't worry about me, go to sleep."

As they drove, he looked out the side window into the darkness. Thinking about the night and how much fun it was to be with everyone. How nice it was knowing Paula had enjoyed her birthday evening. Noah arched up to see the lights of a small town approaching. He felt somewhat relieved, the encounter would break up the moonless monotony of the trip. As the van strolled into Kinston, the streetlights slowly lit up the inside of the van and gave him a change in scenery, looking at the buildings of the town as they passed by. A small town of typical rural blend coffee. Do you like it strong, or weak? With or without cream and sugar? As they approached the main street, the specialty shops, along with "Mom-and-Pop" restaurants, peaked through the large oak trees that flanked both sides of the road. The turn of the century brick buildings displaying their spring flowers and flags created a welcome site for most; but Noah knew better. He grew up in a town just like this. A town where everyone seemed to know one another and where most of its residents would spend their entire life. These small towns that held so much original charm and nostalgia were becoming increasingly obsolete with urban sprawl and the invention of the strip mall. Their struggle against economic decline was matched only by their resistance to new ideas and change. White picket fences, garage sales and community gatherings served to hide the implicit bigotry towards those outside the norm. Christian white conformity was the rule; act the part or remain silent. It was easy to romanticize about the quaint charm of the town, but Noah also knew the views of most of its citizens had remained nostalgic as well. Ms. Delta's voice broke the sound of hum and soft music. She was thinking out loud, "I love these little towns. They're so cute!" Noah spoke out loud, "Somethings look better, when just passing through." He knew any new way of thinking, or being the wrong color, race, or religion would quickly put you at odds with most of the towns smiling faces. The transition of flashing lights and shadows had woken Marie briefly to ask Delta if she was ok and it brought Noah's attention back to the inside of the van. As he looked around inside the van, he realized he, and all the passengers in the van were completely at odds with all that was nostalgic outside. Although he had left his childhood town long ago, he was still haunted by its memories and longed for its nostalgia. Yet things back then were not as they appeared, and his rose-colored glasses no longer fit. Would they ever be welcome in these small, antiquated towns, or would it always be that they would only feel safe as passengers in a van, just passing by? In this new world he found himself living in, he wondered if any future days of nostalgia would happen, or would he be left with only the good memories of days gone by? The glow of the streetlights slowly faded back to darkness leaving the town and were replaced by the beams of the vans headlamps as it opened the road from the abyss in front of them once gain.

It had been twenty minutes or so since they had left Kinston and the haze was clearing allowing the moon and stars to faintly luminate the wire fence lines alongside the road. The trees and shrubbery cast their shadows into shapes left to one's imagination. The homes were placed sporadically. The darkness was interrupted by an occasional twinkle of some far-off light in the distance. They were now just a few miles from Delta's house. It was late night, and Noah found himself fading in and out of sleep. Only to realize he might be dozing; he would quickly shake his head and once again ask, "Delta are you doing alright?" Just as he started to fade again, everyone in the van was startled awake with a quick jar and a bump out of nowhere. Delta hollered out, "Holy Shit, what the hell was that?" As she hit the brakes, the van came quickly to a screeching halt. Everyone was now awake, shaken, and wondering what the hell had just happened. Paula, from the back, "Delta are you alright?" Noah looking around to see if everyone was ok, quickly asked, "Ms. Delta what's going on?" Marie, concerned about everyone's well being asked, "Everybody ok?" All were shaken from the sudden stop and responded with various answers. Vee, who had been slouched down in the seat with her knees propped up on the seat in front of her and hat pulled over her eyes, was now sitting up and adjusting her hat while looking around, "I'm awake, I'm awake." Bob, sitting in the back, had pretty much slept the entire trip but was now wide awake, "If you count shitting my pants fine, then yeah, I'm ok." Sunny spoke out to Delta, "What the hell girl, you fall asleep?" Delta still staring forward seemed a bit spooked, "I think I hit …something, but I'm not quite sure." They all looked at each other confused, at which point Noah chimed in, "What do you mean you think you hit something? You either hit something or you didn't." Vee snapped up from a slumber and leaned to Delta, "Girl this van jumped and swayed, ...I got news for you… You hit something!" Delta hanging on to the steering wheel, shifted to park, before turning her head slowly to the right to make sure her voice could be heard, "I hit something, but I don't know what it was, …I think…, I mean it might have been, it looked like, …an alien…" The van sat quiet. Giselle heard her, sat straight up, looked to Vee, and rolled his eyes. Vee, in disbelief, quickly asked, "What the hell do you mean? … you think you hit an alien, …Is this the twilight zone? Shit, girl quit messing with us!" Marie looked over to Delta, realized she was scared and not joking. "Listen you all calm down; Delta now again what happened?" Delta started recapping her actions, "I was just driving along, and the radio was fuzzy, so I went to adjust it. I looked at it just for a second, and when I looked back up at the road something came out of nowhere from my side and hit the front of the car. All I could see was two big eyes and a little head looking at me through the windshield, and it wasn't human. It looked like an alien. The next thing I know, I hit the brakes and it went down under the car. I ran over it and the car screeched and came to a halt." Vee, listening intensely, quickly came back, "Girl why the hell you keep saying alien? You know damn well that shit don't exist. You're starting to spook me." Delta in defense, "Look all I can tell you is what I saw. It looked like one of those little freak'en space men you see on them shows all the time on TV. I'm telling yah, a damn alien." Sunny, from the back, "Hey ya'll, not trying to break up your party. But we're in the road case you forgot, and I have got to pee. Can we get this thing moving or back on the road, because I have gotta go, and it ain't gonna be pretty if I have to go here!" Delta, looking in her rearview mirror, "Alright ya'll, but I gotta check to see if I can drive this thing the rest of the way home first." Sunny impatiently, "Awe, come on Vee let me out, I can't wait, I'll piss alongside the road." She started tapping the back of the seat, "Come on Vee let me out. Hurry up I got to go!" Marie, trying to speed things up, "Ok Vee, let her out, while she's doing her thang, we can look at the van. Delta, you stay here, case we might need you to move it." Noah chimed in, "I can give you a hand Marie." Vee opened the side back door of the van, when out of nowhere a small head with two big eyes, and a long neck came up from below the door. Vee, starting to get out, was startled, reacting with a jump back in the van landing on Giselle and Noah. "What, … thee, … Hell!!!" Sunny who was attempting to get out, seen it as well, "What the…?" as she turned away in shock and began to scramble along with Paula and Bob to get to the far back corner of the van. Marie had turned completely around in the front seat, looking back in shock. Delta turned to see everyone scattering when she realized whatever she had hit was still under the van. She leaned in to get a closer look when the creature brought its head up and almost inside the door. She could now see the head and eyes clearly. She screamed, "I told you it was an alien, I told you it was an alien!" as she scrambled to open her door to get out. Everyone sat in silence looking out the passenger door. They waited for a moment or two to see if it would move again. Vee was still blocking Noah and Giselle as they started to move. "Don't move, don't move! I don't want to get close to that thing." Noah, feeling claustrophobic and trapped, "Look we can't stay in here all night." Marie moved over to the driver side and exited the van to go calm Delta. Noah moved to get out through the front, pushing Giselle and Vee out of the way and the creature started moving again. Noah quickly moved through the center of the van and out the driver's door, with Giselle and Vee right behind him. When they got out, they could see the van had come to a halt slightly off the right side of the road. Noah looked around and, Ms. Delta and Marie were across the street in the grass holding each other. Noah hollered over to Ms. Delta "Do you have a flashlight." Delta responded, "There's one in the back Noah, you might have to hunt for it, cause I don't know what's back there." He went to the back and opened the door. Paula, Sunny, and Bob were pressing against it from the inside, and stumbled over each other trying to exit the van. Sunny agitated, "It's about damn time! Ain't no way we were going to try to pass that thing." After they were out of the way, he found the flashlight. He quickly turned it on and slowly walked around the van to see the group now huddled with Ms. Delta and Marie. Everyone was now out of the van. He spoke out walking to the group, "Well, what do you all want to do?" Sunny spoke up immediately, "I'm going to piss," as she and Paula walked into the bushes close by. Paula laughed, "You sure you haven't peed on yourself already." Delta stood with Marie's arms around her. Giselle spoke walking off, "The girls got the right idea, this can wait a minute." Noah, looking at the van, "Who wants to do a walk around with me and find out what's going on?" Bob quickly spoke up, "Gurl, I ain't getting anywhere near that thing!" Marie looked at Ms. Delta, "One of us has got to see what kind of damage is going on with the van. Bob, you stay here with Ms. Delta." Marie and Noah approached the front of the van, they could see there was some minor damage to the grill, but still looked drivable. As they continued their walk to the passenger side Marie told Noah, "Let's move a little further away and put some distance between us and whatever is underneath there." They arrived at the passenger side back door, kneeling they shined the light underneath the van. A small head and long neck quickly turned to look at them and started squabbling beneath the vehicle. Still not quite sure what it was, they

moved in closer. Both almost simultaneously "Are you serious?"
with a bit of chuckle, Noah spoke out loud "What the …?" Marie in
disbelief, "You mean, how the freak'n hell?" Noah looked at Marie
"Are you seeing what I'm seeing? Is that a bird? Is that a giant ass
bird?" Maria responded, "It looks like it to me." Both, confused,
moved a bit closer, before stopping when the bird started to move
and get rowdy. Noah spoke out to try and calm it "Whoa girl, Whoa,
calm down. We'll stay right here. We ain't going to come no
further…" They both stopped, fearing getting closer would excite it,
causing it to hurt itself even further. Marie laid down trying to look
beyond the head of the bird, "How does a giant bird get out here in
the middle of nowhere? It looks like an ostrich." Noah replied, "I
know right?" Marie backing up a bit, sat up to her knees. "Whatever
kind'a bird it is, there is no way we can move the van without
hurting it. Hell, it may be seriously hurt already." Marie got up from
her knees and walked back to the front and yelled, "It's ok ya'll! It's
not an alien, jeeze…" With a chuckle she continued to the rest of the
crew. "You all ain't going to believe this, it's an ostrich, a giant
bird!" About that time, you could hear them all starting to laugh as
they walked over to the van. Marie spoke up, "An alien Delta? How
the hell you gonna get a freak'n alien from an ostrich?" Delta spoke
out, "Listen, you all need to calm the hell down. I'm the one who
was driving the damn van, while you all's happy asses slept. That
thing damn near gave me a heart attack. What the hell Marie? How
do I know? I'm not thinking ostrich in the middle of the night. How
in the hell does an ostrich get in the middle of no-fucking-where
North Carolina? Shit, out here it might as well be a freak'n alien."
Vee started laughing. "I hears yah Ms. Delta! Girl let me tell yah, I
thought you was crazy. I knew there weren't no alien. But I tell you
what, when I opened that door, and that head came up. I about shit
myself and damn near fell out trying to get the hell out the way,
cause I thought for sure it might be! ...Lord have mercy! … What…
thee… hell?" She continued to laugh while walking over to Delta
and giving her hug. The two sat, chuckled, cracking up laughing
with relief. Sunny spoke out, "Is it alright?" Marie responded, "I
don't know, but it's sure the hell stuck under the van." Paula
inquisitively concerned, "What are we going to do ya'll, about

getting outta here? We can't move the van with that thing under there." Sunny adding on, "Those things can hurt you if you don't know what you're doing. They can kick the shit out of you, if not peck the hell out of you. Poor thing is hurt and afraid. I think it's too dangerous for us to try." After contemplating a while, the group agreed with Marie's plan; "Look, Delta you stay here. You haven't been drinking, and you'll need to drive the van home. Someone will need to stay here with her, so she isn't alone. The house is maybe a mile or two at best. I'll walk to the house, call the sheriff, and get a wrecker out here. I'll need someone to walk with me cause this late at night I'm not walking alone." Ms. Delta was worried about the sheriff coming, "Marie, I don't know, are you sure we want the Sheriff out her?" Marie smirked not worried, "Don't worry, you ain't been drinking. Besides, we'll need the report for the insurance company, cause they sure the hell ain't going to believe this shit." Vee spoke up. "Hah, Hah, can hear you telling the Sheriff you hit an ostrich. They'll probably think it's a prank phone call." Laughing, "Girl, I'm a stay right here with Ms. Delta. I wanna see this crazy shit through to the end." Noah spoke up, "Me and Giselle will stay behind with Ms. Delta as well." Sunny, Paula, and Bob agreed to walk with Marie to get help.

While waiting, Noah and Delta walked around the van to assess the situation. Noah told Delta, "Let me know if you see any fluid or blood." Noah got down on the driver side with the light and looked to see if the bird was bleeding or badly hurt. He spoke to Ms. Delta, "I don't see any blood, but she might be hurt internally. Right now, she just looks trapped and scared." Ms. Delta sarcastically, "Do you think? And how the hell do you know it's not a guy?" As the two stood up, Noah told her, "I don't, just a figure of speech. But I do know the last thing we want to do is upset it, and to keep it from hurting itself any further. If we stay out of view, it should remain calm, at least until the Sheriff gets here." Delta, looked at Noah sympathetically with guilt, "Noah you know I would never hurt a flea, man that thing just came out of nowhere." She grabbed the light from Noah and got down to look at the bird, "I'm so sorry Buddy, I would never want to hurt you." She started to get back up, "Noah give my fat ass a hand I'm stuck." Noah gave her a hand as she got up. Wondering how long it might be before help would arrive, he asked Delta, "How long do you think it'll be?" Delta threw her hands up, "Awe man, who knows. It's a twenty-minute walk at least to get home and call. The sheriff is a half hour if not longer. Knowing them country ass jack legs in Kinston, shit, then the wrecker, hell we're probably here all night." Noah reached over and patted her on the back. "It's all right, just think of all the bragging rights from this. There will be shit talking for years to come." Vee overhearing Noah, "You got that right! I'll be telling my grandkids about Ms. Delta's crazy ass hitting an alien." As she burst out laughing along with the rest of the group. Giselle added to the laughs, "Yeah, the night Ms. Delta killed E.T." The humor added a brief release from the stress and tension. Delta shut the van down and turned on the flashers and set a couple flares out on the road. The four congregated alongside the road in front of the van taking a seat on the gravel's edge. The dim light of early morning was starting to reveal the green pastures and pine trees in the distance, but still no car from either direction. The conversation was starting to get sparse. Giselle had laid down and started to doze. An occasional laugh would break the silence, along with the question of, "Anyone coming yet?" accompanied with a look in either direction to see if any movement or traffic might be visible.

The morning was starting to take hold, when Delta noticed a car coming from the direction of her house. "Hey ya'll, someone is coming. Get up, we don't want to get hit, and we need to try and slow them down, so they don't hit the van." Getting up Delta recognized the car. "Ya'll that's Marie." Upon Marie's arrival, the group walked over to her. "The Sheriff is on his way, man he was laughing his ass off." The group let out hoots and cheers. "He wanted to know if everybody was ok. I told him yeah, …just the bird, it's stuck under the van." Ms. Delta asked, "Did he say how long it would be?" Marie shook her head no, "He said he'll be here shortly, didn't give me a time; told me he wasn't surprised though. There's an ostrich farm out here and them damn birds get out all the time. He was getting hold of the wrecker and the bird owner. Said the farmer is a nice guy and can try and help get the damn bird out from under the car."

It wasn't long before the morning sun appeared, along with the Sherriff, the wrecker, and the ostrich farmer and a farmhand. All were on the scene working to get the bird out from under the van. The group looked on as each member of the team did their part of the rescue. The Sheriff stood by and observed, while simultaneously directing the occasional car or looky-loo passing by. The farmer covered the birds head with a bag and put a rope around its neck. The wrecker driver blocked the back wheels and started to jack up the car. The van slowly lifted upwards and soon the Ostrich was more visible but wasn't moving. The farmer and his farmhand, with two long cushioned poles, pushed the bird from behind. The group could see the ostrich slowly appear. Just as the bird cleared the van it flocked a bit and immediately found its footing and was standing. The group let out a sigh of relief and applauded to see the bird rise. The farmer came around and grabbed the rope that had been previously attached to its neck, along with the farmhand pushing from behind, they guided the bird safely into the trailer. The group standing off to the side of the road by Marie's car started to disassemble. Marie was not happy about the treatment of the bird or why there was even a farm. "What the hell are they doing with ostriches here in North Carolina?" Noah taking a guess, "I don't know probably selling their eggs or raising them for meat." Ms. Delta a bit disappointed, "Child I don't how much good we did, after seeing that thing tied up by the neck and a hood put over its head, it looked like a damn prisoner." Marie sympathetically, "The pitiful thing knows it don't belong here. What are they going to do take it back to a cage? It just wants to be a free bird." Vee, who had been listening to the conversation wasn't feeling the same and decided to make light of the situation. "Oh goddamn, what we gonna do, break out some "Lynyrd Skynyrd." In song she started singing. "Fly High, Oh Free Bird yeah…, What the hell? It's a goddamn bird! …and it ran the fuck out in front of you, get the fuck over it." The group turned to her in shock. It was as though she had slapped them back to reality. Delta was offended, "Vee, I swear you are just evil, …with your obnoxious ass, you just miss the point!" Vee questioning Ms. Delta's judgement, "What am I miss'n, Ms. Delta? …I ain't miss'n anything, but my bed! We been up all damn night with this crazy fucking bird, shit! You know I loves yah, but Honey it's time to move on. Fuck that bird and fuck that farmer too. I'm ready to get outta here and get home!" Ms. Delta, shaking her head waving her hand in the air, while walking away, "You know what? I ain't got time to argue with your stupid ass right now. Come on ya'll." The crew scattered to get in the van. Ms. Delta, lagging a bit behind, had stopped briefly to speak to the Sheriff. Within minutes she was in the van and the crew was once again on their way.

Looking out the window as they passed the trailer, the ostrich was now standing with its head outside the railing and the hood removed. Noah shook his head in disbelief as he turned his head forward with his thoughts of what a strange and long night it had been. How much did they have in common with the ostrich now inside the trailer, still at odds and out of place in the new world he now found himself in. He glanced over to his traveling buddies of misfits and refugees. Like him, they would never be accepted there, not in that small town and not in that America. Their silence can only hold for so long. A knowing smile came across his face, they had each other for now. Regardless, it was time to get home and get some much-needed rest. The van and its crew moved onward on the back roads of North Carolina.

Chapter 40

The Wizard of Hurricanes

Noah arrived early, ordered his latte, and sat at the bar talking to Sophie. He looked out the window as he watched Gina pull up in her Jaguar. She hopped out wearing a light blue suit dressed to the tens. She was known for always being impeccable in her appearance. Although she was Hispanic, Noah couldn't help but think how much she fit the role of a mobster's wife. She was married to a former Marine, Tony, who got out and opened a business in the local community. He was a nice guy, Italian and originally from New York. He owned and managed a local nightclub called "Mystic." Although Noah never really questioned her on it, there was talk that had floated around about his connections and was revered as someone to respect and not take lightly. Whether he was, or wasn't mafia, he had always treated Noah well. Gina came in and gave both him and Sophie a hug, before ordering her drink. Both paused when the TV had an update about the missing Marine on base. Sophie turned up the volume. The news anchor spoke, "It is now day 18 since anyone has known the whereabouts of Master Gunnery Sergeant Theodore Phobos. He last spoke to his family on Saturday evening, the 21st of August, when he left to go to run an errand, and stop by a local store. Video tapes were checked, and no evidence suggests he ever made it to the store. It's reported the Marine and his wife were having some personal problems and were currently living apart. He may have wandered off on his own. Foul play has not been ruled out at this time. The family and the Police are asking ..." Lowering the volume, Sophie spoke out. "I bet the wife killed him. It's always someone in the home." Both Noah and Gina looked at each other, knowing his background and what was going on. They both simultaneously replied, "I think you're right." Gina shook her head to shake it off. "So, now what I came in here for." Noah couldn't help but wonder how timely this was, knowing the conversation he previously had with Gina. "Gina, don't you find it a bit suspicious, I mean him coming up missing?" Gina shrugged her shoulders, "No, he was a creep! I'm not surprised at all. Somebody was going to get him! It's karma taking hold!" Something was off, it just didn't sit right with Noah. "Gina, look at me. Tell me you don't know what happened to him?" Gina sat quiet, almost annoyed, "I think what they call it, 'Don't Ask, Don't Tell,' right? So now can we get to why I asked you here?" Noah thought it odd, but was sure nothing probably happened, so he let it go. Gina was busy out doing work for the radio station and took a break to talk to Noah about the next playhouse production, "The Wizard of Oz." Knowing his background, she was wondering if he might direct the play. Noah was in awe. What a gift! Did she not know this was a gay man's dream? Of course, Noah said yes immediately. The two sat down over the next few days and brainstormed, getting the leg work done to have the production set up by Thanksgiving. The good news was it was going to be in the large main side Camp Lejeune Base Theater that could sit 3000 people. The theater had been around since the forties and had a complete fly system that was designed for live theater productions. It had many famous stars cross its stage back in the day, and it would be a privilege for the playhouse to perform there. It was currently being used as a movie theater, and they would not gain access until one week prior to opening. The sad news was the little Midway Park theater they had called home, was being taken away from the playhouse, and it too was going to be converted into a movie theater. The base moral welfare and recreation department was reviewing all programs to see where cuts could be made. The playhouse was one of the programs under review. The higher ups were saying it did not appeal to the entire community as a whole and having a move theater in their place might serve the community better. They were saying live theater was considered an over inflated expense, being a thing of the past, and no longer relevant. They were being given a trial run in the big theater to see if it was even possible at this venue. This meant it could be the final performance for the playhouse. Gina and Noah, along with several other playhouse members, talked it over and agreed to make it their mission the playhouse would not close on their watch. The fall production was a make-or-break situation.

Auditions were just underway when news of a Hurricane might be headed their way. Bertha was a Cat 2 hurricane and was expected to make landfall somewhere on the North Carolina coast within the next week. Noah's attention was now back at work. Standard operating procedure for the TV station was to become part of the emergency broadcast crew for the base. This meant go home and get your belongings needed to hunker down at the station until the storm passed over. The station ran news updates 24/7 until the storm was over. This was Noah's first time being in the way of a hurricane. He had no idea what to expect. He went home and moved things away from the windows, grabbed a sleeping bag and change of clothes, stopping by the local store grabbing enough munchies to get him through the storm before returning to base.

Once in place, the crew took time sharing the responsibilities of running the switcher, and as information came in from the base control center, they would do live updates. Folding cots had been provided to sleep on, and different ones found nooks and crannies to claim as their territory for the duration. The good thing was they had a backup generator in the event the lights went out. When it wasn't their shift, the crew would pass time playing cards, reading books, or telling stories. They had set a TV up to watch CNN and other local networks to see the live footage of the wrath of Bertha's assault on the coast. Four days went by before the crew was able to stand down as the emergency broadcast. Bertha had hit, and now the helos were in the air, flying over to document the damage and destruction.

After the stand down, Noah made it home to find everything intact, no major damage at his place. The electricity was out, the banks and ATMs were down due to no electricity. The gas stations were all closed, and for some, the gas was contaminated due to flooding water getting into the tanks. Most of the grocery stores were down, and many routes were closed due to fallen debris. Noah noticed he only had forty dollars in cash on him, a half tank of gas, and few groceries at home. No batteries, so he would run the car a little to try and get any news or information off the radio. Hopefully, these conditions wouldn't last too long. One thing was for sure, if he ever had to go through this again, he would take it seriously and heed the warning to make sure he didn't end up in this situation again. He had made several friends by now. Jorge lived close by and was a Corporal stationed at New River Air Station. He had been in the Marine Corps for a couple of years. Noah had met him out at the local gay bar, and they shared several common friends. Jorge was originally from Puerto Rico, but prior to joining had lived in the Atlanta, and Knoxville areas. The two were able to pull together resources and survived quite nicely until things returned to a state of normalcy. Of course, that didn't last long, before another hurricane named Fran had formed just off the coast and was headed almost in the same path as Bertha. Sure enough, almost within a month of each other, they were back to the same routine of sheltering in place. This time Noah took it seriously and had a full tank of gas, groceries, with a radio and plenty of batteries. He had gone down the check list to make sure he had done everything to be prepared for the emergency response. Two hurricanes back-to-back can make you an expert on what to expect or very stupid. Noah was staying because of his work; he couldn't understand others staying to just to ride it out. Noah, if given the option, would rather have left, and come back after the storm.

The effects of the two hurricanes left much of the vegetation stripped. In some cases, entire trees were ripped right from the ground. Downed power lines, and flood zones, like Topsail, where entire homes were destroyed. Several friends experienced damage. Paula and Sunny had just bought a home and one of the large walnut trees in their yard fell smack between theirs and the neighbor's house. It caused some roof damage but getting someone to come out to clear it was proving impossible with so many people needing help. An entire group of friends, both straight and gay, probably 20 people or so, got together and commenced to helping them out. Different ones brought drinks and various dishes making a potluck. They played music and worked until the place looked normal again. It took a good day to cut up the tree, and have it removed. While it was happening one of the guys called it the gay version of seven brides for seven brothers and a hoe down and barn raising event. Paula and Sunny were ever so grateful.

There was good that came during all the destruction. Noah found out he had been selected for the rank of Gunnery Sergeant and would soon be pinning it on. It seemed just like yesterday that he had made Staff Sergeant, but now he was going to be a Gunny. He was thrilled but couldn't help thinking of most of the Gunnies he knew, they were all old and crusty. The inside joke with the younger gay Marines was the term, "Gunny Butt." Referring to the age when a Marines' ass starts sagging. Noah chuckled, he didn't care, Gunny was one of the coolest ranks in the Marine Corps. It was where all the shit stopped!

The other good news came for the playhouse. Camp Lejeune had a pier at a place called Marston's Pavilion. The hurricanes had partially destroyed it and the remains had washed ashore. It wasn't salvageable and the entire thing would need to be rebuilt. The playhouse needed wood to build sets. The playhouse was given permission to take whatever they might need from the wreckage debris to use for the playhouse. One Saturday morning, playhouse members, their husband, and wives, even some of their children, gathered to salvage what they could for further productions. It was perfect timing for the Playhouse's fall production "Wizard of Oz."

Word had gotten out about the production, and soon there was a buzz about the base, and people were interested in helping. The playhouse had not been known for big productions. This one was not supposed to be any different. Although it was going to be at the Main Theater on base, the budget remained the same. Between Noah and Gina, they started pulling strings, and recruiting all the help and resources they could. When people found out, they were more than ready to help the playhouse. The playhouse couldn't accept money, however there were ways to donate services. The base Exchange allowed them to raid their prop storage and take whatever they needed for the set. They made a list, and it was delivered to the theater. A costume store out in town had been around for years and allowed them to come in and fit as many people in costumes as needed, because of so many costumes they were given an extreme discount. And wouldn't you know it, they just happened to have costumes for the "Wizard of Oz." A friend of Gina's owned a local make-up chain, donated makeup, and her services to the cast. Sophie from the coffee shop was incredibly young in appearance and could sing like a bird. Her red hair was short, but with a bit of makeup and a wig she made the perfect Dorothy. Josh, a long-time member of the playhouse, was a bit on the heavy side and a wonderful actor and singer, along with his "shucks" and "put'm up, put'm up" made the perfect Lion. Gina was pretty, but with a bit of green makeup and the right costume, she transformed bringing the Wicked Witch of the West to life. A guy Noah worked with, was nicknamed the scarecrow at work. In fact, at first glance he looked like him. Noah asked him if he had ever acted before, and he had not. He was a bit nervous, but Noah got him to come and give an audition. When he saw the excitement from his kids knowing Daddy might be the Scarecrow, he was all on board. His audition was a smash, and for the first time out he gave it all he had. Now the only leading role was to find someone to play the tin man. Over and over, they looked but couldn't find the right guy. Finally, a member of the playhouse, named Tara, came to see everyone, and find out if maybe there was a part for her in the up-and-coming production, if nothing else she just wanted to help. She was wearing a leg brace. Tara had a deep raspy voice but could really belt out a song. Noah had seen her on stage, and she could really get the audience's attention. Noah got the idea from the leg brace she wore; how perfect it would fit into the costume of the Tinman. The lights went off in his head, "What about making it the Tin woman?" After all, what was a woman without a heart? However, the true magic came when the four main characters came together to sing. Gina, Noah, and Harold, the music Director, sat in the room together as the four leads sang 'Somewhere Over the Rainbow' in harmony. It brought goose bumps and almost tears as the three looked at each other in amazement. When it was over, everyone in the room knew this show was going to be a hit. Harold was in disbelief, "Wow, what talent the Marine Corps has brought together, all at one time. Can you believe it, right here at Camp Lejeune!" Although the playhouse was flying under the radar with the higher ups on the base, the playhouse kept working hard. As the rehearsals went on, the cast grew stronger and stronger. Butch, who was a Marine on base, was also a master carpenter. He volunteered his services to help build the sets. They had an extremely low budget, but by the time it was over the sets were flawless. Wives were sewing, band members offered their musical skills, even one of the local dance academies offered their students to play the munchkins. The production was bringing the entire community together. It was bringing out the true meaning of a community theater. Even his friend Delta wanted to help. She was an old hat in the theater, with Gina in the production, he needed someone to be an Assistant Director and Delta fit the spot.

Noah was sitting at his desk in the TV production Unit, when Lt Colonel Brocks, the new Officer in Charge of the Training and Audiovisual Support Center, walked in. This was an unusual visit. He informed Noah he needed to report to the Battalion immediately to see Colonel Holden, the Battalion Commander. When Noah started to ask what it was for, he was quickly dismissed by the Lt Colonel and told he would find out once he got there. This was unexpected and highly irregular. Noah had no idea, things this abrupt, usually meant it wasn't good news. He was being blindsided. Had he messed up? Had they found out he was gay? Had a family member passed, and they were trying to get word to him? It was never really a good situation.

Noah grabbed his cover and headed to the Battalion. Once there, he reported to the Colonels office where he was told to have a seat, and she would be with him shortly. As he sat there, the Battalion Chaplain came through and went into her office. He was really worried now. They usually brought in the Chaplain when there has been a death of a family member. If it was so, why hadn't anyone from home called him, they had his work number. Noah's mind began to play tricks, and he became very anxious. All the things running through his mind needed to stop.

The door opened and the Chaplain called Noah into the Colonels office. He came in and centered on the desk before the Colonel quickly put him at ease, telling him to have a seat. When he turned to take a seat, he noticed a Navy Doctor sitting behind him in a corner chair. How did he not notice this guy when he came in. The Chaplain closed the door to the office. With the Navy Doctor in the room, Noah anticipated what he was about to be told. He had figured it out. He had heard stories from friends who had gone through the same thing. He was about to be told he was HIV positive. He did not agree with the way the military handled it, but then again it wasn't his choice. This thing of being told by the Command that one was HIV positive. If he were a civilian, it would be between himself and his doctor. But, no, not in the military, they required the Commanding Officer of each Marine who popped positive be informed. The reasoning was for readiness, who was and who was not deployable. Mission ready, so to speak. HIV positive Marines were non-deployable. Noah kept his composure.

The Colonel spoke. "I want you to know, you are not alone in this. The Command does not judge you or ask questions. But I am required to tell you, you recently gave blood for a medical exam for recruiting duty. This might come as good news; you won't be going on recruiting duty. However, your blood work came back, and you have tested positive for the Human Immunodeficiency Virus."

Noah sat in the chair quietly. What was he supposed to say? He was in a room of strangers, and this is how he was being informed. What did they expect him to say? He couldn't be open about his feelings. Did they think he would even begin to trust them? Part of him felt guilty, like he had let himself down and all of those who had suffered from this disease prior to him. Like Glenn, who told him to pay attention and do better. He had been looked at as a dinosaur by so many of his friends, he had made it this far without catching it. So many things, people, friends, family, the Marines, what was he to say. Yet surprisingly there was some sense of relief. The shadow he had been running from for so many years had finally caught him. This was a time he would most definitely remain silent.

The Colonel had started speaking again explaining the process he would be going under, needing to report to Bethesda Maryland Naval Medical Center for further evaluation. He was to leave immediately. Noah was in shock, "What, I'm sorry Ma'am, …what did you say? … Did you just say immediately" Noah was starting to panic a bit, "No, no, no disrespect Ma'am, but can I, …can I have a moment?"

The Colonel paused. This all seemed to be going a bit faster than Noah was comprehending. The Chaplain spoke up, "Ma'am maybe we can postpone this meeting until tomorrow? Until Gunny has had time to process this news, …give him a moment to think about it, and maybe speak to his family?" The Colonel realized she was basically dumping all this information on Noah. She paused and changed her tone, "You know, …I think you're right. I don't see any reason why we can't do this, say, tomorrow morning. We can meet back here and finish this then. That is, if you tell me Gunnery Sergeant, that you won't do anything crazy?" Noah looked at her. He knew she was thinking he might take himself out over this. Noah nodded his head, "No Ma'am, I think I still want to live." The Colonel quickly replied, "Good, then we will meet in the morning. Gunnery Sergeant, you can go ahead and take the rest of the day off. No need to report back to the Audiovisual Center. I'll let your work know you won't be returning, and you will be reporting directly to me for the next couple of days. You're welcome to go, you are dismissed, and I'll see everyone here say 0900." Noah stood up, "Good Day Ma'am!" He nodded at the Doctor, and the Chaplain, as he was leaving, the Chaplain handed him a business card, "Call me if you feel like you need to talk. It doesn't matter what time."

Once outside the office, Noah couldn't wait to get out of the building. It was suffocating and he felt like it was closing in. He just wanted outside, and away from everyone. As he exited the building, an Officer was just coming in. Noah rendered the appropriate salute and hurried down the steps. Confused, he stopped, looking in both directions, before looking back where he had just come from. He was outside in the fresh air. Outside and away, just away. He didn't know where he was going. He just wanted away. It didn't matter where. He turned back around as he heard someone approaching from behind. Two young Marines were coming his way. He moved forward nodding his head as he passed by. He still had no idea where he was going, but he kept walking. He had walked to Battalion and his car was still back at work. He headed that way. Finding his car, he hopped in and sat for a minute before driving away.

He lost track of what time it was driving around J-Ville. He eventually landed at the beach where he had gotten out and sat for a while. How long he sat there, he didn't know. He was just thinking and contemplating, before finally deciding to drive home and call it a day. He had made up his mind, he wasn't going to tell anyone, at least not until he had more information. It was bedtime and although he didn't think he could sleep, he tried laying down, tossing, and turning until he dozed, in and out of slumber. Not getting much rest, he was feeling strung out when he turned to see the faint glow of the sun making its appearance from behind the blinds. He lay there on the bed in a daze before finding the motivation to get up and get ready.

Traffic at the main gate of Camp Lejeune in the morning was not for the faint at heart. If one didn't know better, they might think they were in the middle of downtown L.A. Noah suffered the traffic calmly, before finally making it through. Arriving at the Battalion early, he sat in the parking lot with music low on the radio and listened to it play. When it was finally time, he shut it down, hopped out and closed the door. Looking at his reflection in the window, making sure he was squared away, he headed in.

He entered the office, giving the appropriate morning greetings, and sat as he listened to what the Colonel had to say. Noah was paying close attention this time. He was being instructed to report for evaluation to the National Naval Medical Center, Bethesda Maryland, without delay. The Navy Medical Doctor in the room, advised him, to have no sexual contact with anyone, and if so, he was required to tell them of his medical situation. Not doing so was punishable by the UCMJ. He would be retested upon his arrival at the medical center to make sure it wasn't a false positive. The stent at the hospital would be a three week stay. The results of his evaluation and his current state of health would determine if he would be able to remain on active duty. The Colonel, on a nicer note, let him know he was not alone. There were others in the Battalion who were in the same situation and been allowed to remain in the service. A couple of them had agreed to make themselves available to anyone who might become positive.

Noah was glad to hear there was some sort of support group and was ready to find out his current state of health. The only concern was how was he going to explain to Gina and the rest of the playhouse crew that he couldn't be there for the play opening two weeks away. Noah looked at the Colonel, "Ma'am I know this might be out of the question but is it possible to postpone the evaluation. I mean, at least for a couple of weeks. I am the director of the upcoming fall production at the base theater's playhouse. Our opening date is less than two weeks." The Colonel paused for a moment, "The Marine Corps takes these things seriously, and has extremely strict protocol we must follow. I can tell you if you were deployed, with these results, you would have been medevaced to Bethesda immediately." She turned to the Naval Doctor. "Do you have any comment or objection to this?"

The Naval Doctor rustled in his chair being put on the spot. "Well, the orders to handle this situation are quite clear, they say immediately. But what does that exactly mean? Immediately schedule an appointment, or immediately send to Bethesda to the infectious disease clinic for evaluation. I think the reasoning behind this, is to get the patient medically triaged as quickly as possible to define a path for treatment. With this particular disease, earlier promotes a better outcome. So, if the patient is willing to wait a couple of weeks, I think it would be fine. Of course, we would want to call and schedule his arrival date to let them know he is inbound."

The Colonel turned to address Noah. "Gunnery Sergeant, I have heard many great things about you. You are well liked, and from what I am told, you are thought of highly by your peers. Colonel Stalion, I think you know of whom I speak. He is the one in charge of MWR and I believe the playhouse falls underneath his authority. I have a great working relationship with him. If I were to take you away from the playhouse right now, I think he would understand." She paused looking at Noah's disappointment, "...But I don't think he would ever forgive me. What do you say...let's make this play happen!" Noah's heart just lifted. He thought surely, she would send him on his way. "I say thank you Ma'am." The Colonel smiled, before getting serious again. "Look, focus on this play, make it happen. Enjoy it! You have bigger things to deal with coming your way." She addressed the Naval doctor. "Let's get this appointment scheduled. I think that will do, and Gunnery Sergeant any questions or concern please keep me posted."

After the meeting, Noah was in a bit of denial. There would be time to deal with it later. For now, he put it in the back of his mind, and thought of the upcoming production just a few weeks away.

Close to opening, after the cast had their parts spot on, they made an appearance on the Liberty Call show where they did a sample of their performance. They were also allowed to go to the schools on base and give sample performances inviting everyone to come to the show. The base, wanting to be a good neighbor to the community of Jacksonville, decided to open the event to the public. A friend of Noah's was the manager of one of the main anchor stores in the local Jacksonville mall, and he helped the playhouse finagle a promotional performance at the Jacksonville mall. At lunch time, they were able to set up inside the main exchange and give a sample to the shoppers. The uncanny resemblance of the cast, and their talent was getting around and was creating quite a hype.

The week prior to opening, they were given the keys to the main theater and moved in. Rehearsals and preparations started immediately for opening night. It wasn't uncommon to see some of the higher ups in the chain of command of Morale Welfare and Recreation showing up unexpectedly to see how things were coming along. Colonel Stalion, the Commanding Officer of MWR, had sat in the back seat of the theater a couple of nights observing the rehearsals. There had been a few bumps in dress rehearsal with lighting and sound. But the kinks had been worked out and the play was ready to stand on its own. Noah had done his part and it was now up to the cast.

Larry, the lighting guy, and Butch, the set guy, had just finished making some final adjustments, when they hollered to Noah that they were going home. Everyone had left and Noah was now in the theater alone. With so much activity, Noah, for the most part, had no time to dwell on his medical situation. Rehearsals had been a distraction. However, it was there, still lurking in the background. At times he would find himself starting to feel melancholy, and sorry for himself. At one point, he started questioning if this play would not only be the last for the playhouse, but also for himself as well. All of that would change during rehearsals, when he would see the excitement and energy from the cast. Something special was being created here, and he had been a big part of it. He walked up on the stage, which had been set for the opening scene, and sat down on the porch of the farmhouse, as he looked around the theater. His one hope was the cast and crew would have fond memories and be proud of the time they had spent with the playhouse. The opening verse of somewhere over the Rainbow came to mind. "When all the world is a hopeless jumble, and the raindrops tumble all around. Heaven opens a magic lane…" The playhouse had been that for him. He chuckled to himself, thinking it funny how fate had brought him to this point in time. Whatever was about to happen, it was up to fate and the cast. The play was ready to stand up. For himself, there had been bumps in the road, but he had the time of his life.

Finally, opening night had arrived. Noah sat in the control booth in the back of the Theater going over everything one more time. As he looked up, he could see they were performing to a full house. One final review and it was time to walk back to the green room and address the cast one final time. As he stood up, Colonel Stalion approached him. He stopped Noah. "Quite a showing. Is everything ready?" Noah assured him, "I believe so, it's now or never, Sir." The Colonel seemed a bit bemused looking around as the crowd came in. "I am quite impressed with the turnout. I don't think we have ever had an opening quite so big. It is more than anyone had anticipated." He sharply turned to Noah. "With this many people, I hope we don't let them down." He grabbed Noah by the shoulder, "I can tell you're busy, go on, break a leg." Noah was bewildered by the Colonel and felt the pressure had just intensified. He smiled. "Thank you, Sir." Noah decided it best to keep a low profile and get out of the main corridor before being stopped by anyone else.

Back behind stage, Delta came across the headset, "Noah the cast is ready." Noah climbed the stairs and entered the green room. All was surprisingly calm. The room quieted as he entered. As he looked around, he could feel the excitement in the air. They were looking for a few words of encouragement "Well it is here; this is the moment! If you are going to shine, make it happen now." One of the cast members interrupted. "What kind of audience do we have?" Noah looked at him, knowing some of the actors had stage fright if they thought about the audience. They preferred not to know. Noah decided to focus his comment back to the play. "You have a good house, but seriously, don't think of the crowd, …Play for me, just like you have done through all these rehearsals. You have an audience of one. …Me …Just think of it as me out there, (pausing before he chuckled) …Well, and maybe some of my closest friends." The room chuckled with him. He glanced around the room at each one of them. "No more words, …come on, …everyone, grab hands, …take a deep breath, …hold it, …let it out, …center, …now a moment of silence." The cast huddled in a circle, hand in hand, some with bowed heads in silence. After a moment, Noah raised his head. "Now, what do we say? …Not good luck, but what?" The cast all in unison, "Break a leg," as they dispersed. Before heading back to his place on the tech board, Noah walked over to Gina as she got ready to take her place. They both smiled at each other, giving a hug, he grabbed and squeezed her hand before letting go. Both knew the high stakes that were at play. They both had put it all on the line. It was time to find out if it would pay off. It was show time.

Noah made it back to the control booth, gave the five-minute warning and did a quick review of his notes. The lights in the theater went dark and the overture started. As it played, Noah looked around the auditorium at the silhouettes of the heads in front of him. The music lowered when Dorothy surprised the audience appearing from behind, walking up one of the aisles calling for Toto. Once she arrived at the orchestra pit, Toto was let out one of the side doors and came running to her. She picked the dog up, giving him hugs, "There you are, there you are." The audience began to applaud. Dorothy turned and climbed a few steps and walked across one of the three bridges that were built over the orchestra pit, while the curtains opened for her to walk into the family farm in Kansas. The play was underway, and the audience was enthralled. All the marks were being hit, and the audience was responding and laughing in places Noah had never dreamed of. The actors were finding themselves having to pause, waiting for the applause to dissipate. It was a success. The actors could feel the positive energy coming from the audience, and it made them perform even better. Noah sat calling every mark in his head. One by one until it was time for the entr'acte.

The lights came up, and Noah headed to the green room, stopping by the stage along the way. Ms. Delta was busy shuffling props and talking with a couple of stagehands. Seeing Noah, she paused long enough to kiss him on the cheek, "Darling you're the best! We can hear the applause clear back here. They're loving it." Noah gave her a hug. "Thank you, Hun, but you all are the ones doing all the work. You guys have hit every mark. Keep running a tight ship." Once in the green room, the actors were all busy touching up makeup and changing into costumes, replenishing with water, from the heat that came down from the lights. Noah was just a presence to let them know he was still there if they needed him. Different ones would talk about their part and how it was received. Noah spoke up letting them know after the show there would be no meeting for notes until the morning. So many in the cast had family members, friends, and guests and he knew they wanted to enjoy their time with them. He made it back down to the auditorium to tech and took his place. The orchestra fired up, and the lights dimmed. The second act of the show began.

The second act was received just as well as the first. By the end of the show, Noah could see different ones wiping their eyes from tears. Noah knew the cast had struck the heart strings of those in the audience. The end was a standing ovation. The cast sang the lead song in harmony as they did the final curtain call. Sophie was center stage with roses being laid at her feet. The music ended and the cast came forward to greet the audience. To their surprise, so many parents wanted pictures of their kids taken with the cast.

Noah sat in tech for a while before emerging, letting the cast get their dues. He decided to walk down and congratulate them, but was stopped, in his tracks when the cast noticed him coming to the stage, they all started applauding, and whistling, and bowing as if they were not worthy as he made it their way. Once upon them, he thanked each of them before he turned to have Colonel Stalion standing in front of him. Noah stood tall. The Colonel spoke, "I want to personally thank you! Along with all those from MWR. You have put together an absolutely amazing show. My wife and I loved it, it brought her to tears, they had done so well. Please give my regards to all the cast, but I would like to meet the four leads and thank them myself." All four of them came over and the Colonel greeted and thanked each of them, before saying his farewell. The lines lasted for a time before the cast was finally able to return to their dressing rooms for the night.

The next morning the reviews were out, and they were riveting. One wrote, "Knowing the fate of the playhouse was up for review, if it ever needed a wizard, it was now. From the director to the cast, that is exactly what they got." The show was a smash, and a much-needed hit. The rest of the shows were received just as well. When the final ticket sales were counted, the show that was not supposed to make a profit, had the largest ticket sales of any show before it. All the naysayers, and critics, were now believers wanting more. Even the prior Director, who had left the playhouse in shambles, and broken, was trying to find her way back in the door. Gina and Noah had succeeded. Being so busy for the last few months, both had family, obligations, and things that had been neglected. They both needed to get their affairs in order, before contemplating what would be their encore.

Chapter 41

Could it get any worse?

Walking down the long, lonely corridor, the double doors to the right flung open, and two people walked out from the morgue. Startling Noah, it set an ominous feeling as he continued on to the Bethesda Infectious Disease Clinic. It sat separately from the main area of the hospital.

Noah continued on, finding his way through the corridors, and finally up a flight of stairs where a sign hung from the ceiling, Infectious Disease Clinic. Behind the counter was a handsome gentleman in a tie and dress pants, with a long sleeve shirt, and a couple of corpsmen working diligently. Noah walked to the counter and stood waiting. The gentleman looked up, "Can I help you?" Noah smiled, "Yes I am supposed to be reporting in here I believe." The gentleman asked for his I.D and ran it across a list in front of him. "Yes, we have you scheduled; you'll be here for the next three weeks. Have you already gotten a place to stay?" Noah smiled, "Yes, I'll be staying at the Navy lodge." The young man stood up, "Great, then let's get you started. I'm Fred and I am the administrator for the clinic. If you have any questions, or concerns during your stay, Gunnery Sergeant, please don't hesitate to ask. I will also be the coordinator, and liaison with the Marine Corps during your visit. You are now attached to the clinic, until we say otherwise. Please fill out these forms, when you are done, bring them back." (He pointed) "There is a waiting room right over there." Noah started to walk away, "By the way, for privacy concerns, we like to go by first names here. It puts everyone at the same level and also keeps your rank and last name private. It's up to you if you choose to share. Also, no uniforms, only civilian attire."

Noah sat in the clinic. As he filled out the questionnaire, he noticed those around him. One guy in a wheelchair, and, what appeared to be his partner, sitting in a chair beside him. The man in the wheelchair was so thin, and was wrapped in a blanket, wearing a face mask. His I.V. bag attached and dripped into his arm, as he sat slightly asleep. His partner was not much better, health wise, and was just as skinny. Yet he was still pushing this guy around. There must be some dedication to each other going on. Then it occurred to Noah, this could be his fate. Was he ready for the journey that had just begun? The thought of so many of his friends who had already struggled with this disease came flooding back to him. He had missed the front row seat on so many of them, barely even a spectator. Now after all these years, it caught up to him and he was center stage. Seeing these people, here in the clinic, at all different levels of progression with this disease was reality at its best. He still wasn't sure where he might have caught it, at this point it didn't matter. So many questions were to remain unanswered. He was scared, but now was not the time to panic. It would not change things.

The gentleman in the wheelchair coughed, catching Noah's attention. Noah must have been staring because the gentleman with him spoke. "Don't worry, he's not contagious! You can do more harm to him than he can to you…" Noah was a bit embarrassed, but also this guy was a bit presumptuous. It wasn't what Noah was thinking. "Sorry, didn't mean to be staring, …that wasn't what I was thinking. Is he alright?" The gentleman was defensive, "Don't ask me, he's not dead yet, ask him." Noah didn't know what to say, it seemed he was just digging a hole. After a brief pause, the guy in the wheelchair, still with his head down spoke, "Goddammit Jerry, quit being a bitch!" He raised his head, "I'm fine, Thank you!" He coughed, "Jerry here, sometimes forgets there are those of us still on the same side." Noah smiled briefly. "No worries." The gentleman continued, "You been here before, I don't believe I've seen you?" Noah shook his head no. "This is my first visit, just getting here." The gentleman spoke. "I've been…" and was interrupted by a coughing fit. Jerry grabbed a bottle of water, and stood up, "See you get to talk'n too much, then you choke." He pulled the mask from the gentleman's face, "Here, Eddie, take a drink of this." After he calmed, he tried speaking again, while still a bit raspy. "I ain't dead yet." He juggled the water and mask while putting it back on his face. He continued on in his thought. "I've been coming here since the late eighties. Seen a lot of 'em come and go. This place sure has changed, but they still keep us close to the morgue. What does that tell yah? Oh, it's gotten better in some ways. They used to be afraid to touch us. Come in a room all bundled up. Mask, and then another in case that one would fall off. Hell, I don't even know how they could do anything, gloves, masks, gowns, and such. They put us down here away from everybody…treated like a leper colony. They said it was for our protection, but the real reason, they were afraid of us. Closer to the morgue so they wouldn't have to carry the body too far." He chuckled, with a cough.

Fred, the admin came to the door, "Eddie, are you behaving in here?" Eddie looked over his shoulder, "Who the hell wants to behave?" Fred laughed, "I can tell you're doing fine. The doctor is ready for you, you want me to help you back?" Eddie pointed to Jerry. "I got Jerry here, he can take me back." Fred looked at Jerry, "He's in room three today, the nurse will walk back with you." Jerry wheeled him out, and Fred stepped back in the room. "Gunnery Sergeant Barlow you doing, ok? I hope Eddie didn't scare you too much! He's a fighter. It can be a bit overwhelming here in the clinic the first time." Noah smiled and handed him the clip board, "I'm ok…, I think." With a chuckle and raised eyebrows, he sighed, "So yes, … finished, I was just getting ready to bring it back up to you." Fred reviewed it. "Ok, this looks good, come on with me. We are going to get you started. First thing is blood draws, a brief checkup with Doctor Larken, and then we'll go from there. I hope you have patience! You have a busy three weeks ahead of you. However, just out of scheduling problems, there can be a whole lot of hurry up and wait." As they walked Noah smiled, "I'm a Marine, I'm use to a whole lot of hurry up and wait!" Fred gave him a smile "We try our best, but sometimes it just can't be avoided."

Two weeks had passed, and Noah had already had his fill of HIV. Tired of things he never wanted to know about, or things he never knew existed: ELISA test, …Western Blot, …T-4 helper cell, …viral burden load, …percentages, ... Opportunistic infections, …Marine Corps order on this, …DOD order on that, …sign this stating, …safe sex practice …your responsibility, …wear a condom, … better yet, don't have sex, …and God knows what else. It was just becoming too much. All the many counseling sessions; …how was he feeling, …did he have hope, …listen to other people's stories, …being asked to share when he didn't know what he was supposed to be sharing, etc. The military required all this other stuff. When ultimately, all he wanted to know, …how he was, … and was he going to live. He still had another week to go.

Noah sat in the exam room, waiting for the doctor to arrive. It was Tuesday, and today he would be given a full briefing on his medical status. He knew his results for the second positive test had come back and confirmed a definite positive for HIV. Now he sat waiting for his T-cell count, along with how much virus was actually in his body, with results from what they called a 'Viral Burden Load' test. The two tests, along with any symptoms of opportunistic infections would give the doctor a snapshot of Noah's current state of health, and how the disease was progressing.

The door opened and a tall, slender, black haired man wearing glasses walked in the room. "Good morning Mr. Barlow, I take it you're almost at the end of your first visit?" Noah smiled, "That's what they tell me." Taking up a stool and pulling it over to Noah's side, he didn't waste any time getting to work. "I've had the time to review your record, and I must tell you, things are not where we would like them to be." Noah, a little nervous, continued to listen. "Your viral burden load came back, and there isn't a real high amount of the virus in your system, but that is what concerns me. What virus is there, has already caused a significant amount of damage on your immune system. Your T-4 helper cells have plummeted." Noah nodded, "So what does this all mean?" Dr. Larken pushed away, "Well, you were given the class on how the virus works, and what the difference is between HIV and full-blown AIDS. Your T-Cells have dropped below the required level to continue to classify you as HIV, technically we are supposed to classify you as a person with AIDS." Noah bowed his head. This was really bad news. He made no comment. Dr. Larken put his hand on Noah's shoulder. "I know, it's not a diagnosis anyone wants to hear. But I must tell you I am not here to mislead you. At this point I would make sure your loved ones or close relatives know. Also, I would start getting your personal affairs in order."

Dr. Larken went over Noah's charts again, while Noah sat absorbing the news. Before taking a deep breath and blew out. "So, definitely wasn't what I was expecting! I thought coming here, maybe I might have it, but I would have a little more time to adjust to it. I mean with the Marine Corps, …am I being thrown out? I don't have any idea what I will do. This has been my career. Things were looking good. I just got a promotion. Isn't there some form of treatment, or something at this point, it's been going on since the eighties, I mean…?" Doctor Larken looked back up in silence but was listening closely as Noah spoke. Noah could tell he was racking his brain in thought and could almost see the gears grinding in his head. "The military says I am to recommend you for medical retirement with numbers like these. …I tell you what, if you are willing to work with me, I think I might be able to help." Noah sat up to listen as Dr. Larken continued. "I will sit on these numbers; I have time to delay them. There are some new drugs that are experimental, and some already approved. You might have heard of them, because they have been working miracles on some of the most severe patients. We can give them a try. They can be a bit harsh, and not everyone has been able to tolerate them. Just so you know, it is an extremely strict regimen. Once you go on, there will be no coming off, they have to be adhered to. No missing doses. Do you think you can do that?" Noah was torn, "I have barely been able to take a vitamin a day, but I don't see I have a choice." Dr. Larken continued, "It's very common to be hesitant, it's a lot to take in all at once. So why don't we do this. It is my duty to prescribe you the pills. It is your choice to take them. Pick them up from the pharmacy, take them home with you. Give it a couple of days, even a couple of weeks. But do yourself a favor and start taking them. Oh, when you do, you'll want to eat something fatty, like twinkies, cake, something with high fat, it will help the body to absorb it better. Give me a call when you start. Any side effects let me know. Once you start, we'll schedule another appointment. If your numbers are above the threshold, I'll throw these out and we'll use those as your first set."

Although Noah wasn't ecstatic about the news, it was better than the alternative. At least, there was a possibility in delaying, or even reversing the current trajectory of the situation. Dr. Larken stood up and started to walk out, paused and turned to Noah, "If you need any motivation, …if you think I'm trying to scare you, I am! I can't be any more serious, …if you don't take those pills, at this rate of progression, and from my experience dealing with other patients, you won't be around a year, or year and a half from now to talk about it!"

It had come time to say goodbye to the three weeks stay at Bethesda. Several from the clinic gathered one more time at a bar called The Fireplace. It was a quaint little corner bar, in the gay district of D.C. Spending the last three weeks together at the clinic created new friendships and bonds. The bar was starting to clear out. Noah sat alone watching the fireplace that gave the bar its name. It sat in the corner and was see through to the outside. Since it was early December; it was already getting a bit brisk on the outside. The nice warmth of the bar, beat the boring hotel room.

He sat lost in thought with all that had taken place over the last weeks, occasionally taking note of what the tv was playing. At the other side of the bar, he heard a familiar voice. One from his past, he knew very well, and was almost impossible to forget. Noah sat at the end of the bar by a column tucked away. He leaned forward hoping to be more obscured and out of site. He didn't even want to turn and look to verify for sure, for the fear of being recognized. It was too late. "Well, of all people who I never thought

I would see again, look who is sitting there!" Noah still didn't turn to acknowledge him. Hoping he would go away. The bar stool next to him pulled out and he heard, "What you still not going to talk to me, even after all these years?" Noah turned; it was exactly who he thought it was. Dodge Strumen stood next to him leaning against the bar. As if he hadn't already had enough bad news over the last three weeks, now this.

Noah couldn't believe it. Could it get any worse? He forced the words out to speak, just, to be cordial. "Hello Dodge!" Dodge sat on the stool and ordered a drink. So typical of him, to just assume he was welcome to sit, without even asking Noah if it was ok. It was a public bar, there was nothing for Noah to say. Dodge got his drink and sat quietly. He was wanting to talk, but Noah's silence, and cold shoulder was bothering him. "I, I, don't really know what to say, or even begin. ...I, ...I kind of want to say I'm sorry, but then again, ...yeah, it's like, ...maybe, I don't know..." Noah turned to look at him as he spoke. He was just as handsome as ever, a little aged, which made him look better, but Noah would never let him know. He turned to Noah, each locking eyes. What was there to say. Noah began, "Dodge, that was a whole lifetime ago. ...If you think I'm looking for an apology, or expect one, ..." (Noah turned and looked away) I'm just as stunned as you. I never wanted to see you again." Dodge grinned, "So you are glad to see me?" Noah shook his head in disbelief, "Really? ... I always thought if I saw you first, you would never see me! So, thrilled to see you, ... No." Dodge nodded his head and took a drink, and sarcastically answered his own question, "I'll take that as, YOU SURE ARE!" and grinned. "I can't say I don't blame you!" Noah chuckled in disbelief, "You know my dad had a saying; When you set the garbage out, you don't go out to the curb and bring it back in!" Dodge turned and stuck his hand up. "Whoa, whoa, whoa! That is not what I'm trying to do here! I live just around the corner here, and this is my local bar. The last thing I ever expected was for you to show up in here. Sure, I have thought about you over the years. I have always wondered how you were. I wondered, if it had been different circumstances, if we might have made it! I always thought if I saw you again, I would make it right! I found out you were right on many things, and it was me. I had a lot of issues I needed to work on. Still do!" Noah took a sip, "Well, if that is an apology, I'll accept it, …and I probably owe you one too. So, accept mine, in that I was too young and naive, to really understand your wants and needs. I just wasn't capable of a relationship with anyone. Regardless, of how much either of us wanted it. No one could make me stay, not you, not even me."

Noah took a drink, and both turned to the news on the TV. It was a report of another missing body part being found. When it finished, Dodge made an off-color joke, "Must be a jealous boyfriend." He laughed at his own joke. Noah was not amused. "That's not very funny Dodge." Dodge smirked, "I was just…" Noah interrupted, "I know what you were implying, you the jealous boyfriend, when we were together. Is that what you mean? Hah, Hah, very funny!" Noah took another drink. He was starting to feel a little creepy talking to him again. Dodge continued on, "Chill out, I was just having a little fun. Besides, if you have been following this story, they have been finding one body part at a time in the park, and around the area." Noah curious, "I don't live here, I just came up on business. I don't know anything about the story. What park? What area?" Dodge continued, "Oh man, they're talking about that park right across the street," and he pointed out the window. Noah sat in shock. "That park right across the road? I'm parked right beside the park, just down the road. Do they think it's a serial killer?" Dodge laughed at Noah, clearly concerned and frightened. "They haven't said whether the body parts belong to the same victim, or to others." Noah shook, and shivered, "That's just too creepy." He finished his drink and stood up. "What, that did it, you're leaving?" Dodge made booboo lips. Noah put his coat on, "No, that's not it. I have to get up early in the morning for a day of travel, and I've already stayed longer than I had planned."

Noah stood and started putting on his coat when Dodge said, "Here I'll walk you to your car!" Noah abruptly replied, "No, …no, no, I'm good." Dodge paused, realizing this was it, "Well here, at least let me give you my phone number. If you ever make it back, maybe…" Noah accepted his card not wanting to be rude, besides, he didn't trust him to not make a scene.

Dodge sarcastically, "Oh, sorry to hear about your friend, Glenn…, I still stay in contact with Patsy, she told me about it. By the way, you never did say what kind of business brought you here? Or where you live now?" Noah was hesitant, "You notice the hair, right?" Dodge looked, and then it dawned on him, "Oh my god you are still in the Marines?" Noah chuckled, at Dodge's amazement, "Oh my God, …you must be getting up in rank by now? I have been out nearly 10 years. Where are you stationed?" Noah letting his guard down, "Camp Lejeune, been there a couple years, I'm a Gunny!" Dodge smiled, "That's great, that's great. Who knows I might see you down there some time? Remember my dad was in, they still live in that area." Noah smiled, "I really need to get going Dodge. It was nice seeing you!" Dodge was glassy eyed, "You know you have only gotten better with age; you're looking good!" Noah had a bit of a blush, "Well, I hate to admit it, when I saw you, I thought the same. You're just as handsome as ever!" Dodge moved into give a hug, and Noah unconsciously pulled away. "Thanks, but I think it's time to go."

Two weeks had gone by since his return to Lejeune. He had contacted Dr. Larken and let him know, today was the day he had started the new meds. He stocked up on Twinkies, Ho-Hos, and a few other kinds of fatty foods. His motivation was high, as he started this new chapter in his life. The next 30 days were going to be strict and about him, no distractions. Three different meds, and 27 pills a day, if that was what it was going to take, then so be it.

The first week wasn't too bad. The pills were large and took some getting used to. He didn't really notice any difference. The second week however, things started changing. He could tell he was getting energy back that he didn't even know he had lost. He wasn't feeling as drained. He started noticing he was a bit nauseous in the mornings, and his dreams were more frequent and very real. At work, it was hard to explain where he had been for the last three weeks. Lieutenant Colonel Brocks must have known, because he kept his distance from Noah when entering the room. Noah didn't like the policy that the command had to know. Regardless, they did. It was supposed to be the Commanding Officer only, however, Noah was sure, just by his actions, that Colonel Holden had shared it with him in confidence for whatever reason. Anyone who has dealt with such a life threating disease, can tell when someone finds out.

Some people are not very good at covering up. Some ask questions out of the ordinary, think you won't notice, like, "Are you ok? You're not looking very well!" You're like, "Of course I'm well!" but then you start questioning yourself and might even look in the mirror to see if there are any visible signs you might be sick. But what's even worse, when there are no visible signs, and you realize someone has told them or they found out somehow. The question is do you open up and share with them, or do you ignore it, remain silent and move on. Even a slight bit of weakness could contribute to someone saying oh he's not able to do his job. Noah didn't want any of it. He didn't want sympathy, he definitely didn't want the fear from someone thinking they might get the disease, and he didn't want anyone thinking he was not able to perform his job. He was still a Marine, and as long as he was on active duty, he would keep pulling his own weight.

It had been six weeks since Noah's last checkup, and he now sat in Doctor Larken's office waiting for the results of his last blood draws. Hopefully, it would be good news. He was vigilant in sticking to the regimen, and never missed a dose, doing exactly what the Doctor had ordered. He was starting to get a little concerned though. He couldn't keep eating the junk food. He still had the Marine Corps standards to adhere to. No fatties in the Marine Corps.

Dr. Larken came in and sat behind the computer. "Let's see if our plan worked. Have you been taking your meds regularly?" Noah answered, "Yes, along with the twinkies." Dr Larken turned and looked at him with a smile, "Come on, most people would love to have an excuse to eat that stuff." Noah smiled and continued, "I have no problem, but the Marine Corps might if I can't fit into my uniform." Dr. Larken tilted his head, "Let me worry about the Marine Corps, we can work around that, you just focus on taking those meds. Speaking of, let's find out if they are working for you." He turned and started going over the numbers reading them out loud, "Blood sugar is good, white blood cell, cholesterol, bilirubin, liver, and boom, there it is. T-4 helper cell, 680, percentage is 48%. That is well on its way to being where we want. That is good news! So, we can just forget about those first numbers, and focus at keeping you headed in the right direction." Noah wasn't quite clear what he was saying, "So does that mean I'll be able to stay on active duty?" Dr. Larken chuckled, "Yes, with numbers like they are, there is no grounds for discharge. Matter of fact, I wouldn't be allowed to refer you for medical retirement. The DOD policy forbids it unless you are diagnosed with AIDS. Just a few years ago, if you were "HIV", they could get rid of you. Now they have set a standard because too many people are getting out and still living. So, you are in, Buddy!" Noah responded, "YES!" Dr. Larken continued, "Here is what is going to happen. I'll see you back in three months. Get used to a visit up here. Once we know you are stable, and the drugs are going to work for you, you'll only be coming up twice a year, or every six months. Any major health concerns, contact us. You can still go to your local doctor, but any major issues, we need to be kept in the loop. You are not like others now; this is still a new disease and not every doctor knows how to deal with patients in your condition. When anything goes wrong, it has to be addressed immediately, to prevent it from taking a toll, on your already challenged immune system."

Noah sat in the clinic waiting for his release papers, along with a couple of others watching the TV.

The program was interrupted with a local breaking news. One of the guys reached and turned it up as a reporter spoke:

"Just in, an arrest has been made in the case of missing body parts being found in P Street Beach Park, and Dupont Circle. The police have taken into custody, a guy by the name of Dodge Strumen."

The news showed Dodge, being led out from an apartment building, in hand cuffs, with his head held low. The news continued:

"We must tell you what we are about to report is quite gruesome. Our sources say he was brought in and questioned, when his roommate, Michael Sovern, was reported missing from family members, after not hearing from their loved one for more than a month. Strumen was brought in for questioning, where he confessed to killing Michael Sovern, and agreed to cooperate. Police obtained a warrant, and upon investigating the apartment, it is said, remaining body parts were found in the freezer, and are believed to be that of the missing person. We'll have more as the story unfolds."

Noah was shocked. The others in the room were speaking, but Noah's mind was lost to the point of almost being paralyzed. How did he not see this coming? The facts were there all along. His hunch years ago, when the two were a couple, was correct. The many times Dodge had threatened him. Holding a knife to his throat. Saying he would kill Noah and take his own life. They were not hollow threats. Noah never believed they were. He always believed Dodge was capable of doing something like this. He had brought it up with Glenn back in the day, but there was no one to turn to. Both agreed they could not take it to the military. If Noah went to the civilian authorities back then, they would have turned it over to the Marine Corps, or it would have come out on the morning Military Police blog of off base incidents. Noah always felt Dodge needed help, more than Noah was capable. He needed professional help. If they had been a straight couple, they might have been able to seek out couples counseling on base. The family service center offered it to couples in peril. However, there was no safe haven for Noah, and no help center for Dodge. But now, this poor guy, killed by Dodge! Noah remembered being with him in the bar just a month ago. Strumen was the one telling him all about the murder. Even jokingly commented, "Must be a jealous boyfriend," and then chuckled. Noah thought he was referring to him, when he made the comment, but he was wrong. He was making fun of the situation, knowing full well, he was the one who had been committing this macabre act. Noah somehow felt connected, and unfortunately partially responsible. Was there anything he could have done to get Dodge the help he needed? What was wrong with Dodge, making him feel so threatened, to do such a heinous crime. Something like this, was not an accidental murder, being so violent it had to be a crime of passion. Noah contemplated going to the police and report his involvement with Dodge from years ago. If he did, he would have to expose himself, and once again he would be outing himself to the Marine Corps. Was this a time to keep low, and remain silent? Dodge had already admitted to the crime. Was there anything else that needed to be added?

****

It had now been a year since Noah had found out he was positive, and the horrific news of the downfall of Dodge. Things had started out a bit rough, and the meds took some getting used to but, for the most part, all had turned back to normal. Noah was now filling the position as the Staff Non-Commissioned Officer of the Combat Visual Information Center. Noah was getting close to doing a move back across country. He had received orders to Marine Corps Air Station, Yuma, Arizona. He was on easy street and his time at Camp Lejeune was winding down, just a few more weeks and he would be gone. Lejeune had been a great experience but in order to advance his career, it was time to move on.

Walking back from the coffee mess, Noah overheard Staff Sgt Vronsky speaking to another Marine in the hall, "Don't worry, I'll handle it. I'll let Gunny know." Noah continued on to his office, sat down and fired up his computer, when he heard the tap on his door. "Gunny you got a minute?" Noah continued working, "I suppose this has something to do with the conversation I just overheard in the hall. Come on in and pull up a seat" Staff Sergeant Vronsky entered, closing the door behind him, and took a seat across from Noah's desk. Noah sat back in his chair. "So, what's going on?"

The Staff Sergeant took a deep breath and began. "Well, you know it's inventory time." Noah shook his head, as the Staff Sergeant continued, "Well we were doing inventory and it turns out we have a missing computer." Noah shook his head, "What do you mean by missing? Can't find it, lost it, someone stole it, what? Did you check all the serial numbers on other computers?" Staff Sergeant continued, "That's just it, it was a brand-new computer, not even out of the box. When we got all those computers a couple of weeks ago, we sat them in the backroom when we unloaded them off the truck. As people came in for an exchange, we put the old one on one pallet, and they would take a new one." Noah sat listening, "Ok, so what does that have to do with anything?" "Well, it is a new one that is missing." Noah thinking out loud, "Ok, so someone probably forgot to record that they issued it." Staff Sergeant continued. "It's not that easy, Gunny. I don't think so, …see the box was there, and someone had made sure it was taped up to look like it had never been opened. It wasn't until this morning, when we went to go issue it, that we realized the box was empty. Someone made a deliberate attempt to cover it up." Gunny sat contemplating. "Well, the good news is, there was no classified information on it then. Who signed for them when they first arrived? Check to see if it might have come in empty. Also, you have until the end of the day to tell me where that computer is at. I want anyone in the building who has had access or knew those were back there questioned. We got security cameras, have you pulled them?" Staff Sergeant shook his head, "I pulled the tapes, nothing, that area is a blind spot."

Noah, in disbelief, "This is all I need, right before I'm finally supposed to be getting out of this place. This better not get me on legal hold."

"By the way, while I have you here. I've been meaning to talk to you about that. You know I have orders to Yuma?" Staff Sergeant was surprised, "No, well maybe, I might have heard about it." Noah continued, "So yeah, I will be leaving in about a month or so, early December. My replacement won't be here until about a week before I leave. So, there won't be much of a turnover between the two of us. I'll need you to step up and help until he gets his feet on the ground"

Staff Sergeant curiously, "You said he, …you never said a name, who is it?" Noah chuckled, "Gunny Little, from over at division. He and the Gunner over there don't get along, he is begging to get out of there. From what he says, he can't leave soon enough. Says Gunner Bolton is a religious fanatic, calls him in the office and wants him to pray with him." Staff Sergeant laughed, "I have heard that from others. He holds formation and asks everyone to bow and pray. Isn't that like not allowed?" Noah chuckled, "Look, I knew him back as a Sergeant, he was a fanatic back then. One of the guys we worked with was having an extra marital affair. He found out and turned him in. The command busted him down. He became a shit bird, and eventually got out. So, no I don't think it's legal, but who knows, how he might get away with it. But anyways, back to this computer. If we don't have an answer by this afternoon, I'm going to have to call the Military Police, which means NCIS will get involved. Let me tell you, that is the last thing anyone wants. So, find that computer."

2000's

Chapter 42

Y2K Cal Happy New Year

Noah had made the trek across country and was now back on the west coast. He had checked into Yuma, to an unwelcome check in from the Commanding Officer. He was made aware of Noah's Medical status prior to arrival and made his opinion clear to Noah. "Why you are allowed to continue to be on active duty is beyond me, but trust me, You don't belong in my Marine Corps, and I'll do what I can to get you out!" If the CO had his way Noah wouldn't be in the Marine Corps.

It was just after Christmas, Noah had to report in for a check-up at the I.D. clinic in San Diego. He stood at the receptionist center at Balboa Naval Hospital waiting on his final papers for checkout. The last time he had been in this clinic was when he was here to say goodbye to Glenn. The Infectious Disease Clinic was quiet; it was the Christmas and New Year Holiday season. The receptionist behind the counter handed Noah his papers, "Here you are Gunny Barlow, once again, Welcome to the Balboa I.D clinic. I have made copies of all your blood work and scheduled your next appointments. Oh, I also added some brochures for you of resources in the local community. They can be a great source of information and sometimes can be more up to date than the clinic here. Anyways, do with it as you will. Just thought it might be of help" She gave a big smile. Noah really liked her; she was very welcoming. "Thank you," he smiled and walked down the hall. It was New Year's Eve. He was in San Diego, and he wasn't driving back to Yuma and spending the night alone. Hopefully it wasn't too late to get a hotel room. Hell, he thought, I'll sleep in my car if I have to. Driving around Hillcrest he remembered Hotel Circle, and the hotel where they all stayed back in the day. It was close by, and would be perfect, maybe they might have a room available.

Noah unlocked the door and juggled his luggage into the room. This would be home for the next couple of days. He sat his luggage down and looked out over the balcony. The ghosts came rushing in. He could remember his first visit to this hotel. It was Halloween, and Glenn and Telly, along with the rest of the crew brought him down to experience Hillcrest. He could hear the echoes of laughter coming back to him. He smiled and returned to the room settling in. He decided to relax and rest a bit. Noah remembered the good times they all had. He looked across the room and the package from the hospital lay on the counter. It was such a shame they couldn't have made it just a few more years, to when the new meds had come about. Noah grabbed the packets and sat back down reviewing them. One he was taken aback from. "Say what?" He spoke out to himself. The package had a safe sex brochure of two guys kissing on the cover. "Wow!" he thought. They actually gave this to him at the military hospital. This was a big step in acknowledging the gay community. At least someone in the military was not living in a fantasy world. The brochures listed local HIV support groups and out resources in the San Diego community. Noah tucked it away back in his folder. This was something he felt would be helpful and didn't want it to be lost. Time to take a nap, it was millennium New Years, and whatever he did he was going to be ready and well rested.

****

Cal entered the door to Numbers. He and a few others had just finished dinner and were out for drinks and dancing to bring in the New Year. Numbers was a fairly new bar on the scene in San Diego. It hadn't quite caught on yet, which meant it didn't require having to wait in a long line to get in. Grabbing a beer, he mixed and mingled, recognizing a few people, and old acquaintances, as he worked his way to the dance floor. Time to stake out his claim before it got too busy.

The real estate next to the dance floor was highly sought after. Standing next to the rail, by the wall, Cal took inventory of those around him. Slowly gazing around the room, "Let the music play, so he won't get away…," squelched all other noise in the room. One could barely hear themselves think. The flashing lights, and the occasional fog release across the dance floor, created a very hypnotic haze. Between the flashes of light, across the dance floor, Cal noticed a guy. He reminded him of a sports caster on TV. A tall, handsome, blonde, with a military haircut, standing by the wall looking out watching those on the dance floor. Cal moved slightly to get a better look. The gentleman moved away like he was going to the bar. Cal waited to see what his next move would be.

The guy ordered a drink, and then moved on to the side where Cal had been standing, just a short distance to Cal's left. Cal watched to see if the guy was even aware he was standing there. The guy had yet to look in his direction. Cal took stock of those around him, to see if anyone else noticed how good looking this guy was. One younger guy came up and spoke to the stranger briefly, before the guy smiled and turned and moved away. From the looks of him, Cal was sure he probably got hit on all the time and was capable of steering off any unwanted suitors. Cal turned away trying not to look so obvious that he was checking this guy out. When he turned to take another look at him, ...he had gone. Cal looked around the room, quickly and to the exit. Nothing, ...the guy had just disappeared. Oh well, probably best anyway, guys like that usually have attitude, and were stuck on themselves. Cal returned his gaze to the lights of, the now full, dance floor.

A few minutes passed, when he heard a voice from behind, "You going to stand there all night watching everyone else have all the fun?" Cal thought it was directed to someone else and ignored it. Then he heard someone clear their throat behind him. He turned, and there stood the stranger, back from out of nowhere. "I was saying, are you going to let everyone else have all the fun?" Being taller than Cal, he looked up to see the stranger smiling, and looked him straight into the pearl blue eyes. Cal paused, and all the world paused with him. The stranger continued, "I noticed you've been standing and watching for a while. I just thought maybe you would like to join in on the fun?" Cal smiled, "Is that an easy way of asking me to dance, I barely know you." The stranger grinned, "Who, me? ...no! It was just an observation, it just looked like you might want to join in." and chuckled. Cal smiled at him. "I'm good, thank you, but glad to know you're concerned about my happiness!" The stranger chuckled, "You're welcome, here come on, let me help you pick one out. I don't think you'll have any problem finding one. I've seen several guys walking by and checking you out." The stranger pointed to another guy in the bar. "What about that one?" Cal laughed, this guy was definitely not shy, and a bit crazy, what the hell was he thinking? Cal decided to play along with it. "No, not my type." The stranger pointed to another, and Cal checked him out. "No too old, not bad just don't like'm that old." The stranger pointed to another, "Aha, what about that one, not bad." Cal smiled, "You better try again, the guy's boyfriend showed up. I don't think his boyfriend would appreciate it." The stranger laughed, "Then again, you never know, he might like it!" The two looked at each other smiling and took a drink.

They both were enjoying the banter. The stranger smiled, "Rats, just when I thought I almost had you married for the night!" Cal looked at him, "Only for the night, how do you know I'm not a long-term kind of guy?" The stranger shrugged his shoulders and smirked, "Well, I don't know. So, are you?" Cal continued, feeling the guy out. "It depends, …I can be, for the right guy, …when he comes along. But I'll kiss a few toads until then." The stranger nodded his head, "Well then I have one more pick for you, … What about me?" Cal smiled, "Like I said, I barely know you." The stranger stepped back and stuck out his hand. "Well then let me, … I'm sorry I never got your name?" Cal looked at him, "That's because I never gave it to you. I'm Cal." The stranger continued, "Well Cal, I'm Noah, nice to meet you!" Cal didn't think of anyone he had met before with that name "I'm sorry, but can you repeat that again? I thought you said Noah." Noah smiled; he already knew the next seven questions that were going to happen. "You heard me right. The name is Noah." Cal continued, "Really, I don't think I have ever met anyone by that name. So, I got to ask, the question is just begging me! What is your middle name?" Noah laughed he didn't go down the normal list of questions. But Noah was ready for him and wanted to have some fun with it. "Goliath." Cal stood there, for a moment, contemplating. "No way, you're just fucking with me now. I thought you were a nice guy. Are you serious, Noah Goliath?" Noah nodded his head. Cal was stunned and didn't want to insult him if it was really his name. "So, what were your parents like, really religious or something? There, Noah Goliath?" Noah tried to hold a straight face but couldn't help but start laughing. Cal realized he was being messed with. "What, your name isn't even Noah, is it?" Noah was laughing, knowing Cal was getting a bit agitated. He better act quick. "No, no, no, my real name is Noah, but my middle name is not Goliath. I was just messing with you on that one." Cal was confused, "Ok, that's it, pull out your ID. I want to see, ...I've already lost trust in you." Noah pulled open his wallet and showed him his military ID. Cal wasn't sure what it was. "What, what form of ID is this?" Noah, who was normally cautious about sharing he was in the military, threw caution to the wind. "It's a military ID. ...I'm a Marine?" Cal read, it, gave it back to Noah. "Ok that's it you're with me, there, 'NOAH GERARD!' If anyone even looks like they are getting close to you tonight, they'll have to go through me!" Noah laughed. "So, I guess that means we can dance?"

The two danced for a couple of songs, and then went to a quieter area of the bar. Laughing and talking for almost the rest of the evening, it was getting close to midnight before they headed back to the dance floor with their champagne. It was a rare occurrence to be able to bring in a millennium, 1999 to 2000. The countdown began, "...4, 3, 2, 1, Happy New Year!" Noah and Cal were a little embarrassed but were both smiling. Noah looked into Cal's eyes, "It's not right unless you get kissed on New Year's Eve!" A disco version of "Auld Lang Syne" began to play. Cal grabbed Noah and the two embraced in a kiss, in the middle of the dance floor. They remained and danced enjoying the night.

Last call was sounded, Cal sighed, "Already, it still seems so early." Noah looked around noticing they were one of the last few still there, "You know how long it's been since I closed a bar?" Cal laughed, "I know, right? So, what are your plans from here? Would you like to go for a bite, or come back to my place? Come on, say yes! ... the night is still young!" Noah laughed, "Oh, I like the way you just casually slipped in, or come back to my place. Very sly." Cal, blushed, "Well, what do you say?" Noah stepped back, jokingly gave Cal the once over, "I don't know, …let me get a good look at you. I don't even know what you look like because we have been in this dim lighting…" Cal was stunned, "What, you been talking to me all night!" Noah laughed and grabbed Cal's hand, "Come on, go with me." Noah led Cal by the hand into the bathroom, turned and looked at Cal like he was inspecting him. "There, now I can see you, Aha…You're a pretty good-looking fella." Cal smiled. What the hell was this guy doing. Noah commented, "Wow, you even got all your teeth!" Cal gave Noah a weird frown, "Ugh, yeah, what did you expect?" Noah laughed "Yeah, I can do it, …let's go get a bite to eat!"

Noah and Cal spent the next few days touring San Diego and hanging out, until it was time for Noah to return to Yuma. Cal had driven through Yuma a couple of times and had a favorite joke he liked to share. Waiting for the right moment he sprang it on Noah as he got ready to pull away. "What's a matter have you lost your since of Yuma?"

Chapter 43

Yuma Investigation

Walking into the office, the lights flickered before coming to a steady glow. Noah walked over to his desk and set his backpack down on the floor before sitting and firing up his computer. These were the few moments, in the morning, that he enjoyed and needed the most to start his workday out properly. It was quiet as he walked out into the hall, and ventured further into the building, turning on lights and awakening the building as he went. Stopping in the break room he started a pot of coffee before continuing on. This was the time he was able to make observations and take notes of the upkeep of the buildings. The Marines had not yet arrived, but soon the building would be bustling with the day's activity. Noah was often the last one to leave and usually the first one to arrive, except on the days when there might be an early job requiring the Marines to come in early. For the most part, the Marines often wondered if Noah lived there, he would hear them whispering to each other, "Does he ever go home?"

As he arrived in the video production section, he turned on the lights and looked around. At one of the desks, he paused looking at the handwritten schedule on the calendar before moving on to programming and distribution. He checked out the auto programming schedule on the computer screen, scrolling through to make sure all was well, before removing the video tapes from the machine and filing them back into the completed rack. The MoPic section held a special place in his heart. It reminded him of the days coming up through the ranks. This is where his heart was. He remembered how his old boss would say, "Be careful, you'll find yourself getting promoted out of a job." Noah would chuckle, and comment, "If only!" He never really understood what Gunny was saying, until now. It had been several months since his arrival at

Yuma. As the senior Gunny, he was no longer just in charge of TV, but was now the Staff Non-Commissioned Officer for the entire Combat Visual Information Center. For the next month or so, he would be the acting officer in charge until the new OIC arrived. He was no longer involved in the creative process and making of films and television productions. Everything was now from a bird's eye view.

He worked his way back to his office, grabbing a cup of coffee along the way. Just as he arrived back at the office, the outside door flung open and the Marines one by one started walking in. Noah stood by the door as each passed. They would straighten up to almost a march as they walked by, "Good morning, Gunny," greeting him before they continued their way.

Noah was sitting at his desk going over correspondence and answering emails when a knock on the hatch caused him to look up. In the doorway was SSgt Martin. "Excuse me Gunny, getting ready to hold formation. Any word to pass?" Noah shook his head no, "No not at this time, but just a reminder, I have a 0900 meeting at NCIS, …not sure how long I'll be out, so you'll need to make sure you're around." The Staff Sergeant nodded, "You got it Gunny," as he turned and headed out the door.

Noah returned to his work, contemplating the meeting with NCIS. It was about a computer that came up missing back at Lejeune. This was normal routine to get called back in after one reported something missing or stolen. They would often have you make a statement again to see if you might have remembered something not already reported and cross-reference your statement with the last to see if there was any flaw or that you might not have been forth coming on your report. Either way, he didn't like it. No matter how innocent one might be, they always seemed to treat you like you might be the culprit, dishonest, or hiding something.

Arriving at the NCIS office about 10 minutes early, Noah walked up to the customer service desk, signed in, and the clerk took his name and called someone on the phone letting them know he had arrived. Noah took a seat and started thumbing through one of the magazines from the table nearby.

A few minutes went by before a 30's something, slender, medium height, blonde headed guy walked out. Noah noticed the mirrored window next to the door. He figured everyone in the room was probably being observed. The gentleman walked to the front desk and was pointed to Noah from the receptionist. He approached, "Good morning, Gunnery Sergeant Barlow, thank you for coming in today. I'm Agent Bowker," and shook Noah's hand. He then asked him to follow him back into his office area.

At his cubical, he offered Noah a seat. "Can I get you a water or something to drink?" Noah quickly realized this guy was a bit overly friendly, "No, no I'm good," as he sat down. Agent Bowker pulled out a folder, opened it and started reviewing the paperwork inside.

Noah sat quietly observing the belongings on the desk. There was a small bible, a picture of Agent Bowker and his family, and a necklace with a cross hanging over the photo frame. Noah's first thought, ...this guy is a bible thumper. He tried to push the thought from his mind, by looking away, but ended up working a complete scenario out in his mind. This guy had the wife, the kid, the two-car garage, probably went to church every Sunday, and stood for everything Noah wasn't. Self-righteous, and if he were to find out Noah was gay, he would hang Noah on the cross himself.

Noah sat quietly and did not care to make any kind of small talk. The agent finally lifted his head and spoke. "You are probably wondering why you are here. You filed a report back at Camp Lejeune about a missing computer and we are following up." The agent pulled out a tape recorder and asked if Noah had any objection to being recorded. Noah nodded he had no problem. The agent turned to his computer and asked Noah to tell him about the incident in question. As they continued, he asked questions. The process continued for several minutes before they had completed. When they were done, the agent printed off a copy handing it to Noah. "Go ahead and read it, ...if you agree with it, go ahead and sign it." Once signed, he took the statement and walked into what appeared to be his boss's office. He returned shortly and sat down. "Ok, the statement is good. We don't believe you had anything to do with the missing computer. However, to be sure we'll need your permission to go to your house and check to make sure the computer isn't there. It's no big deal, just routine, so we can close this case." Noah clarifying what the agent was saying, "So you want to come to my house and verify that it is not there?" Agent Bowker replied, "Correct. We'd like to go right now and get this behind us." Noah thought for a moment. He had nothing to hide, so let them come look for it, just as he started to respond the agent spoke. "Look, it's not uncommon when someone gets ready to transfer, ...that is usually when they will take something. It's the perfect opportunity, ...knowing it will likely be some time before anyone might notice it's missing." Noah looked at him hesitantly. He really didn't like the feeling of this but knew they would be relentless if he said no. "Ok, no problem come look." The Agent pulled out a form and filled in the information. It stated they had permission to come in and look for a computer. He handed it to Noah to sign. As soon as it was signed the agent grabbed his keys "Ok, let's go take a look." Noah wasn't surprised how quickly this guy reacted; they were going now.

As they walked out, Noah pointed to his car, "That's my car, you can follow me there." The agent turned to Noah, "Oh, I'm sorry, you'll have to ride with us. We can't allow you to get there before we arrive." Noah frowned; this was getting a bit odd. Noah hopped in the agent's car and sat quiet the entire ride. When they pulled into the apartment complex, they parked in front of his apartment. Noah walked up with the agent and unlocked the door to let him inside.

Once unlocked, Noah stepped aside, when up came four more Agents entering the apartment. Noah walked in and noticed they all had dispersed into different rooms, and were going through drawers, cupboards, closets, and such. They were even going through the silverware drawer and opening his photo albums. They went through the nightstands by his bed. Every bit of his private life and belongings were being violated. Noah started getting nauseous.

It was as though they were raping him. He stepped outside and threw-up on the ground.

This was not what he expected. He thought they would do a walk through, look at any computers, verify they weren't the missing computer and be on their way. This was something else. He suddenly realized there was an ulterior motive. The computer was an excuse to get in to search the apartment. Could he tell them to stop? What were his rights? He had no idea. He sat down on the steps in disbelief and shock. How had he been so naive.

Noah wasn't sure how long he had sat there before Agent Bowker and the rest left his apartment. Agent Bowker asked him to come with him, to give him a ride back to the base. Noah sat silent humiliated and pissed at what just took place. Once they arrived back to the NCIS building, the Agent asked Noah to come back in, he had some final things to go over with him.

Once inside, the Agent went into the office area, and asked Noah to sit down in the lobby. After about 10 minutes or so, he returned and asked Noah to come back and have a seat at his desk again. As Noah sat, Agent Bowker spoke. "Well, we know you didn't take the computer, so we are done with that and will respond to the Lejeune office that we looked, and you don't have it" Noah nodded his head but could tell the Agent had something else to say. Agent Bowker began, "However, there was something else that came up while we were there. We saw some things that we need your permission to go back in and get. I could have taken them, but I wanted to check with my boss, before getting them."

Noah knew immediately where this was going. This was a witch hunt; this whole thing was about getting information trying to prove he was gay. Noah looked at the Agent, "Really, what things are you talking about? I thought this was about a missing computer?" Noah was standing his ground. Agent Bowker spoke, "You know, things, you know like…" trying to get Noah to say things about him being gay. Noah played dumb. "No, I don't know what you're talking about, and if you can't tell me what you want, then no, you don't have permission to go back in." Agent Bowker spoke, "You know we saw some pictures and sexual items that might mean you are a homosexual." Noah looked to the bible on his desk, and the family picture with the cross. This was definitely a witch hunt and there was no way that he would allow them to go back into his apartment.

Noah quickly invoked his right to no longer talk. "Look I don't know what you think you saw, but I can tell you, as of right now, this conversation is over, and absolutely, you do not have my permission to go back into my apartment. So, unless you have something else, or you're going to charge me, then I'm leaving. I want an Attorney and representation present." Agent Bowker's mild demeanor changed as he pulled back from Noah. He was a bit at a loss for words, stunned that Noah had stood his ground. He sat and looked at him for a second before replying, "You know we can get a search warrant to go in and get the things." Noah, still in defiance, "Well I suggest you do, because you don't have my permission." Noah stood up and started to leave when Agent Bowker spoke out, "Hold on! No one gave you permission to leave!" Noah stopped and looked at him, "Are you arresting me?" Agent Bowker quickly responded, "No, we are detaining you to further our investigation, if you leave, we'll charge you with interference!" Noah was hesitant, and paused, when Agent Bowker asked him to sit back down. He needed to speak with his Boss before he could let him leave.

Noah sat down in the chair, while Agent Bowker went into the door behind him. Although Noah sat quietly, his mind was racing. Was this legal? What were his rights? Was this against the "Don't Ask, Don't Tell" policy? He needed a lawyer and needed one now. What was his plan if they come back out and wanted him to talk? What was in the apartment that made them think he's homosexual? He couldn't think of anything other than the workout poster he had pinned on the mirror as a daily reminder of his goal to achieve that level of fitness. None of that mattered the plan now was to use their own law against them. They were asking, but Noah was going to remain silent, and stick to the "Don't tell" part. After all, if they wanted him out, they needed to prove it, and right now they had nothing. So let them work for it, but it wouldn't be from his own admittance.

Agent Bowker came out and asked Noah to come with him, his boss wanted a word. Noah followed Agent Bowker through the door as he spoke, "It is Warrant Officer Haggard, you'll need to report into him."

The office was full of cigarette smoke, thick enough to cut with a knife, even though smoking was prohibited in government buildings. Noah thought, well this guy really doesn't care much about government policy or regs, definitely a "Do as I say, not as I do," kinda guy. Camouflage netting hung on the walls with various plaques and achievements. Green field mount-out boxes were set around for furniture, and Noah noted a packed ALICE pack in the corner. This guy was obviously caught up on trying to prove he was a Marine's Marine. In Noah's experience, most of these guys felt underachieved which usually meant a power complex of something to prove. Noah lined up center of the desk, on the other side, sat a crusty older blondish-gray haired man in a wrinkled camouflage uniform. Noah noticed a smoldering crushed out cigarette in a dusty ash tray sitting next to a steaming cup of coffee. What really caught Noah's attention was the bayonet knife laying center on the desk in front of him. Noah sounded off. "Gunnery Sergeant Barlow reporting as ordered Sir."

The Warrant Officer sat up and leaned on his desk. "So, you're Gunnery Sergeant Barlow. The one who doesn't want to talk or cooperate with my Agents. Stand at ease." The Warrant Officer grabbed the bayonet knife from his desk, sat back and began to speak, while picking his teeth with the bayonet, and waving it and pointing it at Noah. "So, listen here Gunny, … I have been in the business for a long time. I know how these things go. You can make it hard, or you can make it easy, but in the end, it will all be the same. We can go the hard way, which means we are going to investigate you. We'll find the evidence to prove it, and you'll be on your way. Or you could save us a lot of time. I have illegals coming across the border and drugs being smuggled, so do us a favor and just tell us you're a homosexual. I'm finding dead illegals every day, so let us get back to the real business, …not this bullshit, …So what do yah say, just tell us you're a homosexual."

Noah stood quiet, how could he even consider responding, this guy was picking his teeth with a bayonet. Was he going to come across this desk if Noah said anything he didn't like? The Warrant Officer asked again, "Well, I believe I asked you a question Gunny? Last time I checked when an Officer asks a question, you're supposed to answer?" The Warrant Officer was agitated. Noah thought quickly, "Sir, no disrespect, but I believe you are not allowed to ask me that under the "Don't Ask, Don't Tell" policy, and like I told Agent Bowker, I choose to remain silent. If I'm being charged with something, I would like my council present if I'm going to be questioned."

The Warrant Officer became furious and stood up taking the knife, stabbing it into the desk in front of them. "… I don't have time to deal with some pansy, homosexual, who wants to hide behind some lame ass policy that says I'm not supposed to ask if he is queer! Lock your body while I'm talking to you! Let me tell you something, this is a small base, and can be made pure hell for you! I tried to make it easy for you, but you want to play it your way, that is fine! Agent Bowker read him his rights, let his company CO know he is confined to base, until I give the authorization he can go, and let's start working on getting a search warrant." Noah remained at attention as the Warrant Officer continued, "I'm sick of looking at you, get out of my office you piece of shit!" Noah stepped back and did an about face and left the office.

Agent Bowker stopped by the desk, "Have a seat." He began informing Noah of his legal rights and they had him sign a document saying he had them read to him, and that he was being investigated for being a homosexual. Once finished, he told Noah he could go back to work but was not allowed to leave the base until told otherwise by NCIS or by his Company Commander. If so, he would be charged with violation of a lawful order.

Noah exited the building and went immediately to his car. Grabbing his cell phone confused, not knowing who to call. He decided to go by base legal to speak to an attorney about his rights.

He signed into the list at the reception desk in the lobby, only slightly briefing the clerk his reason for being there. Noah had a seat and waited for an hour or so before a Major appeared from the hall and asked for him.

Once in the office he introduced himself as Major Calum, and although he wouldn't be the one representing him, he could give him temporary council until one could be appointed. Noah explained the events that transpired throughout the day. The thing that stuck with Noah was his initial comment, "I won't be the lawyer representing you." Noah finished, the Major sat for a moment, before speaking, "Well it seems like it's been a rough day for you, are you doing alright?" Noah was surprised by the concern of his wellbeing. "Yes, I'm a bit taken by surprise, but I'm alright. I just wasn't expecting this…" The Major continued on, "I'm sure, Warrant Officer Haggard can be a bit over the top, but he's good at what he does. There is a military Navy Officer in San Diego, that specializes in this. I recommend he should be brought in. However, the question that needs to be answered is, Are you gay?"

Noah was immediately uncomfortable; did he really just ask him if he was gay? Noah sat for a moment and looked him in the eye, "Excuse me Sir, didn't you tell me you're not my Attorney, and if I said yes, couldn't you report it?" The Major sat back; a bit surprised Noah caught on. "Let me make it clear, I represent the command here at Yuma. Whoever is appointed is going to ask if you are gay or not, they'll want to know what they are dealing with. If you like, you can request to have an attorney appointed, but it will probably take a week or two before you get one. Just my experience, you'll probably want to get a civilian attorney." Noah stood up, "Well thank you Sir for your advice, I'll take note of it." The Major stood up, "Just so you know, you'll need to make an appointment to get assistance with council, or have a civilian attorney, to work with your military appointed one. It's late, you'll need to call back to set an appointment up."

Noah left the legal building confused and now a bit paranoid. These guys were closing ranks on him quick. The Major wanted him to admit he was gay, then he could turn it over to NCIS and their case was closed. It was time to not trust anyone! He almost believed this guy was on his side. He sat in his car contemplating what was the next move. He thought a bit, before remembering a legal group that represented military members being pursued for being gay. Who would know how to get a hold of them? Only if he had a gay rag, they always ran an advertisement for military members needing help. Noah headed back to work and decided he would hang out there. Who knew how long he could be confined to base?

Yu-must be out of your office

A week had passed since the showdown in the NCIS office. Noah arrived at work just round 6:30am and the new Warrant Officer had arrived and was already in his office. When Noah passed, he stuck his head in briefly to say hello. The Warrant Officer thanked him again, ahead of time, for doing him the favor of riding over to Miramar/San Diego for the day. Noah was to attend a Combat Camera meeting for him. Because he was so new and still checking in, the Warrant Officer had asked Noah to go in his stead, telling him to give his regards to the others. Going to the meeting meant Noah would be out of office the entire day. He didn't mind. It would give him time away from all the ignorance and stress of the investigation. Most importantly it would be an opportunity to meet with his friend Joe later in the evening. Noah went to his office to check his emails and grab his briefcase when Gunnery Sergeant Woods knocked on the door. "Anything I need to be aware of, or you want to pass on before heading out?" Gunny would be filling in for him while he was away. Noah smiled, "No, not really, … just check with the company to see if there is any word to pass. Also, the new rifle range details are posted, so make sure the troops know their dates. Oh, check in with the Warrant Officer to see if he needs anything and keep him posted of your whereabouts. I'll call later today to check in. I'll have my cell with me if anything comes up, don't hesitate to call. Any questions?" Noah stood up, grabbed his things, and the two headed out.

As they walked down the hall, "We're good," Gunnery Sergeant Woods smiled, "I would be glad to be going, you get out of Yuma for a day. This place is crazy." About that time, at the end of the hall Agent Bowker along with two other NCIS agents headed into the Warrant Officer's office. Noah stopped in his tracks, recognizing the one who had ransacked his house. "What the fuck are they doing here?" Gunnery Sergeant Woods turned to Noah, "I didn't want to say anything, ...thought it might upset you." Noah was angry and stunned, "What, you knew?" Gunnery Sergeant Woods backed up a bit, and was hesitant, as he began to speak slowly, "...That right there is why I didn't say anything! ...What was I supposed to say?" as he shook his hands up in the air. "Man, this is the Marine Corps, ...these people are going to do what they want to do. I can't stop them!" Noah calmed a bit, "I know, I know, I'm not pissed at you...," Gunnery Sergeant Woods continued, "They're here to talk to the troops, they are setting up in your office, and will be calling each Marine in individually to ask them about you, including me."

Noah turned to look down the hall in disbelief and realized this whole trip to Miramar was a ruse. "The Warrant Officer, ...fuck, ...he knew. That is why he asked me to go to Miramar for him, to get me out of the office. So, I wouldn't be around while they're here.... It's fucked up man, he knew and acted like I was doing him a favor. That piece of shit didn't even have the guts to tell me. Typical, Officers, they all like to close ranks when it comes to doing the shitty work, don't they?" Gunnery Sergeant Woods frowned, not knowing how to respond. "That or get someone else to do their bidding for them. NCIS. They will throw you to the wolves in a heartbeat!" he put his hand on Noah's shoulder, "Man, go on...get outta here, I got this! Enjoy yourself, get your mind off things around here. You need a day away from this place!" Noah nodded, "Thanks man I appreciate it!"

Gunnery Sergeant Woods and he walked on down the hall. Once outside, Gunnery Sergeant Woods looked around making sure no one was close enough to hear. "Look, we all know what is going on. This base is small, and people like to talk, … I know you man. I got you, and so do the troops. They like you man, and so do a lot of other people. We know what they are trying to do to you, and we got your back. The Colonel here, he is a big fish in a small pond trying to have his way. Not just with you, I've seen him try to do shit to others, …eat'm up, and go unchecked. No one to challenge him. You just got to remind him there are bigger fish in the rivers and streams feeding this pond. Fuck these Mother Fuckers!"

The drive to San Diego and Miramar was roughly three hours. Noah had developed a routine, having driven it many times. He learned to time it by the changes in landscape and terrain. He put on some music and allowed his mind to wonder and escape. Nothing like a drive cross country or day trip to ease the mind. It was always a picturesque drive he enjoyed. Starting on the US 8 heading west right outside of Yuma, Noah passed the large sand dunes, flanking the freeway. There wasn't a time he could pass by without thinking of Jedd and skipping down the freeway. Eventually the dunes would break into desert land filled with sage brush. It remained that way till somewhere around El Centro where the desert quickly sprang to life with agricultural farmlands. This seemed so out of place the first time he saw it, but learned it was made possible by the creation of the Hoover Dam system, and the Army Corps of Engineers. The dams were developed to control the sporadic meandering Colorado river. The once barren land was now part of the US food basket and helped feed the country and the world.

Noah stopped briefly to fuel up, grab a coffee, and was soon back on the road. He tried to block out what was taking place back at his office, but it kept coming back to him. How humiliating, degrading and compromising it was to know they would be asking his troops, his peers, everyone he worked with about him. Most importantly, exactly what was it they were asking? The thought of the whole thing was overwhelming. He pulled onto one of the overpasses and parked the SUV off to the side of the road. He hopped out, walking to the side, and leaned on the window and spit, lowering his head in his arms. What the fuck was he doing? He stood there with his head lowered just shaking his head. What the fuck was he going to do? What happens if they succeed? He had nothing to fall back on. He couldn't go home, at least not to his father's house. What about medical, would he be able to find a job if he were to get a dishonorable discharge. If he stayed in, it would never be the same. From now on, no matter where he was to go or who he worked with, he would always be labeled the homosexual in whispers behind his back. He turned to look out at the landscape around him. He looked down the road, before going to the passenger side door and opened it up and grabbed his phone. He looked through it, contemplating who to call, before he threw it back into the front seat. He stumbled back a few steps and leaned back on to the SUV looking out, wiping tears from his eyes, even then, trying to hold back from a total breakdown. He looked around and there was nothing but farmland. No one to call, no one, ...did anyone even care. He felt totally isolated. With tears falling down his face, he was no longer holding back. He looked out to the blue sky, and stood hollering to the heavens, "What, …, What, …tell me? What, … is it? Is this what it's all about? What happened to "Don't Ask, Don't Tell?" cause they're sure asking, … Is this how it is supposed to end?" He leaned back up against the SUV, as he cried with his head lowered before looking back up, almost begging, "Tell me something, ...give me something, …give me a sign, give me some direction, anything, cause I'm at a loss here. … I have no fucking direction to go!" Noah looked down at the ground, as he continued to sob. He stayed there, quietly sobbing, before raising his head and looking around. Wiping his face free of tears, he stepped out from the vehicle and looked around to see if anyone might have watched his little fit, before chuckling to himself. He chuckled a couple more times, then realized he needed to get back on the road after looking at his watch. As he drove off, he looked out in all directions before pulling back onto the road. Once on the road safely, he spoke out loud. "Don't ask, Don't tell, ...Huh, …my ass. Fuck those motherfuckers. You want a fight, ok Mother Fuckers, …what do you got when you got nothing else to lose!"

The farmland continued for some distance before turning back into desert. Soon the horizon gave way to some quickly rising mountains. This was about the midway point of the drive. Once at the base of the mountains, the incline was rapid. Noah thought of this area as a Mars alien environment. Barren, with steep red mountains, large boulders lying next to the treacherous, steep inclines, and winding roads. Passing the Desert View Tower, somewhere in the middle of the sharp turns and twists, he found himself in San Diego County. As he continued working through the climb and elevation, it had a gradual way of turning into a plateau of green pastures, lakes, and pine trees of the high desert. The plateau, with an occasional valley, continued for miles before a slight descent back down into the El Cajon valley. Just west of El Cajon, Noah took the exit to the US 15 north and soon found himself at the gates of Miramar.

Noah arrived just as the meeting was starting, taking a seat in the back of the classroom. One by one each participant stood and introduced themselves. Noah took a glance around the room and knew almost everyone in the room. A few he was aware of but had never met them. Eventually it was his turn to stand and introduce himself. As soon as he stood and said his name, several of those not paying attention, suddenly stopped what they were doing and turned to look. He could tell immediately those familiar with him, were surprised to see him there. He gaged from their unsettling mood, word had gotten out and they were aware of the accusations and the ongoing investigation.

The meeting was being led by Major Lemond, and various topics of concern were being discussed. The meeting seemed to go by quickly. During the first break, Noah hit the head and got a drink of water, avoiding the coffee mess where most were congregating. As he walked back into the room, a small group was huddled talking and stopped once he entered the room. This was totally unfamiliar, that no one was even trying to approach him to speak. Normally he would be approached and all subject matters pertaining to the occ field would be discussed. His opinion had always been valued. He could see the avoidance being taken; he was being shunned. He chuckled as he sat down and thought, well you find out in times like these who your real friends are. He said to himself… Oh well, hold your head high! No time to feel small here. The last of the crowd returned, the door closed, and the meeting continued. Noah tried to stay focused, but he found himself wondering off to what was taking place, back at Yuma. What was being said. Any one of the troops could say anything, even make it up, and their word would be taken seriously. It was a flat-out witch hunt to find anything, literally anything, to support their claim and give reason to get rid of him. After all, the law doesn't say must have committed homosexual acts, it says, "Have the propensity." What a big word. Prior to this, he didn't even know what it meant. He had to look it up in the dictionary to find the meaning. "An inclination or natural tendency to behave in a particular way..." in this case homosexual. Even the dictionary says a natural tendency, but yet they call it unnatural, funny how they can choose to flip, and coerce the meaning to meet their needs. Finally, the last of the topics of the meeting were being discussed. Major Lemond had taken the helm, "Any final questions, going once..., Going twice..., Gone! That will be it. Thank you everyone for attending."

Noah started gathering his things when Master Gunnery Sergeant Rizzio approached him. "Glad to see you could make it today," as he held out his hand. Noah stood and shook his hand, as Master Gunny Sergeant continued. "I want to thank you for what you are doing out there in Yuma. You know you were hand selected by Captain Rogers. He wanted to have a strong SNCO to be able to help with the young new Warrant Officer. We knew he would be going there and wanted to team him with someone who knows the field. He is new to the field himself, even though he is a Warrant Officer, he has spent most of his time on the drill field and B billets and doesn't really know much about running an information center. We thought you would be a good trainer for him with your expertise." Noah lifted his eyebrow, "Thank you for the vote of confidence in me, but I'm sure he'll be fine. From what I've seen, I don't think he listens too much to anyone but himself." Master Gunny chuckled, "So I see you understand him already. He can be a bit thick in the skull, but he needs help. I know he doesn't think so, but you're a strong SNCO, you'll find a way to get through!"

By the time Noah finished the meeting and made it back to the hotel room to change over, he had just enough time to get to the Hillcrest coffee shop, where he was to meet with his friend Joe.

Joe was at one point in the Marine Corps but had long been retired. He was now an attorney in the local community with strong ties to an organization called Service Men and Women's Legal Defense Network. An organization formed to specifically advocate for and offer guidance to, service members being persecuted under the "Don't Ask, Don't Tell" policy. He had already spoken to Joe and the two had agreed to meet up over coffee in San Diego. It would be good to get his insight on how to handle the investigation and how to move forward.

As they sat at the coffee shop, Joe didn't waste any time getting to the point of what lay ahead for Noah. Joe quickly explained. "If you have any intention of beating this, it will require more people to get involved. It might be uncomfortable, but you'll need to ask your mom, dad, siblings, friends, anybody you can trust. They will need to advocate for you. We'll need them to reach out to Senators and Congressmen. No worries, we can help them with what to say. If need be, you can create the letter and they'll just need to sign it and mail it in. They can also call their offices. The idea is if you, along with enough people, contact your Reps, it will get them to act on your part and request a Congruent investigation on the command. Now you must know, this may not stop the investigation, but will require them to play by the law and answer the question as to why they had grounds to investigate to begin with. Sometimes just the outside pressure alone is enough to scare them into halting the investigation. This would be the best option, Noah, to have a fair chance to win and see it through to its end. Is this something you think you can do? Do you think this is something you would be willing to do? And can you get enough people to respond, especially your mother? Politicians always pay attention to mothers."

Noah sighed and exhaled in exhaustion. Lowering his head, to take in all that had just been said, before raising it. "This is so much at once, but I don't think I have a choice. The only other possibility is to let them win. So yes, I'll have to make it happen." Joe looked Noah in the eye, with a brief smile. "You will need to work along with the Service Men and Women's Legal Defense

Network to make this happen. They will send a letter to the command, as well as your elected officials, requesting the investigation be stopped, explaining your rights under the law of "Don't Ask, Don't Tell" are being violated." Noah was becoming overwhelmed and choked up a bit. "Joe, … I just, … I mean, I'm like, …Wow! Just wow, here! What kind of fucking alternate universe did I step off in? I feel like I am in some bad dream, and it's a loop that keeps playing over and over in my head! I go to sleep, and I wake up to another piece of the shit show being revealed!" Before Joe finished, he grabbed Noah's hand, "Stay strong brother, you have a long and rough road ahead of you. There are no guarantees, but if we do everything we are supposed to, it will give us a fighting chance. Remember, you are not alone in this. Any questions, big or small, call me or SLDN, don't hesitate! Most importantly, when dealing with your command, use your right to stay SILENT! … No matter how they try to coerce you."

Chapter 44

SLDN

Waiting by the phone, watching the clock, Noah's thoughts were running rampant. He was worried, and his lack of ability to concentrate was becoming normal. The longer this investigation went on, the more frustrated he became. Looking at his clock one more time. "Come on, hurry up," he said as he paced the floor. It was becoming crunch time, any longer and work would start noticing him missing. He reviewed his notes again, making sure he would be able to ask any questions, and nothing was left out or forgotten. All the important things were written down.

Finally, the phone rang, and Noah picked up on the first ring. "Hello?" The voice on the other end spoke, "Hello this is Kevin. I'm calling to speak to Noah, is he available?" Noah relieved, "Yes, this is Noah speaking." "Hi Noah, I'm one of the legal advocates that will be assisting you with your case. Thank you for taking my call. I have reviewed your written statements and correspondence with us, and I'm so sorry you are having to go through this. I must tell you things don't look good and can go south in a hurry when dealing with a small, isolated command such as Yuma. Being so isolated can give the commanding officer a false sense of power, and they often step out of bounds with their authority, thinking no one is looking. I want you to know here, at the Men's and Women's Legal Defense Network, we are on your side, and with your permission, we plan on sending a letter to your Commanding Officer. We would like to remind him of his responsibility to abide by the laws, including that of "Don't Ask, Don't Tell," which he is violating and, clearly overstepping. We also would like him to know people are looking, and our goal is to let him know we have contacted your Senators, and Representatives in Congress. Our goal is to bring this injustice to their attention and get them to react by putting a congruent on the command. So, we reverse the role, and now the Commander is being investigated. That usually is enough to scare the Commanders and shut the whole thing down. If he doesn't, at least everything will be by the book, and if there are no grounds, he'll have to shut it down. Now in order for all this to happen, I have sent you some documents, saying we have a right to act on your behalf. Also, I am going to draft a letter for you to send to anyone who is willing to complete it and send it to your elected officials. Remember, the squeaky hinge gets the oil. But what I need right now is a verbal confirmation to get this going. Action and speed is of the essence when dealing with these things." Noah didn't hesitate, "Yes, I want your help, and you have my permission to go forward with this on my behalf." Kevin replied, "Congratulations, I will send over an email with privacy waiver/authorization for the USMC to communicate with SLDN and fax it back to me ASAP. Great talking to you Noah, and remember, you are not alone on this, any questions call. Once again, Thank you for your service to our country."

After the phone call, Noah checked his emails and there it was, just like Kevin had promised.

Date: Wednesday, August 9, 2000

Noah,

Nice chatting with you over the phone. Please print out the waiver/authorization for the USMC to communicate with SLDN and fax back to me ASAP.

Note: Don't panic over the "News media" language in the waiver. I put it there ONLY to make the USMC believe that you are considering going to the news media (Note: I am NOT suggesting that you go public). If they think you are considering this, they "may" go slower OR think twice about continuing. SLDN will do NOTHING on your behalf without you and Captain Jamison's full, prior consent/approval.

Best Regards,

Kevin

Noah continued to read the privacy statement:

I, Noah Barlow, (Gunnery Sergeant, United States Marine Corps), hereby authorize the Servicemembers Legal Defense Network (SLDN) to communicate with the United States Marine Corps, the Naval Criminal Investigative Service

(NCIS), the Department of Defense, members of the United States Congress and the news media on all matters relating to my military service and all ongoing legal matters pertaining to my service.

I further authorize the United States Marine Corps, through its employees and personnel, to release information contained in its records relating to my military service and service-related legal matters to representatives of the Servicemembers Legal Defense Network (SLDN) and to communicate with SLDN on all such matters.

This authorization waives protections afforded me by the privacy Act of 1974, 5 U.S.C. SS 552a. as amended.

Noah reviewed, signed, and dated it August 10, 2000. He received an email back from Kevin letting him know they had received it. A week or so went by, when the phone rang. It was Kevin. "Hey Noah wanted to let you know, we have been working on your case, and composed a letter on your behalf. We will be sending it out tomorrow to all pertinent parties. Trust me this will start rattling some heads and if all goes well, we should start seeing some results. It is addressed to your Commanding Officer, but we included all of whom we are communicating with in the letter, so the command knows we are not fly by night small town attorneys. It will be going to all members in the Chain of Command, and your U.S. Elected Officials as well. Just so you know, the Command may want to speak to you, just decline and invoke your rights, and refer them to us, or your defense attorney. Whatever they say, keep track of it and let us know. Best of luck."

Letters of request, and intent etc. ...

Noah continued with the homework he had been tasked to do by his attorney, and SLDN's. He made a form letter to send to his family and friends to fill out and send to his elected officials in protest of the actions being taken against him. He himself sent letters to both his U.S. Senators, informing them of the unjust policy and actions being taken against him. He was new to all of this and had no idea what to expect. Much to his surprise, a few days had gone by and in the mail were letters of response from both United States Senators, Dan Boyd, and Victor G. Logan.

First letter from Senator Boyd:

United States Senate
WASHINGTON, DC 20510-1401

August 14, 2000

Dear Noah:

Thank you for your recent mail. I am sincerely sorry to hear of the difficulties you have encountered with the Marine Corps and appreciate that you have taken the time to bring this matter to my attention.

In an effort to be of assistance to you, I will be happy to contact the appropriate officials on your behalf to request their review of this matter. Before I can do this, however, I will need for you to sign and complete the enclosed consent form in order to meet the provisions of the 1974 Privacy Act.

If you return this form to me, I will initiate an inquiry on your behalf. I look forward to hearing from you.

Best wishes,

Dan Boyd

Then shortly thereafter a letter response from Senator Victor G. Logan:

United States Senate
WASHINGTON, DC 20510-1401

August 14, 2000

Dear Mr. Barlow

Thank you for your inquiry regarding your concerns about harassment. I appreciate the time you have taken to notify me of your concerns.

My military and veteran's affairs specialist, Angie Roman, is working with me to investigate your concern. She has contacted the United States Marine Corps on your behalf. I will notify you as soon as I obtain further information on your case.

If you have any additional questions, please do not hesitate to write, or phone Angie. Again, thank you for your requesting my assistance in this matter.

Sincerely,

Victor G Logan

SLDN Letter of request and intent, to all pertinent parties involved

Lt Col Segall sat at his desk opening the registered correspondence addressed to him specifically. Noting the return address, he pulled out the letter and began to read:

Servicemembers Legal Defense Network

Date, August 17, 2000

Dear Lt. Col. Segall

I write at the request of Gunnery Sergeant Noah Barlow (encl.) to express concern over what appears to be an improper investigation into Gunnery Sergeant Barlow's private life in direct violation of the "Don't Ask, Don't Tell, Don't Pursue, Don't Harass" policy. As there is no basis for this inquiry, it should be halted immediately.

According to Gunnery Sergeant Barlow, on July 5, 2000, CID questioned him regarding a missing office computer. Gunnery Sergeant Barlow consented to a CID request to search his off-base living quarters. According to Gunnery Sergeant Barlow, CID-while authorized only to search for a computer- proceeded to conduct a search of his privately owned vehicle, his wallet, and every portion of his apartment, to include rifling through his photo albums, personal files, and private letters. Afterwards, CID reportedly told Gunnery Sergeant Barlow they did not believe Gunnery Sergeant Barlow had the missing computer.

The CID agents then escorted Gunnery Sergeant Barlow back to their Marine Corps Air Station (MCAS) Yuma Office and attempted to interrogate him about non-criminal matters unrelated to the missing computer. According to Gunnery Sergeant Barlow, CID agents requested his permission to return to his apartment because they claimed that, while searching for the missing computer, they saw personal items, unrelated to the missing computer, that CID wanted to confiscate.

Gunnery Sergeant Barlow reports that he was taken into a CID office where CID Warrant Officer Haggard questioned him while the Warrant Officer was picking his teeth with a "K-Bar type military knife". According to Gunnery Sergeant Barlow, the Warrant Officer stated, "It's not really my job to get into people's lifestyles, why don't you go ahead and just tell us about it." The CID agents informed Gunnery Sergeant Barlow that they saw items inside his apartment suggesting that Gunnery Sergeant Barlow may be gay. The agents reportedly further told Gunnery Sergeant Barlow, "We need to keep these things quiet." At this point, Gunnery Sergeant Barlow invoked his article 31 right and asked to speak with a defense attorney.

"Don't Ask, Don't Tell, Don't Purse, Don't Harass" allows an inquiry only if a service member engages in "homosexual conduct." The policy defines "homosexual conduct" as either a (1) statement by member that he is gay. (2) a "homosexual act" by the member or (3) the member engages in a gay marriage. (ref.1)
Ref.1 Marine Corps Separation Manual (MARCORSEPMAN) MCO P1900.16E. 6207, Homosexual Conduct.

The inquiry into Gunnery Sergeant Barlow's private life is improper. There is no evidence that Gunnery Sergeant Barlow stated that he was gay or engaged in a gay "act" or marriage.

Gunnery Sergeant Barlow states that during the CID search of his quarters, the agent may have viewed some publications that provide information on HIV/AIDS resources, as well as updates on HIV disease treatment and health management matters. "Don't Ask, Don't Tell, Don't Pursue, Don't Harass" allows all Marines to possess publications that may be considered gay related; the policy prohibits an inquiry based upon an allegation that a Marine possesses HIV or gay related publications (ref 2)
Ref. 2 Id. DoDD 1332.14, Enlisted Administrative Separations, Inquiry Guidelines E (4), "Credible information does not exist ...when the only information known is an associational activity such as ...reading homosexual publications..."

Gunnery Sergeant Barlow states that the command is aware that he is HIV positive, and he fears the command is using the CID computer investigation as a ruse to discover whether he is gay. The intent of "Don't Ask, Don't Tell, Don't Pursue, Don't Harass" is to respect the private lives of all service personnel, regardless of their sexual orientation. (ref.3)
Ref.3 "There will be a decent regard to the legitimate privacy and associational rights of all service members." President William J. Clinton, Text of Remarks Announcing the New Policy, The Washington Post A12 (July 20, 1993).

Military criminal investigative organizations are prohibited from conducting investigations to determine the sexual orientation of a service member. (Ref. 4)
Ref.4 DoD Instruction 5505.8: "No Defense criminal investigative organization or other DoD law enforcement organization will conduct an investigation solely to determine a servicemembers' sexual orientation," Secretary of Defense Les Aspin, News Release: Secretary Aspin Releases New Regulations on Homosexual Conduct in the Armed Forces, December 22, 1993.

It appears that CID was deliberately "searching" for something other than a missing computer in Gunnery Sergeant Barlow's home. Although Gunnery Sergeant Barlow has a personal computer, he reports that the CID agents, surprisingly did not seem interested in his computer and did not inspect the computer's serial numbers. Further, according to Gunnery Sergeant Barlow, the agent looking through his personal photographs asked him whether he "is a model?" Gunnery Sergeant Barlow believed this CID agent was fishing for information about sexual orientation.

Speculation about a Marines' sexual orientation is not a basis to investigate the Marine's private life. (Ref. 5)

Ref.5 DoDD 1332.14, Inquiry Guidelines E (2)(3), "Credible information does not exist when the only information is the opinions of others that a member is a homosexual [or] when the inquiry would be based on rumor, suspicion, or capricious claims concerning a member's sexual orientation."

It appears to be the case, CID entered Gunnery Sergeant Barlow's home for the covert purpose of collecting information to bolster their suspicion that he may be gay, and this represents an egregious Violation of "Don't Ask, Don't Tell, Don't Pursue, Don't Harass."

Further, the CID search of Gunnery Sergeant Barlow's quarters greatly exceeded the scope of the consent Gunnery Sergeant Barlow granted. CID did not have the authority to search Gunnery Sergeant Barlow's vehicle glove compartment, or his wallet, or his photo albums, or his personal files, or read his private letters because a computer could not be hidden in those places. This unusual CID behavior towards an exemplary senior enlisted Marine strongly suggests that the agents were more interested in snooping into Gunnery Sergeant Barlow's personal life rather than actually searching for a missing computer.

My understanding is that Gunnery Sergeant Barlow is an outstanding noncommissioned officer with over 17 years of service to our country. There is no reason to investigate Gunnery Sergeant Barlow's private life.

I ask that the inquiry concerning Gunnery Sergeant Barlow's private life be halted immediately, and that no further administrative actions be taken against him on the basis of perceptions of his sexual orientation.

Sincerely,

Anna L. Christian, Esq.

Legal Director

Chapter 45

Someone is listening

Still not comfortable about taking personal calls in his own office for fear of who might be listening, Noah stepped outside into the morning breeze and felt the warmth of an early rising Yuma sun on his face. He was expecting a phone call from the office of Senator Victor Logan. Noah knew it was about his DADT request but wasn't exactly sure what more they might need to know. He was told the Senator wanted to speak to him directly.

Answering the phone, it was an Assistant and put Noah on hold. Soon, Noah heard a male voice. "Gunny Barlow, this is Senator Victor Logan, how are you?" Noah calmly spoke, "Fine thank you Sir." The Senator continued, "Great, great. First, I want to thank you for your service to this country. You have a lot of people concerned about you. My office has received quite a bit of mail concerned about your wellbeing. I have reviewed your records and they are impressive. It would be of great loss to lose such a fine Marine over this nonsense. So, I must say, I look forward to your continued service. Yes, you heard that right, I said continued service. Listen, my office has done an inquiry and we find no reason for this to continue. I have demanded an end to it. I have already spoken to several people in your chain of command including the Inspector General's office. I want you to know you should be getting a phone call, if you haven't received one already, very shortly. Your Commanding Officer should be giving you an apology on his behalf, as well for the United States Marine Corps. I have further instructed an after action as to why this happened in the first place and want to know what will be done to prohibit this from happening in the future. I can't change the harassment you have already endured, but we can stop it from happening again. I think your Commanding Officer, and a few others for that matter, need to be reschooled on the policy of "Don't Ask, Don't Tell". Regardless of one's opinion, it's the law, and must be adhered to. Furthermore, I can't understand why we are wasting time, and taxpayers' money, investigating the personal life of an impeccable Marine with nearly 18 years of service. Surely, there are better ways to apply the resources of the American people. If he is not capable of doing that, he can step aside, or we can arrange that for him. Because of the damage, I have tasked my military and veteran's affairs specialist to work with the United States Marine Corps officials. They tell me they can accommodate you on your wishes, if you decide to stay at Yuma, or if you plan on leaving." Noah spoke up, "I would prefer transferring, Sir. I think this would be a toxic environment for me to stay in. Especially with this Commanding Officer." Senator Logan, continued, "I couldn't agree more. I'm sure we can arrange for that to happen. But something tells me, your Commanding Officer will be changing soon. Just so you know, you are the one who was done an injustice here, and it's not you that has to go. I will pass this information on to my Assistant. She will be the liaison, working with The United States Marine Corps, and the Inspector General's Office, to make sure your request is taken care of. Any concerns let her know. I have spoken to Senator Dan Boyd, and I think it is safe to say we agree on this. Once again Gunny Barlow, my apologies for the harassment you have endured. It's not often I can speak one on one with my constituents from the great state of Indiana, but it's opportunities like this, where I am able to make a difference, that I most enjoy. I thank you for your outstanding service and your choice to serve as a career Marine." Noah was ecstatic, but at the same time didn't want to lose his bearing. "Thank you, Sir. I'm sure this would have taken a different path without your help. I can't tell you how grateful I am to hear this."

Noah hung up the phone. Was this for real? As he sat in disbelief. He just spoke to Senator Logan. All his letters, his family, and friend's letters, had paid off. He thought it was a "Hail Mary" chance to make this go away. He had almost resigned to being put out, thinking no one would pay any attention. For once in his life someone was taking note. SLDN's guidance and plan had paid off.

He needed to call and tell Kevin at SLDN and let him know the great news. He had been there for Noah since the beginning of this mess.

Kevin was elated to hear the news. Like Noah, he was surprised to know Senator Logan himself contacted Noah. Without being a kill joy, Kevin quickly brought Noah back into reality. He still needed to face the Command, or more importantly, he had to stand at attention in front of a Colonel who ended up with egg on his face. Although unlikely, retribution was still possible, and Noah was still within the Colonel's reach. Heeding Kevin's advice to play it cool, when he was finally called in, was the plan. Kevin told him, "Act as though you know nothing, and he is the one breaking the news the investigation is over for the first time. And by all means do not gloat. Keep your military bearing. Although, it was a triumph on this battle, there were still other fronts he can go after you. Disrespect does not need to be one of them."

The Sergeant Major opened his door and glanced outside seeing Gunny Barlow, asked him to come in and have a seat. Closing the door behind him, the SgtMaj took his place behind his desk. "You must really know some people in high places. I've not seen heads fly like they have around here in the last few days. Trust me, this guy who sits behind that desk in there, was hell bent on getting you thrown out of the Marine Corps. He has gained a whole new attitude. I personally felt like they were headed down the wrong path on this from the beginning. But my job is to advise, I gave my opinion, but he had the ultimate say. I have to know, how did you come into contact with this organization, but most importantly, how did you get your Senators involved?" Noah still guarded, and also aware he had not been officially informed the investigation was over. "Sergeant Major, I appreciate your interest, but my legal counsel still requires me to not talk about the case." The SgtMaj nodded his head, "I understand you being distant, and hesitant to talk. I think you'll find out here shortly, this whole thing is over. But do me a favor, for other Marines. Can you get me the right contacts if this happens again? I can steer them in the right direction. I have seen this happen before, not just here but other Commands. You are the first one I have seen that will remain in the Marine Corps. So, if you like, and when you are comfortable, I would like to offer help to others who find themselves in your situation. I also know several other Sergeant Majors, who would put that information to good use. Now, I need to let the Colonel know you are here."

Entering the room, Noah saw the Colonel sitting at his desk, looking down at some paperwork. Off to his left was the Major who was assigned to be the investigating officer. Noah positioned himself front and center of the Colonel's desk and reported in. The Colonel looked up briefly and gave him a once over before he was quickly put at ease. Once the Colonel began to speak, he never looked directly at Noah again.

Looking at the paper on his desk he picked it up. "Gunny I think you know why we have called you in here today. It is my good news to tell you that the investigation into your personal life has been brought to a halt. The Major here tells me, as I read it here in this final report, so I get it right. No evidence of homosexual activity, nor evidence to believe he has propensity to commit such acts. Now you know and I know, we never really got to the bottom of this. You got some hotshot lawyers and cried out and the higher ups listened. So now I am being directed to shut it all down, and apologize on behalf of the Marine Corps. So, with that being said, I'll set aside my personal beliefs and do what I'm told. On behalf of the United States Marine Corps, we are sorry for the violation of rights, you might feel you have incurred. Because we recognize these infractions have happened, the Marine Corps has directed me to offer you a couple solutions. One, you are welcome to stay here at MCAS Yuma. However, if you choose to do so, the Marine Corps will have to work with you to create what is considered a nonhostile environment. Which means removing or replacing personnel, myself included. We can't take back the professional damage you have incurred, when we so-called, "interrogated" your troops. So, they too would be subject to being replaced. Even so, I'm afraid no matter how much we sanitize, the gossip mill on such a small installation works rapidly. I believe the stigma would precede you wherever you might go. Of course, with these types of allegations it can be expected. So, the other alternative, you choose to go to another installation of your choice. Now rest assured I am not saying you have to go. The Marine Corps considers you the victim here, and those around you are the ones to be relieved. I can't tell you what to do, but surely you could see the benefits if you decided to go to another command and make a fresh start."

Noah looked at him directly and with a cold face. "The Marine Corps didn't have my welfare or concern when it started all of this. However, I can see the benefits of both options. As for reputation, and humiliation, that will never be repaired. The Marine Corps is small, my occupational field is smaller, and word has already traveled fast. You're right, Sir. The stigma will precede me, not just here at Yuma, but no matter where I go. However, I have no good memories here at Yuma. I think personalities, and a toxic environment, would only end badly if I stay. I think a fresh start would be best for myself and all parties involved."

The Colonel looked away, biting his tongue, …ignoring what Noah had to say. Standing in front of this guy watching his actions, Noah realized there was something more personal going on. This guy was not sincere in his apology, nor humbled. When Noah spoke, he tried his best to stay within the lines of respect and not appear to gloat. However, he wanted it known he was not a push over, nor afraid of this guy. This guy might be Noah's superior officer, but by no means was he a superior human being! It was obvious he was avoiding eye contact. He wasn't upset that he had to apologize. He couldn't look at Noah out of fear. Fear, because Noah could see him for what he really was. He wasn't a leader. He was a bigoted middle-aged man, with no courage, who, left to his own devices, chose to use his entrusted authority, to practice prejudice and hate. He was the bully, and all it took was one person to stand up to make everyone see. Noah accepted orders to Miramar, California. It was a good fit. If nothing else, it would suffice for the next few years until he hit the twenty mark and could retire.

The transfer was effective immediately. By the end of the week Noah would be on his way to Miramar. As he made his last rounds, finishing his checkout process on Yuma, he had one last stop he wanted to make, now that he had his orders in hand. Noah pulled up in front of the squadron admin office. Inside he knocked on the Sgt. Major's door. "Come in," he heard from inside. Noah walked in carrying a stack of business cards. "Good afternoon, Sergeant Major, I was just stopping by to say farewell!" Sergeant Major stood and shook his hand. "Well, I'm sorry things couldn't have gone better with you while here. But I know you're glad to be going. I really do hope your next duty station works out better for you!" Noah smiled, "Thank you Sergeant Major, I appreciate that, I really do. I also wanted to stop by to give you these cards. They are little cheat cards, with the contact info of the legal network I used. It explains what to do if you are accused of being a homosexual. You asked if I could pass on the information, well there it is."

The Sergeant Major took a look at them and set them on his desk. He told Noah to come in and closed the door behind him. "There is something I've been meaning to tell you but was waiting for the right time. My son is gay, and I am very proud of him. He has often wanted to join the Marines; you know follow in his father's footsteps. I have advised him against it. His mother and I both have known for some time. Well, in the middle of all this going on with you, without telling us, he surprised us and joined the Marines. He will be graduating in a few short weeks. When all this was going on, I couldn't help but think of him. My own son being put through what you have had to deal with. You are a Gunny and a seasoned Marine, but he, …he is just a boy. So, I have to say thank you for opening this old Sergeant Major's eyes. I worry about him, along with his mother. I'll be attending his graduation as a proud father, but I'll make sure he keeps one of those cards right there on him at all times." Noah was in tears with how candid and open the Sergeant

Major was being. He had been an ally the whole time, but out of fear, was still having to remain silent.

Chapter 46

I'm still here

Seeing Yuma in the rearview mirror couldn't happen quick enough. The move to San Diego was a welcomed one. He had plenty of friends in the area and establishing himself again would be easy. He would be working at Combat Camera, with the wing. Checking in, he was reviewed, and welcomed by his Commanding Officer, Captain Stern. He let Noah know he was aware of the misfortunes that had taken place at Yuma and told him he was glad to have him on board. If he did his job, there would be no problems. Reviewing his records, the captain noted Noah had not completed the Advanced Course, and immediately wanted to get him scheduled. By going, he would be highly qualified for the next promotion cycle. Noah felt welcomed, and more importantly, the captain made him feel like he had a future to gain in the Marine Corps.

Sure enough, within a year, Noah received word he would be attending the Advanced Staff Noncommissioned Officer Course at Camp Pendleton. The course was a six-week course refreshing and teaching military subjects, for the advanced enlisted ranks of the Marine Corps. The purpose was to better assist the Commander and the unit mission at a company level. Noah was familiar with most of the material, but it added to and reinforced what knowledge he had already attained. In the final week, it was mostly testing, inspections, and close outs. It was final inspection morning, and Noah arrived at the barracks early to get a head start. The light had just came on in the barracks as Noah walked up the stairs. He arrived at his cubicle, opened his wall locker, and began working on his uniform. The Marines were all hustling and bustling around getting things ready when a distraction on the TV caught their attention. All paused as one of the guys turned up the volume. The news reported, "An airplane has flown into one of the towers of the World Trade

Center." Some of the Marines speculated, it was just a small commuter plane, others paid it no mind and continued on. Everyone came to a halt again when came the news of a second plane. Before long, word was given for everyone to report to the classroom. Noah, along with all the other students, sat anxiously, while being informed the base was in shut down. No one would be allowed to go home. The inspection would continue as planned. The decision, on being recalled to their units, would still need to be made. If so, it was the last week and they would still graduate.

Arriving back to Miramar, word had been given to start preparing for a contingency of conflict. Plans were not definite, but the quotes had come in. The captain approached Noah and gave him the responsibility of choosing what Marines would be going to Iraq, and Afghanistan, along with getting their cameras and equipment ready. Some of the decisions were made easy by those volunteering. Others, however, were hard, knowing it would be someone's husband, father, son, or daughter. Worse yet, sending those he felt were not responsible enough, or ready for combat. If something happened, he would carry with him the thought that he was the one who chose to put them in harm's way. He himself wanted to volunteer, but the quota was for someone junior his rank. Out of all the decisions he had to make throughout his career, he felt this one was the most difficult. Regardless, when the time came, the Marines deployed. Noah joined their spouses and families at 3:30 am on the flight line to see them off and prayed each one would make it back safely.

Amongst all the turmoil, Noah had forgotten he was up for promotion. The day after they left, the captain came and handed Noah a message. It was the promotion roster. Noah, reviewing it carefully, came across his name, he had been selected to the rank of Master Sergeant. He was a bit perplexed. He had been concerned about the investigation, and all the difficulties, and troubles he had faced. Not knowing if it would follow him the rest of his career, he had wondered if he would ever see a promotion again. This was welcomed, and good news! Wow, he could hardly believe it. Master Sergeant, or as some called it, Top. He still had to wait to pin it on but being selected was "AMAZING!"

****

November had come and Noah decided to go home for Thanksgiving. When Noah learned of Jedd not having any plans, he insisted he come back to Indiana with him. It was the Wednesday before Thanksgiving when they arrived. First stopping at Lois's house, the hub of all activity. She always had family and friends stopping by. Add in her own kids, and her husband's family, it was sure to be bustling for the holiday. Noah sat at the table in amusement watching the interaction that was taking place in the room. Earl, her husband, was a bit of a comedian, and pretty much had no filter. Noah watched Jedd as he sat observing all that was taking place. Lois curiously entertained him, by asking about his family, and all they did for the holidays. Jedd spoke, "Oh, my family? ...it's small. Dad has been gone for years. My mother is the only one left, and she is off traveling this year. My brother is married and spending the holiday with his wife's family." Lois smiled, "Well, we're glad you came back to visit! We are a big family, and crazy, you can see or hear anything, so don't be scared." Lois, turned to Noah, "Have you told him about Gertie yet?" Noah laughed, "No, I figure there is no way of telling anyone about her. I'll just let him enjoy the experience." Jedd chuckled. The phone rang, Lois looked at it. "Speaking of, I bet that's her. She's Miss Nosey. She's probably seen your car out front, she lives just across the street, so I lay money she wants to know who's here." Lois answered, "Hello, ...What? ...No, that is a friend of Earl's car out front, our brother is not here." Noah laughed in the background, along with Jedd as Lois continued, "Have you got your turkeys out of the freezer yet? Ok, that's good Gertie, they need to be out and thawing. Ok, good, once they are thawed out, they'll be ready to cook. ...Ok, is that Aunt Biffy I hear in the background? ...Ask her, she knows what she's doing, she can help. Nollie says to tell you he'll be over later. I know, we were just messing with you, …and don't call me bitch!" As Lois hung up the phone, "I swear, that girl worries me sometimes." Lois looked at Jedd. "She's our older sister, but she is a little special if you know what I mean. That's why she lives right across the street. She can live on her own, but sometimes she needs a little help. We look out for her. She can be a little lazy, so I have to keep on her about things."

The conversation with Lois had dwindled down. Noah yawned and stood up. "I think, we're going to go to Gertie's and get that knocked out of the way. Besides, Aunt Biffy is over there, I would like to see her before she takes off." Lois laughed, "Oh, you'll be fine, she is there for the night. She is doing all her cooking over there. So, she isn't home alone. I think she practically lives over there." Lois grabbed her coat, "Come on, I'll walk over with you! I'm going to check Ms. Daisy out and see how her cooking is coming along." The three headed out. On the walk over, Noah and Lois prepared Jedd for what he was about to experience. Gertie was not a good housekeeper, and things tended to be a bit uncouth. "Gertie doesn't drive," Lois explained, "So, I take her everywhere she needs to go. That's why I call her Ms. Daisy, like in the movie, and yes, she can be very bossy!"

Noah looked at Jedd and smiled. Jedd was grinning and chuckling listening to Lois rattle. He could tell Jedd was enjoying himself, knowing he had never been around such a large family. Since it was just Jedd and his brother; he never had the experience of dealing with sisters. The three arrived at the door and opened it. Lois looked at Jedd, "Here we go."

Lois walked in first, and there was clutter, and clothes on the living room chairs, as they made their way to the kitchen. Lois started in, "Gertie, why is that living room a mess? My God, Nollie has brought his friend here all the way from California. He doesn't want to see your dirty undies. You need to get this place cleaned up." Gertie in defense, "They're not dirty, I just pulled them out of the dryer, Lois. I just haven't got around to folding them." Aunt

Biffy chimed in, "Gertie, quit your lying! I've been here since this morning, and they were there when I came in." Gertie ignored them and came around the table, "You better give your big See-ster a hug! God, I've missed you!" Noah gave her a hug, and then she introduced herself, to Jedd, "Hi, I'm Gertie, I'm his big sister. You wouldn't know it though. Him and Lois think they are the boss of me!" Gertie looked at Noah, "Oh, he's purdeeeee"!" Noah laughed, "Alright Gertie …."

The group gathered around the table and visited for a while, catching up on family gossip, and going over plans for the next few days. There was going to be an extended get together for Aunts, Uncles, and Cousins, and then Gabbi was going to be hosting the immediate family gathering this year, at her house. Jedd had stepped away for a minute to go to the restroom, when he caught Noah's attention across the living room. He was motioning for Noah to come.

Noah quietly got up and went into the living room. Jedd looked at him, "Come on man you got to see this?" Noah followed him into the restroom, where there were two turkeys floating in the dirty bathtub. The turkeys were out of there wrappers and floating around. Noah looked at the tub. It was utterly and completely disgusting. There was a scum ring around it, along with pubic hairs floating along with the turkeys. Dirty, mildewy wash cloths and towels, sitting on its edge. Soiled underwear lay on the floor, and the trash can was overflowing. Noah was embarrassed. "Oh my God! … what the fuck is she thinking? And she is going to be serving those for Thanksgiving tomorrow." Noah took off out of the bathroom, and back to the kitchen. "Gertie, what the hell are you thinking? What are you doing with those turkeys in the tub in there?" Gertie looked at him, "Lois told me to put them in the tub to thaw, so they won't take up the kitchen sink!" Lois looked at him, "That's normal, we do it all the time. Why?" Noah looked at Lois, "Go in there and take a look." Lois got up and went to the bathroom, knowing immediately what Noah was talking about. Noah spoke out. "Now, would you want to eat those turkeys, knowing they were soaking in a tub where Gertie, and everyone else washed their ass?" Lois chuckled. "I told her to put them in here. I didn't tell her to take them out of the wrapper, and I didn't realize I had to tell her to make sure it was cleaned." Jedd watched in amazement, Lois grinned, "Well, I told you be prepared for anything!" The three chuckled, while Noah tried to make the best of it, "Well, there is nothing we can do about it now. Maybe the heat will kill any germs. But still though, …we just won't eat turkey at tomorrow's aunt's and uncle's gathering." Noah looked at Jedd, "We'll just wait to eat at Gabbi's…"

The next day Noah and Jedd stopped briefly to say hello to his father, Claudia, and all his distant relatives at the aunt's and uncle's gathering. The two sat at Beck's table. Only having drinks, Claudia noticed. "Noah, you boys best get up there and grab something to eat before it's all gone." Noah cleared his throat, "No, I think we're good! We'll be eating at Gabbi's later, you know the Marine Corps, and the uniforms, we got to watch what we eat." Beck chimed in, "We'll be heading out there later, but I am starved, I can't wait!" Jedd looked at Noah and turned away suppressing his laugh.

Gabbi lived out in the country. This time of year, the fields had all been plowed for the oncoming winter. The land was frosted, desolate, and barren. The large white barn and outbuildings gave back drop to the nestled Bedford ranch style home. The chimney smoke rising, was a warm welcoming to Noah and Jedd as they arrived.

Hopping out, their breath could be seen as they made their way to the front door. Gabbi was standing in the doorway ready to greet them. "Hurry up, you better get in here, it's cold out there!" The two hustled in blowing on their hands. Once in, their coats off and warm, Gabbi toured them around her home. While she commented on all the work her and her husband had been doing to the place, Jedd noticed a picture of Rodney hanging on the wall. "That's Rod!" Gabbi looked at him surprised, "Yes, that's my son, you know him?" Jedd smiled, "Yeah, he used to be over at Noah's all the time." Gabbi continued, "Oh yes he and that daughter of mine, they were both in the Marine Corps. They followed in their Uncle Nollie's footsteps. Rod's up in Seattle now. My daughter got out, but she married a Marine, and they, along with my grand brats, are stationed up in North Carolina." Gabbi heard a timer go off in the kitchen. "Oh, hold up, let me get out there and get that. Otherwise, we'll be having burnt turkey." Noah and Jedd followed her into the kitchen. Noah watched her pull the turkey from the oven. "You didn't soak that in the bathtub, did you?" Gabbi looked at him like he was crazy. "What? …what do you mean soak it in the tub?" Noah and Jedd laughed, before they explained the story to her. She laughed, "That's your crazy relatives, …Huh, …No, I did not soak it in the bathtub, my god, she's silly!"

The house began to fill, Noah and Jedd sat in the living room chatting, as other family and guests arrived. Birdy sitting in the kitchen, hollered out, "Dads here, someone needs to go out and help him in." Noah and Jedd went out and walked him up to the house. Claudia was ranting about something as she walked frantic ahead of them. Claudia came into the kitchen. "I swear, I don't know what I'm going to do with him! You can't take him anywhere!" Gabbi pulled out the chair for Beck to sit down in, when Claudia hollered, "Stop, he's peed all over himself! He'll ruin your furniture, he'll just have to stand, until we get his pee-pad changed." Claudia's comments were embarrassing and belittled Beck. Gabbi noticed and became agitated, "That's my father, he can sit anywhere he likes. I don't give a shit!" Claudia grabbed her purse "Well, don't say I didn't warn you!" and moved on into the living room. Gabbi looked at Beck. "I swear, the older she gets, the more hateful she becomes. Sometimes, I'd like to bust her right in the face! Why she feels like she has to embarrass you, I don't know!" Beck spoke up, "Don't let her get to you!" Gabbi looked at him. "You're my dad, you can sit anywhere you like! You don't have anything to be ashamed of, she's silly! She isn't smart enough to know when to keep her mouth shut. There are some things that are just a part of life, you don't need to tell the world about them!"

****

Captain Stern, called Noah front and center. Once there, the reading of the promotion warrant began. "To all who shall see these present greetings..." Noah was holding back his emotions and held his head proudly, thinking of all the humiliation he had undergone to get here. He wasn't gloating but was respecting the moment, knowing how fragile things were under "Don't Ask, Don't Tell." Regardless of how far he had come since the days of being a private, he was still just as vulnerable, as the day he arrived at recruit training. All he had attained and worked for could be taken away in a moment's notice, if the Marines found out he was gay.

When they finished reading the warrant, Captain Stern called for Mr. Barlow to come forward to pin the Master Sergeant chevron on to his son's collar. Beck, on his walker, left it behind and hobbled up to meet the captain and the two pinned the chevrons on Noah. Beck had not made it to Noah's recruit graduation, but at least he was able to make it to what might be Noah's last promotion. Beck was proud, he had never before been a part of a major Marine Corps formation. He was put at the center of attention. The Captain put everyone at rest, he thanked Beck, "It's not often we get to have a family member other than maybe a wife or husband here to pin a stripe on. So, it's especially nice Mr. Barlow, as a father to have you here." He turned to Noah, "Let me be the first to call you, Master Sergeant, and tell you congratulations!" The room applauded. "Unfortunately, as much as I'm glad to see you get promoted, I know we will be saying goodbye, being it also comes with a new duty station. It's just up the street, at MCRD, so I hope you stop by and see us every so often. Once again congratulations Master Sergeant Barlow!"

Afterword's, some of the guests in attendance, stopped to congratulate Noah and thank Beck for his attendance, as well as, Claudia, and his sisters Birdy, and Beulah. They were there mainly to assist Beck in getting around. Since 9/11, the airports could be difficult and Claudia had refused to come, without having help in supporting Beck's needs. The Colonel stopped by to congratulate

Noah, meet Beck and the rest of the family, and offered them front row seats to the Marine Corps Silent Drill team and Drum and Bugle Corps performance, which happened to be occurring that very day. Noah accepted his offer. Before leaving, Noah showed them around the studio and gave them a chance to see firsthand what he did for a living.

On the way out, the ladies went to the restroom and Noah and Beck waited outside. As they stood and waited, Beck turned to him, "I still see that little boy in you. I know you're a man, but I still remember you telling me you wanted to be a Combat Photojournalist when you were just a kid." Beck chuckled, as he grabbed a wad of chewing tobacco and put it in his mouth, "Hell, I didn't even know what it was. I know, I usually say, your mom would be proud of you, and I'm sure she would, but I want you to know I'm proud of you. You went after your dream!" They made it to the parade deck. As they sat and watched, Noah could tell his dad felt like royalty. Never had someone rolled out the red carpet for him. He was proud, and more importantly, he was proud of Noah. Not the Marine Corps investigation, not Claudia, or being gay, not any of it could take that away. His Dad had been paying attention all these years.

****

The tall canary palm trees accented the yellow stucco and red terra cotta tiled roof buildings of the Marine Corps Recruit Depot. Noah had finished his checking-in process and was now ready to fulfill his responsibility as the new Combat Visual Information Chief of the Marine Corps Recruit Depot and Western Recruiting Region. It was surreal being back here. The very building, he worked in was the same building he entered into the first night of recruit training. Then, it was the barber shop and receiving center for recruits. They built the new receiving center some years ago, and the current building was converted into the Combat Visual Information Center. Never in his mind did he think he would ever work in the building, and definitely not when he entered it for the first time. The ghosts the building held were immeasurable.

Master Sergeant Barlow was in his office getting things organized when Gunny Johnson came in asking if he had a moment. Noah agreed, and Gunny closed the door behind him and took a seat. Gunny began to speak, "I'm not sure how to approach this, so I guess I'll just start. I was talking to the OIC, Mr. Lassiter, and we were discussing your medical situation. I just want you to know I talked and agreed, I can continue to run the place, and you can be kind of a figure head. You know, take it easy and stuff, you know, because of your medical condition." Noah sat quietly. His mind was doing everything to keep from exploding and blasting this guy through the wall. "So, you and Mr. Lassiter talked, and you two made the decision?" Noah shook his head; Gunny had no idea what was coming next when Noah cut loose. "Who in the fuck do you think you are? Don't you have some big balls! First of all, Gunny, last time I checked, I believe a Master Sergeant is higher than a Gunny. I don't believe you will be telling me what to do. Furthermore, how, or why you seem to think you know something about my health, is beyond me. Unless you have been snooping into my medical record. Which if you have, by the way is illegal. So, what you think you know, is beyond me. Oh, if it were true, whatever it is you think is wrong with me, I'm glad you and Mr. Lassiter have decided to take my personal medical issues into your concern. But let me make something clear. Whatever it is, you can just delete it out of your mind. I am a Master Sergeant in the Marine Corps. Last time I checked, it wasn't your signature, or for that matter, Mr. Lassiter's, on the warrant. Someone way higher than you seems to think I'm capable of doing this job, and as long as I'm here and on active duty, I plan on doing it! I'M STILL HERE! Furthermore, if you feel compelled to talk to Mr. Lassiter, I'll save you the trouble, because as soon as you leave, I plan on doing it myself. Also, I think the command might need to hear the two of yours concern. And maybe they would like to know how you came across such privileged information."

Once Gunny was out of the office, Noah made a beeline to Mr. Lassiter's office. Knocking on the door, he went in. Mr. Lassiter sat at his computer. Noah briefed him on the entire conversation, and schooled him on the Marine Corps, and DOD policy in regard to his medical situation. Mr. Lassiter became concerned. "The Colonel isn't the one who told me, I was told by Captain Stern. When I found out you were inbound, I called him wanting to know about you, and it came up in our conversation." Noah was agitated. Why was this allowed to happen. People who had no reason to know were being informed about his medical situation. Noah continued to speak, "Although, you might have found out, Sir. It was not Captain Stern's information to share. It really is not any of your concern. The Colonel is the only one who is required to know. The policy, intentionally, does not require OIC's to know, for the possibility of retaliation. It is also a privacy matter. I thank you for the placed concern on my health. Just so you know, I take one pill a day. Other than a routine checkup, every six months, there is really nothing for you to worry about. If this is going to be an issue, then let me know now. I'll be glad to speak to the Colonel about the situation." Mr. Lassiter was nervous, "It was unintentional, and, by no means did I mean any harm. You're right, I should have not shared it with anyone, especially not Gunny." Noah left the office.

This was beginning to have the same stink of Yuma, and he wasn't going to sit by and allow it to happen. He was no longer naive in believing people had good intentions. If they didn't like him, fuck'em! He was not going to take a back seat and let it play out. Time to nip it in the butt now! Noah put a call into Battalion Colonel's office. When he was checking in, she let him know she had an open-door policy with dealing with the subject of HIV, and if he ever encountered any resistance, let her know.

The Colonel took Noah's call. "Good afternoon, Ma'am, this is Master Sergeant Barlow. Thank you for taking my call." After briefing her, the Colonel sat quietly on the phone before speaking. "Top, I am so sorry this is happening to you. I can assure you no one from the Battalion has spoken to Mr. Lassiter, or anyone. I take this issue and your privacy very seriously! I plan to rectify the situation and have Mr. Lassiter and Gunny Johnson pay me a visit. Maybe he can explain to me his bad judgement in bringing Gunny Johnson, one of your juniors, in on this conversation. Although I can't stop what has already been said, I can demand professionalism from all who might have been told. I will not accept any form of retaliation on you. You are a valued addition to the Battalion, and a much-welcomed part of the team." When Noah hung up the phone, he was still not comfortable. Could he trust the Colonel? Maybe it was just his past experience, and he was being paranoid, but it was time to start documenting and writing everything down.

Chapter 47

When two worlds divide

Claudia finished getting Beck situated, closed the car door, and came around and hopped into the driver seat. It was early in the morning and the sun was just peeking over the treetops in the distance. "I thought you might like this as a surprise, us being able to go off to the riverboat." She reached over and patted his hand that lay on the console between them. The river boat was in southern Indiana on the Ohio river and was about a three-hour drive. As the two roamed over the back country roads, they sat and reminisced about all the good times they had spent together. All the many trips they had taken, and of course the one-time Beck had hit the jackpot for $14,000 at the very river boat they were going to. Before they knew it, they were walking up the ramp to board the Riverboat Casino. Beck, on his walker, hobbled along, and Claudia, walking eagerly in front of him. "Come on now Beck, I can hear those slot machines calling!"

****

It had now been almost a year since Noah's transfer to MCRD. Turns out Gunny Johnson, after getting over Noah's vocal blast, fell in line like all good Marines, and he and Noah were getting along. Over a beer, they had even joked about the entire incident. Gunny Johnson claiming Noah was nothing like what he had expected. They had just finished running PT and Noah stopped at the front entrance of the grinder. "The run was a kicker…,"as he leaned over panting, out of breath. Gunny Johnson walked by and slapped Noah on the back, "All in a days' work, right?" Noah hobbled up, "I'm getting too old for this shit! I don't know how much longer I can keep this up for…" Gunny Johnson laughed, as the two continued to walk, cooling down. "Have you done the Martial arts training, yet?" Noah frowned, "You got to be kidding me. What grown man, at the age of forty, would just say, ok I'm going to just fall down? That ain't right! Who the hell do they have making this shit up?" Gunny Johnson chuckled, and chimed in, "I thought I broke a rib, or two from that shit." Noah shook his head, "I think the instructor went a little easy on me, but being a Master Sergeant, you know everyone else was checking me out to make sure I was doing it. I don't care how bad it hurt; I wasn't going to let it show. I earned that belt!" The two arrived at the cars. Gunny turned "You headed back in or are you done for the day?" Noah looked at his clock, "No, I'm out of here, anything that needs to be done can wait until tomorrow." Gunny walked on, "I've got to get a few things outta my office, I'll see you in the AM Top."

Noah drove with the windows down, letting the breeze cool him. Once close to home, he stopped at the local store to pick up a drink. While standing in line, he realized he was still in the Marine Corps PT uniform. "Oh shit! Hope no one walks in that might know…" Here he was 23 years in, and a Master Sergeant still worried about getting his ass chewed for not being in the proper attire. "Oh well, integrity is doing what was right even when no one's looking."

****

It was late afternoon when Beck and Claudia decided to call it quits. He was looking at her and smiled, "Have I told you how pretty you are lately!" She blushed, "Beck, come on now, let's get you home." Beck chuckled, and put out his hand, holding a thousand dollars. "Here, put that in your purse, I wouldn't want it to get lost." Claudia took it and started counting, "Oh my goodness, where did you get that?" He chuckled, "I won it while you were downstairs on the other slots." She giggled and tucked it in her purse and the two headed home. Occasionally, Beck would doze off, but the two sat and held hands in silence. Beck had known he had not fully appreciated what he had in Claudia. At times, he even felt guilty thinking he never really lived up to what she expected from him. However, it was a day like this he was content. Especially when at one point Claudia patted his hand and said, "You're a good husband!"

It was just starting to turn dark, when the two made it back home. Upon arriving, Claudia pulled under the carport and hopped out. "I'll be back in a minute; you wait here while I get the other walker and the door unlocked." Claudia disappeared into the house, while Beck sat patiently waiting. He was in good thoughts. Today had been a good day for the two of them. The driver side door flung open, and Claudia threw keys at Beck, shouting, "I'm done, have a good life!" Beck was stunned. "What the hell, what's a matter with you? Have you lost your mind?" He turned to see her hurry across the lawn, hop in the Cadillac and take off. Was this some kind of joke? He sat in the car quiet, wondering if she was coming back. Finally, after several minutes, he managed to get himself out of the car. He hobbled around to the house door, which was still left open from Claudia's dramatic, yet hustled, exit. He stood on the step just outside the door and looked into an empty house. Baffled, everything had been taken. There was no furniture, nothing, all was gone. All he had worked for his entire life, gone.

****

Noah sat in the car contemplating going in. A combination of letting go of work and going into the loneliness of an empty house led to his procrastination. For some reason the phone call he had received from his stepmother, the week prior was not sitting well with him. She was sending papers for his review and signature regarding the guardianship of his father. She was saying, it wasn't necessary right at this moment, his dad's stability and health were in decline. He would eventually need to go into a nursing home. Noah couldn't understand why she might need his signature, or even permission, and most importantly, did his dad even know or have a say in it. There was one statement she glossed over which he thought out of place. "You know I did what you asked and sent a letter to that senator." What was she trying to get at? Was her action transactional, or quid pro quo? Surely, she wouldn't be naive to think he wouldn't be concerned about his father. Besides, she would need his other sibling's involvement as well. So, nothing of the like would happen, getting all of them to agree on anything would prove impossible. Over the weekend he would reach out to some of the others to get their take on it.

He set his belongings down as he juggled to unlock the door. As he entered the apartment, the phone was ringing causing him to do a panicked rush. He gave up and let the phone machine answer. The phone rang and rang but the machine wasn't answering. Noah looked on to realize it was full. He had twenty-two messages. Grabbing his mobile phone, he realized it was off. Turning it on, it was the same, full of messages. Something was going on. He listened to his messages, most were his sister Lois, and few from his sister Birdy, finally, the last two were from his father. "Noah, you get this, call home." Noah had no idea what to make of it, something bad must have happened, to be getting these many calls.

Noah grabbed his cell phone and started pacing the floor between the kitchen and living room. He thought it best to call his father first, one ring, two ring, three… The phone picked up, it was his sister Lois, "Hello." Noah thought he had dialed the wrong number, "Hey it's Nollie, I thought I was calling Dad's. Sorry, I must have hit your number instead. …Do you know what's going on back there, my phone has been blowing up?" Lois did not hesitate. "You called Dad's, I'm out here, give me a second," Noah could hear her speaking in the background, "Dad, here, it's your son, do you want to speak?" Noah could hear her give him the phone. "Nollie is that you?" Noah baited with anticipation, "Hey! What's going on?" Noah could hear his father sobbing on the other end "She's gone, …(sob) … She's gone, …. she's left me, …(sob)." Noah was confused. "Dad what do you mean she's gone? Who's gone, what are you trying to say?" Noah could barely make out what he was saying, from the sobbing, "Claudia, she's gone, she left me. ………All I know we went to the river boat today, and she kept telling me how much she loved me."

Noah sat in astonishment. His sister Lois picked up the phone, "Nollie, you still there?" Noah replied, "Yeah, yeah, … I'm still here. Lois is this all true?" She calmly spoke, "Yeah, give me one second while I step outside." Noah could hear his other sister Birdy in the background talking to his father. Lois continued, "Yeah, so I was at home, and I see dad's name come across the caller I.D., … I'm like what? … Dad hardly ever calls me. So, I picked up the phone. He was crying. I got him calmed down, and he told me she had left and taken everything. I was the only number he could get on his phone. I called the others. We are here now."

Noah didn't know what to make of the whole thing, "What was she thinking? I mean come on; she couldn't have let one of us know?" Lois continued, "Oh Nollie, she has taken everything! And the way she did it, she is a heartless bitch. She had this planned the whole time. They were at the river boat all day, dad said she was all Lovie Dovie, knowing her kids were back here moving all her things out of the house. There is not even a bed for him to sleep in. We just didn't think someone would leave after 30 years. I mean who does that? We all got a letter from her attorney wanting us to sign over rights to guardianship to him, and none of us would sign it. Birdy came out to talk to her about it, and she said it was just in case. I think, she was planning on putting him in a home, and thought we all would go along with it. When we wouldn't, she took off."

Noah's thinking became clear, the phone call he had with her the week prior. "Oh my God Lois, she had contacted me, about a week ago telling me to expect papers. I questioned her on it. I asked if she had spoken to Birdy, or any of the other kids. She got really defensive, and started rattling, telling me, it didn't matter whether we signed it or not, she could put him in a home on her own. I just don't get why now? … Dad ain't a saint, and by no means is he easy to live with. But come on, he's almost on his death bed, you spend thirty years, why take off now." Lois who had been sitting quiet spoke out, "Because she is a cold-hearted bitch!" Birdy was in the background eavesdropping, "That's to say the least! …Here, let me talk to him."

Birdy's voice came over the phone. "Are you coming home? This place is a complete disaster! Nollie, there are papers strung everywhere. He doesn't even know what meds he is supposed to be taking. She did all that for him." Noah was anxious, "I'll need to check with my boss, …I'm pretty sure I can, …I mean, it's a family emergency for Pete's sake." Birdy continued, "You got to Nollie! There is so much that needs to be done. I did not know things had gotten this bad out here, with him, or the house. The plumbing under the house is broken and the dogs in the kennels have not been taken care of. Why he is still running a kennel I do not know. This should have been stopped years ago. Let me tell you what happened tonight. I go out there with him, to feed. I'm walking along and there is a dead dog in one of them. So, I tell him, …Dad, that dog is dead, how long has he been there? ...He looked at me and said, 'I don't know, feed him anyway.'" Noah sat in shock as she continued. "So, I think what we are going to have to do, ... He can't stay here by himself. I'm going to find a place over by me, where I can look after him. The dogs are gone as of tomorrow. It's not fair to them. There is so much to figure out, I need you back here to help!" Noah sat quietly allowing Birdy to get it all out, before speaking. "Sis, it might take me a week or so to get things sorted out on my end, but I promise I'll be there."

****

The flight home was filled with all kinds of emotions. This was something he never expected, for that matter, no one expected. They, all his sibling, had gotten used to Claudia handling everything. Even if they tried to help or find out what was going on, they were pushed out. It was always hush, hush. No one questioned it, after all, she was his wife, and they had been married for so long. Beck was definitely not ready for a nursing home, but he was at a point he needed help with day-to-day activities. He was resisting every bit of help. He was set on blaming them for his break from Claudia. If he could only talk to her, she would listen and come back to him. Mad at her, he was taking his anger out on them.

Noah thought about the phone call he had with Birdy. Birdy explained Claudia had gotten a restraining order on Beck. They had a preliminary hearing in front of the divorce judge. He directed there be no contact between Beck and Claudia. She stated in court, "He was wanting some peaches one day, and I told him no. The doctors say you can't because of his sugar. He became violent and threatened me. He told me if he could shoot me and get by with it, he would. Then he would like to cut my head off and throw it in the side ditch." The judge asked Beck if it were true, he said he didn't remember. The judge, not totally oblivious to the situation, commented. "Well Mrs. Barlow, I'm sure he probably said some things out of anger, at times we all have. As for how much of a threat Mr. Barlow is, …I don't know, …he can barely walk. Unless you got to within a few feet of him, I don't think there is too much to worry about. However, I will ask that all guns be confiscated from the house, and grant your request there be a restraining order put in place."

Birdy had continued to explain to Noah, they took the keys from Beck, after he drove into the front of a convenience store. He apparently thought he had put it in reverse and actually had it in drive. He hit the gas a little too heavy, and before he knew what had happened, the lady at the cash register was running for the back door seeing the truck come barreling through the store.

Noah could tell immediately the house was in disarray when pulling into the driveway. Repairs on the barn had not been taken care of. The yard was overgrown, and things were shuffled and lay where they were last used. He parked and opened the door to get out when his father appeared in the doorway, holding onto his walker. It was all the two could do to hold back the tears. Noah didn't want to cry in front of his father. Now was the time to be strong, for him! No words were spoken as the two embraced in a hug. Beck's hold was tight, long, and unusual. Noah could sense the fear and vulnerability through his embrace. Beck was not a touchy, feely type of guy. If he hugged, he meant it.

Letting go, Beck hobbled back into the house, where Birdy and Gabbi stood waiting. Both gave hugs, before they all sat down to review the current situation. It had now been almost two weeks since the breakup, and the assessment of the damage, was much clearer. Simply put, the house was in a bad state of disrepair, and Beck would have to move. Beck and Birdy had already met with an attorney and were now following his guidance. Birdy had found a small house just a few doors down from her, and he would be looked after and safe there. Unbeknownst to Beck, Claudia had taken a mortgage out for full equity on the home and had overextended his credit with cards, and personal loans. All were in Beck's name alone; he was in financial ruin. The attorney asked to see all the bills, and Beck was instructed to not use any cards he might still have. The homestead needed to be made ready for sale, or worse it may have to be given back to the bank. Birdy was furious when she spoke. "This bitch knew what she was doing. She had this planned out years ago!" Beck still heartbroken, "I trusted her…" Gabbi patted him on the back, "I know Dad, we all did!" Birdy had already contacted the local animal shelter. They, along with the help of a few friends, managed for the dogs to find new homes.

The next week was spent mainly trying to get things settled and organized. Separating what Beck would need at the new house, and what to do with everything else that would be left. All was going well, other than a minor set-back from Beck who was still being resistant. A police officer called and made an appointment to show up to confiscate his rifles. When he arrived, Birdy had been there along with Beulah, they had removed the rifles and signed an affidavit stating there were none on the premises. On the way out, Beck decided to plead with the officer about Birdy and Beulah's behavior. "Officer, I want you to arrest these two. They're keeping me hostage. They shouldn't be in charge of me! They're both drunks, and that one can't wait to get home to her boyfriend and suck his dick. The other one right there is married and cheating on her husband, she's a whore and always looking for her next victim." The police officer was taken aback by what Beck was saying.

"Mister Barlow these two ladies are your daughters." Beck stood in defiance and ducked his head. "Yes, Officer I know, and I am ashamed to say it." The officer shook his head, and chuckled. "Mr. Barlow I'm sure things will be ok. You listen to these two ladies you hear? I don't want to have to come back out here because you don't want to mind. They're looking out for you" He nodded his head, "Ladies, …Mr. Barlow, you all have a nice day."

Needed repairs to the house were a priority on the list, some of which Noah could do. So, they headed to the hardware store. After getting the needed items, Birdy, Beck and Noah loaded the counter. The attendant rang them up. "That will be two hundred and eighty dollars." Beck went to pay, and didn't have the cash, so he grabbed a credit card. Birdy noticed. "Dad you can't pay with that. I thought you gave me all your cards to put away." Beck became agitated, "Why can't I use it … it's mine! If I want to pay with it, I will!" Birdy took the card from him and pulled her own card from her purse and paid. Beck was furious and started fussing. "I'm not a little kid, goddammit, and don't treat me like one! … you're just as bad as her!" Noah spoke up, noticing they were making a scene and holding the line up. "Dad, we got this, just go on, we can talk about it later." Beck, on an electric scooter, pulled off in a hurry. He almost hit a lady when he rushed out the door full speed.

Walking out to the car pushing the cart, Birdy intentionally walked slowly. "I don't know how much more I can take of this. Look at him. He is just sitting there storming. He is mad but wants to blame us for what she has done. Nollie, I'm trying my best. It breaks my heart, but I can't be his punching bag. Does he not see we're all trying to figure this out?" Noah remained silent as she spoke, but grew more and more angry about the whole mess they found themselves in. He had now witnessed the way his father had been treating everyone firsthand. The blow ups at home, the embarrassment with the police officer, and now here at the store. Something had to give. He understood the lack of trust with Beulah because their relationship was already strained from things in the past. But Birdy, he had always trusted her, why was he treating her like this now? She was the one person he still had in his corner.

Noah finished getting Beck in the car while Birdy loaded all the items into the trunk. As Noah maneuvered trying to get him buckled in. Beck continued to speak, "Who in the hell does she think she is? It's my damn card, if I want to use it, I will! Who in the hell is she to tell me what I can and can't do! Piss on her, I'm tired of her shit, she ain't my boss." Noah tried to ignore him but wanted him to understand where she was coming from. "Dad, I think she is just following orders from the attorney. He doesn't want you using those cards. If you do, you will become responsible for them in the divorce." Beck smirked, "What do I care, that bitch has already taken everything from me anyways!" Noah, along with Birdy, hopped in and soon they were on their way.

The air could be cut with a knife, the tension was so thick. Everyone remained silent. Noah had just made the final turn on to the country road where his father's home was. Birdy in the back, spoke up. "Nollie, I won't be able to stay long. Tim will be off soon, and I promised I would be home tonight, to make dinner. I haven't slept in my own bed in over a week. I need to do laundry, and get more clothes, but I'll be back tomorrow." The comment was enough to set Beck off one more time. "Why is it you always gotta get home to him? Why you always gotta get back there to him? Can't he do shit on his own?" Noah was taken aback at the way he lashed out. Noah noticed Birdy was almost in tears in the rear-view mirror. She started to speak, "Dad, I just need…." She was interrupted by Beck hollering, "I'm so sick of this! What about me, who's going to cook my dinner? Ain't nobody cares about me! Claudia was right, …I should have listened to her all along! You kids don't care about anything but yourselves!" That clenched it for Noah. He was furious.

Noah slammed on the brakes and pulled over the car. He got out and slammed the door. "I'm so fucking tired of this shit…" ranting as he stormed around to the passenger side door. He flung it open. "Get out! Get out now or I swear I will pull you out! I've had enough of this. I'm so fucking sick of your shit." Birdy pleaded from the back, "Nollie don't, …he…" Noah spoke over her. "You never think of anybody or anyone except yourself! Hell, no wonder Claudia left you, you never loved her, you told me so! She was convenient, a paycheck, she finally figured you out and she left! As long as she had a good job, you were willing to put us and everyone else on hold. So, you listen here buddy, if it weren't for that lady right there in that back seat, you wouldn't have anything or anybody rooting for you right now. We're your last straw! Do you think we wanted to land here? Do you think we wanted to be the ones in charge of you? Hell no! You've always pushed us out, …pushed us away, always to put other women's kids first, … in front of us. So, when we finally accepted that we were never going to be anything in your life, after so many times of being rejected, Boom! Oh, but isn't it ironic, look who's here now! Here we sit, and you're old and all alone in your life, … and now we're the ones expected to come in and take care of you! After all these years, US…, we're the ones supposed to take care of you, but who took care of us! So, you just sit there and think about that! There is no rulebook here! Her leaving, it doesn't just affect you it affects all of us! You're mad, …we're mad, … we're all mad! But at the same time, you have a whole lot of responsibility in this yourself! You need to do some soul searching, because this one ain't on us! We all have our own lives. I'm tired of keeping my mouth shut, we all are! I came here all the way across the country, giving up vacation time to help you. Birdy is giving up time away from her husband and her family! You are not alone, but you will be if you can't get it together!"

Beck sat in the car looking down the road as Noah closed the door and came around and climbed back into the driver seat. As he headed down the road, Beck looked out the passenger side window stunned and quiet before he spoke. "I didn't know you all felt that way! I'm sorry!" Noah looked into the rearview mirror seeing Birdy wipe tears from her eyes with a tissue. Enough had been said for one day.

Looking up at the cracks in the plastered ceiling that needed repaired, Noah lay in bed. He remembered when the addition to the house was built, and the reason for it. Dad had married Claudia and to accommodate the combined families, the old farmhouse had to be increased in size. That was now thirty years ago. It had served its purpose. All the life it had seen reflected on its walls, both joy and sorrow, of so many Christmases, Thanksgivings, and Birthdays. The memories of teenagers growing into adults, …their children, …and even now, some great grandchildren. Leaving to go back to San Diego today, would be the last time he would step foot in this house. It just didn't seem right. His thoughts were interrupted when he heard voices coming from outside the door. As much as he wanted to hold on to time, the day had already begun.

Emerging from the room, his brother-in-law Walt was helping his father get ready for church. Beck, just out of the shower, was standing in the middle of the living room in his tighty-whities, Walt was bent down trying to get him to step into his trousers. "Beck, if you don't hurry up, we're going to be late. You got to work with me now old timer!" Gabbi was hollering from the kitchen, "Does he have his trousers on yet? Is it ok to come out?" Noah thought the whole thing was comical. Once the trousers were on, Beck noticed Noah. "You going to make it to church with us this morning? I've been telling everyone about you. My preacher, he was in the Marines. He used to volunteer with me when I would dress up as Santa Clause for Toys-4-Tots. He always asks when that Marine son of mine is going to come home?" Noah listened to his father talk as he fixed his coffee from the kitchen. Gabbi joined him. "You going to go to church this morning? Walt is going to take him. I'm expecting a phone call from that son of mine all the way over in Germany." Noah took a sip of coffee and sat down at the kitchen table. Gabbi asked "When's the last time you talked to him?" Noah though for a moment, "It's been a couple of months. He called once he got over there." Gabbi continued, "You might want to give him a call. He is going to Iraq at the end of the month." Those words caused Noah to pause, "What? Rod is headed to Iraq. When did you find this out?"

Walt's voice could be heard from the living room "Beck, if you don't help me with these shoes, you ain't never going to get to church? Now push!" Gabbi stood up and walked to the kitchen door, "Dad you gotta work with Walt, the ladies at the church are going to make all over you when he gets done with you!"

Gabbi returned chuckling, "No, I spoke to Rod last Sunday, he calls me every weekend. I'm scared, I don't like it! It's not safe over there!" Noah sipping his coffee, "Rod's a warrior. He knows what he signed up for!" Gabbi sat calmly, almost in a daze, "I know, I asked him if he was worried, and he told me he wasn't going to back out now!"

Walt appeared, "We're ready, man it's like trying to dress a three-year-old with him. He focuses on everything else in sight, except the task at hand." Beck hobbled up next to him, "Noah you going to make it, I would love to have you!" Noah sat calmly. The words and thoughts from the day before were still haunting the air. He could tell his dad was trying to get back into his good graces. "Dad, I don't think so. Besides I'm not even close to being ready." Beck spoke up, "Well maybe you can make it after Sunday school. Service doesn't start until eleven." Noah was pretty adamant, "Dad, I really don't think so, please don't make me say anything more?" Walt gave Gabbi a kiss, "Love you honey, Beck lets go." Gabbi was taking off at the same time and gave Noah a hug goodbye. "What time you fly out?" Noah responded "Not until 5pm. Oh, you still have some time then. Alright, I'm heading out, you have a safe flight home. I'll tell Rod you love him, and you make sure to give him a call! God forbid anything ever happens, but you never know! Love yah!"

Once Gabbi left, Noah sat in the kitchen with the entire house to himself. It was totally quiet. How strange this whole thing was turning out to be. Finishing his coffee, he headed to his room to pack, when a picture sitting on the dining room buffet caught his attention. It was of his father, dressed up as Santa Claus, with a lady dressed as a helper, along with a Marine in dress blues. It must have been taken at a Toys-4-Tots fund drive. How did he miss this picture before? Did his dad just place it out there, or had it been there all along? It brought a smile to his face. He spoke out loud, "You Old Kook!"

Beck sat on the church pew. The choir was just finishing the opening song when the doors in back of the sanctuary opened and Noah walked down the center aisle. Normally he would try not to make a scene, but he was wearing his dress blues, there was no getting around it. If there is a Marine in dress blues in the room, everyone will notice. Noah figured he might as well exploit it. Besides his dad would love it. Noah looked around until he saw his father from behind, and marched forward. Without Beck knowing, he made it to his pew. Beck turned to see Noah standing there, he mustered up the strength to do an awkward stand. Beck had tears in his eyes. Noah shuffled down the pew past a few of the congregants. Arriving at his father, he grasped Beck by the shoulder, and patted it with one hand. Walt, from the other side, reached out and shook Noah's hand. The three took their seats just as the sermon began. Beck noticed the preacher looking on, smiling. Beck mouthed to him and pointed to Noah. "That's my son."

Chapter 48

Give our heroes a welcome home!

The May gray, and June gloom, had given way to a beautiful sunny July day in San Diego. The dust from the shock of the breakup between Beck and Claudia was settling in. Although things were not perfect, slowly, the needed adjustments were being made. Noah was on his lunch break headed out the back gate of MCRD to go meet Jedd for lunch. He was in town for the week, and they were taking a moment to catch up. The news on the radio, was giving updates about the current situation in Iraq. One of the stories had gotten his attention of a blast that had taken place in Iraq. A suicide bomber broke through a gate and ran into a barracks of sleeping US military personnel. It had killed five, and many others were injured. Rodney was now in country, and any news of a bombing quickly grabbed his attention.

Arriving at B Street Deli's, he was in luck. Doris Day parking, right in front, how lucky! He could see Jedd sitting at one of the tables on the sidewalk. This would be their first visit in some time. Jedd, recently returned from a six-month stint in Iraq, and Noah was glad he had made it home. He was in uniform, so Noah opted to skip the hug for a handshake. Jedd had already ordered, "I ordered for the two of us, I figure you're a creature of habit, Pastrami on Rye with everything, right?" Noah jokingly commented, "Aah man, a Pastrami and Rye, …am I that predictable?" Jedd quickly tried to correct it, "No, no it's ok man, …if you don't want it, I can get it to go, and you can order something else?" Noah laughed, "Jedd, it's ok. I'm just messing with you! You're right, I would have ordered it myself!" The outdoor TV, hung on the wall, and was playing CNN, with the report of the same story he had just heard on the radio of the bombing. Jedd shook his head. "Why is everyone so obsessed with this shit! I just wish this shit would be over! Every fucking where I go, it's Iraq. I mean I get it, support the troops and all, but come on, …You really want to support the troops, then get us the fuck out of there!" Noah was shocked at Jedd's stance, "Why Jedd, there might be hope for you after all! I always thought you were a little more on the conservative side. You know, Republican. Be careful, you almost sound like a Democrat. Keep that up, I'll have you going to a rally with me before too long!" Jedd rolled his eyes, "Don't get your hopes up, I'm not either. I did my time over there; I can say that. I hated it, we were not wanted, and we knew it. We didn't fit in. I couldn't wait to get home. The last thing I want is to see it over here! I'm beginning to wonder if I fit in here anymore?" "Noah was at a loss for words, what could he say? He knew Jedd was jaded these days. He had already been to Iraq twice. He just wanted some peace at home, and a moment to get his mind off it! "Jedd I can ask them to turn it off, or we can go elsewhere if you like? I know the owner, he's a cool guy. I'm sure he won't mind" Jedd in disregard, "No, I'm cool. But really, …now I sound like an asshole." Noah chuckled, "Buddy what do you mean now?" Jedd laughed, "I know right? But you get what I'm saying. The last thing I want to be is difficult!"

Noah smiled, as their sandwiches were being placed in front of him. "Thank you! You guys are the best. Can you believe how quick they are here; I swear I love this place." Noah was trying to lighten up the conversation. Jedd was no longer the sweet young man he had first met. He was now a jaded combat veteran of both Desert Shield, and Desert Storm, along with Operation Iraqi Freedom with two tours under his belt. Noah could only listen when he complained. After all, Jedd had a right to. He was beginning to wonder if Jedd may need some professional help.

Noah spoke cautiously, "Jedd, don't take this the wrong way, but have you ever thought about maybe speaking to someone, you know a counselor, or someone?" Jedd smirked, "Come on man, don't do that to me. I'm alright, let me deal with it in my own way. Don't make it like I'm going to go all harry carry, or some shit! I just have zero tolerance for bullshit anymore. So, change of topic. You know Tom and I broke up. He's on ship somewhere in the

Mediterranean right now, …haven't seen each other in more than a year. Between his deployments, and mine, we just kept passing the key to the neighbor, until the other one could pick it up when they get home. He sent me a Dear John letter, saying he couldn't deal with the long-distance stuff anymore. I don't blame him; he beat me to the point. Besides, I don't have to worry about being a home wrecker anymore, if he decided to come out to his wife and kids. Maybe in another universe it might have worked." Jedd broke out in song when he realized he might be getting a bit mushy. "Somewhere, somehow, we'll find a new way of living!" Noah laughed, "Aah, Barbra, I was beginning to wonder if I was going to have to pull your gay card. There you go buddy, let it go."

Jedd started laughing, "You know Noah, I've missed you!" Jedd continued, "So enough about me! …wait, wait, what about, … more about me?" Noah laughed. "Right, aha, I got your number…" Jedd chuckled, "No seriously, what about you? How are you?" Noah shook his head, and smirked, he wasn't one to share a whole lot. "Ah, I don't know, where do I begin. Let's see, you already knew I got promoted, let's see, what else, …oh, oh, maaan, I know what to tell you. My dad and stepmother broke up!" Jedd was surprised. "Say whaaaat? Claudia the evil twin of the wicked witch of the west?" Noah continued, "Yeah I know right? So, I had to go back to Indy for a while, to help my sisters get dad situated. It still is fresh, so we are kind of feeling our way around that one right now. Don't know what is going to happen with that. Let's see, my nephew is in Iraq, you remember Rod?" Jedd chuckled, "Of course I do, that little shit, …the runner! How the hell is he? I didn't realize he was still in." Noah shook his head. "Yeah, well, not in the Marines. He jumped ship and joined the Army. That is who he is with now." Jedd laughed, "Well you tell your little bro, that Jedd said hello! And keep an eye out over there, …you can't trust'm!" Noah nodded, "I sure will."

The two finished their sandwiches. Noah continued, "So how long you in town for?" Jedd laughed, "It depends…" Noah was a bit confused, "What do you mean?" Jedd laughed, "It depends how long you let me stay at your apartment!" Noah laughed, "Jedd, Jedd, Jedd, …Stay as long as you like! You know where I keep the extra key. You butt! Listen, I got to get going. I'll see you later, yes?" Jedd smiled, "Absolutely!" Noah looked at his watch, threw a twenty down. "Can you take care of that for me Buddy!" and headed to the car.

While unlocking his car, he heard a commotion back at the deli. He turned to see Jedd standing up and yelling in the face of the waiter. "What the hell is that about?" Noah quickly took off, back to Jedd, only hearing the end of Jedd's rant. "Next time don't just take for granted that I'm done. How about asking me, before you swipe up everything!" Jedd continued, but Noah really didn't care what it was about. Jedd was making a scene. The owner had come from inside, and the other customers were staring. Jedd was making a spectacle of himself. Noah reacted, putting his hand on Jedd's shoulder. "Jedd, Jedd, it's me, listen, listen, calm down man, come on now. It's no big deal, we got this, it was a simple mistake" Noah pushed back with his other hand looking at the owner, letting him know he had it under control. Jedd was angry and shouted at Noah, "What, … you think you're coming in and going to save the day? Fuck this, like I can't make up my own mind or some shit! What, are you siding with them?" Noah tried to remain calm. "Jedd, just stop!" Jedd stood staring at Noah like he wasn't going to budge. Finally, he threw his hands in the air, "Fuck it!" and walked away.

Noah watched as Jedd walked down the street. By the time Noah settled up with the owner and apologized, Jedd had disappeared. Hopping in the car, Noah drove by looking for him, but he was gone.

Heading home, he couldn't help but think about how the whole thing had played out. It was like it came from out of nowhere. They were just joking and had a good lunch. Now running late, he arrived at his apartment, with just enough time to change over into his PT gear and make it back for the Battalion run. At the gate to MCRD, he sat in traffic, watching as the security guards waved each car in, one by one, doing a thorough check on each vehicle. It was normal procedure, since 9/11. Anytime there was a bombing on U.S. personnel, the base went into heightened security. With this last bombing taking place in Iraq, the heightened security was no surprise for Noah. Once through the gate, Noah was enroute when the phone rang. He looked at the caller I.D. It was his sister Birdy. He let it ring and go to voicemail and continued on his way. Whatever was happening with Dad would have to wait. As he pulled into park, the phone started ringing again. Another look, and it was Birdy once again. He might as well go ahead and answer, it might be something important. If not, at least he could let her know he would call her later.

Iraqi National Guard Headquarters, Samarra 2004

It was 10am and Rod had just finished coming off watch. Glad to be back inside the barracks and out of the 120-degree heat. It didn't take him long to unload, settle in, and hit the rack. It had been a long watch, and the crew was tired and all they wanted to do was rest. It was their break, halfway through a 48-hour watch. A couple of hours of sleep and they would be right back at it. Johnson, one of the guys in Rod's platoon, was unable to sleep, and decided to take the opportunity for some personnel hygiene. He grabbed his shaving gear and headed out. Using a mirror off one of the Humvees, he began to shave. About halfway through, for some reason he noticed an Iraqi police truck at the entrance. It was nothing unusual, but at the same time he felt a chill. The Iraqi guard pulled open the concertina wire gate. Johnson heard the tires screech, taking off. Once clear, the driver hit the gas pedal, full speed ahead straight for the barracks 50 meters away, where the rest of the platoon was sleeping. Johnson turned to run, toward the barracks hollering…. The truck slammed into the barracks. It was too late. Johnson fell to his knees. The truck did not explode instantly. It looked just like a wreck, right before the explosion. Boom! Johnson was knocked to the ground. When the dust cleared, the smoke and smell of explosives filled the air. Complete chaos was under way. Johnson picked himself up, other than a ringing in his ear, and some scrapes he was ok. The Lt had ordered a MEDIVAC and recover, and rescue was under way. Johnson started going after those he could help. One by one, rushing into the rubble and returning with another soldier. Soon there were others joining him in the effort. Johnson heard a voice from under the rubble, and went to it to start digging, it was Sergeant Dalton. Rod, who was barely alive, was down below. He was crying out for help. Johnson continued to dig, tossing rocks off the pile. Johnson continued hollering to let him know they were working, and help was on the way. Johnson worked frantically in hopes of saving him. His hope turned to fear after a few minutes, when Rod's cries for help stopped.

Blotch, Indiana

Noah sat on the church pew, listening to Rod's friend Capt. Campbell finishing his eulogy to Rod. Noah was nervous, hoping he would be able to make Rod proud, and do him justice in remembering him. Capt. Campbell finished, and Noah took to the podium. Looking out to the crowd, he tried not to focus on his sister Gabbi, or any of the rest of the family, knowing his emotions would overwhelm him, and he would not be able to deliver his message. Choked up, he paused, getting the first word out was the hardest. The tension and mood in the air was somber and thick. Rod was such an upbeat, and fun guy! Full of energy, this would not be how he would have wanted to be remembered. Noah felt he needed to break the atmosphere. He set the prepared speech aside on the podium and began. "This may be a little unorthodox, but Rod is a hero! He is our hero. Now I know when hero's come home from war, they deserve a standing ovation. So, I'm going to ask you to stand with me and give our hero a warm Indiana welcome home!" The crowd stood and cheered and applauded in Rod's honor. Noah smiled, with tears in his eyes, as he looked upon the flag draped coffin that lay center of the alter. Breaking the tension, Noah was able to continue Rod's eulogy.

Jedd and Noah cruised along just a few cars back from the hearse in the funeral procession. Passing those along the side of the road who had come to pay their last respects as the hearse with Rod in it passed by. Upon entering the cemetery, the police and firefighters stood guard, and rendered a salute under the giant American flag. The flag hung from one of the fire engines ladders and waved gently in the breeze. The city really took out all stops in paying respects to their fallen hero Rod.

After final taps and the presenting of the colors to Rod's wife, and his mother Gabbi, the crowd began to disperse. Jedd, Noah, Adrian, and Brock all stood at the grave. All four were Marines looking upon the grave of their fallen comrade. Jedd broke the silence. "You know, it's ironic. They always say the Marines are the first to die. This happened while Rod was in the Army." Noah made no comment, but looked at Adrian and Brock briefly, before the four moved on.

****

Beck sat in the back of the police car, while the officer waited for Jimmy, Beulah's son, to get help on the phone. The officer was a friend of the family, and knew Beck, along with other family members. Jimmy tried calling his mother Beulah, Birdy, Noah, any number he had on his phone, until he could find someone to pick up. He knew they all were probably already at Rod's funeral. Jimmy was the one tasked with getting Beck ready and driving him to the service. When Jimmy arrived, Beck was already sitting in the back of the police car. The police officer was driving by, when he noticed Beck trying to walk down the street on his walker with a rifle. When he stopped him, the officer ran a check and realized Beck was in violation of a court order and wasn't supposed to have a gun. When he asked Beck where he was headed off to in such a hurry on his walker, he couldn't answer and seemed confused. The officer didn't want to take him in, but if a family member couldn't vouch for him, he was either going to take him to the hospital to the mental ward, or he would have to take him to jail. Jimmy finally contacted Aunt Biffy and she spoke to the officer on the phone. They had no idea where Beck had got the gun. The police officer let her speak to her brother Beck. She asked what he was thinking, and what he wanted done. Beck admitted, he had found out where Claudia was, and he was going to bring her home. Beck was furious about the whole thing, and mad he was stopped by the police. Biffy was exasperated, "Beck, oh no!" she cried. When the policeman got back on the phone, Biffy asked he be taken to the hospital, under the current situation. He wasn't in his right mind. The police informed her if he did, Beck would be on twenty-four-hour lock down with no visitors, until the next day.

Chapter 49

The meek shall inherit the earth…

The next few weeks at work were filled with people paying their respects, and condolences as they learned it was Noah's nephew who was killed in harm's way. Noah did his best to try and focus on the task at hand. He even increased his workout routine. There was something missing now. He was having trouble finding his motivation. Noah had started attending a church regularly again. MCC, San Diego, (Metropolitan Community Church) was an open and affirming church and was accepting of gays. With all the turmoil taking place in the family, he was searching for answers, trying to lean into something bigger. Tonight, was Friday night, and the church was having a bonfire on the beach, for their fall celebration. Noah had invited Jedd down to go with him; some uplifting people might do him some good. Just that day, Noah had received word, he would probably be in the promotion zone, and it got him thinking. He wanted someone to talk to, someone he could trust, and he knew he could rely on Jedd.

It was dark on the beach, and the fire's light bounced off the faces of those gathered around it with a mystic glow. The heat felt good on the chilly evening. Several were seated watching the flames, and embers, rise and fall. An occasional chuckle, and someone walking into the circle, or away kept things interesting. One of the musicians had brought his guitar and strummed softly. Noah and Jedd sat in their beach chairs, joining in on this ancient ritual. Noah had already told Jedd about his possible promotion. "You know, if I do get selected, they will expect me to transfer to Quantico." Jedd listening, "Why Quantico, why not stay out here? You're a west coast guy?" Noah agreed, "That's what I was thinking. But you know how it goes. The needs of the Marine Corps. At this rank, you're expected to fall in line. I would be working as the Senior enlisted lead in the field." Jedd looking into the fire, "It sounds good, what's the issue?" Noah continued, "Yeah, that's the catch. See the guy I would be working for, Major Bolton, is a religious fanatic. We were troops together back in the day. He went Warrant Officer, and later LDO. We didn't see eye to eye back then, and we sure to hell don't see eye to eye now. Let's just say he likes to wear his religion on his sleeve. I think he lets it get in his way of thinking or leading? It would only be a matter of time before we bump heads, and he would start questioning and butting into my personal life."

Jedd threw a piece of kindling he had been playing with onto the fire. "Yeah, that's not good man, but you shouldn't allow him to stop you. That's not like you!" Noah smirked, "You're right, but there is so much more to it than that! I mean, I got so much shit going through my mind right now. I don't know what the fuck I'm doing!" Jedd leaned forward and grabbed Noah's knee, "Lighten up man, you got this! I've known you to go through some serious shit before, you can hang!"

Noah wanted to talk, he wanted to be heard. "That's just it Jedd, Fuck that! I'm tired of all the bullshit. I'm tired of all the lying and cover up. I'm tired of hiding who I am. I'm ready to let the rainbow flag fly! Jedd, just listen to me, I got to get this out, I need someone as a sounding board, just listen to me?" Jedd, looked at him, "I'm here, preach brother, like you said, …let that flag fly." Noah began, "My dad's situation isn't getting any better. I've considered a move back to Indiana." Jedd interrupted, "Well I can't blame you there, you know I had to do that once already in my life. I get it." Noah continued, "As much as I hate to admit it, I actually missed being able to call home, even though it would be Claudia most of the time, hearing her voice meant stability. I didn't always agree with her, but her being there was affirming you know, …things were in good hands." Jedd made a weird face in surprise, "Wow, I didn't see that one coming. Look, she was a big part of your life. What she did hurt. She didn't just up an take off from your dad, it might have been directed at him, but man she abandoned the hole family. It's natural to want to know the other side of the story."

Noah relied on Jedd, and he was making sense. "Not now, but one day, if she would allow, I would like to sit down with her. I mean in many ways; I feel like I owe her a debt of gratitude." Jedd patted him on the knee again. "It's ironic, when all else fails, and slips away, it brings forward what, and who, is most important in life." Noah nodded and glazed into the fire. "Well, here is what I really wanted to get at… the effect of Rod's death on the entire family. Watching it unfold, this family has paid enough. I never want to put them through that again. If I stay in, with these non-stop wars, it's possible, and I don't want to be a part of that." Jedd agreed, looking on into the fire, "I mean, you never know, but you're right there! If you don't get on the wagon, you're not going anywhere!" Noah shook his head, "What the hell does that mean?" Jedd chuckled and gave him a look, "What? … I'm just saying, if you're not in the Corps, you're not going to be going to a war front anytime soon, … right?" Noah smirked, "I guess." As he continued, "I've missed out on so many important parts of my family's lives. I've been gone for so long and missed out on so much. Hell, I got nieces and nephews, that were just babies when I left, some weren't even born, and now they're all grown up. But the thing that bothers me the most. After all these years, it doesn't matter what rank I've attained. How good I have done my job, one slip up and if it was found out that I was gay, my entire career would be over. I'd be sent packing! …Nothing, …not a pension, …not anything. At this stage in life, I've got too much to lose. I can't risk it anymore. I don't have anyone to fall back on. My support system, it's gone. If I get thrown out, I end up with nothing. It's time to collect my toys and go home. I gain nothing by sticking around. It's time to say goodbye and hang up the uniform."

Jedd sat quiet for a moment before speaking. "Are you looking for some one's approval? Only you have the answer. You know what you have to do, now do it." Noah chuckled as Jedd continued. "So, you get it all out? How long you been holding on to that speech?" Noah shook his head, before he started to laugh.

Jedd's comment was untimely, but it was exactly what Noah needed to hear. He was right, Noah already knew the answer.

Retirement Ceremony

Noah gave a once over to his Charlie uniform. He remembered the first time he was called a Marine on the grinder right outside his office. He was wearing the Charlie uniform. How appropriate, for it to be the last uniform he would wear. He stepped out of his office and was on his way.

The command museum was just a few buildings down, the arrangements were made, and all he had to do was show up. Upon arrival, he met with his guests, and mixed and mingled, before Gunny Johnson came to his side. "Master Sergeant it's time." Noah nodded and took his seat.

The ceremony began. All the thoughts, and memories started to flood in. It was happening, he was finally going to say goodbye! A sweet sorrow, this love-hate relationship he had with this organization called the United States Marine Corps, for the last twenty some odd years. It had been his life; it was embedded into the very fiber of who he was. Although the Marine Corps picked him up and polished him off, he was, in so many ways, still that little midwestern boy from Indiana. It was time for Noah to step up and the orders to be read. He walked front and center of Major Bead, who stood in front of the color guard. His old friend of many years, Major Bead was officiating the ceremony. She and Noah were, at one time, both Sergeants together as Combat Motion Picture Photographers. Noah asked if she would officiate, and she accepted. Noah stood as the letters and awards were read. Once finished, Major Bead made a few comments, and then the microphone was handed to him. It was time for Noah to make a speech. Starting out with the proper protocol of thanking the high-ranking officers, and dignitaries, and special guests, he turned to the Marines behind him. "I want to say thank you to each and every one of you. Above all else, you took an oath, and, for whatever reason, answered your country's call. Take your time and enjoy the journey, it may seem like it goes slow, but trust me, one day you will be where I'm standing. Once again, I thank each of you, for allowing this old Master Sergeant the privilege of serving with you. I can remember all the way back in recruit training, my drill instructor told me, 'Private Barlow you need to learn to speak up! The meek shall inherit the earth, but not in the Marine Corps. If you want to make it in the Marine Corps, you better find your voice and learn to speak out fast.' I wasn't sure at the time what he meant. So, I just sounded off louder! I can't tell you how many times that has come back to haunt me. Now, standing on this end of my journey, I now know what he meant. I was on the fence. I needed to decide who I was. I needed to make a choice, be decisive, and act. Or as we say in the Marine Corps, lead, follow, or get the hell out of the way. You need to keep moving. So, there are many times you will need to find your voice, and so many times you will lose it. If you want to survive, you'll need to find it again."

Noah turned to the guests. "They say normal people can do extraordinary things. In the Marines, extraordinary is a daily routine. I have been through more in my life than I could have ever dreamt. Both good, bad, and, in some cases, right out evil! For every mountain climbed, to every valley I have crossed, for every blister, lesson, or fall, I am grateful. That includes every friendship, and every enemy, and trust me I have made a few. All this has been the steppingstones that led me to where I am right now."

"I have been asked, what my plans will be now, what is the next chapter? Well, there are a few people that could not be here today, and I plan on paying them a visit. All those tasks that have been on delay, I will finally have the time to do them. But I don't believe I will ever do anything greater than becoming a Marine. It is embedded in my heart and tattooed in my soul! I'm not sure what the future holds. However, I know it will require faith for me to take some chances. I have found my voice, and I plan to use it. I thank you all for coming out here today to send me off. It is a sweet sorrow that I must say "Fair Winds and Following Seas! Semper Fi!"

Chapter 50

Thank you for remembering me

This was Noah's first trip to Little Rock, Arkansas, and he was still learning his way around. Pulling onto Ash Street, Noah went slowly, looking at the addresses. As he approached a small white craftsman style house, he could read the name Hall. This was it. He stopped and parked the car. Noah stepped out of the car, reached back to grab his cover. Putting it on, he checked out his reflection in the car window. The yellow and red chevrons filled the sleeve of his dress blue uniform. Sometimes it was hard to believe he was the one wearing all those stripes, but today was not about him. As he walked around the car, he looked up and down the street. The small house sat on the corner and had a front porch running the full width. As he looked closer, he could see through the screen door into the house. It was good news, because someone was home with the front door open. He took a second glance at the written address and compared it to the numbers on the mailbox. Hopefully this was the correct place. He tucked away the paper and straightened out his uniform and stepped off toward the door.

****

Late spring days in Blotch, Indiana were hit and miss. An occasional frost was rare, and, for most parts, all signs of summer were on the way with the foliage just beginning to sprout, and the fields showing the first signs of the year's new bounty. Today was exceptional as Birdy and Beck rode out of the Root Beer stand with the windows down, enjoying the warm sunny day. Beck had asked Birdy to drive by the old factory, just to reminisce about his days in the Union, and how he had negotiated to save jobs with his time spent in the UAW. Birdy smiled "No problem, but just remember I got an appointment to get you to." Beck was up in years now, and

Birdy knew these times were going to be far and few. As they drove by, he told her stories of different people and the adventures they had. "Alright Dad we have to get going or we'll be late." Beck sat quietly as she drove, before he noticed she wasn't headed to the doctor, "Where you headed, the doctor's office isn't out here?" Birdy smiled, "We're headed to a different one Dad, trust me, I got this, you just sit back." Beck sat quietly in his seat as she turned the corner and drove on. A little way down the street, he spoke again, "I use to know someone who lived on this street years ago."

****

As Noah approached the door, he could hear the television playing from inside, and whatever was cooking, sure did smell good and was making its way to the door. Noah rang the doorbell. "One second," came from deep in the house. Noah stood waiting patiently, but could see movement in the house, as a tall, graying older black woman came to the door. At first, she started to say "Can I help …" but stopped herself mid-sentence and stepped back from the door. "Haw…," She caught her breath and clasped her chest. "Oh, oh my…" The lady at the door was at a loss for words. Noah wasn't sure what to do, "Uh, I'm sorry Ma'am! …I didn't mean to startle you. It's just that I'm looking for the Hall residence, I hope this is the right place?" The woman, in silence, looked at him and pushed the door open as she stepped forward to come outside. Noah stepped back. She stood and looked at him for a moment almost as if she were in a trance. A tear fell down her face as she reached to Noah's hand and grasped it. "Child you got the right address." Noah started to introduce himself, before she interrupted, "I remember who you are, now you don't have to say another word. Thank you for remembering an old Marine's Mom."

****

Birdy drove up in front of the small brick ranch style home and stopped the car. Beck panicked, "What are you doing, you can't stop here…" Birdy got out of the car and walked around, grabbed his walker, and opened his door. "Come on, get out, …" He was half turned looking at her, "I can't, we just can't do this…" Birdy smiled with a chuckle, "Trust me we can, now you're getting out of that car or I'm pulling you out, and that isn't going to look good for either one of us." Beck turned, grabbed the edge of the car, and stood up. As he grabbed the walker, Birdy stepped out of the way.

In front of him, at the front door was La Mora, now an older woman. She still had her shoulder length black hair, and in Beck's mind she was just as beautiful as he had remembered. All else around the two had stopped, the only thing the two saw was each other. Beck slowly walked up the sidewalk not letting her out of his sight, mesmerized without saying a word, as if she was a magnet pulling him nearby. "La Mora is that you? …Is that really you?" La Mora came down from the step to his side, "Yes, you old fool, it's my house, who else would it be!" Beck stopped and held her by the hand, "Let me look at you…. You're just as beautiful as I remember." La Mora reached up with both hands and held his head as the two gazed, both with tears of joy running down." Beck spoke, "I never thought I would see you again, …La Mora I'm sorry." La Mora spoke, "Hush, no need for that now." They leaned on to each other with a gentle embrace.

As the two held each other, Birdy looked on, wiping the tears from her eyes. Not wanting to interrupt the two, she spoke softly. "Dad, I'll leave you two alone for a while, I know you have a lot of catching up. I'll be back in a bit to get you." Beck looked to La Mora, "So you already knew about this." La Mora reached down grabbing him by the arm. "I did, but it's that wonderful daughter of yours. She asked if I would see you. I had only one choice, to say yes." She smiled, "What about you, are you ok with it?" Beck smiled with glazed over eyes. "Am I ok with it, …. Huh, if you knew how many times, and how long I've dreamed of this happening, …I wouldn't want to be anywhere else in the world!" La Mora chuckled, "…Good, come on now, let's get you in the house."

****

Noah enjoyed his hour or so visit with Mrs. Hall. She gave him the directions to the graveyard. When he left, he hugged her, and as he was walking out, she spoke. "When I see you, it reminds me of how old Glenn would be, ... If he would not have passed away. Oh, ...I'm sorry, ...Please don't take it the wrong way, it's just I can't help but wonder how he might have aged, and how young he really was." Noah smiled, "No need to apologize." He tipped his hat, "It was nice seeing you Ma'am!" Noah turned to walk away. At the steps, from behind, he heard her say. "You know he is looking down from wherever he might be! Master Sergeant, isn't it?" Noah nodded his head, "Yes Ma'am." She smiled, "You did him proud!"

After leaving, Noah drove around looking at the area and seeing all the places Glenn had spoken of. His high school, church, local neighborhood, etc. He could imagine Glenn growing up here. But now it was time to find his way to the last location before going home. Mrs. Hall's directions led him right to the graveyard and Glenn's resting place. Noah had already prepared what he was going to do. As he approached the grave marker, Noah could read his full name and to his surprise, it was a veteran's tombstone. "Sergeant Glenn. A Hall." Noah knelt and paid his respects, touching the stone, before speaking, holding back the tears, "I didn't forget you Buddy..." After a few moments, he stood and took in the surroundings. Although it was not a veteran's cemetery, his grave was surrounded by other veterans. Noah assumed this must be the veterans' section. Noah came to attention and saluted the grave, "Goodbye old friend," placing a quarter on the headstone, he walked away.

****

Birdy pulled up in front of La Mora's house and shortly the two emerged from the door. As Beck struggled down the walk with his walker, La Mora walked beside him. Once almost to the car Beck stopped and turned to her. "Well, ...I guess this is it?" La Mora grabbed his hand, "I had a wonderful time Beck." Beck smiled, "That makes me happy, ...La Mora I'm so sorry if I ever did anything to hurt you. It's just that it was a different place, a different time." Beck patted her hand, "You know I really did love you, ... I just wish I had been stronger, a better man. You deserved that. I let too many other people get in our way. I let them rob me of a life of happiness. I should have stayed. I should have fought for you." La

Mora frowned a bit, "Don't you think I had a say in all this!" She looked on, "I know Beck. I was there. I lived through it too. You don't think I could have done more. Who knows what might have been had we been born twenty years later? We can't change what has happened. I really did love you; I still do. But look at us we are up in years. Neither one of us is going to up and jump and change our lives now. You got yours and I got mine, and other than an occasional visit, dinner, or date with maybe a peck on the cheek, that's all we are ever going to be." She paused and moved in close, grabbing Beck by both hands. "Beck you're a good man, I have had a good life. Sometimes it's best to remember, embrace and be thankful for what time we had!" Beck's eyes filled with sadness realizing what she was saying, but his heart was filled with joy just knowing he had got to tell her one more time how he felt. La Mora had a tear roll down her cheek as Beck spoke with a crack in his voice, "I don't want to go, but I know I have too." La Mora feathered her hand across his hair line, landing it on his cheek, before giving him a gentle kiss. "We'll be alright!"

Chapter 51

Go to the light...

Noah picked up the phone on the first ring. It was Birdy, "Nollie, it's time, you need to come home!" Noah knew exactly what she was talking about. "Oh, ok, I'm on my way."

Pulling up in front of the little white house, where his father now lived, it was evening. The gold glow of the late spring bounced in the air, as he stepped from the car into the humid and sweaty air. They didn't get this kind of humidity in southern California. His sister Gabbi was on the small front porch as he walked up the steps. She was talking on the phone and drinking a beer. Hearing the last of her conversation, "My brothers here, I'll let you go." She hung up. "You made it?" as she greeted him with a hug on the front steps. "You sure you're ready for this?" Noah wasn't sure of anything, "I don't think anyone can say they're ready for this..." Gabbi continued talking as she stepped out of the way. "Brace yourself, before you go in. He's right in there. The bedroom was too small, so his bed is in the living room. They had to place it out there, so it is easier for us, and hospice to be able to take care of him. He sleeps most of the time now. The nurse said it won't be long. All we can do is keep him comfortable." Noah was feeling a bit numb from the jet lag, and no sleep, tossing and turning in anticipation of coming home. Gabbi looked in through the front screen door, and came back to where Noah was standing, "Geeeeez, that girl won't give anyone a moment alone with him. She's getting on my nerves. She keeps hovering over him. (Gabbi mocked her in a whiney voice) 'Go to the light Grandpa, go to the light!' it just makes me want to bust her in the face!" Noah wanted to laugh, but under the circumstance thought best to hold out. "Who are you talking about?" Gabbi being agitated, "Halo, ...that daughter of Beulah's."

Noah opened the door and stepped in. In front of him lay his father with Halo holding his hand. "Go to the light Grandpa, Go to the light!" Noah, in his mind, was wondering what the hell she was thinking. His father was asleep as he approached the foot of the bed. He stood there for a moment watching him. He seemed at peace. He was barely making a sound. Noah couldn't help but remember how he normally snored, and loudly. Their father would fall asleep watching TV when they were kids. They would all laugh as he would ramp up in his lazy chair, before it got so loud, he would startle himself. But now, he could barely be heard. Halo paused her chant. "Grandpa, your son Nollie is here!"

Noah didn't know what to make of her. What was this role she was assuming? Was she his translator, his host, the welcoming committee? Whatever it was he wanted a moment with his father. "Halo, if you don't mind, can we have a moment to ourselves?" She smiled, "Grandpa, I'm going to go now, but I'll be back in a minute. Your son is here, and he wants to talk to you?" Noah smiled and thanked her as she walked away.

Stepping to the side of the bed, Noah spoke out. "Hey old timer! I think that's what we're calling it now?" Noah paused. He wasn't sure his father knew he was there. Was he completely unconscious? "Hey old man can you hear me?" Noah grabbed his hand, and Beck opened his eyes, "Is she gone?" his father asked. Noah looked at him, and let out a small laugh, but muzzled it not to draw attention. "You been awake this whole time!" Beck laughed, "Shush, I figured if I acted like I was asleep, she would go away, but she stayed, then she started doing her crazy chants!" Noah chuckled, "Well I'm glad you're awake." Beck struggled to speak, "I'm glad you made it son!" He gripped Noah's hand. "Look, without saying much. You know what to do. Everything has been taken care of, I'm counting on you! Don't let me down." Noah teared up. "You don't have to worry; we'll be fine here!" Beck relaxed his head, closed his eyes, and fell asleep holding Noah's hand.

Noah stood there when Birdy came and stood next to him. She put her arm around his shoulder. "I think he was holding out for you. Now you're here, I don't think it will be long."

Outside Noah sat with the rest of the family. Different ones were taking turns standing vigil beside Beck's bed. Distant relatives and friends provided food to the family in light of the situation. It had now been 24 hours since Noah's arrival, and Beck had not spoken to anyone since their conversation. Noah remembered Beck's words, "I'm counting on you, don't let me down." He knew exactly what he was talking about. A few months prior, Beck contacted him. He had created his Last Will and Testament, assigning Noah as the executor. Beck had told Noah of his last wishes, and Noah agreed he would see it through. The only problem was, he also told everyone else, which had created animosity and a rift between him and a few of his siblings. Mainly Beulah, who felt Noah should not be in charge of anything.

As the night went on, the siblings agreed on a plan. With so many family members standing by, the small house had become too crowded. Birdy opened her house up for extended family, and only the siblings would be staying to hold vigil. Those who stayed, tried to find a place to call their own, and catch sleep. Noah sat in the dining room, along with Jimmy, Beulah's son, and Herman her husband. The phone rang and it was Halo, wondering if she should return. Jimmy asked Noah, "Hey, its Halo, mom's asleep, she wants to know if it's alright for her to return?" Noah shrugged his shoulder, "How should I know? I'm not the gate keeper here. When we all talked earlier, we agreed, extended family would be down at Birdy's home. But it's up to your mom if she wants Halo here." Noah got up and went outside for a breath of fresh air.

Noah leaned on his father's truck and ducked his head. He was exhausted, but not able to sleep. Aunt Biffy was sitting on a lawn chair, and a few other relatives sat around a picnic table. Noah contemplated what was to be taking place over the next few days. He was on auto pilot at this point. The retirement from the Marine Corps, Rod's death, Claudia, and Beck's break up, and now his father at deaths door. Noah had already scanned over Beck's will. He knew what was inside of it. He brought it with him, and it was tucked away safely in his briefcase. Noah anticipated chaos once his father passed. If not immediately, definitely once the Will was read. Beck had intentionally cut Beulah from the will. A few years prior, he leant Beulah a large sum of money. When she wouldn't pay it back, he took her to court. When the Judge, a friend of Beck's deemed she was liable and had to pay it back, she threw a rant in court. In front of everyone she screamed, "I'll piss on your grave you old son of a bitch! You were never a father to me!" Beck's feelings were hurt, and because it was in front of his friend, he never forgave her. Over the last few months, she had tried to get back in his good graces, by helping out with his care. But he never told Noah he had changed the will. Noah had even asked him at one point if he was sure about Beulah. His words were, "Absolutely, she isn't nothing but a troublemaker, and doesn't care about anything but herself. Piss on my grave, I don't want her to have a dime!" Noah didn't agree with it, but Beck could be very stubborn. For whatever reason, the Will Noah had would be Beck's final. He crossed his arms on the top of the side bed of the truck and lay his head down.

Noah stumbled, almost falling asleep, leaning on the truck. Aunt Biffy noticed. "Nollie, why don't you come over here and sit down. It could be a long night." Noah looked at his watch, …it was now 11 pm. With a bam, and a screech, the back door flew open startling everyone. "Who the hell says my kids can't be here?" It caught everyone's attention. Beulah stood on the back porch, twitching like one of the bugs that gathered around the light behind her. She was oozing with anger and her glare was directed at Noah. Noah started to speak, "Beulah, that is not what I said…" Beulah interrupted, "That's not what Herman, or Jimmy told me. If I want my kids here, they will be here. You ain't the boss around here!" Noah looked at her, knowing whatever he was to say after would be disputed, why bother he thought. He turned away, only to here. "I'm so fucking sick of that faggot, he's a disgrace!" Noah heard it and turned, sarcastically, "Oh, that's an original, you should try something better, I wear that badge with honor! … you know like you wear Bitch!" Jimmy who was standing at the front of the truck came at Noah. "Don't you call my mom a bitch!" Noah seeing his fist coming, stepped back and he missed. Noah couldn't believe his own nephew would try and hit him. Jimmy stumbled, then got his footing only to try and hit Noah again. Noah realized this 20s something guy wasn't going to quit. Noah backed up when Jimmy took another swing, ducked, and Noah came back and knocked him to the ground, when out of nowhere, he was tackled by Herman, Beulah's husband. Before he knew what was happening, Aunt Biffy, and the entire family were in an all-out brawl. Beulah, still on the porch, started screaming, ran and grabbed the phone and called the police. Hearing the police might be coming, Herman, Beulah's husband took off, for fear, he might be arrested knowing he had outstanding warrants.

Finally, between Aunt Biffy, and the rest of the family, the fight was broken up. Birdy got Noah into the house, and tried to separate him from Beulah, who was following behind them ranting. Noah sat down in the living room. Beulah stood in the kitchen hollering insanities across the house. Gabbi stood in the doorway between the kitchen and dining room, blocking her from going any further. "It's all his fault!" she yelled. In the midst of all this, Noah looked to see his father still unconscious. Beulah had no respect for him, or anyone. Beck was right all along. It was as though he could hear his father saying, "See I told you so." Noah could almost hear his father laugh about the whole episode that had just happened.

When the police arrived, they took statements down, and Noah and Beulah sat in the living room, as the police spoke to different ones. Finally, one police officer who knew Gabbi personally asked her, "I can't leave here, and have to come back later. So, who is leaving?" Noah overheard, "Sir, I can leave if it will calm the situation down. I just want my father to go in peace." Gabbi looked at Noah, "Like hell you are. You came here all the way from California, you haven't done shit!" Gabbi turned to the Officer, "Officer, that's my brother, and his son. He hasn't done anything." Gabbi pointed to Beulah, "She is the one who caused all this trouble. Her, her husband, and her son." The officer started to speak to Beulah, "Ma'am, is that the case?" Beulah, who had been on her best behavior since the police's arrival, was a ticking time bomb. Hearing what Gabbi had just said, and the officer's question, she exploded. "You need to arrest him! I knew I would be the one who would get the blame. Officer, he is a disgrace, He ain't nothing but a goddamn faggot! He's a queer! …not only that, but he also has AIDS!" The officer was jolted, from the explosion in her personality. The rest sat and watched as she spiraled out of control. The officer spoke, "Ma'am calm down. I didn't say I was taking you in. I simply want…" Beulah interrupted him screaming at Noah, "You think this is funny, you make me sick. Dad was ashamed of you; you make me sick, you fucking faggot!" The Officer spoke. "I think we have heard enough here. I can tell who will be the one leaving." The officer moved forward and asked her to turn around. Beulah tried to resist, before long another police officer was in the room, and she was up against the wall, being handcuffed, while still screaming profanities. On the way out, she passed by Noah, "I hope you die of AIDS!"

Once Beulah was removed, the rest of the family calmed and focused their attention back on Beck. All were wide awake at this point. Beck lay in bed, his breathing shallowed, and his life was slowly fading from his body. It was about 2 a.m. when Gabbi called everyone to his bedside. Birdy put a Johnny Cash gospel CD on, since Beck was a fan. They watched as Beck slipped into another place, peacefully. The man they all struggled to gain his love. The man that joined them together, the man they all shared a common bond of calling Dad, was gone.

The next morning, the family gathered at the funeral home to make arrangements. When Noah arrived, Beulah was parked out front of the building, standing beside her car. Noah ignored her and went inside. Birdy arrived, and Beulah stopped her on her way in. "Am I allowed to come in, or am I going to be barred from the funeral as well?" Birdy shook her head and raised her hand waving Beulah off. "Don't start your shit this morning Beulah! I don't know." Birdy stopped and looked at her and lit a cigarette. "Can you keep your mouth shut and get along?" as she took a hit of her cigarette. Beulah started in. "I'm not the one, …that fag…" Birdy interrupted her. "I take it, that's a no! …You know what kind of bird don't fly, …you'll find out if you keep that up, …a jail bird dumb ass! I'm not in charge, that guy you keep calling that disgusting name is. If you want to be a part of this, then I would learn to keep my mouth shut for once!" Gabbi arrived and joined them. "Is everyone here already?" She lit a cigarette as Birdy answered her, "I don't know, I haven't been in there yet. I don't see Lois's car." Beulah spoke up. "Only the queer, I haven't seen anybody else." Gabbi gave her a frown, looked at Birdy, and rolled her eyes. Lois pulled in and the three joined her and headed in. When they entered, Noah was standing next to the office, waving for them to come over.

Gabbi under her breath. "You better not say a word Beulah, I swear I will bust you in the face this morning, and they will take me to jail!" Birdy, stepped in front of her. "That goes for me as well, if you so much as even say a word"

The family sat around a large circular table finishing the final arrangements. One by one the funeral director asked if there was any more questions. Beulah spoke up, wanting to know about a fingerprint necklace. The director said he had no problem, but being Noah was the one in charge, he told her, "You'll need to ask your brother?" That set Beulah off, "He ain't my brother!" Gabbi stood up, "What did I tell you!" Noah realized things were about to get out of control. "Gabbi it's alright!" Noah looked at Beulah, "As much as you and I would like to change it, the one thing we can never change is the fact I will always be your brother."

The funeral went peacefully. In typical Beulah fashion, she acted as though all those hateful words were never said. However, Noah never forgot. She even offered for him to go to dinner with her family. The same family where the son, and father had doubled up to physically beat Noah the night his father had died. Noah answered her sarcastically. "Why yes, I would love to be there…" as he walked away. His thoughts were, No, …just flat out No! His presence was never to be at their dining room table again!

The backbone of the family was gone. Dad was the common bond that kept them all united. Noah couldn't help but wonder if his father's acceptance of him being gay was what protected him, at least within the family. With him being gone, he didn't know if things would ever be the same. One ugly monster had already reared its head. Hopefully, there were no more hidden monsters waiting.

After the funeral, Noah returned to his father's house, away from everyone. He sat quietly remembering all that had taken place over the last few days. The phone rang, Noah answered, "Hello." He heard the familiar voice coming from the other end, it was Jedd. "Hey, how's it going?" Noah explained without going into great detail what had happened. Jedd was a great friend, and he needed that right now. Noah explained, "You know Jedd, no matter what, no matter how good, fair or decent of a human being we might be, there will always be someone, who can't see past us being gay. Like

Beulah, it is a go to… you know, when they can't find anything else, they grab the straight trophy, and hold it overhead claiming, "I'm straight, I'm straight!" No matter how much of a horrible human being they might be, they're like I'm still better than you, you're gay!"

Jedd's reassuring voice spoke on the other end, "Look, get out of your head. They don't define you! Pick yourself back up and just do what you always do. Hold your head high, stand your ground, and keep moving on! They can only control you if you give them the power, …SO DON'T!"

Chapter 52

I hope I served the ghost well!

Noah sat impatiently at the computer, while Cal read the last of the manuscript. Noah decided to check his emails and noticed "Joel Hammond's" name once again. This must be in response from the previous conversation. Noah was curious how things had been going with him. After all, it was Joel who caused Noah to take pause and rethink the whole "Don't Ask, Don't Tell" thing. Noah opened up the correspondence.

Master Sergeant Barlow,

Thank you so much for your sincerity! You bring a lot of interesting points that I would not have otherwise considered. I've always respected your opinion, and I appreciate your perspective on this subject. I keep reading what you wrote over and over and can't help but feel angry and upset! I quite honestly don't even know how to reply, but to say thank you, thank you for your service and conducting yourself honorably during your years of service, and during the time I worked for you. I look up to you for your leadership as a Marine Master Sergeant and your courage regarding the aforementioned subject. Your insight will be very helpful, thank you!

PS. What are you doing these days.

Best Regards,

Joel

Noah sat for a moment and looked out the window, before reading Joel's email once again. Joel had given Noah faith and hope in his letter. He was a nice guy, and it was nice to know, Joel was never swayed from all the accusations and bigotry he witnessed Noah go through. Noah smiled and wrote:

Joel,

Your comments are very kind, but no thank you is necessary! It was my honor to serve! As for what I'm doing these days. I have decided to speak out and write a book. Your correspondence motivated me to reconsider, and visit the subject of "Don't Ask, Don't Tell" once again. I had pushed it aside and accepted silence. Your interest, along with the ban being lifted, has brought me to the conclusion, my time of being silent is over!

Once again, thank you for your interest. It was great hearing from you, and I wish you great success in your endeavors.
Semper Fi,

Noah

Cal sat back in his chair, as he finished reading the final chapter of Noah's manuscript. "That's a lot to take in, are you sure about this?" Noah looked on in anticipation, "I know, right? ...It's been a long journey. I think I have the gist of it all down on paper." Cal hesitated with concern, "...it will take courage." Noah nodded his head in agreement. It was a big step and took a lot of courage to revisit the old memories. "You're right, but I actually think it was cathartic, but more importantly, I hope I served the ghost well!" Cal still concerned, "Even still, with the ban lifted, ...Do you think they can come back on you? Don't get me wrong, ...I think people should hear this!" Noah sighed, "I know, and I hear what you're saying! By "they," I assume you mean the Marine Corps. Even with the ban lifted, the fear the Marine Corps can come in and take everything is still there. So yeah, ...I'm still guarded, ...I think! So many of us, those who served under 'Don't ask Don't tell' share some form of PTSD. Especially the ones who were in it for the long hall. After all, we were fighting a war, it's just that it was with our own country. There were those who were open, and on the outside, in the foreground leading the charge. Then there were those like us, ...the ones on the inside, ...the underground." Cal, being inquisitive, asked, "You never said what happened to that Phobos guy? You know the rapist. Did they ever find him?" Noah smirked, "I don't believe they ever found out what happened to him." Cal looking at Noah, was trying not to think the worst, but still had to ask. "Noah, you don't know anything about what happened to him do you?" Noah had a pregnant pause, as he thought carefully before answering. "No, of course not, come on, really? I'm sure someone does, but then again, one never knows about these things. It was 'Don't Ask, Don't Tell!' You know, you have to be careful when asking someone to keep a secret, THEY can become good at it..."

Chapter 53

What really happened, 1998

Other than her husband Tony's Jag at the far end, the parking lot was almost empty when Gina pulled into Club Mystic. Speaking out loud, "This is going to work!" as she backed her purple Range Rover in, parked and sat in the car waiting.

The afternoon had already turned to evening and the night was setting in. Tuesday nights were not busy for Club Mystic. The reflection of the blue and yellow neon sign glistened on the pavement now that the rain had stopped. Soon she saw an old farm truck pull in. She wasn't familiar with it and spoke out loud. "Who the hell is this? I hope it isn't someone going to mess things up."

It pulled in, backed up and parked next to her. Hickman (Hick) hopped out and gave a scan of the parking lot. Noticing how empty it was, he worked his way to her. Recognizing him, she rolled down the window to speak. "What the hell are you driving?" Hick laughed, "It's an old farm truck, Bob brought it over for me to drive back." Hick was a bit anxious, "You sure about this? You know we can still call it off." Gina frowned, "I told you Hick, for me this is it! There is no other option." Hickman looked around the parking lot, "Still no sign of the others, huh? You don't think they backed out? What if…" Gina interrupted, "Hick, we got this! Calm down, we have thought it through, and it will all work out!" Hickman blew out some air and sighed. Looking at his watch, "Where are they, weren't they supposed to be here by now?" Gina rolled her eyes, "Hick, really? They'll be here!"

Gina took a glance at her watch and turned looking toward the entrance. She was starting to wonder herself if the others were going to make it, it was getting late. A few guests had pulled into the parking lot and had already gone into the bar. Gina looked at Hickman, "Don't worry, Tony has got things under control, he knows what he's doing. All the guests are being directed to the main area, but when our guest arrives, he'll be told there is a special event going on and be directed into the smaller bar. He'll be isolated from everyone else. The other guests will not even have a chance to see him. It's not unheard of anyways. He normally sits in the smaller bar when he comes in. Besides, it will look better when he shows up, that there are other people in the bar.

Hickman's head perked up when he saw the black cargo van pull in. "Is that them?" Gina looked over, "Yep, Alabama license plates, it has to be." The van pulled in front of them and stopped. The window rolled down, it was Bob from Toadvine, he grinned, "Can't a girl get a kiss around here?" Hickman and Gina laughed. Hickman walked over as Bob hopped out and gave him a hug. From the passenger side of the van, Giselle hopped out and joined the rest.

After the greetings, Hickman stepped back, "Man, you all were giving me a scare." Gina quickly turned to business, "Ok guys, listen up, we have got to make this happen quickly. We all have gone over this, and it looks like tonight will be the night. Go ahead and pull the van to the back door and knock on it. Tony will be there… he has agreed to help us out. After I told him about this guy and what he did to his own little girl, Tony was sickened. Being a father himself, to his own little girl, he signed on! The security system is shut down. Trust me without going too far into it, this is not Tony's first trip to the circus. You're all ready for this right?" Hickman spoke up, "If you want out, now is the time, just walk away! No questions asked, and we'll call it off. It's all of us or nothing. If one bails, we all bail. No hard feelings, no nothing. But just know, if you're in, after this, there will be no turning back. You'll have to see it to the end." Giselle asked, "What about the other lady, she in?" Gina answered, "I've contacted her, and felt the situation out. She's good. I trust her." Hickman spoke, "Ok, one more time, in front of the group. I'm going to ask each of you one at a time. Yes or no." he turned, "Gina, you in?" Gina didn't hesitate, "Oh, I'm in!" Hickman turned, "Bob, you in?" Bob spitting his chewing tobacco, "You know, … society believes in giving second chances. We've all seen guys like this walk scot-free. Oh, they'll say, 'We re-haw-bill-itated him.' And you know in my "opinion" that is, …pardon my language Ms. Gina, …but it's kinda like trying to clean the shit off of used toilet paper, (*the others laughed*) …it just ain't going to happen! So, this guy has had his second chances.

Hell, matter of fact, third and fourth! So, you ask me if I'm in? HELL YES! I'M IN! …and I can't wait to get my hands on that motherfucker!" Giselle was next. Hickman asked, "Giselle, you in?" Giselle spoke, "There ain't a day goes by, that I don't remember what he done to me! To know he did it to others, … it just makes me sick! I only wish I had done something sooner! So yes, I'm in!" Gina turned to Hickman, "Hick, we haven't heard your answer yet, are you in?" Hickman paused briefly, "I believe in the law, and don't like this vigilante thing, but in this case, I agree with Bob, I think the law has let us down. So yes, I am in!"

Master Gunny Phobos walked in the front door to the Mystic lounge, when he was quickly directed over into the small bar seating area. Tony, Gina's husband, was working the bar, "What'll you have tonight fella, the usual?" Master Gunny spoke, "Yeah, straight up vodka martini, if you don't mind?" Tony created the drink and sat it on the bar. Master Gunny spoke, "Quiet tonight over here. I see you have some kind of event going on in the other room." Tony, continued on doing makeshift work, "Yeah, I think it's some kind of corporate event, just getting started." Master Gunny downed his drink and ordered another. Tony noticed how easy he threw it back. "Rough week, that one seemed to go down pretty quick." He fetched the martini glass from the bar. Master Gunny replied, "Every week is a rough week in my world these days. Are we still allowed to smoke in this joint? I forget, so many places don't allow it anymore!" Tony just finishing his drink, stuck a mickey in it, before sitting it on the bar. "Smoke'm if you got'm! That's what they use to say when I was in the Marine Corps." Master Gunny laughed, the comment made him feel at ease, "I believe they still do." He lit up a cigarette and Tony sat an ashtray in front of him. He then turned to the doorman and nodded his head giving him a signal. The doorman acknowledged, and left the room momentarily, before Gina entered. The door man returned and closed the wooden double doors behind her, once she sat down at the bar a few stools away from Master Gunny. Tony acted as though he never knew her, and she ordered a drink. It wasn't long before Master Gunny made his move and spoke. "What's a pretty lady like you doing in here all by yourself?" Gina smiled, "I'm not by myself, I was just next door, and decided to take a break, and come in here where it is a bit quieter. The music can be so loud." Master Gunny smiled, "Have we met before, you look a bit familiar?" Gina grinned, "I don't know, have we?" Master Gunny took a hit of his cigarette and blew it out, racking his brain as to why she might look so familiar. Gina noticing the cigarette, "You smoke, …awe, a cigarette, can I get one from you?" He held up the pack, "Come and get it." Gina was putting on her best show, she understood the undertone of his remark, and played along. "Oh, thank you!" She stood up, making sure he seen her mini skirt had risen up, showing a bit of panty, "Oh, excuse me…" giggling, she grabbed her drink and wiggled over to sit next to him. He gave her a cigarette and lit it for her. "Thank you, I normally don't smoke, but sometimes when I drink, I'll have one." He grinned and finished his martini, before ordering he asked, "Can I buy you a drink?" Gina giggled, "Oh, I think I've had enough, I'm starting to feel a little tipsy." He grinned, "Are you sure?" She hesitated, "All right, I guess one more will be ok. But that is it, or I'll have to find a ride home." He smiled, "I'm pretty sure we can find a way for you to get home all right." Master Gunny waved for another round of drinks. Tony was watching everything going on, made the drinks and returned. The two did a toast, "Cheers!" Master Gunny kept looking at her but couldn't place where he might know her from. The two chatted a bit longer when Master Gunny started slurring his speech.

Gina noticed and nodded to Tony and gave him a thumbs up. He looked to the back door at the doorman and gave him the go ahead. That was when Gina started her speech.

"You know I do think we have met before." Master Gunny was feeling a little lightheaded and confused, "What? You do, where?" "I was stationed on main side up on base years ago, back in the late 80's." Master Gunny in surprise, "You were in the Marines?" Gina laughed, "Um, I still am?" He shook his head, "Really…" Gina continued, "So yeah, see I had a roommate who came home one night, telling me all about you." Master Gunny grinned, "I hope it was all good, but we never did meet, right?" Gina continued, "Oh yes, honey we've met. …I remember you being on duty and seeing you at the E-Club that night. I left, but my friend stayed, you gave her a ride home. She had been drinking and she trusted you. Do you remember any of this?"

Master Gunny grabbed his martini and downed it, went to stand up, but the effects of the mickey were kicking in and he staggered. From behind, Hickman and Bob stood without him knowing. "What kinda shit you trying to pull" and started to leave before he had to sit back down. Gina continued, "See you raped my friend! And the Marine Corps belittled her, and let you get away with it. You and all your cronies just laughed and tucked it away."

Master Gunny was trying to focus, but was still hearing what she was saying, "It's all lies, that girl wanted it! She was all over me in the car. It was all a lie." That was when Giselle came from behind Hickman and Bob.

Giselle started walking and speaking, "Isn't that getting old there, Gunny? You heard me right, I said Gunny, after all that was your rank, when you did the same to me." Master Gunny turned to see Giselle standing. Giselle continued, "You remember me, right? The one you were going to help out on an inspection. The one you raped, and then the next day, failed me on inspection. The one you told, 'I'll just deny it if you turn me in.' You know after all; the Marine Corps would never believe this little old Lance Corporal."

Master Gunny shouted, "STOP! …stop! What kind of shit fucking game is this, you people are playing?" He looked to Tony, "You, …you're a part of this?" Tony laughed in his face, "She's my wife you sick fuck! Do you think she would even give you the time of day? Hell yeah, I'm in on it! I have seen that disgusting tape of what you did to your daughter! What kind of sick fuck are you? That alone in my book is enough to take you out! I put a mickey in your drink, you sick bastard, you won't be walking outta here!"

Master Gunny, still struggling, looked to see if anyone in the room might help. He grabbed his head, ranting, "Who are you people? Who are you people? Why? Why, are you doing this to me?" With his back up against the bar, he bent over, "Why are you doing this to me?" He started crying as he fell to his knees, and soon was laid out cold on the floor.

It was only a moment before Hickman and Bob, along with the others tied him up and gagged him. They dragged him through the back and out the door, loading him into the back of the black cargo van. The group all clustered one more time. Bob spoke, "Me and Giselle will be taking the back roads, we don't want anybody seeing Giselle driving Master Gunn's car." Gina was curious. "What about gas? All these gas stations now have video, they can record it." Bob chuckled. "Hold on Ms. Gina. We're one step ahead of you. Ole Hick, he'll be driving my big old farm truck behind us. It's got the gas pump in the back, and it's full. We won't even have to stop to get gas. So, we got you covered in our old Marine Corps, 5 paragraph order." Gina chuckled, as Bob continued, "The plan is, we'll be meeting you at the farm in about three days. Don't worry about old shit head in there. He'll be there when you get there!" Hickman smiled, "This is it guys, it's only forward from here! No looking back." Gina gave them all hugs, "Bob, we owe you! You really are the guy to call when in trouble. You guys be safe, and we'll see you on the other end. Oh, I almost forgot, I have a pit stop to make before I get there. So, I might be a little late. But don't do anything until I arrive." Bob, Giselle, and Hickman pulled away.

****

Bob, digging with his shovel threw the last bit of dirt from inside the grave. He had finished his digging. "That my boys, is deep enough!" as he stuck his hand out for help out of the grave. Hickman grabbed it and pulled him forward. The three, Hickman, Bob, and Giselle, looked back at it. Giselle spoke, "Never dug one before, this is the first!" Bob patted him on the shoulder, "Well, for the amount of digging you did, you can still say you never dug one. Hell, me and Hick did most of it!" Hickman and Giselle laughed. Bob continued, "Any word yet from Gina?" Hickman checked his phone, "No. ... If she did try and call, we're not going to get it here, the signal is too weak!" Bob looked out to the black cargo van. "I'm going to have to get that back before too long, or we're going to get charged another day. Don't let me forget to put the original license plates back on it. Those there are the stolen ones." Giselle looking down the road, seen dust flying high. "There comes someone, it better be her." Bob and Hickman both looked, holding their hands over their eyes trying to keep the sun glare down. "Giselle, you and Hickman go and keep our friend in the barn company. If he even looks like he is going to try and make a sound, you take the butt of that rifle of yours, and bash him in the face to shut him up." The two headed out, while Bob went on up to the house.

Bob sat down on his porch, until he could see the vehicle approaching clearly. Once close enough, he hollered to the barn, "It's her, …It's that goddam bright purple Range Rover! …I swear I think that is the ugliest car I have ever seen." Hickman and Giselle came from the barn as Gina pulled up. Bob noticed someone in the car, besides her. She wasn't alone. "Who she got with her? What the hell is she thinking?" Hickman stood next to him. "It's ok, it'll all make sense in a minute." Gina got out of the car. "We made it! Now come on you all give me a hug!" She made her rounds, and then motioned for the passenger in the car to get out.

An African American woman with long braids pulled back in a ponytail, opened the door, and got out, fluffing her hair, and pulling her shirt down at the waist. As she came around the front of the car, Gina spoke, "You all this is my old roommate and friend, from back in the day. Lance Corporal Shalika Davis." Bob was still confused, "Who?" Hickman leaned in, "That is the one that asshole raped back in the day." Bob, "Oh, oh," …he stuck out his hand, "Nice to meet you! Well maybe not so nice of an occasion. Well, …you know what I mean." Hickman and the others followed suit.

Once the introductions were over, Gina sighed, "Well, where we at with all of this? I didn't drive all this way to give hugs, let's get to work!" Bob led them around and showed them the property, ending at the family graveyard. As they stood at the grave, Shalika who had been very quiet, spoke, "Let's do this. It has taken up enough space in my life! Let's make it happen, come on now, let's get it over!" Giselle standing next to her, gave her a hug. "I hear you sister, my thoughts exactly."

Bob and Hickman went to the barn and brought Master Gunny Phobos to the grave. His hands tied and a bag over his head, they forced him to kneel at the end of the grave.

Gina spoke, "How we going to do this? Are we all going to take a whack at him, or what?" Hickman started to speak, "Well I

figured, since Giselle, and Shalika were the most effected by…"
BAM! a blast was fired.

The group all flinched and stepped back from the grave.
Blood had splattered on them. They looked to Master Gunny
Phobos, he was still at the foot of the grave, but now shot in the
head. They looked behind, and there stood Shalika holding a gun,
still pointed at Master Gunny. She spoke, "It's done. He's dead!"

Bob, looking at Master Gunny and then back at her. "Damn
girl, you could have hit any one of us!" She moved the gun and
pointed it to him. "Oh, ok, I see how it is, …never mind, we're good,
we're good!"

Bob moved over to the grave, as Shalika spoke, "I'm an
expert with my pistol! One shot one kill, he's dead. You don't think
I was going to allow anyone else to take this away?"

Giselle calmly walked over to Master Gunny's body, reached
down, and felt his pulse. "He's dead." Bob looked at Giselle and
spoke sarcastically, "You think, … what gave you the first clue?
Hell, half his face is gone." Giselle looked at Bob, "Just making
sure," as he pushed the body into the grave.

The crew huddled around the grave as the last shovels of dirt
were thrown on. Hickman confirming with Bob one more time.
"You sure no one will find him here?" Bob nodded his head, "Yeah,
that bag of bones I threw on top of him, that was my old great, great,
Grandpa. That's his tombstone right there. They'll have to go
through him first. Ain't nobody going to find him here!"

Gina stuck her hand out over the grave, "Well this is it you
all! He'll never be able to hurt anyone again. It's up to us now, you
all know what we have to do!" Giselle put his hand on top, "It is our
secret, …" Shalika, put her hand in, "to never telling…" Hickman
put his hand on top. "Anyone ever ask, or comes looking, you know
what we have to do." Bob stuck his hand on top. "We all know how
it works, hell, we've been doing it for years. Here's to "Semper
Silence.""

The End

Epilogue

President Barrack Obama, Secretary of Defense, Leon Panetta, and Chairman of the Joint Chiefs of Staff Admiral Mike Mullen sent certification to congress on July 22, 2011, which set the end of "Don't Ask Don't Tell". The ban was lifted September 20, 2011.

In the case Obergefell v. Hodges, the U.S. Supreme Court struck down all state bans on same-sex marriage, legalized it in all fifty stars, and required states to honor out-of-state same-sex marriage licenses on June 26, 2015.

Although the "Don't Ask, Don't Tell," ban was lifted in 2011, Transgenders were still discriminated against and banned from serving in their true sexual identity. March 2021, The Pentagon announced new policies undoing the Trump-era rules that effectively banned transgender people from serving in the military. The Department of Defense instruction states, the policies are based on the conclusion that service by transgender persons, who are subject to the same high standards and procedures as other Service members, is constant with military service and readiness. The policies became effective April 30, 2021.

The Defense Department Inspector General found in a report released in November 2021, all branches of the Armed forces, are not getting military victims of domestic violence, child abuse, and sexual assault the help of special criminal investigators and prosecutors they're entitled to under federal law. The report also stated, the DOD cannot ensure that all commanders and investigators are making decisions based on the best possible information because of, among other things, inexperienced or untrained prosecutors. The number of unrestricted reports of sexual assault in the military more than doubled between 2011 and 2019. The violence includes, hazing, rape, and murder. Lawmakers have become frustrated by the military's lack of progress, despite efforts and support for a major overhaul of the uniform Code of Military Justice.

The call for changes have reached a tipping point as Congress continues to debate the issues.

The I am Vanessa Guillen Act was included in the Defense Authorization Act of Dec 2021. It will transform how the military handles and prosecutes allegations of sexual assault and misconduct. The cases will now be turned over to independent military prosecutors and taken out of the chain of command.

Many battles may have been won, ...the struggle continues.

About the Author…

"I'm just a small town, midwestern boy, who wanted to see the world…"

M.G. Rigau is an Author, and Artist. He grew up as the youngest child of a large family of eleven, in a small midwestern town in Indiana. Busting at the seams to see the world, he was barely eighteen when he joined the U.S. Marines, serving more than 25 years, as a Combat Motion Picture Photographer. His inspiration pulls from a life of love, hardship, adventure, and imagination. He brings fictional characters and stories to life, as only he can, from diverse experience and world views. Semper Silence is his breakout novel and has been one of his life's passions in the making!

A note from the Author…

Hey ya'll! I hope you like the book! You know I'm a small-town boy in the big city, and I love to hear from people all around the world. I'll be the first to tell you, I'm not for everyone, and that's ok, but I'd still like to hear from you anyways. Especially if you like my books-tell me why? Positive feedback keeps me going! Be nice now, after all when we can't be anything else, we can always be nice! If you like what you read tell someone! Your word is important to us!

Best Regards,

M.G. Rigau

Follow our journey,

If you would like to know more or find out about an M.G. Rigau book signing event, or schedule one, visit us on our website; Sempersilence.com, or our Semper Silence Facebook. Email: sempersilence@gmail.com

Professional credits...

Front Cover Photographer: <u>Michael Murphy</u>
Photographic Imaging Studio, 261 NE 32nd Ct, Oakland Park, FL 33334, Email: michael@michaelmurphy.com

Front Cover Model: Shawn Weese, Ft Lauderdale, FL

Back Cover Photographer: Melodie Barnhisel, Jacksonville, NC

Back Cover Model: Kylie Lewis, Jacksonville, NC

www.ingramcontent.com/pod-product-compliance
Lightning Source LLC
Chambersburg PA
CBHW032256020726
47495CB00001B/131